DRACULA,
DRACULA'S GUEST
and Other Stories

DRACULA, DRACULA'S GUEST

and Other Stories

Bram Stoker

with Introductions by
DAVID ROGERS *and*
DAVID STUART DAVIES

WORDSWORTH EDITIONS

For my husband
ANTHONY JOHN RANSON
with love from your wife, the publisher
Eternally grateful for your
unconditional love

Readers who are interested in other titles from
Wordsworth Editions are invited to visit our
website at www.wordsworth-editions.com

This joint edition first published 2009
by Wordsworth Editions Limited
8B East Street, Ware, Hertfordshire SG12 9HJ

ISBN 978 1 84022 627 0

Text © Wordsworth Editions Limited 1993, 2000, 2006, 2009
Introduction and notes to *Dracula* © David Rogers 2000
Introduction to *Dracula's Guest and Other Stories*
© David Stuart Davies 2006

Wordsworth® is a registered trademark of
Wordsworth Editions Limited

Wordsworth Editions is
the company founded in 1987 by
MICHAEL TRAYLER

Typeset in Great Britain by Antony Gray
Printed and bound by Clays Ltd, St Ives plc

DRACULA

Bram Stoker

with an Introduction by
DAVID ROGERS
Kingston University

INTRODUCTION

Dracula is one of the greatest horror stories in English literature. Bram Stoker first began taking notes for it on 8 March 1890 while on holiday in Whitby, origin of Captain Cook's famous Pacific voyages. He entered his last note six years later and published the novel with Constable in the Diamond Jubilee Year 1897, dedicating it to his 'dear friend Hommy-Beg', the best-selling novelist Hall Caine ('Hommy Beg', meaning 'little Tommy', is a Manx term of endearment). Late-Victorian audiences loved vampire stories and, although no American publisher accepted it until Doubleday & McClure in 1899, the novel almost immediately sold well both in England and later on the Continent, its first translation, *Makt Mgrkanna* meaning *The Prince of Darkness*, appearing in Iceland in 1898. Since that beginning, Stoker's story, which appeared in a poor quality yellow binding due to the extra cost involved in a last-minute change to its title, has been translated into forty-three more languages. Having never once been out of print, it has had an impact on twentieth-century popular culture that has proved little short of phenomenal. Indeed, with the possible exception of Mary Shelley's monster in *Frankenstein* and the Devil himself ('Dracula' means 'devil' in the Wallachian language), Stoker's neck-biting, blood-sucking, ubiquitous Count has probably been the most widely popularised anti-hero in the whole of Western culture. More than two hundred and fifty films and innumerable stories and comics owe their inspiration to his figure and testify to the almost universal way in which his erotic, sometimes camp, adventures have continued to frighten, attract and, often, amuse audiences of all ages.

For all of the novel's appeal, however, given the bare facts of his life, Stoker generally seems a rather unlikely creator of such an enduring figure and tale. The third of seven children born to Anglo-Irish parents in Clontarf, in the northern suburbs of Dublin, in 1847, Stoker could not stand upright until he was six. He nevertheless later developed into an accomplished all-round athlete and walker, winning the athletic championship at Trinity College, Dublin. He later earned an honours degree in mathematics at Trinity, serving as president of the university's Philosophical Society, into which he introduced Oscar Wilde, at whose parents' home in the prestigious Merrion Square in Dublin Stoker regularly attended *soirées* and listened to Wilde's father William give accounts of Egyptian adventures. After graduation, Stoker was called before both the Irish and English bars and then, in 1870, followed his father Abraham, a third-class clerk-in-chief in the office of the secretary in Dublin Castle, into the Irish civil service (his grand father William had previously been an ordinance clerk). There the young Stoker worked as inspector of petty services and, after publishing his first short story 'The Crystal Cup' in *The London Society* in 1872, placed his first horror story 'The Chain of Destiny' in four instalments in the weekly *Shamrock* newspaper in 1875. Stoker then published his first book, entitled *The Duties of the Inspector of Petty Services*, in December 1879.

By that time, however, Stoker's life had taken a decisive turn. In 1877, the young civil servant met Henry Irving, the most famous English actor of the time. The occasion was a reading Irving gave at Trinity that Stoker covered as an unpaid drama critic for a local paper. So impressed was Stoker by Irving's commanding performance, that he quit his job within a year, married Florence Balcombe, whom Oscar Wilde once described as an 'exquisitely pretty girl' with the 'most perfect face' he had ever seen, and moved to London. There he served as Irving's manager and front-of-house at the Lyceum Theatre for the remaining twenty-eight years of the actor's life.[1] During that time, which included periods of travel both in England and Europe and across the United States, Stoker managed to publish a collection of nightmarishly allegorical stories for children, *Under the Sunset* (1881), and no fewer than ten novels in addition to *Dracula*. He also wrote a two-volume account of his relationship with Irving, *Personal Reminiscences of Henry Irving*, that appeared in 1906. Although one or two of these texts may have drawn praise from certain critical circles, none really suggests that Stoker had the potential to write the classic for which he is now rightly remembered. Each may still hold some interest for the

---

1 Stoker's claim that his relationship with Irving was as 'profound, as close, as lasting as can be between two men' has, given Irving's growing and tempermental dependence on Stoker, encouraged some critics to read *Dracula* as a narrative of the writer-manager's repressed feelings for revenge or possibly same-sex desire. They read it as evidence that Stoker was unaware of the many sexual innuendoes that appear in the novel, as were reviewers at the time.

most dedicated Stoker fans and scholars.[2] But the novelist, who died at the age of sixty-four on 20 April 1912, quite possibly, according to his grand-nephew Daniel Farson, of complications from tertiary syphilis contracted in 1896 after a 'loveless, frigid marriage' and a lifetime of affairs, will, one suspects, forever owe his fame to a single astonishing work.[3]

How then should we account for the singular quality of Stoker's *Dracula*? What, other than the uncharacteristically meticulous care Stoker took with the book, may have been responsible for inspiring a writer of apparently modest talent and limited imagination to produce not only a perpetually captivating story but also a telling cultural docu-ment, a text that both exposes the particular anxieties of its immediate period and marks a vital moment in the paradigm shift that defines the modern age? What allowed Stoker to produce a text that is often almost embarrassing in its treatment of the sexual and the erotic, and yet, at the same time, increasingly provocative in an intellectual sense, meaningful and expressive to so many successive generations; in short, what makes *Dracula* a classic?

The answer lies partly in the novel's most central narrative opposition. Narratives constructed upon a clash between polar forces such as those of Good and Evil are as old as narrative itself, and Stoker generally follows this time-honoured tradition by pitting Dracula against a group of unam-biguously 'manly' men whose qualities, actions and outlook seem to contrast him in virtually every way. For this reason the novel potentially provides many different, if possibly overlapping, allegorical readings.

2 *The Snake's Pass*, serialised in *People* in 1889 and published as a book in 1890; *The Watter's Mou'*, a melodrama about Cruden Bay during the smuggling era that served in 1895 as a companion volume to Arthur Conan Doyle's *The Parasite*; *The Shoulder of Shasta*, which also appeared in 1895; *Miss Betty*, published in *The Era* in 1898; *The Mystery of the Sea*, considered one of Stoker's best efforts when it appeared in 1902; *The Jewel of the Seven Stars*, 1903; *The Man*, paradoxically about a New Woman heroine, 1905; *Snowbound: The Record of a Theatrical Touring Party*, a short story collection written while travelling in America in 1908; *The Lady of the Shroud*, 1909; and, probably the most intriguing of all, *The Lair of the White Worm*, published in November 1911 and the source of the 1988 Ken Russell film of the same name.

3 Barbara Bedford, Stoker's most recent biographer, doubts Farson's sensational account. She believes that the medical evidence behind Farson's claim is inconclu-sive, not least because, Stoker having died at home, no medical records were made of his death. She concedes that nineteenth-century doctors often used the cause of death listed on Stoker's death certificate – 'locomotor ataxi' – as a euphemism for tertiary syphilis. But she believes the novelist never showed the signs of dementia and psychosis usually seen in syphilis patients. For her, death followed from conse-quences of Stoker's two previous strokes.

There are, for example, Marxist readings associated with class struggle (1897, we should note, is the same year that Lenin announced Western imperialism had reached its zenith). There are also Freudian ones highlighting Oedipal concerns and issues of the unconscious, 1897 also being the year in which Freud began his research into psychoanalysis. Finally, there are allegorical readings potentially drawn from a number of conceptual polarities, including reason and intuition, rationality and irrationality, the visible and the invisible, free will and determination. There are those that might arise from nineteenth-century debates concerning the struggle between the social or the altruistic and the egotistical, the single-mindedness of the selfish, increasingly democratised, individual.[4]

Yet the real answer to the novel's remarkable power more probably lies in the subtle ways in which Stoker exploits the traditions of Dracula himself and the mysteries and latent implications that surrounded him. Vampirism, in some form or another, has appeared in all cultures, in all times, or, as Professor Van Helsing puts it in the novel, 'everywhere that men have been' (p. 198).[5] Very often, however, as with the AIDS and hepatitis C viruses in our own time and syphilis during Stoker's, the vampiric cult has emerged during periods of strangely spreading infection and disease. Or again, as now, its popularity has resurfaced at the end of millennia and periods of perceived social change and anxiety over the future, as the successes of novelists such as Stephen King and Anne Rice imply and Frances Ford Coppola's popular 1995 film *Bram Stoker's Dracula* confirms. (Indeed, as the last millennium came to an end, the original 1931 Bela Lagosi film was rereleased with a modernised score by the experimental composer Philip Glass.)

In England the specific tradition of the modern vampire story, to which *Dracula* is so central, developed as a sub-genre within the Gothic tradition. That tradition began with Horace Walpole's *The Castle of Otranto* in

4 For examples of such readings, see Maurice Richardson, 'The Psychoanalysis of Count Dracula', Christopher Frayling (ed.), *Vampyres: Lord Byron to Count Dracula*, Faber and Faber, London, pp. 418–22; Mark M. Hennelly, Jr., '*Dracula*: The Gnostic Quest and the Victorian Wasteland', *English Literature in Transition*, 20, 1977; Thomas B. Byers, 'Good Men & Monsters: The Defenses of Dracula', *Literature and Psychology*, 31, No. 4, 1981; Burton Hatlen, 'The Return of the Repressed/Oppressed', *Minnesota Review*, 15, 1980; and Pericles Lewis, 'Dracula and the Epistemology of the Victorian Gothic Novel', Elizabeth Miller (ed.), *Dracula: The Shade and the Shadow*, Desert Island Books, Westcliff-on-Sea 1998, pp. 71–81.

5 Although Stoker may not have known about vampires as a child, he may have learned of similar cults in his childhood, for his mother especially immersed him in the rich folk culture and superstitions of his native Ireland.

1765 and later found expression in such examples as *The Mysteries of Udolpho* by Ann Radcliffe (1794), *Melmoth the Wanderer* by Charles Maturin (1820), and Emily Brontë's *Wuthering Heights* (1848). The first English vampire story, appropriately called *The Vampyre*, was written by John Polidori, the one-time personal physician to Lord Byron, who, like Stoker, is destined to be remembered largely for a single creation, Polidori having died mysteriously at the age of twenty-six. Published in 1819, but written three years earlier under the same circumstances of composition at Percy Shelley's rented villa on Lake Geneva that inspired the poet's wife Mary to write *Frankenstein*, Polidori's tale, which appeared in the *New Monthly Magazine* and was later adapted for the stage under the title *The Vampire or The Bride of the Isle*, left two important legacies. It established the vampiric villain as anti-bourgeois (vampires before then had not been consistently linked with an established class), and it aligned the nineteenth-century vampire with the perceived threat of unbridled romanticism and a sexual potency that ensured neither society ladies nor innocent girls could resist his advances.

Polidori's Bryonic stereotype remained largely unchanged until the publication of *Varney the Vampire*, which appeared in 1846. Variously attributed to James Madison Rymer and to Thomas Preston Priest, *Varney the Vampire or The Feast of Blood*, is, in contrast to Polidori's short work, typically Victorian in length. Its original edition numbers over 750,000 words and runs to 868 double-columned pages. The novel may have little more than subject matter in common with *Dracula*, but Stoker, as we will see, used to wonderfully unsettling effect its most important variation for the genre – a sub-plot, full of comic tones, involving a Hungarian vampire who visits England and initiates one of the novel's heroines and whose nature is defined by an unpredictability that can be temporarily combated by the methods of science. Stoker also, however, borrowed much of the main plot of his narrative from an anonymous German story translated into English in 1860 as *The Mysterious Stranger*, and he incorporated elements of the erotic from Sheridan Le Fanu's mixture of vampirism and lesbianism in *Carmilla* (1871). Moreover, he relied heavily on non-fiction sources, one of which was his brother George's *With the Unspeakables; or Two Years Campaigning in European and Asiatic Turkey* (1878). A second was Emily Gerard's popular book *The Land Beyond the Forest* (1887). One of the innumerable Victorian travel books written to satisfy the period's enormous desire for knowledge about unknown and exotic people and places, Gerard's text introduced Stoker to the real-life fifteenth-century prince or *viovode* of Wallachia, Vlad the Impaler, whose notorious reputation for staking his enemies to death provided Stoker with a further model for his Count.

Yet Stoker's Dracula exceeds the sum of these various parts. As one of the Undead, Dracula, as every filmgoer knows, exists in the novel somewhere indefinably between two states of being.[6] The most nebulous of presences, he casts no shadow and reflects no image in a mirror. He is, moreover, virtually plastic. He can change himself into an almost infinite number of shapes, most familiarly those of wolves and bats and dogs, and into the airy nothingness of a tellingly *grey* mist, the colour of which implies both this essential in-between-ness and the air of uncertainty that Dracula casts about the affairs and understanding of the other characters in the novel.

In keeping with such an in-between-ness, what contemporary theorists such as Alice Jardine have often generally referred to as a 'trans-positionality',[7] Stoker's Dracula does not reside simply in a place that defines the East as if fundamentally different from the West. Instead, living 'just on the borders of three states, Transylvania, Moldavia, and Bukovina' (p. 3), he makes it impossible for the young solicitor Jonathan Harker 'to light on any map or work giving the exact locality of the Castle Dracula' (p. 3). For this reason, Harker's first meeting with the Count acts as a metonym for the entire text, suggesting with its indistinguishable location the potential creation of a 'Mittel Land' (p. 8) between reality and illusion, a land neither wholly material and locatable nor defined by the strict negations of those terms. To complicate matters even further, the Count also blurs the distinction between conventionally gendered identity. He appears as if androgyn-ous, his luscious mouth with his sharp protruding (and penetrating) teeth combining the symbolic shape of the feminine with a signifier of masculine phallic power to provide, as Christopher Craft has argued, only the most conspicuous of many signs of his figurative bisexuality.[8]

By radically defying the strict binaries that distinguished the gender- and class-conscious England of the novel, Dracula thus configures the novel's engagement with the paradigm struggle that characterises its specific historical context. *Fin-de-siècle* England was outwardly a relatively stable society compared to other Western societies of the time and its

---

6 In early drafts Stoker used *The Dead Undead* as a possible title for the novel. A few weeks before publication, the title of the manuscript remained simply *The Undead*.

7 Alice A. Jardine, *Gynesis: Configurations of Woman and Modernity*, Cornell University Press, Ithaca 1985

8 Christopher Craft, 'Kiss Me with Those Red Lips: Gender and Inversion in Bram Stoker's *Dracula*', *Representations*, 8, 1984, pp. 107–33

cultural and political disputes were usually conducted within acknowledged premises. Nevertheless, energetic discussions took place across a
wide range of social issues, none of which was more impassioned than the
one concerning gender laws. Indeed, as Elaine Showalter writes, 'all the
laws that governed sexual identity and behaviour seemed to be breaking
down'.[9] From the late 1880s, there was, for example, an unprecedented
amount of public discussion and criticism of marriage and the family in
the press, in literature and in pamphlets. Reform began to make inroads
into the patriarchal English legal system with the passage of acts such as
the Married Woman's Property Act (1882) that permitted wives, who had
previously gained the right in 1880 to retain any earnings or property
acquired after marriage, to retain possessions they had owned at the time
of their union. Marriage thus began to seem less a relationship of patriarchal dominance and female dependence and more one involving
reciprocal rights and duties between husband and wife. The word 'femi-
nism', as well as 'homosexual' (and 'unemployment'), first came into use.

At the centre of these debates were the so-called New Women
novelists.[10] These novelists, whose texts, wrote Lady Laura Riding in
her 1896 essay 'What Should Women Read?', were 'morbid, pessimistic,
coarse, flippant, irreverent [. . .] bigoted [and] controversial', usually
advocated intellectual achievements for women and competition with
men.[11] They often dramatised marital breakdowns and adultery in their
stories. They ridiculed the family and marriage, and, perhaps most
controversially of all, they questioned the sanctity of motherhood at a
time when conservative groups in the country were demanding more
and better mothers, worried that declining birth rates were eroding the
general health of the national stock and the continuation of English
economic and military superiority.

As a sign of the intensity of their fear of such women novelists, tradi-
tionalists frequently represented the New Woman in contradictory ways.
On the one hand, they pictured her as a nervous type, often anorexic, a
neurasthenic woman, prone to hysteria, for whom intellectual activity
could have debilitating physiological effects; on the other, they cast her as
a highly sexual creature, whose permissiveness undermined social stabil-
ity by breaking down the vital bonds of state and culture and by inciting

9 Elaine Showalter, *Sexual Anarchy: Gender and Culture at the Fin de Siècle*,
Bloomsbury, London 1991

10 The term, first used by Sarah Grand in her novel *The Heavenly Twins* (1893), was
popular among journalists and novelists in the 1890s.

11 See Kate Flint, *The Woman Reader 1837–1914*, Clarendon Press, Oxford 1993

selfish behaviour, and, though the idea is hardly ever acknowledged
explicitly, the apparently random fecundity of a Darwinian world.

Stoker follows the former lead by having Mina Harker cry uncontrol-
lably after she is first bitten by Dracula: 'There now, crying again!' Mina
writes in her journal:

> I wonder what has come over me today. I must hide it from Jonathan,
> for if he knew that I had been crying twice in one morning – I, who
> never cried on my own account, and whom he has never caused to
> shed a tear – the dear fellow would fret his heart out. I shall put a bold
> face on, and if I do feel weepy, he shall never see it. I suppose it is one
> of the lessons that we poor women have to learn . . . '   [p. 214]

More importantly, following *Varney*, Stoker depicts the second type in
Lucy Westenra. Susceptible enough to the influences of the liberated
woman to admit to Mina that she would like to be able to marry three
men, Lucy is transformed by Dracula from a conventional figure of the
West's ideal Woman, characterised by her 'sweetness' and 'purity', into a
Darwinian one, a figure whose 'heartless cruelty' and 'voluptuous wantonness' (p. 175) connote the brutal promiscuity of the world depicted by
nineteenth-century natural history. With this change, Stoker situates
Lucy within the many unmarried, pregnant women who begin to people
the Anglo-American novels of the century. These figures, which include
Ruth from Elizabeth Gaskell's novel of the same name, Hester Prynne
from Nathaniel Hawthorne's *The Scarlet Letter* and, most famously,
Thomas Hardy's 'spouseless mother' Tess, act individually and collectively to displace both the figure of the virgin and the figure of the earth
mother that had underpinned the Judaeo-Christian Platonism of most
Victorian writers. Rejecting the hierarchy and gender polarities that had
characterised that pre-Darwinian world view, these figures suggest a
world that is, in the conventional terms, no longer 'natural'. And like
Lucy, who acquires from Dracula the ability to assume different shapes
and sizes and to appear and disappear as if out of thin air, they reveal how
the contest over the representative and symbolic value of Woman fundamentally challenged late nineteenth-century culture's understanding of
the material world.[12] For the world that these unwed mothers imply is,
ultimately, not even wholly material. It is a world turned upside down, a
world made *perverse* (according to the *Oxford English Dictionary*, 'to per-

---

12 Stoker's one real innovation for the genre was to have Dracula's victims turn into
vampires themselves. The detail adds to the sense that Dracula has a potentially
pervasive effect on the West.

vert' means 'to turn upside down', or 'to lead astray'; 'to turn aside from a right religious belief or system'). Indeed, given the in-between-ness of Dracula, from whom this perversion follows, it is a world, we might say, that is best characterised as naturally perverse or perversely natural, an oscillation between the two phrases suggesting the need to avoid defining one of the terms in strict opposition to the other.[13]

In threatening to infect the country with a pervasive sense of perversity, Dracula, described by Dr Seward as 'the father or furtherer of a new order of beings, whose road must lead through Death, not Life' (p. 251), therefore not only complicates the gender of these newly represented figures of women; but he also potentially undermines – *deconstructs* – the metaphysical views of the novel's England: the belief in a world created by God and governed by rational laws. In keeping with his suspension between conventional genders, he therefore also emerges as the last important nineteenth-century male figure of the cultural outsider or 'other' in the Gothic tradition of Emily Brontë's Heathcliff and in the line of conventional figures such as Frank Churchill from Jane Austen's *Emma* and Will Ladislaw from George Eliot's *Middlemarch*. Like these figures, who are also conveyed as mysterious in origin and possessed of an excessive imagination, and, in Heathcliff's case, hysteria and insanity, Dracula is aligned with qualities at odds with the prevailing gender-defined attitudes within the novel. And, like them, he is contrasted to Victorian ideals of masculinity typically aligned with clear-sightedness and emotional control.[14]

13 For deconstructionists, a 'perverse dynamic' characterises all systems of thought. Doubly insurgent because it operates, as does Dracula once he begins to transform his English victims, as if both from the outside in and the inside out, this dynamic represents the most potent threat to conventional Western beliefs of rationality and idealism. For it is not simply alien to those beliefs but imbedded in the ideas of the authentic upon which those beliefs rest. For a greater discussion of this idea, see Jonathan Dollimore, *Sexual Dissidence: Augustine to Wilde, Freud to Foucault*, Clarendon Press, Oxford 1991.

14 Dracula also anticipates the androgyne figures so prevalent in modernism. More specifically, he directly 'foreshadows' the transpositional figures of men and women in the novels of the American novelist William Faulkner. These Faulknerian figures, exemplified across the length of Faulkner's canon by such figures as Margaret Mahon in *Soldiers' Pay*, Dilsey in *The Sound and the Fury*, Lena Grove in *Light in August* and V. K. Ratliff in the Snopes trilogy, defy the polarities traditionally used to contrast values of the 'masculine' and the 'feminine' and the premises with which they are convention-ally assigned. Across his novels, Faulkner completes the process of de-naturalisation along gender lines in which Stoker's creation plays such a vital part. He eventually transfers the concept of subjectivity from the masculine to the feminine.

As such an outsider, Dracula therefore represents ('embodies' would obviously be the wrong word here) those forces and implications of impending social change that so many English writers throughout the century had been forced to confront because they were thought to undermine prevailing assumptions and the dichotomies that underpinned them. For nineteenth-century writers, on both sides of the Atlantic, such perverse forces included romanticism; democratic theories, individualism and ideas of women's rights imported from the social and political revolutions in France and America; and radical discoveries of science, particularly in areas of geology and natural history. In revealing new qualities of the material universe and offering new explanations for the age and manner of the world, these forces threatened the cultural authority of the Bible. Hence, they steadily undermined the authority of an hierarchical, class-structured society that empowered propertied men at the expense of all groups and consigned women like Lucy to the role of symbolic objects for universal Purity and God-given Truth. All, in their own ways, tended to endorse the openness of the individual to the uncertainties of experience and the validity of individual perceptions and intuition instead of the ideals of common sense and reason so central to eighteenth-century rationalism and nineteenth-century utilitarianism and positivist theories. All acted to privilege the subjectivity of experience and the metaphorical, hybrid quality of truth, the premise that chance and individual rights rather than Providence and traditional social deference determined the course of events and human experience. All struck at the heart (it's hard not to pun when referring to this novel) of metaphysical certainty while appearing to promote an antisocial egotism and potentially to unravel the social fabric of the country.

At first glance, Stoker, who once publicly stated that 'the ideal man is entirely or almost entirely masculine and the ideal woman is entirely or almost entirely feminine' but that the 'great mass' of people 'close to the borderline' are 'easily satisfied to mate with anyone', appears to side with the opponents of such controversial representations. He seems to offer a misogynistic, as well as xenophobic, reaction against such forces. His Dracula – so singular and selfish in his pursuits, so comprehensively aligned to an excess of imagination and a lack of sufficient reason – is finally driven from England and destroyed by the group of 'manly' men to whom I've referred. Individually, these men hold various professions and social roles. Collectively, they represent the restorative powers of traditional patriarchal rule and the metaphysical world-view that rule accompanies. There is the man of law, the young solicitor Harker; there is the man of science, the psychol-ogist Dr Seward, in whose care resides the psychotic patient Renfield who is under Dracula's spell (psychiatrists in England classified one kind of male neurotic whose mind lacked sufficient 'controlling power' as a 'borderline'); there is the man of aristocratic privilege and financial might, Lord Godalming, Lucy's fiancé, the name for whom Stoker invites us to read as Lord God Almighty or even Lord Gold Aiming, the aim of his affection being the blonde, 'pure' Lucy; and, finally, there is the American Quincey Morris, a man of the New-World virility and rugged male companionship Stoker openly admired in the American poet Walt Whitman. (Stoker famously once wrote an unsolicited letter of praise to Whitman that he never mailed. Later he became acquainted with the poet, the fact that Whitman was gay having subsequently allowed further speculation about Stoker's sexual orientation.)[15] Leading the group is Dr Abraham Van Helsing, who, as a medical doctor, a doctor of philosophy and literature *and* a knowledgeable para-legalist carrying Stoker's own given name, is Dracula's opposite and double, at least in many overt ways.

Stoker's narrative strategy (taken, as an early reviewer noted, from Wilkie Collins's *The Woman in White*, but also a variation on the Gothic tradition of telling a story without one central, omniscient narrative voice) appears to confirm further the traditional Victorian ideology implicit in the success of Van Helsing's men in first understanding the whereabouts and movements of Dracula, then tracking him down, and destroying him.[16] *Dracula* is comprised of a series of mostly first-person accounts of events. Among these narratives are journal and diary entries kept by the principal characters (with the important exception of Dracula, of course, who speaks as if to us as readers only once, after his successful seduction of Mina), letters, newspaper articles, ships' logs and personal interviews. Some are written in shorthand, others dictated on to a phonograph (the book gives a wonderful insight into the emerging technology of the period

15 Stoker wrote the letter on 18 February 1872. He first met Whitman, with Henry Irving, while on tour with the actor in America on 20 March 1884. The two literary men reputedly got along well, Stoker referring to Whitman as the 'Master', the same term he has Renfield use for Dracula.

16 Stoker also employs the Gothic convention of providing allegedly factual documents on which his story is based, prefacing the narrative with an explanation about the nature and sequencing of the 'papers' that comprise the text. For an analysis of Stoker's use of this convention and the narrative structure of the novel, see David Schmid, 'Is the Pen Mightier than the Sword', Elizabeth Miller (ed.), *Dracula: The Shade and the Shadow*, Desert Island Books, Westcliff-on-Sea 1998, pp. 119–29. See too David Seed, 'The Narrative Method of Dracula', *Nineteenth Century Fiction*, 40, No.1, 1985, pp. 61–75.

and its perceived implications). All of these first-person narratives rest upon the premise, largely shared by nineteenth-century positivists, that reality conforms to that which we observe and then faithfully and meticulously record. They assume that words derive their meanings from a natural, inherent link with the material world. Indeed, for Harker, as it is increasingly for others, describing events and ideas in language, especially when that language appears to be part of what seems a common cultural narrative, not only acts as an aid to memory, but also keeps the writer sane. It re-enforces the idea that there is a solid world 'out there' that we can know completely and record. The written word for Stoker's gang carries more weight than does the spoken.

As if to endorse this view, which was challenged at the time by a theory of language called semiotics that holds that language is a system of signs in which meaning is not fixed but arbitrary, a function of the relationships among signs rather than their inherent link to a world beyond or outside language, individual characters slowly but surely share their personal records with each other. By virtue of their communal ethos, they create a single, apparently coherent narrative from the various potentially subjective or unreliable accounts, what Dr Seward calls 'a whole connected narrative' (p. 187). This collective coherence, possible only because of Mina's skill with the new technologies, appears to authenticate their separate experiences and therefore to prevent their separate drifts into isolation and madness. Their success implies that it was still possible to construct a cultural coherence in the face of the perversity Dracula represents. It also makes it possible for the protagonists in the novel to reduce their nemesis to a set of predictable movements and so defeat him.

The most formal effect of this strategy is to transform the nature of the discourse of the novel itself, shifting it paradoxically from the literary – which in the works of Thomas Hardy and Henry James, to name two, had begun to represent the world as ambiguous and only subjectively known – to the scientific with its premises of truth and objectivity, its belief in the possibility of rational explanation. It is, in this sense, as if Stoker sought to transfuse the former with the latter, slowly replacing the (conventionally feminine) connotations of the literary with those of the (more masculine) scientific. It is as if he wished to suggest such displacement analogously through the scenes in the novel when each of the men gives his blood in turn to Lucy in an attempt to counter the effect of Dracula's equally sexual but much more horrific penetration.

For all of these signs, however, to read the novel simply as reactionary is to do it scant justice. Indeed, the attentive reader can't help but notice how often Stoker either calls attention to or dramatises the way in which an arresting, perhaps even pervasive, irony compromises the actions of the characters. The transfusions for Lucy, for instance, all fail. Not even collectively can their attempted reversals of Dracula's influence save her in the end. What Van Helsing refers to it as 'the grim irony of it all' attends their joint efforts of restoration (p. 146). The men not only change Lucy into the very figure of perversity that they are trying to fight off, but, as Van Helsing illustrates, they also subvert their own moral position: 'Then this so sweet maid is a polyandrist,' reflects the old Professor, 'and me, with my poor wife dead to me, but alive by Church's law, though no wits, all gone – even I, who am faithful husband to this now-no-wife, am bigamist.' (p. 146).[17]

Later, a different, equally disturbing irony also characterises Dracula's initial attack on Mina. The first to learn the secrets of the journals of others, Mina is, for the first time in the novel, excluded from the actions of the group of men. The reason is specifically that she is a woman and so unsuited to such actions, or to the discussions concerning them. As a consequence, however, Mina lies defenceless when Dracula attacks her, for her would-be guardians are at the same time searching for the Count at 'Carfax', his London hideaway. Their need to re-establish traditional gender dichotomies again leads, in other words, to the very thing they wish to prevent. Because of this need, they allow Mina to fall victim to Dracula, and when Harker returns and expresses his concern about his wife's welfare, Stoker victimises him in turn with a stroke of spoken irony: 'I am truly thankful,' Harker says unknowingly, 'that she is to be left out of our future work, and even of our deliberations' (p. 211). Mina, however, rightly, voices the novel's most self-conscious general expression of its ironical view: 'Everything that one does,' she laments, 'seems, no matter how right it might be, to bring on the very thing which is most to be deplored' (p. 214).

Just how central such irony may be to the novel – and to our appreciation of Stoker's (sometimes quite humorous) cultural critique – is dramatised in what might otherwise seem a rather minor incident. Throughout the novel, Stoker presents us with instances when characters are involved in some type of search. Often these searches are searches for ways of physical escape. Their object is therefore a literal key. Harker, for example, searches Dracula's body in an attempt to find the key with which to unlock Dracula's castle and set himself free. Just as often, however,

17 A polyandrist is a woman who is married to more than one man at the same time. She thus represents the female equivalent of a bigamist.

Stoker's searches represent escapes of a different type. Here again, the object of such searches may be a literal key; but in such instances the key in question is also metaphorical. It signifies a clue, the need to discover the meaning of that which is being sought – the desire, more specifically, on the part of all of the protagonists in the novel to unravel the mystery that is Dracula and all he represents. It implies the desire to control the world, to re-right it, to rid it of the perversity Dracula connotes.

And, by the end of the novel, the men, with Mina's help, would seem to discover that metaphorical key. They figure Dracula out. They understand his movements, and, because of this understanding, they find and defeat him. Yet at the very instant when, as Van Helsing observes, they 'in all probable' face 'the *key* [to] the[ir] situation', the men experience a disturbing and generally unnoticed irony that seems once again to qualify their victories and undo their system of belief (p. 243; my emphasis). For in order to gain access into Dracula's home in Piccadilly to destroy the remaining coffins into which the Count may still retire, the erstwhile restorers must employ a locksmith to provide them with a key with which to break into the house. Rather than hide their criminal activity, however, the men decide to conduct their illegal entry during the day and in plain view of passers-by. Yet, in adopting this strategy, they contradict their own rationalist premises. In successfully fooling those who witness their actions, they demonstrate the fallacy of their fundamental belief in the truth of the record of things seen. In being taken for the rightful owners of the house, in other words, in being accepted for what they are not, they become ironically aligned with their enemy. They implicitly expose the potential inadequacy of collective observation, of supposedly clear-sighted reason and scientific proof.

The men thus only superficially succeed with their search. They find their key, in both senses of the word, but only by denying the possibility of any ultimate understanding. In the process of trying to reassert the validity of the discourse of reason and scientific explanation, that is, they cause the opposite. They, not Dracula, now connote the mysterious, rather than the fully known. That which the eye sees, their success demonstrates, provides, in other words, no reliable window to the truth. Subjective interpretation, not objective fact, provides the basis for their victory.

The irony of this scene may, of course, be simply another unconscious joke at Stoker's expense. It may simply represent an artistic oversight. Yet to dismiss it – and Stoker – too easily, whatever our reason, is surely to miss the subtle cultural critique available in the novel's modernist commitment to irony and paradox and ambiguity. It is to overlook evidence of the novel's own moment of potential deconstruction and to dismiss one of the many rhetorical resemblances that complicate the more overt allegiances of the novel. Yet whatever one's views about Stoker's or the novel's final stance towards gender and social change or towards ambiguous sexual roles, which for so many late Victorians symbolised the period's apocalyptic nature; whatever one's final opinion about sources of the novel's greatness or its longevity, *Dracula* remains what it has been for over a century now: a delightfully suspenseful and wonderfully atmospheric (and often surprisingly poetic) novel, a story which, as we enter the new millennium, is still enormous fun to read. It remains a text that continues to teach us, not only about the specific historical time in which it was written, but also, in these days of gender debates, ethnic conflicts and ever more rapid electronic advances, much about our own.

DAVID ROGERS
Principal Lecturer
Kingston University

BIBLIOGRAPHY

Barbara Belford, *Dracula's Secrets: The World of Bram Stoker*, Alfred A. Knopf, New York and Weidenfeld & Nicolson, London 1995; the latest and most reliable of the many biographies on Stoker

Paul V. Barker, *Vampires, Burial and Death: Folklore and Reality*, Yale University Press, New Haven and London 1998

Margaret L. Carter (ed.), *Dracula: The Vampire and the Critics*, UMI Research Press, Ann Arbor 1988; this collection contains many insightful essays.

Gail Cunningham, *The New Woman and the Victorian Novel*, Barnes and Noble, New York 1978

Christopher Craft, 'Kiss Me with Those Red Lips: Gender and Inversion in Bram Stoker's *Dracula*,' *Representations* 8, 1984, 107–33

Marianne DeKoven, *Rich and Strange: Gender, History, Modernism*, Princeton University Press, Princeton 1991; DeKoven does not discuss *Dracula* specifically, but her study implicitly gives a good sense of the way in which the novel anticipates many important developments in modernism.

Bram Dijkstra, *Idols of Perversity: Fantasies of Evil in Fin-de-Siècle Culture*, Oxford University Press, New York 1986

Jonathan Dollimore, *Sexual Dissidence: Augustine to Wilde, Freud to Foucault*, Clarendon Press, Oxford 1991

Linda Dowling, 'The Decadent and the New Woman in the 1890s', *Nineteenth-Century Fiction*, 33, 1979, pp. 434-53

Daniel Farson, *The Man Who Wrote Dracula: A Biography of Bram Stoker*, St Martin's Press, New York 1975

Kate Flint, *The Woman Reader 1837–1914*, Clarendon Press, Oxford 1993

Christopher Frayling, *Vampires: Lord Byron to Count Dracula*, Faber & Faber, London and Boston 1991

Alice Jardine, *Gynesis: Configurations of Woman and Modernity*, Cornell University Press, Ithaca 1985

Clive Leatherdale, *Dracula – The Novel and the Legend: A Study of Bram Stoker's Gothic Masterpiece*, Aquarian Press, Wellingborough, Northamptonshire 1986

Harry Ludlam, *A Biography of Dracula: The Life Story of Bram Stoker*, W. Foulsham & Co. Ltd, London 1962

Raymond T. McNally and Radu Florescu, *In Search of Dracula: A True History of Dracula and the Vampire Legend*, New English Library, London 1975

Elaine Showalter, *Sexual Anarchy: Gender and Culture at the Fin de Siècle*, Bloomsbury, London 1991

David J. Skal, *Hollywood Gothic: The Tangled Web of 'Dracula' from Novel to Stage to Screen*, André Deutsch, London 1990

Montague Summers, *The Vampire in Europe*, Columbia University Press, New York 1968

James B. Twitchell, *The Living Dead: A Study of the Vampire in Romantic Literature*, Duke University Press, Durham, North Carolina 1981

Leonard Wolf (ed.), *The Essential Dracula*, Plume, London 1993

Dracula's Homepage: http://www.ucs.mun.ca/~emiller

Bram Stoker's Homepage: http://userwww.sfsu.edu/~arf/

CONTENTS

How these papers have been placed in sequence will be made manifest in the reading of them. All needless matters have been eliminated, so that a history almost at variance with the possibilites of latter-day belief may stand forth as simple fact. There is throughout no statement of past things wherein memory may err, for all the records chosen are exactly contemporary, given from the stand-points and within the range of knowledge of those who made them.

Chapter 1

JONATHAN HARKER'S JOURNAL (*kept in shorthand*)

3 May. Bistritz.[1] – Left Munich at 8.35 p.m. on 1st May, arriving at Vienna early next morning; should have arrived at 6.46, but train was an hour late. Buda-Pesth[2] seems a wonderful place, from the glimpse which I got of it from the train and the little I could walk through the streets. I feared to go very far from the station, as we had arrived late and would start as near the correct time as possible. The impression I had was that we were leaving the West and entering the East; the most Western of splendid bridges over the Danube,[3] which is here of noble width and depth, took us among the traditions of Turkish rule.

We left in pretty good time, and came after nightfall to Klausenburgh.[4] Here I stopped for the night at the Hotel Royale. I had for dinner, or rather supper, a chicken done up some way with red pepper, which was very good but thirsty. (*Mem.*, get recipe for Mina.) I asked the waiter, and he said it was called *paprika hendl*, and that, as it was a national dish, I should be able to get it anywhere along the Carpathians. I found my smattering of German very useful here; indeed, I don't know how I should be able to get on without it.

Having some time at my disposal when in London, I had visited the British Museum,[5] and made search among the books and maps in the library regarding Transylvania; it had struck me that some foreknowledge of the country could hardly fail to have some importance in dealing with a noble of that country. I find that the district he named is in the extreme east of the country, just on the borders of three states, Transylvania, Moldavia, and Bukovina,[6] in the midst of the Carpathian mountains; one of the wildest and least known portions of Europe. I was not able to light on any map or work giving the exact locality of the Castle Dracula, as there are no maps of this country as yet to compare with our own Ordnance Survey maps;[7] but I found that Bistritz, the post town named by Count Dracula, is a fairly well-known place. I shall enter here some of my notes, as they may refresh my memory when I talk over my travels with Mina.

In the population of Transylvania there are four distinct nationalities: Saxons in the south, and mixed with them the Wallachs, who are the descendants of the Dacians; Magyars in the west, and Szekelys[8] in the east and north. I am going among the latter, who claim to be descended from Attila and the Huns. This may be so, for when the Magyars conquered the country in the eleventh century they found the Huns settled in it. I read that every known superstition in the world is gathered into the horseshoe of the Carpathians, as if it were the centre of some sort of imaginative whirlpool; if so my stay may be very interesting. (*Mem.*, I must ask the Count all about them.)

I did not sleep well, though my bed was comfortable enough, for I had all sorts of queer dreams. There was a dog howling all night under my window, which may have had something to do with it; or it may have been the paprika, for I had to drink up all the water in my carafe, and was still thirsty. Towards morning I slept and was wakened by the continuous knocking at my door, so I guess I must have been sleeping soundly then. I had for breakfast more paprika, and a sort of porridge of maize flour which they said was *mamaliga*, and egg-plant stuffed with forcemeat,[9] a very excellent dish, which they call *impletata*. (*Mem.*, get recipe for this also.) I had to hurry breakfast, for the train started a little before eight, or rather it ought to have done so, for after rushing to the station at 7.30 I had to sit in the carriage for more than an hour before we began to move. It seems to me that the further East you go the more unpunctual are the trains. What ought they to be in China?

All day long we seemed to dawdle through a country which was full of beauty of every kind. Sometimes we saw little towns or castles on the top of steep hills such as we see in old missals; sometimes we ran by rivers and streams which seemed from the wide stony margin on each side of them to be subject to great floods. It takes a lot of water, and running strong, to sweep the outside edge of a river clear. At every station there were groups of people, sometimes crowds, and in all sorts of attire. Some of them were just like the peasants at home or those I saw coming through France and Germany, with short jackets and round hats and home-made trousers; but others were very picturesque. The women looked pretty, except when you got near them, but they were very clumsy about the waist. They had all full white sleeves of some kind or other, and most of them had big belts with a lot of strips of something fluttering from them like the dresses in a ballet, but of course petticoats under them. The strangest figures we saw were the Slovaks, who are more barbarian than the rest, with their big cowboy hats, great baggy dirty-white trousers, white linen shirts, and enormous heavy leather belts, nearly a foot wide, all studded over with brass nails. They wore high boots, with their trousers tucked into them, and had long black hair and heavy black moustaches. They are very picturesque, but do not look prepossessing. On the stage they would be set down at once as some old Oriental band of brigands. They are, however, I am told, very harmless and rather wanting in natural self-assertion.

It was on the dark side of twilight when we got to Bistritz, which is a very interesting old place. Being practically on the frontier – for the Borgo Pass leads from it into Bukovina – it has had a very stormy existence, and it certainly shows marks of it. Fifty years ago a series of great fires took place, which made terrible havoc on five separate occasions. At the very beginning of the seventeenth century it underwent a siege of three weeks and lost 13,000 people, the casualties of war proper being assisted by famine and disease.

Count Dracula had directed me to go to the Golden Krone Hotel, which I found, to my great delight, to be thoroughly old-fashioned, for of course I wanted to see all I could of the ways of the country. I was evidently expected, for when I got near the door I faced a cheery-looking elderly woman in the usual peasant dress – white undergarment with long double apron, front, and back, of coloured stuff fitting almost too tight for modesty. When I came close she bowed, and said: 'The Herr Englishman?' 'Yes,' I said, 'Jonathan Harker.' She smiled, and gave some message to an elderly man in white shirt-sleeves, who had followed her to the door. He went, but immediately returned with a letter:

MY FRIEND, – Welcome to the Carpathians. I am anxiously expecting you. Sleep well tonight. At three tomorrow the diligence will start for Bukovina; a place on it is kept for you. At the Borgo Pass my carriage will await you and will bring you to me. I trust that your journey from London has been a happy one, and that you will enjoy your stay in my beautiful land. –

Your friend,

DRACULA.

4 May. – I found that my landlord had got a letter from the Count, directing him to secure the best place on the coach for me; but on making inquiries as to details he seemed somewhat reticent, and pretended that he could not understand my German. This could not be true, because up to then he had understood it perfectly; at least, he answered my questions exactly as if he did. He and his wife, the old lady who had received me, looked at each other in a frightened sort of way. He mumbled out that the money had been sent in a letter, and that was all he knew. When I asked him if he knew Count Dracula, and could tell me anything of his castle, both he and his wife crossed themselves, and, saying that they knew nothing at all, simply refused to speak further. It was so near the time of starting that I had no time to ask anyone else, for it was all very mysterious and not by any means comforting.

Just before I was leaving, the old lady came up to my room and said in a very hysterical way:

'Must you go? Oh! young Herr, must you go?' She was in such an excited state that she seemed to have lost her grip of what German she knew, and mixed it all up with some other language which I did not know at all. I was just able to follow her by asking many questions. When I told her that I must go at once, and that I was engaged on important business, she asked again:

'Do you know what day it is?' I answered that it was the fourth of May. She shook her head as she said again:

'Oh, yes! I know that, I know that! but do you know what day it is?' On my saying that I did not understand, she went on:

'It is the eve of St George's Day. Do you not know that tonight when the clock strikes midnight, all the evil things in the world will have full sway? Do you know where you are going, and what you are going to?' She was in such evident distress that I tried to comfort her, but without effect. Finally she went down on her knees and implored me not to go; at least to wait a day or two before starting. It was all very ridiculous, but I did not feel comfortable. However, there was business to be done, and I could allow nothing to interfere with it. I therefore tried to raise her up, and said, as gravely as I could, that I thanked her, but my duty was imperative, and that I must go. She then rose and dried her eyes, and taking a crucifix from her neck offered it to me. I did not know what to do, for, as an English Churchman,[10] I have been taught to regard such things as in some measure idolatrous, and yet it seemed so ungracious to refuse an old lady meaning so well and in such a state of mind. She saw, I suppose, the doubt in my face, for she put the rosary round my neck, and said, 'For your mother's sake,' and went out of the room. I am writing up this part of the diary whilst I am waiting for the coach, which is, of course, late; and the crucifix is still round my neck. Whether it is the old lady's fear, I do not know, but I am not feeling nearly as easy in my mind as usual. If this book should ever reach Mina before I do, let it bring my good-bye. Here comes the coach!

5 May. – The Castle – The grey of the morning has passed and the sun is high over the distant horizon which seems jagged, whether with trees or hills I know not, for it is so far off that big things and little are

mixed. I am not sleepy, and, as I am not to be called till I awake, naturally I write till sleep comes. There are many odd things to put down, and, lest who reads them may fancy that I dined too well before I left Bistritz, let me put down my dinner exactly. I dined on what they call 'robber steak' – bits of bacon, onion, and beef, seasoned with red pepper, and strung on sticks and roasted over the fire, in the simple style of the London cat's-meat! The wine was Golden Mediasch, which produces a queer sting on the tongue, which is, however, not disagreeable. I had only a couple of glasses of this, and nothing else.

When I got on the coach the driver had not taken his seat, and I saw him talking with the landlady. They were evidently talking of me, for every now and then they looked at me, and some of the people who were sitting on the bench outside the door – which they call by a name meaning 'word-bearer' – came and listened, and then looked at me, most of them pityingly. I could hear a lot of words often repeated, queer words, for there were many nationalities in the crowd; so I quietly got my polyglot dictionary from my bag and looked them out. I must say they were not cheering to me, for amongst them were *Ordog* – Satan, *pokol* – hell, *stregoica* – witch, *vrolok* and *vlkoslak* – both of which mean the same thing, one being Slovak and the other Servian for something that is either were-wolf or vampire. (*Mem.*, I must ask the Count about these superstitions.)

When we started, the crowd round the inn door, which had by this time swelled to a considerable size, all made the sign of the cross and pointed two fingers towards me. With some difficulty I got a fellow-passenger to tell me what they meant; he would not answer at first, but on learning that I was English, he explained that it was a charm or guard against the evil eye. This was not very pleasant for me, just starting for an unknown place to meet an unknown man; but everyone seemed so kind-hearted, and so sorrowful, and so sympathetic that I could not but be touched. I shall never forget the last glimpse which I had of the inn-yard and its crowd of picturesque figures, all crossing themselves, as they stood round the wide archway, with its background of rich foliage of oleander and orange trees in green tubs clustered in the centre of the yard. Then our driver, whose wide linen drawers covered the whole front of the box-seat – *gotza* they call them – cracked his big whip over his four small horses, which ran abreast, and we set off on our journey.

I soon lost sight and recollection of ghostly fears in the beauty of the scene as we drove along, although had I known the language, or rather languages, which my fellow-passengers were speaking, I might not have been able to throw them off so easily. Before us lay a green sloping land full of forests and woods, with here and there steep hills, crowned with clumps of trees or with farmhouses, the blank gable end to the road. There was everywhere a bewildering mass of fruit blossom – apple, plum, pear, cherry; and as we drove by I could see the green grass under the trees spangled with the fallen petals. In and out amongst these green hills of what they call here the 'Mittel Land' ran the road, losing itself as it swept round the grassy curve, or was shut out by the straggling ends of pine woods, which here and there ran down the hillsides like tongues of flame. The road was rugged, but still we seemed to fly over it with a feverish haste. I could not understand then what the haste meant, but the driver was evidently bent on losing no time in reaching Borgo Prund.[11] I was told that this road is in summer-time excellent, but that it had not yet been put in order after the winter snows. In this respect it is different from the general run of roads in the Carpathians, for it is an old tradition that they are not to be kept in too good order. Of old the Hospadars[12] would not repair them, lest the Turk should think that they were preparing to bring in foreign troops, and so hasten the war which was always really at loading point.

Beyond the green swelling hills of the Mittel Land rose mighty slopes of forest up to the lofty steeps of the Carpathians themselves. Right and left of us they towered, with the afternoon sun falling full upon them and bringing out all the glorious colours of this beautiful range, deep blue and purple in the shadows of the peaks, green and brown where grass and rock mingled, and an endless perspective of jagged rock and pointed crags, till these were themselves lost in the distance, where the snowy peaks rose grandly. Here and there seemed mighty rifts in the mountains, through which, as the sun began to sink, we saw now and again the white gleam of falling water. One of my companions touched my arm as we swept round the base of a hill and opened up the lofty, snow-covered peak of a mountain, which seemed, as we wound on our serpentine way, to be right before us:

'Look! *Isten szek!*' – 'God's seat!' – and he crossed himself reverently. As we wound on our endless way, and the sun sank lower and lower behind us, the shadows of the evening began to creep round us. This was emphasised by the fact that the snowy mountain-top still held the sunset, and seemed to glow out with a delicate cool pink. Here and there we passed Cszeks and Slovaks, all in picturesque attire, but I noticed that goitre was painfully prevalent. By the roadside were many crosses, and as we swept by, my companions all crossed themselves. Here and there was a peasant man or woman kneeling before a shrine, who did not even turn round as we approached, but seemed in the self-surrender of devotion to have neither eyes nor ears for the outer world. There were many things new to me: for instance, hay-ricks in the trees, and here and there very beautiful masses of weeping birch, their white stems shining like silver through the delicate green of the leaves. Now and again we passed a *leiterwagon* – the ordinary peasant's cart, with its long, snake-like vertebra, calculated to suit the inequalities of the road. On this were sure to be seated quite a group of home-coming peasants, the Cszeks with their white, and the Slovaks with their coloured, sheepskins, the latter carrying lance-fashion their long staves, with axe at end. As the evening fell it began to get very cold, and the growing twilight seemed to merge into one dark mistiness the gloom of the trees, oak, beech, and pine, though in the valleys which ran deep between the spurs of the hills, as we ascended through the Pass, the dark firs stood out here and there against the background of late-lying snow. Sometimes, as the road was cut through the pine woods that seemed in the darkness to be closing down upon us, great masses of greyness, which here and there bestrewed the trees, produced a peculiarly weird and solemn effect, which carried on the thoughts and grim fancies engendered earlier in the evening, when the falling sunset threw into strange relief the ghost-like clouds which amongst the Carpathians seem to wind ceaselessly through the valleys. Sometimes the hills were so steep that, despite our driver's haste, the horses could only go slowly. I wished to get down and walk up them, as we do at home, but the driver would not hear of it. 'No, no,' he said; 'you must not walk here; the dogs are too fierce,' and then he added, with what he evidently meant for grim pleasantry – for he looked round to catch the approving smile of the rest – 'and you may have enough of such matters before you go to sleep.' The only stop he would make was a moment's pause to light his lamps.

When it grew dark there seemed to be some excitement amongst the passengers, and they kept speaking to him, one after the other, as though urging him to further speed. He lashed the horses unmercifully with his long whip, and with wild cries of encouragement urged them on to further exertions. Then through the darkness I could see a sort of patch of grey light ahead of us, as though there were a cleft in the hills. The excitement of the passengers grew greater; the crazy coach rocked on its great leather springs, and swayed like a boat tossed on a stormy sea. I had to hold on. The road grew more level, and we appeared to fly along. Then the mountains seemed to come nearer to us on each side and to frown down upon us; we were entering the Borgo Pass. One by one several of the passengers offered me gifts, which they pressed upon me with an earnestness which would take no denial; these were certainly of an odd and varied kind, but each was given in simple good faith, with a kindly word, and a blessing, and that strange mixture of fear-meaning movements which I had seen outside the hotel at Bistritz – the sign of the cross and the guard against the evil eye. Then, as we flew along, the driver leaned forward, and on each side the passengers, craning over the edge of the coach, peered eagerly into the darkness. It was evident that something very exciting was either happening or expected, but though I asked each passenger, no one would give me the slightest explanation. This state of excitement kept on for some little time; and at last we saw before us the Pass opening out on the eastern side. There were dark, rolling clouds overhead, and in the air the heavy, oppressive sense of thunder. It seemed as though the mountain range had separated two atmospheres, and that now we had got into the thunderous one. I was now myself looking out for the conveyance which was to take me to the Count. Each moment I expected to see the glare of lamps through the blackness; but all was dark. The only light was the flickering rays of our own lamps, in which steam from our hard-driven hoses rose in a white cloud. We could now see the sandy road lying white before us, but there was on it no sign of a vehicle. The passengers drew back with a sigh of gladness, which seemed to mock my own disappointment. I was already thinking what I had best do, when the driver, looking at his watch, said to the others something which I could hardly hear, it was spoken so quietly and in so low a tone; I thought it was, 'An hour less than the time.' Then, turning to me, he said in German worse than my own:

'There is no carriage here. The Herr is not expected, after all. He will now come on to Bukovina, and return tomorrow or the next day; better the next day.' Whilst he was speaking the horses began to neigh and snort and plunge wildly, so that the driver had to hold them up. Then, amongst a chorus of screams from the peasants and a universal crossing of themselves, a calèche, with four horses, drove up behind us, overtook us, and drew up beside the coach. I could see from the flash of our lamps, as the rays fell on them, that the horses were coal-black and splendid animals. They were driven by a tall man, with a long brown beard and a great black hat, which seemed to hide his face from us. I could only see the gleam of a pair of very bright eyes, which seemed red in the lamplight, as he turned to us. He said to the driver:

'You are early tonight, my friend.' The man stammered in reply:

'The English Herr was in a hurry,' to which the stranger replied:

'That is why, I suppose, you wished him to go on to Bukovina. You cannot deceive me, my friend; I know too much, and my horses are swift.' As he spoke he smiled, and the lamplight fell on a hard-looking mouth, with very red lips and sharp-looking teeth, as white as ivory. One of my companions whispered to another the line from Burger's *Lenore*:

> *Denn die Todten*[13] *reiten schnell. –*
> (For the dead travel fast.)

The strange driver evidently heard the words, for he looked up with a gleaming smile. The passenger turned his face away, at the same time putting out his two fingers and crossing himself. 'Give me the Herr's luggage,' said the driver; and with exceeding alacrity my bags were handed out and put in the calèche. Then I descended from the side of the coach, as the calèche was close alongside, the driver helping me with a hand which caught my arm in a grip of steel; his strength must have been prodigious. Without a word he shook his reins, the horses turned, and we swept into the darkness of the Pass. As I looked back I saw the steam from the horses of the coach by the light of the lamps, and projected against it the figures of my late companions crossing themselves. Then the driver cracked his whip and called to his horses, and off they swept on their way to Bukovina.

As they sank into the darkness I felt a strange chill, and a lonely feeling came over me; but a cloak was thrown over my shoulders, and a rug across my knees, and the driver said in excellent German:

'The night is chill, mein Herr, and my master the Count bade me take all care of you. There is a flask of *slivovitz* [the plum brandy of the country] underneath the seat, if you should require it.' I did not take any, but it was a comfort to know it was there, all the same. I felt a little strangely, and not a little frightened. I think had there been any alternative I should have taken it, instead of prosecuting that unknown night journey. The carriage went at a hard pace straight along, then we made a complete turn and went along another straight road. It seemed to me that we were simply going over and over the same ground again; and so I took note of some salient point, and found that this was so. I would have liked to have asked the driver what this all meant, but I really feared to do so, for I thought that, placed as I was, any protest would have had no effect in case there had been an intention to delay. By and by, however, as I was curious to know how time was passing, I struck a match, and by its flame looked at my watch; it was within a few minutes of midnight. This gave me a sort of shock, for I suppose the general superstition about midnight was increased by my recent experiences. I waited with a sick feeling of suspense.

Then a dog began to howl somewhere in a farmhouse far down the
road – a long, agonised wailing, as if from fear, The sound was taken up
by another dog, and then another and another, till, borne on the wind
which now sighed softly through the Pass, a wild howling began, which
seemed to come from all over the country, as far as the imagination
could grasp it through the gloom of the night. At the first howl the
horses began to strain and rear, but the driver spoke to them soothingly,
and they quieted down, but shivered and sweated as though after a
runaway from sudden fright. Then, far off in the distance, from the
mountains on each side of us began a louder and a sharper howling –
that of wolves – which affected both the horses and myself in the same
way – for I was minded to jump from the calèche and run, whilst they
reared again and plunged madly, so that the driver had to use all his
great strength to keep them from bolting. In a few minutes, however,
my own ears got accustomed to the sound, and the horses so far became
quiet that the driver was able to descend and to stand before them. He
petted and soothed them, and whispered something in their ears, as I
have heard of horse-tamers doing, and with extraordinary effect, for
under his caresses they became quite manageable again, though they
still trembled. The driver again took his seat, and shaking his reins,
started off at a great pace. This time, after going to the far side of the
Pass, he suddenly turned down a narrow roadway which ran sharply to
the right.

Soon we were hemmed in with trees, which in places arched right
over the roadway till we passed as through a tunnel; and again great
frowning rocks guarded us boldly on either side. Though we were in
shelter, we could hear the rising wind, for it moaned and whistled
through the rocks, and the branches of the trees crashed together as we
swept along. It grew colder and colder still, and fine, powdery snow
began to fall, so that soon we and all around us were covered with a
white blanket. The keen wind still carried the howling of the dogs,
though this grew fainter as we went on our way. The baying of the
wolves sounded nearer and nearer, as though they were closing round
on us from every side. I grew dreadfully afraid, and the horses shared
my fear; but the driver was not in the least disturbed. He kept turning
his head to left and right, but I could not see anything through the
darkness.

Suddenly, away on our left, I saw a faint flickering blue flame.[14] The
driver saw it at the same moment; he at once checked the horses and,
jumping to the ground, disappeared into the darkness. I did not know
what to do, the less as the howling of the wolves grew closer; but while I

wondered the driver suddenly appeared again, and without a word took his seat, and we resumed our journey. I think I must have fallen asleep and kept dreaming of the incident, for it seemed to be repeated endlessly, and now, looking back, it is like a sort of awful nightmare. Once the flame appeared so near the road that even in the darkness around us I could watch the driver's motions. He went rapidly to where the blue flame arose – it must have been very faint, for it did not seem to illumine the place around it at all – and gathering a few stones, formed them into some device. Once there appeared a strange optical effect: when he stood between me and the flame he did not obstruct it, for I could see its ghostly flicker all the same. This startled me, but as the effect was only momentary, I took it that my eyes deceived me straining through the darkness. Then for a time there were no blue flames, and we sped onwards through the gloom, with the howling of the wolves around us, as though they were following in a moving circle.

At last there came a time when the driver went further afield than he had yet gone, and during his absence the horses began to tremble worse than ever and to snort and scream with fright. I could not see any cause for it, for the howling of the wolves had ceased altogether; but just then the moon, sailing through the black clouds, appeared behind the jagged crest of a beetling, pine-clad rock, and by its light I saw around us a ring of wolves, with white teeth and lolling red tongues, with long, sinewy limbs and shaggy hair. They were a hundred times more terrible in the grim silence which held them than even when they howled. For myself, I felt a sort of paralysis of fear. It is only when a man feels himself face to face with such horrors that he can understand their true import.

All at once the wolves began to howl as though the moonlight had had some peculiar effect on them. The horses jumped about and reared, and looked helplessly round with eyes that rolled in a way painful to see; but the living ring of terror encompassed them on every side, and they had perforce to remain within it. I called to the coachman to come, for it seemed to me that our only chance was to try to break out through the ring and to aid his approach. I shouted and beat the side of the calèche, hoping by the noise to scare the wolves from that side, so as to give him a chance of reaching the trap. How he came there, I know not, but I heard his voice raised in a tone of imperious command, and looking towards the sound, saw him stand in the roadway. As he swept his long arms, as though brushing aside some impalpable obstacle, the wolves fell back and back further still. Just then a heavy cloud passed across the face of the moon, so that we were again in darkness.

When I could see again the driver was climbing into the calèche, and the wolves had disappeared. This was all so strange and uncanny that a dreadful fear came upon me, and I was afraid to speak or move. The time seemed interminable as we swept on our way, now in almost complete darkness, for the rolling clouds obscured the moon. We kept on ascending, with occasional periods of quick descent, but in the main always ascending. Suddenly I became conscious of the fact that the driver was in the act of pulling up the horses in the courtyard of a vast ruined castle, from whose tall black windows came no ray of light, and whose broken battlements showed a jagged line against the moonlit sky.

Chapter 2

JONATHAN HARKER'S JOURNAL (continued)

5 May. – I must have been asleep, for certainly if I had been fully awake I must have noticed the approach to such a remarkable place. In the gloom the courtyard looked of considerable size, and as several dark ways led from it under great round arches it perhaps seemed bigger than it really is. I have not yet been able to see it by daylight.

When the calèche stopped the driver jumped down, and held out his hand to assist me to alight. Again I could not but notice his prodigious strength. His hand actually seemed like a steel vice that could have crushed mine if he had chosen. Then he took out my traps, and placed them on the ground beside me as I stood close to a great door, old and studded with large iron nails, and set in a projecting doorway of massive stone. I could see even in the dim light that the stone was massively carved, but that the carving had been much worn by time and weather. As I stood, the driver jumped again into his seat and shook the reins; the horses started forward, and trap and all disappeared down one of the dark openings.

I stood in silence where I was, for I did not know what to do. Of bell or knocker there was no sign; through these frowning walls and dark window openings it was not likely that my voice could penetrate. The time I waited seemed endless, and I felt doubts and fears crowding upon me. What sort of place had I come to, and among what kind of people? What sort of grim adventure was it on which I had embarked? Was this a customary incident in the life of a solicitor's[15] clerk sent out to explain the purchase of a London estate to a foreigner? Solicitor's clerk! Mina would not like that. Solicitor – for just before leaving London I got word that my examination was successful; and I am now a full-blown solicitor! I began to rub my eyes and pinch myself to see if I were awake. It all seemed like a horrible nightmare to me, and I expected that I should suddenly awake, and find myself at home, with the dawn struggling in through the windows, as I had now and again felt in the morning after a day of overwork. But my flesh answered the pinching test, and my eyes were not to be deceived. I was indeed awake and among the Carpathians. All I could do now was to be patient, and to wait the coming of the morning.

Just as I had come to this conclusion I heard a heavy step approaching behind the great door, and saw through the chinks the gleam of a coming light. Then there was the sound of rattling chains and the clanking of massive bolts drawn back. A key was turned with the loud grating noise of long disuse, and the great door swung back.

Within, stood a tall old man, clean-shaven save for a long white moustache, and clad in black from head to foot, without a single speck of colour about him anywhere. He held in his hand an antique silver lamp, in which the flame burned without chimney or globe of any kind, throwing long, quivering shadows as it flickered in the draught of the open door. The old man motioned me in with his right hand with a courtly gesture, saying in excellent English, but with a strange intonation:

'Welcome to my house! Enter freely and of your own will!' He made no motion of stepping to meet me, but stood like a statue, as though his gesture of welcome had fixed him into stone. The instant, however, that I had stepped over the threshold, he moved impulsively forward, and holding out his hand grasped mine with a strength which made me wince, an effect which was not lessened by the fact that it seemed as cold as ice – more like the hand of a dead than a living man. Again he said:

'Welcome to my house. Come freely. Go safely. And leave something of the happiness you bring!' The strength of the handshake was so much akin to that which I had noticed in the driver, whose face I had not seen, that for a moment I doubted if it were not the same person to whom I was speaking; so, to make sure, I said interrogatively:

'Count Dracula?' He bowed in a courtly way as he replied:

'I am Dracula. And I bid you welcome, Mr Harker, to my house. Come in; the night air is chill, and you must need to eat and rest.' As he was speaking he put the lamp on a bracket on the wall, and stepping out, took my luggage; he had carried it in before I could forestall him. I protested, but he insisted:

'Nay, sir, you are my guest. It is late, and my people are not available. Let me see to your comfort myself.' He insisted on carrying my traps along the passage, and then up a great winding stair, and along another great passage, on whose stone floor our steps rang heavily. At the end of this he threw open a heavy door, and I rejoiced to see within a well-lit room in which a table was spread for supper, and on whose mighty hearth a great fire of logs flamed and flared.

The Count halted, putting down my bags, closed the door, and crossing the room, opened another door, which led into a small octagonal room lit by a single lamp, and seemingly without a window of any sort. Passing through this, he opened another door, and motioned me to enter. It was a welcome sight; for here was a great bedroom well lighted and warmed with another log fire, which sent a hollow roar up the wide chimney. The Count himself left my luggage inside and withdrew, saying, before he closed the door:

'You will need, after your journey, to refresh yourself by making your toilet. I trust you will find all you wish. When you are ready come into the other room, where you will find your supper prepared.'

The light and warmth and the Count's courteous welcome seemed to have dissipated all my doubts and fears. Having then reached my normal state, I discovered that I was half-famished with hunger; so making a hasty toilet, I went into the other room.

I found supper already laid out. My host, who stood on one side of the great fireplace, leaning against the stone-work, made a graceful wave of his hand to the table, and said:

'I pray you, be seated and sup how you please. You will, I trust, excuse me that I do not join you; but I have dined already, and I do not sup.'

I handed to him the sealed letter which Mr Hawkins had entrusted to me. He opened it and read it gravely; then, with a charming smile, he handed it to me to read. One passage of it, at least, gave me a thrill of pleasure:

I much regret that an attack of gout, from which malady I am a constant sufferer, forbids absolutely any travelling on my part for some time to come; but I am happy to say I can send a sufficient substitute, one in whom I have every possible confidence. He is a young man, full of energy and talent in his own way, and of a very faithful disposition. He is discreet and silent, and has grown into manhood in my service. He shall be ready to attend on you when you will during his stay, and shall take your instructions in all matters.

The Count himself came forward and took off the cover of a dish, and

I fell to at once on an excellent roast chicken. This, with some cheese and a salad and a bottle of old Tokay,[16] of which I had two glasses, was my supper. During the time I was eating it the Count asked me many questions as to my journey, and I told him by degrees all I had experienced.

By this time I had finished my supper, and by my host's desire had drawn up a chair by the fire and begun to smoke a cigar which he offered me, at the same time excusing himself that he did not smoke. I had now an opportunity of observing him, and found him of a very marked physiognomy.

His face was a strong – a very strong – aquiline, with high bridge of the thin nose and peculiarly arched nostrils; with lofty domed forehead, and hair growing scantily round the temples, but profusely elsewhere. His eyebrows were very massive, almost meeting over the nose, and with bushy hair that seemed to curl in its own profusion. The mouth, so far as I could see it under the heavy moustache, was fixed and rather cruel-looking, with peculiarly sharp white teeth; these protruded over the lips, whose remarkable ruddiness showed astonishing vitality in a man of his years. For the rest, his ears were pale and at the tops extremely pointed; the chin was broad and strong, and the cheeks firm though thin. The general effect was one of extraordinary pallor.

Hitherto I had noticed the backs of his hands as they lay on his knees in the firelight, and they had seemed rather white and fine; but seeing them now close to me, I could not but notice that they were rather coarse – broad, with squat fingers. Strange to say, there were hairs in the centre of the palm. The nails were long and fine, and cut to a sharp point. As the Count leaned over me and his hands touched me, I could not repress a shudder. It may have been that his breath was rank, but a horrible feeling of nausea came over me, which, do what I would, I could not conceal. The Count, evidently noticing it, drew back; and with a grim sort of smile, which showed more than he had yet done his protuberant teeth, sat himself down again on his own side of the fireplace. We were both silent for a while; and as I looked towards the window I saw the first dim streak of the coming dawn. There seemed a strange stillness over everything; but as I listened I heard, as if from down below in the valley, the howling of many wolves. The Count's eyes gleamed, and he said:

'Listen to them – the children of the night. What music they make!' Seeing, I suppose, some expression in my face strange to him, he added:

'Ah, sir, you dwellers in the city cannot enter into the feelings of the hunter.' Then he rose and said:

'But you must be tired. Your bedroom is all ready, and tomorrow you shall sleep as late as you will. I have to be away till the afternoon; so sleep well and dream well!' and, with a courteous bow, he opened for me himself the door to the octagonal room, and I entered my bedroom . . .

I am all in a sea of wonders. I doubt; I fear; I think strange things which I dare not confess to my own soul. God keep me, if only for the sake of those dear to me!

7 *May.* – It is again early morning, but I have rested and enjoyed the last twenty-four hours. I slept till late in the day, and awoke of my own accord. When I had dressed myself I went into the room where we had supped, and found a cold breakfast laid out, with coffee kept hot by the pot being placed on the hearth. There was a card on the table, on which was written:

'I have to be absent for a while. Do not wait for me. – D.' So I set to and enjoyed a hearty meal. When I had done, I looked for a bell, so that I might let the servants know I had finished – but I could not find one. There are certainly odd deficiencies in the house, considering the extraordinary evidences of wealth which are round me. The table service is of gold, and so beautifully wrought that it must be of immense value. The curtains and upholstery of the chairs and sofas and the hangings of my bed are of the costliest and most beautiful fabrics, and must have been of fabulous value when they were made, for they are centuries old, though in excellent order. I saw something like them in Hampton Court,[17] but there they were worn and frayed and moth-eaten. But still in none of the rooms is there a mirror. There is not even a toilet glass on my table, and I had to get the little shaving-glass from my bag before I could either shave or brush my hair. I have not yet seen a servant anywhere, or heard a sound near the castle except the howling of wolves. When I had finished my meal – I do not know whether to call it breakfast or dinner, for it was between five and six o'clock when I had it – I looked about for something to read, for I did not like to go about the castle until I had asked the Count's permission. There was absolutely nothing in the room, book, newspaper, or even writing materials; so I opened another door in the room and found a sort of library. The door opposite mine I tried, but found it locked.

In the library I found, to my great delight, a vast number of English books, whole shelves full of them, and bound volumes of magazines and newspapers. A table in the centre was littered with English magazines and newspapers, though none of them were of very recent date. The books were of the most varied kind – history, geography, politics, political economy, botany, geology, law – all relating to England and

English life and customs and manners. There were even such books of reference as the *London Directory*, the 'Red' and 'Blue' books, *Whitaker's Almanack*, the Army and Navy Lists, and – it somehow gladdened my heart to see it – the Law List.[18]

Whilst I was looking at the books, the door opened, and the Count entered. He saluted me in a hearty way, and hoped that I had had a good night's rest. Then he went on:

'I am glad you found your way in here, for I am sure there is much that will interest you. These friends' – and he laid his hand on some of the books – 'have been good friends to me and for some years past, ever since I had the idea of going to London, have given me many, many hours of pleasure. Through them I have come to know your great England; and to know her is to love her. I long to go through the crowded streets of your mighty London, to be in the midst of the whirl and rush of humanity, to share its life, its change, its death, and all that makes it what it is. But alas! as yet I only know your tongue through books. To you, my friend, I look that I know it to speak.'

'But, Count,' I said, 'you know and speak English thoroughly!' He bowed gravely.

'I thank you, my friend, for your all too flattering estimate, but yet I fear that I am but a little way on the road I would travel. True, I know the grammar and the words, but yet I know not how to speak them.'

'Indeed,' I said, 'you speak excellently.'

'Not so,' he answered. 'Well I know that, did I move and speak in your London, none there are who would not know me for a stranger. That is not enough for me. Here I am noble; I am *boyar*; [19]the common people know me, and I am master. But a stranger in a strange land,[20] he is no one; men know him not – and to know not is to care not for. I am content if I am like the rest, so that no man stops if he see me, or pause in his speaking if he hear my words, to say, "Ha, ha! a stranger!" I have been so long master that I would be master still – or at least that none other should be master of me. You come to me not alone as agent of my friend Peter Hawkins, of Exeter, to tell me all about my new estate in London. You shall, I trust, rest here with me a while, so that by our talking I may learn the English intonation; and I would that you tell me when I make error, even of the smallest, in my speaking. I am sorry that I had to be away so long today; but you will, I know, forgive one who has so many important affairs in hand.'

Of course I said all I could about being willing, and asked if I might come into that room when I chose. He answered: 'Yes, certainly,' and added:

'You may go anywhere you wish in the castle, except where the doors are locked, where of course you will not wish to go. There is reason that all things are as they are, and did you see with my eyes and know with my knowledge, you would perhaps better understand.' I said I was sure of this, and then he went on:

'We are in Transylvania; and Transylvania is not England. Our ways are not your ways, and there shall be to you many strange things. Nay, from what you have told me of your experiences already, you know something of what strange things here may be.'

This led to much conversation. And as it was evident that he wanted to talk, if only for talking's sake, I asked him many questions regarding things that had already happened to me or come within my notice. Sometimes he sheered off the subject, or turned the conversation by pretending not to understand; but generally he answered all I asked most frankly. Then as time went on, and I had got somewhat bolder, I asked him of some of the strange things of the preceding night, as, for instance, why the coachman went to the places where we had seen the blue flames. Was it indeed true that they showed where gold was hidden? He then explained to me that it was commonly believed that on a certain night of the year – last night, in fact, when all evil spirits are supposed to have unchecked sway – a blue flame is seen over any place where treasure has been concealed. 'That treasure has been hidden,' he went on, 'in the region through which you came last night, there can be but little doubt; for it was the ground fought over for centuries by the Wallachian, the Saxon, and the Turk. Why, there is hardly a foot of soil in all this region that has not been enriched by the blood of men, patriots or invaders. In old days there were stirring times, when the Austrian and the Hungarian came up in hordes, and the patriots went out to meet them – men and women, the aged and the children too – and waited their coming on the rocks above the passes, that they might sweep destruction on them with their artificial avalanches.[21] When the invader was triumphant he found but little, for whatever there was had been sheltered in the friendly soil.'

'But how,' said I, 'can it have remained so long undiscovered, when there is a sure index to it if men will but take the trouble to look?' The Count smiled, and as his lips ran back over his gums, the long, sharp, canine teeth showed out strangely; he answered:

'Because your peasant is at heart a coward and a fool! Those flames only appear on one night. And on that night no man of this land will, if he can help it, stir without his doors. And, dear sir, even if he did he would not know what to do. Why, even the peasant that you tell me of who marked the place of the flame would not know where to look in daylight even for his own work. You would not, I dare be sworn, be able to find these places again?'

'There you are right,' I said. 'I know no more than the dead where even to look for them.' Then we drifted into other matters.

'Come,' he said at last, 'tell me of London and of the house which you have procured for me.' With an apology for my remissness, I went into my own room to get the papers from my bag. Whilst I was placing them in order I heard a rattling of china and silver in the next room, and as I passed through, noticed that the table had been cleared and the lamp lit, for it was by this time deep into the dark. The lamps were also lit in the study or library, and I found the Count lying on the sofa, reading, of all things in the world, an English *Bradshaw's Guide*.[22] When I came in he cleared the books and papers from the table; and with him I went into plans and deeds and figures of all sorts. He was interested in everything, and asked me a myriad questions about the place and its surroundings. He clearly had studied beforehand all he could get on the subject of the neighbourhood, for he evidently at the end knew very much more than I did. When I remarked this, he answered:

'Well, but, my friend, is it not needful that I should? When I go there I shall be all alone, and my friend Harker Jonathan – nay, pardon me, I fall into my country's habit of putting your patronymic first – my friend Jonathan Harker will not be by my side to correct and aid me. He will be in Exeter, miles away, probably working at papers of the law with my other friend, Peter Hawkins. So!'

We went thoroughly into the business of the purchase of the estate at Purfleet.[23] When I had told him the facts and got his signature to the necessary papers, and had written a letter with them ready to post to Mr Hawkins, he began to ask me how I had come across so suitable a place. I read to him the notes which I had made at the time, and which I inscribe here:

'At Purfleet, on a by-road, I came across just such a place as seemed to be required, and where was displayed a dilapidated notice that the place was for sale. It is surrounded by a high wall, of ancient structure, built of heavy stones, and has not been repaired for a large number of years. The closed gates were of heavy old oak and iron, all eaten with rust.

'The estate is called Carfax, no doubt a corruption of the old *Quatre Face*, as the house is four-sided, agreeing with the cardinal points of the compass. It contains in all some twenty acres, quite surrounded by the solid stone wall above mentioned. There are many trees on it, which make it in places gloomy, and there is a deep, dark-looking pond or small lake, evidently fed by some springs, as the water is clear and flows away in a fair-sized stream. The house is very large and of all periods back, I should say, to mediæval times, for one part is of stone immensely thick, with only a few windows high up and heavily barred with iron. It looks like part of a keep, and is close to an old chapel or church. I could not enter it, as I had not the key of the door leading to it from the house, but I have taken with my Kodak[24] views of it from various points. The house has been added to, but in a very straggling way, and I can only guess at the amount of ground it covers, which must be very great. There are but few houses close at hand, one being a very large house only recently added to and formed into a private lunatic asylum. It is not, however, visible from the grounds.'

When I had finished, he said:

'I am glad that it is old and big. I myself am of an old family, and to live in a new house would kill me. A house cannot be made habitable in a day; and, after all, how few days go to make up a century. I rejoice also that there is a chapel of old times. We Transylvanian nobles love not to think that our bones may be amongst the common dead. I seek not gaiety nor mirth, not the bright voluptuousness of much sunshine and sparkling waters which please the young and gay. I am no longer young. And my heart, through weary years of mourning over the dead, is not attuned to mirth. Moreover, the walls of my castle are broken; the shadows are many, and the wind breathes cold through the broken battlements and casements. I love the shade and the shadow, and would be alone with my thoughts when I may.'

Somehow his words and his look did not seem to accord, or else it was that his cast of face made his smile look malignant and saturnine.

Presently, with an excuse, he left me, asking me to put all my papers together. He was some little time away, and I began to look at some of the books around me. One was an atlas, which I found opened naturally at England, as if that map had been much used. On looking at it I found in certain places little rings marked, and on examining these I noticed that one was near London on the east side, manifestly where his new estate was situated; the other two were Exeter, and Whitby on the Yorkshire coast.

It was the better part of an hour when the Count returned. 'Aha!' he said; 'still at your books? Good! But you must not work always. Come; I am informed that your supper is ready.' He took my arm, and we went into the next room, where I found an excellent supper ready on the table. The Count again excused himself, as he had dined out on his being away from home. But he sat as on the previous night, and chatted whilst I ate. After supper I smoked, as on the last evening, and the Count stayed with me, chatting and asking questions on every conceivable subject, hour after hour. I felt that it was getting very late indeed, but I did not say anything, for I felt under obligation to meet my host's wishes in every way. I was not sleepy, as the long sleep yesterday had fortified me; but I could not help experiencing that chill which comes over one at the coming of the dawn, which is like, in its way, the turn of the tide. They say that people who are near death die generally at the change to the dawn or at the turn of the tide; anyone who has, when tired, and tied as it were to his post, experienced this change in the atmosphere can well believe it. All at once we heard the crow of a cock coming up with preternatural shrillness through the clear morning air; Count Dracula, jumping to his feet, said:

'Why, there is the morning again! How remiss I am to let you stay up so long. You must make your conversation regarding my dear new country of England less interesting, so that I may not forget how time flies by us,' and, with a courtly bow, he left me.

I went into my own room and drew the curtains, but there was little to notice; my window opened into the courtyard, all I could see was the warm grey of quickening sky. So I pulled the curtains again, and have written of this day.

8 May. – I began to fear as I wrote in this book that I was getting too diffuse; but now I am glad that I went into detail from the first, for there is something so strange about this place and all in it that I cannot but feel uneasy. I wish I were safe out of it or that I had never come. It may be that this strange night-existence is telling on me; but would that that were all! If there were anyone to talk to I could bear it, but there is no one. I have only the Count to speak with, and he! – I fear I am myself the only living soul within the place. Let me be prosaic so far as facts can be; it will help me to bear up, and imagination must not run riot with me. If it does I am lost. Let me say at once how I stand – or seem to.

I only slept a few hours when I went to bed, and feeling that I could not sleep any more, got up. I had hung my shaving-glass by the window, and was just beginning to shave. Suddenly I felt a hand on my shoulder, and heard the Count's voice saying to me, 'Good morning.' I started, for it amazed me that I had not seen him, since the reflection of the glass covered the whole room behind me. In starting I had cut myself slightly, but did not notice it at the moment. Having answered the Count's salutation, I turned to the glass again to see how I had been mistaken. This time there could be no error, for the man was close to me, and I could see him over my shoulder. But there was no reflection of him in the mirror! The whole room behind me was displayed; but there was no sign of a man in it, except myself. This was startling, and, coming on the top of so many strange things, was beginning to increase that vague feeling of uneasiness which I always have when the Count is near but at that instant I saw that the cut had bled a little, and the blood was trickling over my chin. I laid down the razor, turning as I did so half-round to look for some sticking-plaster. When the Count saw my face, his eyes blazed with a sort of demoniac fury, and he suddenly made a grab at my throat. I drew away, and his hand touched the string of beads which held the crucifix. It made an instant change in him, for the fury passed so quickly that I could hardly believe that it was ever there.

'Take care,' he said, 'take care how you cut yourself. It is more dangerous than you think in this country.' Then seizing the shaving-glass, he went on: 'And this is the wretched thing that has done the mischief. It is a foul bauble of man's vanity. Away with it!' and opening the heavy window with one wrench of his terrible hand, he flung out the glass, which was shattered into a thousand pieces on the stones of the courtyard far below. Then he withdrew without a word. It is very annoying, for I do not see how I am to shave, unless in my watch-case or the bottom of the shaving-pot, which is, fortunately, of metal.

When I went into the dining-room, breakfast was prepared; but I could not find the Count anywhere. So I breakfasted alone. It is strange that as yet I have not seen the Count eat or drink. He must be a very peculiar man! After breakfast I did a little exploring in the castle. I went out on the stairs and found a room looking towards the south. The view was magnificent, and from where I stood there was every opportunity of seeing it. The castle is on the very edge of a terrible precipice. A stone falling from the window would fall a thousand feet without touching anything! As far as the eye can reach is a sea of green tree-tops, with occasionally a deep rift where there is a chasm. Here and there are silver threads where the rivers wind in deep gorges through the forests.

But I am not in heart to describe beauty, for when I had seen the view I explored further; doors, doors, doors everywhere, and all locked and bolted. In no place save from the windows in the castle walls is there an available exit.

The castle is a veritable prison, and I am a prisoner!

Chapter 3

JONATHAN HARKER'S JOURNAL (*continued*)

WHEN I FOUND that I was a prisoner a sort of wild feeling came over me. I rushed up and down the stairs, trying every door and peering out of every window I could find; but after a little the conviction of my helplessness overpowered all other things. When I look back after a few hours I think I must have been mad for the time, for I behaved much as a rat does in a trap. When, however, the conviction had come to me that I was helpless I sat down quietly – as quietly as I have ever done anything in my life – and began to think over what was best to be done. I am thinking still, and as yet have come to no definite conclusion. Of one thing only am I certain: that it is no use making my ideas known to the Count. He knows well that I am imprisoned; and as he has done it himself, and has doubtless his own motives for it; he would only deceive me if I trusted him fully with the facts. So far as I can see, my only plan will be to keep my knowledge and my fears to myself, and my eyes open. I am, I know, either being deceived, like a baby, by my own fears, or else I am in desperate straits; and if the latter be so, I need, and shall need, all my brains to get through. I had hardly come to this conclusion when I heard the great door below shut, and knew that the Count had returned. He did not come at once into the library, so I went cautiously to my own room and found him making the bed. This was odd, but only confirmed what I had all along thought – that there were no servants in the house. When later I saw him through the chink of the hinges of the door laying the table in the dining-room, I was assured of it; for if he does himself all these menial offices, surely it is proof that there is no one else to do them. This gave me a fright, for if there is no one else in the castle, it must have been the Count himself who was the driver of the coach that brought me here. This is a terrible thought; for if so, what does it mean that he could control the wolves, as he did, by only holding up his hand in silence? How was it that all the people at Bistritz and on the coach had some terrible fear for me? What meant the giving of the crucifix, of the garlic, of the wild rose, of the mountain ash? Bless that good, good woman who hung the crucifix round my neck! for it is a comfort and a strength to me whenever I touch it. It is odd that a thing which I have been taught to regard with disfavour and as idolatrous should in a time of loneliness and trouble be of help. Is it that there is something in the essence of the thing itself, or that it is a medium, a tangible help, in conveying memories of sympathy and comfort? Some time, if it may be, I must examine this matter and try to make up my mind about it. In the meantime I must find out all I can about Count Dracula, as it may help me to understand. Tonight he may talk of himself, if I turn the conversation that way. I must be very careful, however, not to awake his suspicion.

Midnight. – I have had a long talk with the Count. I asked him a few questions on Transylvanian history, and he warmed up to the subject wonderfully. In his speaking of things and people, and especially of battles, he spoke as if he had been present at them all. This he afterwards explained by saying that to a *boyar* the pride of his house and name is his own pride, that their glory is his glory, that their fate is his fate. Whenever he spoke of his house he always said 'we,' and spoke almost in the plural, like a king speaking. I wish I could put down all he said exactly as he said it, for to me it was most fascinating. It seemed to have in it a whole history of the country. He grew excited as he spoke, and walked about the room pulling his great white moustache and grasping anything on which he laid his hands as though he would crush it by main strength. One thing he said which I shall put down as nearly as I can; for it tells in its way the story of his race:

'We Szekelys have a right to be proud, for in our veins flows the blood of many brave races who fought as the lion fights, for lordship. Here, in the whirlpool of European races, the Ugric tribe[25] bore down from Iceland the fighting spirit which Thor and Wodin gave them, which their Berserkers[26] displayed to such fell intent on the seaboards of Europe, aye, and of Asia and Africa, too, till the peoples thought that the were-wolves themselves had come. Here, too, when they came, they found the Huns, whose warlike fury had swept the earth like a living flame, till the dying peoples held that in their veins ran the blood of those old witches, who, expelled from Scythia,[27] had mated with the devils in the desert. Fools, fools! What devil or what witch was ever so great as Attila, whose blood is in these veins?' He held up his arms. 'Is it a wonder that we were a conquering race; that we were proud; that when the Magyar, the Lombard, the Avar, the Bulgar, or the Turk poured his thousands on our frontiers, we drove them back? Is it strange that when Arpad and his legions swept through the Hungarian father-land he found us here when he reached the frontier; that the Honofoglalas[28] was completed there? And when the Hungarian flood swept eastward, the Szekelys were claimed as kindred by the victorious

Magyars, and to us for centuries was trusted the guarding of the frontier of Turkey-land; aye, and more than that, endless duty of the frontier guard, for, as the Turks say, "water sleeps, and enemy is sleepless". Who more gladly than we throughout the Four Nations received the "bloody sword" or at its warlike call flocked quicker to the standard of the King? When was redeemed that great shame of my nation, the shame of Cassova,[29] when the flags of the Wallach and the Magyar went down beneath the Crescent; who was it but one of my own race who as Viovode[30] crossed the Danube and beat the Turk on his own ground! This was a Dracula indeed. Who was it that his own unworthy brother,[31] when he had fallen, sold his people to the Turk and brought the shame of slavery on them! Was it not this Dracula, indeed, who inspired that other of his race who in a later age again and again brought his forces over the great river into Turkey-land; who, when he was beaten back, came again, and again, and again, though he had to come alone from the bloody field where his troops were being slaughtered, since he knew that he alone could ultimately triumph? They said that he thought only of himself. Bah! what good are peasants without a leader? Where ends the war without a brain and heart to conduct it? Again, when, after the battle of Mohacs,[32] we threw off the Hungarian yoke, we of the Dracula blood were amongst their leaders, for our spirit would not brook that we were not free. Ah, young sir, the Szekelys – and the Dracula as their heart's blood, their brains, and their swords – can boast a record that mushroom growths like the Hapsburgs and the Romanoffs[33] can never reach. The warlike days are over. Blood is too precious a thing in these days of dishonourable peace; and the glories of the great races are as a tale that is told.'

It was by this time close on morning, and we went to bed. (*Mem.*, this diary seems horribly like the beginning of the *Arabian Nights*, for everything has to break off at cockcrow – or like the ghost of Hamlet's father.)

12 May. – Let me begin with facts – bare, meagre facts, verified by books and figures, and of which there can be no doubt. I must not confuse them with experiences which will have to rest on my own observation or my memory of them. Last evening when the Count came from his room he began by asking me questions on legal matters and on the doing of certain kinds of business. I had spent the day wearily over books, and, simply to keep my mind occupied, went over some of the matters I had been examined in at Lincoln's Inn.[34] There was a certain method in the Count's inquiries, so I shall try to put them down in sequence; the knowledge may somehow or some time be useful to me.

First, he asked if a man in England might have two solicitors, or more. I told him he might have a dozen if he wished, but that it would not be wise to have more than one solicitor engaged in one transaction, as only one could act at a time, and that to change would be certain to militate against his interest. He seemed thoroughly to understand, and went on to ask if there would be any practical difficulty in having one man to attend, say, to banking, and another to look after shipping, in case local help were needed in a place far from the home of the banking solicitor. I asked him to explain more fully, so that I might not by any chance mislead him, so he said:

'I shall illustrate. Your friend and mine, Mr Peter Hawkins, from under the shadow of your beautiful cathedral at Exeter, which is far from London, buys for me through your good self my place at London. Good! Now here let me say frankly, lest you should think it strange that I have sought the services of one so far off from London instead of someone resident there, that my motive was that no local interest might be served save my wish only; and as one of London resident might, perhaps, have some purpose of himself or friend to serve, I went thus afield to seek my agent, whose labours should be only to my interest. Now, suppose I, who have much of affairs, wish to ship goods, say, to Newcastle, or Durham, or Harwich, or Dover, might it not be that it could with more ease be done by consigning to one in these ports?' I answered that certainly it would be most easy, but that we solicitors had a system of agency one for the other, so that local work could be done locally on instruction from any solicitor, so that the client, simply placing himself in the hands of one man, could have his wishes carried out by him without further trouble.

'But,' said he, 'I could be at liberty to direct myself. Is it not so?'

'Of course,' I replied, 'and such is often done by men of business, who do not like the whole of their affairs to be known by any one person.'

'Good!' he said, and then went on to ask about the means of making consignments and the forms to be gone through, and of all sorts of difficulties which might arise, but by forethought could be guarded against. I explained all these things to him to the best of my ability, and he certainly left me under the impression that he would have made a wonderful solicitor, for there was nothing that he did not think of or foresee. For a man who was never in the country, and who did not evidently do much in the way of business, his knowledge and acumen were wonderful. When he had satisfied himself on these points of which he had spoken, and I had verified all as well as I could by the books available, he suddenly stood up and said:

'Have you written since your first letter to our friend Mr Peter Hawkins, or to any other?' It was with some bitterness in my heart that I answered that I had not, that as yet I had not seen any opportunity of sending letters to anybody.

'Then write now, my young friend,' he said, laying a heavy hand on my shoulder; 'write to our friend and to any other; and say, if it will please you, that you shall stay with me until a month from now.'

'Do you wish me to stay so long?' I asked, for my heart grew cold at the thought.

'I desire it much; nay, I will take no refusal. When your master, employer, what you will, engaged that someone should come on his behalf, it was understood that my needs only were to be consulted. I have not stinted. Is it not so?'

What could I do but bow acceptance? It was Mr Hawkins's interest, not mine, and I had to think of him, not myself; and besides, while Count Dracula was speaking, there was that in his eyes and in his bearing which made me remember that I was a prisoner, and that if I wished it I could have no choice. The Count saw his victory in my bow, and his mastery in the trouble of my face, for he began at once to use them, but in his own smooth, resistless way:

'I pray you, my good young friend, that you will not discourse of things other than business in your letters. It will doubtless please your friends to know that you are well, and that you look forward to getting home to them. Is it not so?' As he spoke he handed me three sheets of notepaper and three envelopes. They were all of the thinnest foreign post, and looking at them, then at him, and noticing his quiet smile, with the sharp, canine teeth lying over the red under-lip, I understood as well as if he had spoken that I should be careful what I wrote, for he would be able to read it. So I determined to write only formal notes now, but to write fully to Mr Hawkins in secret, and also to Mina, for to her I could write in shorthand, which would puzzle the Count, if he did see it. When I had written my two letters I sat quiet, reading a book whilst the Count wrote several notes referring as he wrote them to some books on his table. Then he took up my two and placed them with his own, and put by his writing materials, after which, the instant the door had closed behind him, I leaned over and looked at the letters, which were face down on the table. I felt no compunction in doing so, for under the circumstances I felt that I should protect myself in every way I could.

One of the letters was directed to Samuel F. Billington, No. 7, The Crescent, Whitby, another to Herr Leutner, Varna; the third was to

Coutts & Co., London, and the fourth to Herren Klopstock & Billreuth, bankers, Buda-Pesth. The second and fourth were unsealed. I was just about to look at them when I saw the door-handle move. I sank back in my seat, having just had time to replace the letters as they had been and to resume my book before the Count, holding still another letter in his hand, entered the room. He took up the letters on the table and stamped them carefully, and then, turning to me, said:

'I trust you will forgive me, but I have much work to do in private this evening. You will, I hope, find all things as you wish.' At the door he turned and after a moment's pause said:

'Let me advise you, my dear young friend – nay, let me warn you with all seriousness, that should you leave these rooms you will not by any chance go to sleep in any other part of the castle. It is old, and has many memories, and there are bad dreams for those who sleep unwisely. Be warned! Should sleep now or ever overcome you, or be like to do, then haste to your own chamber or to these rooms, for your rest will then be safe. But if you be not careful in this respect, then – ' He finished his speech in a gruesome way, for he motioned with his hands as if he were washing them. I quite understood; my only doubt was as to whether any dream could be more terrible than the unnatural, horrible net of gloom and mystery which seemed closing round me.

Later. – I endorse the last words written, but this time there is no doubt in question. I shall not fear to sleep in any place where he is not. I have placed the crucifix over the head of my bed – I imagine that my rest is thus freer from dreams; and there it shall remain.

When he left me I went to my room. After a little while, not hearing any sound, I came out and went up the stone stair to where I could look out towards the south. There was some sense of freedom in the vast expanse, inaccessible though it was to me, as compared with the narrow darkness of the courtyard. Looking out on this, I felt that I was indeed in prison, and I seemed to want a breath of fresh air, though it were of the night. I am beginning to feel this nocturnal existence tell on me. It is destroying my nerve. I start at my own shadow, and am full of all sorts of horrible imaginings. God knows that there is ground for any terrible fear in this accursed place! I looked out over the beautiful expanse, bathed in soft yellow moonlight till it was almost as light as day. In the soft light the distant hills became melted, and the shadows in the valleys and gorges of velvety blackness. The mere beauty seemed to cheer me; there was peace and comfort in every breath I drew. As I leaned from the window my eye was caught by something moving a story below me, and somewhat to my left, where I imagined, from the lie of the rooms, that the windows of the Count's own room would look out. The window at which I stood was tall and deep, stone-mullioned, and though weather-worn, was still complete; but it was evidently many a day since the case had been there. I drew back behind the stonework, and looked carefully out.

What I saw was the Count's head coming out from the window. I did not see the face, but I knew the man by the neck and the movement of his back and arms. In any case, I could not mistake the hands which I had had so many opportunities of studying. I was at first interested and somewhat amused, for it is wonderful how small a matter will interest and amuse a man when he is a prisoner. But my very feelings changed to repulsion and terror when I saw the whole man slowly emerge from the window and begin to crawl down the castle wall over that dreadful abyss, *face down* with his cloak spreading out around him like great wings. At first I could not believe my eyes. I thought it was some trick of the moonlight, some weird effect of shadow; but I kept looking, and it could be no delusion. I saw the fingers and toes grasp the corners of the stones, worn clear of the mortar by the stress of years, and by thus using every projection and inequality move downwards with considerable speed, just as a lizard moves along a wall.

What manner of man is this, or what manner of creature is it in the semblance of man? I feel the dread of this horrible place overpowering me; I am in fear – in awful fear – and there is no escape for me; I am encompassed about with terrors that I dare not think of . . .

15 May. – Once more have I seen the Count go out in his lizard fashion. He moved downwards in a sidelong way, some hundred feet down, and a good deal to the left. He vanished into some hole or window. When his head had disappeared I leaned out to try and see more, but without avail – the distance was too great to allow a proper angle of sight. I knew he had left the castle now, and thought to use the opportunity to explore more that I had dared to do as yet. I went back to the room, and taking a lamp, tried all the doors. They were all locked as I had expected and the locks were comparatively new; but I went down the stone stairs to the hall where I had entered originally. I found I could pull back the bolts easily enough and unhook the great chains; but the door was locked, and the key was gone! That key must be in the Count's room; I must watch should his door be unlocked, so that I may get it and escape. I went on to make a thorough examination of the various stairs and passages, and to try the doors that opened from them. One or two small rooms near the hall were open, but there was nothing to see in them except old furniture, dusty with age and moth-eaten. At last, however, I found one door at the top of a stairway which, though it seemed to be locked, gave a little under pressure. I tried it harder, and found that it was not really locked, but that the resistance came from the fact that the hinges had fallen somewhat, and the heavy door rested on the floor. Here was an opportunity which I might not have again, so I exerted myself, and with many efforts forced it back so that I could enter. I was now in a wing of the castle further to the right than the rooms I knew and a story lower down. From the windows I could see that the suite of rooms lay along to the south of the castle, the windows of the end room looking out both west and south. On the latter side, as well as to the former, there was a great precipice. The castle was built on the corner of a great rock, so that on three sides it was quite impregnable, and great windows were placed here where sling, or bow, or culverin[35] could not reach, and consequently light and comfort, impossible to a position which had to be guarded, were secured. To the west was a great valley, and then, rising far away, great jagged mountain fastnesses, rising peak on peak, the sheer rock studded with mountain ash and thorn, whose roots clung in cracks and crevices and crannies of the stone. This was evidently the portion of the castle occupied in bygone days, for the furniture had more air of comfort than any I had seen. The windows were curtainless, and the yellow moonlight, flooding in through the diamond panes, enabled one to see even colours, whilst it softened the wealth of dust which lay over all and disguised in some measure the ravages of time and the moth. My lamp seemed to be of little effect in the brilliant moonlight, but I was glad to have it with me, for there was a dread loneliness in the place which chilled my heart and made my nerves tremble. Still, it was better than living alone in the rooms which I had come to hate from the presence of the Count, and after trying a little to school my nerves, I found a soft quietude come over me. Here I am, sitting at a little oak table where in old times possibly some fair lady sat to pen, with much thought and many blushes, her ill-spelt love-letter, and writing in my diary in shorthand all that has happened since I closed it last. It is nineteenth century up-to-date with a vengeance. And yet, unless my senses deceive me, the old centuries had, and have, powers of their own which mere 'modernity' cannot kill.

Later: the Morning of 16 May. – God preserve my sanity, for to this I am reduced. Safety and the assurance of safety are things of the past. Whilst I live on here there is but one thing to hope for: that I may not go mad, if, indeed, I be not mad already. If I be sane, then surely it is maddening to think that of all the foul things that lurk in this hateful place the Count is the least dreadful to me; that to him alone I can look for safety, even though this be only whilst I can serve his purpose. Great God! merciful God! Let me be calm, for out of that way lies madness indeed. I begin to get new lights on certain things which have puzzled me. Up to now I never quite knew what Shakespeare meant when he made Hamlet say:

> 'My tablets! quick, my tablets!
> 'Tis meet that I put it down,' etc.,[36]

for now, feeling as though my own brain were unhinged or as if the shock had come which must end in its undoing, I turn to my diary for repose. The habit of entering accurately must help to soothe me.

The Count's mysterious warning frightened me at the time; it frightens me more now when I think of it, for in future he has a fearful hold upon me. I shall fear to doubt what he may say!

When I had written in my diary and had fortunately replaced the book and pen in my pocket, I felt sleepy. The Count's warning came into my mind, but I took a pleasure in disobeying it. The sense of sleep was upon me, and with it the obstinacy which sleep brings as outrider. The soft moonlight soothed, and the wide expanse without gave a sense of freedom which refreshed me. I determined not to return tonight to the gloom-haunted rooms, but to sleep here, where of old ladies had sat and sung and lived sweet lives whilst their gentle breasts were sad for their menfolk away in the midst of remorseless wars. I drew a great couch out of its place near the corner, so that, as I lay, I could look at the lovely view to east and south, and unthinking of and uncaring for the dust, composed myself for sleep.

I suppose I must have fallen asleep; I hope so, but I fear, for all that followed was startlingly real – so real that now, sitting here in the broad, full sunlight of the morning, I cannot in the least believe that it was all sleep.

I was not alone. The room was the same, unchanged in any way since I came into it; I could see along the floor, in the brilliant moonlight, my own footsteps marked where I had disturbed the long accumulation of dust. In the moonlight opposite me were three young women, ladies by their dress and manner. I thought at the time that I must be dreaming when I saw them, for, though the moonlight was behind them, they threw no shadow on the floor. They came close to me and looked at me for some time, and then whispered together. Two were dark, and had high aquiline noses, like the Count, and great dark, piercing eyes, that seemed to be almost red when contrasted with the pale yellow moon.

The other was fair, as fair as can be, with great, wavy masses of golden hair and eyes like pale sapphires. I seemed somehow to know her face, and to know it in connection with some dreamy fear, but I could not recollect at the moment how or where. All three had brilliant white teeth, that shone like pearls against the ruby of their voluptuous lips. There was something about them that made me uneasy, some longing and at the same time some deadly fear. I felt in my heart a wicked, burning desire that they would kiss me with those red lips. It is not good to note this down, lest some day it should meet Mina's eyes and cause her pain; but it is the truth. They whispered together, and then they all three laughed – such a silvery, musical laugh, but as hard as though the sound never could have come through the softness of human lips. It was like the intolerable, tingling sweetness of water-glasses when played on by a cunning hand. The fair girl shook her head coquettishly, and the other two urged her on. One said:

'Go on! You are first, and we shall follow; yours is the right to begin.' The other added:

'He is young and strong; there are kisses for us all.' I lay quiet, looking out under my eyelashes in an agony of delightful anticipation. The fair girl advanced and bent over me till I could feel the movement of her breath upon me. Sweet it was in one sense, honey-sweet, and sent the same tingling through the nerves as her voice, but with a bitter underlying the sweet, a bitter offensiveness, as one smells in blood.

I was afraid to raise my eyelids, but looked out and saw perfectly under the lashes. The fair girl went on her knees, and bent over me, fairly gloating. There was a deliberate voluptuousness which was both thrilling and repulsive, and as she arched her neck she actually licked her lips like an animal, till I could see in the moonlight the moisture shining on the scarlet lips and on the red tongue as it lapped the white sharp teeth. Lower and lower went her head as the lips went below the range of my mouth and chin and seemed about to fasten on my throat. Then she paused, and I could hear the churning sound of her tongue as it licked her teeth and lips, and could feel the hot breath on my neck. Then the skin of my throat began to tingle as one's flesh does when the hand that is to tickle it approaches nearer – nearer. I could feel the soft, shivering touch of the lips on the supersensitive skin of my throat, and the hard dents of two sharp teeth, just touching and pausing there. I closed my eyes in a languorous ecstasy and waited – waited with beating heart.

But at that instant another sensation swept through me as quick as lightning. I was conscious of the presence of the Count, and of his being as if lapped in a storm of fury. As my eyes opened involuntarily I saw his strong hand grasp the slender neck of the fair woman and with giant's power draw it back, the blue eyes transformed with fury, the white teeth champing with rage, and the fair cheeks blazing red with passion. But the Count! Never did I imagine such wrath and fury even in the demons of the pit. His eyes were positively blazing. The red light in them was lurid, as if the flames of hell-fire blazed behind them. His face was deathly pale, and the lines of it were hard like drawn wires; the thick eyebrows that met over the nose now seemed like a heaving bar of white-hot metal. With a fierce sweep of his arm, he hurled the woman from him, and then motioned to the others, as though he were beating them back; it was the same imperious gesture that I had seen used to the wolves. In a voice which, though low and almost a whisper, seemed to cut through the air and then ring round the room, he exclaimed:

'How dare you touch him, any of you? How dare you cast eyes on him when I had forbidden it? Back, I tell you all! This man belongs to me! Beware how you meddle with him, or you'll have to deal with me.' The fair girl, with a laugh of ribald coquetry, turned to answer him:

'You yourself never loved; you never love!' On this the other women joined, and such a mirthless, hard, soulless laughter rang through the room that it almost made me faint to hear; it seemed like the pleasure of fiends. The Count turned, after looking at my face attentively, and said in a soft whisper:

'Yes, I too can love; you yourselves can tell it from the past. Is it not so? Well, now I promise you that when I am done with him, you shall kiss him at your will. Now go! go! I must awaken him, for there is work to be done.'

'Are we to have nothing tonight?' said one of them, with a low laugh, as she pointed to the bag which he had thrown upon the floor, and which moved as though there were some living thing within it. For answer he nodded his head. One of the women jumped forward and opened it. If my ears did not deceive me there was a gasp and a low wail, as of a half-smothered child. The women closed round, whilst I was aghast with horror but as I looked they disappeared, and with them the dreadful bag. There was no door near them, and they could not have passed me without my noticing. They simply seemed to fade into the rays of the moonlight and pass out through the window, for I could see outside the dim, shadowy forms for a moment before they entirely faded away.

Then the horror overcame me, and I sank down unconscious.

Chapter 4

I AWOKE in my own bed. If it be that I had not dreamt, the Count must have carried me here. I tried to satisfy myself on the subject, but could not arrive at any unquestionable result. To be sure, there were certain small evidences, such as that my clothes were folded and laid by in a manner which was not my habit. My watch was still unwound, and I am rigorously accustomed to wind it the last thing before going to bed, and many such details. But these things are no proof, for they may have been evidences that my mind was not as usual, and, from some cause or another, I had certainly been much upset. I must watch for proof. Of one thing I am glad: if it was the Count that carried me here and undressed me, he must have been hurried in his task, for my pockets are intact. I am sure this diary would have been a mystery to him which he would not have brooked. He would have taken or destroyed it. As I look round this room, although it has been to me so full of fear, it is now a sort of sanctuary, for nothing can be more dreadful than those awful women, who were – who *are* waiting to suck my blood.

18 May. – I have been down to look at that room again in daylight, for I must know the truth. When I got to the doorway at the top of the stairs, I found it closed. It had been so forcibly driven against the jamb that part of the woodwork was splintered. I could see that the bolt of the lock had not been shot, but the door is fastened from the inside. I fear it was no dream, and must act on this surmise.

19 May. – I am surely in the toils.[37] Last night the Count asked me in the suavest tones to write three letters, one saying that my work here was nearly done, and that I should start for home within a few days, another that I was starting on the next morning from the time of the letter, and the third that I had left the castle and arrived at Bistritz. I would fain have rebelled, but felt that in the present state of things it would be madness to quarrel openly with the Count whilst I am so absolutely in his power; and to refuse would be to excite his suspicion and to arouse his anger. He knows that I know too much, and that I must not live, lest I be dangerous to him; my only chance is to prolong my opportunities. Something may occur which will give me a chance to escape. I saw in his eyes something of that gathering wrath which was

manifest when he hurled that fair woman from him. He explained to me
that posts were few and uncertain, and that my writing now would
ensure ease of mind to my friends; and he assured me with so much
impressiveness that he would countermand the later letters, which
would be held over at Bistritz until due time in case chance would admit
of my prolonging my stay, that to oppose him would have been to
create new suspicion. I therefore pretended to fall in with his views, and
asked him what dates I should put on the letters. He calculated a
minute, and then said:

'The first should be June 12, the second June 19, and the third
June 29.'

I know now the span of my life. God help me!

28 May. – There is a chance of escape, or at any rate of being able to
send word home. A band of Szgany[38] have come to the castle, and are
encamped in the courtyard. These Szgany are gipsies; I have notes of
them in my book. They are peculiar to this part of the world, though
allied to the ordinary gipsies all the world over. There are thousands of
them in Hungary and Transylvania, who are almost outside all law.
They attach themselves as a rule to some great noble or *boyar*, and call
themselves by his name. They are fearless and without religion, save
superstition, and they talk only their own varieties of the Romany
tongue.

I shall write some letters home, and shall try to get them to have them
posted. I have already spoken to them through my window to begin an
acquaintanceship. They took their hats off and made obeisance and
many signs, which, however, I could not understand any more than I
could their spoken language . . .

I have written the letters. Mina's is in shorthand, and I simply ask Mr
Hawkins to communicate with her. To her I have explained my
situation, but without the horrors which I may only surmise. It would
shock and frighten her to death were I to expose my heart to her.
Should the letters not carry, then the Count shall not yet know my
secret or the extent of my knowledge . . .

I have given the letters; I threw them through the bars of my window
with a gold piece, and made what signs I could to have them posted.
The man who took them pressed them to his heart and bowed, and then
put them in his cap. I could do no more. I stole back to the study and
began to read. As the Count did not come in, I have written here . . .

The Count has come. He sat down beside me, and said in his
smoothest voice as he opened two letters:

'The Szgany has given me these, of which, though I know not whence they come, I shall, of course, take care. See!' – he must have looked at it – 'one is from you, and to my friend Peter Hawkins; the other' – here he caught sight of the strange symbols as he opened the envelope, and the dark look came into his face, and his eyes blazed wickedly – 'the other is a vile thing, an outrage upon friendship and hospitality! It is not signed. Well! so it cannot matter to us.' And he calmly held letter and envelope in the flame of the lamp till they were consumed. Then he went on:

'The letter to Hawkins – that I shall, of course, send on, since it is yours. Your letters are sacred to me. Your pardon, my friend, that unknowingly I did break the seal. Will you not cover it again?' He held out the letter to me, and with a courteous bow handed me a clean envelope. I could only redirect it and hand it to him in silence. When he went out of the room I could hear the key turn softly. A minute later I went over and tried it, and the door was locked.

When, an hour or two after, the Count came quietly into the room, his coming wakened me, for I had gone to sleep on the sofa. He was very courteous and very cheery in his manner and seeing that I had been sleeping, he said:

'So, my friend, you are tired? Get to bed. There is the surest rest. I may not have the pleasure to talk tonight, since there are many labours to me; but you will sleep, I pray.' I passed to my room and went to bed, and, strange to say, slept without dreaming. Despair has its own calms.

31 May. – This morning when I woke I thought I would provide myself with some paper and envelopes from my bag and keep them in my pocket, so that I might write in case I should get an opportunity; but again a surprise, again a shock!

Every scrap of paper was gone, and with it all my notes, my memoranda relating to railways and travel, my letter of credit, in fact, all that might be useful to me were I once outside the castle. I sat and pondered a while, and then some thought occurred to me, and I made search of my portmanteau and in the wardrobe where I had placed my clothes.

The suit in which I had travelled was gone, and also my overcoat and rug; I could find no trace of them anywhere. This looked like some new scheme of villainy . . .

17 June. – This morning, as I was sitting on the edge of my bed cudgelling my brains, I heard without a cracking of whips and pounding and scraping of horses' feet up the rocky path beyond the courtyard. With joy I hurried to the window, and saw drive into the yard two great *leiterwagons*, each drawn by eight sturdy horses, and at the head of each pair a Slovak, with his wide hat, great, nail-studded belt, dirty sheepskin, and high boots. They had also their long staves in hand. I ran to the door, intending to descend and try and join them through the main hall, as I thought that way might be opened for them. Again a shock: my door was fastened on the outside.

Then I ran to the window and cried to them. They looked up at me stupidly and pointed, but just then the *hetman*[39] of the Szgany came out, and seeing them pointing to my window, said something, at which they laughed. Henceforth, no effort of mine, no piteous cry or agonised entreaty, would make them even look at me. They resolutely turned away. The *leiterwagons* contained great, square boxes, with handles of thick rope; these were evidently empty by the ease with which the Slovaks handled them, and by their resonance as they were roughly moved. When they were all unloaded and packed in a great heap in one corner of the yard, the Slovaks were given some money by the Szgany, and spitting on it for luck, lazily went each to his horse's head. Shortly afterwards I heard the cracking of their whips die away in the distance.

24 June, before morning. – Last night the Count left me early, and locked himself into his own room. As soon as I dared, I ran up the winding stair, and looked out of the window which opened south. I thought I would watch for the Count, for there is something going on. The Szgany are quartered somewhere in the castle, and are doing work of some kind. I know it, for now and then I hear a far-away, muffled sound as of mattock and spade and, whatever it is, it must be to the end of some ruthless villainy.

I had been at the window somewhat less than half an hour, when I saw something coming out of the Count's window. I drew back and watched carefully, and saw the whole man emerge. It was a new shock to me to find that he had on the suit of clothes which I had worn whilst travelling here, and slung over his shoulder the terrible bag which I had seen the women take away. There could be no doubt as to his quest, and in my garb, too! This, then, is his new scheme of evil: that he will allow others to see me, as they think, so that he may both leave evidence that I have been seen in the towns or villages posting my own letters, and that any wickedness which he may do shall by the local people be attributed to me.

It makes me rage to think that this can go on, and whilst I am shut up here, a veritable prisoner, but without that protection of the law which is even a criminal's right and consolation.

I thought I would watch for the Count's return, and for a long time sat doggedly at the window. Then I began to notice that there were some quaint little specks floating in the rays of the moonlight. They were like the tiniest grains of dust, and they whirled round and gathered in clusters in a nebulous sort of way. I watched them with a sense of soothing, and a sort of calm stole over me. I leaned back in the embrasure in a more comfortable position, so that I could enjoy more fully the aerial gambolling.

Something made me start up, a low, piteous howling of dogs somewhere far below in the valley, which was hidden from my sight. Louder it seemed to ring in my ears, and the floating motes of dust to take new shapes to the sound as they danced in the moonlight. I felt myself struggling to awake to some call of my instincts; nay, my very soul was struggling, and my half-remembered sensibilities were striving to answer the call. I was becoming hypnotised! Quicker and quicker danced the dust, and the moonbeams seemed to quiver as they went by me into the mass of gloom beyond. More and more they gathered till they seemed to take dim phantom shapes. And then I started, broad awake and in full possession of my senses, and ran screaming from the place. The phantom shapes, which were becoming gradually material- ised from the moonbeams, were those of the three ghostly women to whom I was doomed. I fled, and felt somewhat safer in my own room, where there was no moonlight and where the lamp was burning brightly.

When a couple of hours had passed I heard something stirring in the Count's room, something like a sharp wail quickly suppressed; and then there was silence, deep, awful silence, which chilled me. With a beating heart, I tried the door; but I was locked in my prison, and could do nothing. I sat down and simply cried.

As I sat I heard a sound in the courtyard without – the agonised cry of a woman. I rushed to the window, and throwing it up, peered out between the bars. There, indeed, was a woman with dishevelled hair, holding her hands over her heart as one distressed with running. She was leaning against a corner of the gateway. When she saw my face at the window she threw herself forward, and shouted in a voice laden with menace:

'Monster, give me my child!'

She threw herself on her knees, and raising up her hands, cried the same words in tones which wrung my heart. Then she tore her hair and beat her breast, and abandoned herself to all the violences of extrava- gant emotion. Finally she threw herself forward, and, though I could not see her, I could hear the beating of her naked hands against the door.

Somewhere high overhead, probably on the tower, I heard the voice of the Count calling in his harsh, metallic whisper. His call seemed to be answered from far and wide by the howling of wolves. Before many minutes had passed a pack of them poured, like a pent-up dam when liberated, through the wide entrance into the courtyard.

There was no cry from the woman, and the howling of the wolves was but short. Before long they streamed away singly, licking their lips.

I could not pity her, for I knew now what had become of her child, and she was better dead.

What shall I do? what can I do? How can I escape from this dreadful thrall of night and gloom and fear?

25 June, morning. – No man knows till he has suffered from the night how sweet and how dear to his heart and eye the morning can be. When the sun grew so high this morning that it struck the top of the great gateway opposite my window, the high spot which it touched seemed to me as if the dove from the ark had lighted there. My fear fell from me as if it had been a vaporous garment which dissolved in the warmth. I must take action of some sort while the courage of the day is upon me. Last night one of my post-dated letters went to post, the first of that fatal series which is to blot out the very traces of my existence from the earth.

Let me not think of it. Action!

It has always been at night-time that I have been molested or threatened, or in some way in danger or in fear. I have not yet seen the Count in the daylight. Can it be that he sleeps when others wake, that he may be awake whilst they sleep? If I could only get into his room! But there is no possible way. The door is always locked, no way for me.

Yes, there is a way, if one dares to take it. Where his body has gone why may not another body go? I have seen him myself crawl from his window; why should not I imitate him, and go in by his window? The chances are desperate, but my need is more desperate still. I shall risk it. At the worst it can only be death. And a man's death is not a calf's, and the dread Hereafter may still be open to me. God help me in my task! Good-bye, Mina if I fail; good-bye, my faithful friend and second father, good-bye, all, and last of all Mina!

Same day, later. – I have made the effort, and, God helping me, have come safely back to this room. I must put down every detail in order. I went whilst my courage was fresh straight to the window on the south side, and at once got outside on the narrow ledge of stone which runs round the building on this side. The stones were big and roughly cut, and the mortar had by process of time been washed away between them. I took off my boots, and ventured out on the desperate way. I looked down once, so as to make sure that a sudden glimpse of the awful depth

would not overcome me, but after that kept my eyes away from it. I
knew pretty well the direction and distance of the Count's window, and
made for it as well as I could, having regard to the opportunities
available. I did not feel dizzy – I suppose I was too excited – and the time
seemed ridiculously short till I found myself standing on the windowsill
and trying to raise up the sash. I was filled with agitation, however,
when I bent down and slid feet foremost in through the window. Then I
looked around for the Count, but, with surprise and gladness, made a
discovery. The room was empty! It was barely furnished with odd
things, which seemed to have never been used; the furniture was
something the same style as that in the south rooms, and was covered
with dust. I looked for the key, but it was not in the lock, and I could not
find it anywhere. The only thing I found was a great heap of gold in one
corner – gold of all kinds, Roman, and British, and Austrian, and
Hungarian, and Greek and Turkish money, covered with a film of dust,
as though it had lain long in the ground. None of it that I noticed was
less than three hundred years old. There were also chains and ornaments, some jewelled but all of them old and stained.

At one corner of the room was a heavy door. I tried it, for, since I
could not find the key of the room or the key of the outer door, which
was the main object of my search, I must make further examination, or
all my efforts would be in vain. It was open, and led through a stone
passage to a circular stairway, which went steeply down. I descended,
minding carefully where I went, for the stairs were dark, being only lit
by loopholes in the heavy masonry. At the bottom there was a dark,
tunnel-like passage, through which came a deathly, sickly odour, the
odour of old earth newly turned. As I went through the passage the
smell grew closer and heavier. At last I pulled open a heavy door which
stood ajar, and found myself in an old, ruined chapel, which had
evidently been used as a graveyard. The roof was broken, and in two
places were steps leading to vaults, but the ground had recently been
dug over, and the earth placed in great wooden boxes, manifestly those
which had been brought by the Slovaks. There was nobody about, and I
made search for any further outlet, but there was none. Then I went
over every inch of the ground, so as not to lose a chance. I went down
even into the vaults, where the dim light struggled, although to do so
was a dread to my very soul. Into two of these I went, but saw nothing
except fragments of old coffins and piles of dust; in the third, however, I
made a discovery.

There, in one of the great boxes, of which there were fifty in all, on a
pile of newly dug earth, lay the Count! He was either dead or asleep, I

could not say which – for the eyes were open and stony, but without the glassiness of death – and the cheeks had the warmth of life through all their pallor, and the lips were as red as ever. But there was no sign of movement, no pulse, no breath, no beating of the heart. I bent over him, and tried to find any sign of life, but in vain. He could not have lain there long, for the earthy smell would have passed away in a few hours. By the side of the box was its cover, pierced with holes here and there. I thought he might have the keys on him, but when I went to search I saw the dead eyes, and in them, dead though they were, such a look of hate, though unconscious of me or my presence, that I fled from the place, and leaving the Count's room by the window, crawled again up the castle wall. Regaining my own chamber, I threw myself panting upon the bed and tried to think . . .

29 June. – Today is the date of my last letter, and the Count has taken steps to prove that it was genuine, for again I saw him leave the castle by the same window, and in my clothes. As he went down the wall, lizard fashion, I wished I had a gun or some lethal weapon, that I might destroy him; but I fear that no weapon wrought alone by man's hand would have any effect on him. I dared not wait to see him return, for I feared to see those weird sisters.[40] I came back to the library, and read there till I fell asleep.

I was awakened by the Count, who looked at me as grimly as a man can look as he said:

'Tomorrow, my friend, we must part. You return to your beautiful England, I to some work which may have such an end that we may never meet. Your letter home has been despatched; tomorrow I shall not be here, but all shall be ready for your journey. In the morning come the Szgany, who have some labours of their own here, and also come some Slovaks. When they have gone, my carriage shall come for you, and shall bear you to the Borgo Pass to meet the diligence from Bukovina to Bistritz. But I am in hopes that I shall see more of you at Castle Dracula.' I suspected him, and determined to test his sincerity. Sincerity! It seems like a profanation of the word to write it in connection with such a monster, so I asked him point-blank:

'Why may I not go tonight?'

'Because, dear sir, my coachman and horses are away on a mission.'

'But I would walk with pleasure. I want to get away at once.' He smiled, such a soft, smooth, diabolical smile that I knew there was some trick behind his smoothness. He said:

'And your baggage?'

'I do not care about it. I can send for it some other time.'

The Count stood up, and said, with a sweet courtesy which made me rub my eyes, it seemed so real:

'You English have a saying which is close to my heart, for its spirit is that which rules our *boyars:* "Welcome the coming, speed the parting guest."[41] Come with me, my dear young friend. Not an hour shall you wait in my house against your will, though sad am I at your going, and that you so suddenly desire it. Come!' With a stately gravity, he, with the lamp, preceded me down the stairs and along the hall. Suddenly he stopped.

'Hark!'

Close at hand came the howling of many wolves. It was almost as if the sound sprang up at the raising of his hand, just as the music of a great orchestra seems to leap under the bâton of the conductor. After a pause of a moment, he proceeded, in his stately way, to the door, drew back the ponderous bolts, unhooked the heavy chains, and began to draw it open.

To my intense astonishment I saw that it was unlocked. Suspiciously I looked all round, but could see no key of any kind.

As the door began to open, the howling of the wolves without grew louder and angrier; their red jaws, with champing teeth, and their blunt-clawed feet as they leaped, came in through the opening door. I knew that to struggle at the moment against the Count was useless. With such allies as these at his command, I could do nothing. But still the door continued slowly to open, and only the Count's body stood in the gap. Suddenly it struck me that this might be the moment and the means of my doom; I was to be given to the wolves, and at my own instigation. There was a diabolical wickedness in the idea great enough for the Count, and as a last chance I cried out:

'Shut the door; I shall wait till morning!' and covered my face with my hands to hide my tears of bitter disappointment. With one sweep of his powerful arm, the Count threw the door shut, and the great bolts clanged and echoed through the hall as they shot back into their places.

In silence we returned to the library, and after a minute or two I went to my own room. The last I saw of Count Dracula was his kissing his hand to me with a red light of triumph in his eyes, and with a smile that Judas in hell might be proud of.

When I was in my room and about to lie down, I thought I heard a whispering at my door. I went to it softly and listened. Unless my ears deceived me, I heard the voice of the Count:

'Back, back, to your own place! Your time is not yet come. Wait. Have patience. Tomorrow night, tomorrow night, is yours!' There was a low, sweet ripple of laughter, and in a rage I threw open the door, and saw without the three terrible women licking their lips. As I appeared they all joined in a horrible laugh, and ran away.

I came back to my room and threw myself on my knees. It is then so near the end? Tomorrow! tomorrow! Lord, help me, and those to whom I am dear!

30 June, morning. – These may be the last words I ever write in this diary. I slept till just before the dawn, and when I woke threw myself on my knees, for I determined that if Death came he should find me ready.

At last I felt that subtle change in the air and knew that the morning had come. Then came the welcome cock-crow and I felt that I was safe. With a glad heart, I opened my door and ran down to the hall. I had seen that the door was unlocked and now escape was before me. With hands that trembled with eagerness, I unhooked the chains and drew back the massive bolts.

But the door would not move. Despair seized me. I pulled and pulled at the door, and shook it till, massive as it was, it rattled in its casement. I could see the bolt shot. It had been locked after I left the Count.

Then a wild desire took me to obtain that key at any risk, and I determined then and there to scale the wall again and gain the Count's room. He might kill me, but death now seemed the happier choice of evils. Without a pause I rushed up to the east window and scrambled down the wall, as before, into the Count's room. It was empty but that was as I expected. I could not see a key anywhere but the heap of gold remained. I went through the door in the corner and down the winding stair and along the dark passage to the old chapel. I knew now well enough where to find the monster I sought.

The great box was in the same place, close against the wall, but the lid was laid on it, not fastened down, but with the nails ready in their places to be hammered home. I knew I must search the body for the key, so I raised the lid and laid it back against the wall; and then I saw something which filled my very soul with horror. There lay the Count, but looking as if his youth had been half-renewed, for the white hair and moustache were changed to dark iron-grey; the cheeks were fuller, and the white skin seemed ruby-red underneath; the mouth was redder than ever, for on the lips were gouts of fresh blood, which trickled from the corners of the mouth and ran over the chin and neck. Even the deep, burning eyes seemed set amongst swollen flesh, for the lids and pouches underneath were bloated. It seemed as if the whole awful creature were simply gorged with blood; he lay like a filthy leech, exhausted with his repletion. I shuddered as I bent over to touch him, and every sense in me revolted at the contact; but I had to search, or I was lost. The coming night might see my own body a banquet in a similar way to those horrid three. I felt all over the body, but no sign could I find of the key. Then I stopped and looked at the Count. There was a mocking smile on the bloated face which seemed to drive me mad. This was the being I was helping to transfer to London, where, perhaps for centuries to come, he might, amongst its teeming millions, satiate his lust for blood, and create a new and ever-widening circle of semi-demons to batten on the helpless. The very thought drove me mad. A terrible desire came upon me to rid the world of such a monster. There was no lethal weapon at hand, but I seized a shovel which the workmen had been using to fill the cases, and lifting it high struck, with the edge downward, at the hateful face. But as I did so the head turned, and the eyes fell full upon me, with all their blaze of basilisk horror. The sight seemed to paralyse me, and the shovel turned in my hand and glanced from the face, merely making a deep gash above the forehead. The shovel fell from my hand across the box, and as I pulled it away the flange of the blade caught the edge of the lid, which fell over again, and hid the horrid thing from my sight. The last glimpse I had was of the bloated face, bloodstained and fixed with a grin of malice which would have held its own in the nethermost hell.

I thought and thought what should be my next move, but my brain seemed on fire, and I waited with a despairing feeling growing over me. As I waited I heard in the distance a gipsy song sung by merry voices coming closer, and through their song the rolling of heavy wheels and the cracking of whips; the Szgany and the Slovaks of whom the Count had spoken were coming. With a last look around and at the box which contained the vile body, I ran from the place and gained the Count's room, determined to rush out at the moment the door should be opened. With strained ears I listened, and heard downstairs the grinding of the key in the great lock and the falling back of the heavy door. There must have been some other means of entry, or someone had a key for one of the locked doors. Then there came the sound of many feet tramping and dying away in some passage which sent up a clanging echo. I turned to run down again towards the vault, where I might find the new entrance; but at that moment there seemed to come a violent puff of wind, and the door to the winding stair blew to with a shock that set the dust from the lintels flying. When I ran to push it open, I found that it was hopelessly fast. I was again a prisoner, and the net of doom was closing round me more closely.

As I write there is in the passage below a sound of many tramping feet and the crash of weights being set down heavily, doubtless the boxes, with their freight of earth. There is a sound of hammering; it is the box being nailed down. Now I can hear the heavy feet tramping again along the hall, with many other idle feet coming behind them.

The door is shut, and the chains rattle; there is a grinding of the key in the lock; I can hear the key withdrawn; then another door opens and shuts; I hear the creaking of lock and bolt.

Hark! in the courtyard and down the rocky way the roll of heavy wheels, the crack of whips, and the chorus of the Szgany as they pass into the distance.

I am alone in the castle with those awful women. Faugh! Mina is a woman, and there is nought in common. They are devils of the Pit!

I shall not remain alone with them; I shall try to scale the castle wall farther than I have yet attempted. I shall take some of the gold with me, lest I want it later. I may find a way from this dreadful place.

And then away for home! away to the quickest and nearest train! away from this cursed spot, from this cursed land, where the devil and his children still walk with earthly feet!

At least God's mercy is better than that of these monsters, and the precipice is steep and high. At its foot a man may sleep – as a man. Good-bye, all! Mina!

Chapter 5

Letter from Miss Mina Murray to Miss Lucy Westenra

9 May

MY DEAREST LUCY, –

Forgive my long delay in writing, but I have been simply over-whelmed with work. The life of an assistant schoolmistress is sometimes trying. I am longing to be with you, and by the sea, where we can talk together freely and build our castles in the air. I have been working very hard lately, because I want to keep up with Jonathan's studies, and I have been practising shorthand very assiduously. When we are married I shall be able to be useful to Jonathan, and if I can stenograph well enough I can take down what he wants to say in this way and write it out for him on the typewriter,[42] at which I am also practising very hard. He and I sometimes write letters in shorthand, and he is keeping a stenographic journal of his travels abroad. When I am with you I shall

keep a diary in the same way. I don't mean one of those two-pages-to-
the-week-with-Sunday-squeezed-in-a-corner diaries, but a sort of journal which I can write in whenever I feel inclined. I do not suppose there
will be much of interest to other people; but it is not intended for them.
I may show it to Jonathan some day if there is in it anything worth
sharing, but it is really an exercise-book. I shall try to do what I see lady
journalists do: interviewing and writing descriptions and trying to
remember conversations. I am told that, with a little practice, one can
remember all that goes on or that one hears said during a day. However,
we shall see. I shall tell you all my little plans when we meet. I have just
had a few hurried lines from Jonathan from Transylvania. He is well,
and will be returning in about a week. I am longing to hear all his news.
It must be so nice to see strange countries. I wonder if we – I mean
Jonathan and I – shall ever see them together. There is the ten o'clock
bell ringing. Good-bye.

   Your loving

                                                             Mina

   Tell me all the news when you write. You have not told me anything
for a long time. I hear rumours, and especially of a tall, handsome,
curly-haired man???

Letter, Lucy Westenra to Mina Murray

                                                   17 Chatham Street,
                                                   Wednesday

My dearest Mina, –

   I must say you tax me *very* unfairly with being a bad correspondent. I
wrote to you *twice* since we parted, and your last letter was only your
second. Besides, I have nothing to tell you. There is really nothing to
interest you. Town is very pleasant just now, and we go a good deal to
picture-galleries and for walks and rides in the park. As to the tall, curly-
haired man, I suppose it was the one who was with me at the last Pop.[43]
Someone has evidently been telling tales. That was Mr Holmwood. He
often comes to see us, and he and mamma get on very well together;
they have so many things to talk about in common. We met some time
ago a man that would just *do for you*, if you were not already engaged to
Jonathan. He is an excellent *parti*,[44] being handsome, well off, and of
good birth. He is a doctor and really clever. Just fancy! He is only nine-
and-twenty, and he has an immense lunatic asylum all under his own
care. Mr Holmwood introduced him to me, and he called here to see us,
and often comes now. I think he is one of the most resolute men I ever

saw, and yet the most calm. He seems absolutely imperturbable. I can fancy what a wonderful power he must have over his patients. He has a curious habit of looking one straight in the face, as if trying to read one's thoughts. He tries this on very much with me, but I flatter myself he has got a tough nut to crack. I know that from my glass. Do you ever try to read your own face? *I do*, and I can tell you it is not a bad study, and gives you more trouble than you can well fancy if you have never tried it. He says that I afford him a curious psychological study and I humbly think I do. I do not, as you know, take sufficient interest in dress to be able to describe the new fashions. Dress is a bore. That is slang again, but never mind; Arthur says that every day. There, it is all out. Mina, we have told all our secrets to each other since we were *children;* we have slept together and eaten together, and laughed and cried together; and now, though I have spoken, I would like to speak more. Oh, Mina, couldn't you guess? I love him. I am blushing as I write, for although I *think* he loves me, he has not told me so in words. But, oh, Mina, I love him; I love him; I love him! There, that does me good. I wish I were with you, dear, sitting by the fire undressing, as we used to sit; and I would try to tell you what I feel. I do not know how I am writing this even to you. I am afraid to stop, or I should tear up the letter, and I don't want to stop, for I *do so* want to tell you all. Let me hear from you *at once*, and tell me all that you think about it. Mina, I must stop. Good-night. Bless me in your prayers; and, Mina, pray for my happiness.

LUCY.

P.S. – I need not tell you this is a secret. Good-night again.

L.

Letter, Lucy Westenra to Mina Murray

24 May.

MY DEAREST MINA, –

Thanks, and thanks, and thanks again for your sweet letter! It was so nice to be able to tell you and to have your sympathy.

My dear, it never rains but it pours. How true the old proverbs are. Here am I, who will be twenty in September, and yet I never had a proposal till today, not a real proposal, and today I have had three. Just fancy! THREE proposals in one day! Isn't it awful! I feel sorry, really and truly sorry, for two of the poor fellows. Oh, Mina, I am so happy that I don't know what to do with myself. And three proposals! But, for goodness' sake, don't tell any of the girls, or they would be getting all sorts of extravagant ideas and imagining themselves injured and slighted if in their very first day at home they did not get six at least. Some girls are so vain. You and I, Mina dear, who are engaged and are going to settle down soon soberly into old married women, can despise vanity. Well, I must tell you about the three, but you must keep it a secret, dear, from *everyone*, except, of course, Jonathan. You will tell him because I would, if I were in your place, certainly tell Arthur. A woman ought to tell her husband everything – don't you think so, dear? – and I must be fair. Men like women, certainly their wives, to be quite as fair as they are; and women, I am afraid, are not always quite as fair as they should be. Well, my dear, number one came just before lunch. I told you of him, Dr John Seward, the lunatic-asylum man, with the strong jaw and the good forehead. He was very cool outwardly, but was nervous all the same. He had evidently been schooling himself as to all sorts of little things, and remembered them; but he almost managed to sit down on his silk hat, which men don't generally do when they are cool, and then when he wanted to appear at ease he kept playing with a lancet in a way that made me nearly scream. He spoke to me, Mina, very straightforwardly. He told me how dear I was to him, though he had known me so little, and what his life would be with me to help and cheer him. He was going to tell me how unhappy he would be if I did not care for him, but when he saw me cry he said that he was a brute and would not add to my present trouble. Then he broke off and asked if I could love him in time; and when I shook my head his hands trembled, and then with some hesitation he asked me if I cared already for anyone else. He put it very nicely, saying that he did not want to wring my confidence from me, but only to know, because if a woman's heart was free a man might have hope. And then, Mina, I felt it a sort of duty to tell him that there was someone. I only told him that much, and then he stood up, and he looked very strong and very grave as he took both my hands in his and said he hoped I would be happy, and that if I ever wanted a friend I must count him one of my best. Oh, Mina dear, I can't help crying; and you must excuse this letter being all blotted. Being proposed to is all very nice and all that sort of thing, but it isn't at all a happy thing when you have to see a poor fellow, whom you know loves you honestly, going away and looking all broken-hearted, and to know that, no matter what he may say at the moment, you are passing quite out of his life. My dear, I must stop here at present, I feel so miserable, though I am so happy.

Evening.

Arthur has just gone, and I feel in better spirits than when I left off, so I can go on telling you about the day. Well, my dear, number two came after lunch. He is such a nice fellow, an American from Texas, and he looks so young and so fresh that it seems almost impossible that he has been to so many places and has had such adventures. I sympathise with poor Desdemona[45] when she had such a dangerous stream poured in her ear, even by a black man. I suppose that we women are such cowards that we think a man will save us from fears, and we marry him. I know now what I would do if I were a man and wanted to make a girl love me. No, I don't, for there was Mr Morris telling us his stories, and Arthur never told any, and yet – My dear, I am somewhat previous. Mr Quincey P. Morris found me alone. It seems that a man always does find a girl alone. No, he doesn't, for Arthur tried twice to *make* a chance, and I helping him all I could; I am not ashamed to say it now. I must tell you beforehand that Mr Morris doesn't always speak slang – that is to say, he never does so to strangers or before them, for he is really well educated and has exquisite manners – but he found out that it amused me to hear him talk American slang, and whenever I was present, and there was no one to be shocked, he said such funny things. I am afraid, my dear, he has to invent it all, for it fits exactly into whatever else he has to say. But this is a way slang has. I do not know myself if I shall ever speak slang; I do not know if Arthur likes it, as I have never heard him use any as yet. Well, Mr Morris sat down beside me and looked as happy and jolly as he could, but I could see all the same that he was very nervous. He took my hand in his, and said ever so sweetly:

'Miss Lucy, I know I ain't good enough to regulate the fixin's of your little shoes, but I guess if you wait till you find a man that is you will go join them seven young women with the lamps when you quit. Won't you just hitch up alongside of me and let us go down the long road together driving in double harness?'

Well, he did look so good-humoured and so jolly that it didn't seem half so hard to refuse him as it did poor Dr Seward, so I said, as lightly as I could, that I did not know anything of hitching, and that I wasn't broken to harness at all yet. Then he said that he had spoken in a light manner, and he hoped that if he had made a mistake in doing so on so grave, so momentous, an occasion for him, I would forgive him. He really did look serious when he was saying it, and I couldn't help feeling a bit serious, too. I know, Mina, you will think me a horrid flirt – though I couldn't help feeling a sort of exultation that he was number two in one day. And then, my dear, before I could say a word he began pouring out a perfect torrent of love-making, laying his very heart and soul at my feet. He looked so earnest over it that I shall never again think that a man must be playful always, and never earnest, because he is merry at times. I suppose he saw something in my face which checked him, for he suddenly stopped, and said with a sort of manly fervour that I could have loved him for if I had been free:

'Lucy, you are an honest-hearted girl, I know. I should not be here speaking to you as I am now if I did not believe you clean grit, right through to the very depths of your soul. Tell me, like one good fellow to another, is there anyone else that you care for? And if there is, I'll never trouble you a hair's breadth again, but will be, if you will let me, a very faithful friend.'

My dear Mina, why are men so noble when we women are so little worthy of them? Here was I almost making fun of this great-hearted, true gentleman. I burst into tears – I am afraid, my dear, you will think this is a very sloppy letter in more ways than one – and I really felt very badly. Why can't they let a girl marry three men, or as many as want her, and save all this trouble? But this is heresy, and I must not say it. I am glad to say that, though I was crying, I was able to look into Mr Morris's brave eyes, and I told him out straight:

'Yes, there is someone I love, though he has not told me yet that he even loves me.' I was right to speak to him so frankly, for quite a light came into his face, and he put out both his hands and took mine – I think I put them into his – and said in a hearty way:

'That's my brave girl. It's better worth being late for a chance of winning you than being in time for any other girl in the world. Don't cry, my dear. If it's for me, I'm a hard nut to crack; and I take it standing up. If that other fellow doesn't know his happiness, well, he'd better look for it soon, or he'll have to deal with me. Little girl, your honesty and pluck have made me a friend, and that's rarer than a lover; it's more unselfish anyhow. My dear, I'm going to have a pretty lonely walk between this and Kingdom Come. Won't you give me one kiss? It'll be something to keep off the darkness now and then. You can, you know, if you like, for that other good fellow – he must be a good fellow, my dear, and a fine fellow or you could not love him – hasn't spoken yet.' That quite won me, Mina, for it *was* brave and sweet of him, and noble, too, to a rival – wasn't it? – and he so sad; so I leant over and kissed him. He stood up with my two hands in his, and as he looked down into my face – I am afraid I was blushing very much – he said:

'Little girl, I hold your hand, and you've kissed me, and if these things don't make us friends nothing ever will. Thank you for your sweet honesty to me, and good-bye.' He wrung my hand, and taking up his hat, went straight out of the room without looking back, without a tear or a quiver or a pause; and I am crying like a baby. Oh, why must a man like that be made unhappy when there are lots of girls about who would worship the very ground he trod on? I know I would if I were free – only I don't want to be free. My dear, this quite upset me, and I feel I cannot write of happiness just at once, after telling you of it; and I don't wish to tell of the number three till it can be all happy. – Ever your loving

LUCY.

P.S. – Oh, about number three – I needn't tell you of number three, need I? Besides, it was all so confused; it seemed only a moment from his coming into the room till both his arms were round me, and he was kissing me. I am very, very happy, and I don't know what I have done to deserve it. I must only try in the future to show that I am not ungrateful for all His goodness to me in sending to me such a lover, such a husband, and such a friend.

Good-bye.

DR SEWARD'S DIARY (*kept in phonograph*)[46]

25 April. – Ebb tide in appetite today. Cannot eat, cannot rest, so diary instead. Since my rebuff of yesterday I have a sort of empty feeling; nothing in the world seems of sufficient importance to be worth the doing . . . As I knew that the only cure for this sort of thing was work, I went down amongst the patients. I picked out one who has afforded me a study of much interest. He is so quaint in his ideas, and so unlike the normal lunatic, that I have determined to understand him as well as I can. Today I seemed to get nearer than ever before to the heart of his mystery.

I questioned him more fully than I had ever done, with a view to making myself master of the facts of his hallucination. In my manner of doing it there was, I now see, something of cruelty. I seemed to wish to keep him to the point of his madness – a thing which I avoid with the patients as I would the mouth of hell. (*Mem.*, under what circumstances would I *not* avoid the pit of hell?) *Omnia Romæ vernalia sunt.*[47] Hell has its price! *verb. sap.*[48] If there be anything behind this instinct it will be valuable to trace it afterwards *accurately*, so I had better commence to do so, therefore –

R. M. Renfield, *ætat.* 59[49] – Sanguine temperament; great physical strength; morbidly excitable; periods of gloom ending in some fixed idea which I cannot make out. I presume that the sanguine temperament itself and the disturbing influence end in a mentally-accomplished finish; a possibly dangerous man, probably dangerous if unselfish. In selfish men caution is as secure an armour for their foes as for themselves. What I think of on this point is, when self is the fixed point the centripetal force is balanced with the centrifugal: when duty, a cause, etc., is the fixed point, the latter force is paramount, and only accident or a series of accidents can balance it.

Letter, Quincey P. Morris to Hon. Arthur Holmwood

25 May.

MY DEAR ART, –

We've told yarns by the camp-fire in the prairies; and dressed one another's wounds after trying a landing at the Marquesas;[50] and drunk healths on the shore of Titicaca.[51] There are more yarns to be told, and other wounds to be healed, and another health to be drunk. Won't you let this be at my camp-fire tomorrow night? I have no hesitation in asking you, as I know a certain lady is engaged to a certain dinner-party, and that you are free. There will only be one other, our old pal at the Korea,[52] Jack Seward. He's coming, too, and we both want to mingle our weeps over the wine-cup, and to drink a health with all our hearts to the happiest man in all the wide world, who has won the noblest heart that God has made and the best worth winning. We promise you a hearty welcome, and a loving greeting, and a health as true as your own right hand. We shall both swear to leave you at home if you drink too deep to a certain pair of eyes. Come!

Yours, as ever and always,

QUINCEY P. MORRIS.

Telegram from Arthur Holmwood to Quincey P. Morris

26 May.

Count me in every time. I bear messages which will make both your ears tingle.

ART.

Chapter 6

MINA MURRAY'S JOURNAL

24 July. Whitby.[53] – Lucy met me at the station, looking sweeter and lovelier than ever, and we drove up to the house at the Crescent, in which they have rooms. This is a lovely place. The little river, the Esk, runs through a deep valley, which broadens out as it comes near the harbour. A great viaduct runs across, with high piers, through which the view seems, somehow, farther away than it really is. The valley is beautifully green and it is so steep that when you are on the high land on either side you look right across it, unless you are near enough to see down. The houses of the old town – the side away from us – are all red-roofed, and seem piled up one over the other anyhow, like the pictures we see of Nuremberg. Right over the town is the ruin of Whitby Abbey,[54] which was sacked by the Danes, and which is the scene of part of 'Marmion',[55] where the girl was built up in the wall. It is a most noble ruin, of immense size, and full of beautiful and romantic bits; there is a legend that a white lady is seen in one of the windows. Between it and the town there is another church, the parish one, round which is a big graveyard, all full of tombstones. This is, to my mind, the nicest spot in Whitby, for it lies right over the town and has a full view of the harbour and all up the bay to where the headland called Kettleness stretches out into the sea. It descends so steeply over the harbour that part of the bank has fallen away, and some of the graves have been destroyed. In one place part of the stonework of the graves stretches out over the sandy pathway far below. There are walks, with seats beside them, through the churchyard; and people go and sit there all day long looking at the beautiful view and enjoying the breeze. I shall come and sit here very often myself and work. Indeed, I am writing now, with my book on my knee, and listening to the talk of three old men who are sitting beside me. They seem to do nothing all day but sit up here and talk.

The harbour lies below me, with, on the far side, one long granite wall stretching out into the sea, with a curve outwards at the end of it in the middle of which is a lighthouse. A heavy sea-wall runs along outside of it. On the near side, the sea-wall makes an elbow crooked inversely, and its end too has a lighthouse. Between the two piers there is a narrow opening into the harbour, which then suddenly widens.

It is nice at high tide; but when the tide is out it shoals away to nothing, and there is merely the stream of the Esk, running between banks of sand, with rocks here and there. Outside the harbour on this side there rises for about half a mile a great reef, the sharp edge of which runs straight out from behind the south lighthouse. At the end of it is a buoy with a bell, which swings in bad weather, and sends in a mournful sound on the wind. They have a legend here that when a ship is lost bells are heard out at sea. I must ask the old man about this; he is coming this way . . .

He is a funny old man. He must be awfully old, for his face is all gnarled and twisted like the bark of a tree. He tells me that he is nearly a hundred, and that he was a sailor in the Greenland fishing fleet when Waterloo[56] was fought. He is, I am afraid, a very sceptical person, for when I asked him about the bells at sea and the White Lady at the abbey he said very brusquely:

'I wouldn't fash masel'[57] about them, miss. Them things be all wore out. Mind, I don't say that they never was, but I do say that they wasn't in my time. They be all very well for comers and trippers an' the like, but not for a nice young lady like you. Them feet-folks[58] from York and Leeds[59] that be always eatin' cured herrin's an' drinkin' tea an' lookin' out to buy cheap jet would creed aught. I wonder masel' who'd be bothered tellin' lies to them – even the newspapers, which is full of fool-talk.' I thought he would be a good person to learn interesting things from, so I asked him if he would mind telling me something about whale-fishing in the old days. He was just settling himself to begin when the clock struck six, whereupon he laboured to get up, and said:

'I must gang ageeanwards home now, miss. My granddaughter doesn't like to be kept waitin' when the tea is ready, for it takes me time to crammle aboon the grees,[60] for there be a many of 'em; an', miss, I lack belly-timber[61] sairly by the clock.'

He hobbled away, and I could see him hurrying, as well as he could, down the steps. The steps are a great feature of the place. They lead from the town up to the church, there are hundreds of them – I do not know how many – and they wind up in a delicate curve; the slope is so gentle that a horse could easily walk up and down them. I think they must originally have had something to do with the Abbey. I shall go home too. Lucy went out visiting with her mother, and as they were only duty calls, I did not go. They will be home by this.

1 August. – I came up here an hour ago with Lucy, and we had a most interesting talk with my old friend and the two others who always come and join him. He is evidently the Sir Oracle[62] of them, and I should think must have been in his time a most dictatorial person. He will not admit anything, and downfaces everybody. If he can't out-argue them he bullies them, and then takes their silence for agreement with his views. Lucy was looking sweetly pretty in her white lawn frock; she has got a beautiful colour since she has been here. I noticed that the old men did not lose any time in coming up and sitting near her when we sat down. She is so sweet with old people; I think they all fell in love with her on the spot. Even my old man succumbed and did not contradict her, but gave me double share instead. I got him on the subject of the legends, and he went off at once into a sort of sermon. I must try to remember it and put it down:

'It be all fool-talk, lock, stock, and barrel; that's what it be, an' nowt else. These bans an' wafts an' boh-ghosts an' bar-guests and bogles an' all anent them is only fit to set bairns an' dizzy women a-belderin'.[63] They be nowt but air-blebs! They, an' all grims an' signs an' warnin's, be all invented by parsons an' illsome beuk-bodies[64] an' railway touters to skeer an' scunner hafflin's,[65] an' to get folks to do somethin' that they don't other incline to. It makes me ireful to think o' them. Why, it's them that, not content with printin' lies on paper an' preachin' them out of pulpits, does want to be cuttin' them on the tombstones. Look here all round you in what airt ye will; all them steans, holdin' up their heads as well as they can out of their pride, is acant – simply tumblin' down with the weight o' the lies wrote on them, "Here lies the body" or "Sacred to the memory" wrote on all of them, an' yet in nigh half of them there bean't no bodies at all; an' the memories of them bean't cared a pinch of snuff about, much less sacred. Lies all of them, nothin' but lies of one kind or another! My gog, but it'll be a quare scowderment[66] at the Day of Judgment when they come tumblin' up here in their death-sarks, all jouped together an' tryin' to drag their tombsteans with them to prove how good they was; some of them trimmlin' and ditherin', with their hands that dozzened an' slippy from lyin' in the sea that they can't even keep ther grup o' them.'

I could see from the old fellow's self-satisfied air and the way in which he looked round for the approval of his cronies that he was 'showing off', so I put in a word to keep him going:

'Oh, Mr Swales, you can't be serious. Surely these tombstones are not all wrong?'

'Yabblins![67] There may be a poorish few not wrong, savin' where they make out the people too good, for there be folk that do think a balm-bowl be like the sea, if only it be their own. The whole thing be only lies. Now look you here; you come here a stranger, an' you see this kirk-garth.' I nodded for I thought it better to assent, though I did not quite understand his dialect. I knew it had something to do with the church. He went on: 'And you consate that all these steans be aboon folk that be happed here, snod an' snog?" I assented again. 'Then that be just where the lie comes in. Why, there be scores of these lay-beds that be toom as old Dun's bacca-box on Friday night.' He nudged one of his companions, and they all laughed. 'And my gog! how could they be otherwise? Look at that one, the aftest abaft the bier-bank; read it!' I went over and read:

'Edward Spencelagh, master mariner, murdered by pirates off the coast of Andres, April, 1854, *æt*. 30.' When I came back Mr Swales went on:

'Who brought him home, I wonder, to hap him here? Murdered off the coast of Andres! an' you consated his body lay under! Why, I could name ye a dozen whose bones lie in the Greenland seas above' – he pointed northwards – 'or where the currents may have drifted them. There be the steans around ye. Ye can, with your young eyes, read the small print of the lies from here. This Braithwaite Lowrey – I knew his father, lost in the *Lively* off Greenland in '20; or Andrew Woodhouse, drowned in the same seas in 1777; or John Paxton, drowned off Cape Farewell a year later; or old John Rawlings, whose grandfather sailed with me, drowned in the Gulf of Finland in '50. Do ye think that all these men will have to make a rush to Whitby when the trumpet sounds? I have me antherums[68] aboot it! I tell ye that when they got here they'd be jommlin'[69] an' jostlin' one another that way that it 'ud be like a fight up on the ice in the old days, when we'd be at one another from daylight to dark, an' tryin' to tie up our cuts by the light of the aurora borealis.' This was evidently local pleasantry, for the old man cackled over it, and his cronies joined in with gusto.

'But,' I said, 'surely you are not quite correct, for you start on the assumption that all the poor people, or their spirits, will have to take their tombstones with them on the Day of Judgment. Do you think that will be really necessary?'

'Well, what else be they tombsteans for? Answer me that, miss!'

'To please their relatives, I suppose.'

'To please their relatives, you suppose!' This he said with intense scorn. 'How will it pleasure their relatives to know that lies is wrote over them, and that everybody in the place knows that they be lies?' He pointed to a stone at our feet which had been laid down as a slab, on which the seat was rested close to the edge of the cliff. 'Read the lines on that thruffstean,'[70] he said. The letters were upside down to me from where I sat, but Lucy was more opposite to them, so she leant over and read:

' "Sacred to the memory of George Canon, who died, in the hope of a glorious resurrection, on July 29, 1873, falling from the rocks at Kettleness. This tomb is erected by his sorrowing mother to her dearly beloved son." He was the only son of his mother, and she was a widow. Really, Mr Swales, I don't see anything very funny in that!' She spoke her comment very gravely and somewhat severely.

'Ye don't see aught funny! Ha! ha! But that's because ye don't gawm[71] the sorrowin' mother was a hell-cat that hated him because he was acrewk'd[72] – a regular lamiter[73] he was – an' he hated her so that he committed suicide in order that she mightn't get an insurance she put on his life. He blew nigh the top of his head off with an old musket that they had for scarin' the crows with. 'Twarn't for crows then, for it brought the clegs and the dowps[74] to him. That's the way he fell off the rocks. And, as to hopes of a glorious resurrection, I've often heard him say masel' that he hoped he'd go to hell, for his mother was so pious that she'd be sure to go to heaven, an' he didn't want to addle[75] where she was. Now isn't that stean at any rate' – he hammered it with his stick as he spoke – 'a pack of lies? and won't it make Gabriel keckle[76] when Geordie comes pantin' up the grees with the tombstean balanced on his hump, and asks it to be took as evidence!'

I did not know what to say, but Lucy turned the conversation as she said, rising up:

'Oh, why did you tell us of this? It is my favourite seat, and I cannot leave it; and now I find I must go on sitting over the grave of a suicide.'

'That won't harm ye, my pretty, an' it may make poor Geordie gladsome to have so trim a lass sittin' on his lap. That won't hurt ye. Why, I've sat here off an' on for nigh twenty years past, an' it hasn't done me no harm. Don't ye fash about them as lies under ye, or that doesn' lie there either! It'll be time for ye to be getting scart when ye see the tombsteans all run away with, and the place as bare as a stubble-field. There's the clock, an' I must gang. My service to ye, ladies!' And off he hobbled.

Lucy and I sat awhile, and it was all so beautiful before us that we took hands as we sat; and she told me all over again about Arthur and their coming marriage. That made me just a little heart-sick, for I haven't heard from Jonathan for a whole month.

The same day. – I came up here alone, for I am very sad. There was no letter for me. I hope there cannot be anything the matter with Jonathan. The clock has just struck nine. I see the lights scattered all over the town, sometimes in rows where the streets are, and sometimes singly; they run right up the Esk and die away in the curve of the valley. To my left the view is cut off by a black line of roof of the old house next the Abbey. The sheep and lambs are bleating in the fields away behind me, and there is a clatter of a donkey's hoofs up the paved road below. The band on the pier is playing a harsh waltz in good time, and farther along the quay there is a Salvation Army meeting in a back street. Neither of the bands hears the other, but up here I hear and see them both. I wonder where Jonathan is and if he is thinking of me! I wish he were here.

Dr Seward's Diary

5 June. – The case of Renfield grows more interesting the more I get to understand the man. He has certain qualities very largely developed: selfishness, secrecy, and purpose. I wish I could get at what is the object of the latter. He seems to have some settled scheme of his own, but what it is I do not yet know. His redeeming quality is a love of animals, though, indeed, he has such curious turns in it that I sometimes imagine he is only abnormally cruel. His pets are of odd sorts. Just now his hobby is catching flies. He has at present such a quantity that I have had myself to expostulate. To my astonishment, he did not break out into a fury, as I expected, but took the matter in simple seriousness. He thought for a moment, and then said: 'May I have three days? I shall clear them away.' Of course, I said that would do. I must watch him.

18 June. – He has turned his mind now to spiders, and has got several very big fellows in a box. He keeps feeding them with his flies, and the number of the latter is becoming sensibly diminished, although he has used half his food in attracting more flies from outside to his room.

1 July. – His spiders are now becoming as great a nuisance as his flies, and today I told him that he must get rid of them. He looked very sad at this, so I said that he must clear out some of them, at all events. He cheerfully acquiesced in this, and I gave him the same time as before for reduction. He disgusted me much while with him, for when a horrid blow-fly, bloated with some carrion food, buzzed into the room, he caught it, held it exultingly for a few moments between his finger and thumb and, before I knew what he was going to do, put it in his mouth and ate it. I scolded him for it but he argued quietly that it was very good and very wholesome; that it was life, strong life, and gave life to him. This gave me an idea, or the rudiment of one. I must watch how he gets rid of his spiders. He has evidently some deep problem in his mind, for he keeps a little note-book in which he is always jotting down something. Whole pages of it are filled with masses of figures, generally single numbers added up in batches, and then the totals added in batches again as though he were 'focusing' some account, as the auditors put it.

8 July. – There is a method in his madness,[77] and the rudimentary idea in my mind is growing. It will be a whole idea soon, and then, oh, unconscious cerebration! you will have to give the wall to your conscious brother. I kept away from my friend for a few days, so that I might notice if there were any change. Things remain as they were except that he has parted with some of his pets and got a new one. He has managed to get a sparrow, and has already partially tamed it. His means of taming is simple, for already the spiders have diminished. Those that do remain, however, are well fed, for he still brings in the flies by tempting them with his food.

19 July. – We are progressing. My friend has now a whole colony of sparrows, and his flies and spiders are almost obliterated. When I came in he ran to me and said he wanted to ask me a great favour – a very, very great favour; and as he spoke he fawned on me like a dog. I asked him what it was, and he said with a sort of rapture in his voice and bearing:

'A kitten, a nice little, sleek, playful kitten, that I can play with, and teach, and feed – and feed – and feed!' I was not unprepared for this request, for I had noticed how his pets went on increasing in size and vivacity, but I did not care that his pretty family of tame sparrows should be wiped out in the same manner as the flies and the spiders, so I said I would see about it, and asked him if he would not rather have a cat than a kitten. His eagerness betrayed him as he answered:

'Oh, yes I would like a cat! I only asked for a kitten lest you should refuse me a cat. No one would refuse me a kitten, would they?' I shook my head, and said that at present I feared it would not be possible, but that I would see about it. His face fell, and I could see a warning of danger in it, for there was a sudden fierce, sidelong look which meant killing. The man is an undeveloped homicidal maniac. I shall test him with his present craving and see how it will work out; then I shall know more.

10 p.m. – I have visited him again and found him sitting in a corner brooding. When I came in he threw himself on his knees before me and implored me to let him have a cat, that his salvation depended upon it. I was firm, however, and told him that he could not have it, whereupon he went without a word, and sat down, gnawing his fingers, in the corner where I had found him. I shall see him in the morning early.

20 July. – Visited Renfield very early, before the attendant went his rounds. Found him up and humming a tune. He was spreading out his sugar, which he had saved, in the window, and was manifestly beginning his fly-catching again; and beginning it cheerfully and with a good grace. I looked around for his birds, and not seeing them, asked him where they were. He replied, without turning round, that they had all flown away. There were a few feathers about the room and on his pillow a drop of blood. I said nothing, but went and told the keeper to report to me if there were anything odd about him during the day.

11 a.m. – The attendant has just been to me to say that Renfield has been very sick and has disgorged a whole lot of feathers. 'My belief is, doctor,' he said, 'that he has eaten his birds, and that he just took and ate them raw!'

11 p.m. – I gave Renfield a strong opiate tonight, enough to make even him sleep, and took away his pocket-book to look at it. The thought that has been buzzing about my brain lately is complete, and the theory proved. My homicidal maniac is of a peculiar kind. I shall have to invent a new classification for him, and call him a zoophagous (life-eating) maniac; what he desires is to absorb as many lives as he can, and he has laid himself out to achieve it in a cumulative way. He gave many flies to one spider and many spiders to one bird, and then wanted a cat to eat the many birds. What would have been his later steps? It would almost be worth while to complete the experiment. It might be done if there were only a sufficient cause. Men sneered at vivisection, and yet look at its results today! Why not advance science in its most difficult and vital aspect – the knowledge of the brain? Had I even the secret of one such mind – did I hold the key to the fancy of even one lunatic – I might advance my own branch of science to a pitch compared with which Burdon-Sanderson's physiology or Ferrier's brain-knowledge[78] would be as nothing. If only there were a sufficient cause! I must not think too much of this, or I may be tempted; a good cause might turn the scale with me, for may not I too be of an exceptional brain, congenitally?

How well the man reasoned! Lunatics always do within their own scope. I wonder at how many lives he values a man, or if at only one. He has closed the account most accurately, and today begun a new record. How many of us begin a new record with each day of our lives?

To me it seems only yesterday that my whole life ended with my new hope, and that truly I began a new record. So it will be until the Great Recorder sums me up and closes my ledger account with a balance to profit or loss. Oh, Lucy, Lucy, I cannot be angry with you, nor can I be angry with my friend whose happiness is yours; but I must only wait on hopeless and work. Work! work!

If I only could have as strong a cause as my poor mad friend there, a good, unselfish cause to make me work, that would be indeed happiness.

Mina Murray's Journal

26 July. – I am anxious, and it soothes me to express myself here; it is like whispering to one's self and listening at the same time. And there is also something about the shorthand symbols that makes it different from writing. I am unhappy about Lucy and about Jonathan. I had not heard from Jonathan for some time, and was very concerned; but yesterday dear Mr Hawkins, who is always so kind, sent me a letter from him. I had written asking him if he had heard, and he said the enclosed had just been received. It is only a line dated from Castle Dracula, and says that he is just starting for home. That is not like Jonathan; I do not understand it, and it makes me uneasy. Then, too, Lucy, although she is so well, has lately taken to her old habit of walking in her sleep. Her mother has spoken to me about it, and we have decided that I am to lock the door of our room every night. Mrs Westenra has got an idea that sleep-walkers always go out on roofs of houses and along the edges of cliffs, and then get suddenly wakened and fall over with a despairing cry that echoes all over the place. Poor dear, she is naturally anxious about Lucy, and she tells me that her husband, Lucy's father, had the same habit; that he would get up in the night and dress himself and go out, if he were not stopped. Lucy is to be married in the autumn, and she is already planning out her dresses and how her house is to be arranged. I sympathise with her, for I do the same, only Jonathan and I will start in life in a very simple way, and shall have to try to make both ends meet. Mr Holmwood – he is the Hon. Arthur Holmwood, only son of Lord Godalming – is coming up here very shortly – as soon as he can leave town, for his father is not very well, and I think dear Lucy is counting the moments till he comes. She wants to take him up to the seat on the churchyard cliff and show him the beauty of Whitby. I daresay it is the waiting which disturbs her; she will be all right when he arrives.

27 July. – No news from Jonathan. I am getting quite uneasy about him, though why I should I do not know; but I *do* wish that he would write, if it were only a single line. Lucy walks more than ever, and each night I am awakened by her moving about the room. Fortunately, the weather is so hot that she cannot get cold; but still the anxiety and the perpetually being wakened is beginning to tell on me, and I am getting nervous and wakeful myself. Thank God, Lucy's health keeps up. Mr Holmwood has been suddenly called to Ring to see his father, who has been taken seriously ill. Lucy frets at the postponement of seeing him, but it does not touch her looks; she is a trifle stouter, and her cheeks are a lovely rose pink. She has lost that anæmic look which she had. I pray it will all last.

3 August. – Another week gone, and no news from Jonathan, not even to Mr Hawkins, from whom I have heard. Oh, I do hope he is not ill. He surely would have written. I look at that last letter of his, but somehow it does not satisfy me. It does not read like him, and yet it is his writing. There is no mistake of that. Lucy has not walked much in her sleep the last week, but there is an odd concentration about her which I do not understand; even in her sleep she seems to be watching me. She tries the door, and finding it locked, goes about the room searching for the key.

6 August. – Another three days, and no news. This suspense is getting dreadful. If I only knew where to write to or where to go to, I should feel easier; but no one has heard a word of Jonathan since that last letter. I must only pray to God for patience. Lucy is more excitable than ever, but is otherwise well. Last night was very threatening, and the fishermen say that we are in for a storm. I must try to watch it and learn the weather signs. Today is a grey day, and the sun as I write is hidden in thick clouds, high over Kettleness. Everything is grey – except the green grass, which seems like emerald amongst it; grey earthy rock; grey clouds, tinged with the sunburst at the far edge, hang over the grey sea, into which the sand-points stretch like grey fingers. The sea is tumbling in over the shallows and the sandy flats with a roar, muffled in the sea-mists drifting inland. The horizon is lost in a grey mist. All is vastness; the clouds are piled up like giant rocks, and there is a 'brool'[79] over the sea that sounds like some presage of doom. Dark figures are on the beach here and there, sometimes half shrouded in the mist, and seem 'men like trees walking'.[80] The fishing-boats are racing for home, and rise and dip in the ground swell as they sweep into the harbour, bending to the scuppers.[81] Here comes old Mr Swales. He is making straight for me, and I can see, by the way he lifts his hat, that he wants to talk . . .

I have been quite touched by the change in the poor old man. When he sat down beside me, he said in a very gentle way:

'I want to say something to you, miss.' I could see he was not at ease, so I took his poor old wrinkled hand in mine and asked him to speak fully; so he said, leaving his hand in mine:

'I'm afraid, my deary, that I must have shocked you by all the wicked things I've been sayin' about the dead, and suchlike, for weeks past; but I didn't mean them, and I want you to remember that when I've gone. We aud folks that be daffled, and with one foot abaft the krok-hooal,[82] don't altogether like to think of it, and we don't want to feel scart of it; an' that's why I've took to makin' light of it, so that I'd cheer up my own heart a bit. But, Lord love ye, miss, I ain't afraid of dyin' not a bit; only I don't want to die if I can help it. My time must be nigh at hand now, for I be aud, and a hundred years is too much for any man to expect; and I'm so nigh it that the Aud Man is already whettin' his scythe. Ye see, I can't get out o' the habit of caffin''[83] about it all at once; the chafts[84] will wag as they be used to. Some day soon the Angel of Death will sound his trumpet for me. But don't ye dooal an' greet, my deary!' – for he saw that I was crying – 'if he should come this very night I'd not refuse to answer his call. For life be, after all, only a waitin' for somethin' else than what we're doin'; and death be all that we can rightly depend on. But I'm content, for it's comin' to me, my deary, and comin' quick. It may be comin' while we be lookin' and wonderin'. Maybe it's in that wind out over the sea that's bringin' with it loss and wreck, and sore distress and sad hearts. Look! look!' he cried suddenly. 'There's something in that wind and in the hoast beyont that sounds, and looks, and tastes, and smells like death. It's in the air, I feel it comin'. Lord, make me answer cheerful when my call comes!' He held up his arms devoutly, and raised his hat. His mouth moved as though he were praying. After a few minutes' silence, he got up, shook hands with me, and blessed me, and said good-bye, and hobbled off. It all touched me, and upset me very much. I was glad when the coastguard came along, with his spy-glass under his arm. He stopped to talk with me, as he always does, but all the time kept looking at a strange ship.

'I can't make her out,' he said; 'she's a Russian, by the look of her; but she's knocking about in the queerest way. She doesn't know her mind a bit; she seems to see the storm coming, but can't decide whether to run up north in the open, or to put in here. Look there again! She is steered mighty strangely, for she doesn't mind the hand on the wheel; changes about with every puff of wind. We'll hear more of her before this time tomorrow.'

Chapter 7

CUTTING FROM THE *Dailygraph*, 8 AUGUST
(pasted in Mina Murray's Journal)

From a Correspondent

Whitby.

ONE OF THE GREATEST and suddenest storms on record has just been experienced here, with results both strange and unique. The weather had been somewhat sultry, but not to any degree uncommon in the month of August. Saturday evening was as fine as was ever known, and the great body of holiday-makers set out yesterday for visits to Mulgrave Woods, Robin Hood's Bay, Rig Mill, Runswick, Staithes,[85] and the various trips in the neighbourhood of Whitby. The steamers *Emma* and *Scarborough* made excursions along the coast, and there was an unusual amount of 'tripping' both to and from Whitby. The day was unusually fine till the afternoon, when some of the gossips who frequent the East Cliff churchyard, and from that commanding eminence watch the wide sweep of sea visible to the north and east, called attention to a sudden show of 'mares'-tails' high in the sky to the north-west. The wind was then blowing from the south-west in the mild degree which in barometrical language is ranked 'No. 2: light breeze.' The coastguard on duty at once made report, and one old fisherman, who for more than half a century has kept watch on weather signs from the East Cliff, foretold in an emphatic manner the coming of a sudden storm. The approach of sunset was so very beautiful, so grand in its masses of splendidly-coloured clouds, that there was quite an assemblage on the walk along the cliff in the old churchyard to enjoy the beauty. Before the sun dipped below the black mass of Kettleness, standing boldly athwart the western sky, its downward way was marked by myriad clouds of every sunset-colour – flame, purple, pink, green, violet, and all the tints of gold; with here and there masses not large, but of seemingly absolute blackness, in all sorts of shapes, as well outlined as colossal silhouettes. The experience was not lost on the painters, and doubtless some of the sketches of the 'Prelude to the Great Storm' will grace the R.A. and R.I.[86] walls in May next. More than one captain made up his mind then and there that his 'cobble' or his 'mule', as they term the different classes of boats, would remain in the harbour till the storm had passed. The wind fell away entirely during the evening, and at midnight there was a dead calm, a sultry heat, and that prevailing intensity which, on the approach of thunder, affects persons of a sensitive nature. There were but few lights in sight at sea, for even the coasting steamers, which usually 'hug' the shore so closely, kept well to seaward, and but few fishing-boats were in sight. The only sail noticeable was a foreign schooner with all sails set, which was seemingly going westwards. The foolhardiness or ignorance of her officers was a prolific theme for comment whilst she remained in sight, and efforts were made to signal her to reduce sail in face of her danger. Before the night shut down she was seen with sails idly flapping as she gently rolled on the undulating swell of the sea.

As idle as a painted ship upon a painted ocean.[87]

Shortly before ten o'clock the stillness of the air grew quite oppressive, and the silence was so marked that the bleating of a sheep inland or the barking of a dog in the town was distinctly heard, and the band on the pier, with its lively French air, was like a discord in the great harmony of nature's silence. A little after midnight came a strange sound from over the sea, and high overhead the air began to carry a strange, faint hollow booming.

Then without warning the tempest broke. With a rapidity which, at the time, seemed incredible, and even afterwards is impossible to realise, the whole aspect of nature at once became convulsed. The waves rose in growing fury, each overtopping its fellow, till in a very few minutes the lately glassy sea was like a roaring and devouring monster. White-crested waves beat madly on the level sands and rushed up the shelving cliffs, others broke over the piers, and with their spume swept the lanthorns of the lighthouses which rise from the end of either pier of Whitby Harbour. The wind roared like thunder, and blew with such force that it was with difficulty that even strong men kept their feet, or clung with grim clasp to the iron stanchions. It was found necessary to clear the entire piers from the mass of onlookers, or else the fatalities of the night would have been increased manyfold. To add to the difficulties and dangers of the time, masses of sea-fog came drifting inland – white, wet clouds, which swept by in ghostly fashion, so dank and damp and cold that it needed but little effort of imagination to think that the spirits of those lost at sea were touching their living brethren with the clammy hands of death, and many a one shuddered as the wreaths of sea-mist swept by. At times the mist cleared, and the sea for some distance could be seen in the glare of the lightning which now came thick and fast followed by such sudden peals of thunder that the whole sky overhead seemed trembling under the shock of the footsteps of the storm. Some of the scenes thus revealed were of immeasurable grandeur and of absorbing interest – the sea, running mountains high, threw skywards with each wave mighty masses of white foam, which the tempest seemed to snatch at and whirl away into space; here and there a fishing-boat, with a rag of sail, running madly for shelter before the blast; now and again the white wings of a storm-tossed sea-bird. On the summit of the East Cliff the new searchlight was ready for experiment, but had not yet been tried. The officers in charge of it got it into working order, and in the pauses of the inrushing mist swept with it the surface of the sea. Once or twice its service was most effective, as when a fishing-boat, with gunwale[88] under water, rushed into the harbour, able, by the guidance of the sheltering light, to avoid the danger of dashing against the piers. As each boat achieved the safety of the port there was a shout of joy from the mass of people on shore, a shout which for a moment seemed to cleave the gale and was then swept away in its rush. Before long the searchlight discovered some distance away a schooner with all sails set, apparently the same vessel which had been noticed earlier in the evening. The wind had by this time backed to the east, and there was a shudder amongst the watchers on the cliff as they realised the terrible danger in which she now was. Between her and the port lay the great flat reef on which so many good ships have from time to time suffered, and, with the wind blowing from its present quarter, it would be quite impossible that she should fetch the entrance of the harbour. It was now nearly the hour of high tide, but the waves were so great that in their troughs the shallows of the shore were almost visible, and the schooner, with all sails set, was rushing with such speed that, in the words of one old salt, 'she must fetch up somewhere, if it was only in hell.' Then came another rush of sea-fog, greater than any hitherto mass of dank mist, which seemed to close on all things like a grey pall, and left available to men only the organ of hearing, for the roar of the tempest, and the crash of the thunder, and the booming of the mighty billows came through the damp oblivion even louder than before. The rays of the searchlight were kept fixed on the harbour mouth across the East Pier, where the shock was expected, and men waited breathless. The wind suddenly shifted to the north-east, and the remnant of the sea-fog melted in the blast; and then, *mirabile dictu*,[89] between the piers, leaping from wave to wave as it rushed at headlong speed, swept the strange schooner before the blast, with all sail set, and gained the safety of the harbour. The searchlight followed her, and a shudder ran through all who saw her, for lashed to the helm was a corpse, with drooping head, which swung horribly to and fro at each motion of the ship. No other form could be seen on deck at all. A great awe came on all as they realised that the ship, as if by a miracle, had found the harbour, unsteered save by the hand of a dead man! However, all took place more quickly than it takes to write these words. The schooner paused not, but rushing across the harbour, pitched herself on that accumulation of sand and gravel washed by many tides and many storms into the south-east corner of the pier jutting under the East Cliff, known locally as Tate Hill Pier.

There was of course a considerable concussion as the vessel drove up on the sand-heap. Every spar, rope, and stay was strained, and some of the 'top-hammer'[90] came crashing down. But, strangest of all, the very instant the shore was touched, an immense dog sprang up on deck from below, as if shot up by the concussion, and running forward, jumped from the bow on to the sand. Making straight for the steep cliff, where the churchyard hangs over the laneway to the East Pier so steeply that some of the flat tombstones – 'thruff-steans' or 'through-stones', as they call them in the Whitby vernacular – actually project over where the sustaining cliff has fallen away, it disappeared in the darkness, which seemed intensified just beyond the focus of the searchlight.

It so happened that there was no one at the moment on Tate Hill Pier, as all those whose houses are in close proximity were either in bed or were out on the heights above. Thus the coastguard on duty on the eastern side of the harbour, who at once ran down to the little pier was the first to climb on board. The men working the searchlight, after scouring the entrance of the harbour without seeing anything, then turned the light on the derelict and kept it there. The coastguard ran aft, and when he came beside the wheel, bent over to examine it and recoiled at once as though under some sudden emotion. This seemed to pique the general curiosity, and quite a number of people began to run. It is a good way round from the West Cliff by the Drawbridge to Tate Hill Pier, but your correspondent is a fairly good runner, and came well ahead of the crowd. When I arrived, however, I found already assembled on the pier a crowd, whom the coastguard and police refused to allow to come on board. By the courtesy of the chief boatman, I was, as your correspondent, permitted to climb on deck, and was one of a small group who saw the dead seaman whilst actually lashed to the wheel.

It was no wonder that the coastguard was surprised, or even awed, for not often can such a sight have been seen. The man was simply fastened by his hands, tied one over the other, to a spoke of the wheel. Between the inner hand and the wood was a crucifix, the set of beads on which it was fastened being around both wrists and wheel, and all kept fast by the binding cords. The poor fellow may have been seated at one time, but the flapping and buffeting of the sails had worked through the rudder of the wheel and dragged him to and fro, so that the cords with which he was tied had cut the flesh to the bone. Accurate note was made of the state of things, and a doctor – Surgeon J. M. Caffyn, of 33, East Elliot Place – who came immediately after me, declared, after making examination, that the man must have been dead for quite two days. In his pocket was a bottle, carefully corked, empty save for a little roll of paper, which proved to be the addendum to the log. The coastguard said the man must have tied up his own hands, fastening the knots with his teeth. The fact that a coastguard was the first on board may save some complications, later on, in the Admiralty Court; for the coast-guards cannot claim the salvage which is the right of the first civilian entering on a derelict. Already, however, the legal tongues are wagging, and one young law student is loudly asserting that the rights of the owner are already completely sacrificed, his property being held in contravention of the statutes of mortmain,[91] since the tiller, as emblemship, if not proof, of delegated possession, is held in a *dead hand*. It is needless to say that the dead steersman has been reverently removed from the place where he held his honourable watch and ward till death – a steadfastness as noble as that of the young Casabianca [92] – and placed in the mortuary to await inquest.

Already the sudden storm is passing, and its fierceness is abating; the crowds are scattering homewards, and the sky is beginning to redden over the Yorkshire wolds.[93] I shall send, in time for your next issue, further details of the derelict ship which found her way so miraculously into harbour in the storm.

Whitby.

9 August. – The sequel to the strange arrival of the derelict in the storm last night is almost more startling than the thing itself. It turns out that the schooner is a Russian from Varna and is called the *Demeter*.[94] She is almost entirely in ballast of silver sand, with only a small amount of cargo – a number of great wooden boxes filled with mould. This cargo was consigned to a Whitby solicitor, Mr S. F. Billington, of 7, The Crescent, who this morning went aboard and formally took possession of the goods consigned to him. The Russian consul, too, acting for the charter-party, took formal possession of the ship, and paid all harbour dues, etc.

Nothing is talked about here today except the strange coincidence; the officials of the Board of Trade have been most exacting in seeing that every compliance has been made with existing regulations. As the matter is to be a 'nine days' wonder', they are evidently determined that there shall be no cause of after complaint. A good deal of interest was abroad concerning the dog which landed when the ship struck, and more than a few of the members of the S.P.C.A., which is very strong in Whitby, have tried to befriend the animal. To the general disappointment, however, it was not to be found; it seems to have disappeared entirely from the town. It may be that it was frightened and made its way on to the moors, where it is still hiding in terror. There are some who look with dread on such a possibility, lest later on it should in itself become a danger, for it is evidently a fierce brute. Early this morning a large dog, a half-bred mastiff, belonging to a coal merchant close to Tate Hill Pier, was found dead in the roadway opposite its master's yard. It had been fighting, and manifestly had had a savage opponent, for its throat was torn away, and its belly was slit open as if with a savage claw.

Later. – By the kindness of the Board of Trade inspector I have been permitted to look over the log-book of the *Demeter*, which was in order up to within three days, but contained nothing of special interest except as to facts of missing men. The greater interest, however, is with regard to the paper found in the bottle, which was today produced at the inquest; and a more strange narrative than the two between them unfold it has not been my lot to come across. As there is no motive for concealment, I am permitted to use them, and accordingly send you a rescript, simply omitting technical details of seamanship and supercargo. It almost seems as though the captain had been seized with some kind of mania before he had got well into blue water, and that this had developed persistently throughout the voyage. Of course my statement must be taken *cum grano*,[95] since I am writing from the dictation of a clerk of the Russian consul, who kindly translated for me, time being short.

LOG OF THE 'DEMETER' (*Varna to Whitby*)

Written 18 July, things so strange happening, that I shall keep accurate note henceforth till we land.

On 6 July we finished taking in cargo, silver sand and boxes of earth. At noon set sail. East wind, fresh. Crew, five hands . . . two mates, cook, and myself (captain).

On 11 July at dawn entered Bosphorus. Boarded by Turkish Customs officers. Backsheesh.[96] All correct. Under way at 4 p.m.

On 12 July through Dardanelles. More Customs officers and flagboat of guarding squadron. Backsheesh again. Work of officers thorough, but quick. Want us off soon. At dark passed into Archipelago.

On 13 July passed Cape Matapan. Crew dissatisfied about something. Seemed scared, but would not speak out.

On 14 July was somewhat anxious about crew. Men all steady fellows, who sailed with me before. Mate could not make out what was wrong; they only told him there was *something* aboard and crossed themselves. Mate lost temper with one of them that day and struck him. Expected fierce quarrel, but all was quiet.

On 16 July mate reported in the morning that one of crew, Petrofsky, was missing. Could not account for it. Took larboard watch eight bells last night; was relieved by Abramoff, but did not go to bunk. Men more downcast than ever. All said they expected something of the kind, but would not say more than that there was *something* aboard. Mate getting very impatient with them; feared some trouble ahead.

On 17 July, yesterday, one of the men, Olgaren, came to my cabin, and in an awestruck way confided to me that he thought there was a strange man aboard the ship. He said that in his watch he had been sheltering behind the deck-house, as there was a rain-storm, when he saw a tall, thin man, who was not like any of the crew, come up the companion way, and go along the deck forward, and disappear. He followed cautiously, but when he got to bows found no one, and the hatchways were all closed. He was in a panic of superstitious fear, and I am afraid the panic may spread. To allay it, I shall today search entire ship carefully from stem to stern.

Later in the day I got together the whole crew, and told them, as they evidently thought there was someone in the ship, we should search from stem to stem. First mate angry; said it was folly, and to yield to such foolish ideas would demoralise the men; said he would engage to keep them out of trouble with a handspike. I let him take the helm , while the rest began thorough search, all keeping abreast, with lanterns; we left no corner unsearched. As there were only the big wooden boxes, there were no odd corners where a man could hide. Men much relieved when search over, and went back to work cheerfully. First mate scowled, but said nothing.

22 July. – Rough weather last three days, and all hands busy with sails – no time to be frightened. Men seem to have forgotten their dread. Mate cheerful again, and all on good terms. Praised men for work in bad weather. Passed Gibraltar and out through Straits. All well.

24 July – There seems some doom over this ship. Already a hand short, and entering on the Bay of Biscay with wild weather ahead, and yet last night another man lost – disappeared. Like the first, he came off his watch and was not seen again. Men all in a panic of fear; sent a round robin,[97] asking to have double watch, as they fear to be alone. Mate violent. Fear there will be some trouble, as either he or the men will do some violence.

28 July. – Four days in hell, knocking about in a sort of maelstrom, and the wind a tempest. No sleep for anyone. Men all worn out. Hardly know how to set a watch since no one fit to go on. Second mate volunteered to steer and watch, and let men snatch a few hours' sleep. Wind abating; seas still terrific, but feel them less, as ship is steadier.

29 July. – Another tragedy. Had single watch tonight, as crew too tired to double. When morning watch came on deck could find no one except steersman. Raised outcry, and all came on deck. Thorough search, but no one found. Are now without second mate, and crew in a panic. Mate and I agreed to go armed henceforth and wait for any sign of cause.

30 July. – Last night. Rejoiced we are nearing England. Weather fine, all sails set. Retired worn out; slept soundly; awaked by mate telling me that both men of watch and steersman missing. Only self and mate and two hands left to work ship.

1 August. – Two days of fog, and not a sail sighted. Had hoped when in the English Channel to be able to signal for help or get in somewhere. Not having power to work sails, have to run before wind. Dare not lower, as could not raise them again. We seem to be drifting to some terrible doom. Mate now more demoralised than either of them. His stronger nature seems to have worked inwardly against himself. Men are beyond fear, working stolidly and patiently, with minds made up to worst. They are Russian, he Roumanian.

2 August, midnight. – Woke up from few minutes' sleep by hearing a cry, seemingly outside my port. Could see nothing in fog. Rushed on deck, and ran against mate. Tells me heard cry and ran, but no sign of man on watch. One more gone. Lord, help us! Mate says we must be past Straits of Dover, as in a moment of fog lifting he saw North Foreland just as he heard the man cry out. If so we are now off in the North Sea, and only God can guide us in the fog, which seems to move with us; and God seems to have deserted us.

3 August. – At midnight I went to relieve the man at the wheel, but when I got to it found no one there. The wind was steady, and as we ran before it there was no yawing.[98] I dared not leave it, so shouted for the mate. After a few seconds he rushed up on deck in his flannels. He looked wild-eyed and haggard, and I greatly fear his reason has given way. He came close to me and whispered hoarsely, with his mouth to my ear, as though fearing the very air might hear: 'It is here; I know it, now. On the watch last night I saw It, like a man, tall and thin, and ghastly pale. It was in the bows, and looking out. I crept behind It, and gave It my knife; but the knife went through It, empty as the air.' And as he spoke he took his knife and drove it savagely into space. Then he went on: 'But It is here, and I'll find it. It is in the hold, perhaps, in one of those boxes. I'll unscrew them one by one and see. You work the helm.' And, with a warning look and his finger on his lip, he went below. There was springing up a choppy wind, and I could not leave the helm. I saw him come out on deck again with a tool-chest and a lantern, and go down the forward hatchway. He is mad, stark, raving mad, and it's no use my trying to stop him. He can't hurt those big boxes: they are invoiced as 'clay', and to pull them about is as harmless a thing as he can do. So here I stay, and mind the helm, and write these notes. I can only trust in God and wait till the fog clears. Then if I can't steer to any harbour with the wind that is, I shall cut down sails and lie by, and signal for help . . .

It is nearly all over now. Just as I was beginning to hope that the mate would come out calmer – for I heard him knocking away at something in the hold, and work is good for him – there came up the hatchway a sudden, startled scream, which made my blood run cold, and up on the deck he came as if shot from a gun – a raging madman, with his eyes rolling and his face convulsed with fear. 'Save me! save me!' he cried, and then looked round on the blanket of fog. His horror turned to despair, and in a steady voice he said: 'You had better come too captain, before it is too late. *He* is there. I know the secret now. The sea will save me from Him, and it is all that is left!' Before I could say a word, or move forward to seize him, he sprang on the bulwark and deliberately threw himself into the sea. I suppose I know the secret too, now. It was this madman who had got rid of the men one by one, and now he has followed them himself. God help me! How am I to account for all these horrors when I get to port? *When* I get to port! Will that ever be?

4 August. – Still fog, which the sunrise cannot pierce. I know there is sunrise because I am a sailor, why else I know not. I dared not go below, I dared not leave the helm so here all night I stayed, and in the dimness of the night I saw It – Him! God forgive me, but the mate was right to jump overboard. It is better to die like a man; to die like a sailor in blue water no man can object. But I am captain, and I must not leave my ship. But I shall baffle this fiend or monster, for I shall tie my hands to

the wheel when my strength begins to fail, and along with them I shall
tie that which He – It! – dare not touch; and then, come good wind or
foul, I shall save my soul, and my honour as a captain. I am growing
weaker, and the night is coming on. If He can look me in the face again,
I may not have time to act . . . If we are wrecked, mayhap this bottle may
be found and those who find it may understand; if not, . . . well, then all
men shall know that I have been true to my trust. God and the Blessed
Virgin and the saints help a poor ignorant soul trying to do his duty . . .

Of course the verdict was an open one. There is no evidence to adduce;
and whether or not the man himself committed the murders there is
now none to say. The folk hold almost universally here that the captain
is simply a hero, and he is to be given a public funeral. Already it is
arranged that his body is to be taken with a train of boats up the Esk for
a piece and then brought back to Tate Hill Pier and up the Abbey steps;
for he is to be buried in the churchyard on the cliff. The owners of more
than a hundred boats have already given in their names as wishing to
follow him to the grave.

No trace has ever been found of the great dog; at which there is much
mourning, for, with public opinion in its present state, he would, I
believe, be adopted by the town. Tomorrow will see the funeral; and so
will end this one more 'mystery of the sea'.

MINA MURRAY'S JOURNAL

8 August. – Lucy was very restless all night, and I, too, could not sleep.
The storm was fearful, and as it boomed loudly among the chimney-
pots, it made me shudder. When a sharp puff came it seemed to be like
a distant gun. Strangely enough, Lucy did not wake; but she got up
twice and dressed herself. Fortunately, each time I awoke in time, and
managed to undress her without waking her, and got her back to bed. It
is a very strange thing, this sleep-walking, for as soon as her will is
thwarted in any physical way, her intention, if there be any, disappears,
and she yields herself almost exactly to the routine of her life.

Early in the morning we both got up and went down to the harbour
to see if anything had happened in the night. There were very few
people about, and though the sun was bright, and the air clear and fresh,
the big, grim-looking waves, that seemed dark themselves because the
foam that topped them was like snow, forced themselves in through the
narrow mouth of the harbour – like a bullying man going through a
crowd. Somehow I felt glad that Jonathan was not on the sea last night,

but on land. But, oh, is he on land or sea? Where is he, and how? I am
getting fearfully anxious about him. If I only knew what to do, and
could do anything!

10 August. – The funeral of the poor sea-captain today was most
touching. Every boat in the harbour seemed to be there, and the coffin
was carried by captains all the way from Tate Hill Pier up to the
churchyard. Lucy came with me, and we went early to our old seat,
whilst the cortège of boats went up the river to the Viaduct and came
down again. We had a lovely view, and saw the procession nearly all the
way. The poor fellow was laid to rest quite near our seat, so that we
stood on it when the time came and saw everything. Poor Lucy seemed
much upset. She was restless and uneasy all the time, and I cannot but
think that her dreaming at night is telling on her. She is quite odd in
one thing: she will not admit to me that there is any cause for
restlessness; or if there be, she does not understand it herself. There is
an additional cause in that poor old Mr Swales was found dead this
morning on our seat, his neck being broken. He had evidently, as the
doctor said, fallen back in the seat in some sort of fright, for there was a
look of fear and horror on his face that the men said made them
shudder. Poor dear old man! Perhaps he had seen Death with his dying
eyes! Lucy is so sweet and sensitive that she feels influences more
acutely than other people do. Just now she was quite upset by a little
thing which I did not much heed, though I am myself very fond of
animals. One of the men who come up here often to look for the boats
was followed by his dog. The dog is always with him. They are both
quiet persons, and I never saw the man angry, nor heard the dog bark.
During the service the dog would not come to its master, who was on
the seat with us, but kept a few yards off, barking and howling. Its
master spoke to it gently, and then harshly, and then angrily; but it
would neither come nor cease to make a noise. It was in a sort of fury,
with its eyes savage, and all its hairs bristling out like a cat's tail when
puss is on the war-path. Finally the man, too, got angry, and jumped
down and kicked the dog, and then took it by the scruff of the neck and
half dragged and half threw it on the tombstone on which the seat is
fixed. The moment it touched the stone the poor thing became quiet
and fell all into a tremble. It did not try to get away, but crouched down,
quivering and cowering, and was in such a pitiable state of terror that I
tried, though without effect, to comfort it. Lucy was full of pity, too, but
she did not attempt to touch the dog, but looked at it in an agonised sort
of way. I greatly fear that she is of too super-sensitive a nature to go
through the world without trouble. She will be dreaming of this

tonight, I am sure. The whole agglomeration of things – the ship steered into port by a dead man; his attitude, tied to the wheel with a crucifix and beads; the touching funeral; the dog, now furious and now in terror – will all afford material for her dreams.

I think it will be best for her to go to bed tired out physically, so I shall take her for a long walk by the cliffs to Robin Hood's Bay and back. She ought not to have much inclination for sleep-walking then.

Chapter 8

MINA MURRAY'S JOURNAL

Same day, 11 o'clock p.m. – Oh, but I am tired! If it were not that I have made my diary a duty I should not open it tonight. We had a lovely walk. Lucy, after a while, was in gay spirits, owing, I think, to some dear cows who came nosing towards us in a field close to the lighthouse and frightened the wits out of us. I believe we forgot everything, except, of course, personal fear, and it seemed to wipe the slate clean and give us a fresh start. We had a capital 'severe tea' at Robin Hood's Bay in a sweet little old-fashioned inn, with a bow-window right over the seaweed-covered rocks of the strand. I believe we should have shocked the 'New Woman' with our appetites. Men are more tolerant, bless them! Then we walked home with some, or rather many, stoppages to rest, and with our hearts full of a constant dread of wild bulls. Lucy was really tired, and we intended to creep off to bed as soon as we could. The young curate came in, however, and Mrs Westenra asked him to stay for supper. Lucy and I had both a fight for it with the dusty miller;[99] I know it was a hard fight on my part, and I am quite heroic. I think that some day the bishops must get together and see about breeding up a new class of curates, who don't take supper, no matter how they may be pressed to, and who will know when girls are tired. Lucy is asleep and breathing softly. She has more colour in her cheeks than usual, and looks, oh, so sweet. If Mr Holmwood fell in love with her seeing her only in the drawing-room, I wonder what he would say if he saw her now. Some of the 'New Woman' writers will some day start an idea that men and women should be allowed to see each other asleep before proposing or accepting. But I suppose the New Woman won't condescend in future to accept; she will do the proposing herself. And a nice job she will make of it, too! There's some consolation in that. I am so happy tonight, because dear Lucy seems better. I really believe she has turned the corner, and that we are over her troubles with dreaming. I should be quite happy if I only knew if Jonathan . . . God bless and keep him.

11 August, 3 a.m. – Diary again. No sleep now, so I may as well write. I am too agitated to sleep. We have had such an adventure, such an agonising experience. I fell asleep as soon as I had closed my diary . . . Suddenly I became broad awake, and sat up, with a horrible sense of fear upon me, and of some feeling of emptiness around me. The room was dark, so I could not see Lucy's bed, I stole across and felt for her. The bed was empty. I lit a match, and found that she was not in the room. The door was shut, but not locked, as I had left it. I feared to wake her mother, who has been more than usually ill lately, so threw on some clothes and got ready to look for her. As I was leaving the room it struck me that the clothes she wore might give me some clue to her dreaming intention. Dressing-gown would mean house; dress, outside. Dressing-gown and dress were both in their places. 'Thank God,' I said to myself, 'she cannot be far, as she is only in her nightdress.' I ran downstairs and looked in the sitting-room. Not there! Then I looked in all the other open rooms of the house, with an ever-growing fear chilling my heart. Finally I came to the hall-door and found it open. It was not wide open, but the catch of the lock had not caught. The people of the house are careful to lock the door every night, so I feared that Lucy must have gone out as she was. There was no time to think of what might happen; a vague, over-mastering fear obscured all details. I took a big, heavy shawl and ran out. The clock was striking one as I was in the Crescent, and theré was not a soul in sight. I ran along the North Terrace, but could see no sign of the white figure which I expected. At the edge of the West Cliff above the pier I looked across the harbour to the East Cliff, in the hope or fear – I don't know which – of seeing Lucy in our favourite seat. There was a bright full moon, with heavy black, driving clouds, which threw the whole scene into a fleeting diorama[100] of light and shade as they sailed across. For a moment or two I could see nothing, as the shadow of a cloud obscured St Mary's Church and all around it. Then as the cloud passed I could see the ruins of the Abbey coming into view; and as the edge of a narrow band of light as sharp as a sword-cut moved along, the church and the churchyard became gradually visible. Whatever my expectation was, it was not disappointed, for there, on our favourite seat, the silver light of the moon struck a half-reclining figure, snowy white. The coming of the cloud was too quick for me to see much, for shadow shut down on light almost immediately; but it seemed to me as though something dark stood behind the seat where the white figure shone, and bent over it. What it was, whether man or beast, I could not tell; I did not wait to catch another glance, but flew down the steep steps to the pier and along by the fish-market to the bridge which was the only way to reach the East Cliff. The town seemed as dead, for not a soul did I see – I rejoiced that it was so, for I wanted no witness of poor Lucy's condition. The time and distance seemed endless, and my knees trembled and my breath came laboured as I toiled up the endless steps to the Abbey. I must have gone fast, and yet it seemed to me as if my feet were weighted with lead, and as though every joint in my body were rusty. When I got almost to the top I could see the seat and the white figure, for I was now close enough to distinguish it even through the spells of shadow. There was undoubtedly something, long and black, bending over the half-reclining white figure. I called in fright, 'Lucy! Lucy!' and something raised a head, and from where I was I could see a white face and red, gleaming eyes. Lucy did not answer, and I ran on to the entrance of the churchyard. As I entered, the church was between me and the seat, and for a minute or so I lost sight of her. When I came in view again the cloud had passed, and the moonlight struck so brilliantly that I could see Lucy half-reclining with her head lying over the back of the seat. She was quite alone, and there was not a sign of any living thing about.

When I bent over her I could see that she was still asleep. Her lips were parted, and she was breathing – not softly, as usual with her, but in long, heavy gasps, as though striving to get her lungs full at every breath. As I came close, she put up her hand in her sleep and pulled the collar of her nightdress close round her throat. Whilst she did so there came a little shudder through her, as though she felt the cold. I flung the warm shawl over her, and drew the edges tight round her neck, for I dreaded lest she should get some deadly chill from the night air, unclad as she was. I feared to wake her all at once, so, in order to have my hands free that I might help her, I fastened the shawl at her throat with a big safety-pin; but I must have been clumsy in my anxiety and pinched or pricked her with it, for by-and-by, when her breathing became quieter, she put her hand to her throat again and moaned. When I had her carefully wrapped up I put my shoes on her feet, and then began very gently to wake her. At first she did not respond; but gradually she became more and more uneasy in her sleep, moaning and sighing occasionally. At last, as time was passing fast, and for many other reasons, I wished to get her home at once, I shook her more forcibly, till finally she opened her eyes and awoke. She did not seem surprised to see me, as, of course, she did not realise all at once where she was. Lucy always wakes prettily, and even at such a time, when her body must have

been chilled with cold, and her mind somewhat appalled at waking
unclad in a churchyard at night, she did not lose her grace. She
trembled a little, and clung to me; when I told her to come at once with
me home she rose without a word, with the obedience of a child. As we
passed along, the gravel hurt my feet, and Lucy noticed me wince. She
stopped and wanted to insist upon my taking my shoes; but I would not.
However, when we got to the pathway outside the churchyard, where
there was a puddle of water remaining from the storm, I daubed my feet
with mud, using each foot in turn on the other, so that as we went home
no one, in case we should meet anyone, should notice my bare feet.

Fortune favoured us, and we got home without meeting a soul. Once
we saw a man, who seemed not quite sober, passing along a street in
front of us; but we hid in a door till he had disappeared up an opening
such as there are here, steep little closes, or 'wynds', as they call them in
Scotland. My heart beat so loud all the time that sometimes I thought I
should faint. I was filled with anxiety about Lucy, not only for her
health lest she should suffer from the exposure, but for her reputation in
case the story should get wind. When we got in, and had washed our
feet, and had said a prayer of thankfulness together, I tucked her into
bed. Before falling asleep she asked – even implored – me not to say a
word to anyone, even her mother, about her sleep-walking adventure. I
hesitated at first to promise; but on thinking of the state of her mother's
health and how the knowledge of such a thing would fret her, and
thinking, too, of how such a story might become distorted – nay,
infallibly would – in case it should leak out I thought it wiser to do so. I
hope I did right. I have locked the door, and the key is tied to my wrist,
so perhaps I shall not be again disturbed. Lucy is sleeping soundly; the
reflex of the dawn is high and far over the sea . . .

Same day, noon. – All goes well. Lucy slept till I woke her, and seemed
not to have even changed her side. The adventure of the night does not
seem to have harmed her; on the contrary, it has benefited her, for she
looks better this morning than she has done for weeks. I was sorry to
notice that my clumsiness with the safety-pin hurt her. Indeed, it might
have been serious, for the skin of her throat was pierced. I must have
pinched up a piece of loose skin and have transfixed it, for there are two
little red points like pin-pricks, and on the band of her nightdress was a
drop of blood. When I apologised and was concerned about it, she
laughed and petted me, and said she did not even feel it. Fortunately it
cannot leave a scar, as it is so tiny.

Same day, night. – We passed a happy day. The air was clear, and the
sun bright, and there was a cool breeze. We took our lunch to Mulgrave

Woods, Mrs Westenra driving by the road and Lucy and I walking by the cliff-path and joining her at the gate. I felt a little sad myself, for I could not but feel how *absolutely* happy it would have been had Jonathan been with me. But there! I must only be patient. In the evening we strolled in the Casino Terrace, and heard some good music by Spohr and Mackenzie,[101] and went to bed early. Lucy seems more restful than she has been for some time, and fell asleep at once. I shall lock the door and secure the key the same as before, though I do not expect any trouble tonight.

12 August. – My expectations were wrong, for twice during the night I was awakened by Lucy trying to get out. She seemed, even in her sleep, to be a little impatient at finding the door shut, and went back to bed under a sort of protest. I woke with the dawn, and heard the birds chirping outside of the window. Lucy woke, too, and, I was glad to see, was even better than on the previous morning. All her old gaiety of manner seemed to have come back, and she came and snuggled in beside me, and told me all about Arthur; I told her how anxious I was about Jonathan, and then she tried to comfort me. Well, she succeeded somewhat, for, though sympathy can't alter facts, it can help to make them more bearable.

13 August. – Another quiet day, and to bed with the key on my wrist as before. Again I woke in the night, and found Lucy sitting up in bed, still asleep pointing to the window. I got up quietly, and pulling aside the blind, looked out. It was brilliant moonlight, and the soft effect of the light over the sea and sky – merged together in one great, silent mystery – was beautiful beyond words. Between me and the moonlight flitted a great bat, coming and going in great, whirling circles. Once or twice it came quite close, but was, I suppose, frightened at seeing me, and flitted away across the harbour towards the Abbey. When I came back from the window Lucy had lain down again, and was sleeping peacefully. She did not stir again all night.

14 August. – On the East Cliff, reading and writing all day. Lucy seems to have become as much in love with the spot as I am, and it is hard to get her away from it when it is time to come home for lunch or tea or dinner. This afternoon she made a funny remark. We were coming home for dinner, and had come to the top of the steps up from the West Pier and stopped to look at the view, as we generally do. The setting sun, low down in the sky, was just dropping behind Kettleness; the red light was thrown over on the East Cliff and the old Abbey, and seemed to bathe everything in a beautiful rosy glow. We were silent for a while, and suddenly Lucy murmured as if to herself:

'His red eyes again! They are just the same.' It was such an odd expression, coming *apropos* of nothing, that it quite startled me. I slewed round a little, so as to see Lucy well without seeming to stare at her, and saw that she was in a half-dreamy state, with an odd look on her face that I could not quite make out; so I said nothing, but followed her eyes. She appeared to be looking over at our own seat, whereon was a dark figure seated alone. I was a little startled myself, for it seemed for an instant as if the stranger had great eyes like burning flames; but a second look dispelled the illusion. The red sunlight was shining on the windows of St Mary's Church behind our seat, and as the sun dipped there was just sufficient change in the refraction and reflection to make it appear as if the light moved. I called Lucy's attention to the peculiar effect, and she became herself with a start, but she looked sad all the same; it may have been that she was thinking of that terrible night up there. We never refer to it; so I said nothing, and we went home to dinner. Lucy had a headache and went early to bed. I saw her asleep, and went out for a little stroll myself; I walked along the cliffs to the westward, and was full of sweet sadness, for I was thinking of Jonathan. When coming home – it was then bright moonlight, so bright that, though the front of our part of the Crescent was in shadow, everything could be well seen – I threw a glance up at our window, and saw Lucy's head leaning out. I thought that perhaps she was looking out for me, so I opened my handkerchief and waved it. She did not notice or make any movement whatever. Just then, the moonlight crept round an angle of the building, and the light fell on the window. There distinctly was Lucy with her head lying up against the side of the windowsill and her eyes shut. She was fast asleep, and by her, seated on the window-sill, was something that looked like a good-sized bird. I was afraid she might get a chill, so I ran upstairs, but as I came into the room she was moving back to her bed, fast asleep, and breathing heavily; she was holding her hand to her throat, as though to protect it from cold. I did not wake her, but tucked her up warmly, I have taken care that the door is locked and the window securely fastened.

She looks so sweet as she sleeps; but she is paler than is her wont, and there is a drawn, haggard look under her eyes which I do not like. I fear she is fretting about something. I wish I could find out what it is.

15 *August*. – Rose later than usual. Lucy was languid and tired, and slept on after we had been called. We had a happy surprise at breakfast. Arthur's father is better, and wants the marriage to come off soon. Lucy is full of quiet joy, and her mother is glad and sorry at once. Later on in the day she told me the cause. She is grieved to lose Lucy as her very

own, but she is rejoiced that she is soon to have someone to protect her. Poor dear, sweet lady! She confided to me that she has got her death-warrant. She has not told Lucy, and made me promise secrecy; her doctor told her that within a few months, at most, she must die, for her heart is weakening. At any time, even now, a sudden shock would be almost sure to kill her. Ah, we were wise to keep from her the affair of the dreadful night of Lucy's sleep-walking.

17 August. – No diary for two whole days. I have not had the heart to write. Some sort of shadowy pall seems to be coming over our happiness. No news from Jonathan, and Lucy seems to be growing weaker, whilst her mother's hours are numbering to a close. I do not understand Lucy's fading away as she is doing. She eats well and sleeps well, and enjoys the fresh air; but all the time the roses in her cheeks are fading, and she gets weaker and more languid day by day; at night I hear her gasping as if for air. I keep the key of our door always fastened to my wrist at night, but she gets up and walks about the room, and sits at the open window. Last night I found her leaning out when I woke up, and when I tried to wake her I could not; she was in a faint. When I managed to restore her she was as weak as water, and cried silently between long, painful struggles for breath. When I asked her how she came to be at the window she shook her head and turned away. I trust her feeling ill may not be from that unlucky prick of the safety-pin. I looked at her throat just now as she lay asleep, and the tiny wounds seem not to have healed. They are still open, and, if anything, larger than before, and the edges of them are faintly white. They are like little white dots with red centres. Unless they heal within a day or two, I shall insist on the doctor seeing about them.

Letter, Samuel F. Billington & Son, Solicitors, Whitby,
to Messrs. Carter, Paterson & Co., London

17 August.

DEAR SIRS, –

Herewith please receive invoice of goods sent by Great Northern Railway. Same are to be delivered at Carfax near Purfleet, immediately on receipt at goods station King's Cross. The house is at present empty, but enclosed please find keys, all of which are labelled.

You will please deposit the boxes, fifty in number, which form the consignment, in the partially ruined building forming part of the house and marked 'A' on rough diagram enclosed. Your agent will easily recognise the locality, as it is the ancient chapel of the mansion. The goods leave by the train at 9.30 tonight, and will be due at King's Cross at 4.30 tomorrow afternoon. As our client wishes the delivery made as soon as possible, we shall be obliged by your having teams ready at King's Cross at the time named and forthwith conveying the goods to destination. In order to obviate any delays possible through any routine requirements as to payment in your departments, we enclose cheque herewith for ten pounds (£10) receipt of which please acknowledge. Should the charge be less than this amount, you can return balance; if greater, we shall at once send cheque for difference on hearing from you. You are to leave the keys on coming away in the main hall of the house, where the proprietor may get them on his entering the house by means of his duplicate key.

Pray do not take us as exceeding the bounds of business courtesy in pressing you in all ways to use the utmost expedition.

We are dear Sirs,
Faithfully yours,

SAMUEL F. BILLINGTON & SON.

Letter, Messrs. Carter. Paterson & Co., London,
to Messrs. Billington and Son, Whitby

21 August.

DEAR SIRS, –

We beg to acknowledge £10 received and to return cheque £1 17s. 9d., amount of overplus, as shown in receipted account herewith. Goods are delivered in exact accordance with instructions , and keys left in parcel in main hall, as directed.

We are, dear Sirs,
Yours respectfully,

PRO CARTER, PATERSON & CO.

MINA MURRAY'S JOURNAL

18 August. – I am happy today, and write sitting on the seat in the churchyard. Lucy is ever so much better. Last night she slept well all night, and did not disturb me once. The roses seem coming back already to her cheeks, though she is still sadly pale and wan-looking. If she were in any way anæmic I could understand it, but she is not. She is in gay spirits and full of life and cheerfulness. All the morbid reticence seems to have passed from her, and she has just reminded me, as if I needed any reminding, of *that* night, and that it was here, on this very seat, I found her asleep. As she told me she tapped playfully with the heel of her boot on the stone slab and said:

'My poor little feet didn't make much noise then! I daresay poor old Mr Swales would have told me that it was because I didn't want to wake up Geordie.' As she was in such a communicative humour, I asked her if she had dreamed at all that night. Before she answered, that sweet, puckered look came into her forehead, which Arthur – I call him Arthur from her habit – says he loves; and, indeed, I don't wonder that he does. Then she went on in a half-dreaming kind of way, as if trying to recall it to herself: 'I didn't quite dream; but it all seemed to be real. I only wanted to be here in this spot – I don't know why, for I was afraid of something – I don't know what. I remember, though I suppose I was asleep, passing through the streets and over the bridge. A fish leaped as I went by, and I leaned over to look at it, and I heard a lot of dogs howling – the whole town seemed as if it must be full of dogs all howling at once – as I went up the steps. Then I have a vague memory of something long and dark with red eyes, just as we saw in the sunset, and something very sweet and very bitter all around me at once; and then I seemed sinking into deep green water, and there was a singing in my ears, as I have heard there is to drowning men; and then everything seemed passing away from me; my soul seemed to go out from my body and float about the air. I seemed to remember that once the West Lighthouse was right under me, and then there was a sort of agonising feeling, as if I were in an earthquake, and I came back and found you shaking my body. I saw you do it before I felt you.'

Then she began to laugh. It seemed a little uncanny to me, and I listened to her breathlessly. I did not quite like it and thought it better not to keep her mind on the subject, so we drifted on to other subjects, and Lucy was like her old self again. When we got home the fresh breeze had braced her up, and her pale cheeks were really more rosy. Her mother rejoiced when she saw her, and we all spent a very happy evening together.

19 August. – Joy, joy, joy! although not all joy. At last, news of Jonathan. The dear fellow has been ill, that is why he did not write. I am not afraid to think it or to say it, now that I know. Mr Hawkins sent me on the letter, and wrote himself, oh, so kindly. I am to leave in the morning and to go over to Jonathan and to help to nurse him if necessary, and to bring him home. Mr Hawkins says it would not be a bad thing if we were to be married out there. I have cried over the good Sister's letter till I can feel it wet against my bosom, where it lies. It is of Jonathan, and must be next my heart, for he is in my heart. My journey is all mapped out, and my luggage ready. I am only taking one change of dress; Lucy will bring my trunk to London and keep it till I send for it, for it may be that . . . I must write no more; I must keep it to say to Jonathan, my husband. The letter that he has seen and touched must comfort me till we meet.

Letter, Sister Agatha, Hospital of St Joseph and Ste Mary,
Buda-Pesth, to Miss Wilhelmina Murray

12 August

Dear Madam, –

I write by desire of Mr Jonathan Harker, who is himself not strong enough to write, though progressing well, thanks to God and St Joseph and Ste Mary. He has been under our care for nearly six weeks, suffering from a violent brain fever. He wishes me to convey his love, and to say that by this post I write for him to Mr Peter Hawkins, Exeter, to say, with his dutiful respects, that he is sorry for his delay, and that all his work is completed. He will require some few weeks' rest in our sanatorium in the hills, but will then return. He wishes me to say that he has not sufficient money with him, and that he would like to pay for his staying here, so that others who need shall not be wanting for help.
    Believe me,
    Yours, with sympathy and all blessings,

Sister Agatha

P.S. My patient being asleep, I open this to let you know something more. He has told me all about you, and that you are shortly to be his wife. All blessings to you both! He has had some fearful shock – so says our doctor – and in his delirium his ravings have been dreadful; of wolves and poison and blood; of ghosts and demons; and I fear to say of what. Be careful with him always that there may be nothing to excite him of this kind for a long time to come; the traces of such an illness as his do not lightly die away. We should have written long ago, but we knew nothing of his friends, and there was on him nothing that anyone could understand. He came in the train from Klausenburgh, and the guard was told by the station-master there that he rushed into the station shouting for a ticket for home. Seeing from his violent demeanour that he was English, they gave him a ticket for the farthest station on the way thither that the train reached.
    Be assured that he is well cared for. He has won all hearts by his sweetness and gentleness. He is truly getting on well, and I have no doubt will in a few weeks be as himself. But be careful of him for safety's sake. There are, I pray God and St Joseph and Ste Mary, many, many happy years for you both.

Dr Seward's Diary

19 August. – Strange and sudden change in Renfield last night. About eight o'clock he began to get excited and to sniff about as a dog does when setting. The attendant was struck by his manner and knowing my interest in him, encouraged him to talk. He is usually respectful to the attendant, and at times servile; but tonight, the man tells me, he was quite haughty. Would not condescend to talk with him at all. All he would say was:

'I don't want to talk to you: you don't count now; the Master is at hand.'

The attendant thinks it is some sudden form of religious mania which has seized him. If so, we must look out for squalls, for a strong man with homicidal and religious mania at once might be dangerous. The combination is a dreadful one. At nine o'clock I visited him myself. His attitude to me was the same as that to the attendant; in his sublime self-feeling the difference between myself and attendant seemed to him as nothing. It looks like religious mania, and he will soon think that he himself is God. These infinitesimal distinctions between man and man are too paltry for an Omnipotent being. How these madmen give themselves away! The real God taketh heed lest a sparrow fall; but the God created from human vanity sees no difference between an eagle and a sparrow. Oh, if men only knew!

For half an hour or more Renfield kept getting excited in greater and greater degree. I did pretend not to be watching him, but I kept strict observation all the same. All at once that shifty look came into his eyes which we always see when a madman has seized an idea, and with it the shifty movement of the head and back which asylum attendants come to know so well. He became quite quiet, and went and sat on the edge of his bed resignedly, and looked into space with lack-lustre eyes. I thought I would find out if his apathy were real or only assumed, and tried to lead him to talk of his pets, a theme which had never failed to excite his attention. At first he made no reply, but at length said testily:

'Bother them all! I don't care a pin about them.'

'What?' I said. 'You don't mean to tell me that you don't care about spiders?' (Spiders at present are his hobby, and the note-book is filling up with columns of small figures.) To this he answered enigmatically:

'The bride-maidens rejoice [102] the eyes that wait the coming of the bride; but when the bride draweth nigh, then the maidens shine not to the eyes that are filled.'

He would not explain himself, but remained obstinately seated on his bed all the time I remained with him.

I am weary tonight and low in spirits. I cannot but think of Lucy, and how different things might have been. If I don't sleep at once, chloral, the modern Morpheus[103] – $C_2HCl_3O.H_2O$! I must be careful not to let it grow into a habit. No, I shall take none tonight! I have thought of Lucy, and I shall not dishonour her by mixing the two. If need be, tonight shall be sleepless . . .

Glad I made the resolution; gladder that I kept to it. I had lain tossing about, and had heard the clock strike only twice, when the night-watchman came to me, sent up from the ward, to say that Renfield had escaped. I threw on my clothes and ran down at once; my patient is too dangerous a person to be roaming about. Those ideas of his might work out dangerously with strangers. The attendant was waiting for me. He said he had seen him not ten minutes before, seemingly asleep in his bed, when he had looked through the observation-trap in the door. His attention was called by the sound of the window being wrenched out. He ran back and saw his feet disappear through the window, and had at once sent up for me. He was only in his night-gear, and cannot be far off. The attendant thought it would be more useful to watch where he should go than to follow him, as he might lose sight of him whilst getting out of the building by the door. He is a bulky man, and couldn't get through the window. I am thin, so, with his aid, I got out, but feet foremost, and, as we were only a few feet above ground, landed unhurt. The attendant told me the patient had gone to the left and had taken a straight line, so I ran as quickly as I could. As I got through the belt of trees I saw a white figure scale the high wall which separates our grounds from those of the deserted house.

I ran back at once, and told the watchman to get three or four men immediately and follow me into the grounds of Carfax, in case our friend might be dangerous. I got a ladder myself, and crossing the wall, dropped down on the other side. I could see Renfield's figure just disappearing behind the angle of the house, so I ran after him. On the far side of the house I found him pressed close against the old iron-bound oak door of the chapel. He was talking, apparently to someone, but I was afraid to go near enough to hear what he was saying, lest I might frighten him, and he should run off. Chasing an errant swarm of bees is nothing to following a naked lunatic when the fit of escaping is upon him! After a few minutes, however, I could see that he did not take note of anything around him, and so ventured to draw nearer to him – the more so as my men had now crossed the wall and were closing him in. I heard him say:

'I am here to do Your bidding, Master. I am Your slave, and You will reward me, for I shall be faithful. I have worshipped You long and afar off. Now that You are near I await Your commands, and You will not pass me by, will You, dear Master, in Your distribution of good things?'

He *is* a selfish old beggar anyhow. He thinks of the loaves and fishes[104] even when he believes he is in a Real Presence. His manias make a startling combination. When we closed in on him he fought like a tiger. He is immensely strong, and he was more like a wild beast than a man. I never saw a lunatic in such a paroxysm of rage before; and I hope I shall not again. It is a mercy that we have found out his strength and his danger in good time. With strength and determination like his, he might have done wild work before he was caged. He is safe now at any rate. Jack Sheppard himself couldn't get free from the strait-waistcoat that keeps him restrained, and he's chained to the wall in the padded room. His cries are at times awful, but the silences that follow are more deadly still, for he means murder in every turn and movement.

Just now he spoke coherent words for the first time:

'I shall be patient, Master. It is coming – coming – coming!'

So I took the hint, and came too. I was too excited to sleep, but this diary has quieted me, and I feel I shall get some sleep tonight.

Chapter 9

Letter, Mina Harker to Lucy Westenra

Buda-Pesth, 24 August.

My dearest Lucy, –

I know you will be anxious to hear all that has happened since we parted at the railway station at Whitby. Well, my dear, I got to Hull all right, and caught the boat to Hamburg,[105] and then the train on here. I feel I can hardly recall anything of the journey, except that I knew I was coming to Jonathan, and that, as I should have to do some nursing, I had better get all the sleep I could . . . I found my dear one, oh, so thin and pale and weak-looking. All the resolution has gone out of his dear eyes, and that quiet dignity which I told you was in his face has vanished. He is only a wreck of himself, and he does not remember anything that has happened to him for a long time past. At least, he wants me to believe so, and I shall never ask. He has had some terrible shock and I fear it might tax his poor brain if he were to try to recall it. Sister Agatha, who is a good creature and a born nurse, tells me that he raved of dreadful things whilst he was off his head. I wanted her to tell me what they were; but she would only cross herself and say she would never tell; that the ravings of the sick were the secrets of God, and that if a nurse through her vocation should hear them, she should respect her trust. She is a sweet good soul, and the next day, when she saw I was troubled, she opened up the subject again, and after saying that she could never mention what my poor dear raved about, added: 'I can tell you this much, my dear: that it was not about anything which he has done wrong himself; and you, as his wife to be, have no cause to be concerned. He has not forgotten you or what he owes to you. His fear was of great and terrible things, which no mortal can treat of.' I believe the dear soul thought I might be jealous lest my poor dear should have fallen in love with any other girl. The idea of *my* being jealous about Jonathan! And yet, my dear, let me whisper, I felt a thrill of joy through me when I *knew* that no other woman was a cause of trouble. I am now sitting by his bedside, where I can see his face while he sleeps. He is waking! . . . When he woke he asked me for his coat, as he wanted to get something from the pocket; I asked Sister Agatha, and she brought all his things. I saw that amongst them was his note-book, and was going to ask him to let me look at it – for I knew then that I might find some clue to his trouble – but I suppose he must have seen my wish in my eyes for he sent me over to the window, saying he wanted to be quite alone for a moment. Then he called me back, and when I came he had his hand over the note-book and he said to me very solemnly:

'Wilhelmina' – I knew then that he was in deadly earnest, for he has never called me by that name since he asked me to marry him –'you know, dear, my ideas of the trust between husband and wife: there should be no secret, no concealment. I have had a great shock, and when I try to think of what it is I feel my head spin round, and I do not know if it was all real or the dreaming of a madman. You know I have had brain fever, and that is to be mad. The secret is here, and I do not want to know it. I want to take up my life here, with our marriage.' For, my dear, we had decided to be married as soon as the formalities are complete. 'Are you willing, Wilhelmina, to share my ignorance? Here is the book. Take it and keep it, read it if you will, but never let me know; unless, indeed, some solemn duty should come upon me to go back to the bitter hours, asleep or awake, sane or mad, recorded here.' He fell back, exhausted, and I put the book under his pillow, and kissed him. I have asked Sister Agatha to beg the Superior to let our wedding be this afternoon, and am waiting her reply . . .

She has come and told me that the chaplain of the English mission church has been sent for. We are to be married in an hour, or as soon after as Jonathan awakes . . .

Lucy, the time has come and gone. I feel very solemn, but very, very happy. Jonathan woke a little after the hour, and all was ready, and he sat up in bed, propped up with pillows. He answered his 'I will' firmly and strongly. I could hardly speak; my heart was so full that even these words seemed to choke me. The dear Sisters were so kind. Please God, I shall never, never forget them, nor the grave and sweet responsibilities I have taken upon me. I must tell you of my wedding present. When the chaplain and the Sisters had left me alone with my husband – oh, Lucy, it is the first time I have written the words 'my husband' – left me alone with my husband, I took the book from under his pillow, and wrapped it up in white paper, and tied it with a little bit of pale blue ribbon which was wound round my neck, and sealed it over the knot with sealing-wax, and for my seal I used my wedding ring. Then I kissed it and showed it to my husband, and told him that I would keep it so, and then it would be an outward and visible sign for us all our lives that we trusted each other; that I would never open it unless it were for his own dear sake, or for the sake of some stern duty. Then he took my hand in his, and oh,

Lucy, it was the first time he took *his wife's* hand, and said that it was the dearest thing in all the wide world, and that he would go through all the past again to win it, if need be. The poor dear meant to have said a part of the past; but he cannot think of time yet, and I shall not wonder if at first he mixes up not only the month, but the year.

Well, my dear, what could I say? I could only tell him that I was the happiest woman in all the wide world, and that I had nothing to give him except myself, my life, and my trust, and that with these went my love and duty for all the days of my life. And, my dear, when he kissed me, and drew me to him with his poor weak hands, it was like a very solemn pledge between us ...

Lucy dear, do you know why I tell you all this? It is not only because it is all sweet to me, but because you have been, and are, very dear to me. It was my privilege to be your friend and guide when you came from the schoolroom to prepare for the world of life. I want you to see now, and with the eyes of a very happy wife, whither duty has led me; so that in your own married life you too may be all happy as I am. My dear, please Almighty God, your life may be all it promises: a long day of sunshine, with no harsh wind, no forgetting duty, no distrust. I must not wish you no pain, for that can never be; but I do hope you will be *always* as happy as I am *now*. Goodbye, my dear. I shall post this at once, and, perhaps, write you very soon again. I must stop, for Jonathan is waking – I must attend to my husband!

Your ever-loving

MINA HARKER.

Letter, Lucy Westenra to Mina Harker

Whitby, 30 August.[106]

MY DEAREST MINA, –

Oceans of love and millions of kisses, and may you soon be in your own home with your husband. I wish you could be coming home soon enough to stay with us here. This strong air would soon restore Jonathan; it has quite restored me. I have an appetite like a cormorant, am full of life, and sleep well. You will be glad to know that I have quite given up walking in my sleep. I think I have not stirred out of my bed for a week, that is, when I once got into it at night. Arthur says I am getting fat. By the way, I forgot to tell you that Arthur is here. We have such walks and drives, and rides, and rowing, and tennis, and fishing together; and I love him more than ever. He tells me that he loves me more, but I doubt that, for at first he told me that he couldn't love me

more than he did then. But this is nonsense. There he is, calling to me.
So no more just at present from your loving

LUCY

P.S. – Mother sends her love. She seems better, poor dear.
P.P.S. – We are to be married on 28 September.

DR SEWARD'S DIARY

20 August. – The case of Renfield grows even more interesting. He has
now so far quieted that there are spells of cessation from his passion.
For the first week after his attack he was perpetually violent. Then one
night, just as the moon rose, he grew quiet, and kept murmuring to
himself: 'Now I can wait; now I can wait.' The attendant came to tell
me, so I ran down at once to have a look at him. He was still in the
strait-waistcoat and in the padded room, but the suffused look had
gone from his face and his eyes had something of their old pleading – I
might almost say, 'cringing' – softness. I was satisfied with his present
condition, and directed him to be relieved. The attendants hesitated,
but finally carried out my wishes without protest. It was a strange
thing that the patient had humour enough to see their distrust, for,
coming close to me, he said in a whisper all the while looking furtively
at them:

'They think I could hurt you! Fancy *me* hurting *you*! The fools!'

It was soothing, somehow, to the feelings to find myself dissociated
even in the mind of this poor madman from the others; but all the same
I do not follow his thought. Am I to take it that I have anything in
common with him, so that we are, as it were, to stand together; or has
he to gain from me some good so stupendous that my well-being is
needful to him? I must find out later on. Tonight he will not speak.
Even the offer of a kitten or even a full-grown cat will not tempt him.
He will only say: 'I don't take any stock in cats. I have more to think of
now, and I can wait; I can wait.'

After a while I left him. The attendant tells me that he was quiet until
just before dawn, and then he began to get uneasy, and at length violent,
until at last he fell into a paroxysm which exhausted him so that he
swooned into a sort of coma.

. . . Three nights has the same thing happened – violent all day, then
quiet from moonrise to sunrise. I wish I could get some clue to the
cause. It would almost seem as if there was some influence which came
and went. Happy thought! We shall tonight play sane wits against mad
ones. He escaped before without our help; tonight he shall escape with

it. We shall give him a chance, and have the men ready to follow in case they are required . . .

23 August. – 'The unexpected always happens.' [107] How well Disraeli knew life! Our bird when he found the cage open would not fly, so all our subtle arrangements went for nought. At any rate, we have proved one thing: that the spells of quietness last a reasonable time. We shall in future be able to ease his bonds for a few hours each day. I have given orders to the night attendant merely to shut him in the padded room, when once he is quiet, until an hour before sunrise. The poor soul's body will enjoy the relief even if his mind cannot appreciate it. Hark! The unexpected again! I am called; the patient has once more escaped.

Later. – Another night adventure. Renfield artfully waited until the attendant was entering the room to inspect. Then he dashed out past him and flew down the passage. I sent word for the attendants to follow. Again he went into the grounds of the deserted house, and we found him in the same place, pressed against the old chapel door. When he saw me he became furious, and had not the attendants seized him in time, he would have tried to kill me. As we were holding him a strange thing happened. He suddenly redoubled his efforts, and then as suddenly grew calm. I looked round instinctively, but could see nothing. Then I caught the patient's eye and followed it, but could trace nothing as it looked into the moonlit sky except a big bat, which was flapping its silent and ghostly way to the west. Bats usually wheel and flit about, but this one seemed to go straight on, as if it knew where it was bound for or had some intention of its own. The patient grew calmer every instant, and presently said:

'You needn't tie me; I shall go quietly!' Without trouble we came back to the house. I feel there is something ominous in his calm, and shall not forget this night . . .

Lucy Westenra's Diary

Hillingham, 24 August. – I must imitate Mina, and keep writing things down. Then we can have long talks when we do meet. I wonder when it will be. I wish she were with me again, for I feel so unhappy. Last night I seemed to be dreaming again just as I was at Whitby. Perhaps it is the change of air, or getting home again. It is all dark and horrid to me, for I can remember nothing; but I am full of vague fear, and I feel so weak and worn out. When Arthur came to lunch he looked quite grieved when he saw me, and I hadn't the spirit to be cheerful. I wonder if I could sleep in mother's room tonight. I shall make an excuse and try.

25 *August*. – Another bad night. Mother did not seem to take to my proposal. She seems not too well herself, and doubtless she fears to worry me. I tried to keep awake, and succeeded for a while; but when the clock struck twelve it waked me from a doze, so I must have been falling asleep. There was a sort of scratching or flapping at the window, but I did not mind it, and as I remember no more, I suppose I must then have fallen asleep. More bad dreams. I wish I could remember them. This morning I am horribly weak. My face is ghastly pale, and my throat pains me. It must be something wrong with my lungs, for I don't seem ever to get air enough. I shall try to cheer up when Arthur comes, or else I know he will be miserable to see me so.

Letter, Arthur Holmwood to Dr Seward

Albemarle Hotel, 31 August.

MY DEAR JACK, –

I want you to do me a favour. Lucy is ill; that is, she has no special disease, but she looks awful, and is getting worse every day. I have asked her if there is any cause; I do not dare to ask her mother, for to disturb the poor lady's mind about her daughter in her present state of health would be fatal. Mrs Westenra has confided to me that her doom is spoken – disease of the heart – though poor Lucy does not know it yet. I am sure that there is something preying on my dear girl's mind. I am almost distracted when I think of her; to look at her gives me a pang. I told her I should ask you to see her, and though she demurred at first – I know why, old fellow – she finally consented. It will be a painful task for you, I know, old friend, but it is for *her* sake, and I must not hesitate to ask, or you to act. You are to come to lunch at Hillingham tomorrow, two o'clock, so as not to arouse any suspicion in Mrs Westenra, and after lunch Lucy will take an opportunity of being alone with you. I shall come in for tea, and we can go away together. I am filled with anxiety, and want to consult with you alone as soon as I can after you have seen her. Do not fail!

ARTHUR

Telegram, Arthur Holmwood to Seward

1 September.

Am summoned to see my father, who is worse. Am writing. Write me fully by tonight's post to Ring. Wire me if necessary.

Letter from Dr Seward to Arthur Holmwood

2 September.

MY DEAR OLD FELLOW, —

With regard to Miss Westenra's health, I hasten to let you know at once that in my opinion there is not any functional disturbance or any malady that I know of. At the same time, I am not by any means satisfied with her appearance, she is woefully different from what she was when I saw her last. Of course you must bear in mind that I did not have full opportunity of examination such as I should wish; our very friendship makes a little difficulty which not even medical science or custom can bridge over. I had better tell you exactly what happened, leaving you to draw, in a measure, your own conclusions. I shall then say what I have done and propose doing.

I found Miss Westenra in seemingly gay spirits. Her mother was present, and in a few seconds I made up my mind that she was trying all she knew to mislead her mother and prevent her from being anxious. I have no doubt she guesses, if she does not know, what need of caution there is. We lunched alone, and as we all exerted ourselves to be cheerful, we got, as some kind of reward for our labours, some real cheerfulness amongst us. Then Mrs Westenra went to lie down, and Lucy was left with me. We went into her boudoir, and till we got there her gaiety remained, for the servants were coming and going. As soon as the door was closed, however, the mask fell from her face, and she sank down into a chair with a great sigh, and hid her eyes with her hand. When I saw that her high spirits had failed, I at once took advantage of her reaction to make a diagnosis. She said to me very sweetly:

'I cannot tell you how I loathe talking about myself.' I reminded her that a doctor's confidence was sacred, but that you were grievously anxious about her. She caught on to my meaning at once, and settled that matter in a word. 'Tell Arthur everything you choose. I do not care for myself, but all for him!' So I am quite free.

I could easily see that she is somewhat bloodless, but I could not see the usual anæmic signs, and by a chance I was actually able to test the quality of her blood, for in opening a window which was stiff a cord gave way, and she cut her hand slightly with broken glass. It was a slight matter in itself, but it gave me an evident chance, and I secured a few drops of the blood and have analysed them. The qualitative analysis gives a quite normal condition, and shows, I should infer, in itself a vigorous state of health. In other physical matters I was quite satisfied that there is no need for anxiety; but as there must be a cause somewhere, I have come to the conclusion that it must be something mental. She complains of difficulty in breathing satisfactorily at times, and of heavy, lethargic sleep, with dreams that frighten her, but regarding which she can remember nothing. She says that as a child she used to walk in her sleep, and that when in Whitby the habit came back, and that once she walked out in the night and went to the East Cliff, where Miss Murray found her: but she assures me that of late the habit has not returned. I am in doubt, and so have done the best thing I know of: I have written to my old friend and master, Professor Van Helsing, of Amsterdam, who knows as much about obscure diseases as anyone in the world. I have asked him to come over, and as you told me that all things were to be at your charge, I have mentioned to him who you are and your relations to Miss Westenra. This, my dear fellow, is only in obedience to your wishes, for I am only too proud and happy to do anything I can for her. Van Helsing would, I know, do anything for me for a personal reason. So, no matter on what ground he comes, we must accept his wishes. He is a seemingly arbitrary man, but this is because he knows what he is talking about better than anyone else. He is a philosopher and a metaphysician, and one of the most advanced scientists of his day; and he has, I believe, an absolutely open mind. This, with an iron nerve, a temper of the ice-brook,[108] an indomitable resolution, self-command and toleration exalted from virtues to bless-ings, and the kindliest and truest heart that beats – these form his equipment for the noble work that he is doing for mankind – work both in theory and practice, for his views are as wide as his all-embracing sympathy. I tell you these facts that you may know why I have such confidence in him. I have asked him to come at once. I shall see Miss Westenra tomorrow again. She is to meet me at the Stores,[109] so that I may not alarm her mother by too early a repetition of my call.

Yours always,

JOHN SEWARD.

Letter, Abraham Van Helsing, M.D., D.Ph., D.Litt., etc., etc.
to Dr Seward

2 September.

MY GOOD FRIEND, –
    When I have received your letter I am already coming to you. By good fortune I can leave just at once, without wrong to any of those who have trusted me. Were fortune other, then it were bad for those who

have trusted, for I come to my friend when he call me to aid those he holds dear. Tell your friend that when that time you suck from my wound so swiftly the poison of the gangrene from that knife that our other friend, too nervous, let slip, you did more for him when he wants my aids and you call for them than all his great fortune could do. But it is pleasure added to do for him, your friend; it is to you that I come. Have then rooms for me at the Great Eastern Hotel, so that I may be near to hand, and please it so arrange that we may see the young lady not too late on tomorrow, for it is likely that I may have to return here that night. But if need be I shall come again in three days, and stay longer if it must. Till then good-bye, my friend John.

Van Helsing

Letter, Dr Seward to Hon. Arthur Holmwood

3 September.

My dear Art, –

Van Helsing has come and gone. He came on with me to Hillingham, and found that, by Lucy's discretion, her mother was lunching out, so that we were alone with her. Van Helsing made a very careful examination of the patient. He is to report to me, and I shall advise you, for of course I was not present all the time. He is, I fear, much concerned, but says he must think. When I told him of our friendship and how you trust to me in the matter, he said: 'You must tell him all you think. Tell him what I think, if you can guess it, if you will. Nay, I am not jesting. This is no jest, but life and death, perhaps more.' I asked what he meant by that, for he was very serious. This was when we had come back to town, and he was having a cup of tea before starting on his return to Amsterdam. He would not give me any further clue. You must not be angry with him, Art, because his very reticence means that all his brains are working for her good. He will speak plainly enough when the time comes, be sure. So I told him I would simply write an account of our visit, just as if I were doing a descriptive special article for the *Daily Telegraph*. He seemed not to notice, but remarked that the smuts[110] in London were not quite so bad as they used to be when he was a student here. I am to get his report tomorrow if he can possibly make it. In any case I am to have a letter.

Well as to the visit. Lucy was more cheerful than on the day I first saw her, and certainly looked better. She had lost something of the ghastly look that so upset you, and her breathing was normal. She was very sweet to the Professor (as she always is), and tried to make him feel at ease; though I could see that the poor girl was making a hard struggle for it. I believe Van Helsing saw it, too, for I saw the quick look under his bushy brows that I knew of old. Then he began to chat of all things except ourselves and diseases, and with such an infinite geniality that I could see poor Lucy's pretence of animation merge into reality. Then, without any seeming change, he brought the conversation gently round to his visit, and suavely said:

'My dear young miss, I have the so great pleasure because you are much beloved. That is much, my dear, even were there that which I do not see. They told me you were in the spirit, and that you were of a ghastly pale. To them I say: "Pouf!" ' And he snapped his fingers at me and went on: 'But you and I shall show them how wrong they are. How can he' – and he pointed at me with the same look and gesture as that with which once he pointed me out to his class, on, or rather after, a particular occasion which he never fails to remind me of –'know anything of a young ladies? He has his madmans to play with, and to bring them back to happiness and to those that love them. It is much to do, and, oh, but there are rewards, in that we can bestow such happiness. But the young ladies! He has no wife nor daughter, and the young do not tell themselves to the young, but to the old, like me, who have known so many sorrows and the causes of them. So, my dear, we will send him away to smoke the cigarette in the garden, whiles you and I have little talk all to ourselves.' I took the hint, and strolled about, and presently the Professor came to the window and called me in. He looked grave, but said: 'I have made careful examination, but there is no functional cause. With you I agree that there has been much blood lost; it has been, but is not. But the conditions of her are in no way anæmic. I have asked her to send me her maid, that I may asked just one or two question, that so I may not chance to miss nothing. I know well what she will say. And yet there is cause; there is always cause for everything. I must go back home and think. You must send to me the telegram every day; and if there be cause I shall come again. The disease – for not to be all well is a disease – interest me, and the sweet young dear, she interest me too. She charm me, and for her, if not for you or disease, I come.'

As I tell you, he would not say a word more, even when we were alone. And so now, Art, you know all I know. I shall keep stern watch. I trust your poor father is rallying. It must be a terrible thing to you, my dear old fellow, to be placed in such a position between two people who are both so dear to you. I know your idea of duty to your father, and you are right to stick to it; but, if need be, I shall send you word to come at once to Lucy; so do not be over-anxious unless you hear from me.

Dr Seward's Diary

4 September. – Zoophagous patient still keeps up our interest in him. He had only one outburst, and that was yesterday at an unusual time. Just before the stroke of noon he began to grow restless. The attendant knew the symptoms, and at once summoned aid. Fortunately the men came at a run, and were just in time, for at the stroke of noon he became so violent that it took all their strength to hold him. In about five minutes, however, he began to get more and more quiet, and finally sank into a sort of melancholy, in which state he has remained up to now. The attendant tells me that his screams whilst in the paroxysm were really appalling; I found my hands full when I got in, attending to some of the other patients who were frightened by him. Indeed, I can quite understand the effect, for the sounds disturbed even me, though I was some distance away. It is now after the dinner-hour of the asylum, and as yet my patient sits in a corner brooding, with a dull, sullen, woebegone look in his face, which seems rather to indicate than to show something directly. I cannot quite understand it.

Later. – Another change in my patient. At five o'clock I looked in on him, and found him seemingly as happy and contented as he used to be. He was catching flies and eating them, and was keeping note of his capture by making nail-marks on the edge of the door between the ridges of padding. When he saw me, he came over and apologised for his bad conduct, and asked me in a very humble, cringing way to be led back to his own room and to have his note-book again. I thought it well to humour him; so he is back in his room, with the window open. He has the sugar of his tea spread out on the windowsill, and is reaping quite a harvest of flies. He is not now eating them, but putting them in a box, as of old, and is already examining the corners of his room to find a spider. I tried to get him to talk about the past few days, for any clue to his thoughts would be of immense help to me; but he would not rise. For a moment or two he looked very sad, and said in a sort of far-away voice, as though saying it rather to himself than to me:

'All over! all over! He has deserted me. No hope for me now unless I do it for myself!' Then suddenly turning to me in a resolute way, he said: 'Doctor, won't you be very good to me and let me have a little more sugar? I think it would be good for me.'

'And the flies?' I said.

'Yes! The flies like it, too, and I like the flies; therefore I like it.' And there are people who know so little as to think that madmen do not argue. I procured him a double supply, and left him as happy a man as, I suppose, any in the world. I wish I could fathom his mind.

Midnight. – Another change in him. I had been to see Miss Westenra, whom I found much better, and had just returned, and was standing at our own gate looking at the sunset, when once more I heard him yelling. As his room is on this side of the house, I could hear it better than in the morning. It was a shock to me to turn from the wonderful smoky beauty of a sunset over London, with its lurid lights and inky shadows and all the marvellous tints that come on foul clouds even as on foul water, and to realise all the grim sternness of my own cold stone building, with its wealth of breathing misery, and my own desolate heart to endure it all. I reached him just as the sun was going down, and from his window saw the red disc sink. As it sank he became less and less frenzied; and just as it dipped he slid from the hands that held him, an inert mass, on the floor. It is wonderful, however, what intellectual recuperative power lunatics have, for within a few minutes he stood up quite calmly and looked around him. I signalled to the attendants not to hold him, for I was anxious to see what he would do. He went straight over to the window and brushed out the crumbs of sugar; then he took his fly-box and emptied it outside, and threw away the box; then he shut the window, and crossing over, sat down on his bed. All this surprised me, so I asked him: 'Are you not going to keep flies any more?'

'No,' said he; 'I am sick of all that rubbish!' He certainly is a wonderfully interesting study. I wish I could get some glimpse of his mind or of the cause of his sudden passion. Stop; there may be a clue after all, if we can find why today his paroxysms came on at high noon and at sunset. Can it be that there is a malign influence of the sun at periods which affects certain natures – as at times the moon does others? We shall see.

Telegram, Seward, London, to Van Helsing, Amsterdam

4 September. – Patient still better today.

Telegram, Seward, London, to Van Helsing, Amsterdam

5 September. – Patient greatly improved. Good appetite; sleeps naturally; good spirits, colour coming back.

Telegram, Seward, London, to Van Helsing, Amsterdam

6 September. – Terrible change for the worse. Come at once; do not lose an hour. I hold over telegram to Holmwood till have seen you.

Chapter 10

Letter, Dr Seward to Hon. Arthur Holmwood

6 September.

MY DEAR ART, –

My news today is not so good. Lucy this morning had gone back a bit. There is, however, one good thing which has arisen from it: Mrs Westenra was naturally anxious concerning Lucy, and has consulted me professionally about her. I took advantage of the opportunity, and told her that my old master, Van Helsing, the great specialist, was coming to stay with me, and that I would put her in his charge conjointly with myself; so now we can come and go without alarming her unduly, for a shock to her would mean sudden death, and this, in Lucy's weak condition, might be disastrous to her. We are hedged in with difficulties, all of us, my poor old fellow; but, please God, we shall come through them all right. If any need I shall write, so that, if you do not hear from me, take it for granted that I am simply waiting for news. In haste,

Yours ever

JOHN SEWARD.

DR SEWARD'S DIARY

7 September. – The first thing Van Helsing said to me when we met at Liverpool Street was:

'Have you said anything to our young friend the lover of her?'

'No,' I said. 'I waited till I had seen you, as I said in my telegram. I wrote him a letter simply telling him that you were coming, as Miss Westenra was not so well, and that I should let him know if need be.'

'Right, my friend,' he said, 'quite right! Better he not know as yet; perhaps he shall never know. I pray so; but if it be needed, then he shall know all. And, my good friend John, let me caution you. You deal with the madmen. All men are mad in some way or the other; and inasmuch as you deal discreetly with your madmen, so deal with God's madmen, too – the rest of the world. You tell not your madmen what you do nor why you do it; you tell them not what you think. So you shall keep knowledge in its place, where it may rest – where it may gather its kind around it and breed. You and I shall keep as yet what we know here, and here.' He touched me on the heart and on the forehead, and then touched himself the same way. 'I have for myself thoughts at the present. Later I shall unfold to you.'

'Why not now?' I asked. 'It may do some good; we may arrive at some decision.' He stopped and looked at me, and said:

'My friend John, when the corn is grown,[111] even before it has ripened – while the milk of its mother-earth is in him, and the sunshine has not yet begun to paint him with his gold, the husbandman he pull the ear and rub him between his rough hands, and blow away the green chaff, and say to you: "Look! he's good corn; he will make good crop when the time comes".' I did not see the application, and told him so. For reply he reached over and took my ear in his hand and pulled it playfully, as he used long ago to do at lectures, and said: 'The good husbandman tell you so then because he knows, but not till then. But you do not find the good husbandman dig up his planted corn to see if he grow; that is for the children who play at husbandry, and not for those who take it as of the work of their life. See you now, friend John? I have sown my corn, and Nature has her work to do in making it sprout; if he sprout at all, there's some promise; and I wait till the ear begins to swell.' He broke off, for he evidently saw that I understood. Then he went on, and very gravely:

'You were always a careful student, and your case-book was ever more full than the rest. You were only student then; now you are master, and I trust that good habit have not fail. Remember, my friend, that knowledge is stronger than memory, and we should not trust the weaker. Even if you have not kept the good practice, let me tell you that this case of our dear miss is one that may be – mind, I say *may* be – of such interest to us and others that all the rest may not make him kick the beam, as your peoples say. Take then good note of it. Nothing is too small. I counsel you, put down in record even your doubts and surmises. Hereafter it may be of interest to you to see how true you guess. We learn from failure, not from success!'

When I described Lucy's symptoms – the same as before, but infinitely more marked – he looked very grave, but said nothing. He took with him a bag in which were many instruments and drugs, 'the ghastly paraphernalia of our beneficial trade,' as he once called, in one of his lectures, the equipment of a professor of the healing craft. When we were shown in, Mrs Westenra met us. She was alarmed, but not nearly so much as I expected to find her. Nature in one of her beneficent moods has ordained that even death has some antidote to its own terrors. Here, in a case where any shock may prove fatal, matters

are so ordered that, from some cause or other, the things not personal –
even the terrible change in her daughter to whom she is so attached –
do not seem to reach her. It is something like the way Dame Nature
gathers round a foreign body an envelope of some insensitive tissue
which can protect from evil that which it would otherwise harm by
contact. If this be an ordered selfishness, then we should pause before
we condemn anyone for the vice of egoism, for there may be deeper
roots for its causes than we have knowledge of.

I used my knowledge of this phase of spiritual pathology, and laid
down a rule that she should not be present with Lucy or think of her
illness more than was absolutely required. She assented readily, so
readily that I saw again the hand of Nature fighting for life. Van
Helsing and I were shown up to Lucy's room. If I was shocked when I
saw her yesterday, I was horrified when I saw her today. She was
ghastly, chalkily pale; the red seemed to have gone even from her lips
and gums and the bones of her face stood out prominently; her
breathing was painful to see or hear. Van Helsing's face grew set as
marble, and his eyebrows converged till they almost touched over his
nose. Lucy lay motionless and did not seem to have strength to speak,
so for a while we were all silent. Then Van Helsing beckoned to me,
and we went gently out of the room. The instant we had closed the door
he stepped quickly along the passage to the next door, which was open.
Then he pulled me quickly in with him and closed the door.

'My God!' he said; 'this is dreadful. There is no time to be lost. She
will die for sheer want of blood to keep the heart's action as it should be.
There must be transfusion of blood at once. Is it you or me?'

'I am younger and stronger, Professor. It must be me.'

'Then get ready at once. I will bring up my bag. I am prepared.'

I went downstairs with him, and as we were going there was a knock
at the hall-door. When we reached the hall the maid had just opened
the door, and Arthur was stepping quickly in. He rushed up to me,
saying in an eager whisper:

'Jack, I was so anxious. I read between the lines of your letter, and
have been in an agony. The dad was better, so I ran down here to see for
myself. Is not that gentleman Dr Van Helsing? I am so thankful to you,
sir, for coming.' When first the Professor's eye had lit upon him he had
been angry at any interruption at such a time; but now, as he took in his
stalwart proportions and recognised the strong young manhood which
seemed to emanate from him, his eyes gleamed. Without a pause he
said to him gravely as he held out his hand:

'Sir, you have come in time. You are the lover of our dear miss. She is bad, very, very bad. Nay, my child, do not go like that.' For he suddenly grew pale and sat down in a chair almost fainting. 'You are to help her. You can do more than any that live, and your courage is your best help.'

'What can I do?' asked Arthur hoarsely. 'Tell me, and I shall do it. My life is hers, and I would give the last drop of blood in my body for her.' The Professor has a strongly humorous side, and I could from old knowledge detect a trace of its origin in his answer:

'My young sir, I do not ask so much as that – not the last!'

'What shall I do?' There was fire in his eyes, and his open nostrils quivered with intent. Van Helsing slapped him on the shoulder. 'Come!' he said. 'You are a man, and it is a man we want. You are better than me, better than my friend John.' Arthur looked bewildered, and the Professor went on by explaining in a kindly way:

'Young miss is bad, very bad. She wants blood and blood she must have or die. My friend John and I have consulted; and we are about to perform what we call transfusion of blood – to transfer from full veins of one to the empty veins which pine for him. John was to give his blood, as he is the more young and strong than me' – here Arthur took my hand and wrung it hard in silence – 'but, now you are here, you are more good than us, old or young, who toil much in the world of thought. Our nerves are not so calm and our blood not so bright than yours!' Arthur turned to him and said:

'If you only knew how gladly I would die for her you would understand – '

He stopped, with a sort of choke in his voice.

'God boy!' said Van Helsing. 'In the not-so-far-off you will be happy that you have done all for her you love. Come now and be silent. You shall kiss her once before it is done, but then you must go; and you must leave at my sign. Say no word to Madame; you know how it is with her! There must be no shock; any knowledge of this would be one. Come!'

We all went up to Lucy's room. Arthur by direction remained outside. Lucy turned her head and looked at us, but said nothing. She was not asleep, but she was simply too weak to make the effort. Her eyes spoke to us; that was all. Van Helsing took some things from his bag and laid them on a little table out of sight. Then he mixed a narcotic, and coming over to the bed, said cheerily:

'Now, little miss, here is your medicine. Drink it off, like a good child. See, I lift you so that to swallow is easy. Yes.' She had made the effort with success.

It astonished me how long the drug took to act. This, in fact, marked the extent of her weakness. The time seemed endless until sleep began to flicker in her eyelids. At last, however, the narcotic began to manifest its potency; and she fell into a deep sleep. When the Professor was satisfied he called Arthur into the room, and bade him strip off his coat. Then he added: 'You may take that one little kiss whiles I bring over the table. Friend John, help to me!' So neither of us looked whilst he bent over her.

Van Helsing turning to me, said:

'He is so young and strong and of blood so pure that we need not defibrinate it.'

Then with swiftness, but with absolute method, Van Helsing performed the operation. As the transfusion went on something like life seemed to come back to poor Lucy's cheeks, and through Arthur's growing pallor the joy of his face seemed absolutely to shine. After a bit I began to grow anxious, for the loss of blood was telling on Arthur, strong man as he was. It gave me an idea of what a terrible strain Lucy's system must have undergone that what weakened Arthur only partially restored her. But the Professor's face was set, and he stood watch in hand and with his eyes fixed now on the patient and now on Arthur. I could hear my own heart beat. Presently he said in a soft voice: 'Do not stir an instant. It is enough. You attend him; I will look to her.' When all was over I could see how much Arthur was weakened. I dressed the wound and took his arm to bring him away, when Van Helsing spoke without turning round – the man seems to have eyes in the back of his head:

'The brave lover I think deserve another kiss, which he shall have presently.' And as he had now finished his operation, he adjusted the pillow to the patient's head. As he did so the narrow black velvet band which she seemed always to wear round her throat, buckled with an old diamond buckle which her lover had given her, was dragged a little up, and showed a red mark on her throat. Arthur did not notice it, but I could hear the deep hiss of indrawn breath which is one of Van Helsing's ways of betraying emotion. He said nothing at the moment, but turned to me, saying: 'Now take down our brave young lover, give him of the port wine, and let him lie down a while. He must then go home and rest, sleep much and eat much, that he may be recruited of what he has so given to his love. He must not stay here. Hold a moment. I may take it, sir, that you are anxious of result. Then bring it with you that in all ways the operation is successful. You have saved her life this time, and you can go home and rest easy in mind that all that can be is. I shall tell her all when she is well; she shall love you none the less for what you have done. Good-bye.'

When Arthur had gone I went back to the room. Lucy was sleeping gently, but her breathing was stronger; I could see the counterpane move as her breast heaved. By the bedside sat Van Helsing, looking at her intently. The velvet band again covered the red mark. I asked the Professor in a whisper:

'What do you make of that mark on her throat?'

'What do you make of it?'

'I have not seen it yet,' I answered, and then and there proceeded to loose the band. Just over the external jugular vein there were two punctures, not large, but not wholesome-looking. There was no sign of disease, but the edges were white and worn-looking, as if by some trituration. It at once occurred to me that this wound, or whatever it was, might be the means of that manifest loss of blood, but I abandoned the idea as soon as formed, for such a thing could not be. The whole bed would have been drenched to a scarlet with the blood which the girl must have lost to leave such a pallor as she had before the transfusion.

'Well?' said Van Helsing.

'Well,' said I, 'I can make nothing of it.' The Professor stood up. 'I must go back to Amsterdam tonight,' he said. 'There are books and things there which I want. You must remain here all the night, and you must not let your sight pass from her.'

'Shall I have a nurse?' I asked.

'We are the best nurses, you and I. You keep watch all night; see that she is well fed, and that nothing disturbs her. You must not sleep all the night. Later on we can sleep, you and I. I shall be back as soon as possible. And then we may begin.'

'May begin?' I said. 'What on earth do you mean?'

'We shall see!' he answered as he hurried out. He came back a moment later and put his head inside the door, and said, with warning finger held up:

'Remember, she is your charge. If you leave her, and harm befall, you shall not sleep easy hereafter!'

Dr Seward's Diary (continued)

8 September. – I sat up all night with Lucy. The opiate worked itself off towards dusk, and she waked naturally; she looked a different being from what she had been before the operation. Her spirits even were good, and she was full of a happy vivacity, but I could see evidences of the absolute prostration which she had undergone. When I told Mrs Westenra that Dr Van Helsing had directed that I should sit up with her she almost pooh-poohed the idea, pointing out her daughter's renewed strength and excellent spirits. I was firm, however, and made preparations for my long vigil. When her maid had prepared her for the night I came in, having in the meantime had supper, and took a seat by the bedside. She did not in any way make objection, but looked at me gratefully whenever I caught her eye. After a long spell she seemed sinking off to sleep, but with an effort seemed to pull herself together and shook it off. This was repeated several times, with greater effort and with shorter pauses as the time moved on. It was apparent that she did not want to sleep, so I tackled the subject at once:

'You do not want to go to sleep?'

'No; I am afraid.'

'Afraid to go to sleep! Why so? It is the boon we all crave for.'

'Ah, not if you were like me – if sleep was to you a presage of horror!'

'A presage of horror! What on earth do you mean?'

'I don't know; oh, I don't know. And that is what is so terrible. All this weakness comes to me in sleep; until I dread the very thought.'

'But, my dear girl, you may sleep tonight. I am here watching you, and I can promise that nothing will happen.'

'Ah, I can trust you!' I seized the opportunity, and said: 'I promise you that if I see any evidence of bad dreams I will wake you at once.'

'You will? Oh, will you really? How good you are to me! Then I will sleep!' And almost at the word she gave a deep sigh of relief, and sank back, asleep.

All night long I watched by her. She never stirred, but slept on and on in a deep, tranquil, life-giving, health-giving sleep. Her lips were slightly parted, and her breast rose and fell with the regularity of a pendulum. There was a smile on her face, and it was evident that no bad dreams had come to disturb her peace of mind.

In the early morning her maid came, and I left her in her care and took myself back home, for I was anxious about many things. I sent a short wire to Van Helsing and to Arthur, telling them of the excellent result of the operation. My own work, with its manifold arrears, took me all day to clear off; it was dark when I was able to inquire about my zoophagous patient. The report was good: he had been quite quiet for the past day and night. A telegram came from Van Helsing at Amsterdam whilst I was at dinner, suggesting that I should be at Hillingham tonight, as it might be well to be at hand, and stating that he was leaving by the night mail and would join me early in the morning.

9 September. – I was pretty tired and worn-out when I got to Hillingham. For two nights I had hardly had a wink of sleep, and my brain was beginning to feel that numbness which marks cerebral exhaustion. Lucy was up and in cheerful spirits. When she shook hands with me she looked sharply in my face and said –

'No sitting up tonight for you. You are worn-out. I am quite well again, indeed, I am; and if there is to be any sitting up, it is I who will sit up with you.' I would not argue the point, but went and had my supper. Lucy came with me, and, enlivened by her charming presence, I made an excellent meal, and had a couple of glasses of the more than excellent port. Then Lucy took me upstairs, and showed me a room next her own, where a cosy fire was burning. 'Now,' she said, 'you must stay here. I shall leave this door open and my door too. You can lie on the sofa, for I know that nothing would induce any of you doctors to go to bed whilst there is a patient above the horizon. If I want anything I shall call out, and you can come to me at once.' I could not but acquiesce, for I was 'dog-tired', and could not have sat up had I tried. So, on her renewing her promise to call me if she should want anything, I lay on the sofa, and forgot all about everything.

LUCY WESTENRA'S DIARY

9 September. – I feel so happy tonight. I have been so miserably weak, that to be able to think and move about is like feeling sunshine after a long spell of east wind out of a steel sky. Somehow Arthur feels very, very close to me. I seem to feel his presence warm about me. I suppose it is that sickness and weakness are selfish things and turn our inner eyes and sympathy on ourselves, whilst health and strength give Love rein, and in thought and feeling he can wander where he wills. I know where my thoughts are. If Arthur only knew! My dear, my dear, your ears must tingle as you sleep, as mine do waking. Oh, the blissful rest of last night! How I slept, with that dear, good Dr Seward watching me. And tonight I shall not fear to sleep, since he is close at hand and within call. Thank everybody for being so good to me! Thank God! Good-night Arthur.

DR SEWARD'S DIARY

10 September. – I was conscious of the Professor's hand on my head, and started awake all in a second. That is one of the things that we learn in an asylum, at any rate.

'And how is our patient?'

'Well, when I left her, or rather when she left me,' I answered.

'Come, let us see,' he said. And together we went into the room.

The blind was down, and I went over to raise it gently, whilst Van Helsing stepped, with his soft, cat-like tread, over to the bed.

As I raised the blind, and the morning sunlight flooded the room, I heard the Professor's low hiss of inspiration, and knowing its rarity, a deadly fear shot through my heart. As I passed over he moved back, and his exclamation of horror, 'Gott in Himmel!'[112] needed no enforcement from his agonised face. He raised his hand and pointed to the bed, and his iron face was drawn and ashen white. I felt my knees begin to tremble.

There on the bed, seemingly in a swoon, lay poor Lucy, more horribly white and wan-looking than ever. Even the lips were white, and the gums seemed to have shrunken back from the teeth, as we sometimes see in a corpse after a prolonged illness. Van Helsing raised his foot to stamp in anger, but the instinct of his life and all the long years of habit stood to him, and he put it down again softly. 'Quick!' he said. 'Bring the brandy.' I flew to the dining-room, and returned with the decanter. He wetted the poor white lips with it, and together we rubbed palm and wrist and heart. He felt her heart, and after a few moments of agonising suspense said:

'It is not too late. It beats, though but feebly. All our work is undone; we must begin again. There is no young Arthur here now, I have to call on you yourself this time, friend John.' As he spoke, he was dipping into his bag and producing the instruments for transfusion; I had taken off my coat and rolled up my shirt-sleeve. There was no possibility of an opiate just at present, and no need of one, and so, without a moment's delay, we began the operation. After a time – it did not seem a short time either, for the draining away of one's blood, no matter how willingly it be given, is a terrible feeling – Van Helsing held up a warning finger. 'Do not stir,' he said, 'but I fear that with growing strength she may wake; and that would make danger, oh, so much danger. But I shall precaution take. I shall give hypodermic injection of morphia.' He proceeded then, swiftly and deftly, to carry out his intent. The effect on Lucy was not bad, for the faint seemed to merge subtly into the narcotic sleep. It was with a feeling of personal pride that I could see a faint tinge of colour steal back into the pallid cheeks and lips. No man knows till he experiences it, what it is to feel his own life-blood drawn away into the veins of the woman he loves.

The Professor watched me critically. 'That will do,' he said. 'Already?' I remonstrated. 'You took a great deal more from Art.' To which he smiled a sad sort of smile as he replied:

'He is her lover, her fiancé. You have work, much work, to do for her and for others; and the present will suffice.'

When we stopped the operation, he attended to Lucy, whilst I applied digital pressure to my own incision. I lay down, whilst I waited his leisure to attend to me, for I felt faint and a little sick. By-and-by he bound up my wound, and sent me downstairs to get a glass of wine for myself. As I was leaving the room, he came after me, and half whispered:

'Mind, nothing must be said of this. If our young lover should turn up unexpected, as before, no word to him. It would at once frighten him and enjealous him, too. There must be none. So!'

When I came back he looked at me carefully, and then said:

'You are not much the worse. Go into the room, and lie on your sofa, and rest awhile; then have much breakfast, and come here to me.'

I followed out his orders, for I knew how right and wise they were. I had done my part, and now my next duty was to keep up my strength. I felt very weak, and in the weakness lost something of the amazement at what had occurred. I fell asleep on the sofa, however, wondering over and over again how Lucy had made such a retrograde movement, and how she could have been drained of so much blood with no sign anywhere to show for it. I think I must have continued my wonder in my dreams, for sleeping and waking, my thoughts always came back to the little punctures in her throat and the ragged, exhausted appearance of their edges – tiny though they were.

Lucy slept well into the day; and when she woke she was fairly well and strong, though not nearly so much so as the day before. When Van Helsing had seen her, he went out for a walk, leaving me in charge, with strict injunctions that I was not to leave her for a moment. I could hear his voice in the hall, asking the way to the nearest telegraph office.

Lucy chatted with me freely, and seemed quite unconscious that anything had happened. I tried to keep her amused and interested. When her mother came up to see her, she did not seem to notice any change whatever, but said to me gratefully:

'We owe you so much, Dr Seward, for all you have done but you really must now take care not to overwork yourself. You are looking pale yourself. You want a wife to nurse and look after you a bit; that you do!' As she spoke Lucy turned crimson, though it was only momentarily, for her poor wasted veins could not stand for long such an unwonted drain to the head. The reaction came in excessive pallor as she turned imploring eyes on me. I smiled and nodded, and laid my finger on my lips; with a sigh, she sank back amid her pillows.

Van Helsing returned in a couple of hours, and presently said to me: 'Now you go home, and eat much and drink enough. Make yourself strong. I stay here tonight, and I shall sit up with little miss myself. You and I must watch the case, and we must have none other to know. I have grave reasons. No, do not ask them; think what you will. Do not fear to think even the most not-probable. Good-night.'

In the hall two of the maids came to me, and asked if they or either of them might not sit up with Miss Lucy. They implored me to let them; and when I said it was Dr Van Helsing's wish that either he or I should sit up, they asked me quite piteously to intercede with the 'foreign gentleman'. I was much touched by their kindness. Perhaps it is because I am weak at present, and perhaps it was on Lucy's account that their devotion was manifested, for over and over again have I seen similar instances of woman's kindness. I got back here in time for a late dinner; went my rounds – all well; and set this down whilst waiting for sleep. It is coming.

11 September – This afternoon I went over to Hillingham. Found Van Helsing in excellent spirits, and Lucy much better. Shortly after I had arrived, a big parcel from abroad came for the Professor. He opened it with much impressment – assumed, of course – and showed a great bundle of white flowers.

'These are for you, Miss Lucy,' he said.

'For me? Oh, Dr Van Helsing!'

'Yes, my dear, but not for you to play with. These are medicines.' Here Lucy made a wry face. 'Nay, but they are not to take in a decoction or in nauseous form, so you need not snub that so charming nose, or I shall point out to my friend Arthur what woes he may have to endure in seeing so much beauty that he so loves so much distort. Aha, my pretty miss, that bring the so nice nose all straight again. This is medicinal, but you do not know how. I put him in your window, I make pretty wreath, and hang him round your neck, so that you sleep well. Oh yes! they, like the lotus flower, make your trouble forgotten. It smell so like the waters of Lethe,[113] and of that fountain of youth that the Conquistadores sought for in the Floridas, and find him all too late.'

Whilst he was speaking, Lucy had been examining the flowers and smelling them. Now she threw them down, saying, with half-laughter and half-disgust:

'Oh, Professor, I believe you are only putting up a joke on me. Why, these flowers are only common garlic.'

To my surprise, Van Helsing rose up and said with all his sternness, his iron jaw set and his bushy eyebrows meeting:

'No trifling with me! I never jest! There is grim purpose in all I do; and I warn you that you do not thwart me. Take care, for the sake of others if not for your own.' Then seeing poor Lucy scared, as she might well be, he went on more gently: 'Oh, little miss, my dear, do not fear me. I only do for your good; but there is much virtue to you in those so common flower. See, I place them myself in your room. I make myself the wreath that you are to wear. But hush! no telling to others that make so inquisitive questions. We must obey, and silence is a part of obedience; and obedience is to bring you strong and well into loving arms that wait for you. Now sit still awhile. Come with me, friend John, and you shall help me deck the room with my garlic, which is all the way from Haarlem, where my friend Vanderpool raise herb in his glass-houses all the year. I had to telegraph yesterday, or they would not have been here.'

We went into the room, taking the flowers with us. The Professor's actions were certainly odd, and not to be found in any pharmacopœia that I ever heard of. First he fastened up the windows and latched them securely; next, taking a handful of the flowers, he rubbed them all over the sashes, as though to ensure that every whiff of air that might get in would be laden with the garlic smell. Then with the wisp he rubbed all over the jamb of the door, above, below, and at each side, and round the fireplace in the same way. It all seemed grotesque to me, and presently I said:

'Well, Professor, I know you always have a reason for what you do, but this certainly puzzles me. It is well we have no sceptic here, or he would say that you were working some spell to keep out an evil spirit.'

'Perhaps I am!' he answered quietly as he began to make the wreath which Lucy was to wear round her neck.

We then waited whilst Lucy made her toilet for the night, and when she was in bed he came and himself fixed the wreath of garlic round her neck. The last words he said to her were:

'Take care you do not disturb it; and even if the room feel close, do not tonight open the window or the door.'

'I promise,' said Lucy, 'and thank you both a thousand times for all your kindness to me! Oh, what have I done to be blessed with such friends?'

As we left the house in my fly,[114] which was waiting, Van Helsing said:

'Tonight I can sleep in peace, and sleep I want – two nights of travel, much reading in the day between, and much anxiety on the day to follow, and a night to sit up, without to wink. Tomorrow in the morning early you call for me, and we come together to see our pretty miss, so much more strong for my "spell" which I have work. Ho! ho!'

He seemed so confident that I, remembering my own confidence two nights before and with the baneful result, felt awe and vague terror. It must have been my weakness that made me hesitate to tell it to my friend, but I felt it all the more, like unshed tears.

Chapter 11

LUCY WESTENRA'S DIARY

12 September. – How good they all are to me! I quite love that dear Dr Van Helsing. I wonder why he was so anxious about these flowers. He positively frightened me, he was so fierce. And yet he must have been right, for I feel comfort from them already. Somehow, I do not dread being alone tonight, and I can go to sleep without fear. I shall not mind any flapping outside the window. Oh, the terrible struggle that I have had against sleep so often of late; the pain of the sleeplessness, or the pain of the fear of sleep, with such unknown horrors as it has for me! How blessed are some people, whose lives have no fears, no dreads; to whom sleep is a blessing that comes nightly, and brings nothing but sweet dreams. Well, here I am tonight, hoping for sleep, and lying like Ophelia in the play, with 'virgin crants and maiden strewments'.[115] I never liked garlic before, but tonight it is delightful! There is peace in its smell; I feel sleep coming already. Good-night everybody.

DR SEWARD'S DIARY

13 September. – Called at the Berkeley[116] and found Van Helsing, as usual, up to time. The carriage ordered from the hotel was waiting. The Professor took his bag, which he always brings with him now.

Let all be put down exactly. Van Helsing and I arrived at Hillingham at eight o'clock. It was a lovely morning; the bright sunshine and all the fresh feeling of early autumn seemed like the completion of nature's annual work. The leaves were turning to all kinds of beautiful colours, but had not yet begun to drop from the trees. When we entered we met Mrs Westenra coming out of the morning-room. She is always an early riser. She greeted us warmly and said:

'You will be glad to know that Lucy is better. The dear child is still asleep. I looked into her room and saw her, but did not go in, lest I should disturb her.' The Professor smiled, and looked quite jubilant. He rubbed his hands together, and said: 'Aha! I thought I had diagnosed the case. My treatment is working,' to which she answered:

'You must not take all the credit to yourself, doctor. Lucy's state this morning is due in part to me.'

'How do you mean, ma'am?' asked the Professor.

'Well, I was anxious about the dear child in the night, and went into her room. She was sleeping soundly – so soundly that even my coming did not wake her. But the room was awfully stuffy. There were a lot of those horrible, strong-smelling flowers about everywhere, and she had actually a bunch of them round her neck. I feared that the heavy odour would be too much for the dear child in her weak state, so I took them all away and opened a bit of the window to let in a little fresh air. You will be pleased with her, I am sure.'

She moved off into her boudoir, where she usually breakfasted early. As she had spoken, I watched the Professor's face, and saw it turn ashen grey. He had been able to retain his self-command whilst the poor lady was present, for he knew her state and how mischievous a shock would be; he actually smiled on her as he held open the door for her to pass into her room. But the instant she had disappeared he pulled me, suddenly and forcibly, into the dining-room and closed the door.

Then, for the first time in my life, I saw Van Helsing break down. He raised his hands over his head in a sort of mute despair, and then beat his palms together in a helpless way; finally he sat down on a chair, and putting his hands before his face, began to sob, with loud, dry sobs that seemed to come from the very racking of his heart. Then he raised his arms again, as though appealing to the whole universe. 'God! God! God!' he said. 'What have we done, what has this poor thing done, that we are so sore beset? Is there fate amongst us still, sent down from the pagan world of old, that such things must be, and in such way? This poor mother, all unknowing, and all for the best as she think, does such thing as lose her daughter body and soul; and we must not tell her, we must not even warn her, or she die, and then both die. Oh, how we are beset! How are all the powers of the devils against us!' Suddenly he jumped to his feet. 'Come,' he said, 'come, we must see and act. Devils or no devils, or all the devils at once, it matters not; we fight him all the same.' He went to the hall-door for his bag; and together we went up to Lucy's room.

Once again I drew up the blind, whilst Van Helsing went towards the bed. This time he did not start as he looked on the poor face with the same awful, waxen pallor as before. He wore a look of stern sadness and infinite pity.

'As I expected,' he murmured, with that hissing inspiration of his which meant so much. Without a word he went and locked the door, and then began to set out on the little table the instruments for yet another operation of transfusion of blood. I had long ago recognised the necessity, and begun to take off my coat, but he stopped me with a warning hand. 'No!' he said. 'Today you must operate. I shall provide. You are weakened already.' As he spoke he took off his coat and rolled up his shirt-sleeve.

Again the operation; again the narcotic; again some return of colour to the ashy cheeks, and the regular breathing of healthy sleep. This time I watched whilst Van Helsing recruited himself and rested.

Presently he took an opportunity of telling Mrs Westenra that she must not remove anything from Lucy's room without consulting him; that the flowers were of medicinal value and that the breathing of their odour was a part of the system of cure. Then he took over the care of the case himself, saying that he would watch this night and the next and would send me word when to come.

After another hour Lucy waked from her sleep, fresh and bright, and seemingly not much the worse for her terrible ordeal.

What does it all mean? I am beginning to wonder if my long habit of life amongst the insane is beginning to tell upon my own brain.

Lucy Westenra's Diary

17 *September*. – Four days and nights of peace. I am getting so strong again that I hardly know myself. It is as if I had passed through some long nightmare, and had just awakened to see the beautiful sunshine and feel the fresh air of the morning around me. I have a dim half-remembrance of long, anxious times of waiting and fearing; darkness in which there was not even the pain of hope to make present distress more poignant and then long spells of oblivion, and the rising back to life as a diver coming up through a great press of water. Since, however, Dr Van Helsing has been with me, all this bad dreaming seems to have passed away, the noises that used to frighten me out of my wits – the flapping against the windows, the distant voices which seemed so close to me, the harsh sounds that came from I know not where and commanded me to do I know not what – have all ceased. I go to bed now without any fear of sleep. I do not even try to keep awake. I have grown quite fond of the garlic, and a boxful arrives for me every day from Haarlem. Tonight Dr Van Helsing is going away, as he has to be for a day in Amsterdam. But I need not be watched, I am well enough to be left alone. Thank God for mother's sake, and dear Arthur's, and for all our friends who have been so kind! I shall not even feel the change, for last night Dr Van Helsing slept in his chair a lot of the time. I found him asleep twice when I awoke; but I did not fear to go to sleep again,

although the boughs or bats or something flapped almost angrily against the window-panes.

The Pall Mall Gazette,[117] *18 September*
THE ESCAPED WOLF
PERILOUS ADVENTURE OF OUR INTERVIEWER
Interview with the Keeper in the Zoological Gardens

After many inquiries and almost as many refusals, and perpetually using the words *Pall Mall Gazette* as a sort of talisman, I managed to find the keeper of the section of the Zoological Gardens in which the wolf department is included. Thomas Bilder lives in one of the cottages in the enclosure behind the elephant-house, and was just sitting down to his tea when I found him. Thomas and his wife are hospitable folk, elderly, and without children, and if the specimen I enjoyed of their hospitality be of the average kind, their lives must be pretty comfortable.

The keeper would not enter on what he called 'business' until the supper was over, and we were all satisfied. Then when the table was cleared, and he had lit his pipe, he said:

'Now, sir, you can go on and arsk me what you want. You'll excoose me refoosin' to talk of perfeshunal subjects afore meals. I gives the wolves and the jackals and the hyenas in all our section their tea afore I begins to arsk them questions.'

'How do you mean, ask them questions?' I queried, wishing to get him into a talkative humour.

' 'Ittin' of them over the 'ead with a pole is one way; scratchin' of their hears is another, when gents as is flush wants a bit of a show-orf to their gals. I don't so much mind the fust – the 'ittin' with a pole afore I chucks in their dinner – but I waits till they've 'ad their sherry and kawffee, so to speak, afore I tries on with the ear-scratchin'. Mind you,' he added philosophically, 'there's a deal of the same nature in us as in them there animiles. Here's you a-comin' and arskin' of me questions about my business, and I that grumpy-like that only for your bloomin' arf-quid[118] I'd 'a' seen you blowed fust, 'fore I'd answer. Not even when you arsked me sarcastic-like if I'd like you to arsk the Superintendent if you might arsk me questions. Without offence, did I tell yer to go to 'ell?'

'You did.'

'An' when you said you'd report me for usin' of obscene language that was 'itten' me over the 'ead; but the 'arf-quid made that all right. I weren't a-goin' to fight, so I waited for the food, and did with my 'owl as the wolves, and lions, and tigers does. But, Lor' love yer 'art, now that the old 'ooman has stuck a chunk of her tea-cake in me, an' rinsed me out with her bloomin' old teapot, and I've lit up, you may scratch my ears for all you're worth, and won't get even a growl out of me. Drive along with your questions. I know what yer a-comin' at, that 'ere escaped wolf.'

'Exactly. I want you to give me your view of it. Just tell me how it happened; and when I know the facts I'll get you to say what you consider was the cause of it, and how you think the whole affair will end.'

'All right, guv'nor. This 'ere is about the 'ole story. That 'ere wolf what we called Bersicker was one of three grey ones that came from Norway to Jamrach's, which we bought off him four year ago. He was a nice well-behaved wolf, that never gave no trouble to talk of. I'm more surprised at 'im for wantin' to get out nor any other animile in the place. But, there, you can't trust wolves no more nor women.'

'Don't you mind him, sir!' broke in Mrs Tom, with a cheery laugh. ' 'E's got mindin' the animiles so long that blest if he ain't like a old wolf 'isself! But there ain't no 'arm in 'im.'

'Well, sir, it was about two hours after feedin' yesterday when I first hear any disturbance. I was makin' up a litter in the monkey-house for a young puma which is ill; but when I heard the yelpin' and 'owlin' I kem away straight. There was Bersicker a-tearin' like a mad thing at the bars as if he wanted to get out. There wasn't much people about that day, and close at hand was only one man, a tall, thin chap, with a 'ook nose and a pointed beard, with a few white hairs runnin' through it. He had a 'ard, cold look and red eyes, and I took a sort of mislike to him, for it seemed as if it was 'im as they was hirritated at. He 'ad white kid gloves on 'is 'ands, and he pointed out the animiles to me and says: "Keeper, these wolves seem upset at something."

' "Maybe it's you," says I, for I did not like the airs as he give 'isself. He didn't get angry, as I 'oped he would but he smiled a kind of insolent smile, with a mouth full of white, sharp teeth. "Oh no, they wouldn't like me," 'e says.

' "Ow yes, they would," says I, a-imitatin' of him. "They always likes a bone or two to clean their teeth on about tea-time, which you 'as a bagful."

'Well, it was a odd thing, but when the animiles see us a-talkin' they lay down, and when I went over to Bersicker he let me stroke his ears same as ever. That there man kem over, and blessed but if he didn't put in his hand and stroke the old wolf's ears too!

' "Tyke care," says I. "Bersicker is quick."

' "Never mind," he says. "I'm used to 'em! "

' "Are you in the business yourself?" I says, tyking off my 'at, for a man what trades in wolves, anceterer,[119] is a good friend to keepers.

' "No," says he, "not exactly in the business, but I 'ave made pets of several." And with that he lifts his 'at as perlite as a lord, and walks away. Old Bersicker kep' a-lookin' arter 'im till 'e was out of sight, and then went and lay down in a corner, and wouldn't come hout the 'ole hevening. Well, larst night, so soon as the moon was hup, the wolves here all began a-'owling. There warn't nothing for them to 'owl at. There warn't no one near except someone that was evidently a-callin' a dog somewheres out back of the gardings in the Park road. Once or twice I went out to see that all was right, and it was, and then the 'owling stopped. Just before twelve o'clock I just took a look round afore turnin' in, an', bust me, but when I kem opposite to old Bersicker's cage I see the rails broken and twisted about and the cage empty. And that's all I know for certing.'

'Did anyone else see anything?'

'One of our gard'ners was a-comin' 'ome about that time from a 'armony,[120] when he sees a big grey dog comin' out through the garding 'edges.[121] At least, so he says; but I don't give much for it myself, for if he did 'e never said a word about it to his missis when 'e got 'ome, and it was only after the escape of the wolf was made known, and we had been up all night a-huntin' of the Park for Bersicker, that he remembered seein' anything. My own belief was that the 'armony 'ad got into his 'ead.'

'Now, Mr Bilder, can you account in any way for the escape of the wolf?'

'Well, sir,' he said, with a suspicious sort of modesty, 'I think I can; but I don't know as 'ow you'd be satisfied with the theory.'

'Certainly I shall. If a man like you, who knows the animals from experience, can't hazard a good guess at any rate, who is even to try?'

'Well then, sir, I accounts for it this way; it seems to me that 'ere wolf escaped – simply because he wanted to get out.'

From the hearty way that both Thomas and his wife laughed at the joke I could see that it had done service before, and that the whole explanation was simply an elaborate sell. I couldn't cope in badinage with the worthy Thomas, but I thought I knew a surer way to his heart so I said: 'Now, Mr Bilder, we'll consider that first half-sovereign worked off, and this brother of his is waiting to be claimed when you've told me what you think will happen.'

'Right y'are, sir,' he said briskly. 'Ye'll excoose me, I know, for a-chaffin' of ye, but the old woman here winked at me, which was as much as telling me to go on.'

'Well, I never!' said the old lady.

'My opinion is this: that 'ere wolf is a-'idin' of, somewheres. The gard'ner wot didn't remember said he was a-gallopin' northward faster than a horse could go; but I don't believe him, for yer see, sir, wolves don't gallop no more than dogs does, they not bein' built that way. Wolves is fine things in a story-book, and I dessay when they gets in packs and does be chivvin' somethin' that's more afeared than they is they can make a devil of a noise and chop it up, whatever it is. But, Lor' bless you, in real life a wolf is only a low creature, not half so clever or bold as a good dog; and not half a quarter so much fight in 'im. This one ain't been used to fightin' or even to providin' for hisself, and more like he's somewhere round the Park a-'idin' an' a-shiverin' of, and, if he thinks at all, wonderin' where he is to get his breakfast from; or maybe he's got down some area and is in a coal-cellar. My eye, won't some cook get a rum start when she sees his green eyes a-shining at her out of the dark! If he can't get food he's bound to look for it, and mayhap he may chance to light on a butcher's shop in time. If he doesn't, and some nursemaid goes a'-walkin' orf with a soldier, leavin' of the hinfant in the perambulator – well then I shouldn't be surprised if the census is one babby the less. That's all.'

I was handing him the half-sovereign, when something came bobbing up against the window, and Mr Bilder's face doubled its natural length with surprise.

'God bless me!' he said 'If there ain't old Bersicker come back by 'isself!'

He went to the door and opened it; a most unnecessary proceeding it seemed to me. I have always thought that a wild animal never looks so well as when some obstacle of pronounced durability is between us; a personal experience has intensified rather than diminished that idea.

After all, however, there is nothing like custom, for neither Bilder nor his wife thought any more of the wolf than I should of a dog. The animal itself was as peaceful and well-behaved as that father of all picture-wolves, Red Riding Hood's quondam friend,[122] whilst seeking her confidence in masquerade.

The whole scene was an unutterable mixture of comedy and pathos. The wicked wolf that for half a day had paralysed London and set all the children in the town shivering in their shoes, was there in a sort of penitent mood, and was received and petted like a sort of vulpine prodigal son. Old Bilder examined him all over with most tender solicitude, and when he had finished with his penitent said:

'There, I knew the poor old chap would get into some kind of trouble; didn't I say it all along? Here's his head all cut and full of broken glass. 'E's been a-gettin' over some bloomin' wall or other. It's a shyme that people are allowed to top their walls with broken bottles. This 'ere's what comes of it. Come along, Bersicker.'

He took the wolf and locked him up in a cage, with a piece of meat that satisfied, in quantity at any rate, the elementary conditions of the fatted calf, and went off to report.

I came off, too, to report the only exclusive information that is given today regarding the strange escapade at the Zoo.

Dr Seward's Diary

17 September. – I was engaged after dinner in my study posting up my books, which, through press of other work and the many visits to Lucy, had fallen sadly into arrear. Suddenly the door was burst open, and in rushed my patient, with his face distorted with passion. I was thunder-struck, for such a thing as a patient getting of his own accord into the Superintendent's study is almost unknown. Without an instant's pause he made straight at me. He had a dinner-knife in his hand, and, as I saw he was dangerous, I tried to keep the table between us. He was too quick and too strong for me, however; for before I could get my balance he had struck at me and cut my left wrist rather severely. Before he could strike again, however, I got in my right, and he was sprawling on his back on the floor. My wrist bled freely, and quite a little pool trickled on to the carpet. I saw that my friend was not intent on further effort, and occupied myself binding up my wrist, keeping a wary eye on the prostrate figure all the time. When the attendants rushed in, and we turned our attention to him, his employment positively sickened me. He was lying on his belly on the floor licking up like a dog, the blood which had fallen from my wounded wrist. He was easily secured, and, to my surprise, went with the attendants quite placidly, simply repeating over and over again: 'The blood is the life! the blood is the life!' [123]

I cannot afford to lose blood just at present: I have lost too much of late for my physical good, and then the prolonged strain of Lucy's illness and its horrible phases is telling on me. I am over-excited and weary, and I need rest, rest, rest. Happily Van Helsing has not summoned me, so I need not forgo my sleep; tonight I could not well do without it.

Telegram, Van Helsing, Antwerp, to Seward, Carfax.
(Sent to Carfax, Sussex, as no county given; delivered late
by twenty-two hours.)

17 September. – Do not fail to be at Hillingham tonight. If not watching all the time, frequently visit and see that flowers are as placed; very important; do not fail. Shall be with you as soon as possible after arrival.

Dr Seward's Diary

18 September. – Just off for train to London. The arrival of Van Helsing's telegram filled me with dismay. A whole night lost, and I know by bitter experience what may happen in a night. Of course it is possible that all may be well, but what may have happened? Surely there is some horrible doom hanging over us that every possible accident should thwart us in all we try to do. I shall take this cylinder with me, and then I can complete my entry on Lucy's phonograph.

Memorandum left by Lucy Westenra

17 September. Night. – I write this and leave it to be seen, so that no one may by any chance get into any trouble through me. This is an exact record of what took place tonight. I feel I am dying of weakness and have barely strength to write, but it must be done if I die in the doing.

I went to bed as usual, taking care that the flowers were placed as Dr Van Helsing directed, and soon fell asleep.

I was waked by the flapping at the window, which had begun after that sleep-walking on the cliff at Whitby when Mina saved me, and which now I know so well. I was not afraid, but I did wish that Dr Seward was in the next room – as Dr Van Helsing said he would be – so that I might have called him. I tried to go to sleep, but could not. Then there came to me the old fear of sleep, and I determined to keep awake. Perversely sleep would try to come when I did not want it; so, as I feared to be alone, I opened my door and called out: 'Is there anybody there?' There was no answer. I was afraid to wake mother and so closed my door again. Then outside in the shrubbery I heard a sort of howl like a dog's, but more fierce and deeper. I went to the window and looked out, but could see nothing, except a big bat, which had evidently been buffeting its wings against the window. So I went back to bed again, but determined not to go to sleep. Presently the door opened, and mother looked in; seeing by my moving that I was not asleep, came in, and sat by me. She said to me even more sweetly and softly than her wont:

'I was uneasy about you, darling, and came in to see that you were all right.'

I feared she might catch cold sitting there, and asked her to come in and sleep with me, so she came into bed, and lay down beside me; she did not take off her dressing-gown, for she said she would only stay a while and then go back to her own bed. As she lay there in my arms, and I in hers, the flapping and buffeting came to the window again. She was startled and a little frightened, and cried out: 'What is that?' I tried to pacify her, and at last succeeded, and she lay quiet; but I could hear her poor dear heart still beating terribly. After a while there was the low howl again out in the shrubbery, and shortly after there was a crash at the window, and a lot of broken glass was hurled on the floor. The window blind blew back with the wind that rushed in, and in the aperture of the broken panes there was the head of a great gaunt grey wolf. Mother cried out in a fright, and struggled up into a sitting posture, and clutched wildly at anything that would help her. Amongst other things she clutched the wreath of flowers that Dr Van Helsing insisted on my wearing round my neck, and tore it away from me. For a second or two she sat up, pointing at the wolf, and there was a strange and horrible gurgling in her throat; then she fell over, as if struck with lightning, and her head hit my forehead and made me dizzy for a moment or two. The room and all round seemed to spin round. I kept my eyes fixed on the window, but the wolf drew his head back, and a whole myriad of little specks seemed to come blowing in through the broken window, and wheeling and circling round like the pillar of dust that travellers describe when there is a simoom[124] in the desert. I tried to stir, but there was some spell upon me, and dear mother's poor body, which seemed to grow cold already – for her dear heart had ceased to beat – weighed me down; and I remembered no more for a while.

The time did not seem long, but very, very awful, till I recovered consciousness again. Somewhere near, a passing bell was tolling; the dogs all round the neighbourhood were howling; and in our shrubbery, seemingly just outside, a nightingale was singing. I was dazed and stupid with pain and terror and weakness, but the sound of the nightingale seemed like the voice of my dead mother come back to comfort me. The sounds seemed to have awakened the maids, too, for I could hear their bare feet pattering outside my door. I called to them, and they came in, and when they saw what had happened, and what it was that lay over me on the bed, they screamed out. The wind rushed in through the broken window, and the door slammed to. They lifted off the body of my dear mother and laid her, covered up with a sheet, on the bed after I had got up. They were all so frightened and nervous that I directed them to go to the dining-room and have each a glass of wine. The door flew open for an instant and closed again. The maids shrieked, and then went in a body to the dining-room; and I laid what flowers I had on my dear mother's breast. When they were there I remembered what Dr Van Helsing had told me, but I didn't like to remove them, and, besides, I would have some of the servants to sit up with me now. I was surprised that the maids did not come back. I called them, but got no answer, so I went to the dining-room to look for them.

My heart sank when I saw what had happened. They all four lay helpless on the floor, breathing heavily. The decanter of sherry was on the table half full, but there was a queer, acrid smell about. I was suspicious, and examined the decanter. It smelt of laudanum, and looking on the sideboard, I found that the bottle which mother's doctor uses for her – oh! did use – was empty. What am I to do? What am I to do? I am back in the room with mother. I cannot leave her, and I am alone, save for the sleeping servants, whom someone has drugged. Alone with the dead! I dare not go out, for I can hear the low howl of the wolf through the broken window.

The air seems full of specks, floating and circling in the draught from the window, and the lights burn blue and dim. What am I to do? God shield me from harm this night! I shall hide this paper in my breast, where they shall find it when they come to lay me out. My dear mother gone! It is time that I go too. Good-bye, dear Arthur, if I should not survive this night. God keep you, dear, and God help me!

Chapter 12

Dr Seward's Diary

18 September. – I drove at once to Hillingham and arrived early. Keeping my cab at the gate, I went up the avenue alone. I knocked gently and rang as quietly as possible, for I feared to disturb Lucy or her mother, and hoped to bring only a servant to the door. After a while, finding no response, I knocked and rang again; still no answer. I cursed the laziness of the servants that they should lie abed at such an hour – for it was now ten o'clock – and so rang and knocked again, but more impatiently, and still without response. Hitherto I had blamed only the servants, but now a terrible fear began to assail me. Was this desolation but another link in the chain of doom which seemed drawing tight around us? Was it indeed a house of death to which I had come, too late? I knew that minutes, even seconds, of delay might mean hours of danger to Lucy, if she had had again one of those frightful relapses; and I went round the house to try if I could find by chance an entry anywhere.

I could find no means of ingress. Every window and door was

fastened and locked, and I returned baffled to the porch. As I did so, I heard the rapid pit-pat of a swiftly driven horse's feet. They stopped at the gate, and a few seconds later I met Van Helsing running up the avenue. When he saw me, he gasped out:

'Then it was you, and just arrived. How is she? Are we too late? Did you not get my telegram?'

I answered as quickly and coherently as I could that I had only got his telegram early in the morning and had not lost a minute in coming here, and that I could not make anyone in the house hear me. He paused and raised his hat as he said solemnly:

'Then I fear we are too late. God's will be done!' With his usual recuperative energy, he went on: 'Come. If there be no way open to get in, we must make one. Time is all in all to us now.'

We went round to the back of the house, where there was a kitchen window. The Professor took a small surgical saw from his case, and handing it to me, pointed to the iron bars which guarded the window. I attacked them at once and had very soon cut through three of them. Then with a long, thin knife we pushed back the fastening of the sashes and opened the window. I helped the Professor in and followed him. There was no one in the kitchen or in the servants' rooms, which were close at hand. We tried all the rooms as we went along, and in the dining-room, dimly lit by rays of light through the shutters, found four servant-women lying on the floor. There was no need to think them dead, for their stertorous breathing and the acrid smell of laudanum in the room left no doubt as to their condition. Van Helsing and I looked at each other, and as we moved away he said: 'We can attend to them later.' Then we ascended to Lucy's room. For an instant or two we paused at the door to listen, but there was no sound that we could hear. With white faces and trembling hands, we opened the door gently, and entered the room.

How shall I describe what we saw? On the bed lay two women, Lucy and her mother. The latter lay farthest in, and she was covered with a white sheet, the edge of which had been blown back by the draught through the broken window, showing the drawn, white face, with a look of terror fixed upon it. By her side lay Lucy, with face white and still more drawn. The flowers which had been round her neck we found upon her mother's bosom, and her throat was bare, showing the two little wounds which we had noticed before, but looking horribly white and mangled. Without a word the Professor bent over the bed, his head almost touching poor Lucy's breast; then he gave a quick turn of his head, as of one who listens, and leaping to his feet, he cried out to me:

'It is not yet too late! Quick! Quick! Bring the brandy!'

I flew downstairs and returned with it, taking care to smell and taste it, lest it, too, were drugged like the decanter of sherry which I found on the table. The maids were still breathing, but more restlessly, and I fancied that the narcotic was wearing off. I did not stay to make sure, but returned to Van Helsing. He rubbed the brandy, as on another occasion, on her lips and gums and on her wrists and the palms of her hands. He said to me:

'I can do this, all that can be at the present. You go wake those maids. Flick them in the face with a wet towel, and flick them hard. Make them get heat and fire and a warm bath. This poor soul is nearly as cold as that beside her. She will need be heated before we can do anything more.'

I went at once, and found little difficulty in waking three of the women. The fourth was only a young girl and the drug had evidently affected her more strongly, so I lifted her on the sofa and let her sleep. The others were dazed at first, but as remembrance came back to them they cried and sobbed in a hysterical manner. I was stern with them, however, and would not let them talk. I told them that one life was bad enough to lose, and that if they delayed they would sacrifice Miss Lucy. So, sobbing and crying, they went about their way, half-clad as they were, and prepared fire and water. Fortunately, the kitchen and boiler fires were still alive, and there was no lack of hot water. We got a bath, and carried Lucy out as she was and placed her in it. Whilst we were busy chafing her limbs there was a knock at the hall-door. One of the maids ran off, hurried on some more clothes, and opened it. Then she returned and whispered to us that there was a gentleman who had come with a message from Mr Holmwood. I bade her simply tell him that he must wait, for we could see no one now. She went away with the message, and, engrossed with our work, I clean forgot all about him.

I never saw in all my experience the Professor work in such deadly earnest. I knew – as he knew – that it was a stand-up fight with death, and in a pause told him so. He answered me in a way that I did not understand, but with the sternest look that his face could wear:

'If that were all, I would stop here where we are now, and let her fade away into peace, for I see no light in life over her horizon.' He went on with his work with, if possible, renewed and more frenzied vigour.

Presently we both began to be conscious that the heat was beginning to be of some effect. Lucy's heart beat a trifle more audibly to the stethoscope, and her lungs had a perceptible movement. Van Helsing's face almost beamed, and as we lifted her from the bath and rolled her in a hot sheet to dry her, he said to me:

'The first gain is ours! Check to the king!'

We took Lucy into another room, which had by now been prepared, and laid her in bed and forced a few drops of brandy down her throat. I noticed that Van Helsing tied a soft silk handkerchief round her throat. She was still unconscious, and was quite as bad as, if not worse than, we had ever seen her.

Van Helsing called in one of the women, and told her to stay with her and not to take her eyes off her till we returned, and then beckoned me out of the room.

'We must consult as to what is to be done,' he said as we descended the stairs. In the hall he opened the dining-room door, and we passed in, he closing the door carefully behind him. The shutters had been opened, but the blinds were already down, with that obedience to the etiquette of death which the British woman of the lower classes always rigidly observes. The room was, therefore, dimly dark. It was, however, light enough for our purposes. Van Helsing's sternness was somewhat relieved by a look of perplexity. He was evidently torturing his mind about something, so I waited for an instant and he spoke:

'What are we to do now? Where are we to turn for help? We must have another transfusion of blood, and that soon, or that poor girl's life won't be worth an hour's purchase. You are exhausted already; I am exhausted too. I fear to trust those women, even if they would have courage to submit. What are we to do for someone who will open his veins for her?'

'What's the matter with me, anyhow?'

The voice came from the sofa across the room, and its tones brought relief and joy to my heart, for they were those of Quincey Morris. Van Helsing started angrily at the first sound, but his face softened and a glad look came into his eyes as I cried out: 'Quincey Morris!' and rushed towards him with outstretched hands.

'What brought you here?' I cried as our hands met.

'I guess Art is the cause.'

He handed me a telegram:

'Have not heard from Seward for three days, and am terribly anxious. Cannot leave. Father still in same condition. Send me word how Lucy is. Do not delay. – HOLMWOOD.'

'I think I came just in the nick of time. You know you have only to tell me what to do.'

Van Helsing strode forward and took his hand, looking him straight in the eyes as he said:

'A brave man's blood is the best thing on this earth when a woman is in trouble. You're a man, and no mistake. Well, the devil may work against us for all he's worth, but God sends us men when we want them.'

Once again we went through that ghastly operation. I have not the heart to go through with the details. Lucy had got a terrible shock, and it told on her more than before, for though plenty of blood went into her veins, her body did not respond to the treatment as well as on the other occasions. Her struggle back into life was something frightful to see and hear. However, the action of both heart and lungs improved, and Van Helsing made a subcutaneous injection of morphia, as before, and with good effect. Her faint became a profound slumber. The Professor watched whilst I went downstairs with Quincey Morris, and sent one of the maids to pay off one of the cabmen who were waiting. I left Quincey lying down after having a glass of wine, and told the cook to get ready a good breakfast. Then a thought struck me, and I went back to the room where Lucy now was. When I came softly in, I found Van Helsing with a sheet or two of note-paper in his hand. He had evidently read it, and was thinking it over as he sat with his hand to his brow. There was a look of grim satisfaction in his face, as of one who has had a doubt solved. He handed me the paper saying only: 'It dropped from Lucy's breast when we carried her to the bath.'

When I had read it, I stood looking at the Professor, and after a pause asked him: 'In God's name, what does it all mean? Was she, or is she, mad: or what sort of horrible danger is it?' I was so bewildered that I did not know what to say more. Van Helsing put out his hand and took the paper, saying: 'Do not trouble about it now. Forget it for the present. You shall know and understand it all in good time; but it will be later. And now what is it that you came to me to say?' This brought me back to fact, and I was all myself again.

'I came to speak about the certificate of death. If we do not act properly and wisely, there may be an inquest, and that paper would have to be produced. I am in hopes that we need have no inquest, for if we had it would surely kill poor Lucy, if nothing else did. I know, and you know, and the other doctor who attended her knows, that Mrs Westenra had disease of the heart, and we can certify that she died of it. Let us fill up the certificate at once, and I shall take it myself to the registrar and go on to the undertaker.'

'Good, oh my friend John! Well thought of! Truly Miss Lucy, if she be sad in the foes that beset her, is at least happy in the friends that love her. One, two, three, all open their veins for her, besides one old man. Ah yes, I know, friend John; I am not blind! I love you all the more for it! Now go.'

In the hall I met Quincey Morris, with a telegram for Arthur telling him that Mrs Westenra was dead; that Lucy also had been ill, but was now going on better; and that Van Helsing and I were with her. I told him where I was going, and he hurried me out, but as I was going said:

'When you come back, Jack, may I have two words with you all to ourselves?' I nodded in reply and went out. I found no difficulty about the registration, and arranged with the local undertaker to come up in the evening to measure for the coffin and to make arrangements.

When I got back Quincey was waiting for me. I told him I would see him as soon as I knew about Lucy and went up to her room. She was still sleeping, and the Professor seemingly had not moved from his seat at her side. From his putting his finger to his lips, I gathered that he expected her to wake before long and was afraid of forestalling nature. So I went down to Quincey and took him into the breakfast-room, where the blinds were not drawn down, and which was a little more cheerful, or rather less cheerless, than the other rooms. When we were alone, he said to me:

'Jack Seward, I don't want to shove myself in anywhere where I've no right to be; but this is no ordinary case. You know I loved that girl and wanted to marry her; but, although that's all past and gone, I can't help feeling anxious about her all the same. What is it that's wrong with her? The Dutchman – and a fine old fellow he is; I can see that – said, that time you two came into the room, that you must have *another* transfusion of blood, and that both you and he were exhausted. Now I know well that you medical men speak *in camera*,[125] and that a man must not expect to know what they consult about in private. But this is no common matter, and, whatever it is, I have done my part. Is not that so?'

'That's so,' I said, and he went on:

'I take it that both you and Van Helsing had done already what I did today. Is not that so?'

'That's so.'

'And I guess Art was in it too. When I saw him four days ago down at his own place he looked queer. I have not seen anything pulled down so quick since I was on the Pampas[126] and had a mare that I was fond of go to grass[127] all in a night. One of those big bats that they call vampires had got at her in the night, and, what with his gorge and the vein left open, there wasn't enough blood in her to let her stand up, and I had to put a bullet through her as she lay. Jack, if you may tell me without betraying confidence, Arthur was the first; is not that so?' As he spoke the poor fellow looked terribly anxious. He was in a torture of suspense regarding the woman he loved, and his utter ignorance of the terrible mystery which seemed to surround her intensified his pain. His very heart was bleeding, and it took all the manhood of him and there was a royal lot of it, too – to keep him from breaking down. I paused before answering, for I felt that I must not betray anything which the Professor wished kept secret, but already he knew so much, and guessed so much, that there could be no reason for not answering, so I answered in the same phrase: 'That's so.'

'And how long has this been going on?'

'About ten days.'

'Ten days! Then I guess, Jack Seward, that that poor pretty creature that we all love has had put into her veins within that time the blood of four strong men. Man alive, her whole body wouldn't hold it.' Then, coming close to me, he spoke in a fierce half-whisper: 'What took it out?'

I shook my head. 'That,' I said, 'is the crux. Van Helsing is simply frantic about it, and I am at my wits' end. I can't even hazard a guess. There has been a series of little circumstances which have thrown out all our calculations as to Lucy being properly watched. But these shall not occur again. Here we stay until all be well – or ill.' Quincey held out his hand. 'Count me in,' he said. 'You and the Dutchman will tell me what to do, and I'll do it.'

When she woke late in the afternoon, Lucy's first movement was to feel in her breast, and, to my surprise, produced the paper which Van Helsing had given me to read. The careful Professor had replaced it where it had come from, lest on waking she should be alarmed. Her eye then lit on Van Helsing and on me too, and gladdened. Then she looked round the room, and seeing where she was, shuddered; she gave a loud cry, and put her poor thin hands before her pale face. We both understood what that meant – that she had realised to the full her mother's death; so we tried what we could to comfort her. Doubtless sympathy eased her somewhat, but she was very low in thought and spirit, and wept silently and weakly for a long time. We told her that either or both of us would now remain with her all the time, and that seemed to comfort her. Towards dusk she fell into a doze. Here a very odd thing occurred. Whilst still asleep she took the paper from her breast and tore it in two. Van Helsing stepped over and took the pieces from her. All the same, however, she went on with the action of tearing, as though the material were still in her hands, finally she lifted her hands and opened them as though scattering the fragments. Van Helsing seemed surprised, and his brows gathered as if in thought, but he said nothing.

19 September.[128] – All last night she slept fitfully, being always afraid to sleep, and something weaker when she woke from it. The Professor and I took it in turns to watch, and we never left her for a moment unattended. Quincey Morris said nothing about his intention, but I knew that all night long he patrolled round and round the house.

When the day came, its searching light showed the ravages in poor Lucy's strength. She was hardly able to turn her head, and the little nourishment which she could take seemed to do her no good. At times she slept, and both Van Helsing and I noticed the difference in her, between sleeping and waking. Whilst asleep she looked stronger, although more haggard, and her breathing was softer; her open mouth showed the pale gums drawn back from the teeth, which thus looked positively longer and sharper than usual; when she woke the softness of her eyes evidently changed the expression, for she looked her own self although a dying one. In the afternoon she asked for Arthur, and we telegraphed for him. Quincey went off to meet him at the station.

When he arrived it was nearly six o'clock, and the sun was setting full and warm, and the red light streamed in through the window and gave more colour to the pale cheeks. When he saw her, Arthur was simply choking with emotion, and none of us could speak. In the hours that had passed, the fits of sleep, or the comatose condition that passed for it, had grown more frequent, so that the pauses when conversation was possible were shortened. Arthur's presence, however, seemed to act as a stimulant; she rallied a little, and spoke to him more brightly than she had done since we arrived. He too pulled himself together, and spoke as cheerily as he could, so that the best was made of everything.

It is now nearly one o'clock, and he and Van Helsing are sitting with her. I am to relieve them in a quarter of an hour, and I am entering this on Lucy's phonograph. Until six o'clock they are to try to rest. I fear that tomorrow will end our watching, for the shock has been too great; the poor child cannot rally. God help us all.

Letter, Mina Harker to Lucy Westenra
(unopened by her)

17 September.

MY DEAREST LUCY, –

It seems *an age* since I heard from you, or indeed since I wrote. You will pardon me, I know, for all my faults when you have read all my budget of news. Well, I got my husband back all right; when we arrived at Exeter there was a carriage waiting for us, and in it, though he had an attack of gout, Mr Hawkins. He took us to his own house, where there were rooms for us all nice and comfortable, and we dined together. After dinner Mr Hawkins said:

'My dears, I want to drink your health and prosperity; and may every blessing attend you both. I know you both from children, and have, with love and pride, seen you grow up. Now I want you to make your home here with me. I have left to me neither chick nor child; all are gone, and in my will I have left you everything.' I cried, Lucy dear, as Jonathan and the old man clasped hands. Our evening was a very, very happy one.

So here we are, installed in this beautiful old house, and from both my bedroom and drawing-room I can see the great elms of the cathedral close, with their great black stems standing out against the old yellow stone of the cathedral; and I can hear the rooks overhead cawing and cawing and chattering and gossiping all day, after the manner of rooks – and humans. I am busy, I need not tell you, arranging things and housekeeping. Jonathan and Mr Hawkins are busy all day; for, now that Jonathan is a partner, Mr Hawkins wants to tell him all about the clients.

How is your dear mother getting on? I wish I could run up to town for a day or two to see you, dear, but I dare not go yet, with so much on my shoulders; and Jonathan wants looking after still. He is beginning to put some flesh on his bones again, but he was terribly weakened by the long illness; even now he sometimes starts out of his sleep in a sudden way and awakes all trembling until I can coax him back to his usual placidity. However, thank God, these occasions grow less frequent as the days go on, and they will in time pass away altogether, I trust. And now I have told you my news, let me ask yours. When are you to be married, and where, and who is to perform the ceremony, and what are you to wear, and is it to be a public or a private wedding? Tell me all about it, dear; tell me all about everything, for there is nothing which interests you which will not be dear to me. Jonathan asks me to send his 'respectful duty', but I do not think that is good enough from the junior partner of the important firm of Hawkins and Harker; and so as you love me, and he loves me, and I love you with all the moods and tenses of the verb, I send you simply his 'love' instead. Good-bye, my dearest Lucy, and all blessings on you.

Yours,

MINA HARKER.

Report from Patrick Hennessey, M.D., M.R.C.S.,L.K.Q.C.P.I., etc., etc., [129]
to John Seward, M.D.

20 September.

MY DEAR SIR, –

In accordance with your wishes, I enclose report of the conditions of everything left in my charge . . . With regard to patient, Renfield, there is more to say. He has had another outbreak which might have had a dreadful ending, but which, as it fortunately happened, was unattended with any unhappy results. This afternoon a carrier's cart with two men made a call at the empty house whose grounds abut on ours – the house to which, you will remember, the patient twice ran away. The men stopped at our gate to ask the porter their way, as they were strangers. I was myself looking out of the study window, having a smoke after dinner, and saw one of them come up to the house. As he passed the window of Renfield's room the patient began to rate him from within, and called him all the foul names he could lay his tongue to. The man, who seemed a decent fellow enough, contented himself by telling him to 'shut up for a foul-mouthed beggar', whereon our man accused him of robbing him and wanting to murder him and said that he would hinder him if he were to swing for it. I opened the window and signed to the man not to notice, so he contented himself after looking the place over and making up his mind as to what kind of place he had got to by saying: 'Lor' bless yer, sir, I wouldn't mind what was said to me in a bloomin' madhouse. I pity ye and the guv'nor for havin' to live in the house with a wild beast like that.' Then he asked the way civilly enough, and I told him where the gate of the empty house was; he went away, followed by threats and curses and revilings from our man. I went down to see if I could make out any cause for his anger, since he is usually such a well-behaved man, and except his violent fits nothing of the kind had ever occurred. I found him, to my astonishment, quite composed and most genial in his manner. I tried to get him to talk of the incident, but he blandly asked me questions as to what I meant, and led me to believe that he was completely oblivious of the affair. It was, I am sorry to say, however, only another instance of his cunning, for within half an hour I heard of him again. This time he had broken out through the window of his room, and was running down the avenue. I called to the attendants to follow me, and ran after him, for I feared he was intent on some mischief. My fear was justified when I saw the same cart which had passed before coming down the road, having on it some great wooden boxes. The men were wiping their foreheads, and were flushed in the face, as if with violent exercise. Before I could get up to him the patient rushed at them, and pulling one of them off the cart, began to knock his head against the ground. If I had not seized him just at the moment I believe he would have killed the man there and then. The other fellow jumped down and struck him over the head with the butt-end of his heavy whip. It was a terrible blow; but he did not seem to mind it, but seized him also, and struggled with the three of us, pulling us to and fro as if we were kittens. You know I am no light weight, and the others were both burly men. At first he was silent in his fighting; but as we began to master him, and the attendants were putting a strait-waistcoat on him, he began to shout: 'I'll frustrate them! They shan't rob me! they shan't murder me by inches! I'll fight for my Lord and Master!' and all sorts of similar incoherent ravings. It was with very considerable difficulty that they got him back to the house and put him in the padded room. One of the attendants, Hardy, had a finger broken. However, I set it all right; and he is going on well.

The two carriers were at first loud in their threats of actions for damages, and promised to rain all the penalties of the law on us. Their threats were, however, mingled with some sort of indirect apology for the defeat of the two of them by a feeble madman. They said that if it had not been for the way their strength had been spent in carrying and raising the heavy boxes to the cart they would have made short work of him. They gave as another reason for their defeat the extraordinary state of drouth to which they had been reduced by the dusty nature of their occupation and the reprehensible distance from the scene of their labours of any place of public entertainment. I quite understood their drift, and after a stiff glass of grog,[130] or rather more of the same, and with each a sovereign in hand, they made light of the attack, and swore that they would encounter a worse madman any day for the pleasure of meeting so 'bloomin' good a bloke' as your correspondent. I took their names and addresses, in case they might be needed. They are as follows:Jack Smollet, of Dudding's Rents, King George's Road, Great Walworth, and Thomas Snelling, Peter Parley's Row, Guide Court, Bethnal Green. They are both in the employment of Harris & Sons, Moving and Shipment Company, Orange Master's Yard, Soho.

I shall report to you any matter of interest occurring here, and shall wire you at once if there is anything of importance.

Believe me, dear Sir,

Yours faithfully,

PATRICK HENESSEY.

Letter, Mina Harker to Lucy Westenra
(unopened by her)

18 September.

MY DEAREST LUCY, –

Such a sad blow has befallen us. Mr Hawkins has died very suddenly. Some may not think it so sad for us, but we had both come to so love him that it really seems as though we had lost a father. I never knew either father or mother, so that the dear old man's death is a real blow to me. Jonathan is greatly distressed. It is not only that he feels sorrow, deep sorrow, for the dear, good man who has befriended him all his life, and now at the end has treated him like his own son and left him a fortune which to people of our modest bringing up is wealth beyond the dream of avarice, but Jonathan feels it on another account. He says the amount of responsibility which it puts upon him makes him nervous. He begins to doubt himself. I try to cheer him up, and *my* belief in *him* helps him to have a belief in himself. But it is here that the grave shock that he experienced tells upon him the most. Oh, it is too hard that a sweet, simple, noble, strong nature such as his – a nature which enabled him, by our dear, good friend's aid, to rise from clerk to master in a few years – should be so injured that the very essence of its strength is gone. Forgive me, dear, if I worry you with my troubles in the midst of your own happiness; but, Lucy dear, I must tell someone, for the strain of keeping up a brave and cheerful appearance to Jonathan tries me, and I have no one here that I can confide in. I dread coming up to London, as we must do the day after tomorrow, for poor Mr Hawkins left in his will that he was to be buried in the grave with his father. As there are no relations at all, Jonathan will have to be chief mourner. I shall try to run over to see you, dearest, if only for a few minutes. Forgive me for troubling you. With all blessings,

Your loving

MINA HARKER

DR SEWARD'S DIARY

20 September. – Only resolution and habit can let me make an entry tonight. I am too miserable, too low-spirited, too sick of the world and all in it, including life itself, that I would not care if I heard this moment the flapping of the wings of the angel of death. And he has been flapping those wings to some purpose of late – Lucy's mother and Arthur's father, and now . . . Let me get on with my work.

I duly relieved Van Helsing in his watch over Lucy. We wanted Arthur to go to rest also, but he refused at first. It was only when I told him that we should want him to help us during the day, and that we must not all break down for want of rest, lest Lucy should suffer, that he agreed to go. Van Helsing was very kind to him. 'Come, my child,' he said; 'come with me. You are sick and weak, and have had much sorrow and much mental pain, as well as that tax on your strength that we know of. You must not be alone; for to be alone is to be full of fears and alarms. Come to the drawing-room, where there is a big fire, and there are two sofas. You shall lie on one and I on the other, and our sympathy will be comfort to each other, even though we do not speak, and even if we sleep.' Arthur went off with him, casting back a longing look on Lucy's face, which lay on her pillow, almost whiter than the lawn. She lay quite still, and I looked round the room to see that all was as it should be. I could see that the Professor had carried out in this room, as in the other, his purpose of using the garlic; the whole of the window-sashes reeked with it, and round Lucy's neck, over the silk handkerchief which Van Helsing made her keep on, was a rough chaplet[131] of the same odorous flowers. Lucy was breathing somewhat stertorously, and her face was at its worst, for the open mouth showed the pale gums. Her teeth, in the dim, uncertain light, seemed longer and sharper than they had been in the morning. In particular, by some trick of the light, the canine teeth looked longer and sharper than the rest. I sat down by her, and presently she moved uneasily. At the same moment there came a sort of dull flapping or buffeting at the window. I went over to it softly, and peeped out by the corner of the blind. There was a full moonlight, and I could see that the noise was made by a great bat, which wheeled round – doubtless attracted by the light, although so dim – and every now and again struck the window with its wings. When I came back to my seat I found that Lucy had moved slightly, and had torn away the garlic flowers from her throat. I replaced them as well as I could, and sat watching her.

Presently she woke, and I gave her food, as Van Helsing had prescribed. She took but a little, and that languidly. There did not seem to be with her now the unconscious struggle for life and strength that had hitherto so marked her illness. It struck me as curious that the moment she became conscious she pressed the garlic flowers close to her. It was certainly odd that whenever she got into that lethargic state, with the stertorous breathing, she put the flowers from her; but that when she waked she clutched them close. There was no possibility of making any mistake about this, for in the long hours that followed, she had many spells of sleeping and waking, and repeated both actions many times.

At six o'clock Van Helsing came to relieve me. Arthur had then fallen into a doze, and he mercifully let him sleep on. When he saw Lucy's face I could hear the hissing indraw of his breath, and he said to me in a sharp whisper: 'Draw up the blind; I want light!' Then he bent down, and, with his face almost touching Lucy's, examined her carefully. He removed the flowers and lifted the silk handkerchief from her throat. As he did so he started back, and I could hear his ejaculation, '*Mein Gott!*' as it was smothered in his throat. I bent over and looked too, and as I noticed some queer chill came over me.

The wounds on the throat had absolutely disappeared.

For fully five minutes Van Helsing stood looking at her, with his face at its sternest. Then he turned to me and said calmly:

'She is dying. It will not be long now. It will be much difference, mark me, whether she dies conscious or in her sleep. Wake that poor boy, and let him come and see the last; he trusts us, and we have promised him.'

I went to the dining-room and waked him. He was dazed for a moment, but when he saw the sunlight streaming in through the edges of the shutters he thought he was late, and expressed his fear. I assured him that Lucy was still asleep, but told him as gently as I could that both Van Helsing and I feared that the end was near. He covered his face with his hands, and slid down on his knees by the sofa, where he remained, perhaps a minute, with his head buried, praying, whilst his shoulders shook with grief. I took him by the hand and raised him up. 'Come,' I said, 'my dear old fellow, summon all your fortitude; it will be best and easiest for *her*.'

When we came into Lucy's room I could see that Van Helsing had, with his usual forethought, been putting matters straight and making everything look as pleasing as possible. He had even brushed Lucy's hair, so that it lay on the pillow in its usual shiny ripples. When we came into the room she opened her eyes, and seeing him, whispered softly:

'Arthur! Oh, my love, I am so glad you have come!' He was stooping to kiss her, when Van Helsing motioned him back. 'No,' he whispered, 'not yet! Hold her hand: it will comfort her more.'

So Arthur took her hand and knelt beside her, and she looked her best, with all the soft lines matching the angelic beauty of her eyes. Then gradually her eyes closed, and she sank to sleep. For a little bit her breast heaved softly, and her breath came and went like a tired child's.

And then insensibly there came the strange change which I had noticed in the night. Her breathing grew stertorous, the mouth opened, and the pale gums, drawn back, made the teeth look longer and sharper than ever. In a sort of sleep-waking, vague, unconscious way she opened her eyes, which were now dull and hard at once, and said in a soft voluptuous voice, such as I had never heard from her lips:

'Arthur! Oh, my love, I am so glad you have come! Kiss me!' Arthur bent eagerly over to kiss her; but at that instant Van Helsing, who, like me, had been startled by her voice, swooped upon him, and catching him by the neck with both hands, dragged him back with a fury of strength which I never thought he could have possessed, and actually hurled him almost across the room.

'Not for your life!' he said; 'not for your living soul and hers!' And he stood between them like a lion at bay.

Arthur was so taken aback that he did not for a moment know what to do or say; and before any impulse of violence could seize him he realised the place and the occasion, and he stood silent, waiting.

I kept my eyes fixed on Lucy, as did Van Helsing, and we saw a spasm as of rage flit like a shadow over her face; the sharp teeth champed together. Then her eyes closed, and she breathed heavily.

Very shortly after she opened her eyes in all their softness, and putting out her poor pale, thin hand, took Van Helsing's great brown one; drawing it to her, she kissed it. 'My true friend,' she said, in a faint voice, but with untellable pathos, 'my true friend, and his! Oh, guard him, and give him peace!'

'I swear it!' said he solemnly, kneeling beside her and holding up his hand, as one who registers an oath. Then he turned to Arthur, and said to him: 'Come, my child, take her hand in yours, and kiss her on the forehead, and only once.'

Their eyes met instead of their lips; and so they parted.

Lucy's eyes closed; and Van Helsing, who had been watching closely, took Arthur's arm, and drew him away.

And then Lucy's breathing became stertorous again, and all at once it ceased.

'It is all over, ' said Van Helsing. 'She is dead!'

I took Arthur by the arm, and led him away to the drawing-room, where he sat down, and covered his face with his hands, sobbing in a way that nearly broke me down to see.

I went back to the room, and found Van Helsing looking at poor Lucy, and his face was sterner than ever. Some change had come over her body. Death had given back part of her beauty, for her brow and cheeks had recovered some of their flowing lines; even the lips had lost their deadly pallor. It was as if the blood, no longer needed for the working of the heart had gone to make the harshness of death as little rude as might be.

> We thought her dying whilst she slept,
> And sleeping when she died.[132]

I stood beside Van Helsing, and said: 'Ah, well, poor girl, there is peace for her at last. It is the end!'

He turned to me, and said with grave solemnity: 'Not so; alas! not so. It is only the beginning!'

When I asked him what he meant, he only shook his head and answered: 'We can do nothing as yet. Wait and see.'

Chapter 13

DR SEWARD'S DIARY (continued)

THE FUNERAL WAS arranged for the next succeeding day, so that Lucy and her mother might be buried together. I attended to all the ghastly formalities, and the urbane undertaker proved that his staff were afflicted – or blessed – with something of his own obsequious suavity. Even the woman who performed the last offices for the dead remarked to me, in a confidential brother-professional way, when she had come out from the death-chamber:

'She makes a very beautiful corpse, sir. It's quite a privilege to attend on her. It's not too much to say that she will do credit to our establishment!'

I noticed that Van Helsing never kept far away. This was possible from the disordered state of things in the household. There were no relatives at hand; and as Arthur had to be back the next day to attend at his father's funeral, we were unable to notify anyone who should have been bidden. Under the circumstances, Van Helsing and I took it upon ourselves to examine papers, etc. He insisted upon looking over Lucy's papers himself. I asked him why, for I feared that he, being a foreigner, might not be quite aware of English legal requirements, and so might in ignorance make some unnecessary trouble He answered me:

'I know; I know. You forget that I am a lawyer as well as a doctor. But this is not altogether for the law. You knew that, when you avoided the coroner. I have more than him to avoid. There may be papers – such as this.'

As he spoke he took from his pocket-book the memorandum which had been in Lucy's breast, and which she had torn in her sleep.

'When you find anything of the solicitor who is for the late Mrs Westenra, seal all her papers, and write him tonight. For me, I watch here in the room and in Miss Lucy's old room all night, and I myself search for what may be. It is not well that her very thoughts go into the hands of strangers.'

I went on with my part of the work, and in another half-hour had found the name and address of Mrs Westenra's solicitor and had written to him. All the poor lady's papers were in order; explicit directions regarding the place of burial were given. I had hardly sealed the letter, when, to my surprise, Van Helsing walked into the room, saying:

'Can I help you, friend John? I am free, and if I may, my service is to you.'

'Have you got what you looked for?' I asked, to which he replied:

'I did not look for any specific thing. I only hoped to find, and find I have, all that there was – only some letters and a few memoranda, and a diary new begun. But I have them here, and we shall for the present say nothing of them. I shall see that poor lad tomorrow evening, and, with his sanction, I shall use some.'

When we had finished the work in hand, he said to me:

'And now, friend John, I think we may to bed. We want sleep, both you and I, and rest to recuperate. Tomorrow we shall have much to do, but for the tonight there is no need of us. Alas!'

Before turning in we went to look at poor Lucy. The undertaker had certainly done his work well, for the room was turned into a small *chapelle ardente*.[133] There was a wilderness of beautiful white flowers, and death was made as little repulsive as might be. The end of the winding-sheet was laid over the face; when the Professor bent over and turned it gently back, we both started at the beauty before us, the tall wax candles showing a sufficient light to note it well. All Lucy's loveliness had come back to her in death, and the hours that had passed, instead of leaving traces of 'decay's effacing fingers',[134] had but restored the beauty of life, till positively I could not believe my eyes that I was looking at a corpse.

The Professor looked sternly grave. He had not loved her as I had, and there was no need for tears in his eyes. He said to me: 'Remain till I return,' and left the room. He came back with a handful of wild garlic from the box waiting in the hall, but which had not been opened, and placed the flowers amongst the others on and around the bed. Then he took from his neck, inside his collar, a little golden crucifix, and placed it over the mouth. He restored the sheet to its place, and we came away.

I was undressing in my own room, when, with a premonitory tap at the door, he entered, and at once began to speak:

'Tomorrow I want you to bring me, before night, a set of post-mortem knives.'

'Must we make an autopsy?' I asked.

'Yes, and no. I want to operate, but not as you think. Let me tell you now, but not a word to another. I want to cut off her head and take out her heart. Ah! you a surgeon, and so shocked! You, whom I have seen with no tremble of hand or heart, do operations of life and death that make the rest shudder. Oh, but I must not forget, my dear friend John, that you loved her; and I have not forgotten it, for it is I that shall operate, and you must only help. I would like to do it tonight, but for Arthur I must not; he will be free after his father's funeral tomorrow, and he will want to see her – to see *it*. Then, when she is coffined ready for the next day, you and I shall come when all sleep. We shall unscrew the coffin-lid, and shall do our operation; and then replace all, so that none know, save we alone.'

'But why do it at all? The girl is dead. Why mutilate her poor body without need? And if there is no necessity for a post-mortem and nothing to gain by it – no good to her, to us, to science, to human knowledge – why do it? Without such it is monstrous.'

For answer he put his hand on my shoulder, and said, with infinite tenderness: 'Friend John, I pity your poor bleeding heart; and I love you the more because it does so bleed. If I could, I would take on myself the burden that you do bear. But there are things that you know not, but that you shall know, and bless me for knowing, though they are not pleasant things. John, my child, you have been my friend now many years, and yet did you ever know me to do any without good cause? I may err – I am but man; but I believe in all I do. Was it not for these causes that you send for me when the great trouble came? Yes! Were you not amazed, nay horrified, when I would not let Arthur kiss his love – though she was dying – and snatched him away by all my strength? Yes! And yet you saw how she thanked me, with her so beautiful dying eyes, her voice, too, so weak, and she kiss my rough old hand and bless me? Yes! and did you not hear me swear promise to her, that so she closed her eyes grateful? Yes!

'Well, I have good reason now for all I want to do. You have for many years trust me; you have believe me weeks past, when there be things so strange that you might have well doubt. Believe me yet a

little, friend John. If you trust me not, then I must tell what I think, and that is not perhaps well. And if I work – as work I shall, no matter trust or no trust – without my friend trust in me, I work with heavy heart, and feel oh! so lonely when I want all help and courage that may be! '
He paused a moment, and went on solemnly: 'Friend John, there are strange and terrible days before us. Let us not be two, but one, that so we work to a good end. Will you not have faith in me?'

I took his hand, and promised him. I held my door open as he went away, and watched him go into his room and close the door. As I stood without moving, I saw one of the maids pass silently along the passage – she had her back towards me, so did not see me – and go into the room where Lucy lay. The sight touched me. Devotion is so rare, and we are so grateful to those who show it unasked to those we love. Here was a poor girl putting aside the terrors which she naturally had of death to go watch alone by the bier of the mistress whom she loved, so that the poor clay might not be lonely till laid to eternal rest . . .

I must have slept long and soundly, for it was broad daylight when Van Helsing waked me by coming into my room. He came over to my bedside and said:

'You need not trouble about the knives; we shall not do it.'

'Why not?' I asked. For his solemnity of the night before had greatly impressed me.

'Because,' he said sternly, 'it is too late – or too early. See!' Here he held up the little golden crucifix. 'This was stolen in the night.'

'How stolen,' I asked in wonder, 'since you have it now?'

'Because I get it back from the worthless wretch who stole it, from the woman who robbed the dead and the living. Her punishment will surely come, but not through me; she knew not altogether what she did, and thus unknowing, she only stole. Now we must wait.'

He went away on the word, leaving me with a new mystery to think of, a new puzzle to grapple with.

The forenoon was a dreary time, but at noon the solicitor came: Mr Marquand, of Wholeman, Sons, Marquand and Lidderdale. He was very genial and very appreciative of what we had done, and took off our hands all cares as to details. During lunch he told us that Mrs Westenra had for some time expected sudden death from her heart, and had put her affairs in absolute order; he informed us that, with the exception of a certain entailed property of Lucy's father's which now, in default of direct issue, went back to a distant branch of the family, the whole estate, real and personal, was left absolutely to Arthur Holmwood. When he had told us so much he went on:

'Frankly we did our best to prevent such a testamentary disposition, and pointed out certain contingencies that might leave her daughter either penniless or not so free as she should be to act regarding a matrimonial alliance. Indeed, we pressed the matter so far that we almost came into collision, for she asked us if we were or were not prepared to carry out her wishes. Of course, we had then no alternative but to accept. We were right in principle, and ninety-nine times out of a hundred we should have proved, by the logic of events, the accuracy of our judgment. Frankly, however, I must admit that in this case any other form of disposition would have rendered impossible the carrying out of her wishes. For by her predeceasing her daughter the latter would have come into possession of the property, and, even had she only survived her mother by five minutes, her property would, in case there were no will – and a will was a practical impossibility in such a case – have been treated at her decease as under intestacy. In which case, Lord Godalming, though so dear a friend, would have had no claim in the world; and the inheritors, being remote, would not be likely to abandon their just rights for sentimental reasons regarding an entire stranger. I assure you, my dear sirs, I am rejoiced at the result, perfectly rejoiced.' He was a good fellow, but his rejoicing at the one little part – in which he was officially interested – of so great a tragedy, was an object-lesson in the limitations of sympathetic understanding.

He did not remain long, but said he would look in later in the day and see Lord Godalming. His coming, however, had been a certain comfort to us, since it assured us that we should not have to dread hostile criticism as to any of our acts. Arthur was expected at five o'clock, so a little before that time we visited the death-chamber. It was so in very truth, for now both mother and daughter lay in it. The undertaker, true to his craft, had made the best display he could of his goods, and there was a mortuary air about the place that lowered our spirits at once. Van Helsing ordered the former arrangement to be adhered to, explaining that, as Lord Godalming was coming very soon, it would be less harrowing to his feelings to see all that was left of his *fiancée* quite alone. The undertaker seemed shocked at his own stupidity, and exerted himself to restore things to the condition in which we left them the night before, so that when Arthur came such shocks to his feelings as we could avoid were saved.

Poor fellow! He looked desperately sad and broken; even his stalwart manhood seemed to have shrunk somewhat under the strain of his much-tried emotions. He had, I knew, been very genuinely and devotedly attached to his father; and to lose him, and at such a time, was a bitter blow to him. With me he was warm as ever, and to Van Helsing he was sweetly courteous; but I could not help seeing that there was some constraint with him. The Professor noticed it, too, and motioned me to bring him upstairs. I did so, and left him at the door of the room, as I felt he would like to be quite alone with her; but he took my arm and led me in, saying huskily:

'You loved her too, old fellow; she told me all about it, and there was no friend had a closer place in her heart than you. I don't know how to thank you for all you have done for her. I can't think yet . . . '

Here he suddenly broke down, and threw his arms round my shoulders and laid his head on my breast, crying:

'Oh, Jack, Jack! What shall I do? The whole of life seems gone from me all at once, and there is nothing in the wide world for me to live for.'

I comforted him as well as I could. In such cases men do not need much expression. A grip of the hand, the tightening of an arm over the shoulder, a sob in unison, are expressions of sympathy dear to a man's heart. I stood still and silent till his sobs died away, and then I said softly to him: 'Come and look at her.'

Together we moved over to the bed, and I lifted the lawn from her face. God! how beautiful she was. Every hour seemed to be enhancing her loveliness. It frightened and amazed me somewhat; and as for Arthur, he fell a-trembling, and finally was shaken with doubt as with an ague. At last, after a long pause, he said to me in a faint whisper:

'Jack, is she really dead?'

I assured him sadly that it was so, and went on to suggest – for I felt that such a horrible doubt should not have life for a moment longer than I could help – that it often happened that after death faces became softened and even resolved into their youthful beauty; that this was especially so when death had been preceded by any acute or prolonged suffering. It seemed to quite do away with any doubt, and, after kneeling beside the couch for a while and looking at her lovingly and long, he turned aside. I told him that that must be good-bye, as the coffin had to be prepared; so he went back and took her dead hand in his and kissed it, and bent over and kissed her forehead. He came away, fondly looking back over his shoulder at her as he came.

I left him in the drawing-room, and told Van Helsing that he had said good-bye; so the latter went to the kitchen to tell the undertaker's men to proceed with the preparations and to screw up the coffin. When he came out of the room again I told him of Arthur's question, and he replied:

'I am not surprised. Just now I doubted for a moment myself!'

We all dined together, and I could see that poor Art was trying to make the best of things. Van Helsing had been silent all dinner-time, but when we had lit our cigars he said:

'Lord — ;' but Arthur interrupted him:

'No, no, not that, for God's sake! not yet at any rate. Forgive me, sir: I did not mean to speak offensively; it is only because my loss is so recent.'

The Professor answered very sweetly:

'I only used that name because I was in doubt. I must not call you "Mr", and I have grown to love you – yes, my dear boy, to love you – as Arthur.'

Arthur held out his hand, and took the old man's warmly.

'Call me what you will,' he said. 'I hope I may always have the title of a friend. And let me say that I am at a loss for words to thank you for your goodness to my poor dear.' He paused a moment, and went on: 'I know that she understood your goodness even better than I do; and if I was rude or in any way wanting at that time you acted so – you remember' – the Professor nodded – 'you must forgive me.'

He answered with a grave kindness:

'I know it was hard for you to quite trust me then, for to trust such violence needs to understand; and I take it that you do not – that you cannot – trust me now, for you do not yet understand. And there may be more times when I shall want you to trust when you cannot – and may not – and must not yet understand. But the time will come when your trust shall be whole and complete in me, and when you shall understand as though the sunlight himself shone through. Then you shall bless me from first to last for your own sake, and for the sake of others, and for her dear sake to whom I swore to protect.'

'And, indeed, indeed, sir,' said Arthur warmly, 'I shall in all ways trust you. I know and believe you have a very noble heart, and you are Jack's friend, and you were hers. You shall do what you like.'

The Professor cleared his throat a couple of times, as though about to speak, and finally said:

'May I ask you something now?'

'Certainly.'

'You know that Mrs Westenra left you all her property?'

'No, poor dear; I never thought of it.'

'And as it is all yours, you have a right to deal with it as you will. I want you to give me permission to read all Miss Lucy's papers and letters. Believe me, it is no idle curiosity. I have a motive of which, be sure, she would have approved. I have them all here. I took them before we knew that all was yours, so that no strange hand might touch them – no strange eye look through words into her soul. I shall keep them if I may; even you may not see them yet, but I shall keep them safe. No word shall be lost; and in the good time I shall give them back to you. It's a hard thing I ask, but you will do it, will you not, for Lucy's sake?'

Arthur spoke out heartily, like his old self:

'Dr Van Helsing, you may do what you will. I feel that in saying this I am doing what my dear one would have approved. I shall not trouble you with questions till the time comes.'

The old Professor stood up as he said solemnly:

'And you are right. There will be pain for us all; but it will not be all pain, nor will this pain be the last. We and you too – you most of all, my dear boy – will have to pass through the bitter water before we reach the sweet. But we must be brave of heart and unselfish, and do our duty, and all will be well!'

I slept on a sofa in Arthur's room that night. Van Helsing did not go to bed at all. He went to and fro, as if patrolling the house, and was never out of sight of the room where Lucy lay in her coffin, strewn with the wild garlic flowers, which sent, through the odour of lily and rose, a heavy, overpowering smell into the night.

MINA HARKER'S JOURNAL

22 *September*. – In the train to Exeter. Jonathan sleeping.

It seems only yesterday that the last entry was made, and yet how much between them, in Whitby and all the world before me, Jonathan away and no news of him; and now, married to Jonathan, Jonathan a solicitor, a partner, rich, master of his business, Mr Hawkins dead and buried, and Jonathan with another attack that may harm him. Some day he may ask me about it. Down it all goes. I am rusty in my shorthand – see what unexpected prosperity does for us – it may be as well to freshen it up again with an exercise anyhow . . .

The service was very simple and very solemn. There were only ourselves and the servants there, one or two old friends of his from Exeter, his London agent, and a gentleman representing Sir John Paxton, the President of the Incorporated Law Society. Jonathan and I stood hand in hand, and we felt that our best and dearest friend was gone from us . . .

We came back to town quietly, taking a 'bus to Hyde Park Corner.[135] Jonathan thought it would interest me to go into the Row [136] for a while, so we sat down; but there were very few people there, and it was sad-looking and desolate to see so many empty chairs. It made us think of the empty chair at home; so we got up and walked down Piccadilly.[137]

Jonathan was holding me by the arm, the way he used to in old days before I went to school. I felt it very improper, for you can't go on for some years teaching etiquette and decorum to other girls without the pedantry of it biting into yourself a bit; but it was Jonathan, and he was my husband, and we didn't know anybody who saw us – and we didn't care if they did – so on we walked. I was looking at a very beautiful girl, in a big cart-wheel hat, sitting in a victoria[138] outside Giuliano's, when I felt Jonathan clutch my arm so tight that he hurt me, and he said under his breath: 'My God!' I am always anxious about Jonathan, for I fear that some nervous fit may upset him again; so I turned to him quickly, and asked him what it was that disturbed him.

He was very pale, and his eyes seemed bulging out as, half in terror and half in amazement, he gazed at a tall, thin man, with a beaky nose and black moustache and pointed beard, who was also observing the pretty girl. He was looking at her so hard that he did not see either of us, and so I had a good view of him. His face was not a good face; it was hard, and cruel, and sensual, and his big white teeth, that looked all the whiter because his lips were so red, were pointed like an animal's. Jonathan kept staring at him, till I was afraid he would notice. I feared he might take it ill, he looked so fierce and nasty. I asked Jonathan why he was disturbed, and he answered evidently thinking that I knew as much about it as he did. 'Do you see who it is?'

'No, dear,' I said; 'I don't know him; who is it?' His answer seemed to shock and thrill me, for it was said as if he did not know that it was to me, Mina, to whom he was speaking:

'It is the man himself!'

The poor dear was evidently terrified at something – very greatly terrified; I do believe that if he had not had me to lean on and to support him, he would have sunk down. He kept staring; a man came out of the shop with a small parcel, and gave it to the lady, who then drove off. The dark man kept his eyes fixed on her, and when the carriage moved up Piccadilly he followed in the same direction, and hailed a hansom. Jonathan kept looking after him, and said, as if to himself:

'I believe it is the Count, but he has grown young. My God, if this be so! Oh, my God! my God! If I only knew! if I only knew!' He was distressing himself so much that I feared to keep his mind on the subject by asking him any questions, so I remained silent. I drew him away quietly, and he, holding my arm, came easily. We walked a little further, and then went in and sat for a while in the Green Park.[139] It was a hot day for autumn, and there was a comfortable seat in a shady place. After a few minutes' staring at nothing, Jonathan's eyes closed, and he went quietly into a sleep, with his head on my shoulder. I thought it was the best thing for him, so did not disturb him. In about twenty minutes he woke up, and said to me quite cheerfully:

'Why, Mina, have I been asleep? Oh, do forgive me for being so rude. Come, and we'll have a cup of tea somewhere.' He had evidently forgotten all about the dark stranger, as in his illness he had forgotten all that this episode had reminded him of. I don't like this lapsing into forgetfulness; it may make or continue some injury to the brain. I must not ask him, for fear I shall do more harm than good; but I must somehow learn the facts of his journey abroad. The time is come, I fear, when I must open that parcel and know what is written. Oh, Jonathan you will, I know, forgive me if I do wrong, but it is for your own dear sake.

Later. – A sad home-coming in every way – the house empty of the dear soul who was so good to us; Jonathan still pale and dizzy under a slight relapse of his malady; and now a telegram from Van Helsing, whoever he may be:

'You will be grieved to hear that Mrs Westenra died five days ago, and that Lucy died the day before yesterday. They were both buried today.'

Oh, what a wealth of sorrow in a few words! Poor Mrs Westenra! poor Lucy! Gone, gone, never to return to us! And poor, poor Arthur, to have lost such sweetness out of his life! God help us all to bear our troubles.

DR SEWARD'S DIARY

22 *September*. – It is all over. Arthur has gone back to Ring, and has taken Quincey Morris with him. What a fine fellow is Quincey! I believe in my heart of hearts that he suffered as much about Lucy's death as any of us; but he bore himself through it like a moral Viking. If America can go on breeding men like that, she will be a power in the world indeed. Van Helsing is lying down, having a rest preparatory to his journey. He goes over to Amsterdam tonight, but says he returns tomorrow night; that he only wants to make some arrangements which can only be made personally. He is to stop with me then, if he can; he says he has work to do in London which may take him some time. Poor old fellow! I fear that the strain of the past week has broken down even his iron strength. All the time of the burial he was, I could see, putting some terrible restraint on himself. When it was all over, we were standing beside Arthur, who, poor fellow, was speaking of his part in the operation where his blood had been transfused to his Lucy's veins; I could see Van Helsing's face grow white and purple by turns. Arthur

was saying that he felt since then as if they two had been really married, and that she was his wife in the sight of God. None of us said a word of the other operations, and none of us ever shall. Arthur and Quincey went away together to the station, and Van Helsing and I came on here. The moment we were alone in the carriage he gave way to a regular fit of hysterics. He has denied to me since that it was hysterics, and insisted that it was only his sense of humour asserting itself under very terrible conditions. He laughed till he cried and I had to draw down the blinds lest anyone should see us and misjudge; and then he cried till he laughed again; and laughed and cried together, just as a woman does. I tried to be stern with him, as one is to a woman under the circumstances; but it had no effect. Men and women are so different in manifestations of nervous strength or weakness! Then when his face grew grave and stern again I asked him why his mirth, and why at such a time. His reply was in a way characteristic of him, for it was logical and forceful and mysterious. He said:

'Ah, you don't comprehend, friend John. Do not think that I am not sad, though I laugh. See, I have cried even when the laugh did choke me. But no more think that I am all sorry when I cry, for the laugh he come just the same. Keep it always with you that laughter who knock at your door and say: "May I come in?" is not the true laughter. No! he is a king, and he come when and how he like. He ask no person; he choose no time of suitability. He say: "I am here." Behold, in example, I grieve my heart out for that so sweet young girl; I give my blood for her, though I am old and worn; I give my time, my skill, my sleep; I let my other sufferers want that she may have all. And yet I can laugh at her very grave – laugh when the clay from the spade of the sexton drop upon her coffin and say: "Thud! thud! " to my heart, till it send back the blood from my cheek. My heart bleed for that poor boy – that dear boy so of the age of mine own boy had I been so blessed that he live, and with his hair and eyes the same. There, you know now why I love him so. And yet when he say things that touch my husband-heart to the quick, and make my father-heart yearn to him as to no other man – not even to you, friend John, for we are more level in experiences than father and son – yet even at such moment King Laugh he come to me and shout and bellow in my ear: "Here I am! Here I am!' till the blood come dance back and bring some of the sunshine that he carry with him to my cheek. Oh, friend John, it is a strange world, a sad world, a world full of miseries, and woes, and troubles; and yet when King Laugh come he make them all dance to the tune he play. Bleeding hearts, and dry bones of the churchyard, and tears that burn as they fall – all dance together to the music that he make with that smileless mouth of him. And believe me, friend John, that he is good to come, and kind. Ah, we men and women are like ropes drawn tight with strain that pull us different ways. Then tears come; and, like the rain on the ropes, they brace us up, until perhaps the strain become too great, and we break. But King Laugh he come like the sunshine, and he ease off the strain again; and we bear to go on with our labour, what it may be.'

I did not like to wound him by pretending not to see his idea; but, as I did not yet understand the cause of his laughter, I asked him. As he answered me his face grew stern, and he said in quite a different tone:

'Oh, it was the grim irony of it all – this so lovely lady garlanded with flowers, that looked so fair as life, till one by one we wondered if she were truly dead; she laid in that so fine marble house in that lonely churchyard, where rest so many of her kin, laid there with the mother who loved her, and whom she loved; and that sacred bell going "Toll! toll! toll!" so sad and slow; and those holy men, with the white garments of the angel, pretending to read books, and yet all the time their eyes never on the page; and all us with the bowed head. And all for what? She is dead; so! Is it not?'

'Well, for the life of me, Professor,' I said, 'I can't see anything to laugh at in all that. Why, your explanation makes it a harder puzzle than before. But even if the burial service was comic, what about poor Art and his trouble? Why, his heart was simply breaking.'

'Just so. Said he not that the transfusion of his blood to her veins had made her truly his bride?'

'Yes, and it was a sweet and comforting idea for him.'

'Quite so. But there was a difficulty, friend John. If so that, then what about the others? Ho, ho! Then this so sweet maid is a polyandrist, and me, with my poor wife dead to me, but alive by Church's law, though no wits, all gone – even I, who am faithful husband to this now-no-wife, am bigamist.'

'I don't see where the joke comes in there either!' I said; and I did not feel particularly pleased with him for saying such things. He laid his hand on my arm, and said: 'Friend John, forgive me if I pain. I showed not my feeling to others when it would wound, but only to you, my old friend, whom I can trust. If you could have looked into my very heart then when I want to laugh; if you could have done so when the laugh arrived; if you could do so now, when King Laugh have pack up his crown and all that is to him – for he go far, far away from me, and for a long, long time – maybe you would perhaps pity me the most of all.'

I was touched by the tenderness of his tone, and asked why.

'Because I know!'

And now we are all scattered; and for many a long day loneliness will sit over our roofs with brooding wings. Lucy lies in the tomb of her kin, a lordly death-house in a lonely churchyard away from teeming London; where the air is fresh; and the sun rises over Hampstead Hill, and where wild flowers grow of their own accord.

So I can finish this diary; and God only knows if I shall ever begin another. If I do, or if I ever open this again, it will be to deal with different people and different themes; for here at the end, where the romance of my life is told, ere I go back to take up the thread of my life-work, I say sadly and without hope, FINIS.

The Westminster Gazette,[140] *25 September*

A HAMPSTEAD MYSTERY

The neighbourhood of Hampstead is just at present exercised with a series of events which seem to run on lines parallel to those of what was known to the writers of headlines as 'The Kensington Horror', or 'The Stabbing Woman', or 'The Woman in Black'. During the past two or three days several cases have occurred of young children straying from home or neglecting to return from their playing on the Heath. In all these cases the children were too young to give any properly intelligible account of themselves, but the consensus of their excuses is that they had been with a 'bloofer lady'.[141] It has always been late in the evening when they have been missed, and on two occasions the children have not been found until early in the following morning. It is generally supposed in the neighbourhood that, as the first child missed gave as his reason for being away that a 'bloofer lady' had asked him to come for a walk, the others had picked up the phrase and used it as occasion served. This is the more natural as the favourite game of the little ones at present is luring each other away by wiles. A correspondent writes us that to see some of the tiny tots pretending to be the 'bloofer lady' is supremely funny. Some of our caricaturists might, he says, take a lesson in the irony of grotesque by comparing the reality and the picture. It is only in accordance with general principles of human nature that the 'bloofer lady' should be the popular rôle at these *al fresco* performances. Our correspondent naïvely says that even Ellen Terry[142] could not be so winningly attractive as some of these grubby-faced little children pretend – and even imagine themselves – to be.

There is, however, possibly a serious side to the question, for some of the children, indeed all who have been missed at night have been slightly torn or wounded in the throat. The wounds seem such as might be made by a rat or a small dog, and although of not much importance individually, would tend to show that whatever animal inflicts them has a system or method of its own.

The police of the division have been instructed to keep a sharp lookout for straying children, especially when very young, in and around Hampstead Heath, and for any stray dog which may be about.

The Westminster Gazette, *25 September – Extra Special*

THE HAMPSTEAD HORROR – ANOTHER CHILD INJURED
The 'Bloofer Lady'

We have just received intelligence that another child, missed last night, was only discovered late in the morning under a furze bush at the Shooter's Hill side of Hampstead Heath, which is, perhaps, less frequented than the other parts. It has the same tiny wound in the throat as has been noticed in other cases. It was terribly weak, and looked quite emaciated. It too, when partially restored, had the common story to tell of being lured away by the 'bloofer lady'.

Chapter 14

MINA HARKER'S JOURNAL

23 September. – Jonathan is better after a bad night. I am so glad that he has plenty of work to do, for that keeps his mind off the terrible things; and oh, I am rejoiced that he is not now weighed down with the responsibility of his new position. I knew he would be true to himself, and now how proud I am to see my Jonathan rising to the height of his advancement and keeping pace in all ways with the duties that come upon him. He will be away all day till late, for he said he could not lunch at home. My household work is done, so I shall take his foreign journal, and lock myself up in my room and read it . . .

24 September. – I hadn't the heart to write last night; that terrible record of Jonathan's upset me so. Poor dear! How he must have suffered, whether it be true or only imagination. I wonder if there is any truth in it at all. Did he get his brain fever, and then write all those terrible things; or had he some cause for it all? I suppose I shall never know, for I dare not open the subject to him . . . And yet that man we saw yesterday! He seemed quite certain of him . . . Poor fellow! suppose it was the funeral upset him and sent his mind back on some train of thought . . . He believes it all himself. I remember how on our wedding-day he said: 'Unless some solemn duty come upon me to go back to the bitter hours, asleep or awake, mad or sane.' There seems to be through it all some thread of continuity . . . That fearful Count was coming to London. . . . If it should be, and he came to London, with its teeming millions. . . . There may be a solemn duty; and if it come we must not shrink from it . . . I shall be prepared. I shall get my typewriter this very hour and begin transcribing. Then we shall be ready for other eyes if required. And if it be wanted, then, perhaps, if I am ready, poor Jonathan may not be upset, for I can speak for him and never let him be troubled or worried with it all. If ever Jonathan quite gets over the nervousness he may want to tell me of it all, and I can ask him questions and find out things, and see how I may comfort him.

Letter, Van Helsing to Mrs Harker

24 September. (Confidence.)

DEAR MADAM,

I pray you to pardon my writing, in that I am so far friend as that I sent to you sad news of Miss Lucy Westenra's death. By the kindness of Lord Godalming, I am empowered to read her letters and papers, for I am deeply concerned about certain matters vitally important. In them I find some letters from you, which show how great friends you were and how you love her. Oh, Madam Mina, by that love, I implore you, help me. It is for others' good that I ask – to redress great wrong, and to lift much and terrible troubles – that may be more great than you can know. May it be that I see you? You can trust me. I am a friend of Dr John Seward and of Lord Godalming (that was Arthur of Miss Lucy). I must keep it private for the present from all. I should come to Exeter to see you at once if you tell me I am privilege to come, and where and when. I implore your pardon, madam. I have read your letters to poor Lucy, and know how good you are and how your husband suffer; so I pray you, if it may be, enlighten him not, lest it may harm. Again your pardon, and forgive me.

VAN HELSING

Telegram, Mrs Harker to Van Helsing

25 *September*. – Come today by quarter-past ten train if you can catch it.
Can see you any time you call.

WILHELMINA HARKER.

MINA HARKER'S JOURNAL

25 *September*. – I cannot help feeling terribly excited as the time draws
near for the visit of Dr Van Helsing, for somehow I expect it will throw
some light upon Jonathan's sad experience; and as he attended poor dear
Lucy in her last illness, he can tell me all about her. That is the reason of
his coming; it is concerning Lucy and her sleep-walking, and not about
Jonathan. Then I shall never know the real truth now! How silly I am.
That awful journal gets hold of my imagination and tinges everything
with something of its own colour. Of course it is about Lucy. That habit
came back to the poor dear, and that awful night on the cliff must have
made her ill. I had almost forgotten in my own affairs how ill she was
afterwards. She must have told him of her sleep-walking adventure on
the cliff, and that I knew all about it; and now he wants me to tell him
about it, so that he may understand. I hope I did right in not saying
anything of it to Mrs Westenra; I should never forgive myself if any act
of mine, were it even a negative one, brought harm on poor dear Lucy. I
hope, too, Dr Van Helsing will not blame me; I have had so much
trouble and anxiety of late that I feel I cannot bear more just at present.

I suppose a cry does us all good at times – clears the air as other rain
does. Perhaps it was reading the journal yesterday that upset me, and
then Jonathan went away this morning to stay away from me a whole
day and night, the first time we have been parted since our marriage. I
do hope the dear fellow will take care of himself, and that nothing will
occur to upset him. It is two o'clock, and the doctor will be here soon
now. I shall say nothing of Jonathan's journal unless he asks me. I am so
glad I have type-written out my own journal, so that, in case he asks
about Lucy, I can hand it to him; it will save much questioning.

Later. – He has come and gone. Oh, what a strange meeting and how
it all makes my head whirl round! I feel like one in a dream. Can it be all
possible, or even a part of it? If I had not read Jonathan's journal first, I
should never have accepted even a possibility. Poor, poor, dear Jonathan!
How he must have suffered. Please the good God all this may not upset

him again. I shall try to save him from it; but it may be even a consolation and a help to him – terrible though it be and awful in its consequences – to know for certain that his eyes and ears and brain did not deceive him, and that it is all true. It may be that it is the doubt which haunts him; that when the doubt is removed no matter which – waking or dreaming – may prove the truth, he will be more satisfied and better able to bear the shock. Dr Van Helsing must be a good man as well as a clever one if he is Arthur's friend and Dr Seward's, and if they brought him all the way from Holland to look after Lucy. I feel from having seen him that he *is* good and kind and of a noble nature. When he comes tomorrow I shall ask him about Jonathan; and then, please God, all this sorrow and anxiety may lead to a good end. I used to think I would like to practise interviewing; Jonathan's friend on the *Exeter News* told him that memory was everything in such work – that you must be able to put down exactly almost every word spoken, even if you had to refine some of it afterwards. Here was a rare interview. I shall try to record it *verbatim*.

It was half-past two o'clock when the knock came. I took my courage *à deux mains*[143] and waited. In a few minutes Mary opened the door, and announced, 'Dr Van Helsing.'

I rose and bowed, and he came towards me; a man of medium height, strongly built, with his shoulders set back over a broad, deep chest and a neck well balanced on the trunk as the head is on the neck. The poise of the head strikes one at once as indicative of thought and power, the head is noble, well-sized, broad, and large behind the ears. The face, clean-shaven, shows a hard, square chin, a large, resolute, mobile mouth, a good-sized nose, rather straight, but with quick, sensitive nostrils, that seem to broaden as the big, bushy eyebrows come down and the mouth tightens. The forehead is broad and fine, rising at first almost straight and then sloping back above two bumps or ridges wide apart; such a forehead that the reddish hair cannot possibly tumble over it, but falls naturally back and to the sides. Big, dark blue eyes are set widely apart, and are quick and tender or stern with the man's moods. He said to me:

'Mrs Harker, is it not?' I bowed assent.

'That was Miss Mina Murray?' Again I assented.

'It is Mina Murray that I came to see, that was friend of that poor dear child Lucy Westenra. Madam Mina, it is on account of the dead I come.'

'Sir,' I said, 'you could have no better claim on me than that you were a friend and helper of Lucy Westenra.' And I held out my hand. He took it and said tenderly:

'Oh, Madam Mina, I knew that the friend of that poor lily girl must be good, but I had yet to learn – ' He finished his speech with a courtly bow. I asked him what it was that he wanted to see me about, so he at once began:

'I have read your letters to Miss Lucy. Forgive me, but I had to begin to inquire somewhere, and there was none to ask. I know that you were with her at Whitby. She sometimes kept a diary – you need not look surprised, Madam Mina; it was begun after you had left, and was made in imitation of you – and in that diary she traces by inference certain things to a sleep-walking in which she puts down that you saved her. In great perplexity then I come to you, and ask you out of your so much kindness to tell me all of it that you remember.'

'I can tell you, I think, Dr Van Helsing, all about it.'

'Ah, then you have a good memory for facts, for details? It is not always so with young ladies.'

'No, doctor, but I wrote it all down at the time. I can show it to you if you like.'

'Oh, Madam Mina, I will be grateful; you will do me much favour.' I could not resist the temptation of mystifying him a bit – I suppose it is some of the taste of the original apple that remains still in our mouths – so I handed him the shorthand diary. He took it with a grateful bow, and said:

'May I read it?'

'If you wish,' I answered as demurely as I could. He opened it, and for the instant his face fell. Then he stood up and bowed.

'Oh, you so clever woman!' he said. 'I long knew that Mr Jonathan was a man of much thankfulness; but see, his wife have all the good things. And will you not so much honour me and so help me as to read it for me? Alas! I know not the shorthand.' By this time my little joke was over, and I was almost ashamed; so I took the typewritten copy from my work-basket and handed it to him.

'Forgive me,' I said: 'I could not help it; but I had been thinking that it was of dear Lucy that you wished to ask, and so that you might not have to wait – not on my account, but because I know your time must be precious – I have written it out on the typewriter for you.'

He took it, and his eyes glistened. 'You are so good,' he said. 'And may I read it now? I may want to ask you some things when I have read.'

'By all means,' I said, 'read it over whilst I order lunch; and then you can ask me questions whilst we eat.' He bowed and settled himself in a chair with his back to the light, and became absorbed in the papers, whilst I went to see after lunch, chiefly in order that he might not be disturbed. When I came back I found him walking hurriedly up and

down the room, his face all ablaze with excitement. He rushed up to me
and took me by both hands.

'Oh, Madam Mina,' he said, 'how can I say what I owe to you? This
paper is as sunshine. It opens the gate to me. I am daze, I am dazzle,
with so much light; and yet clouds roll in behind the light every time.
But that you do not, cannot, comprehend. Oh, but I am grateful to you,
you so clever woman. Madam' – he said this very solemnly – 'if ever
Abraham Van Helsing can do anything for you or yours, I trust you will
let me know. It will be pleasure and delight if I may serve you as a
friend; as a friend, but all I have ever learned, all I can ever do, shall be
for you and those you love. There are darknesses in life, and there are
lights; you are one of the lights. You will have happy life and good life,
and your husband will be blessed in you.'

'But, doctor, you praise me too much, and – and you do not know me.'

'Not know you – I, who am old, and who have studied all my life men
and women; I, who have made my specialty the brain and all that
belongs to him and all that follow from him! And I have read your diary
that you have so goodly written for me, and which breathes out truth in
every line. I, who have read your so sweet letter to poor Lucy of your
marriage and your trust, not know you! Oh, Madam Mina, good
women tell all their lives, and by day and by hour and by minute, such
things that angels can read; and we men who wish to know have in us
something of angel's eyes. Your husband is noble nature, and you are
noble too, for you trust, and trust cannot be where there is mean nature.
And your husband – tell me of him. Is he quite well? Is all that fever
gone, and is he strong and hearty?' I saw here an opening to ask him
about Jonathan, so I said:

'He was almost recovered, but he has been greatly upset by Mr
Hawkins' death.'

He interrupted: 'Oh yes, I know, I know. I have read your last two
letters.'

I went on: 'I suppose this upset him, for when we were in town on
Thursday last he had a sort of shock.'

'A shock, and after brain fever so soon! That was not good. What
kind of shock was it?'

'He thought he saw someone who recalled something terrible, something which led to his brain fever.' And here the whole thing seemed to
overwhelm me in a rush. The pity for Jonathan, the horror which he
experienced, the whole fearful mystery of his diary, and the fear that has
been brooding over me ever since, all came in a tumult. I suppose I was
hysterical, for I threw myself on my knees and held up my hands to him,

and implored him to make my husband well again. He took my hands and raised me up, and made me sit on the sofa, and sat by me; he held my hand in his, and said to me with, oh, such infinite sweetness –

'My life is a barren and lonely one, and so full of work that I have not had much time for friendships; but since I have been summoned to here by my friend John Seward I have known so many good people and seen such nobility that I feel more than ever – and it has grown with my advancing years – the loneliness of my life. Believe me, then, that I come here full of respect for you, and you have given me hope – hope, not in what I am seeking of, but that there are good women still left to make life happy – good women, whose lives and whose truths may make good lesson for the children that are to be. I am glad, glad, that I may here be of some use to you; for if your husband suffer, he suffer within the range of my study and experience. I promise you that I will gladly do *all* for him that I can – all to make his life strong and manly, and your life a happy one. Now you must eat. You are overwrought and perhaps over-anxious. Husband Jonathan would not like to see you so pale; and what he like not where he love, is not to his good. Therefore for his sake you must eat and smile. You have told me all about Lucy, and so now we shall not speak of it, lest it distress. I shall stay in Exeter tonight, for I want to think much over what you have told me, and when I have thought I will ask you questions, if I may. And then, too, you will tell me of husband Jonathan's trouble so far as you can, but not yet. You must eat now; afterwards you shall tell me all.'

After lunch, when we went back to the drawing-room he said to me:

'And now tell me all about him.' When it came to speaking to this great, learned man, I began to fear that he would think me a weak fool, and Jonathan a madman – that journal is all so strange – and I hesitated to go on. But he was so sweet and kind, and he had promised to help, and I trusted him, so I said:

'Dr Van Helsing, what I have to tell you is so queer that you must not laugh at me or at my husband. I have been since yesterday in a sort of fever of doubt, you must be kind to me and not think me foolish that I have even half believed some very strange things.' He reassured me by his manner as well as his words when he said:

'Oh, my dear, if you only knew how strange is the matter regarding which I am here, it is you who would laugh. I have learned not to think little of anyone's belief, no matter how strange it be. I have tried to keep an open mind; and it is not the ordinary things of life that could close it, but the strange things, the extraordinary things, the things that make one doubt if they be mad or sane.'

'Thank you, thank you, a thousand times! You have taken a weight off my mind. If you will let me, I shall give you a paper to read. It is long, but I have typewritten it out. It will tell you my trouble and Jonathan's. It is the copy of his journal when abroad, and all that happened. I dare not say anything of it; you will read for yourself and judge. And then when I see you, perhaps, you will be very kind and tell me what you think.'

'I promise,' he said as I gave him the papers; 'I shall in the morning, so soon as I can, come to see you and your husband, if I may.'

'Jonathan will be here at half-past eleven, and you must come to lunch with us and see him then; you could catch the quick 3.34 train, which will leave you at Paddington[144] before eight.' He was surprised at my knowledge of the trains offhand, but he does not know that I have made up all the trains to and from Exeter, so that I may help Jonathan in case he is in a hurry.

So he took the papers with him and went away, and I sit here thinking – thinking I don't know what.

Letter (by hand), Van Helsing to Mrs Harker

25 September, 6 o'clock.

Dear Madam Mina,

I have read your husband's so wonderful diary. You may sleep without doubt. Strange and terrible as it is, it is *true!* I will pledge my life on it. It may be worse for others; but for him and you there is no dread. He is a noble fellow; and let me tell you from experience of men, that one who would do as he did in going down that wall and to that room – ay, and going a second time – is not one to be injured in permanence by a shock. His brain and his heart are all right; this I swear, before I have even seen him; so be at rest. I shall have much to ask him of other things. I am blessed that today I come to see you, for I have learn all at once so much that again I am dazzle – dazzle more than ever, and I must think.

Yours the most faithful,

Abraham Van Helsing.

Letter, Mrs Harker to Van Helsing

25 September, 6.30 p.m.

My dear Dr Van Helsing,

A thousand thanks for your kind letter, which has taken a great weight off my mind. And yet, if it be true, what terrible things there are in the world, and what an awful thing if that man, that monster, be really in London! I fear to think. I have this moment, whilst writing, had a wire from Jonathan, saying that he leaves by the 6.25 tonight from Launceston[145] and will be here at 10.18, so that I shall have no fear tonight. Will you, therefore, instead of lunching with us, please come to breakfast at eight o'clock, if this be not too early for you? You can get away, if you are in a hurry, by the 10.30 train, which will bring you to Paddington by 2.35. Do not answer this, as I shall take it that, if I do not hear, you will come to breakfast.

   Believe me,
   Your faithful and grateful friend,

                                                    MINA HARKER.

JONATHAN HARKER'S JOURNAL

26 September. – I thought never to write in this diary again but the time has come. When I got home last night Mina had supper ready, and when we had supped she told me of Van Helsing's visit, and of her having given him the two diaries copied out, and of how anxious she had been about me. She showed me in the doctor's letter that all I wrote down was true. It seems to have made a new man of me. It was the doubt as to the reality of the whole thing that knocked me over. I felt impotent, and in the dark, and distrustful. But, now that I *know*, I am not afraid, even of the Count. He has succeeded after all, then, in his design in getting to London, and it was he I saw. He has got younger, and how? Van Helsing is the man to unmask him and hunt him out, if he is anything like what Mina says. We sat late, and talked it all over. Mina is dressing and I shall call at the hotel in a few minutes and bring him over . . .

   He was, I think, surprised to see me. When I came into the room where he was, and introduced myself, he took me by the shoulder and turned my face round to the light, and said, after a sharp scrutiny:

   'But Madam Mina told me you were ill, that you had had a shock.' It was so funny to hear my wife called 'Madam Mina' by this kindly, strong-faced old man. I smiled, and said:

   'I *was* ill, I *have* had a shock: but you have cured me already.'

   'And how?'

   'By your letter to Mina last night. I was in doubt, and then everything took a hue of unreality, and I did not know what to trust, even the evidence of my own senses. Not knowing what to trust, I did not know what to do; and so had only to keep on working in what had hitherto been the groove of my life. The groove ceased to avail me, and I mistrusted myself. Doctor, you don't know what it is to doubt everything, even yourself. No, you don't; you couldn't with eyebrows like yours.' He seemed pleased, and laughed as he said: 'So! You are physiognomist. I learn more here with each hour. I am with so much pleasure coming to you to breakfast; and, oh, sir, you will pardon praise from an old man, but you are blessed in your wife.' I would listen to him go on praising Mina for a day, so I simply nodded and stood silent.

'She is one of God's women fashioned by His own hand to show us men and other women that there is a heaven where we can enter, and that its light can be here on earth. So true, so sweet, so noble, so little an egoist – and that, let me tell you, is much in this age, so sceptical and selfish. And you, sir – I have read all the letters to poor Miss Lucy and some of them speak of you, so I know you since some days from the knowing of others; but I have seen your true self since last night. You will give me your hand, will you not? And let us be friends for all our lives.'

We shook hands, and he was so earnest and so kind that it made me quite choky.

'And now,' he said, 'may I ask you for some more help? I have a great task to do, and at the beginning it is to know. You can help me here. Can you tell me what went before your going to Transylvania? Later on I may ask more help and of a different kind; but at first this will do.'

'Look here, sir,' I said, 'does what you have to do concern the Count?'

'It does,' he said solemnly.

'Then I am with you heart and soul. As you go by the 10.30 train, you will not have time to read them; but I shall get the bundle of papers. You can take them with you and read them in the train.'

After breakfast I saw him to the station. When we were parting he said: 'Perhaps you will come to town if I send to you, and take Madam Mina too.'

'We shall both come when you will,' I said.

I had got him the morning papers and the London papers of the previous night, and while we were talking at the carriage window; waiting for the train to start, he was turning them over. His eye suddenly seemed to catch something in one of them, the *Westminster Gazette* – I knew it by the colour – and he grew quite white. He read something intently, groaning to himself: '*Mein Gott! Mein Gott!* So soon! so soon!' I do not think he remembered me at the moment. Just then the whistle blew and the train moved off. This recalled him to himself, and he leaned out of the window and waved his hand, calling out: 'Love to Madam Mina; I shall write so soon as ever I can.'

DR SEWARD'S DIARY

26 September. – Truly there is no such thing as finality. Not a week since I said 'Finis,' and yet here I am starting fresh again, or rather going on with the same record. Until this afternoon I had no cause to think of what is done. Renfield had become, to all intents, as sane as he ever was. He was already well ahead with his fly business; and he had just started in the spider line also; so he had not been any trouble to me. I had a letter from Arthur, written on Sunday, and from it I gather that he is bearing up wonderfully well. Quincey Morris is with him, and that is much of a help, for he himself is a bubbling well of good spirits. Quincey wrote me a line too, and from him I hear that Arthur is beginning to recover something of his old buoyancy; so as to them all my mind is at rest. As for myself, I was settling down to my work with the enthusiasm which I used to have for it, so that I might fairly have said that the wound which poor Lucy left on me was becoming cicatrised. Everything is, however, now reopened; and what is to be the end God only knows. I have an idea that Van Helsing thinks he knows too, but he will only let out enough at a time to whet curiosity. He went to Exeter yesterday, and stayed there all night. Today he came back, and almost bounded into the room at about half-past five o'clock, and thrust last night's *Westminster Gazette* into my hand.

'What do you think of that?' he asked as he stood back and folded his arms.

I looked over the paper, for I really did not know what he meant; but he took it from me and pointed out a paragraph about children being decoyed away at Hampstead. It did not convey much to me, until I reached a passage where it described small punctured wounds on their throats. An idea struck me and I looked up. 'Well?' he said.

'It is like poor Lucy's.'

'And what do you make of it?'

'Simply that there is some cause in common. Whatever it was that injured her has injured them.' I did not quite understand his answer: 'That is true indirectly, but not directly.'

'How do you mean, Professor?' I asked. I was a little inclined to take his seriousness lightly – for, after all, four days of rest and freedom from burning, harrowing anxiety does help to restore one's spirits – but when I saw his face it sobered me. Never, even in the midst of our despair about poor Lucy, had he looked more stern.

'Tell me!' I said. 'I can hazard no opinion. I do not know what to think, and I have no data on which to found a conjecture.'

'Do you mean to tell me, friend John, that you have no suspicion as to what poor Lucy died of; not after all the hints given, not only by events, but by me?'

'Of nervous prostration following on great loss or waste of blood.'

'And how the blood lost or waste?' I shook my head. He stepped over and sat down beside me, and went on:

'You are clever man, friend John; you reason well, and your wit is bold; but you are too prejudiced. You do not let your eyes see nor your ears hear, and that which is outside your daily life is not of account to you. Do you not think that there are things which you cannot understand, and yet which are; that some people see things that others cannot? But there are things old and new which must not be contemplate by men's eyes, because they know – or think they know – some things which other men have told them. Ah, it is the fault of our science that it wants to explain all; and if it explain not, then it says there is nothing to explain. But yet we see around us every day the growth of new beliefs, which think themselves new; and which are yet but the old, which pretend to be young – like the fine ladies at the opera. I suppose now you do not believe in corporeal transference. No? Nor in materialisation. No? Nor in astral bodies. No? Nor in the reading of thought. No? Nor in hypnotism – '

'Yes,' I said. 'Charcot[146] has proved that pretty well.' He smiled as he went on: 'Then you are satisfied as to it. Yes? And of course then you understand how it act, and can follow the mind of the great Charcot – alas that he is no more! – into the very soul of the patient that he influence. No? Then, friend John, am I to take it that you simply accept fact, and are satisfied to let from premise to conclusion be a blank? No? Then tell me – for I am student of the brain – how you accept the hypnotism and reject the thought-reading. Let me tell you, my friend, that there are things done today in electrical science which would have been deemed unholy by the very men who discovered electricity – who would themselves not so long before have been burned as wizards. There are always mysteries in life. Why was it that Methuselah[147] lived nine hundred years, and "Old Parr"[148] one hundred and sixty-nine and yet that poor Lucy, with four men's blood in her poor veins, could not live even one day! For, had she live one more day, we could have save her. Do you know all the mystery of life and death? Do you know the altogether of comparative anatomy, and can say wherefore the qualities of brutes are in some men, and not in others? Can you tell me why, when other spiders die small and soon, that one great spider lived for centuries in the tower of the old Spanish church and grew and grew, till, on descending, he could drink the oil of all the church lamps? Can you tell me why in the Pampas, ay and elsewhere, there are bats that come at night and open the veins of cattle and horses and suck dry their veins; how in some islands of the Western seas there are bats which hang on the trees all day, that those who have seen describe as like giant nuts or pods, and that when the sailors sleep on the deck, because that it is hot, flit down on them, and then – and then in the morning are found dead men, white as even Miss Lucy was?'

'Good God, Professor!' I said, starting up. 'Do you mean to tell me that Lucy was bitten by such a bat; and that such a thing is here in London in the nineteenth century?' He waved his hand for silence, and went on:

'Can you tell me why the tortoise lives more long than generations of men; why the elephant goes on and on till he have seen dynasties; and why the parrot never die only of bite of cat or dog or other complaint? Can you tell me why men believe in all ages and places that there are some few who live on always if they be permit; that there are men and women who cannot die? We all know – because science has vouched for the fact – that there have been toads shut up in rocks for thousands of years, shut in one so small hole that only hold him since the youth of the world. Can you tell me how the Indian fakir can make himself to die and have been buried, and his grave sealed and corn sowed on it, and the corn reaped and be cut and sown and reaped and cut again, and then men come and take away the unbroken seal, and that there lie the Indian fakir, not dead, but that rise up and walk amongst them as before?' Here I interrupted him. I was getting bewildered; he so crowded on my mind his list of nature's eccentricities and possible impossibilities that my imagination was getting fired. I had a dim idea that he was teaching me some lesson, as long ago he used to do in his study at Amsterdam; but he used then to tell me the thing, so that I could have the object of thought in mind all the time. But now I was without his help, yet I wanted to follow him, so I said:

'Professor, let me be your pet student again. Tell me the thesis, so that I may apply your knowledge as you go on. At present I am going in my mind from point to point as a mad man, and not a sane one, follows an idea. I feel like a novice blundering through a bog in a mist, jumping from one tussock to another in the mere blind effort to move on without knowing where I am going.'

'That is good image,' he said. 'Well, I shall tell you. My thesis is this: I want you to believe.'

'To believe what?'

'To believe in things that you cannot. Let me illustrate. I heard once of an American[149] who so defined faith: "that which enables us to believe things which we know to be untrue." For one, I follow that man. He meant that we shall have an open mind, and not let a little bit of truth check the rush of a big truth, like a small rock does a railway truck. We get the small truth first. Good! We keep him, and we value him; but all the same we must not let him think himself all the truth in the universe.'

'Then you want me not to let some previous conviction injure the receptivity of my mind with regard to some strange matter. Do I read your lesson aright?'

'Ah, you are my favourite pupil still. It is worth to teach you. Now that you are willing to understand, you have taken the first step to understand. You think then that those so small holes in the children's throats were made by the same that made the hole in Miss Lucy?'

'I suppose so.' He stood up and said solemnly:

'Then you are wrong. Oh, would it were so! but alas! no. It is worse, far, far worse.'

'In God's name, Professor Van Helsing, what do you mean?' I cried.

He threw himself with a despairing gesture into a chair, and placed his elbows on the table, covering his face with his hands as he spoke:'They were made by Miss Lucy!'

Chapter 15

Dr Seward's Diary (continued)

For a while sheer anger mastered me; it was as if he had during her life struck Lucy on the face. I smote the table hard and rose up as I said to him:

'Dr Van Helsing, are you mad?' He raised his head and looked at me, and somehow the tenderness of his face calmed me at once. 'Would I were!' he said. 'Madness were easy to bear compared with truth like this. Oh, my friend, why, think you, did I go so far round, why take so long to tell you so simple a thing? Was it because I hate you and have hated you all my life? Was it because I wished to give you pain? Was it that I wanted, now so late, revenge for that time when you saved my life, and from a fearful death? Ah no!'

'Forgive me,' said I. He went on:

'My friend, it was because I wished to be gentle in the breaking to you, for I know that you have loved that so sweet lady. But even yet I do not expect you to believe. It is so hard to accept at once any abstract truth, that we may doubt such to be possible when we have always believed the "no" of it; it is more hard still to accept so sad a concrete truth, and of such a one as Miss Lucy. Tonight I go to prove it. Dare you come with me?'

This staggered me. A man does not like to prove such a truth; Byron excepted from the category, jealousy.

And prove the very truth he most abhorred.[150]

He saw my hesitation, and spoke:

'The logic is simple, no madman's logic this time, jumping from tussock to tussock in a misty fog. If it be not true, then proof will be relief; at worst it will not harm. If it be true! Ah, there is the dread; yet very dread should help my cause, for in it is some need of belief. Come, I tell you what I propose: first, that we go off now and see that child in the hospital. Dr Vincent, of the North Hospital, where the papers say the child is, is friend of mine, and I think of yours since you were in class at Amsterdam. He will let two scientists see his case, if he will not let two friends. We shall tell him nothing, but only that we wish to learn. And then – '

'And then?' He took a key from his pocket and held it up. 'And then we spend the night, you and I, in the churchyard where Lucy lies. This is the key that lock the tomb. I had it from the coffin-man to give to Arthur.' My heart sank within me, for I felt that there was some fearful ordeal before us. I could do nothing, however, so I plucked up what heart I could and said that we had better hasten, as the afternoon was passing . . .

We found the child awake. It had had a sleep and taken some food, and altogether was going on well. Dr Vincent took the bandage from its throat, and showed us the punctures. There was no mistaking the similarity to those which had been on Lucy's throat. They were smaller, and the edges looked fresher; that was all. We asked Vincent to what he attributed them, and he replied that it must have been a bite of some animal, perhaps a rat; but, for his own part, he was inclined to think that it was one of the bats which are so numerous on the northern heights of London. 'Out of so many harmless ones,' he said, 'there may be some wild specimen from the South of a more malignant species. Some sailor may have brought one home, and it managed to escape; or even from the Zoological Gardens a young one may have got loose, or one be bred there from a vampire. These things do occur, you know. Only ten days ago a wolf got out, and was, I believe, traced up in this direction. For a week after, the children were playing nothing but Red Riding Hood on the Heath and in every alley in the place until this "bloofer lady" scare came along, since when it has been quite a gala-time with them. Even this poor little mite, when he woke up today, asked the nurse if he might go away. When she asked him why he wanted to go, he said he wanted to play with the "bloofer lady".'

'I hope,' said Van Helsing, 'that when you are sending the child home you will caution its parents to keep strict watch over it. These fancies to stray are most dangerous; and if the child were to remain out another night, it would probably be fatal. But in any case I suppose you will not let it away for some days?'

'Certainly not, not for a week at least; longer if the wound is not healed.'

Our visit to the hospital took more time than we had reckoned on, and the sun had dipped before we came out. When Van Helsing saw how dark it was, he said:

'There is no hurry. It is more late than I thought. Come, let us seek somewhere that we may eat, and then we shall go on our way.'

We dined at 'Jack Straw's Castle'[151] along with a little crowd of bicyclists and others who were genially noisy. About ten o'clock we started from the inn. It was then very dark, and the scattered lamps made the darkness greater when we were once outside their individual radius. The Professor had evidently noted the road we were to go, for he went on unhesitatingly; but, as for me, I was in quite a mix-up as to locality. As we went further, we met fewer and fewer people, till at last we were somewhat surprised when we met even the patrol of horse police going their usual suburban round. At last we reached the wall of the churchyard, which we climbed over. With some little difficulty – for it was very dark, and the whole place seemed so strange to us – we found the Westenra tomb. The Professor took the key, opened the creaky door and standing back, politely, but quite unconsciously, motioned me to precede him. There was a delicious irony in the offer, in the courtliness of giving preference on such a ghastly occasion. My companion followed me quickly, and cautiously drew the door to, after carefully ascertaining that the lock was a falling, and not a spring one. In the latter case we should have been in a bad plight. Then he fumbled in his bag, and taking out a match-box and a piece of candle, proceeded to make a light. The tomb in the daytime, and when wreathed with fresh flowers, had looked grim and gruesome enough; but now, some days afterwards, when the flowers hung lank and dead, their whites turning to rust and their greens to browns; when the spider and the beetle had resumed their accustomed dominance; when time-discoloured stone, and dust-encrusted mortar, and rusty, dank iron, and tarnished brass, and clouded silver-plating gave back the feeble glimmer of a candle, the effect was more miserable and sordid than could have been imagined. It conveyed irresistibly the idea that life – animal life – was not the only thing which could pass away.

Van Helsing went about his work systematically. Holding his candle so that he could read the coffin plates, and so holding it that the sperm dropped in white patches which congealed as they touched the metal, he made assurance of Lucy's coffin. Another search in his bag, and he took out a turnscrew.

'What are you going to do?' I asked.

'To open the coffin. You shall yet be convinced.' Straightway he began taking out the screws, and finally lifted off the lid, showing the casing of lead beneath. The sight was almost too much for me. It seemed to be as much an affront to the dead as it would have been to have stripped off her clothing in her sleep whilst living; I actually took hold of his hand to stop him. He only said: 'You shall see,' and again fumbling in his bag, took out a tiny fret-saw. Striking the turnscrew through the lead with a swift downward stab, which made me wince, he made a small hole, which was, however, big enough to admit the point of the saw. I had expected a rush of gas from the week-old corpse. We doctors, who have had to study our dangers, have to become accustomed to such things, and I drew back towards the door. But the Professor never stopped for a moment; he sawed down a couple of feet along one side of the lead coffin, and then across, and down the other side. Taking the edge of the loose flange, he bent it back towards the foot of the coffin, and holding up the candle into the aperture, motioned to me to look.

I drew near and looked. The coffin was empty.

It was certainly a surprise to me, and gave me a considerable shock, but Van Helsing was unmoved. He was now more sure than ever of his ground, and so emboldened to proceed in his task. 'Are you satisfied now, friend John?' he asked.

I felt all the dogged argumentativeness of my nature awake within me as I answered him:

'I am satisfied that Lucy's body is not in that coffin; but that only proves one thing.'

'And what is that, friend John?'

'That it is not there.'

'That is good logic,' he said, 'so far as it goes. But how do you – how can you – account for it not being there?'

'Perhaps a body-snatcher,' I suggested. 'Some of the undertaker's people may have stolen it.' I felt that I was speaking folly, and yet it was the only real cause which I could suggest. The Professor sighed. 'Ah well!' he said, 'we must have more proof. Come with me.'

He put on the coffin-lid again, gathered up all his things and placed them in the bag, blew out the light, and placed the candle also in the bag. We opened the door, and went out. Behind us he closed the door and locked it. He handed me the key, saying: 'Will you keep it? You had better be assured.' I laughed – it was not a very cheerful laugh, I am bound to say – as I motioned him to keep it. 'A key is nothing,' I said; 'there may be duplicates; and anyhow it is not difficult to pick a lock of that kind.' He said nothing, but put the key in his pocket. Then he told me to watch at one side of the churchyard whilst he would watch at the other. I took up my place behind a yew-tree, and I saw his dark figure move until the intervening headstones and trees hid it from my sight.

It was a lonely vigil. Just after I had taken my place I heard a distant clock strike twelve, and in time came one and two. I was chilled and unnerved, and angry with the Professor for taking me on such an errand and with myself for coming. I was too cold and too sleepy to be keenly observant, and not sleepy enough to betray my trust; so altogether I had a dreary, miserable time.

Suddenly, as I turned round, I thought I saw something like a white streak, moving between two dark yew-trees at the side of the church-yard farthest from the tomb; at the same time a dark mass moved from the Professor's side of the ground, and hurriedly went towards it. Then I too moved; but I had to go round headstones and railed-off tombs, and I stumbled over graves. The sky was overcast, and somewhere far off an early cock crew. A little way off, beyond the line of scattered juniper-trees, which marked the pathway to the church, a white, dim figure flitted in the direction of the tomb. The tomb itself was hidden by trees, and I could not see where the figure disappeared. I heard the rustle of actual movement where I had first seen the white figure, and coming over, found the Professor holding in his arms a tiny child. When he saw me he held it out to me, and said:

'Are you satisfied now?'

'No,' I said, in a way that I felt was aggressive.

'Do you not see the child?'

'Yes, it is a child, but who brought it here? And is it wounded?' I asked.

'We shall see,' said the Professor, and with one impulse we took our way out of the churchyard, he carrying the sleeping child.

When we had got some little distance away, we went into a clump of trees, and struck a match, and looked at the child's throat. It was without a scratch or scar of any kind.

'Was I right?' I asked triumphantly.

'We were just in time,' said the Professor thankfully.

We had now to decide what we were to do with the child, and so consulted about it. If we were to take it to a police station we should have to give some account of our movements during the night; at least, we should have had to make some statement as to how we had come to find the child. So finally we decided that we would take it to the Heath, and when we heard a policeman coming, would leave it where he could not fail to find it; we would then seek our way home as quickly as we could. All fell out well. At the edge of Hampstead Heath we heard a policeman's heavy tramp, and laying the child on the pathway, we waited and watched until he saw it as he flashed his lantern to and fro. We heard his exclamation of astonishment, and then we went away silently. By good chance we got a cab near the 'Spaniards',[152] and drove to town.

I cannot sleep, so I make this entry. But I must try to get a few hours' sleep, as Van Helsing is to call for me at noon. He insists that I shall go with him on another expedition.

27 *September*. – It was two o'clock before we found a suitable opportunity for our attempt. The funeral held at noon was all completed, and the last stragglers of the mourners had taken themselves lazily away, when, looking carefully from behind a clump of alder-trees, we saw the sexton lock the gate after him. We knew then that we were safe till morning did we desire it; but the Professor told me that we should not want more than an hour at most. Again I felt that horrid sense of the reality of things, in which any effort of imagination seemed out of place; and I realised distinctly the perils of the law which we were incurring in our unhallowed work. Besides, I felt it was all so useless. Outrageous as it was to open a leaden coffin, to see if a woman dead nearly a week were really dead, it now seemed the height of folly to open the tomb again, when we knew, from the evidence of our own eyesight, that the coffin was empty. I shrugged my shoulders, however, and rested silent, for Van Helsing had a way of going on his own road, no matter who remonstrated. He took the key, opened the vault, and again courteously motioned me to precede. The place was not so gruesome as last night, but oh, how unutterably mean-looking when the sunshine streamed in. Van Helsing walked over to Lucy's coffin, and I

followed. He bent over and again forced back the leaden flange; and then a shock of surprise and dismay shot through me.

There lay Lucy, seemingly just as we had seen her the night before her funeral. She was, if possible, more radiantly beautiful than ever; and I could not believe that she was dead. The lips were red, nay redder than before; and on the cheeks was a delicate bloom.

'Is this a juggle?' I said to him.

'Are you convinced now?' said the Professor in response, and as he spoke he put over his hand, and in a way that made me shudder, pulled back the dead lips and showed the white teeth.

'See,' he went on, 'see, they are even sharper than before. With this and this' – and he touched one of the canine teeth and that below it – 'the little children can be bitten. Are you of belief now, friend John?' Once more, argumentative hostility woke within me. I *could* not accept such an overwhelming idea as he suggested; so, with an attempt to argue of which I was even at the moment ashamed, I said:

'She may have been placed here since last night.'

'Indeed? That is so, and by whom?'

'I do not know. Someone has done it.'

'And yet she has been dead one week. Most peoples in that time would not look so.' I had no answer for this, so was silent. Van Helsing did not seem to notice my silence; at any rate, he showed neither chagrin nor triumph. He was looking intently at the face of the dead woman, raising the eyelids and looking at the eyes, and once more opening the lips and examining the teeth. Then he turned to me and said:

'Here, there is one thing which is different from all recorded: here is some dual life that is not as the common. She was bitten by the vampire when she was in a trance, sleep-walking – oh you start; you do not know that, friend John, but you shall know it all later – and in trance could he best come to take more blood. In trance she died, and in trance she is Un-Dead, too. So it is that she differ from all other. Usually when the Un-Dead sleep at home' – as he spoke he made a comprehensive sweep of his arm to designate what to a vampire was 'home' – 'their face show what they are, but this so sweet that-was when she not Un-Dead she go back to the nothings of the common dead. There is no malign there, see, and so it make hard that I must kill her in her sleep.' This turned my blood cold, and it began to dawn upon me that I was accepting Van Helsing's theories; but if she were really dead, what was there of terror in the idea of killing her? He looked up at me, and evidently saw the change in my face, for he said almost joyously:

'Ah, you believe now?'

I answered: 'Do not press me too hard all at once. I am willing to accept. How will you do this bloody work?'

'I shall cut off her head and fill her mouth with garlic, and I shall drive a stake through her body.' It made me shudder to think of so mutilating the body of the woman whom I had loved. And yet the feeling was not so strong as I had expected. I was, in fact, beginning to shudder at the presence of this being, this Un-Dead, as Van Helsing called it, and to loathe it. Is it possible that love is all subjective, or all objective?

I waited a considerable time for Van Helsing to begin, but he stood as if wrapped in thought. Presently he closed the catch of his bag with a snap, and said: 'I have been thinking, and have made up my mind as to what is best. If I did simply follow my inclining I would do now, at this moment, what is to be done; but there are other things to follow, and things that are thousand times more difficult in that them we do not know. This is simple. She have yet no life taken, though that is of time; and to act now would be to take danger from her for ever. But then we may have to want Arthur, and how shall we tell him of this? If you, who saw the wounds on Lucy's throat, and saw the wounds so similar on the child's at the hospital, if you, who saw the coffin empty last night and full today with a woman who have not change only to be more rose and more beautiful in a whole week after she die – if you know of this and know of the white figure last night that brought the child to the churchyard, and yet of your own senses you did not believe, how, then, can I expect Arthur, who know none of those things, to believe? He doubted me when I took him from her kiss when she was dying. I know he has forgiven me because in some mistaken idea I have done things that prevent him say good-bye as he ought; and he may think that in some more mistaken idea this woman was buried alive; and that in most mistake of all we have killed her. He will then argue back that it is we, mistaken ones, that have killed her by our ideas; and so he will be much unhappy always. Yet he never can be sure; and that is the worst of all. And he will sometimes think that she he loved was buried alive, and that will paint his dreams with horrors of what she must have suffered; and, again, he will think that we may be right, and that his so beloved was, after all, an Un-Dead. No! I told him once, and since then I learn much. Now, since I know it is all true, a hundred thousand times more do I know that he must pass through the bitter waters to reach the sweet. He, poor fellow, must have one hour that will make the very face of heaven grow black to him; then we can act for good all round and send him peace. My mind is made up. Let us go. You return home for tonight to your asylum, and see that all be well. As for me, I shall spend the night here in this churchyard in my own way. Tomorrow night you will come to me to the Berkeley Hotel at ten of the clock. I shall send for Arthur to come too, and also that so fine young man of America that gave his blood. Later we shall all have work to do. I come with you so far as Piccadilly and there dine, for I must be back here before the sun set.'

So we locked the tomb and came away, and got over the wall of the churchyard, which was not much of a task, and drove back to Piccadilly.

Note left by Van Helsing in his portmanteau, Berkeley Hotel,
directed to John Seward, M.D. (not delivered)

27 September.

FRIEND JOHN, –

I write this in case anything should happen. I go alone to watch in that churchyard. It pleases me that the Un-Dead, Miss Lucy, shall not leave tonight, that so on the morrow night she may be more eager. Therefore I shall fix some things she like not – garlic and a crucifix – and so seal up the door of the tomb. She is young as Un-Dead, and will heed. Moreover, these are only to prevent her coming out; they may not prevail on her wanting to get in; for then the Un-Dead is desperate, and must find the line of least resistance, whatsoever it may be. I shall be at hand all the night from sunset till after the sunrise, and if there be aught that may be learned I shall learn it. For Miss Lucy, or from her, I have no fear: but that other to whom is there that she is Un-Dead, he have now the power to seek her tomb and find shelter. He is cunning, as I know from Mr Jonathan and from the way that all along he have fooled us when he played with us for Miss Lucy's life, and we lost; and in many ways the Un-Dead are strong. He have always the strength in his hand of twenty men; even we four who gave our strength to Miss Lucy it also is all to him. Besides, he can summon his wolf and I know not what. So if it be that he come thither on this night he shall find me; but none other shall – until it be too late. But it may be that he will not attempt the place. There is no reason why he should; his hunting ground is more full of game than the churchyard where the Un-Dead woman sleep, and one old man watch.

Therefore I write this in case . . . Take the papers that are with this, the diaries of Harker and the rest and read them, and then find this great Un-Dead, and cut off his head and burn his heart or drive a stake through it, so that the world may rest from him.

If it be so, farewell.

VAN HELSING

Dr Seward's Diary

28 September. – It is wonderful what a good night's sleep will do for one. Yesterday I was almost willing to accept Van Helsing's monstrous ideas; but now they seem to start out lurid before me as outrages on common sense. I have no doubt that he believes it all. I wonder if his mind can have become in any way unhinged. Surely there must be *some* rational explanation of all these mysterious things. Is it possible that the Professor can have done it himself? He is so abnormally clever that if he went off his head he would carry out his intent with regard to some fixed idea in a wonderful way. I am loath to think it, and indeed it would be almost as great a marvel as the other to find that Van Helsing was mad; but anyhow I shall watch him carefully. I may get some light on the mystery.

29 September, morning. . . . Last night, at a little before ten o'clock, Arthur and Quincey came into Van Helsing's room; he told us all that he wanted us to do, but especially addressing himself to Arthur, as if all our wills were centred in his. He began by saying that he hoped we would all come with him too, 'for,' he said, 'there is a grave duty to be done there. You were doubtless surprised at my letter?' This query was directly addressed to Lord Godalming.

'I was. It rather upset me for a bit. There has been so much trouble around my house of late that I could do without any more. I have been curious, too, as to what you mean. Quincey and I talked it over; but the more we talked, the more puzzled we got, till now I can say for myself that I'm about up a tree as to any meaning about anything.'

'Me, too,' said Quincey Morris laconically.

'Oh,' said the Professor, 'then you are nearer the beginning, both of you, than friend John here, who has to go a long way back before he can even get so far as to begin.'

It was evident that he recognised my return to my old doubting frame of mind without my saying a word. Then, turning to the other two, he said with intense gravity:

'I want your permission to do what I think good this night. It is, I know, much to ask; and when you know what it is I propose to do you will know, and only then, how much. Therefore may I ask that you promise me in the dark, so that afterwards, though you may be angry with me for a time – I must not disguise from myself the possibility that such may be – you shall not blame yourselves for anything.'

'That's frank anyhow,' broke in Quincey. 'I'll answer for the Professor. I don't quite see his drift, but I swear he's honest, and that's good enough for me.'

'I thank you, sir,' said Van Helsing proudly. 'I have done myself the honour of counting you one trusting friend, and such endorsement is dear to me.' He held out a hand, which Quincey took.

Then Arthur spoke out:

'Dr Van Helsing, I don't quite like to buy a "pig in a poke", as they say in Scotland, and if it be anything in which my honour as a gentleman or my faith as a Christian is concerned, I cannot make such a promise. If you can assure me that what you intend does not violate either of these two, then I give my consent at once; though, for the life of me, I cannot understand what you are driving at.'

'I accept your limitation,' said Van Helsing, 'and all I ask of you is that if you feel it necessary to condemn any act of mine, you will first consider it well and be satisfied that it does not violate your reservations.'

'Agreed!' said Arthur; 'that is only fair. And now that the *pourparlers*[153] are over, may I ask what it is we are to do?'

'I want you to come with me, and to come in secret, to the churchyard at Kingstead.'[154]

Arthur's face fell as he said in an amazed sort of way: 'Where poor Lucy is buried?' The Professor bowed. Arthur went on: 'And when there?'

'To enter the tomb!'

Arthur stood up. 'Professor, are you in earnest; or is it some monstrous joke? Pardon me, I see that you are in earnest.' He sat down again, but I could see that he sat firmly and proudly, as one who is on his dignity. There was silence until he asked again:

'And when in the tomb?'

'To open the coffin.'

'This is too much!' he said, angrily rising again. 'I am willing to be patient in all things that are reasonable; but in this – this desecration of the grave – of one who – ' He fairly choked with indignation. The Professor looked pityingly at him.

'If I could spare you one pang, my poor friend,' he said, 'God knows I would. But this night our feet must tread in thorny paths; or later, and for ever, the feet you love must walk in paths of flame!'

Arthur looked up with set, white face and said:

'Take care, sir, take care!'

'Would it not be well to hear what I have to say?' said Van Helsing. 'And then you will at least know the limit of my purpose. Shall I go on?'

'That's fair enough,' broke in Morris.

Afer a pause Van Helsing went on, evidently with an effort:

'Miss Lucy is dead; is it not so? Yes! Then there can be no wrong to her. But if she be not dead – '

Arthur jumped to his feet.

'Good God!' he cried. 'What do you mean? Has there been any mistake; has she been buried alive?' He groaned in anguish that not even hope could soften.

'I did not say she was alive, my child; I did not think it. I go no further than to say that she might be Un-Dead.'

'Un-Dead! Not alive! What do you mean? Is this all a nightmare, or what is it?'

'There are mysteries which men can only guess at, which age by age they may solve only in part. Believe me, we are now on the verge of one. But I have not done. May I cut off the head of dead Miss Lucy?'

'Heavens and earth no!' cried Arthur in a storm of passion. 'Not for the wide world will I consent to any mutilation of her dead body. Dr Van Helsing, you try me too far. What have I done to you that you should torture me so? What did that poor, sweet girl do that you should want to cast such dishonour on her grave? Are you mad that speak such things or am I mad that listen to them? Don't dare to think more of such a desecration; I shall not give my consent to anything you do. I have a duty to do in protecting her grave from outrage and, by God, I shall do it!'

Van Helsing rose up from where he had all the time been seated, and said, gravely and sternly:

'My Lord Godalming, I, too, have a duty to do, a duty to others, a duty to you, a duty to the dead; and, by God, I shall do it! All I ask you now is that you come with me, that you look and listen; and if when later I make the same request you do not be more eager for its fulfilment even than I am, then – then I shall do my duty, whatever it may seem to me. And then, to follow of your Lordship's wishes, I shall hold myself at your disposal to render an account to you, when and where you will.' His voice broke a little, and he went on with an accent full of pity:

'But, I beseech you, do not go forth in anger with me. In a long life of acts which were often not pleasant to do, and which sometimes did wring my heart, I have never had so heavy a task as now. Believe me that if the time comes for you to change your mind towards me, one look from you will wipe away all this so sad hour, for I would do what a man can to save you from sorrow. Just think. For why should I give myself so much of labour and so much of sorrow? I have come here from my own land to do what I can of good, at the first to please my friend John, and then to help a sweet young lady, whom, too, I came to love. For her – I am ashamed to say so much, but I say it in kindness – I gave what you gave: the blood of my veins, I gave it, I, who was not, like you, her lover, but only her physician and her friend. I gave to her my nights and days – before death, after death; and if my death can do her good even now, when she is the dead Un-Dead, she shall have it freely.' He said this with a very grave, sweet pride, and Arthur was much affected by it. He took the old man's hand and said in a broken voice:

'Oh, it is hard to think of it, and I cannot understand; but at least I will go with you and wait.'

Chapter 16

DR SEWARD'S DIARY (*continued*)

IT WAS JUST A quarter before twelve o'clock when we got into the churchyard over the low wall. The night was dark, with occasional gleams of moonlight between the rents of the heavy clouds that scudded across the sky. We all kept somehow close together, with Van Helsing slightly in front as he led the way. When we had come close to the tomb I looked well at Arthur, for I feared that the proximity to a place laden with so sorrowful a memory would upset him; but he bore himself well. I took it that the very mystery of the proceeding tended in some way to counteract his grief. The Professor unlocked the door, and seeing a natural hesitation amongst us for various reasons, solved the difficulty by entering first himself. The rest of us followed, and he closed the door. He then lit a dark lantern and pointed to the coffin. Arthur stepped forward hesitatingly; Van Helsing said to me:

'You were with me here yesterday. Was the body of Miss Lucy in that coffin?'

'It was.' The Professor turned to the rest, saying:

'You hear; and yet there is one who does not believe with me.' He took his screwdriver and again took off the lid of the coffin. Arthur looked on, very pale but silent; when the lid was removed he stepped forward. He evidently did not know that there was a leaden coffin, or, at any rate, had not thought of it. When he saw the rent in the lead, the blood rushed to his face for an instant, but as quickly fell away again, so that he remained of a ghastly whiteness; he was still silent. Van Helsing forced back the leaden flange, and we all looked in and recoiled.

The coffin was empty!

For several minutes no one spoke a word. The silence was broken by Quincey Morris:

'Professor, I answered for you. Your word is all I want. I wouldn't ask such a thing ordinarily – I wouldn't so dishonour you as to imply a doubt; but this is a mystery that goes beyond any honour or dishonour. Is this your doing?'

'I swear to you by all that I hold sacred that I have not removed nor touched her. What happened was this: Two nights ago my friend Seward and I came here – with good purpose, believe me. I opened that coffin, which was then sealed up, and we found it, as now, empty. We then waited, and saw something white come through the trees. The next day we came here in daytime, and she lay there. Did she not, friend John?'

'Yes.'

'That night we were just in time. One more so small child was missing, and we find it, thank God, unharmed amongst the graves. Yesterday I came here before sundown, for at sundown the Un-Dead can move. I waited here all the night till the sun rose, but I saw nothing. It was most probable that it was because I had laid over the clamps of those doors garlic, which the Un-Dead cannot bear, and other things which they shun. Last night there was no exodus, so tonight before the sundown I took away my garlic and other things. And so it is we find this coffin empty. But bear with me. So far there is much that is strange. Wait you with me outside, unseen and unheard, and things much stranger are yet to be. So' – here he shut the dark slide of his lantern – 'now to the outside.' He opened the door and we filed out, he coming last and locking the door behind him.

Oh! but it seemed fresh and pure in the night air after the terror of that vault. How sweet it was to see the clouds race by, and the brief gleams of the moonlight between the scudding clouds crossing and passing – like the gladness and sorrow of a man's life; how sweet it was to breathe the fresh air, that had no taint of death and decay; how humanising to see the red lighting of the sky beyond the hill, and to hear far away the muffled roar that marks the life of a great city. Each in his own way was solemn and overcome. Arthur was silent, and was, I could see, striving to grasp the purpose and the inner meaning of the mystery. I was myself tolerably patient, and half inclined again to throw aside doubt and to accept Van Helsing's conclusions. Quincey Morris was phlegmatic in the way of a man who accepts all things, and accepts them in the spirit of cool bravery, with hazard of all he has to stake. Not being able to smoke, he cut himself a good-sized plug of tobacco and began to chew. As to Van Helsing, he was employed in a definite way. First he took from his bag a mass of what looked like thin, wafer-like biscuit, which was carefully rolled up in a white napkin; next he took out a double-handful of some whitish stuff, like dough or putty. He crumbled the wafer up fine and worked it into the mass between his hands. This he then took, and rolling it into thin strips, began to lay them into the crevices between the door and its setting in the tomb. I was somewhat puzzled at this, and being close, asked him what it was that he was doing. Arthur and Quincey drew near also, as they too were curious. He answered:

'I am closing the tomb, so that the Un-Dead may not enter.'

'And is that stuff you have put there going to do it?' asked Quincey. 'Great Scott! Is this a game?'

'It is.'

'What is that which you are using?' This time the question was by Arthur. Van Helsing reverently lifted his hat as he answered:

'The Host.[155] I brought it from Amsterdam. I have an Indulgence.'[156] It was an answer that appalled the most sceptical of us, and we felt individually that in the presence of such earnest purpose as the Professor's, a purpose which could thus use the to him most sacred of things, it was impossible to distrust. In respectful silence we took the places assigned to us close round the tomb, but hidden from the sight of anyone approaching. I pitied the others, especially Arthur. I had myself been apprenticed by my former visits to this watching horror; and yet I, who had up to an hour ago repudiated the proofs, felt my heart sink within me. Never did tombs look so ghastly white; never did cypress, or yew, or juniper so seem the embodiment of funereal gloom; never did tree or grass wave or rustle so ominously; never did bough creak so mysteriously; and never did the far-away howling of dogs send such a woeful presage through the night.

There was a long spell of silence, a big, aching void, and then from the Professor a keen 'S–s–s–s!' He pointed; and far down the avenue of yews we saw a white figure advance – a dim white figure, which held something dark at its breast. The figure stopped, and at the moment a ray of moonlight fell between the masses of driving clouds and showed in startling prominence a dark-haired woman, dressed in the cerements of the grave. We could not see the face, for it was bent down over what we saw to be a fair-haired child. There was a pause and a sharp little cry, such as a child gives in sleep, or a dog as it lies before the fire and dreams. We were starting forward, but the Professor's warning hand,

seen by us as he stood behind a yew-tree, kept us back; and then as we
looked the white figure moved forward again. It was now near enough
for us to see clearly, and the moonlight still held. My own heart grew
cold as ice, and I could hear the gasp of Arthur as we recognised the
features of Lucy Westenra. Lucy Westenra, but yet how changed. The
sweetness was turned to adamantine, heartless cruelty, and the purity to
voluptuous wantonness. Van Helsing stepped out, and, obedient to his
gesture, we all advanced too; the four of us ranged in a line before the
door of the tomb. Van Helsing raised his lantern and drew the slide; by
the concentrated light that fell on Lucy's face we could see that the lips
were crimson with fresh blood, and that the stream had trickled over
her chin and stained the purity of her lawn death-robe.

We shuddered with horror. I could see by the tremulous light that
even Van Helsing's iron nerve had failed. Arthur was next to me, and if I
had not seized his arm and held him up, he would have fallen.

When Lucy – I call the thing that was before us Lucy because it bore
her shape – saw us she drew back with an angry snarl, such as a cat
gives when taken unawares; then her eyes ranged over us. Lucy's eyes
in form and colour; but Lucy's eyes unclean and full of hell-fire,
instead of the pure, gentle orbs we knew. At that moment the remnant
of my love passed into hate and loathing; had she then to be killed, I
could have done it with savage delight. As she looked, her eyes blazed
with unholy light, and the face became wreathed with a voluptuous
smile. Oh, God, how it made me shudder to see it! With a careless
motion, she flung to the ground, callous as a devil, the child that up to
now she had clutched strenuously to her breast, growling over it as a
dog growls over a bone. The child gave a sharp cry, and lay there
moaning. There was a cold-bloodedness in the act which wrung a
groan from Arthur; when she advanced to him with outstretched arms
and a wanton smile, he fell back and hid his face in his hands.

She still advanced, however, and with a languorous, voluptuous
grace, said:

'Come to me, Arthur. Leave these others and come to me. My arms
are hungry for you. Come, and we can rest together. Come, my
husband, come!'

There was something diabolically sweet in her tones – something of
the tingling of glass when struck – which rang through the brains even
of us who heard the words addressed to another. As for Arthur, he
seemed under a spell; moving his hands from his face, he opened wide
his arms. She was leaping for them, when Van Helsing sprang forward
and held between them his little golden crucifix. She recoiled from it,

and, with a suddenly distorted face, full of rage, dashed past him as if to enter the tomb.

When within a foot or two of the door, however, she stopped as if arrested by some irresistible force. Then she turned, and her face was shown in the clear burst of moonlight and by the lamp, which had now no quiver from Van Helsing's iron nerves. Never did I see such baffled malice on a face; and never, I trust, shall such ever be seen again by mortal eyes. The beautiful colour became livid, the eyes seemed to throw out sparks of hell-fire, the brows were wrinkled as though the folds of the flesh were the coils of Medusa's snakes,[157] and the lovely, blood-stained mouth grew to an open square, as in the passion masks of the Greeks and Japanese. If ever a face meant death – if looks could kill – we saw it at that moment.

And so for full half a minute, which seemed an eternity, she remained between the lifted crucifix and the sacred closing of her means of entry. Van Helsing broke the silence by asking Arthur:

'Answer me, oh my friend! Am I to proceed in my work?'

Arthur threw himself on his knees, and hid his face in his hands, as he answered:

'Do as you will, friend; do as you will. There can be no horror like this ever any more!' and he groaned in spirit. Quincey and I simultaneously moved towards him, and took his arms. We could hear the click of the closing lantern as Van Helsing held it down; coming close to the tomb, he began to remove from the chinks some of the sacred emblem which he had placed there. We all looked on in horrified amazement as we saw, when he stood back, the woman, with a corporeal body as real at the moment as our own, pass in through the interstice where scarce a knife-blade could have gone. We all felt a glad sense of relief when we saw the Professor calmly restoring the strings of putty to the edges of the door.

When this was done, he lifted the child and said:

'Come now, my friends; we can do no more till tomorrow. There is a funeral at noon, so here we shall all come before long after that. The friends of the dead will all be gone by two, and when the sexton lock the gate we shall remain. Then there is more to do; but not like this of tonight. As for this little one, he is not much harm, and by tomorrow night he shall be well. We shall leave him where the police will find him, as on the other night; and then to home.' Coming close to Arthur, he said:

'My friend Arthur, you have had sore trial; but after, when you will look back, you will see how it was necessary. You are now in the bitter waters, my child. By this time tomorrow, you will, please God, have passed them, and have drunk of the sweet waters; so do not mourn overmuch. Till then I shall not ask you to forgive me.'

Arthur and Quincey came home with me, and we tried to cheer each other on the way. We had left the child in safety, and were tired; so we all slept with more or less reality of sleep.

29 September, night.– A little before twelve o'clock we three – Arthur, Quincey Morris, and myself – called for the Professor. It was odd to notice that by common consent we had all put on black clothes. Of course, Arthur wore black, for he was in deep mourning, but the rest of us wore it by instinct. We got to the churchyard by half-past one, and strolled about, keeping out of official observation, so that when the gravediggers had completed their task, and the sexton, under the belief that everyone had gone, had locked the gate, we had the place all to ourselves. Van Helsing, instead of his little black bag, had with him a long leather one, something like a cricketing bag; it was manifestly of fair weight.

When we were alone and had heard the last of the footsteps die out up the road, we silently, and as if by ordered intention, followed the Professor to the tomb. He unlocked the door, and we entered, closing it behind us. Then he took from his bag the lantern, which he lit, and also two wax candles, which, when lighted, he stuck, by melting their own ends, on other coffins, so that they might give light sufficient to work by. When he again lifted the lid off Lucy's coffin we all looked – Arthur trembling like an aspen – and saw that the body lay there in all its death-beauty. But there was no love in my own heart, nothing but loathing for the foul Thing which had taken Lucy's shape without her soul. I could see even Arthur's face grow hard as he looked. Presently he said to Van Helsing:

'Is this really Lucy's body, or only a demon in her shape?'

'It is her body, and yet not it. But wait a while, and you shall see her as she was, and is.'

She seemed like a nightmare of Lucy as she lay there; the pointed teeth, the bloodstained, voluptuous mouth – which it made one shudder to see – the whole carnal and unspiritual appearance, seeming like a devilish mockery of Lucy's sweet purity. Van Helsing, in his methodical manner, began taking the various contents from his bag and placing them ready for use. First he took out a soldering iron and some plumbing solder, and then a small oil-lamp, which gave out, when lit in a corner of the tomb, gas which burned at fierce heat with a blue flame; then his operating knives, which he placed to hand; and last a round wooden stake, some two and a half or three inches thick and about three feet long. One end of it was hardened by charring in the fire, and was sharpened to a fine point. With this stake came a heavy hammer, such as in households is used in the coal-cellar for breaking the lumps. To me, a doctor's preparations for work of any kind are stimulating and bracing, but the effect of these things on both Arthur and Quincey was to cause them a sort of consternation. They both, however, kept their courage, and remained silent and quiet.

When all was ready, Van Helsing said:

'Before we do anything, let me tell you this; it is out of the lore and experience of the ancients and of all those who have studied the powers of the Un-Dead. When they become such, there comes with the change the curse of immortality; they cannot die, but must go on age after age adding new victims and multiplying the evils of the world; for all that die from the preying of the Un-Dead become themselves Un-Dead, and prey on their kind. And so the circle goes on ever widening, like as the ripples from a stone thrown in the water. Friend Arthur, if you had met that kiss which you know of before poor Lucy die; or again, last night when you open your arms to her, you would in time, when you had died, have become *nosferatu*, as they call it in Eastern Europe, and would all time make more of those Un-Deads that so have filled us with horror. The career of this so unhappy dear lady is but just begun. Those children whose blood she suck are not as yet so much the worse, but if she live on, Un-Dead, more and more they lose their blood, and by her power over them they come to her; and so she draw their blood with that so wicked mouth. But if she die in truth, then all cease; the tiny wounds of the throats disappear, and they go back to their plays unknowing ever of what has been. But of the most blessed of all, when this now Un-Dead be made to rest as true dead, then the soul of the poor lady whom we love shall again be free. Instead of working wickedness by night and growing more debased in the assimilation of it by day, she shall take her place with the other Angels. So that, my friend, it will be a blessed hand for her that shall strike the blow that sets her free. To this I am willing; but is there none amongst us who has a better right? Will it be no joy to think of hereafter in the silence of the night when sleep is not: "It was my hand that sent her to the stars, it was the hand of him that loved her best; the hand that of all she would herself have chosen, had it been to her to choose"? Tell me if there be such a one amongst us?'

We all looked at Arthur. He saw, too, what we all did, the infinite kindness which suggested that his should be the hand which would restore Lucy to us as a holy, and not an unholy memory; he stepped forward and said bravely, though his hand trembled, and his face was as pale as snow: 'My true friend, from the bottom of my broken heart I thank you. Tell me what I am to do, and I shall not falter!'

Van Helsing laid a hand on his shoulder, and said: 'Brave lad! A moment's courage, and it is done. This stake must be driven through her. It will be a fearful ordeal – be not deceived in that – but it will be only a short time, and you will then rejoice more than your pain was great; from this grim tomb you will emerge as though you tread on air. But you must not falter when once you have begun. Only think that we, your true friends, are round you, and that we pray for you all the time.'

'Go on,' said Arthur hoarsely. 'Tell me what I am to do.'

'Take this stake in your left hand, ready to place the point over the heart, and the hammer in your right. Then when we begin our prayer for the dead – I shall read him. I have here the book, and the others shall follow – strike in God's name, that so all may be well with the dead that we love, and that the Un-Dead pass away.'

Arthur took the stake and the hammer, and when once his mind was set on action his hands never trembled nor even quivered. Van Helsing opened his missal and began to read, and Quincey and I followed as well as we could. Arthur placed the point over the heart, and as I looked I could see its dint in the white flesh. Then he struck with all his might.

The Thing in the coffin writhed; and a hideous, blood-curdling screech came from the opened red lips. The body shook and quivered and twisted in wild contortions; the sharp white teeth champed together till the lips were cut and the mouth was smeared with a crimson foam. But Arthur never faltered. He looked like a figure of Thor [158] as his untrembling arm rose and fell, driving deeper and deeper the mercy-bearing stake, whilst the blood from the pierced heart welled and spurted up around it. His face was set, and high duty seemed to shine through it; the sight of it gave us courage, so that our voices seemed to ring through the little vault.

And then the writhing and quivering of the body became less, and the teeth ceased to champ, and the face to quiver. Finally it lay still. The terrible task was over.

The hammer fell from Arthur's hand. He reeled and would have fallen had we not caught him. The great drops of sweat sprang out on his forehead, and his breath came in broken gasps. It had indeed been an awful strain on him; and had he not been forced to his task by more than human considerations he could never have gone through with it. For a few minutes we were so taken up with him that we did not look towards the coffin. When we did, however, a murmur of startled surprise ran from one to the other of us. We gazed so eagerly that Arthur rose, for he had been seated on the ground, and came and looked too; and then a glad, strange light broke over his face and dispelled altogether the gloom of horror that lay upon it.

There in the coffin lay no longer the foul Thing that we had so dreaded and grown to hate that the work of her destruction was yielded as a privilege to the one best entitled to it, but Lucy as we had seen her in her life, with her face of unequalled sweetness and purity. True that there were there, as we had seen them in life, the traces of care and pain and waste; but these were all dear to us, for they marked her truth to what we knew. One and all we felt that the holy calm that lay like sunshine over the wasted face and form was only an earthly token and symbol of the calm that was to reign for ever.

Van Helsing came and laid his hand on Arthur's shoulder, and said to him: 'And now. Arthur, my friend, dear lad, am I not forgiven?'

The reaction of the terrible strain came as he took the old man's hand in his, and raising it to his lips, pressed it, saying:'Forgiven! God bless you that you have given my dear one her soul again, and me peace.' He put his hands on the Professor's shoulder, and laying his head on his breast, cried for a while silently, whilst we stood unmoving. When he raised his head Van Helsing said to him:

'And now, my child, you may kiss her. Kiss her dead lips if you will, as she would have you to, if for her to choose. For she is not a grinning devil now – not any more a foul Thing for all eternity. No longer she is the devil's Un-Dead. She is God's true dead, whose soul is with Him!'

Arthur bent and kissed her, and then we sent him and Quincey out of the tomb; the Professor and I sawed the top off the stake, leaving the point of it in the body. Then we cut off the head and filled the mouth with garlic. We soldered up the leaden coffin, screwed on the coffin-lid, and gathering up our belongings, came away. When the Professor locked the door he gave the key to Arthur.

Outside the air was sweet, the sun shone, and the birds sang, and it seemed as if all nature were tuned to a different pitch. There was gladness and mirth and peace everywhere, for we were at rest ourselves on one account, and we were glad, though it was with a tempered joy.

Before we moved away Van Helsing said:

'Now, my friends, one step of our work is done, one the most harrowing to ourselves. But there remains a greater task: to find out the author of all this our sorrow and to stamp him out. I have clues which we can follow; but it is a long task, and a difficult, and there is danger in it, and pain. Shall you not all help me? We have learned to believe, all of us – is it not so? And since so, do we not see our duty? Yes! And do we not promise to go on to the bitter end?'

Each in turn, we took his hand, and the promise was made. Then said the Professor as we moved off: 'Two nights hence you shall meet with me and dine together at seven of the clock with friend John. I shall entreat two others, two that you know not as yet; and I shall be ready to all our work show and our plans unfold. Friend John, you come with me home, for I have much to consult about, and you can help me. Tonight I leave for Amsterdam, but shall return tomorrow night. And then begins our great quest. But first I shall have much to say, so that you may know what is to do and to dread. Then our promise shall be made to each other anew; for there is a terrible task before us, and once our feet are on the ploughshare,[159] we must not draw back.'

Chapter 17

DR SEWARD'S DIARY (continued)

WHEN WE ARRIVED at the Berkeley Hotel, Van Helsing found a telegram waiting for him:

> Am coming up by train. Jonathan at Whitby. Important news.
> MINA HARKER.

The Professor was delighted. 'Ah, that wonderful Madam Mina,' he said, 'pearl among women! She arrive, but I cannot stay. She must go to your house, friend John. You must meet her at the station. Telegraph her *en route*, so that she may be prepared.'

When the wire was despatched he had a cup of tea; over it he told me of a diary kept by Jonathan Harker when abroad and gave me a typewritten copy of it, as also of Mrs Harker's diary at Whitby. 'Take these,' he said, 'and study them well. When I have returned you will be master of all the facts, and we can then better enter on our inquisition. Keep them safe, for there is in them much of treasure. You will need all your faith, even you who have had such an experience as that of today What is here told,' he laid his hand heavily and gravely on the packet of papers as he spoke, 'may be the beginning of the end to you and me and many another; or it may sound the knell of the Un-Dead who walk the earth. Read all, I pray you, with the open mind; and if you can add in any way to the story here told do so, for it is all-important. You have

kept diary of all these so strange things; is it not so? Yes! Then we shall
go through all these together when that we meet.' He then made ready
for his departure, and shortly after drove off to Liverpool Street.[160] I
took my way to Paddington, where I arrived about fifteen minutes
before the train came in.

The crowd melted away, after the bustling fashion common to arrival
platforms; and I was beginning to feel uneasy, lest I might miss my
guest, when a sweet-faced, dainty-looking girl stepped up to me, and,
after a quick glance, said: 'Dr Seward, is it not?'

'And you are Mrs Harker!' I answered at once; whereupon she held
out her hand.

'I knew you from the description of poor dear Lucy but – ' She
stopped suddenly, and a quick blush overspread her face.

The blush that rose to my own cheeks somehow set us both at ease,
for it was a tacit answer to her own. I got her luggage, which included a
typewriter, and we took the Underground to Fenchurch Street,[161] after
I had sent a wire to my housekeeper to have a sitting-room and
bedroom prepared at once for Mrs Harker.

In due time we arrived. She knew, of course, that the place was a
lunatic asylum, but I could see that she was unable to repress a slight
shudder when we entered.

She told me that, if she might, she would come presently to my study,
as she had much to say. So here I am finishing my entry in my
phonograph diary whilst I await her. As yet I have not had the chance of
looking at the papers which Van Helsing left with me, though they lie
open before me. I must get her interested in something, so that I may
have an opportunity of reading them. She does not know how precious
time is, or what a task we have in hand. I must be careful not to frighten
her. Here she is!

MINA HARKER'S JOURNAL

29 September. – After I had tidied myself, I went down to Dr Seward's
study. At the door I paused a moment, for I thought I heard him talking
with someone. As, however, he had pressed me to be quick, I knocked at
the door, and on his calling out, 'Come in,' I entered.

To my intense surprise, there was no one with him. He was quite
alone, and on the table opposite him was what I knew at once from the
description to be a phonograph. I had never seen one, and was much
interested.

'I hope I did not keep you waiting,' I said; 'but I stayed at the door as I heard you talking, and thought there was someone with you.'

'Oh,' he replied, with a smile, 'I was only entering my diary.'

'Your diary?' I asked him in surprise.

'Yes,' he answered. 'I keep it in this.' As he spoke he laid his hand on the phonograph. I felt quite excited over it, and blurted out:

'Why, this beats even shorthand! May I hear it say something?'

'Certainly,' he replied with alacrity, and stood up to put it in train for speaking. Then he paused, and a troubled look overspread his face.

'The fact is,' he began awkwardly, 'I only keep my diary in it; and as it is entirely – almost entirely – about my cases, it may be awkward – that is, I mean – ' He stopped, and I tried to help him out of his embarrassment:

'You helped to attend dear Lucy at the end. Let me hear how she died; for all that I can know of her, I shall be very grateful. She was very, very dear to me.'

To my surprise, he answered, with a horrorstruck look in his face:

'Tell you of her death? Not for the wide world!'

'Why not?' I asked, for some grave, terrible feeling was coming over me. Again he paused, and I could see that he was trying to invent an excuse. At length he stammered out:

'You see, I do not know how to pick out any particular part of the diary.' Even while he was speaking an idea dawned upon him, and he said with unconscious simplicity, in a different voice, and with the naïveté of a child: 'That's quite true, upon my honour. Honest Indian!' I could not but smile, at which he grimaced. 'I gave myself away that time!' he said. 'But do you know that, although I have kept the diary for months past, it never once struck me how I was going to find any particular part of it in case I wanted to look it up?' By this time my mind was made up that the diary of a doctor who attended Lucy might have something to add to the sum of our knowledge of that terrible Being, and I said boldly: 'Then, Dr Seward, you had better let me copy it out for you on my typewriter.'

He grew to a positively deathly pallor as he said: 'No! no! no! For all the world, I wouldn't let you know that terrible story!'

Then it was terrible; my intuition was right! For a moment I thought, and as my eyes ranged the room, unconsciously looking for something or some opportunity to aid me, they lit on the great batch of typewriting on the table. His eyes caught the look in mine, and, without his thinking, followed their direction. As they saw the parcel he realised my meaning.

'You do not know me,' I said. 'When you have read those papers – my own diary and my husband's also, which I have typed – you will know me better. I have not faltered in giving every thought of my own heart in this cause; but, of course, you do not know me – yet; and I must not expect you to trust me so far.'

He is certainly a man of noble nature; poor dear Lucy was right about him. He stood up and opened a large drawer, in which were arranged in order a number of hollow cylinders of metal covered with dark wax, and said:'You are quite right. I did not trust you because I did not know you. But I know you know; and let me say that I should have known you long ago. I know that Lucy told you of me; she told me of you too. May I make the only atonement in my power? Take the cylinders and hear them – the first half-dozen of them are personal to me, and they will not horrify you; then you will know me better. Dinner will by then be ready. In the meantime I shall read over some of these documents, and shall be better able to understand certain things.' He carried the phonograph himself up to my sitting-room and adjusted it for me. Now I shall learn something pleasant, I am sure; for it will tell me the other side of a true love episode of which I know one side already . . .

Dr Seward's Diary

29 September. – I was so absorbed in that wonderful diary of Jonathan Harker and that other of his wife that I let the time run on without thinking. Mrs Harker was not down when the maid came to announce dinner, so I said: 'She is possibly tired; let dinner wait an hour;' and I went on with my work. I had just finished Mrs Harker's diary, when she came in. She looked sweetly pretty, but very sad, and her eyes were flushed with crying. This somehow moved me much. Of late I have had cause for tears, God knows! but the relief of them was denied me; and now the sight of those sweet eyes, brightened with recent tears, went straight to my heart. So I said as gently as I could:

'I greatly fear I have distressed you.'

'Oh no, not distressed me,' she replied, 'but I have been more touched than I can say by your grief. That is a wonderful machine, but it is cruelly true. It told me, in its very tones, the anguish of your heart. It was like a soul crying out to almighty God. No one must hear them spoken ever again! See, I have tried to be useful. I have copied out the words on my typewriter, and none other need now hear your heart beat, as I did.'

'No one need ever know, shall ever know,' I said in a low voice.

She laid her hand on mine and said very gravely: 'Ah, but they must!'

'Must! But why?' I asked.

'Because it is a part of the terrible story, a part of poor dear Lucy's death and all that led to it; because in the struggle which we have before us to rid the earth of this terrible monster we must have all the knowledge and all the help which we can get. I think that the cylinders which you gave me contained more than you intended me to know; but I can see that there are in your record many lights to this dark mystery. You will let me help, will you not? I know all up to a certain point; and I see already, though your diary only took me to 7 September, how poor Lucy was beset, and how her terrible doom was being wrought out. Jonathan and I have been working day and night since Professor Van Helsing saw us. He is gone to Whitby to get more information, and he will be here tomorrow to help us. We need have no secrets amongst us; working together and with absolute trust, we can surely be stronger than if some of us were in the dark.' She looked at me so appealingly, and at the same time manifested such courage and resolution in her bearing, that I gave in at once to her wishes. 'You shall,' I said, 'do as you like in the matter. God forgive me if I do wrong! There are terrible things yet to learn of; but if you have so far travelled on the road to poor Lucy's death, you will not be content, I know, to remain in the dark. Nay, the end – the very end – may give you a gleam of peace. Come, there is dinner. We must keep one another strong for what is before us; we have a cruel and dreadful task. When you have eaten you shall learn the rest, and I will answer any questions you ask – if there be anything which you do not understand, though it was apparent to us who were present.'

Mina Harker's Journal

29 September. – After dinner I came with Dr Seward to his study. He brought back the phonograph from my room, and I took my typewriter. He placed me in a comfortable chair, and arranged the phonograph so that I could touch it without getting up, and showed me how to stop it in case I should want to pause. Then he very thoughtfully took a chair, with his back to me, so that I might be as free as possible, and began to read. I put the forked metal to my ears and listened.

When the terrible story of Lucy's death, and – and all that followed, was done, I lay back in my chair powerless. Fortunately I am not of a fainting disposition. When Dr Seward saw me he jumped up with a horrified exclamation, and hurriedly taking a case-bottle from a cupboard, gave me some brandy, which in a few minutes somewhat restored me. My brain was all in a whirl, and only that there came through all the multitude of horrors, the holy ray of light that my dear,

dear Lucy was at last at peace, I do not think I could have borne it without making a scene. It is all so wild, and mysterious, and strange that if I had not known Jonathan's experience in Transylvania I could not have believed. As it was, I didn't know what to believe and so got out of my difficulty by attending to something else. I took the cover off my typewriter, and said to Dr Seward:

'Let me write this all out now. We must be ready for Dr Van Helsing when he comes. I have sent a telegram to Jonathan to come on here when he arrives in London from Whitby. In this matter dates are everything, and I think if we get all our material ready, and have every item put in chronological order, we shall have done much. You tell me that Lord Godalming and Mr Morris are coming too. Let us be able to tell them when they come.' He accordingly set the phonograph at a slow pace, and I began to typewrite from the beginning of the seventh cylinder. I used manifold, and so took three copies of the diary just as I had done with all the rest. It was late when I got through, but Dr Seward went about his work of going his round of the patients; when he had finished he came back and sat near me, reading, so that I did not feel too lonely whilst I worked. How good and thoughtful he is; the world seems full of good men – even if there *are* monsters in it. Before I left him I remembered what Jonathan put in his diary of the Professor's perturbation at reading something in an evening paper at the station at Exeter; so, seeing that Dr Seward keeps his newspapers, I borrowed the files of the *Westminster Gazette* and the *Pall Mall Gazette* and took them to my room. I remember how much the *Dailygraph* and the *Whitby Gazette*, of which I had made cuttings, helped us to understand the terrible events at Whitby when Count Dracula landed, so I shall look through the evening papers since then, and perhaps I shall get some new light. I am not sleepy, and the work will help to keep me quiet.

Dr Seward's Diary

30 September. – Mr Harker arrived at nine o'clock. He had got his wife's wire just before starting. He is uncommonly clever, if one can judge from his face, and full of energy. If his journal be true – and judging by one's own wonderful experiences, it must be – he is also a man of great nerve. That going down to the vault a second time was a remarkable piece of daring. After reading his account of it I was prepared to meet a good specimen of manhood, but hardly the quiet, business-like gentleman who came here today.

Later. – After lunch Harker and his wife went back to their own room, and as I passed a while ago I heard the click of the typewriter. They are hard at it. Mrs Harker says that they are knitting together in chronological order every scrap of evidence they have. Harker has got the letters between the consignee of the boxes at Whitby and the carriers in London who took charge of them. He is now reading his wife's typescript of my diary. I wonder what they make out of it. Here he is . . .

Strange that it never struck me that the very next house might be the Count's hiding-place! Goodness knows that we had enough clues from the conduct of the patient Renfield! The bundle of letters relating to the purchase of the house were with the typescript. Oh, if we had only had them earlier we might have saved poor Lucy! Stop; that way madness lies! Harker has gone back, and is again collating his material. He says that by dinner-time they will be able to show a whole connected narrative. He thinks that in the meantime I should see Renfield, as hitherto he has been a sort of index to the coming and going of the Count. I hardly see this yet, but when I get at the dates I suppose I shall. What a good thing that Mrs Harker put my cylinders into type! We never could have found the dates otherwise . . .

I found Renfield sitting placidly in his room with his hands folded, smiling benignly. At the moment he seemed as sane as anyone I ever saw. I sat down and talked with him on a lot of subjects, all of which he treated naturally. He then, of his own accord, spoke of going home, a subject he has never mentioned to my knowledge during his sojourn here. In fact he spoke quite confidently of getting his discharge at once. I believe that, had I not had the chat with Harker and read the letters and the dates of his outbursts, I should have been prepared to sign for him after a brief time of observation. As it is, I am darkly suspicious. All those outbreaks were in some way linked with the proximity of the Count. What then does this absolute content mean? Can it be that his instinct is satisfied as to the vampire's ultimate triumph? Stay, he is himself zoophagous, and in his wild ravings outside the chapel door of the deserted house he always spoke of 'master'. This all seems confirmation of our idea. However, after a while I came away; my friend is just a little too sane at present to make it safe to probe him too deep with questions, he might begin to think, and then – ! So I came away. I mistrust these quiet moods of his; so I have given the attendant a hint to look closely after him, and to have a strait-waistcoat ready in case of need.

Jonathan Harker's Journal

29 September in train to London. – When I received Mr Billington's courteous message that he would give me any information in his power, I thought it best to go down to Whitby and make, on the spot, such inquiries as I wanted. It was now my object to trace that horrid cargo of the Count's to its place in London. Later, we may be able to deal with it. Billington junior, a nice lad, met me at the station, and brought me to his father's house, where they had decided that I must stay the night. They are hospitable, with true Yorkshire hospitality: give everything, and leave him free to do as he likes. They all knew that I was busy, and that my stay was short, and Mr Billington had ready in his office all the papers concerning the consignment of boxes. It gave me almost a turn to see again one of the letters which I had seen on the Count's table before I knew of his diabolical plans. Everything had been carefully thought out, and done systematically and with precision. He seemed to have been prepared for every obstacle which might be placed by accident in the way of his intentions being carried out. To use an Americanism, he had 'taken no chances', and the absolute accuracy with which his instructions were fulfilled, was simply the logical result of his care. I saw the invoice, and took note of it: 'Fifty cases of common earth, to be used for experimental purposes'. Also the copy of letter to Carter Paterson, and their reply; of both of these I got copies. This was all the information Mr Billington could give me, so I went down to the port and saw the coastguards, the Customs officers, and the harbour-master. They had all something to say of the strange entry of the ship, which is already taking its place in local tradition; but no one could add to the simple description: 'Fifty cases of common earth'. I then saw the station-master, who kindly put me in communication with the men who had actually received the boxes. Their tally was exact with the list, and they had nothing to add except that the boxes were 'main and mortal heavy', and that shifting them was dry work. One of them added that it was hard lines that there wasn't any gentleman 'such-like as yourself, squire', to show some sort of appreciation of their efforts in a liquid form; another put in a rider that the thirst then generated was such that even the time which had elapsed had not completely allayed it. Needless to add, I took care before leaving to lift, for ever and adequately, this source of reproach.

30 September. – The station-master was good enough to give me a line to his old companion the station-master at King's Cross so that when I arrived there in the morning I was able to ask him about the arrival of the boxes. He, too, put me at once in communication with the proper officials, and I saw that their tally was correct with the original invoice. The opportunities of acquiring an abnormal thirst had been here limited; a noble use of them had, however, been made, and again I was compelled to deal with the result in an *ex post facto* manner.

From thence I went on to Carter Paterson's central office where I met with the utmost courtesy. They looked up the transaction in their day-book and letter-book, and at once telephoned to their King's Cross office for more details. By good fortune, the men who did the teaming were waiting for work, and the official at once sent them over, sending also by one of them the way-bill and all the papers connected with the delivery of the boxes at Carfax. Here again I found the tally agreeing exactly; the carriers' men were able to supplement the paucity of the written words with a few details. These were, I shortly found, connected almost solely with the dusty nature of the job, and of the consequent thirst engendered in the operators. On my affording an opportunity, through the medium of the currency of the realm, of the allaying at a later period this beneficent evil, one of the men remarked:

'That 'ere 'ouse, guv'nor, is the rummiest I ever was in. Blyme! but it ain't been touched sence a hundred years. There was dust that thick in the place that you might have slep' on it without 'urtin' of yer bones; an' the place was that neglected that yer might 'ave smelled ole Jerusalem in it. But the ole chapel – that took the cike, that did! Me and my mate, we thort we wouldn't never git out quick enough. Lor', I wouldn't take less nor a quid a moment to stay there arter dark.' Having been in the house, I could well believe him; but if he knew what I know, he would, I think, have raised his terms.

Of one thing I am now satisfied: that *all* the boxes which arrived at Whitby from Varna in the *Demeter* were safely deposited in the old chapel of Carfax. There should be fifty of them there, unless any have since been removed – as from Dr Seward's diary I fear.

I shall try to see the carter who took away the boxes from Carfax when Renfield attacked them. By following up this clue we may learn a good deal.

Later. – Mina and I have worked all day, and we have put all the papers into order.

MINA HARKER'S JOURNAL

30 September. – I am so glad that I hardly know how to contain myself. It is, I suppose, the reaction from the haunting fear which I have had: that this terrible affair and the reopening of his old wound might act detrimentally on Jonathan. I saw him leave for Whitby with as brave a face as I could, but I was sick with apprehension. The effort has, however, done him good. He was never so resolute, never so strong, never so full of volcanic energy, as at present. It is just as that dear, good Professor Van Helsing said: he is true grit, and he improves under strain that would kill a weaker nature. He came back full of life and hope and determination; we have got everything in order for tonight. I feel myself quite wild with excitement. I suppose one ought to pity anything so hunted as is the Count. That is just it: this Thing is not human – not even beast. To read Dr Seward's account of poor Lucy's death, and what followed, is enough to dry up the springs of pity in one's heart.

Later. – Lord Godalming and Mr Morris arrived earlier than we expected. Dr Seward was out on business and had taken Jonathan with him, so I had to see them. It was to me a painful meeting, for it brought back all poor dear Lucy's hopes of only a few months ago. Of course they had heard Lucy speak of me, and it seemed that Dr Van Helsing too, had been quite 'blowing my trumpet', as Mr Morris expressed it. Poor fellows, neither of them is aware that I know all about the proposals they made to Lucy. They did not quite know what to say or do, as they were ignorant of the amount of my knowledge; so they had to keep on neutral subjects. However, I thought the matter over, and came to the conclusion that the best thing I could do would be to post them in affairs right up to date. I knew from Dr Seward's diary that they had been at Lucy's death – her real death – and that I need not fear to betray any secret before the time. So I told them, as well as I could, that I had read all the papers and diaries, and that my husband and I, having typewritten them, had just finished putting them in order. I gave them each a copy to read in the library. When Lord Godalming got his and turned it over – it does make a pretty good pile – he said:

'Did you write all this, Mrs Harker?'

I nodded, and he went on:

'I don't quite see the drift of it; but you people are all so good and kind, and have been working so earnestly and so energetically, that all I can do is to accept your ideas blindfold and try to help you. I have had one lesson already in accepting facts that should make a man humble to

the last hour of his life. Besides, I know you loved my poor Lucy – '
Here he turned away and covered his face with his hands. I could hear
the tears in his voice. Mr Morris, with instinctive delicacy just laid a
hand for a moment on his shoulder, and then walked quietly out of the
room. I suppose there is something in woman's nature that makes a man
free to break down before her and express his feelings on the tender or
emotional side without feeling it derogatory to his manhood; for when
Lord Godalming found himself alone with me he sat down on the sofa
and gave way utterly and openly. I sat down beside him and took his
hand. I hope he didn't think it forward of me, and that if he ever thinks
of it afterwards he never will have such a thought. There I wrong him; I
know he never will – he is too true a gentleman. I said to him, for I could
see that his heart was breaking:

'I loved dear Lucy, and I know what she was to you, and what you
were to her. She and I were like sisters; and now she is gone, will you
not let me be like a sister to you in your trouble? I know what sorrows
you have had, though I cannot measure the depth of them. If sympathy
and pity can help in your affliction, won't you let me be of some little
service – for Lucy's sake?'

In an instant the poor dear fellow was overwhelmed with grief. It
seemed to me that all that he had of late been suffering in silence found
a vent at once. He grew quite hysterical, and raising his open hands,
beat his palms together in a perfect agony of grief. He stood up and
then sat down again, and the tears rained down his cheeks. I felt an
infinite pity for him, and opened my arms unthinkingly. With a sob he
laid his head on my shoulder, and cried like a wearied child, whilst he
shook with emotion.

We women have something of the mother in us that makes us rise
above smaller matters when the mother-spirit is invoked; I felt this big,
sorrowing man's head resting on me, as though it were that of the baby
that some day may lie on my bosom, and I stroked his hair as though he
were my own child. I never thought at the time how strange it all was.

After a little bit his sobs ceased and he raised himself with an apology,
though he made no disguise of his emotion. He told me that for days
and nights past – weary days and sleepless nights – he had been unable
to speak with anyone, as a man must speak in his time of sorrow. There
was no woman whose sympathy could be given to him, or with whom,
owing to the terrible circumstances with which his sorrow was surrounded, he could speak freely. 'I know now how I suffered,' he said, as
he dried his eyes, 'but I do not know even yet – and none other can ever
know – how much your sweet sympathy has been to me today. I shall

know better in time; and believe me that, though I am not ungrateful now, my gratitude will grow with my understanding. You will let me be like a brother, will you not, for all our lives – for dear Lucy's sake?'

'For dear Lucy's sake,' I said as we clasped hands. 'Ay and for your own sake,' he added, 'for if a man's esteem and gratitude are ever worth the winning, you have won mine today. If ever the future should bring to you a time when you need a man's help, believe me, you will not call in vain. God grant that no such time may ever come to you to break the sunshine of your life; but if it should ever come, promise me that you will let me know.' He was so earnest, and his sorrow was so fresh, that I felt it would comfort him, so I said: 'I promise.'

As I came along the corridor I saw Mr Morris looking out of a window. He turned as he heard my footsteps. 'How is Art?' he said. Then noticing my red eyes, he went on: 'Ah, I see you have been comforting him. Poor old fellow! he needs it. No one but a woman can help a man when he is in trouble of the heart; and he had no one to comfort him.'

He bore his own trouble so bravely that my heart bled for him. I saw the manuscript in his hand, and I knew that when he read it he would realise how much I knew; so I said to him:

'I wish I could comfort all who suffer from the heart. Will you let me be your friend, and will you come to me for comfort if you need it? You will know, later on, why I speak.' He saw that I was in earnest, and stooping, took my hand, and raising it to his lips, kissed it. It seemed but poor comfort to so brave and unselfish a soul, and impulsively I bent over and kissed him. The tears rose in his eyes, and there was a momentary choking in his throat; he said quite calmly:

'Little girl, you will never regret that true-hearted kindness, so long as ever you live!' Then he went into the study to his friend.

'Little girl!' – the very words he had used to Lucy, and oh, but he proved himself a friend!

Chapter 18

DR SEWARD'S DIARY

30 September. – I got home at five o'clock, and found that Godalming and Morris had not only arrived, but had already studied the transcript of the various diaries and letters which Harker and his wonderful wife had made and arranged. Harker had not yet returned from his visit to the carriers' men, of whom Dr Hennessey had written to me. Mrs Harker gave us a cup of tea, and I can honestly say that, for the first time since I have lived in it, this old house seemed like *home*. When we had finished, Mrs Harker said:

'Dr Seward, may I ask a favour? I want to see your patient, Mr Renfield. Do let me see him. What you have said of him in your diary interests me so much!' She looked so appealing and so pretty that I could not refuse her, and there was no possible reason why I should; so I took her with me. When I went into the room, I told the man that a lady would like to see him; to which he simply answered: 'Why?'

'She is going through the house, and wants to see everyone in it,' I answered. 'Oh, very well,' he said; 'let her come in, by all means; but just wait a minute till I tidy up the place.' His method of tidying was peculiar: he simply swallowed all the flies and spiders in the boxes before I could stop him. It was quite evident that he feared, or was jealous of, some interference. When he had got through his disgusting task, he said cheerfully: 'Let the lady come in,' and sat down on the edge of his bed with his head down, but with his eyelids raised so that he could see her as she entered. For a moment I thought that he might have some homicidal intent; I remembered how quiet he had been just before he attacked me in my own study, and I took care to stand where I could seize him at once if he attempted to make a spring at her. She came into the room with an easy gracefulness which would at once command the respect of any lunatic – for easiness is one of the qualities mad people most respect. She walked over to him, smiling pleasantly, and held out her hand.

'Good evening, Mr Renfield,' said she. 'You see, I know you, for Dr Seward has told me of you.' He made no immediate reply, but eyed her all over intently with a set frown on his face. This look gave way to one of wonder, which merged in doubt; then, to my intense astonishment, he said:

'You're not the girl the doctor wanted to marry, are you? You can't be, you know, for she's dead.' Mrs Harker smiled sweetly as she replied:

'Oh no! I have a husband of my own, to whom I was married before I ever saw Dr Seward, or he me. I am Mrs Harker.'

'Then what are you doing here?'

'My husband and I are staying on a visit with Dr Seward.'

'Then don't stay.'

'But why not?' I thought that this style of conversation might not be pleasant to Mrs Harker, any more than it was to me, so I joined in:

'How did you know I wanted to marry anyone?' His reply was simply contemptuous, given in a pause in which he turned his eyes from Mrs Harker to me, instantly turning them back again:

'What an asinine question!'

'I don't see that at all, Mr Renfield,' said Mrs Harker, at once championing me. He replied to her with as much courtesy and respect as he had shown contempt to me:

'You will, of course, understand, Mrs Harker, that when a man is loved and honoured as our host is, everything regarding him is of interest in our little community. Dr Seward is loved not only by his household and his friends, but even by his patients, who, being some of them hardly in mental equilibrium, are apt to distort causes and effects. Since I myself have been an inmate of a lunatic asylum, I cannot but notice that the sophistic tendencies of some of its inmates lean towards the errors of *non causæ* and *ignoratio elenchi*.' [162] I positively opened my eyes at this new development. Here was my own pet lunatic – the most pronounced of his type that I had ever met with – talking elemental philosophy, and with the manner of a polished gentleman. I wonder if it was Mrs Harker's presence which had touched some chord in his memory. If this new phase was spontaneous, or in any way due to her unconscious influence, she must have some rare gift or power.

We continued to talk for some time; and, seeing that he was seemingly quite reasonable, she ventured, looking at me questioningly as she began, to lead him to his favourite topic. I was again astonished, for he addressed himself to the question with the impartiality of the completest sanity; he even took himself as an example when he mentioned certain things.

'Why, I myself am an instance of a man who had a strange belief. Indeed, it was no wonder that my friends were alarmed, and insisted on my being put under control. I used to fancy that life was a positive and perpetual entity, and that by consuming a multitude of live things, no matter how low in the scale of creation, one might indefinitely prolong life. At times I held the belief so strongly that I actually tried to take human life. The doctor here will bear me out that on one occasion I tried to kill him for the purpose of strengthening my vital powers by the assimilation with my own body of his life through the medium of his blood – relying, of course, upon the Scriptural phrase, "For the blood is the life". Though, indeed, the vendor of a certain nostrum has vulgarised the truism to the very point of contempt. Isn't that true, doctor?' I nodded assent, for I was so amazed that I hardly knew what I ought to think or say; it was hard to imagine that I had seen him eat up his spiders and flies not five minutes before. Looking at my watch, I saw that I should go to the station to meet Van Helsing, so I told Mrs Harker that it was time to leave. She came at once, after saying pleasantly to Mr Renfield: 'Good-bye, and I hope I may see you often, under auspices pleasanter to yourself,' to which to my astonishment, he replied:

'Good-bye, my dear. I pray God I may never see your sweet face again. May He bless and keep you!'

When I went to the station to meet Van Helsing I left the boys behind me. Poor Art seemed more cheerful than he has been since Lucy first took ill, and Quincey is more like his own bright self than he has been for many a long day.

Van Helsing stepped from the carriage with the eager nimbleness of a boy. He saw me at once, and rushed up to me, saying:

'Ah, friend John, how goes all? Well? So! I have been busy, for I come here to stay if need be. All affairs are settled with me, and I have much to tell. Madam Mina is with you? Yes. And her so fine husband? And Arthur and my friend Quincey, they are with you, too? Good!'

As I drove to the house I told him of what had passed, and of how my own diary had come to be of some use through Mrs Harker's suggestion; at which the Professor interrupted me:

'Ah, that wonderful Madam Mina! She has man's brain – a brain that a man should have were he much gifted – and woman's heart. The good God fashioned her for a purpose, believe me, when He made that so good combination. Friend John, up to now fortune has made that woman of help to us; after tonight she must not have to do with this so terrible affair. It is not good that she run a risk so great. We men are determined – nay, are we not pledged? – to destroy this monster; but it is no part for a woman. Even if she be not harmed, her heart may fail her in so much and so many horrors; and hereafter she may suffer – both in waking, from her nerves, and in sleep, from her dreams. And, besides, she is a young woman and not so long married; there may be other things to think of some time, if not now. You tell me she has wrote all, then she must consult with us; but tomorrow she say good-bye to this work, and we go alone.' I agreed heartily with him, and then I told him what we had found in his absence: that the house which Dracula had bought was the very next one to my own. He was amazed, and a great concern seemed to come on him. 'Oh that we had known it before!' he said, 'for then we might have reached him in time to save poor Lucy. However, "the milk that is spilt cries not out afterwards", as you say. We shall not think of that, but go on our way to the end.'

Then he fell into a silence that lasted till we entered my own gateway. Before we went to prepare for dinner he said to Mrs Harker:

'I am told, Madam Mina, by my friend John that you and your husband have put up in exact order all things that have been, up to this moment.'

'Not up to this moment, Professor,' she said impulsively, 'but up to this morning.'

'But why not up to now? We have seen hitherto how good light all the little things have made. We have told our secrets, and yet no one who has told is the worse for it.'

Mrs Harker began to blush, and taking a paper from her pocket, she said:

'Dr Van Helsing, will you read this, and tell me if it must go in. It is my record of today. I too have seen the need of putting down at present everything, however trivial; but there is little in this except what is personal. Must it go in?' The Professor read it over gravely, and handed it back, saying:

'It need not go in if you do not wish it; but I pray that it may. It can but make your husband love you the more, and all us, your friends, more honour you – as well as more esteem and love.' She took it back with another blush and a bright smile.

And so now, up to this very hour, all the records we have are complete and in order. The Professor took away one copy to study after dinner, and before our meeting, which is fixed for nine o'clock. The rest of us have already read everything; so when we meet in the study we shall all be informed as to facts, and can arrange our plan of battle with this terrible and mysterious enemy.

Mina Harker's Journal

30 September. – When we met in Dr Seward's study two hours after dinner, which had been at six o'clock, we unconsciously formed a sort of board or committee. Professor Van Helsing took the head of the table, to which Dr Seward motioned him as he came into the room. He made me sit next to him on his right, and asked me to act as secretary; Jonathan sat next to me. Opposite us were Lord Godalming, Dr Seward, and Mr Morris – Lord Godalming being next the Professor, and Dr Seward in the centre. The Professor said:

'I may, I suppose, take it that we are all acquainted with the facts that are in these papers.' We all expressed assent, and he went on:

'Then it were, I think, good that I tell you something of the kind of enemy with which we have to deal. I shall then make known to you something of the history of this man, which has been ascertained for me. So we then can discuss how we shall act, and can take our measure according.

'There are such beings as vampires; some of us have evidence that they exist. Even had we not the proof of our own unhappy experience, the teachings and the records of the past give proof enough for sane peoples. I admit that at the first I was sceptic. Were it not that through long years I have trained myself to keep an open mind, I could not have believed until such time as that fact thunder on my ear. "See! see! I prove; I prove." Alas! Had I known at the first what now I know – nay, had I even guess at him – one so precious life had been spared to many of us who did love her. But that is gone; and we must so work, that other poor souls perish not, whilst we can save. The *nosferatu* do not die like the bee when he sting once. He is only stronger, and being stronger, have yet more power to work evil. This vampire which is amongst us is of himself so strong in person as twenty men; he is of cunning more than mortal, for his cunning be the growth of ages; he have still the aids of necromancy, which is, as his etymology imply, the divination by the dead, and all the dead that he can come nigh to are for him at command; he is brute, and more than brute; he is devil in callous, and the heart of him is not; he can, within limitations, appear at will when, and where, and in any of the forms that are to him; he can, within his range; direct the elements: the storm, the fog, the thunder; he can command all the meaner things: the rat and the owl and the bat – the moth, and the fox, and the wolf; he can grow and become small; and he can at times vanish and come unknown. How then are we to begin our strife to destroy him? How shall we find his where, and having found it how can we destroy? My friends, this is much; it is a terrible task that we undertake, and there may be consequence to make the brave shudder. For if we fail in this our fight he must surely win: and then where end we? Life is nothings! I heed him not. But to fail here, is not mere life or death. It is that we become as him; that we henceforward become foul things of the night like him – without heart or conscience, preying on the bodies and the souls of those we love best. To us for ever are the gates of heaven shut; for who shall open them to us again? We go on for all time abhorred by all; a blot on the face of God's sunshine; an arrow in the side of Him who died for man. But we are face to face with duty; and in such case must we shrink? For me, I say, no; but then I am old, and life, with his sunshine, his fair places, his song of birds, his music, and his love, lie far behind. You others are young. Some have seen sorrow; but there are fair days yet in store. What say you?'

Whilst he was speaking Jonathan had taken my hand. I feared, oh so much, that the appalling nature of our danger was overcoming him when I saw his hand stretch out; but it was life to me to feel its touch – so strong, so self-reliant, so resolute. A brave man's hand can speak for itself; it does not even need a woman's love to hear its music.

When the Professor had done speaking my husband looked in my eyes, and I in his; there was no need for speaking between us.

'I answer for Mina and myself,' he said.

'Count me in, Professor,' said Mr Quincey Morris, laconically as usual.

'I am with you,' said Lord Godalming, 'for Lucy's sake, if for no other reason.'

Dr Seward simply nodded. The Professor stood up, and after laying his golden crucifix on the table, held out his hand on either side. I took his right hand, and Lord Godalming his left; Jonathan held my right with his left and stretched across to Mr Morris. So as we all took hands our solemn compact was made. I felt my heart icy cold, but it did not even occur to me to draw back. We resumed our places, and Dr Van Helsing went on with a sort of cheerfulness which showed that the serious work had begun. It was to be taken as gravely, and in as businesslike a way, as any other transaction of life:

'Well, you know what we have to contend against; but we, too, are not without strength. We have on our side power of combination – a power denied to the vampire kind; we have resources of science; we are free to act and think; and the hours of the day and the night are ours equally. In fact, so far as our powers extend, they are unfettered and we are free to use them. We have self-devotion in a cause, and an end to achieve which is not a selfish one. These things are much.

'Now let us see how far the general powers arrayed against us are restrict, and how the individual cannot. In fine, let us consider the limitations of the vampire in general, and of this one in particular.

'All we have to go upon are traditions and superstitions. These do not at the first appear much, when the matter is one of life and death – nay, of more than either life or death. Yet must we be satisfied; in the first place because we have to be – no other means is at our control – and secondly, because, after all these things – tradition and superstition – are everything. Does not the belief in vampires rest for others – though not, alas! for us – on them? A year ago which of us would have received such a possibility, in the midst of our scientific, sceptical, matter-of-fact nineteenth century? We even scouted a belief that we saw justified under our very eyes. Take it, then, that the vampire, and the belief in his limitations and his cure, rest for the moment on the same base. For, let me tell you, he is known everywhere that men have been. In old Greece, in old Rome; he flourish in Germany all over, in France, in India, even in the Chersonese;[163] and in China, so far from us in all ways, there even is he, and the peoples fear him at this day. He have follow the wake of the berserker Icelander, the devil-begotten Hun, the Slav, the Saxon, the Magyar. So far, then, we have all we may act upon; and let me tell you that very much of the beliefs are justified by what we have seen in our own so unhappy experience. The vampire live on, and cannot die by mere passing of the time; he can flourish when that he can fatten on the blood of the living. Even more, we have seen amongst us that he can even grow younger, that his vital faculties grow strenuous, and seem as though they refresh themselves when his special pabulum is plenty. But he cannot flourish without this diet; he eat not as others. Even friend Jonathan, who lived with him for weeks, did never see him to eat, never! He throws no shadow; he make in the mirror no reflect, as again Jonathan observe. He has the strength of many in his hand – witness again Jonathan when he shut the door against the wolves, and when he help him from the diligence too. He can transform himself to wolf, as we gather from the ship arrival in Whitby, when he tear open the dog; he can be as bat, as Madam Mina saw him on the window at Whitby, and as friend John saw him fly from this so near house, and as my friend Quincey saw him at the window of Miss Lucy. He can come in mist which he create – that noble ship's captain proved him of this; but, from what we know, the distance he can make this mist is limited, and it can only be round himself. He come on moonlight rays as elemental dust – as again Jonathan saw those sisters in the castle of Dracula. He become so small – we ourselves saw Miss Lucy, ere she was at peace, slip through a hair-breadth space at the tomb door. He can, when once he find his way, come out from anything or into anything, no matter how close it be bound or even fused up with fire – solder you call it. He can see in the dark – no small power this, in a world which is one half shut from the light. Ah, but hear me through. He can do all these things, yet he is not free. Nay, he is even more prisoner than the slave of the galley, than the madman in his cell. He cannot go where he lists; he who is not of nature has yet to obey some of nature's laws – why we know not. He may not enter anywhere at the first, unless there be someone of the household who bid him to come; though afterwards he can come as he please. His power ceases, as does that of all evil things, at the coming of the day. Only at certain times can he have limited freedom. If he be not at the place whither he is bound, he can only change himself at noon or at exact sunrise or sunset. These things are we told, and in this record of ours we have proof by inference. Thus, whereas he can do as he will within his limit, when he have his earth-home, his coffin-home, his hell-home, the place unhallowed, as we saw when he went to the grave of the suicide at Whitby; still at other time he can only change when the time come. It is said, too, that he can only pass running water at the slack or the flood of the tide. Then there are things which so afflict him that he has no power, as the garlic that we know of, and as for things sacred, as this symbol, my crucifix, that was amongst us even now when we resolve, to them he is nothing, but in their presence he take his place far off and silent with respect. There are others, too, which I shall tell you of, lest in our seeking we may need them. The branch of wild rose on his coffin keep him that he move not from it; a sacred bullet fired into the coffin kill him so that he be true dead; and as for the stake through him, we know already of its peace; or the cut off head that giveth rest. We have seen it with our eyes.

'Thus when we find the habitation of this man-that-was, we can confine him to his coffin and destroy him, if we obey what we know. But he is clever. I have asked my friend Arminius,[164] of Buda-Pesth University, to make his record; and, from all the means that are, he tell me of what he has been. He must, indeed, have been that Voivode Dracula who won his name against the Turk, over the great river on the very frontier of Turkey-land. If it be so, then was he no common man; for in that time, and for centuries after, he was spoken of as the cleverest and the most cunning, as well as the bravest of the sons of the "land beyond the forest". That mighty brain and that iron resolution went with him to his grave, and are even now arrayed against us. The Draculas were, says Arminius, a great and noble race, though now and again were scions who were held by their coevals to have had dealings with the Evil One. They learned his secrets in the Scholomance,[165] amongst the mountains over Lake Hermanstadt,[166] where the devil claims the tenth scholar as his due. In the records are such words as "stregoica" – witch, "ordog", and "pokol" – Satan and hell; and in one manuscript this very Dracula is spoken of as "wampyr", which we all understand too well. There have been from the loins of this very one great men and good women, and their graves make sacred the earth where alone this foulness can dwell. For it is not the least of its terrors that this evil thing is rooted deep in all good; in soil barren of holy memories it cannot rest.'

Whilst they were talking Mr Morris was looking steadily at the window, and he now got up quietly, and went out of the room. There was a little pause, and then the Professor went on:

'And now we must settle what we do. We have here much data, and we must proceed to lay out our campaign. We know from the inquiry of

Jonathan that from the castle to Whitby came fifty boxes of earth, all of which were delivered at Carfax; we also know that at least some of these boxes have been removed. It seems to me, that our first step should be to ascertain whether all the rest remain in the house beyond that wall where we look today; or whether any more have been removed. If the latter, we must trace – '

Here we were interrupted in a very startling way. Outside the house came the sound of a pistol-shot; the glass of the window was shattered with a bullet, which, ricochetting from the top of the embrasure, struck the far wall of the room. I am afraid I am at heart a coward, for I shrieked out. The men all jumped to their feet; Lord Godalming flew over to the window and threw up the sash. As he did so we heard Mr Morris's voice without: 'Sorry! I fear I have alarmed you. I shall come in and tell you about it.'

A minute later he came in and said: 'It was an idiotic thing of me to do, and I ask your pardon, Mrs Harker, most sincerely; I fear I must have frightened you terribly. But the fact is that whilst the Professor was talking there came a big bat and sat on the window-sill. I have got such a horror of the damned brutes from recent events that I cannot stand them, and I went out to have a shot, as I have been doing of late of evenings whenever I have seen one. You used to laugh at me for it then, Art.'

'Did you hit it?' asked Dr Van Helsing

'I don't know; I fancy not, for it flew away into the wood.'

Without saying any more he took his seat, and the Professor began to resume his statement: 'We must trace each of these boxes; and when we are ready we must either capture or kill this monster in his lair; or we must so to speak, sterilise the earth, so that no more he can seek safety in it. Thus in the end we may find him in his form of man between the hours of noon and sunset, and so engage with him when he is at his most weak.

'And now for you, Madam Mina, this night is the end until all be well. You are too precious to us to have such risk. When we part tonight, you no more must question. We shall tell you all in good time. We are men, and are able to bear; but you must be our star and our hope, and we shall act all the more free that you are not in the danger, such as we are.'

All the men, even Jonathan, seemed relieved; but it did not seem to me good that they should brave danger and, perhaps, lessen their safety – strength being the best safety – through care of me; but their minds were made up, and, though it was a bitter pill for me to swallow, I could say nothing, save to accept their chivalrous care of me.

Mr Morris resumed the discussion: 'As there is no time to lose, I vote we have a look at his house right now. Time is everything with him; and swift action on our part may save another victim.'

I own that my heart began to fail me when the time for action came so close, but I did not say anything, for I had a greater fear that if I appeared as a drag or a hindrance to their work they might even leave me out of their counsels altogether. They have now gone off to Carfax, with means to get into the house.

Manlike, they have told me to go to bed and sleep; as if a woman can sleep when those she loves are in danger! I shall lie down and pretend to sleep, lest Jonathan have added anxiety about me when he returns.

DR SEWARD'S DIARY

1 October, 4 a.m. – Just as we were about to leave the house an urgent message was brought to me from Renfield to know if I would see him at once, as he had something of the utmost importance to say to me. I told the messenger to say that I would attend to his wishes in the morning; I was busy just at the moment. The attendant added:

'He seems very importunate, sir. I have never seen him so eager. I don't know but what, if you don't see him soon, he will have one of his violent fits.' I knew the man would not have said this without some cause, so I said: 'All right; I'll go now;' and I asked the others to wait a few minutes for me, as I had to go and see my patient.

'Take me with you, friend John,' said the Professor. 'His case in your diary interested me much, and it had bearing, too, now and again on *our* case. I should much like to see him and especially when his mind is disturbed.'

'May I come also?' asked Lord Godalming.

'Me too?' said Quincey Morris. I nodded, and we all went down the passage together.

We found him in a state of considerable excitement, but far more rational in his speech and manner than I had ever seen him. There was an unusual understanding of himself, which was unlike anything I had ever met with in a lunatic; and he took it for granted that his reasons would prevail with others entirely sane. We all four went into the room, but none of the others at first said anything. His request was that I would at once release him from the asylum and send him home. This he backed up with arguments regarding his complete recovery, and adduced his own existing sanity. 'I appeal to your friends,' he said; 'they will, perhaps, not mind sitting in judgment on my case. By the way, you have not introduced me.' I was so much astonished, that the oddness of introducing a madman in an asylum did not strike me at the moment; and, besides, there was a certain dignity in the man's manner, so much of the habit of equality, that I at once made the introduction: 'Lord Godalming; Professor Van Helsing; Mr Quincey Morris, of Texas; Mr Renfield.' He shook hands with each of them, saying in turn:

'Lord Godalming, I had the honour of seconding your father at the Windham; I grieve to know, by your holding the title, that he is no more. He was a man loved and honoured by all who knew him; and in his youth was, I have heard, the inventor of a burnt rum punch, much patronised on Derby night.[167] Mr Morris, you should be proud of your great state. Its reception into the Union[168] was a precedent which may have far-reaching effects hereafter, when the Pole and the Tropics[169] may hold allegiance to the Stars and Stripes. The power of Treaty may yet prove a vast engine of enlargement, when the Monroe doctrine[170] takes its true place as a political fable. What shall any man say of his pleasure at meeting Van Helsing? Sir, I make no apology for dropping all forms of conventional prefix. When an individual has revolutionised therapeutics by his discovery of the continuous evolution of brain-matter, conventional forms are unfitting, since they would seem to limit him to one of a class. You gentlemen, who by nationality, by heredity, or by the possession of natural gifts, are fitted to hold your respective places in the moving world, I take to witness that I am as sane as at least the majority of men who are in full possession of their liberties. And I am sure that you, Dr Seward, humanitarian and medico-jurist as well as scientist, will deem it a moral duty to deal with me as one to be considered as under exceptional circumstances.' He made this last appeal with a courtly air of conviction which was not without its own charm.

I think we were all staggered. For my own part, I was under the conviction, despite my knowledge of the man's character and history, that his reason had been restored; and I felt under a strong impulse to tell him that I was satisfied as to his sanity, and would see about the necessary formalities for his release in the morning. I thought it better to wait, however, before making so grave a statement, for of old I knew the sudden changes to which this particular patient was liable. So I contented myself with making a general statement that he appeared to be improving very rapidly; that I would have a longer chat with him in the morning, and would then see what I could do in the direction of meeting his wishes. This did not at all satisfy him, for he said quickly:

'But I fear, Dr Seward, that you hardly apprehend my wish. I desire to go at once – here – now – this very hour – this very moment, if I may. Time presses, and in our implied agreement with the old scytheman it is of the essence of the contract. I am sure it is only necessary to put before so admirable a practitioner as Dr Seward so simple, yet so momentous a wish, to ensure its fulfilment.' He looked at me keenly, and seeing the negative in my face, turned to the others, and scrutinised them closely. Not meeting any sufficient response, he went on:

'Is it possible that I have erred in my supposition?'

'You have,' I said frankly, but at the same time, as I felt, brutally. There was a considerable pause, and then he said slowly:

'Then I suppose I must only shift my ground of request. Let me ask for this concession – boon, privilege, what you will. I am content to implore in such a case, not on personal grounds, but for the sake of others. I am not at liberty to give you the whole of my reasons; but you may, I assure you, take it from me that they are good ones, sound and unselfish, and springing from the highest sense of duty. Could you look, sir, into my heart, you would approve to the full the sentiments which animate me. Nay, more, you would count me amongst the best and truest of your friends.' Again he looked at us all keenly. I had a growing conviction that this sudden change of his entire intellectual method was but yet another form or phase of his madness, and so determined to let him go on a little longer, knowing from experience that he would, like all lunatics, give himself away in the end. Van Helsing was gazing at him with a look of the utmost intensity, his bushy eyebrows almost meeting with the fixed concentration of his look. He said to Renfield in a tone which did not surprise me at the time, but only when I thought of it afterwards – for it was as of one addressing an equal:

'Can you not tell frankly your real reason for wishing to be free tonight? I will undertake that if you will satisfy even me – a stranger, without prejudice, and with the habit of keeping an open mind – Dr Seward will give you, at his own risk and on his own responsibility, the privilege you seek.' He shook his head sadly, and with a look of poignant regret on his face. The Professor went on:

'Come, sir, bethink yourself. You claim the privilege of reason in the highest degree, since you seek to impress us with your complete reasonableness. You do this, whose sanity we have reason to doubt, since you are not yet released from medical treatment for this very defect. If you will not help us in our effort to choose the wisest course, how can we perform the duty which you yourself put upon us? Be wise, and help us; and if we can we shall aid you to achieve your wish.' He still shook his head as he said:

'Dr Van Helsing, I have nothing to say. Your argument is complete, and if I were free to speak I should not hesitate a moment; but I am not my own master in the matter. I can only ask you to trust me. If I am refused, the responsibility does not rest with me.' I thought it was now time to end the scene, which was becoming too comically grave, so I went towards the door, simply saying:

'Come, my friends, we have work to do. Good night.'

As, however, I got near the door, a new change came over the patient. He moved towards me so quickly that for the moment I feared that he was about to make another homicidal attack. My fears, however, were groundless, for he held up his two hands imploringly, and made his petition in a moving manner. As he saw that the very excess of his emotion was militating against him, by restoring us more to our old relations, he became still more demonstrative. I glanced at Van Helsing, and saw my conviction reflected in his eyes; so I became a little more fixed in my manner, if not more stern, and motioned to him that his efforts were unavailing. I had previously seen something of the same constantly growing excitement in him when he had to make some request of which at the time he had thought much, such, for instance, as when he wanted a cat; and I was prepared to see the collapse into the same sullen acquiescence on this occasion. My expectation was not realised, for, when he found that his appeal would not be successful, he got into quite a frantic condition. He threw himself on his knees, and held up his hands, wringing them in plaintive supplication, and poured forth a torrent of entreaty, with the tears rolling down his cheeks and his whole face and form expressive of the deepest emotion:

'Let me entreat you, Dr Seward, oh, let me implore you, to let me out of this house at once. Send me away how you will and where you will, send keepers with me with whips and chains; let them take me in a strait-waistcoat, manacled and leg-ironed even to a gaol; but let me go out of this. You don't know what you do by keeping me here. I am speaking from the depths of my heart – of my very soul. You don't know whom you wrong, or how; and I may not tell. Woe is me! may not tell. By all you hold sacred – by all you hold dear – by your love that is lost – by your hope that lives – for the sake of the Almighty, take me out of this and save my soul from guilt! Can't you hear me, man? Can't you understand? Will you never learn? Don't you know that I am sane and earnest now; that I am no lunatic in a mad fit, but a sane man fighting for his soul? Oh, hear me! hear me! Let me go! let me go! let me go!'

I thought that the longer this went on the wilder he would get, and so would bring on a fit; so I took him by the hand and raised him up.

'Come,' I said sternly, 'no more of this; we have had quite enough already. Get to your bed and try to behave more discreetly.'

He suddenly stopped and looked at me intently for several moments. Then without a word he rose, and moving over, sat down on the side of the bed. The collapse had come, as on former occasions, just as I had expected.

When I was leaving the room, last of our party, he said to me in a quiet, well-bred voice:

'You will, I trust, Dr Seward, do me the justice to bear in mind, later on, that I did what I could to convince you tonight.'

Chapter 19

JONATHAN HARKER'S JOURNAL

1 October, 5 a.m. – I went with the party to the search with an easy mind, for I think I never saw Mina so absolutely strong and well. I am so glad that she consented to hold back and let us men do the work. Somehow, it was a dread to me that she was in this fearful business at all, but now that her work is done, and that it is due to her energy and brains and foresight that the whole story is put together in such a way that every point tells, she may well feel that her part is finished, and that she can henceforth leave the rest to us. We were, I think, all a little upset by the scene with Mr Renfield. When we came away from his room we were silent till we got back to the study. Then Mr Morris said to Dr Seward:

'Say, Jack, if that man wasn't attempting a bluff, he is about the sanest lunatic I ever saw. I'm not sure but I believe that he had some serious purpose, and if he had it was pretty rough on him not to get a chance.' Lord Godalming and I were silent, but Dr Van Helsing added:

'Friend John, you know more of lunatics than I do, and I'm glad of it, for I fear that if it had been to me to decide I would before that last hysterical outburst have given him free. But we live and learn, and in our present task we must take no chance, as my friend Quincey would say. All is best as they are.' Dr Seward seemed to answer them both in a dreamy kind of way:

'I don't know but that I agree with you. If that man had been an ordinary lunatic I would have taken my chance of trusting him; but he seems so mixed up with the Count in an indexy kind of way that I am afraid of doing anything wrong by helping his fads. I can't forget how he prayed with almost equal fervour for a cat, and then tried to tear my throat out with his teeth. Besides, he called the Count "lord and master", and he may want to get out to help him in some diabolical way.

That horrid thing has the wolves and the rats and his own kind to help him, so I suppose he isn't above trying to use a respectable lunatic. He certainly did seem earnest, though. I only hope we have done what is best. These things, in conjunction with the work we have in hand, help to unnerve a man.'

The Professor stepped over, and laying a hand on his shoulder, said in his grave, kindly way: 'Friend John, have no fear. We are trying to do our duty in a very sad and terrible case; we can only do as we deem best. What else have we to hope for, except the pity of the good God?'

Lord Godalming had slipped away for a few minutes, but he now returned. He held up a little silver whistle as he remarked: 'That old place may be full of rats, and if so, I've got an antidote on call.' Having passed the wall, we took our way to the house, taking care to keep in the shadows of the trees on the lawn when the moonlight shone out. When we got to the porch the Professor opened his bag and took out a lot of things, which he laid on the step, sorting them into four little groups, evidently one for each. Then he spoke:

'My friends, we are going into a terrible danger, and we need arms of many kinds. Our enemy is not merely spiritual. Remember that he has the strength of twenty men, and that, though our necks or our windpipes are of the common kind – and therefore breakable or crushable – his is not amenable to mere strength. A stronger man, or a body of men more strong in all than him, can at certain times hold him; but yet they cannot hurt him as we can be hurt by him. We must, therefore, guard ourselves from his touch. Keep this near your heart' – as he spoke he lifted a little silver crucifix and held it out to me, I being nearest to him – 'put these flowers round your neck' – here he handed to me a wreath of withered garlic blossoms – 'for other enemies more mundane, this revolver and this knife; and for aid in all, these so small electric lamps, which you can fasten to your breast; and for all, and above all at the last, this, which we must not desecrate needless.' This was a portion of sacred wafer, which he put in an envelope and handed to me. Each of the others was similarly equipped. 'Now,' he said, 'friend John, where are the skeleton keys? If so that we can open the door, we need not break house by the window, as before at Miss Lucy's.'

Dr Seward tried one or two skeleton keys, his mechanical dexterity as a surgeon standing him in good stead. Presently he got one to suit; after a little play back and forward the bolt yielded, and, with a rusty clang, shot back. We pressed on the door, the rusty hinges creaked, and it slowly opened. It was startlingly like the image conveyed to me in Dr Seward's diary of the opening of Miss Westenra's tomb; I fancy that the same idea seemed to strike the others, for with one accord they shrank back. The Professor was the first to move forward, and stepped into the open door.

'*In manus tuas, Domine*,'[171] he said, crossing himself as he passed over the threshold. We closed the door behind us, lest when we should have lit our lamps we might possibly attract attention from the road. The Professor carefully tried the lock, in case we might not be able to open it from within should we be in a hurry to make our exit. Then we all lit our lamps and proceeded on our search.

The light from the tiny lamps fell in all sorts of odd forms, as the rays crossed each other, or the opacity of our bodies threw great shadows. I could not for my life get away from the feeling that there was someone else amongst us. I suppose it was the recollection, so powerfully brought home to me by the grim surroundings, of that terrible experience in Transylvania. I think the feeling was common to us all, for I noticed that the others kept looking over their shoulders at every sound and every new shadow, just as I felt myself doing.

The whole place was thick with dust. The floor was seemingly inches deep, except where there were recent footsteps, in which on holding down my lamp I could see marks of hobnails where the dust was caked. The walls were fluffy and heavy with dust, and in the corners were masses of spiders' webs, whereon the dust had gathered till they looked like old tattered rags as the weight had torn them partly down. On a table in the hall was a great bunch of keys, with a time-yellowed label on each. They had been used several times, for on the table were several similar rents in the blanket of dust, like that exposed when the Professor lifted the keys. He turned to me and said:

'You know this place, Jonathan. You have copied maps of it, and you know at least more than we do. Which is the way to the chapel?' I had an idea of its direction, though on my former visit I had not been able to get admission to it, so I led the way, and after a few wrong turnings found myself opposite a low, arched oaken door, ribbed with iron bands. 'This is the spot,' said the Professor, as he turned his lamp on a small map of the house, copied from the file of my original correspondence regarding the purchase. With a little trouble we found the key on the bunch and opened the door. We were prepared for some unpleasantness, for as we were opening the door a faint, malodorous air seemed to exhale through the gaps, but none of us ever expected such an odour as we encountered. None of the others had met the Count at all at close quarters, and when I had seen him he was either in the fasting stage of his existence in his rooms or, when he was glutted with fresh blood, in a ruined building open to the air; but here the place was small and close, and the long disuse had made the air stagnant and foul. There was an earthy smell, as of some dry miasma, which came through the fouler air. But as to the odour itself, how shall I describe it? It was not alone that it was composed of all the ills of mortality and with the pungent, acrid smell of blood, but it seemed as though corruption had become itself corrupt. Faugh! it sickens me to think of it. Every breath exhaled by that monster seemed to have clung to the place and intensified its loathsomeness.

Under ordinary circumstances such a stench would have brought our enterprise to an end; but this was no ordinary case and the high and terrible purpose in which we were involved gave us a strength which rose above merely physical considerations. After the involuntary shrinking consequent on the first nauseous whiff, we one and all set about our work as though that loathsome place were a garden of roses.

We made an accurate examination of the place, the Professor saying as we began: 'The first thing is to see how many of the boxes are left; we must then examine every hole and corner and cranny, and see if we cannot get some clue as to what has become of the rest.' A glance was sufficient to show how many remained, for the great earth chests were bulky, and there was no mistaking them.

There were only twenty-nine left out of the fifty! Once I got a fright, for, seeing Lord Godalming suddenly turn and look out of the vaulted door into the dark passage beyond, I looked too, and for an instant my heart stood still. Somewhere, looking out from the shadow, I seemed to see the high lights of the Count's evil face, the ridge of the nose, the red eyes, the red lips, the awful pallor. It was only for a moment, for as Lord Godalming said, 'I thought I saw a face, but it was only the shadows,' and resumed his inquiry, I turned my lamp in the direction, and stepped into the passage. There was no sign of anyone; and as there were no corners, no doors, no aperture of any kind, but only the solid walls of the passage, there could be no hiding-place even for *him*. I took it that fear had helped imagination, and said nothing.

A few minutes later I saw Morris step suddenly back from a corner, which he was examining. We all followed his movements with our eyes, for undoubtedly some nervousness was growing on us, and we saw a whole mass of phosphorescence, which twinkled like stars. We all instinctively drew back. The whole place was becoming alive with rats.

For a moment or two we stood appalled, all save Lord Godalming, who was seemingly prepared for such an emergency. Rushing over to the great iron-bound oaken door, which Dr Seward had described from the outside, and which I had seen myself, he turned the key in the lock, drew the huge bolts, and swung the door open. Then, taking his little silver whistle from his pocket, he blew a low, shrill call. It was answered from behind Dr Seward's house by the yelping of dogs, and after about a minute three terriers came dashing round the corner of the house. Unconsciously we had all moved towards the door, and as we moved I noticed that the dust had been much disturbed: the boxes which had been taken out had been brought this way. But even in the minute that had elapsed the number of the rats had vastly increased. They seemed to swarm over the place all at once, till the lamplight, shining on their moving dark bodies and glittering, baleful eyes, made the place look like a bank of earth set with fireflies. The dogs dashed on, but at the threshold suddenly stopped and snarled, and then simultaneously lifting their noses, began to howl in most lugubrious fashion. The rats were multiplying in thousands, and we moved out.

Lord Godalming lifted one of the dogs, and carrying him in, placed him on the floor. The instant his feet touched the ground he seemed to recover his courage, and rushed at his natural enemies. They fled before him so fast that, before he had shaken the life out of a score, the other dogs, who had by now been lifted in in the same manner, had but small prey ere the whole mass had vanished.

With their going it seemed as if some evil presence had departed, for the dogs frisked about and barked merrily as they made sudden darts at their prostrate foes, and turned them over and over and tossed them in the air with vicious shakes. We all seemed to find our spirits rise. Whether it was the purifying of the deadly atmosphere by the opening of the chapel door, or the relief which we experienced by finding ourselves in the open I know not; but most certainly the shadow of dread seemed to slip from us like a robe, and the occasion of our coming lost something of its grim significance, though we did not slacken a whit in our resolution. We closed the outer door and barred and locked it, and bringing the dogs with us, began our search of the house. We found nothing throughout except dust in extraordinary proportions, and all untouched save for my own footsteps when I had made my first visit. Never once did the dogs exhibit any symptom of uneasiness, and even when we returned to the chapel they frisked about as though they had been rabbit-hunting in a summer wood.

The morning was quickening in the east when we emerged from the front. Dr Van Helsing had taken the key of the hall-door from the bunch, and locked the door in orthodox fashion, putting the key into his pocket when he had done.

'So far,' he said, 'our night has been eminently successful. No harm has come to us such as I feared might be, and yet we have ascertained how many boxes are missing. More than all do I rejoice that this, our first – and perhaps our most difficult and dangerous – step has been accomplished without the bringing thereinto our most sweet Madam Mina or troubling her waking or sleeping thoughts with sights and sounds and smells of horror which she might never forget. One lesson, too, we have learned, if it be allowable to argue *a particulari:* that the brute beasts which are to the Count's command are yet themselves not amenable to his spiritual power; for look, these rats that would come to his call, just as from his castle top he summon the wolves to your going and to that poor mother's cry, though they come to him, they run pell-mell from the so little dogs of my friend Arthur. We have other matters before us, other dangers, other fears; and that monster – he has not used his power over the brute world for the only or the last time tonight. So be it that he has gone elsewhere. Good! It has given us opportunity to cry "check" in some way in this chess game, which we play for the stake of human souls. And now let us go home. The dawn is close at hand, and we have reason to be content with our first night's work. It may be ordained that we have many nights and days to follow, if full of peril; but we must go on, and from no danger shall we shrink.' The house was silent when we got back, save for some poor creature who was screaming away in one of the distant wards, and a low, moaning sound from Renfield's room. The poor wretch was doubtless torturing himself, after the manner of the insane, with needless thoughts of pain.

I came tiptoe into our own room, and found Mina asleep, breathing so softly that I had to put my ear down to hear it. She looks paler than usual. I hope the meeting tonight has not upset her. I am truly thankful that she is to be left out of our future work, and even of our deliberations. It is too great a strain for a woman to bear. I did not think so at first, but I know better now. Therefore I am glad that it is settled. There may be things which would frighten her to hear; and yet to conceal them from her might be worse than to tell her if once she suspected that there was any concealment. Henceforth our work is to be a sealed book to her, till at least such time as we can tell her that all is finished, and the earth free from a monster of the nether world. I daresay it will be difficult to begin to keep silence after such confidence as ours; but I must be resolute and tomorrow I shall keep dark over tonight's doings, and shall refuse to speak of anything that has happened. I rest on the sofa, so as not to disturb her.

1 October, later. – I suppose it was natural that we should have all overslept ourselves, for the day was a busy one, and the night had no rest at all. Even Mina must have felt its exhaustion, for though I slept till the sun was high, I was awake before her, and had to call two or three times before she awoke. Indeed, she was so sound asleep that for a few seconds she did not recognise me, but looked at me with a sort of blank terror, as one looks who has been waked out of a bad dream. She complained a little of being tired, and I let her rest till later in the day. We now know of twenty-one boxes having been removed, and if it be that several were taken in any of these removals we may be able to trace them all. Such will, of course, immensely simplify our labour, and the sooner the matter is attended to the better. I shall look up Thomas Snelling today.

Dr Seward's Diary

1 October. – It was towards noon when I was awakened by the Professor walking into my room. He was more jolly and cheerful than usual, and it is quite evident that last night's work has helped to take some of the brooding weight off his mind. After going over the adventure of the night he suddenly said:

'Your patient interests me much. May it be that with you I visit him this morning? Or if that you are too occupy, I can go alone if it may be. It is a new experience to me to find a lunatic who talk philosophy, and reason so sound.' I had some work to do which pressed, so I told him that if he would go alone I would be glad, as then I should not have to keep him waiting; so I called an attendant and gave him the necessary instructions. Before the Professor left the room I cautioned him against getting any false impression from my patient. 'But,' he answered, 'I want him to talk of himself and of his delusion as to consuming live things. He said to Madam Mina, as I see in your diary of yesterday, that he had once had such a belief. Why do you smile, friend John?'

'Excuse me,' I said, 'but the answer is here.' I laid my hand on the typewritten matter. 'When our sane and learned lunatic made that very statement of how he *used* to consume life, his mouth was actually nauseous with the flies and spiders which he had eaten just before Mrs Harker entered the room.' Van Helsing smiled in turn. 'Good!' he said. 'Your memory is true, friend John. I should have remembered. And yet it is this very obliquity of thought and memory which makes mental disease such a fascinating study. Perhaps I may gain more knowledge out of the folly of this madman than I shall from the teaching of the most wise. Who knows?' I went on with my work, and before long was through that in hand. It seemed that the time had been very short indeed, but there was Van Helsing back in the study. 'Do I interrupt?' he asked politely as he stood at the door.

'Not at all,' I answered. 'Come in. My work is finished, and I am free. I can go with you now, if you like.'

'It is needless; I have seen him!'

'Well?'

'I fear that he does not appraise me at much. Our interview was short. When I entered the room he was sitting on a stool in the centre, with his elbows on his knees, and his face was the picture of sullen discontent. I spoke to him as cheerfully as I could, and with such a measure of respect as I could assume. He made no reply whatever. 'Don't you know me?' I asked. His answer was not reassuring: 'I know you well enough; you are the old fool Van Helsing. I wish you would take yourself and your idiotic brain theories somewhere else. Damn all thickheaded Dutchmen!' Not a word more would he say, but sat in his implacable sullenness as indifferent to me as though I had not been in the room at all. Thus departed for this time my chance of much learning from this so clever lunatic; so I shall go, if I may, and cheer myself with a few happy words with that sweet soul Madam Mina. Friend John, it does rejoice me unspeakable that she is no more to be pained, no more to be worried, with our terrible things. Though we shall much miss her help, it is better so.'

'I agree with you with all my heart,' I answered earnestly, for I did not want him to weaken in this matter. 'Mrs Harker is better out of it. Things are quite bad enough for us, all men of the world, and who have been in many tight places in our time; but it is no place for a woman, and if she had remained in touch with the affair, it would in time infallibly have wrecked her.'

So Van Helsing has gone to confer with Mrs Harker and Harker; Quincey and Art are both out following up the clues as to the earth-boxes. I shall finish my round of work, and we shall meet tonight.

Mina Harker's Journal

1 October. – It is strange to me to be kept in the dark as I am today; after Jonathan's full confidence for so many years, to see him manifestly avoid certain matters, and those the most vital of all. This morning I slept late after the fatigues of yesterday, and though Jonathan was late too, he was the earlier. He spoke to me before he went out, never more sweetly or tenderly, but he never mentioned a word of what had happened in the visit to the Count's house. And yet he must have known how terribly anxious I was. Poor dear fellow! I suppose it must have distressed him even more than it did me. They all agreed that it was best that I should not be drawn further into this awful work, and I acquiesced. But to think that he keeps anything from me! And now I am crying like a silly fool, when I *know* it comes from my husband's great love and from the good, good wishes of those other strong men . . .

That has done me good. Well, some day Jonathan will tell me all; and lest it should ever be that he should think for a moment that I kept anything from him, I still keep my journal as usual. Then if he has doubted of my trust I shall show it to him, with every thought of my heart put down for his dear eyes to read. I feel strangely sad and low-spirited today. I suppose it is the reaction from the terrible excitement.

Last night I went to bed when the men had gone, simply because they told me to. I didn't feel sleepy, and I did feel full of devouring anxiety. I kept thinking over everything that has been ever since Jonathan came to see me in London, and it all seems like a horrible tragedy, with fate pressing on relentlessly to some destined end. Everything that one does seems, no matter how right it may be, to bring on the very thing which is most to be deplored. If I hadn't gone to Whitby, perhaps poor dear Lucy would be with us now. She hadn't taken to visiting the churchyard till I came, and if she hadn't come there in the daytime with me she wouldn't have walked there in her sleep; and if she hadn't gone there at night and asleep, that monster couldn't have destroyed her as he did. Oh, why did I ever go to Whitby? There now, crying again! I wonder what has come over me today. I must hide it from Jonathan, for if he knew that I had been crying twice in one morning – I, who never cried on my own account, and whom he has never caused to shed a tear – the dear fellow would fret his heart out. I shall put a bold face on, and if I do feel weepy, he shall never see it. I suppose it is one of the lessons that we poor women have to learn . . .

I can't quite remember how I fell asleep last night. I remember hearing the sudden barking of the dogs and a lot of queer sounds, like praying on a very tumultuous scale, from Mr Renfield's room, which is somewhere under this. And then there was silence over everything, silence so profound that it startled me, and I got up and looked out of the window. All was dark and silent, the black shadows thrown by the moonlight seeming full of a silent mystery of their own. Not a thing seemed to be stirring, but all to be grim and fixed as death or fate; so that a thin streak of white mist, that crept with almost imperceptible slowness across the grass towards the house, seemed to have a sentience and a vitality of its own. I think that the digression of my thoughts must have done me good, for when I got back to bed I found a lethargy creeping over me. I lay a while, but could not quite sleep, so I got out and looked

out of the window again. The mist was spreading, and was now close up
to the house, so that I could see it lying thick against the wall, as though
it were stealing up to the windows. The poor man was more loud than
ever, and though I could not distinguish a word he said, I could in some
way recognise in his tones some passionate entreaty on his part. Then
there was the sound of a struggle, and I knew that the attendants were
dealing with him. I was so frightened that I crept into bed, and pulled the
clothes over my head, putting my fingers in my ears. I was not then a bit
sleepy, at least so I thought; but I must have fallen asleep, for, except
dreams, I do not remember anything until the morning, when Jonathan
woke me. I think that it took me an effort and a little time to realise
where I was, and that it was Jonathan who was bending over me. My
dream was very peculiar, and was almost typical of the way that waking
thoughts become merged in, or continued in, dreams.

I thought that I was asleep, and waiting for Jonathan to come back. I
was very anxious about him, and I was powerless to act; my feet, and my
hands, and my brain were weighted, so that nothing could proceed at the
usual pace. And so I slept uneasily and thought. Then it began to dawn
upon me that the air was heavy, and dank, and cold. I put back the
clothes from my face, and found, to my surprise, that all was dim around
me. The gaslight which I had left lit for Jonathan, but turned down,
came only like a tiny red spark through the fog, which had evidently
grown thicker and poured into the room. Then it occurred to me that I
had shut the window before I had come to bed. I would have got out to
make certain on the point, but some leaden lethargy seemed to chain my
limbs and even my will. I lay still and endured; that was all. I closed my
eyes, but could still see through my eyelids. (It is wonderful what tricks
our dreams play us, and how conveniently we can imagine.) The mist
grew thicker and thicker, and I could see now how it came in, for I could
see it like smoke – or with the white energy of boiling water – pouring
in, not through the window, but through the joinings of the door. It got
thicker and thicker, till it seemed as if it became concentrated into a sort
of pillar of cloud in the room, through the top of which I could see the
light of the gas shining like a red eye. Things began to whirl through my
brain just as the cloudy column was now whirling in the room, and
through it all came the scriptural words 'a pillar of cloud by day and of
fire by night'.[172] Was it indeed some spiritual guidance that was coming
to me in my sleep? But the pillar was composed of both the day and the
night guiding, for the fire was in the red eye, which at the thought got a
new fascination for me; till, as I looked, the fire divided, and seemed to
shine on me through the fog like two red eyes, such as Lucy told me of in

her momentary mental wandering when, on the cliff, the dying sunlight struck the windows of St Mary's Church. Suddenly the horror burst upon me that it was thus that Jonathan had seen those awful women growing into reality through the whirling mist in the moonlight, and in my dream I must have fainted, for all became black darkness. The last conscious effort which imagination made was to show me a livid white face bending over me out of the mist. I must be careful of such dreams, for they would unseat one's reason if there was too much of them. I would get Dr Van Helsing or Dr Seward to prescribe something for me which would make me sleep, only that I fear to alarm them. Such a dream at the present time would become woven into their fears for me. Tonight I shall strive hard to sleep naturally. If I do not, I shall tomorrow night get them to give me a dose of chloral; that cannot hurt me for once, and it will give me a good night's sleep. Last night tired me more than if I had not slept at all.

2 *October*, 10 *p.m.* – Last night I slept, but did not dream. I must have slept soundly, for I was not waked by Jonathan coming to bed; but the sleep has not refreshed me, for today I feel terribly weak and spiritless. I spent all yesterday trying to read, or lying down dozing. In the afternoon Mr Renfield asked if he might see me. Poor man, he was very gentle, and when I came away he kissed my hand and bade God bless me. Some way it affected me much; I am crying when I think of him. This is a new weakness of which I must be careful. Jonathan would be miserable if he knew I had been crying. He and the others were out until dinner-time, and they all came in tired. I did what I could to brighten them up, and I suppose that the effort did me good, for I forgot how tired I was. After dinner they sent me to bed, and all went off to smoke together, as they said, but I knew that they wanted to tell each other of what had occurred to each during the day; I could see from Jonathan's manner that he had something important to communicate. I was not so sleepy as I should have been; so before they went I asked Dr Seward to give me a little opiate of some kind, as I had not slept well the night before. He very kindly made me up a sleeping draught, which he gave to me, telling me that it would do me no harm, as it was very mild . . . I have taken it, and am waiting for sleep, which still keeps aloof. I hope I have not done wrong, for as sleep begins to flirt with me, a new fear comes: that I may have been foolish in thus depriving myself of the power of waking. I might want it. Here comes sleep. Good-night.

Chapter 20

JONATHAN HARKER'S JOURNAL

1 October, evening. – I found Thomas Snelling in his house at Bethnal Green,[173] but unhappily he was not in a condition to remember anything. The very prospect of beer which my expected coming had opened to him had proved too much, and he had begun too early on his expected debauch. I learned, however, from his wife, who seemed a decent, poor soul, that he was only the assistant to Smollet, who of the two mates was the responsible person. So off I drove to Walworth, and found Mr Joseph Smollet at home and in his shirt-sleeves, taking a late tea out of a saucer. He is a decent, intelligent fellow, distinctly a good, reliable type of workman, and with a headpiece of his own. He remembered all about the incident of the boxes, and from a wonderful dog's-eared notebook, which he produced from some mysterious receptacle about the seat of his trousers, and which had hieroglyphical entries in thick, half-obliterated pencil, he gave me the destinations of the boxes. There were, he said, six in the cartload which he took from Carfax and left at 197 Chicksand Street, Mile End New Town, and another six which he deposited at Jamaica Lane, Bermondsey.[174] If then the Count meant to scatter these ghastly refuges of his over London, these places were chosen at the first of delivery, so that later he might distribute more fully. The systematic manner in which this was done made me think that he could not mean to confine himself to two sides of London. He was now fixed on the far east of the northern shore, on the east of the southern shore, and on the south. The north and west were surely never meant to be left out of his diabolical scheme – let alone the City[175] itself and the very heart of fashionable London in the south-west and west. I went back to Smollet and asked him if he could tell us if any other boxes had been taken from Carfax.

He replied:

'Well, guv'nor, you've treated me wery 'an'some' – I had given him half a sovereign – 'an' I'll tell yer all I know. I heeard a man by the name of Bloxam say four nights ago in the 'Are an' 'Ounds' in Pincher's Alley, as 'ow he an' his mate 'ad 'ad a rare dusty job in a old 'ouse at Purfleet. There ain't a-many such jobs as this 'ere, an' I'm thinkin' that maybe Sam Bloxam could tell ye summut.' I asked if he could tell me where to find him. I told him that if he could get me the address it would be worth another half-sovereign to him. So he gulped down the rest of his tea and stood up, saying that he was going to begin the search then and there. At the door he stopped, and said:

'Look 'ere, guv'nor, there ain't no sense in me a-keepin' you 'ere. I may find Sam soon, or I mayn't; but anyhow he ain't like to be in a way to tell ye much tonight. Sam is a rare one when he starts on the booze. If you can give me a envelope with a stamp on it, and put yer address on it, I'll find out where Sam is to be found and post it ye tonight. But ye'd better be up arter 'im soon in the mornin', or maybe ye won't ketch 'im; for Sam gets off main early, never mind the booze the night afore.'

This was all practical, so one of the children went off with a penny to buy an envelope and a sheet of paper, and to keep the change. When she came back I addressed the envelope and stamped it, and when Smollet had again faithfully promised to post the address when found, I took my way to home. We're on the track anyhow. I am tired tonight, and want sleep. Mina is fast asleep, and looks a little too pale; her eyes look as though she had been crying. Poor dear, I've no doubt it frets her to be kept in the dark, and it may make her doubly anxious about me and the others. But it is best as it is. It is better to be disappointed and worried in such a way now than to have her nerve broken. The doctors were quite right to insist on her being kept out of this dreadful business. I must be firm, for on me this particular burden of silence must rest. I shall not ever enter on the subject with her under any circumstances. Indeed, it may not be a hard task after all, for she herself has become reticent on the subject, and has not spoken of the Count or his doings ever since we told her of our decision.

2 October, evening. – A long and trying and exciting day. By the first post I got my directed envelope with a dirty scrap of paper enclosed, on which was written with a carpenter's pencil in a sprawling hand:

'Sam Bloxam, Korkrans, 4 Poters Cort, Bartel Street, Walworth. Arsk for the depite.'

I got the letter in bed, and rose without waking Mina. She looked heavy and sleepy and pale, and far from well. I determined not to wake her, but that, when I should return from this new search, I would arrange for her going back to Exeter. I think she would be happier in our own home, with her daily tasks to interest her, than in being here amongst us and in ignorance. I only saw Dr Seward for a moment, and told him where I was off to, promising to come back and tell the rest so soon as I should have found out anything. I drove to Walworth and found, with some difficulty, Potter's Court. Mr Smollet's spelling misled me, as I asked for Poter's Court instead of Potter's Court. However, when I had found the court I had no difficulty in discovering Corcoran's lodging-house. When I asked the man who came to the door for the 'depite', he shook his head, and said: 'I dunno 'im. There ain't no such person 'ere; I never 'eard of 'im in all my bloomin' days. Don't believe there ain't nobody of that kind livin' 'ere or anywheres.' I took out Smollet's letter, and as I read it it seemed to me that the lesson of the spelling of the name of the court might guide me. 'What are you?' I asked.

'I'm the depity,' he answered. I saw at once that I was on the right track; phonetic spelling had again misled me. A half-crown tip put the deputy's knowledge at my disposal, and I learned that Mr Bloxam, who had slept off the remains of his beer on the previous night at Corcoran's, had left for his work at Poplar[176] at five o'clock that morning. He could not tell me where the place of work was situated, but he had a vague idea that it was some kind of a 'new-fangled ware'us'; and with this slender clue I had to start for Poplar. It was twelve o'clock before I got any satisfactory hint of such a building, and this I got at a coffee-shop, where some workmen were having their dinner. One of these suggested that there was being erected at Cross Angel Street a new 'cold storage' building; and as this suited the condition of a 'new-fangled ware'us', I at once drove to it. An interview with a surly gatekeeper and a surlier foreman, both of whom were appeased with coin of the realm, put me on the track of Bloxam; he was sent for on my suggesting that I was willing to pay his day's wages to his foreman for the privilege of asking him a few questions on a private matter. He was a smart enough fellow, though rough of speech and bearing. When I had promised to pay for his information and given him an earnest, he told me that he had made two journeys between Carfax and a house in Piccadilly, and had taken from this house to the latter nine great boxes – 'main heavy ones' – with a horse and cart hired by him for this purpose. I asked him if he could tell me the number of the house in Piccadilly, to which he replied:

'Well, guv'nor, I forgits the number, but it was only a few doors from a big white church or somethink of the kind, not long built. It was a dusty old 'ouse, too, though nothin' to the dustiness of the 'ouse we tooked the bloomin' boxes from.'

'How did you get into the houses if they were both empty?'

'There was the old party what engaged me a-waitin' in the 'ouse at Purfleet. He 'elped me to lift the boxes and put them in the dray. Curse me, but he was the strongest chap I ever struck, an' him a old feller, with a white moustache, one that thin you would think he couldn't throw a shadder.'

How this phrase thrilled through me!

'Why, 'e took up 'is end o' the boxes like they was pounds of tea, and me a-puffin' an' a-blowin' afore I could up-end mine anyhow – an' I'm no chicken, neither.'

'How did you get into the house in Piccadilly?' I asked.

'He was there too. He must 'a' started off and got there afore me, for when I rung of the bell he kem an' opened the door 'isself an' 'elped me to carry the boxes into the 'all.'

'The whole nine?' I asked.

'Yus; there was five in the first load an' four in the second. It was main dry work, an' I don't so well remember 'ow I got 'ome.' I interrupted him:

'Were the boxes left in the hall?'

'Yus; it was a big 'all, an' there was nothin' else in it.' I made one more attempt to further matters.

'You didn't have any key?'

'Never used no key nor nothink. The old gent, he opened the door 'isself an' shut it again when I druv off. I don't remember the last time – but that was the beer.'

'And you can't remember the number of the house?'

'No, sir. But ye needn't have no difficulty about that. It's a 'igh 'un with a stone front with a bow on it, and 'igh steps up to the door. I know them steps, 'avin' 'ad to carry the boxes up with three loafers what come round to earn a copper. The old gent give them shillin's, an' they seein' they got so much, they wanted more; but 'e took one of them by the shoulder and was like to throw 'im down the steps, till the lot of them went away cussin'.' I thought that with this description I could find the house, so, having paid my friend for his information, I started off for Piccadilly. I had gained a new painful experience: the Count could, it was evident, handle the earth-boxes himself. If so, time was precious; for, now he had achieved a certain amount of distribution, he could, by choosing his own time, complete the task unobserved. At Piccadilly Circus[177] I discharged my cab, and walked westward; beyond the Junior Constitutional[178] I came across the house described, and was satisfied that this was the next of the lairs arranged by Dracula. The house looked as though it had been long untenanted. The windows were encrusted with dust, and the shutters were up. All the framework was black with time, and from the iron the paint had mostly scaled away. It was evident that up to lately there had been a large notice-board in front of the balcony; it had, however, been roughly torn away, the uprights which had supported it still remaining. Behind the rails of the balcony I saw there were some loose boards, whose raw edges looked white. I would have given a good deal to have been able to see the notice-board intact, as it would, perhaps, have given some clue to the ownership of the house. I remembered my experience of the investigation and purchase of Carfax, and I could not but feel that if I could find the former owner there might be some means of gaining access to the house.

There was at present nothing to be learned from the Piccadilly side, and nothing could be done; so I went round to the back to see if anything could be gathered from this quarter. The mews were active, the Piccadilly houses being mostly in occupation. I asked one or two of the grooms and helpers whom I saw round if they could tell me anything about the empty houses. One of them said he had heard it had lately been taken, but he couldn't say from whom. He told me, however, that up to very lately there had been a notice-board of 'For sale' up, and that perhaps Mitchell, Sons & Candy, the house agents, could tell me something, as he thought he remembered seeing the name of that firm on the board. I did not wish to seem too eager, or to let my informant know or guess too much, so, thanking him in the usual manner, I strolled away. It was now growing dusk, and the autumn night was closing in, so I did not lose any time. Having learned the address of Mitchell, Sons & Candy from a directory at the Berkeley, I was soon at their office in Sackville Street.[179]

The gentleman who saw me was particularly suave in manner, but uncommunicative in equal proportion. Having once told me that the Piccadilly house – which throughout our interview he called a 'mansion' – was sold, he considered my business as concluded. When I asked who had purchased it, he opened his eyes a thought wider, and paused a few seconds before replying:

'It is sold, sir.'

'Pardon me,' I said, with equal politeness, 'but I have a special reason for wishing to know who purchased it.'

Again he paused longer, and raised his eyebrows still more. 'It is sold, sir,' was again his laconic reply.

'Surely,' I said, 'you do not mind letting me know so much.'

'But I do mind,' he answered. 'The affairs of their clients are absolutely safe in the hands of Mitchell, Sons & Candy.' This was manifestly a prig of the first water, and there was no use arguing with him. I thought I had best meet him on his own ground, so I said:

'Your clients, sir, are happy in having so resolute a guardian of their confidence. I am myself a professional man.' Here I handed him my card. 'In this instance I am not prompted by curiosity; I act on the part of Lord Godalming, who wishes to know something of the property which was, he understood, lately for sale.' These words put a different complexion on affairs. He said:

'I would like to oblige you if I could, Mr Harker, and especially would I like to oblige his lordship. We once carried out a small matter of renting some chambers for him when he was the Honourable Arthur Holmwood. If you will let me have his lordship's address I will consult the House on the subject, and will, in any case, communicate with his lordship by tonight's post. It will be a pleasure if we can so far deviate from our rules as to give the required information to his lordship.'

I wanted to secure a friend, and not to make an enemy, so I thanked him, gave the address at Dr Seward's, and came away. It was now dark, and I was tired and hungry. I got a cup of tea at the Aerated Bread Company[180] and came down to Purfleet by the next train.

I found all the others at home. Mina was looking tired and pale, but she made a gallant effort to be bright and cheerful; it wrung my heart to think that I had had to keep anything from her and so caused her disquietude. Thank God, this will be the last night of her looking on at our conferences, and feeling the sting of our not showing our confidence. It took all my courage to hold to the wise resolution of keeping her out of our grim task. She seems somehow more reconciled; or else the very subject seems to have become repugnant to her, for when any accidental allusion is made she actually shudders. I am glad we made our resolution in time, as with such a feeling as this our growing knowledge would be torture to her.

I could not tell the others of the day's discovery till we were alone; so after dinner – followed by a little music to save appearances even amongst ourselves – I took Mina to her room and left her to go to bed. The dear girl was more affectionate with me than ever, and clung to me as though she would detain me; but there was much to be talked of and I came away. Thank God, the ceasing of telling things has made no difference between us.

When I came down again I found the others all gathered round the fire in the study. In the train I had written my diary so far, and simply read it off to them as the best means of letting them get abreast of my own information; when I had finished Van Helsing said:

'This has been a great day's work, friend Jonathan. Doubtless we are on the track of the missing boxes. If we find them all in that house, then our work is near the end. But if there be some missing, we must search until we find them. Then shall we make our final *coup*, and hunt the wretch to his real death.' We all sat silent awhile, and all at once Mr Morris spoke:

'Say! how are we going to get into that house?'

'We got into the other,' answered Lord Godalming quickly.

'But, Art, this is different. We broke house at Carfax, but we had night and a walled park to protect us. It will be a mighty different thing to commit burglary in Piccadilly, either by day or night. I confess I don't see how we are going to get in unless that agency duck can find us a key of some sort; perhaps we shall know when you get his letter in the morning.' Lord Godalming's brows contracted, and he stood up and walked about the room. By-and-by he stopped and said, turning from one to another of us:

'Quincey's head is level. This burglary business is getting serious; we got off once all right; but we have now a rare job on hand – unless we can find the Count's key basket.'

As nothing could well be done before morning, and as it would be at least advisable to wait till Lord Godalming should hear from Mitchell's, we decided not to take any active step before breakfast time. For a good while we sat and smoked, discussing the matter in its various bearings; I took the opportunity of bringing this diary right up to the moment. I am very sleepy and shall go to bed . . .

Just a line. Mina sleeps soundly and her breathing is regular. Her forehead is puckered up into little wrinkles, as though she thinks even in her sleep. She is still too pale, but does not look so haggard as she did this morning. Tomorrow will, I hope, mend all this; she will be herself at home in Exeter. Oh, but I am sleepy!

DR SEWARD'S DIARY

1 October. – I am puzzled afresh about Renfield. His moods change so rapidly that I find it difficult to keep touch with them, and as they always mean something more than his own wellbeing, they form a more than interesting study. This morning, when I went to see him after his repulse of Van Helsing, his manner was that of a man commanding destiny. He was, in fact, commanding destiny – subjectively. He did not really care for any of the things of mere health; he was in the clouds and looked down on all the weaknesses and wants of us poor mortals. I thought I would improve the occasion and learn something, so I asked him:

'What about the flies these times?' He smiled on me in quite a superior sort of way – such a smile as would have become the face of Malvolio[181] – as he answered me:

'The fly, my dear sir, has one striking feature: its wings are typical of the aerial powers of the psychic faculties. The ancients did well when they typified the soul as a butterfly!'

I thought I would push his analogy to its utmost logically, so I said quickly:

'Oh, it is a soul you are after now, is it?' His madness foiled his reason, and a puzzled look spread over his face as shaking his head with a decision which I had but seldom seen in him, he said:

'Oh no, oh no! I want no souls. Life is all I want.' Here he brightened up: 'I am pretty indifferent about it at present. Life is all right; I have all I want. You must get a new patient doctor, if you wish to study zoophagy!'

This puzzled me a little, so I drew him on:

'Then you command life; you are a god, I suppose?' He smiled with an ineffably benign superiority.

'Oh no! Far be it from me to arrogate to myself the attributes of the Deity. I am not even concerned in His especially spiritual doings. If I may state my intellectual position I am, so far as concerns things purely terrestrial, somewhat in the position which Enoch[182] occupied spiritually!' This was a poser to me. I could not at the moment recall Enoch's appositeness; so I had to ask a simple question, though I felt that by so doing I was lowering myself in the eyes of the lunatic:

'And why Enoch?'

'Because he walked with God.' I could not see the analogy, but did not like to admit it; so I harked back to what he had denied:

'So you don't care about life and you don't want souls. Why not?' I put my question quickly and somewhat sternly, on purpose to discon-cert him. The effort succeeded; for an instant he unconsciously relapsed into his old servile manner, bent low before me, and actually fawned upon me as he replied:

'I don't want any souls, indeed, indeed! I don't. I couldn't use them if I had them! they would be no manner of use to me. I couldn't eat them or – ' he suddenly stopped and the old cunning look spread over his face, like a wind-sweep on the surface of the water. 'And, Doctor, as to life, what is it after all? When you've got all you require, and you know that you will never want, that is all. I have friends – good friends – like you, Doctor Seward,' he said with a leer of inexpressible cunning; 'I know that I shall never lack the means of life!'

I think that through the cloudiness of his insanity he saw some antagonism in me, for he at once fell back on the last refuge of such as he – a dogged silence. After a short time I saw that for the present it was useless to speak to him. He was sulky, and so I came away.

Later in the day he sent for me. Ordinarily I would not have come without special reason, but just at present I am so interested in him that I would gladly make an effort. Besides, I am glad to have anything to help to pass the time. Harker is out, following up clues; and so are Lord Godalming and Quincey. Van Helsing sits in my study poring over the record prepared by the Harkers; he seems to think that by accurate knowledge of all details he will light upon some clue. He does not wish to be disturbed in the work, without cause. I would have taken him with me to see the patient, only I thought that after his last repulse he might not care to go again. There was also another reason: Renfield might not speak so freely before a third person as when he and I were alone.

I found him sitting out in the middle of the floor on his stool, a pose which is generally indicative of some mental energy on his part. When I came in, he said at once, as though the question had been waiting on his lips:

'What about souls?' It was evident then that my surmise had been correct. Unconscious cerebration was doing its work, even with the lunatic. I determined to have the matter out. 'What about them yourself?' I asked. He did not reply for a moment but looked all round him, and up and down, as though he expected to find some inspiration for an answer.

'I don't want any souls!' he said in a feeble, apologetic way. The matter seemed preying on his mind, and so I determined to use it – to 'be cruel only to be kind'.[183] So I said:

'You like life, and you want life?'

'Oh yes! but that is all right: you needn't worry about that!'

'But,' I asked, 'how are we to get the life without getting the soul also?' This seemed to puzzle him, so I followed it up:

'A nice time you'll have some time when you're flying out there, with the souls of thousands of flies and spiders and birds and cats buzzing and twittering and miauing all round you. You've got their lives, you know, and you must put up with their souls!' Something seemed to affect his imagination, for he put his fingers to his ears and shut his eyes, screwing them up tightly just as a small boy does when his face is being soaped. There was something pathetic in it that touched me; it also gave me a lesson, for it seemed that before me was a child – only a child, though the features were worn, and the stubble on the jaws was white. It was evident that he was undergoing some process of mental disturbance, and knowing how his past moods had interpreted things seemingly foreign to himself, I thought I would enter into his mind as well as I could and go with him. The first step was to restore confidence, so I asked him speaking pretty loud so that he would hear me through his closed ears:

'Would you like some sugar to get your flies round again?' He seemed to wake up all at once, and shook his head. With a laugh he replied:

'Not much! flies are poor things, after all!' After a pause he added, 'But I don't want their souls buzzing round me all the same.'

'Or spiders?' I went on.

'Blow spiders! What's the use of spiders? There isn't anything in them to eat or – ' he stopped suddenly, as though reminded of a forbidden topic.

'So, so!' I thought to myself, 'this is the second time he has suddenly stopped at the word "drink"; what does it mean?' Renfield seemed himself aware of having made a lapse, for he hurried on, as though to distract my attention from it:

'I don't take any stock at all in such matters. "Rats and mice and such small deer"[184] as Shakespeare has it; "chicken-feed of the larder" they might be called. I'm past all that sort of nonsense. You might as well ask a man to eat molecules with a pair of chop-sticks, as to try to interest me about the lesser carnivora, when I know of what is before me.'

'I see,' I said. 'You want big things that you can make your teeth meet in? How would you like to breakfast on elephant?'

'What ridiculous nonsense you are talking!' He was getting too wide awake, so I thought I would press him hard. 'I wonder,' I said reflectively, 'what an elephant's soul is like!' The effect I desired was obtained, for he at once fell from his high-horse and became a child again.

'I don't want an elephant's soul, or any soul at all!' he said. For a few moments he sat despondently. Suddenly he jumped to his feet, with his eyes blazing and all the signs of intense cerebral excitement. 'To hell with you and your souls!' he shouted. 'Why do you plague me about souls? Haven't I got enough to worry, and pain, and distract me already, without thinking of souls?' He looked so hostile that I thought he was in for another homicidal fit, so I blew my whistle. The instant, however, that I did so he became calm, and said apologetically:

'Forgive me, Doctor; I forgot myself. You do not need any help. I am so worried in my mind that I am apt to be irritable. If you only knew the problem I have to face, and that I am working out, you would pity, and tolerate, and pardon me. Pray do not put me in a strait-waistcoat. I want to think, and I cannot think freely when my body is confined. I am sure you will understand!' He had evidently self-control; so when the attendants came I told them not to mind, and they withdrew. Renfield watched them go; when the door was closed he said, with considerable dignity and sweetness:

'Dr Seward, you have been very considerate towards me. Believe me that I am very very grateful to you!' I thought it well to leave him in this mood, and so I came away. There is certainly something to ponder over in this man's state. Several points seem to make what the American interviewer calls 'a story', if one could only get them in proper order.

Here they are: Will not mention 'drinking'.

Fears the thought of being burdened with the 'soul' of anything.

Has no dread of wanting 'life' in the future.

Despises the meaner forms of life altogether, though he dreads being haunted by their souls.

Logically all these things point one way! he has assurance of some kind that he will acquire some higher life. He dreads the consequence – the burden of a soul. Then it is a human life he looks to!

And the assurance – ?

Merciful God! the Count has been to him, and there is some new scheme of terror afoot!

Later. – I went after my round to Van Helsing and told him my suspicion. He grew very grave; and, after thinking the matter over for a while, asked me to take him to Renfield. I did so. As we came to the door we heard the lunatic within singing gaily, as he used to do in the time which now seems so long ago. When we entered we saw with amazement that he had spread out his sugar as of old; the flies, lethargic with the autumn, were beginning to buzz into the room. We tried to make him talk of the subject of our previous conversation, but he would not attend. He went on with his singing, just as though we had not been present. He had got a scrap of paper and was folding it into a note-book. We had to come away as ignorant as we went in.

His is a curious case indeed; we must watch him tonight.

Letter, Mitchell, Sons & Candy to Lord Godalming

1 October.

MY LORD, –

We are at all times only too happy to meet your wishes. We beg, with regard to the desire of your Lordship, expressed by Mr Harker on your behalf, to supply the following information concerning the sale and purchase of No. 347 Piccadilly. The original vendors are the executors of the late Mr Archibald Winter-Suffield. The purchaser is a foreign nobleman, Count de Ville, who effected the purchase himself, paying the purchase money in notes 'over the counter', if your Lordship will pardon us using so vulgar an expression. Beyond this we know nothing whatever of him. – We are, my Lord,

Your Lordship's humble servants,

MITCHELL, SONS & CANDY.

DR SEWARD'S DIARY

2 October. – I placed a man in the corridor last night, and told him to make an accurate note of any sound he might hear from Renfield's room, and gave him instructions that if there should be anything strange he was to call me. After dinner, when we had all gathered round the fire in the study – Mrs Harker having gone to bed – we discussed the attempts and discoveries of the day. Harker was the only one who had any result, and we are in great hopes that his clue may be an important one.

Before going to bed I went round to the patient's room and looked in through the observation trap. He was sleeping soundly, and his chest rose and fell with regular respiration.

This morning the man on duty reported to me that a little after midnight he was restless and kept saying his prayers somewhat loudly. I asked him if that was all; he replied that it was all he heard. There was something about his manner so suspicious that I asked him point-blank if he had been asleep. He denied sleep, but admitted to having 'dozed' for a while. It is too bad that men cannot be trusted unless they are watched.

Today Harker is out following up his clue, and Art and Quincey are looking after horses. Godalming thinks that it will be well to have horses always in readiness, for when we get the information which we seek there will be no time to lose. We must sterilise all the imported earth between sunrise and sunset; we shall thus catch the Count at his weakest, and without a refuge to fly to. Van Helsing is off to the British Museum, looking up some authorities on ancient medicine. The old physicians took account of things which their followers do not accept, and the Professor is searching for witch and demon cures which may be useful later.

I sometimes think we must be all mad and that we shall wake to sanity in strait-waistcoats.

Later. – We have met again. We seem at last to be on the track, and our work of tomorrow may be the beginning of the end. I wonder if Renfield's quiet has anything to do with this. His moods have so followed the doings of the Count, that the coming destruction of the monster may be carried to him in some subtle way. If we could only get some hint as to what passed in his mind, between the time of my argument with him yesterday and his resumption of fly-catching, it might afford us a valuable clue. He is now seemingly quiet for a spell . . . Is he? – that wild yell seemed to come from his room . . .

The attendant came bursting into my room and told me that Renfield had somehow met with some accident. He had heard him yell; and when he went to him found him lying on his face on the floor, all covered with blood. I must go at once . . .

Chapter 21

Dr Seward's Diary

3 October. – Let me put down with exactness all that happened, as well as I can remember it, since last I made an entry. Not a detail that I can recall must be forgotten; in all calmness I must proceed.

When I came to Renfield's room I found him lying on the floor on his left side in a glittering pool of blood. When I went to move him, it became at once apparent that he had received some terrible injuries; there seemed none of that unity of purpose between the parts of the body which marks even lethargic sanity. As the face was exposed I could see that it was horribly bruised as though it had been beaten against the floor – indeed it was from the face wounds that the pool of blood originated. The attendant who was kneeling beside the body said to me as we turned him over:

'I think, sir, his back is broken. See, both his right arm and leg and the whole side of his face are paralysed.' How such a thing could have happened puzzled the attendant beyond measure. He seemed quite bewildered, and his brows were gathered in as he said:

'I can't understand the two things. He could mark his face like that by beating his own head on the ground. I saw a young woman do it once at the Eversfield Asylum before anyone could lay hands on her. And I suppose he might have broke his back by falling out of bed, if he got in an awkward kink. But for the life of me I can't imagine how the two things occurred. If his back was broke, he couldn't beat his head and if his face was like that before the fall out of bed, there would be marks of it.' I said to him:

'Go to Dr Van Helsing, and ask him to kindly come here at once. I want him without an instant's delay.' The man ran off, and within a very few minutes the Professor, in his dressing-gown and slippers, appeared. When he saw Renfield on the ground, he looked keenly at him a moment and then turned to me. I think he recognised my thought in my eyes, for he said very quietly, manifestly for the ears of the attendant:

'Ah, a sad accident He will need very careful watching, and much attention. I shall stay with you myself; but I shall first dress myself. If you will remain I shall in a few minutes join you.'

The patient was now breathing stertorously, and it was easy to see that he had suffered some terrible injury. Van Helsing returned with extraordinary celerity, bearing with him a surgical case. He had evidently been thinking and had his mind made up; for, almost before he looked at the patient, he whispered to me:

'Send the attendant away. We must be alone with him when he becomes conscious, after the operation.' So I said:

'I think that will do now, Simmons. We have done all that we can at present. You had better go your round, and Dr Van Helsing will operate. Let me know instantly if there be anything unusual anywhere.'

The man withdrew, and we went into a strict examination of the patient. The wounds of the face were superficial; the real injury was a depressed fracture of the skull, extending right up through the motor area. The Professor thought a moment and said:

'We must reduce the pressure and get back to normal conditions, as far as can be; the rapidity of the suffusion shows the terrible nature of his injury. The whole motor area seems affected. The suffusion of the brain will increase quickly, so we must trephine at once or it may be too late.' As he was speaking there was a soft tapping at the door. I went over and opened it and found in the corridor without, Arthur and Quincey in pyjamas and slippers: the former spoke:

'I heard your man call up Dr Van Helsing and tell him of an accident. So I woke Quincey, or rather called for him as he was not asleep. Things are moving too quickly and too strangely for sound sleep for any of us these times. I've been thinking that tomorrow night will not see things as they have been. We'll have to look back – and forward a little more than we have done. May we come in?' I nodded, and held the door open till they had entered; then I closed it again. When Quincey saw the attitude and state of the patient, and noted the horrible pool on the floor, he said softly:

'My God! what has happened to him! Poor, poor devil!' I told him briefly, and added that we expected he would recover consciousness after the operation – for a short time at all events. He went at once and sat down on the edge of the bed, with Godalming beside him; we all watched in patience.

'We shall wait,' said Van Helsing, 'just long enough to fix the best spot for trephining, so that we may most quickly and perfectly remove the blood clot; for it is evident that the hæmorrhage is increasing.'

The minutes during which we waited passed with fearful slowness. I had a horrible sinking in my heart, and from Van Helsing's face I gathered that he felt some fear or apprehension as to what was to come. I dreaded the words that Renfield might speak. I was positively afraid to think; but the conviction of what was coming was on me, as I have read of men who have heard the death-watch. The poor man's breathing came in uncertain gasps. Each instant he seemed as though he would open his eyes and speak; but then would follow a prolonged stertorous breath, and he would relapse into a more fixed insensibility. Inured as I was to sick-beds and death, this suspense grew and grew upon me. I could almost hear the beating of my own heart; and the blood surging through my temples sounded like blows from a hammer. The silence finally became agonising. I looked at my companions, one after another, and saw from their flushed faces and damp brows that they were enduring equal torture. There was a nervous suspense over us all, as though overhead some dread bell would peal out powerfully when we should least expect it.

At last there came a time when it was evident that the patient was sinking fast; he might die at any moment. I looked up at the Professor and caught his eyes fixed on mine. His face was sternly set as he spoke:

'There is no time to lose. His words may be worth many lives; I have been thinking so, as I stood here. It may be there is a soul at stake! We shall operate just above the ear.'

Without another word he made the operation. For a few moments the breathing continued to be stertorous. Then there came a breath so prolonged that it seemed as though it would tear open his chest. Suddenly his eyes opened, and became fixed in a wild, helpless stare. This was continued for a few moments; then it softened into a glad surprise, and from the lips came a sigh of relief. He moved convulsively, and as he did so, said:

'I'll be quiet, Doctor. Tell them to take off the strait-waistcoat. I have had a terrible dream, and it has left me so weak that I cannot move. What's wrong with my face? it feels all swollen, and it smarts dreadfully.' He tried to turn his head; but even with the effort his eyes seemed to grow glassy again, so I gently put it back. Then Van Helsing said in a quiet grave tone:

'Tell us your dream, Mr Renfield.' As he heard the voice his face brightened through its mutilation, and he said:

'That is Dr Van Helsing. How good it is of you to be here. Give me some water, my lips are dry; and I shall try to tell you. I dreamed' – he stopped and seemed fainting. I called quietly to Quincey – 'The brandy – it is in my study – quick!'

He flew and returned with a glass, the decanter of brandy and a carafe of water. We moistened the parched lips, and the patient quickly revived. It seemed, however, that his poor injured brain had been working in the interval, for, when he was quite conscious, he looked at me piercingly with an agonised confusion which I shall never forget, and said:

'I must not deceive myself; it was no dream, but all a grim reality.' Then his eyes roved round the room; as they caught sight of the two figures sitting patiently on the edge of the bed he went on:

'If I were not sure already, I should know from them.' For an instant his eyes closed – not with pain or sleep but voluntarily, as though he were bringing all his faculties to bear; when he opened them he said, hurriedly, and with more energy than he had yet displayed:

'Quick, Doctor, quick. I am dying! I feel that I have but a few minutes; and then I must go back to death – or worse! Wet my lips with brandy again. I have something that I must say before I die; or before my poor crushed brain dies anyhow. Thank you! It was that night after you left me, when I implored you to let me go away. I couldn't speak then, for I felt my tongue was tied; but I was as sane then, except in that way, as I am now. I was in an agony of despair for a long time after you left me, it seemed hours. Then there came a sudden peace to me. My brain seemed to become cool again, and I realised where I was. I heard the dogs bark behind our house, but not where He was!' As he spoke Van Helsing's eyes never blinked, but his hand came out and met mine and gripped it hard. He did not, however, betray himself; he nodded slightly, and said: 'Go on,' in a low voice. Renfield proceeded:

'He came up to the window in the mist, as I had seen Him often before; but He was solid then – not a ghost, and His eyes were fierce like a man's when angry. He was laughing with His red mouth; the sharp white teeth glinted in the moonlight when He turned to look back over the belt of trees, to where the dogs were barking. I wouldn't ask Him to come in at first, though I knew He wanted to – just as He had wanted all along. Then He began promising me things – not in words but by doing them.' He was interrupted by a word from the Professor:

'How?'

'By making them happen; just as He used to send in the flies when the sun was shining. Great big fat ones with steel and sapphire on their wings; and big moths, in the night, with skull and cross-bones on their backs.' Van Helsing nodded to him as he whispered to me unconsciously:

'The *Acherontia atropos of the Sphinges* – what you call the "Death's-head moth"!' The patient went on without stopping.

'Then he began to whisper: "Rat, rats, rats! Hundreds, thousands, millions of them, and every one a life; and dogs to eat them, and cats too. All lives! all red blood, with years of life in it; and not merely buzzing flies!" I laughed at Him, for I wanted to see what He could do. Then the dogs howled, away beyond the dark trees in His house. He beckoned me to the window. I got up and looked out, and He raised His hands, and seemed to call out without using any words. A dark mass spread over the grass, coming on like the shape of a flame of fire; and then He moved the mist to the right and left, and I could see that there were thousands of rats with their eyes blazing red – like His, only smaller. He held up His hand, and they all stopped; and I thought He seemed to be saying: "All these lives will I give you, ay, and many more and greater, through countless ages, if you will fall down and worship me!" And then a red cloud, like the colour of blood, seemed to close over my eyes; and before I knew what I was doing, I found myself opening the sash and saying to Him: "Come in, Lord and Master!" The rats were all gone, but He slid into the room through the sash, though it was only open an inch wide – just as the Moon herself has often come in through the tiniest crack, and has stood before me in all her size and splendour.'

His voice was weaker, so I moistened his lips with the brandy again, and he continued, but it seemed as though his memory had gone on working in the interval, for his story was further advanced. I was about to call him back to the point, but Van Helsing whispered to me: 'Let him go on. Do not interrupt him; he cannot go back, and maybe could not proceed at all if once he lost the thread of his thought.' He proceeded:

'All day I waited to hear from Him, but He did not send me anything, not even a blow-fly, and when the moon got up I was pretty angry with Him. When He slid in through the window, though it was shut, and did not even knock, I got mad with Him. He sneered at me, and His white face looked out of the mist with His red eyes gleaming, and He went on as though He owned the whole place, and I was no one. He didn't even smell the same as He went by me. I couldn't hold Him. I thought that, somehow, Mrs Harker had come into the room.'

The two men sitting on the bed stood up and came over, standing behind him so that he could not see them, but where they could hear better. They were both silent, but the Professor started and quivered; his face, however, grew grimmer and sterner still. Renfield went on without noticing:

'When Mrs Harker came in to see me this afternoon she wasn't the same; it was like tea after the teapot had been watered.' Here we all moved, but no one said a word; he went on:

'I didn't know that she was here till she spoke; and she didn't look the same. I don't care for the pale people, I like them with lots of blood in them, and hers had all seemed to have run out. I didn't think of it at the time; but when she went away I began to think, and it made me mad to know that He had been taking the life out of her.' I could feel that the rest quivered, as I did; but we remained otherwise still. 'So when He came tonight I was ready for Him. I saw the mist stealing in, and I grabbed it tight. I had heard that madmen have unnatural strength; and as I knew I was a madman – at times anyhow – I resolved to use my power. Ay, and He felt it too, for He had to come out of the mist to struggle with me. I held tight; and I thought I was going to win, for I didn't mean Him to take any more of her life, till I saw His eyes. They burned into me and my strength became like water. He slipped through it, and when I tried to cling to Him, He raised me up and flung me down. There was a red cloud before me, and a noise like thunder, and the mist seemed to steal away under the door.' His voice was becoming fainter and his breath more stertorous. Van Helsing stood up instinctively.

'We know the worst now,' he said. 'He is here, and we know his purpose. It may not be too late. Let us be armed – the same as we were the other night, but lose no time; there is not an instant to spare.' There was no need to put our fear, nay our conviction, into words – we shared them in common. We all hurried and took from our rooms the same things that we had when we entered the Count's house. The Professor had his ready and as we met in the corridor he pointed to them significantly as he said:

'They never leave me; and they shall not till this unhappy business is over. Be wise also, my friends. It is no common enemy that we deal with. Alas! alas that that dear Madam Mina should suffer.' He stopped;

his voice was breaking, and I do not know if rage or terror predominated in my own heart.

Outside the Harkers' door we paused. Art and Quincey held back, and the latter said: 'Should we disturb her?'

'We must,' said Van Helsing grimly. 'If the door be locked, I shall break it in.'

'May it not frighten her terribly? It is unusual to break into a lady's room!' Van Helsing said solemnly:

'You are always right; but this is life and death. All chambers are alike to the doctor, and even were they not they are all as one to me tonight. Friend John, when I turn the handle, if the door does not open, do you put your shoulder down and shove; and you too, my friends. Now!'

He turned the handle as he spoke, but the door did not yield. We threw ourselves against it; with a crash it burst open, and we almost fell headlong into the room. The Professor did actually fall, and I saw across him as he gathered himself up from hands and knees. What I saw appalled me. I felt my hair rise like bristles on the back of my neck, and my heart seemed to stand still.

The moonlight was so bright that through the thick yellow blind the room was light enough to see. On the bed beside the window lay Jonathan Harker, his face flushed, and breathing heavily as though in a stupor. Kneeling on the near edge of the bed facing outwards was the white-clad figure of his wife. By her side stood a tall, thin man, clad in black. His face was turned from us, but the instant we saw it we all recognised the Count – in every way, even to the scar on his forehead. With his left hand he held both Mrs Harker's hands, keeping them away with her arms at full tension; his right hand gripped her by the back of the neck, forcing her face down on his bosom. Her white nightdress was smeared with blood, and a thin stream trickled down the man's bare breast, which was shown by his torn-open dress. The attitude of the two had a terrible resemblance to a child forcing a kitten's nose into a saucer of milk to compel it to drink. As we burst into the room, the Count turned his face, and the hellish look that I had heard described seemed to leap into it. His eyes flamed red with devilish passion; the great nostrils of the white aquiline nose opened wide and quivered at the edge; and the white sharp teeth, behind the full lips of the blood-dripping mouth, champed together like those of a wild beast. With a wrench, which threw his victim back upon the bed as though hurled from a height, he turned and sprang at us. But by this time the Professor had gained his feet, and was holding towards him the envelope which contained the Sacred Wafer. The Count suddenly stopped, just as poor Lucy had done outside the tomb, and cowered back. Further and further back he cowered, as we, lifting our crucifixes, advanced. The moonlight suddenly failed, as a great black cloud sailed across the sky; and when the gaslight sprang up under Quincey's match, we saw nothing but a faint vapour. This, as we looked, trailed under the door, which with the recoil from its bursting open had swung back to its old position. Van Helsing, Art and I moved forward to Mrs Harker, who by this time had drawn her breath and with it had given a scream so wild, so ear-piercing, so despairing that it seems to me now that it will ring in my ears till my dying day. For a few seconds she lay in her helpless attitude and disarray. Her face was ghastly, with a pallor which was accentuated by the blood which smeared her lips and cheeks and chin; from her throat trickled a thin stream of blood. Her eyes were mad with terror. Then she put before her face her poor crushed hands, which bore on their whiteness the red mark of the Count's terrible grip, and from behind them came a low desolate wail which made the terrible scream seem only the quick expression of an endless grief. Van Helsing stepped forward and drew the coverlet gently over her body, whilst Art, after looking at her face for an instant despairingly, ran out of the room. Van Helsing whispered to me:

'Jonathan is in a stupor such as we know the Vampire can produce. We can do nothing with poor Madam Mina for a few moments till she recovers herself; I must wake him!' He dipped the end of a towel in cold water and with it began to flick him on the face, his wife all the while holding her face between her hands and sobbing in a way that was heart-breaking to hear. I raised the blind, and looked out of the window. There was much moonshine; and as I looked I could see Quincey Morris run across the lawn and hide himself in the shadow of a great yew-tree. It puzzled me to think why he was doing this; but at the instant I heard Harker's quick exclamation as he woke to partial consciousness, and turned to the bed. On his face, as there might well be, was a look of wild amazement. He seemed dazed for a few seconds, and then full consciousness seemed to burst upon him all at once and he started up. His wife was aroused by the quick movement, and turned to him with her arms stretched out, as though to embrace him; instantly, however, she drew them in again, and putting her elbows together held her hands before her face, and shuddered till the bed beneath her shook.

'In God's name what does this mean?' Harker cried out. 'Dr Seward, Dr Van Helsing, what is it? What has happened? What is wrong? Mina, dear, what is it? What does that blood mean? My God, my God! has it come to this!' and, raising himself to his knees, he beat his hands wildly together. 'Good God help us! help her! oh, help her!' With a quick movement he jumped from bed, and began to pull on his clothes – all the man in him awake at the need for instant exertion. 'What has happened? Tell me all about it!' he cried without pausing. 'Dr Van Helsing, you love Mina, I know. Oh, do something to save her. It cannot have gone too far yet. Guard her while I look for *him*!' His wife, through her terror and horror and distress, saw some sure danger to him; instantly forgetting her own grief, she seized hold of him and cried out:

'No! no! Jonathan, you must not leave me. I have suffered enough tonight, God knows, without the dread of his harming you. You must stay with me. Stay with these friends who will watch over you!' Her expression became frantic as she spoke; and as he yielded to her, she pulled him down sitting on the bedside, and clung to him fiercely.

Van Helsing and I tried to calm them both. The Professor held up his little golden crucifix, and said with wonderful calmness:

'Do not fear, my dear. We are here; and whilst this is close to you no foul thing can approach. You are safe for tonight; and we must be calm and take counsel together.' She shuddered and was silent, holding down her head on her husband's breast. When she raised it, his white night-robe was stained with blood where her lips had touched, and where the thin open wound in her neck had sent forth drops. The instant she saw it she drew back, with a low wail, and whispered, amidst choking sobs:

'Unclean, unclean! I must touch him or kiss him no more. Oh, that it should be that it is I who am now his worst enemy, and whom he may have most cause to fear.' To this he spoke out resolutely:

'Nonsense, Mina. It is a shame to me to hear such a word. I would not hear it of you, and I shall not hear it from you. May God judge me by my deserts, and punish me with more bitter suffering than even this hour, if by any act or will of mine anything ever come between us!' He put out his arms and folded her to his breast; and for a while she lay there sobbing. He looked at us over her bowed head, with eyes that blinked damply above his quivering nostrils; his mouth was set as steel. After a while her sobs became less frequent and more faint, and then he said to me, speaking with a studied calmness which I felt tried his nervous power to the utmost:

'And now, Dr Seward, tell me all about it. Too well I know the broad fact, tell me all that has been.' I told him exactly what had happened, and he listened with seeming impassiveness; but his nostrils twitched and his eyes blazed as I told how the ruthless hands of the Count had held his wife in that terrible and horrid position, with her mouth to the open wound in his breast. It interested me, even at that moment, to see that whilst the face of white set passion worked convulsively over the bowed head, the hands tenderly and lovingly stroked the ruffled hair. Just as I had finished Quincey and Godalming knocked at the door. They entered in obedience to our summons. Van Helsing looked at me questioningly. I understood him to mean if we were to take advantage of their coming to divert if possible the thoughts of the unhappy husband and wife from each other and from themselves; so on my nodding acquiescence to him he asked them what they had seen or done. To which Lord Godalming answered:

'I could not see him anywhere in the passage, or in any of our rooms. I looked in the study, but, though he had been there, he had gone. He had, however – ' He stopped suddenly, looking at the poor drooping figure on the bed. Van Helsing said gravely: 'Go on, friend Arthur. We want no more concealments. Our hope now is in knowing all. Tell freely!' So Art went on:

'He had been there and though it could only have been for a few seconds, he made rare hay of the place. All the manuscript had been burned, and the blue flames were flickering amongst the white ashes; the cylinders of your phonograph too were thrown on the fire, and the wax had helped the flames.' Here I interrupted. 'Thank God there is the other copy in the safe!' His face lit for a moment, but fell again as he went on: 'I ran downstairs then, but could see no sign of him. I looked into Renfield's room; but there was no trace there except – !' Again he paused. 'Go on,' said Harker hoarsely; so he bowed his head, and moistening his lips with his tongue, added: 'except that the poor fellow is dead.' Mrs Harker raised her head, looking from one to the other of us as she said solemnly:

'God's will be done!' I could not but feel that Art was keeping back something; but, as I took it that it was with a purpose, I said nothing. Van Helsing turned to Morris and asked:

'And you, friend Quincey, have you any to tell?'

'A little,' he answered. 'It may be much eventually, but at present I can't say. I thought it well to know if possible where the Count would go when he left the house. I did not see him; but I saw a bat rise from Renfield's window, and flap westward. I expected to see him in some shape go back to Carfax; but he evidently sought some other lair. He will not be back tonight; for the sky is reddening in the east, and the dawn is close. We must work tomorrow!'

He said the latter words through his shut teeth. For a space of perhaps a couple of minutes there was silence, and I could fancy that I could hear the sound of our hearts beating; then Van Helsing said, placing his hand very tenderly on Mrs Harker's head:

'And now, Madam Mina – poor, dear, dear Madam Mina – tell us exactly what happened. God knows that I do not want that you be pained; but it is need that we know all. For now more than ever has all work to be done quick and sharp, and in deadly earnest. The day is close to us that must end all, if it may so be; and now is the chance that we may live and learn.'

The poor, dear lady shivered, and I could see the tension of her nerves as she clasped her husband closer to her and bent her head lower and lower still on his breast. Then she raised her head proudly, and held out one hand to Van Helsing, who took it in his, and, after stooping and kissing it reverently, held it fast. The other hand was locked in that of her husband, who held his other arm thrown round her protectingly. After a pause in which she was evidently ordering her thoughts, she began:

'I took the sleeping draught which you had so kindly given me, but for a long time it did not act. I seemed to become more wakeful, and myriads of horrible fancies began to crowd in upon my mind – all of them connected with death, and vampires; with blood, and pain, and trouble.' Her husband involuntarily groaned as she turned to him and said lovingly: 'Do not fret, dear. You must be brave and strong, and help me through the horrible task. If you only knew what an effort it is to me to tell of this fearful thing at all, you would understand how much I need your help. Well, I saw I must try to help the medicine to its work with my will, if it was to do me any good, so I resolutely set myself to sleep. Sure enough sleep must soon have come to me, for I remember no more. Jonathan coming in had not waked me, for he lay by my side when next I remember. There was in the room the same thin white mist that I had before noticed. But I forget now if you know of this; you will find it in my diary which I shall show you later. I felt the same vague terror which had come to me before, and the same sense of some presence. I turned to wake Jonathan, but found that he slept so soundly that it seemed as if it was he who had taken the sleeping draught and not I. I tried, but I could not wake him. This caused me a great fear, and I looked around terrified. Then indeed my heart sank within me: beside the bed, as if he had stepped out of the mist – or rather as if the mist had turned into his figure, for it had entirely disappeared – stood a tall, thin man, all in black. I knew him at once from the descriptions of the others. The waxen face; the high aquiline nose, on which the light fell in a thin white line; the parted red lips, with the sharp white teeth showing between; and the red eyes that I had seemed to see in the sunset on the windows of St Mary's Church at Whitby. I knew, too, the red scar on his forehead where Jonathan had struck him. For an instant my heart stood still, and I would have screamed out, only that I was paralysed. In the pause he spoke in a sort of keen, cutting whisper, pointing as he spoke to Jonathan:

' "Silence! If you make a sound I shall take him and dash his brains out before your very eyes." I was appalled and was too bewildered to do or say anything. With a mocking smile, he placed one hand upon my shoulder and, holding me tight, bared my throat with the other, saying as he did so: "First, a little refreshment to reward my exertions. You may as well be quiet; it is not the first time, or the second, that your veins have appeased my thirst!" I was bewildered, and, strangely enough, I did not want to hinder him. I suppose it is a part of the horrible curse that this happens when his touch is on his victim. And oh, my God, my God, pity me! He placed his reeking lips upon my throat!' Her husband groaned again. She clasped his hand harder, and looked at him pityingly, as if he were the injured one, and went on:

'I felt my strength fading away, and I was in a half-swoon. How long this horrible thing lasted I know not; but it seemed that a long time must have passed before he took his foul, awful sneering mouth away. I saw it drip with the fresh blood!' The remembrance seemed for a while to overpower her, and she drooped and would have sunk down but for her husband's sustaining arm. With a great effort she recovered herself and went on:

'Then he spoke to me mockingly: "And so you, like the others, would play your brains against mine. You would help these men to hunt me and frustrate me in my designs! You know now, and they know in part already, and will know in full before long, what it is to cross my path. They should have kept their energies for use closer to home. Whilst they played wits against me – against me who commanded nations, and intrigued for them, and fought for them, hundreds of years before they were born I was countermining them. And you, their best beloved one, are now to me, flesh of my flesh;[185] blood of my blood; kin of my kin; my bountiful wine-press for a while; and shall be later on my companion and my helper. You shall be avenged in turn; for not one of them but shall minister to your needs. But as yet you are to be punished for what you have done. You have aided in thwarting me; now you shall come to my call. When my brain says "Come!" to you, you shall cross land or sea to do my bidding; and to that end this! With that he pulled open his shirt, and with his long sharp nails opened a vein in his breast. When the blood began to spurt out, he took my hands in one of his, holding them tight, and with the other seized my neck and pressed my mouth to the wound, so that I must either suffocate or swallow some of the – Oh, my God, my God! what have I done? What have I done to deserve such a fate, I who have tried to walk in meekness and righteousness all my days? God pity me! Look down on a poor soul in worse than mortal peril; and in mercy pity those to whom she is dear!' Then she began to rub her lips as though to cleanse them from pollution.

As she was telling her terrible story, the eastern sky began to quicken, and everything became more and more clear. Harker was still and quiet; but over his face, as the awful narrative went on, came a grey look which deepened and deepened in the morning light, till when the first red streak of the coming dawn shot up, the flesh stood darkly out against the whitening hair.

We have arranged that one of us is to stay within call of the unhappy pair till we can meet together and arrange about taking action.

Of this I am sure: the sun rises today on no more miserable house in all the great round of its daily course.

Chapter 22

JONATHAN HARKER'S JOURNAL

3 October. – As I must do something or go mad, I write this diary. It is now six o'clock, and we are to meet in the study in half an hour and take something to eat; for Dr Van Helsing and Dr Seward are agreed that if we do not eat we cannot work our best. Our best will be, God knows, required today. I must keep writing at every chance, for I dare not stop to think. All, big and little, must go down; perhaps at the end the little things may teach us most. The teaching, big or little, could not have landed Mina or me anywhere worse than we are today. However, we must trust and hope. Poor Mina told me just now, with the tears running down her dear cheeks, that it is in trouble and trial that our faith is tested – that we must keep on trusting; and that God will aid us up to the end. The end! oh, my God! what end? . . . To work! To work!

When Dr Van Helsing and Dr Seward had come back from seeing poor Renfield, we went gravely into what was to be done. First, Dr Seward told us that when he and Dr Van Helsing had gone down to the room below they had found Renfield lying on the floor, all in a heap. His face was all bruised and crushed in, and the bones of the neck were broken.

Dr Seward asked the attendant who was on duty in the passage if he had heard anything. He said that he had been sitting down – he confessed to half dozing – when he heard loud voices in the room, and then Renfield had called out loudly several times, 'God! God! God!' After that there was a sound of falling, and when he entered the room he found him lying on the floor, face down, just as the doctors had seen him. Van Helsing asked if he had heard 'voices' or 'a voice', and he said he could not say; that at first it had seemed to him as if there were two, but as there was no one in the room it could have been only one. He could swear to it, if required, that the word 'God' was spoken by the patient. Dr Seward said to us, when we were alone, that he did not wish to go into the matter; the question of an inquest had to be considered, and it would never do to put forward the truth, as no one would believe it. As it was, he thought that on the attendant's evidence he could give a certificate of death by misadventure in falling from bed. In case the coroner should demand it, there would be a formal inquest, necessarily to the same result.

When the question began to be discussed as to what should be our next step, the very first thing we decided was that Mina should be in full confidence; that nothing of any sort – no matter how painful – should be kept from her. She herself agreed as to its wisdom, and it was pitiful to see her so brave and yet so sorrowful, and in such a depth of despair. 'There must be no more concealment,' she said. 'Alas! we have had too much already. And besides there is nothing in all the world that can give me more pain than I have already endured – than I suffer now! Whatever may happen, it must be of new hope or of new courage to me!' Van Helsing was looking at her fixedly as she spoke, and said, suddenly but quietly:

'But, dear Madam Mina, are you not afraid; not for yourself, but for others from yourself, after what has happened?' Her face grew set in its lines, but her eyes shone with the devotion of a martyr as she answered:

'Ah no! for my mind is made up!'

'To what?' he asked gently, whilst we were all very still; for each in our own way we had a sort of vague idea of what she meant. Her answer came with direct simplicity, as though she were simply stating a fact:

'Because if I find in myself – and I shall watch keenly for it – a sign of harm to any that I love, I shall die!'

'You would not kill yourself?' he asked hoarsely.

'I would; if there were no friend who loved me, who would save me such a pain, and so desperate an effort!' She looked at him meaningly as she spoke. He was sitting down; but now he rose and came close to her and put his hand on her head as he said solemnly:

'My child, there is such an one if it were for your good. For myself I could hold it in my account with God to find such an euthanasia for you, even at this moment, if it were best. Nay, were it safe! But, my child – ' for a moment he seemed choked, and a great sob rose in his throat; he gulped it down and went on:

'There are here some who would stand between you and death. You must not die. You must not die by any hand; but least of all by your own. Until the other, who has fouled your sweet life, is true dead you must not die; for if he is still with the quick Un-Dead, your death would make you even as he is. No, you must live! You must struggle and strive to live, though death would seem a boon unspeakable. You must fight Death himself, though he come to you in pain or in joy; by the day, or the night; in safety or in peril! In your living soul I charge you that you do not die – nay, nor think of death – till this great evil be past.' The poor dear grew white as death, and shook and shivered, as I have seen a quicksand shake and shiver at the incoming of the tide. We were all silent; we could do nothing. At length she grew more calm, and turning to him said, sweetly, but oh! so sorrowfully, as she held out her hand:

'I promise you, my dear friend, that if God will let me live, I shall strive to do so; till, if it may be in His good time, this horror may have passed away from me.' She was so good and brave that we all felt that our hearts were strengthened to work and endure for her, and we began to discuss what we were to do. I told her that she was to have all the papers in the safe, and all the papers or diaries and phonographs we might hereafter use; and was to keep the record as she had done before. She was pleased with the prospect of anything to do – if 'pleased' could be used in connection with so grim an interest.

As usual Van Helsing had thought ahead of everyone else, and was prepared with an exact ordering of our work.

'It is perhaps well,' he said, 'that at our meeting after our visit to Carfax we decided not to do anything with the earth-boxes that lay there. Had we done so, the Count must have guessed our purpose, and would doubtless have taken measures in advance to frustrate such an effort with regard to the others; but now he does not know our intentions. Nay more, in all probability he does not know that such a power exists to us as can sterilise his lairs, so that he cannot use them as of old. We are now so much further advanced in our knowledge as to their disposition, that, when we have examined the house in Piccadilly we may track the very last of them. Today, then, is ours; and in it rests our hope. The sun that rose on our sorrow this morning guards us in its course. Until it sets tonight, that monster must retain whatever form he now has. He is confined within the limitations of his earthly envelope. He cannot melt into thin air nor disappear through cracks or chinks or crannies. If he go through a doorway, he must open the door like a mortal. And so we have this day to hunt out all his lairs and sterilise them. So we shall, if we have not yet catch him and destroy him, drive him to bay in some place where the catching and the destroying shall be, in time, sure.' Here I started up, for I could not contain myself at the thought that the minutes and seconds so preciously laden with Mina's life and happiness were flying from us, since whilst we talked action was possible. But Van Helsing held up his hand warningly. 'Nay, friend Jonathan,' he said, 'in this, the quickest way home is the longest way, so your proverb say. We shall all act, and act with desperate quick, when the time has come. But think, in all probable the key of the situation is in that house in Piccadilly. The Count may have many houses which he has bought. Of them he will have deeds of purchase, keys and other things. He will have paper that he write on; he will have his book of cheques. There are many belongings that he must have somewhere; why not in this place so central, so quiet, where he come and go by the front or the back at all hour, when in the very vast of the traffic there is none to notice. We shall go there and search that house; and when we learn what it holds, then we do what our friend Arthur call, in his phrases of hunt, "stop the earth", and so we run down our old fox – so? is it not?'

'Then let us come at once,' I cried; 'we are wasting the precious, precious time!' The Professor did not move, but simply said:

'And how are we to get into that house in Piccadilly?'

'Any way!' I cried. 'We shall break in if need be.'

'And your police; where will they be, and what will they say?'

I was staggered; but I knew that if he wished to delay he had a good reason for it. So I said, as quietly as I could:

'Don't wait more than need be; you know, I am sure, what torture I am in.'

'Ah, my child, that I do; and indeed there is no wish of me to add to your anguish. But just think, what can we do, until all the world be at movement. Then will come our time. I have thought and thought, and it seems to me that the simplest way is the best of all. Now we wish to get into the house, but we have no key; is it not so?' I nodded.

'Now suppose that you were, in truth, the owner of that house, and could not still get it; and think there was to you no conscience of the housebreaker, what would you do?'

'I should get a respectable locksmith, and set him to work to pick the lock for me.'

'And your police, they would interfere, would they not?'

'Oh, no! not if they knew the man was properly employed.'

'Then,' he looked at me keenly as he spoke, 'all that is in doubt is the conscience of the employer, and the belief of your policemen as to whether or no that employer has a good conscience or a bad one. Your police must indeed be zealous men and clever – oh, so clever! – in reading the heart, that they trouble themselves in such matter. No, no, my friend Jonathan, you go take the lock off a hundred empty house in this your London, or of any city in the world; and if you do it as such things are rightly done, and at the time such things are rightly done, no one will interfere. I have read of a gentleman who owned a so fine house in your London, and when he went for months of summer to Switzerland and lock up his house, some burglar came and broke window at back and got in. Then he went and made open the shutters in front and walk out and in through the door, before the very eyes of the police. Then he have an auction in that house, and advertise it, and put up big notice; and when the day come he sell off by a great auctioneer all the goods of that other man who own them. Then he go to a builder, and he sell him that house, making an agreement that he pull it down and take all away within a certain time. And your police and other authority help him all they can. And when that owner come back from his holiday in Switzerland he find only an empty hole where his house had been. This was all done *en règle*;[186] and in our work we shall be *en règle* too. We shall not go so early that the policeman who have then little to think of, shall deem it strange; but we shall go after ten o'clock when there are many about, and when such things would be done were we indeed owners of the house.'

I could not but see how right he was, and the terrible despair of Mina's face became relaxed as though there was hope in such good counsel. Van Helsing went on:

'When once within that house we may find more clues; at any rate some of us can remain there whilst the rest find the other places where there be more earth-boxes – at Bermondsey and Mile End.'

Lord Godalming stood up. 'I can be of some use here,' he said. 'I shall wire to my people to have horses and carriage where they will be most convenient.'

'Look here, old fellow,' said Morris, 'it is a capital idea to have all ready in case we want to go horsebacking; but don't you think that one of your snappy carriages with its heraldic adornments in a byeway of Walworth or Mile End would attract too much attention for our purposes? It seems to me that we ought to take cabs when we go south or east; and even leave them somewhere near the neighbourhood we are going to.'

'Friend Quincey is right!' said the Professor. 'His head is what you call in plane with the horizon. It is a difficult thing that we go to do, and we do not want no peoples to watch us if so it may.'

Mina took a growing interest in everything, and I was rejoiced to see that the exigency of affairs was helping her to forget for a time the terrible experience of the night. She was very, very pale – almost ghastly, and so thin that her lips were drawn away, showing her teeth somewhat prominently. I did not mention this last, lest it should give her needless pain; but it made my blood run cold in my veins to think of what had occurred with poor Lucy when the Count had sucked her blood. As yet there was no sign of the teeth growing sharper; but the time as yet was short, and there was time for fear.

When we came to the discussion of the sequence of our efforts and of the disposition of our forces, there were new sources of doubt. It was finally agreed that before starting for Piccadilly we should destroy the Count's lair close at hand. In case he should find it out too soon, we should thus be still ahead of him in our work of destruction; and his presence in his purely material shape, and at his weakest, might give us some new clue.

As to the disposal of forces, it was suggested by the Professor that, after our visit to Carfax, we should all enter the house in Piccadilly; that the two doctors and I should remain there, whilst Lord Godalming and Quincey found the lairs at Walworth and Mile End and destroyed them. It was possible, if not likely, the Professor urged, that the Count might appear in Piccadilly during the day, and that if so we might be able to cope with him then and there. At any rate we might be able to follow him in force. To this plan I strenuously objected, in so far as my going was concerned, for I said that I intended to stay and protect Mina. I thought that my mind was made up on the subject but Mina would not listen to my objection. She said that there might be some law matter in which I could be useful; that amongst the Count's papers might be some clue which I could understand out of my experience in Transylvania; and that, as it was, all the strength we could muster was required to cope with the Count's extraordinary power. I had to give in, for Mina's resolution was fixed; she said that it was the last hope for *her* that we should all work together. 'As for me,' she said, 'I have no fear. Things have been as bad as they can be; and whatever may happen must have in it some element of hope or comfort. Go, my husband! God can, if He wishes it, guard me as well alone as with anyone present.' So I started up, crying out: 'Then in God's name let us come at once, for we are losing time. The Count may come to Piccadilly earlier than we think.'

'Not so!' said Van Helsing, holding up his hand.

'But why?' I asked.

'Do you forget,' he said, with actually a smile, 'that last night he banqueted heavily, and will sleep late?'

Did I forget! shall I ever – can I ever! Can any of us ever forget that terrible scene! Mina struggled hard to keep her brave countenance; but the pain overmastered her and she put her hands before her face, and shuddered whilst she moaned. Van Helsing had not intended to recall her frightful experience. He had simply lost sight of her and her part in the affair in his intellectual effort. When it struck him what he had said, he was horrified at his thoughtlessness and tried to comfort her. 'Oh Madam Mina,' he said, 'dear, dear Madam Mina, alas! that I of all who so reverence you, should have said anything so forgetful. These stupid old lips of mine and this stupid old head do not deserve so; but you will forget it, will you not?' He bent low beside her as he spoke; she took his hand, and looking at him through her tears, said hoarsely:

'No, I shall not forget, for it is well that I remember, and with it I have so much in memory of you that is sweet, that I take it all together. Now, you must all be going soon. Breakfast is ready, and we must all eat that we may be strong.'

Breakfast was a strange meal to us all. We tried to be cheerful and encourage each other, and Mina was the brightest and most cheerful of us. When it was over, Van Helsing stood up and said:

'Now, my dear friends, we go forth to our terrible enterprise. Are we all armed, as we were on that night when first we visited our enemy's lair; armed against ghostly as well as carnal attack?' We all assured him. 'Then it is well. Now, Madam Mina, you are in any case *quite* safe here until the sunset; and before then we shall return – if – We shall return! But before we go let me see you armed against personal attack. I have myself, since you came down, prepared your chamber by the placing of the things of which we know, so that He may not enter. Now let me guard yourself. On your forehead I touch this piece of Sacred Wafer in the name of the Father, the Son and – '

There was a fearful scream which almost froze our hearts to hear. As he had placed the Wafer on Mina's forehead, it had seared it – had burned into the flesh as though it had been a piece of white-hot metal.

My poor darling's brain told her the significance of the fact as quickly as her nerves received the pain of it: and the two so overwhelmed her that her overwrought nature had its voice in that dreadful scream. But the words to her thought came quickly; the echo of the scream had not ceased to ring on the air when there came the reaction, and she sank on her knees on the floor in an agony of abasement. Pulling her beautiful hair over her face, as the leper of old his mantle, she wailed out:

'Unclean! Unclean! [187] Even the Almighty shuns my polluted flesh! I must bear this mark of shame upon my forehead until the Judgment Day.' They all paused. I had thrown myself beside her in an agony of helpless grief, and putting my arm around held her tight. For a few minutes our sorrowful hearts beat together, whilst the friends around us turned away their eyes that ran tears silently. Then Van Helsing turned and said gravely; so gravely that I could not help feeling that he was in some way inspired and was stating things outside himself:

'It may be that you may have to bear that mark till God Himself see fit, as He most surely shall, on the Judgment Day to redress all wrongs of the earth and of His children that He has placed thereon. And oh, Madam Mina, my dear, my dear may we who love you be there to see, when that red scar, the sign of God's knowledge of what has been, shall pass away and leave your forehead as pure as the heart we know. For so surely as we live, that scar shall pass away when God see right to lift the burden that is hard upon us. Till then we bear our Cross, as His Son did in obedience to His will. It may be that we are chosen instruments of His good pleasure and that we ascend to His bidding as that other through stripes and shame; through tears and blood; through doubts and fears, and all that makes the difference between God and man.'

There was hope in his words, and comfort; and they made for resignation. Mina and I both felt so, and simultaneously we each took one of the old man's hands and bent over and kissed it. Then without a word we all knelt down together, and, all holding hands, swore to be true to each other. We men pledged ourselves to raise the veil of sorrow from the head of her whom, each in his own way, we loved; and we prayed for help and guidance in the terrible task which lay before us.

It was then time to start. So I said farewell to Mina, a parting which neither of us shall forget to our dying day; and we set out.

To one thing I have made up my mind: if we find out that Mina must be a vampire in the end, then she shall not go into that unknown and terrible land alone. I suppose it is thus that in old times one vampire meant many; just as their hideous bodies could only rest in sacred earth, so the holiest love was the recruiting sergeant for their ghastly ranks.

We entered Carfax without trouble and found all things the same as on the first occasion. It was hard to believe that amongst so prosaic surroundings of neglect and dust and decay there was any ground for such fear as we already knew. Had not our minds been made up, and had there not been terrible memories to spur us on, we could hardly have proceeded with our task. We found no papers, nor any sign of use in the house and in the old chapel the great boxes looked just as we had seen them last. Dr Van Helsing said to us solemnly as we stood before them:

'And now, my friends, we have a duty here to do. We must sterilise this earth, so sacred of holy memories, that he has brought from a far distant land for such fell use. He has chosen this earth because it has been holy. Thus we defeat him with his own weapon, for we make it more holy still. It was sanctified to such use of man, now we sanctify it to God.' As he spoke he took from his bag a screw-driver and a wrench, and very soon the top of one of the cases was thrown open. The earth smelled musty and close; but we did not somehow seem to mind, for our attention was concentrated on the Professor. Taking from his box a piece of the Sacred Wafer he laid it reverently on the earth and then shutting down the lid began to screw it home, we aiding him as he worked.

One by one we treated in the same way each of the great boxes, and left them as we had found them to all appearance but in each was a portion of the Host.

When we closed the door behind us, the Professor said solemnly:

'So much is already done. If it may be that with all the others we can be so successful, then the sunset of this evening may shine on Madam Mina's forehead all white as ivory and with no stain!'

As we passed across the lawn on our way to the station to catch our train we could see the front of the asylum. I looked eagerly, and in the window of my own room saw Mina. I waved my hand to her, and nodded to tell that our work there was successfully accomplished. She nodded in reply to show that she understood. The last I saw, she was waving her hand in farewell. It was with a heavy heart that we sought the station and just caught the train, which was steaming in as we reached the platform.

I have written this in the train.

Piccadilly, 12.30 o'clock. – Just before we reached Fenchurch Street Lord Godalming said to me:

'Quincey and I will find a locksmith. You had better not come with us in case there should be any difficulty; for under the circumstances it wouldn't seem so bad for us to break into an empty house. But you are a solicitor, and the Incorporated Law Society might tell you that you should have known better.' I demurred as to my not sharing any danger even of odium, but he went on: 'Besides, it will attract less attention if there are not too many of us. My title will make it all right with the locksmith, and with any policeman that may come along. You had better go with Jack and the Professor and stay in the Green Park, somewhere in sight of the house; and when you see the door opened and the smith has gone away, do you all come across. We shall be on the look-out for you, and will let you in.'

'The advice is good!' said Van Helsing, so we said no more. Godalming and Morris hurried off in a cab, we following in another. At the corner of Arlington Street our contingent got out and strolled into the Green Park. My heart beat as I saw the house on which so much of our hope was centred, looming up grim and silent in its deserted condition amongst its more lively and spruce-looking neighbours. We sat down on a bench within good view, and began to smoke cigars so as to attract as little attention as possible. The minutes seemed to pass with leaden feet as we waited for the coming of the others.

At length we saw a four-wheeler drive up. Out of it, in leisurely fashion, got Lord Godalming and Morris; and down from the box descended a thick-set working man with his rush-woven basket of tools. Morris paid the cabman, who touched his hat and drove away. Together the two ascended the steps, and Lord Godalming pointed out what he wanted done. The workman took off his coat leisurely and hung it on one of the spikes of the railing, saying something to a policeman who just then sauntered along. The policeman nodded acquiescence, and the man kneeling down placed his bag beside him. After searching through it, he took out a selection of tools which he proceeded to lay beside him in orderly fashion. Then he stood up, looked into the keyhole, blew into it, and, turning to his employers, made some remark. Lord Godalming smiled, and the man lifted a good-sized bunch of keys; selecting one of them, he began to probe the lock, as if feeling his way with it. After fumbling about for a bit he tried a second, and then a third. All at once the door opened under a slight push from him, and he and the two others entered the hall. We sat still; my own cigar burnt furiously, but Van Helsing's went cold altogether. We waited patiently as we saw the workman come out and bring in his bag. Then he held the door partly open, steadying it with his knees, whilst he fitted a key to the lock. This he finally handed to Lord Godalming, who took out his purse and gave him something. The man touched his hat, took his bag, put on his coat and departed; not a soul took the slightest notice of the whole transaction.

When the man had fairly gone, we three crossed the street and knocked at the door. It was immediately opened by Quincey Morris, beside whom stood Lord Godalming lighting a cigar.

'The place smells so vilely,' said the latter as we came in. It did indeed smell vilely – like the old chapel at Carfax – and with our previous experience it was plain to us that the Count had been using the place pretty freely. We moved to explore the house, all keeping together in case of attack; for we knew we had a strong and wily enemy to deal with, and as yet we did not know whether the Count might not be in the house. In the dining-room, which lay at the back of the hall, we found eight boxes of earth. Eight boxes only out of the nine which we sought! Our work was not over, and would never be until we should have found the missing box. First we opened the shutters of the window which looked out across a narrow stone-flagged yard at the blank face of a stable, pointed to look like the front of a miniature house. There were no windows in it, so we were not afraid of being overlooked. We did not lose any time in examining the chests. With the tools which we had brought with us we opened them, one by one, and treated them as we had treated those others in the old chapel. It was evident to us that the Count was not at present in the house, and we proceeded to search for any of his effects.

After a cursory glance at the rest of the rooms from basement to attic, we came to the conclusion that the dining-room contained any effects which might belong to the Count; and so we proceeded to minutely examine them. They lay in a sort of orderly disorder on the great dining-room table. There were title-deeds of the Piccadilly house in a great bundle; deeds of the purchase of the houses at Mile End and Bermondsey; notepaper, envelopes, and pens and ink. All were covered up in thin wrapping paper to keep them from the dust. There were also a clothes brush, a brush and comb, and a jug and basin – the latter containing dirty water which was reddened as if with blood. Last of all was a little heap of keys of all sorts and sizes, probably those belonging to the other houses. When we had examined this last find, Lord Godalming and Quincey Morris, taking accurate notes of the various addresses of the houses in the East and the South, took with them the keys in a great bunch, and set out to destroy the boxes in these places. The rest of us are, with what patience we can, waiting their return – or the coming of the Count.

Chapter 23

Dr Seward's Diary

3 October. – The time seemed terribly long whilst we were waiting for the coming of Godalming and Quincey Morris. The Professor tried to keep our minds active by using them all the time. I could see his beneficent purpose, by the side glances which he threw from time to time at Harker. The poor fellow is overwhelmed in a misery that is appalling to see. Last night he was a frank, happy-looking man, with strong youthful face, full of energy, and with dark brown hair. Today he is a drawn, haggard, old man, whose white hair matches well with the hollow burning eyes and grief-written lines of his face. His energy is still intact; in fact he is like a living flame. This may yet be his salvation, for, if all goes well, it will tide him over the despairing period; he will then, in a kind of way, wake again to the realities of life. Poor fellow, I thought my own trouble was bad enough, but his – ! The Professor knows this well enough, and is doing his best to keep his mind active. What he has been saying was, under the circumstances, of absorbing interest. As well as I can remember, here it is:

'I have studied, over and over again since they came into my hands, all the papers relating to this monster; and the more I have studied, the greater seems the necessity to utterly stamp him out. All through there are signs of his advance; not only of his power, but of his knowledge of it. As I learned from the researches of my friend Arminius of Buda-Pesth, he was in life a most wonderful man. Soldier, statesman, and alchemist – which latter was the highest development of the science-knowledge of his time. He had a mighty brain, a learning beyond compare, and a heart that knew no fear and no remorse. He dared even to attend the Scholomance, and there was no branch of knowledge of his time that he did not essay. Well, in him the brain powers survived the physical death; though it would seem that memory was not all complete. In some faculties of mind he has been, and is, only a child; but he is growing, and some things that were childish at the first are now of man's stature. He is experimenting, and doing it well; and if it had not been that we have crossed his path he would be yet – he may be yet if we fail – the father or furtherer of a new order of beings, whose road must lead through Death, not Life.'

Harker groaned and said, 'And this is all arrayed against my darling!
But how is he experimenting? The knowledge may help us to defeat
him!'

'He has all along, since his coming, been trying his power, slowly but
surely; that big child-brain of his is working. Well for us, it is, as yet, a
child-brain; for had he dared, at the first, to attempt certain things he
would long ago have been beyond our power. However, he means to
succeed, and a man who has centuries before him can afford to wait and
to go slow. *Festina lente* [188] may well be his motto.'

'I fail to understand,' said Harker wearily. 'Oh, do be more plain to
me! Perhaps grief and trouble are dulling my brain.' The Professor laid
his hand tenderly on his shoulder as he spoke:

'Ah, my child, I will be plain. Do you not see how, of late, this
monster has been creeping into knowledge experimentally. How he
has been making use of the zoophagous patient to effect his entry into
friend John's home; for your Vampire, though in all afterwards he can
come when and how he will must at the first make entry only when
asked thereto by an inmate. But these are not his most important
experiments. Do we not see how at the first all these so great boxes
were moved by others. He knew not then but that must be so. But all
the time that so great child-brain of his was growing, and he began to
consider whether he might not himself move the box. So he begin to
help; and then, when he found that this be all right, he try to move
them all alone. And so he progress, and he scatter these graves of him;
and none but he know where they are hidden. He may have intend to
bury them deep in the ground. So that he only use them in the night,
or at such time as he can change his form, they do him equal well; and
none may know these are his hiding place! But my child, do not
despair; this knowledge come to him just too late! Already all of his
lairs but one be sterilise as for him; and before the sunset this shall be
so. Then he have no place where he can move and hide. I delayed this
morning that so we might be sure. Is there not more at stake for us
than for him? Then why we not be even more careful than him? By
my clock it is one hour, and already, if all be well, friend Arthur and
Quincey are on their way to us. Today is our day, and we must go sure,
if slow, and lose no chance. See! there are five of us when those absent
ones return.'

Whilst he was speaking we were startled by a knock at the hall door,
the double postman's knock of the telegraph boy. We all moved out to
the hall with one impulse, and Van Helsing, holding up his hand to us
to keep silence, stepped to the door and opened it. The boy handed in a

despatch. The Professor closed the door again and, after looking at the direction, opened it and read it aloud:

'Look out for D. He has just now, 12.45, come from Carfax hurriedly and hastened towards the south. He seems to be going the round and may want to see you. – MINA.'

There was a pause, broken by Jonathan Harker's voice:

'Now, God be thanked, we shall soon meet!' Van Helsing turned to him quickly and said:

'God will act in His own way and time. Do not fear, and do not rejoice as yet; for what we wish for at the moment may be our undoings.'

'I care for nothing now,' he answered hotly, 'except to wipe out this brute from the face of creation. I would sell my soul to do it!'

'Oh, hush, hush, my child!' said Van Helsing, 'God does not purchase souls in this wise; and the Devil, though he may purchase, does not keep faith. But God is merciful and just, and knows your pain and your devotion to that dear Madam Mina. Think you, how her pain would be doubled, did she but hear your wild words. Do not fear any of us; we are all devoted to this cause, and today shall see the end. The time is coming for action; today this Vampire is limit to the powers of man, and till sunset he may not change. It will take him time to arrive here – see, it is twenty minutes past one – and there are yet some times before he can hither come, be he never so quick. What we must hope for is that my Lord Arthur and Quincey arrive first.'

About half an hour after we had received Mrs Harker's telegram, there came a quiet resolute knock at the hall door. It was just an ordinary knock, such as is given hourly by thousands of gentlemen, but it made the Professor's heart and mine beat loudly. We looked at each other, and together moved out into the hall; we each held ready to use our various armaments – the spiritual in the left hand, the mortal in the right. Van Helsing pulled back the latch, and, holding the door half open, stood back, having both hands ready for action. The gladness of our hearts must have shown upon our faces when on the step, close to the door, we saw Lord Godalming and Quincey Morris. They came quickly in and closed the door behind them, the former saying, as they moved along the hall:

'It is all right. We found both places; six boxes in each, and we destroyed them all!'

'Destroyed?' asked the Professor.

'For him!' We were silent for a minute, and then Quincey said:

'There's nothing to do but to wait here. If, however, he doesn't turn up by five o'clock, we must start off; for it won't do to leave Mrs Harker alone after sunset.'

'He will be here before long now,' said Van Helsing, who had been consulting his pocket-book. '*Nota bene*,[189] in Madam's telegram he went south from Carfax, that means he went to cross the river, and he could only do so at slack of tide, which should be something before one o'clock. That he went south has a meaning for us. He is as yet only suspicious; and he went from Carfax first to the place where he would suspect interference least. You must have been at Bermondsey only a short time before him. That he is not here already shows that he went to Mile End next. This took him some time; for he would then have to be carried over the river in some way. Believe me, my friends, we shall not have long to wait now. We should have ready some plan of attack, so that we may throw away no chance. Hush, there is no time now. Have all your arms! Be ready!' He held up warning hand as he spoke, for we all could hear a key softly inserted in the lock of the hall door.

I could not but admire, even at such a moment, the way in which a dominant spirit asserted itself. In all our hunting parties and adventures in different parts of the world, Quincey Morris had always been the one to arrange the plan of action, and Arthur and I had been accustomed to obey him implicitly. Now the old habit seemed to be renewed instinctively. With a swift glance round the room, he at once laid out our plan of attack, and, without speaking a word, with a gesture, placed us each in position. Van Helsing, Harker, and I were just behind the door so that when it was opened the Professor could guard it whilst we two stepped between the incomer and the door. Godalming behind and Quincey in front stood just out of sight ready to move in front of the window. We waited in a suspense that made the seconds pass with nightmare slowness. The slow, careful steps came along the hall; the Count was evidently prepared for some surprise – at least he feared it.

Suddenly with a single bound he leaped into the room, winning a way past us before any of us could raise a hand to stay him. There was something so panther-like in the movement – something so unhuman, that it seemed to sober us all from the shock of his coming. The first to act was Harker, who, with a quick movement, threw himself before the door leading into the room in the front of the house. As the Count saw us, a horrible sort of snarl passed over his face, showing the eye-teeth long and pointed; but the evil smile as quickly passed into a cold stare of lion-like disdain. His expression again changed, as, with a single impulse, we all advanced upon him. It was a pity that we had not some

better organised plan of attack, for even at the moment I wondered
what we were to do. I did not myself know whether our lethal weapons
would avail us anything. Harker evidently meant to try the matter, for
he had ready his great Kukri knife, and made a fierce and sudden cut at
him. The blow was a powerful one; only the diabolical quickness of the
Count's leap back saved him. A second less and the trenchant blade had
shorn through his heart. As it was, the point just cut the cloth of his
coat, making a wide gap whence a bundle of bank-notes and a stream of
gold fell out. The expression of the Count's face was so hellish, that for
a moment I feared for Harker, though I saw him throw the terrible
knife aloft again for another stroke. Instinctively I moved forward with a
protective impulse, holding the crucifix and wafer in my left hand. I felt
a mighty power fly along my arm; and it was without surprise that I saw
the monster cower back before a similar movement made spontaneously
by each one of us. It would be impossible to describe the expression of
hate and baffled malignity – of anger and hellish rage – which came over
the Count's face. His waxen hue became greenish-yellow by the
contrast of his burning eyes, and the red scar on the forehead showed
on the pallid skin like a palpitating wound. The next instant, with a
sinuous dive he swept under Harker's arm, ere his blow could fall, and,
grasping a handful of the money from the floor, dashed across the
room, and threw himself at the window. Amid the crash and glitter of
the falling glass, he tumbled into the flagged area below. Through the
sound of the shivering glass I could hear the 'ting' of the gold, as some
of the sovereigns fell on the flagging.

We ran over and saw him spring unhurt from the ground. He,
rushing up the steps, crossed the flagged yard, and pushed open the
stable door. There he turned and spoke to us:

'You think to baffle me you – with your pale faces all in a row, like
sheep in a butcher's. You shall be sorry yet, each one of you! You think
you have left me without a place to rest; but I have more. My revenge is
just begun! I spread it over centuries, and time is on my side. Your girls
that you all love are mine already; and through them you and others
shall yet be mine – my creatures, to do my bidding and to be my jackals
when I want to feed. Bah!' With a contemptuous sneer, he passed
quickly through the door, and we heard the rusty bolt creak as he
fastened it behind him. A door beyond opened and shut. The first of us
to speak was the Professor, as, realising the difficulty of following him
through the stable, we moved towards the hall.

'We have learnt something – much! Notwithstanding his brave
words, he fears us; he fear time, he fear want! For if not, why he hurry

so? His very tone betray him, or my ears deceive. Why take that money? You follow quick. You are hunters of wild beast, and understand it so. For me, I make sure that nothing here may be of use to him, if so that he return.' As he spoke he put the money remaining into his pocket; took the title-deeds in the bundle as Harker had left them; and swept the remaining things into the open fireplace, where he set fire to them with a match.

Godalming and Morris had rushed out into the yard, and Harker had lowered himself from the window to follow the Count. He had, however, bolted the stable door; and by the time they had forced it open there was no sign of him. Van Helsing and I tried to make inquiry at the back of the house; but the mews was deserted and no one had seen him depart.

It was now late in the afternoon, and sunset was not far off. We had to recognise that our game was up; with heavy hearts we agreed with the Professor when he said:

'Let us go back to Madam Mina – poor, poor, dear Madam Mina. All we can do just now is done; and we can there, at least, protect her. But we need not despair. There is but one more earth-box, and we must try to find it; when that is done all may yet be well.' I could see that he spoke as bravely as he could to comfort Harker. The poor fellow was quite broken down; now and again he gave a low groan which he could not suppress – he was thinking of his wife.

With sad hearts we came back to my house, where we found Mrs Harker awaiting us, with an appearance of cheerfulness which did honour to her bravery and unselfishness. When she saw our faces, her own became as pale as death; for a second or two her eyes were closed as if she were in secret prayer; and then she said cheerfully:

'I can never thank you all enough. Oh, my poor darling!' As she spoke, she took her husband's grey head in her hands and kissed it – 'Lay your poor head here and rest it. All will yet be well, dear! God will protect us if He so will it in His good intent.' The poor fellow only groaned. There was no place for words in his sublime misery.

We had a sort of perfunctory supper together, and I think it cheered us all up somewhat. It was, perhaps, the mere animal heat of food to hungry people – for none of us had eaten anything since breakfast – or the sense of companionship may have helped us; but anyhow we were all less miserable, and saw the morrow as not altogether without hope. True to our promise, we told Mrs Harker everything which had passed; and although she grew snowy white at times when danger had seemed to threaten her husband, and red at others when his devotion to her was

manifested, she listened bravely and with calmness. When we came to
the part where Harker had rushed at the Count so recklessly, she clung
to her husband's arm, and held it tight as though her clinging could
protect him from any harm that might come. She said nothing,
however, the narration was all done, and matters had been brought
right up to the present time. Then without letting go her husband's
hand she stood up amongst us and spoke. Oh! that I could give any idea
of the scene; of that sweet, sweet, good, good woman in all the radiant
beauty of her youth and animation, with the red scar on her forehead of
which she was conscious, and which we saw with grinding of our teeth –
remembering whence and how it came; her loving kindness against our
grim hate; her tender faith against all our fears and doubting; and we,
knowing that, so far as symbols went, she with all her goodness and
purity and faith was outcast from God.

'Jonathan,' she said, and the word sounded like music on her lips, it
was so full of love and tenderness, 'Jonathan dear, and you all, my true,
true friends, I want you to bear something in mind through all this
dreadful time. I know that you must fight – that you must destroy even
as you destroyed the false Lucy so that the true Lucy might live
hereafter; but it is not a work of hate. That poor soul who has wrought
all this misery is the saddest case of all. Just think what will be his joy
when he too is destroyed in his worser part that his better part may have
spiritual immortality. You must be pitiful to him too, though it may not
hold your hands from his destruction.'

As she spoke I could see her husband's face darken and draw together,
as though the passion in him were shrivelling his being to its core.
Instinctively the clasp on his wife's hand grew closer till his knuckles
looked white. She did not flinch from the pain which I knew she must
have suffered, but looked at him with eyes that were more appealing
than ever. As she stopped speaking he leaped to his feet, almost tearing
his hand from hers as he spoke:

'May God give him into my hand just for long enough to destroy that
earthly life of him which we are aiming at. If beyond it I could send his
soul for ever and ever to burning hell I would do it!'

'Oh, hush! oh, hush! in the name of the good God. Don't say such
things, Jonathan, my husband; or you will crush me with fear and
horror. Just think, my dear – I have been thinking all this long, long day
of it – that . . . perhaps . . . some day . . . I too may need such pity; and
that some other like you and with equal cause for anger – may deny it to
me! Oh, my husband! my husband, indeed I would have spared you
such a thought had there been another way; but I pray that God may

not have treasured your wild words, except as the heart-broken wail of a very loving and sorely stricken man. Oh, God, let these poor white hairs go in evidence of what he has suffered, who all his life has done no wrong, and on whom so many sorrows have come.'

We men were all in tears now. There was no resisting them, and we wept openly. She wept too, to see that her sweeter counsels had prevailed. Her husband flung himself on his knees beside her, and putting his arms round her, hid his face in the folds of her dress. Van Helsing beckoned to us and we stole out of the room, leaving the two loving hearts alone with God.

Before they retired the Professor fixed up the room against any coming of the Vampire, and assured Mrs Harker that she might rest in peace. She tried to school herself to the belief and, manifestly for her husband's sake, tried to seem content. It was a brave struggle; and was, I think and believe, not without its reward. Van Helsing had placed at hand a bell which either of them was to sound in case of any emergency. When they had retired, Quincey, Godalming, and I arranged that we should sit up, dividing the night between us, and watch over the safety of the poor stricken lady. The first watch falls to Quincey, so the rest of us will be off to bed as soon as we can. Godalming has already turned in, for his is the second watch. Now that my work is done I, too, shall go to bed.

JONATHAN HARKER'S JOURNAL

3 – 4 October, close to midnight. – I thought yesterday would never end. There was over me a yearning for sleep in some sort of blind belief that to wake would be to find things changed, and that any change must now be for the better. Before we parted, we discussed what our next step was to be, but we could arrive at no result. All we knew was that one earth-box remained, and that the Count alone knew where it was. If he chooses to lie hidden, he may baffle us for years; and in the meantime! – the thought is too horrible, I dare not think of it even now. This I know: that if ever there was a woman who was all perfection, that one is my poor wronged darling. I love her a thousand times more for her sweet pity of last night, a pity that made my own hate of the monster seem despicable. Surely God will not permit the world to be the poorer by the loss of such a creature. This is hope to me. We are all drifting reefwards now, and faith is our only anchor. Thank God! Mina is sleeping, and sleeping without dreams. I fear what her dreams might be like, with such terrible memories to ground them in. She has not been so calm, within my seeing, since the sunset. Then for a while, there came over her face a repose which was like spring after the blasts of March. I thought at the time that it was the softness of the red sunset on her face, but somehow now I think it had a deeper meaning. I am not sleepy myself, though I am weary – weary to death. However, I must try to sleep; for there is tomorrow to think of, and there is no rest for me until . . .

Later. – I must have fallen asleep, for I was awakened by Mina, who was sitting up in bed, with a startled look on her face. I could see easily, for we did not leave the room in darkness; she had placed a warning hand over my mouth, and now she whispered in my ear:

'Hush! there is someone in the corridor!' I got up softly, and, crossing the room, gently opened the door.

Just outside, stretched on a mattress, lay Mr Morris, wide awake. He raised a warning hand for silence as he whispered to me:

'Hush! go back to bed; it is all right. One of us will be here all night. We don't mean to take any chances!'

His look and gesture forbade discussion, so I came back and told Mina. She sighed, and positively a shadow of a smile stole over her poor, pale face as she put her arms round me and said softly:

'Oh, thank God for good brave men!' With a sigh she sank back again to sleep. I write this now as I am not sleepy, though I must try again.

4 October, morning. – Once again during the night I was wakened by Mina. This time we had all had a good sleep, for the grey of the coming dawn was making the windows into sharp oblongs, and the gas flame was like a speck rather than a disc of light. She said to me hurriedly:

'Go call the Professor. I want to see him at once.'

'Why?' I asked.

'I have an idea. I suppose it must have come in the night, and matured without my knowing it. He must hypnotise me before the dawn, and then I shall be able to speak. Go quick, dearest; the time is getting close.' I went to the door. Dr Seward was resting on the mattress, and, seeing me, he sprang to his feet.

'Is anything wrong?' he asked, in alarm.

'No,' I replied; 'but Mina wants to see Dr Van Helsing at once.'

'I will go,' he said, and hurried into the Professor's room.

Two or three minutes later Van Helsing was in the room in his dressing-gown, and Mr Morris and Lord Godalming were with Dr Seward at the door asking questions. When the Professor saw Mina a smile – a positive smile – ousted the anxiety of his face; he rubbed his hands as he said:

'Oh, my dear Madam Mina, this is indeed a change. See! friend Jonathan, we have got our dear Madam Mina, as of old, back to us today!' Then turning to her, he said cheerfully: 'And what am I do for you? For at this hour you do not want me for nothings.'

'I want you to hypnotise me!' she said. 'Do it before the dawn, for I feel that then I can speak, and speak freely. Be quick, for the time is short!' Without a word he motioned her to sit up in bed.

Looking fixedly at her, he commenced to make passes in front of her, from over the top of her head downward, with each hand in turn. Mina gazed at him fixedly for a few minutes during which my own heart beat like a trip hammer, for I felt that some crisis was at hand. Gradually her eyes closed, and she sat, stock still; only by the gentle heaving of her bosom could one know that she was alive. The Professor made a few more passes and then stopped, and I could see that his forehead was covered with great beads of perspiration. Mina opened her eyes; but she did not seem the same woman. There was a faraway look in her eyes, and her voice had a sad dreaminess which was new to me. Raising his hand to impose silence, the Professor motioned to me to bring the others in. They came on tip-toe, closing the door behind them, and stood at the foot of the bed, looking on. Mina appeared not to see them. The stillness was broken by Van Helsing's voice speaking in a low level tone which would not break the current of her thoughts:

'Where are you?' The answer came in a neutral way:

'I do not know. Sleep has no place it can call its own.' For several minutes there was silence. Mina sat rigid, and the Professor stood staring at her fixedly; the rest of us hardly dared to breathe. The room was growing lighter; without taking his eyes from Mina's face, Dr Van Helsing motioned me to pull up the blind. I did so, and the day seemed just upon us. A red streak shot up, and a rosy light seemed to diffuse itself through the room. On the instant the Professor spoke again:

'Where are you now?' The answer came dreamily, but with intention; it was as though she were interpreting something. I have heard her use the same tone when reading her notes.

'I do not know. It is all strange to me!'

'What do you see?'

'I can see nothing; it is all dark.'

'What do you hear?' I could detect the strain in the Professor's patient voice.

'The lapping of water. It is gurgling by, and little waves leap. I can hear them on the outside.'

'Then you are on a ship?' We all looked at each other, trying to glean something each from the other. We were afraid to think. The answer came quick: 'Oh, yes!'

'What else do you hear?'

'The sound of men stamping overhead as they run about. There is the creaking of a chain, and the loud tinkle as the check of the capstan falls into the ratchet.'

'What are you doing?'

'I am still – oh, so still. It is like death!' The voice faded away into a deep breath as of one sleeping, and the open eyes closed again.

By this time the sun had risen, and we were all in the full light of day. Dr Van Helsing placed his hands on Mina's shoulders, and laid her head down softly on her pillow. She lay like a sleeping child for a few moments, and then, with a long sigh, awoke and stared in wonder to see us all around her. 'Have I been talking in my sleep?' was all she said. She seemed, however, to know the situation without telling; though she was eager to know what she had told. The Professor repeated the conversation, and she said:

'Then there is not a moment to lose: it may not be yet too late!' Mr Morris and Lord Godalming started for the door, but the Professor's calm voice called them back:

'Stay, my friends. That ship, wherever it was, was weighing anchor whilst she spoke. There are many ships weighing anchor at the moment in your so great Port of London. Which of them is it that you seek? God be thanked that we have once again a clue, though whither it may lead us we know not. We have been blind somewhat; blind after the manner of men, since when we can look back we see what we might have seen looking forward if we had been able to see what we might have seen! Alas! but that sentence is a puddle; is it not? We can know now what was in the Count's mind when he seize that money, though Jonathan's so fierce knife put him in the danger that even he dread. He meant escape. Hear me, ESCAPE! He saw that with but one earth-box left, and a pack of men following like dogs after a fox, this London was no place for him. He have take his last earth-box on board a ship, and he leave the land. He think to escape, but no! we follow him. Tally ho! as friend Arthur would say when he put on his red frock! Our old fox is wily; oh; so wily, and we must follow with wile. I too am wily and I think his mind in a little while. In meantime we may rest and in peace, for there are waters between us which he do not want to pass, and which he could not if he would – unless the ship were to touch the land, and then only at full or slack tide. See, and the sun is just rose, and all day to sunset is to us. Let us take bath, and dress, and have breakfast which we all need, and which we can eat comfortable since he be not in the same land with us.' Mina looked at him appealingly as she asked:

'But why need we seek him further, when he is gone away from us?' He took her hand and patted it as he replied:

'Ask me nothings as yet. When we have breakfast, than I answer all questions.' He would say no more, and we separated to dress.

After breakfast Mina repeated her question. He looked at her gravely for a minute and then said sorrowfully:

'Because, my dear, dear Madam Mina, now more than ever must we find him even if we have to follow him to the jaws of Hell!' She grew paler as she asked faintly:

'Why?'

'Because,' he answered solemnly, 'he can live for centuries and you are but mortal woman. Time is now to be dreaded – since once he put that mark upon your throat.'

I was just in time to catch her as she fell forward in a faint.

Chapter 24

Dr Seward's Phonograph Diary, spoken by Van Helsing

This to Jonathan Harker.

You are to stay with your dear Madam Mina. We shall go to make our search – if I can call it so, for it is not search but knowing, and we seek contamination only. But do you stay and take care of her today. This is your best and most holiest office. This day nothing can find him here. Let me tell you that so you will know what we four know already, for I have tell them. He, our enemy, have gone away; he have gone back to his Castle in Transylvania. I know it so well, as if a great hand of fire wrote it on the wall. He have prepare for this in some way, and that last earth-box was ready to ship somewhere. For this he took the money; for this he hurry at the last, lest we catch him before the sun go down. It was his last hope, save that he might hide in the tomb, that he think poor Miss Lucy, being as he thought like him, keep open to him. But there was not of time. When that fail he make straight for his last resource – his last earthwork I might say did I wish *double entente*.[190] He is clever, oh, so clever! he know that his game here was finish; and so he decide he go back home. He find ship going by the route he came, and he go in it. We go off now to find what ship, and whither bound, when we have discover that, we come back and tell you all. Then we will comfort you and poor dear Madam Mina with new hope. For it will be hope when you think it over: that all is not lost. This very creature that we pursue, he take hundreds of years to get so far as London; and yet in one day, when we know of the disposal of him we drive him out. He is finite, though he is powerful to do much harm and suffers not as we do. But we are strong, each in our purpose; and we are all more strong together. Take heart afresh, dear husband of Madam Mina. This battle is but begun, and in the end we shall win – so sure as that God sits on high to watch over His children. Therefore be of much comfort till we return.

VAN HELSING

JONATHAN HARKER'S JOURNAL

4 October. – When I read to Mina Van Helsing's message in the phonograph, the poor girl brightened up considerably. Already the certainty that the Count is out of the country has given her comfort; and comfort is strength to her. For my own part, now that this horrible danger is not face to face with us, it seems almost impossible to believe in it. Even my own terrible experiences in Castle Dracula seem like a long-forgotten dream. Here in the crisp autumn air in the bright sunlight –

Alas! how can I disbelieve! In the midst of my thought my eye fell on the red scar on my poor darling's white forehead. Whilst that lasts, there can be no disbelief. And afterwards the very memory of it will keep faith crystal clear. Mina and I fear to be idle so we have been over all the diaries again and again. Somehow, although the reality seems greater each time, the pain and the fear seem less. There is something of a guiding purpose manifest throughout, which is comforting. Mina says that perhaps we are the instruments of ultimate good. It may be! I shall try to think as she does. We have never spoken to each other yet of the future. It is better to wait till we see the Professor and the others after their investigations.

The day is running by more quickly than I ever thought a day could run for me again. It is now three o'clock.

Mina Harker's Journal

5 October, 5 p.m. - Our meeting for report. Present: Professor Van Helsing, Lord Godalming, Dr Seward, Mr Quincey Morris, Jonathan Harker, Mina Harker.

Dr Van Helsing described what steps were taken during the day to discover on what boat and whither bound Count Dracula made his escape:

'As I knew that he wanted to get back to Transylvania, I felt sure that he must go by the Danube mouth; or by somewhere in the Black Sea, since by that way he come. It was a dreary blank that was before us. *Omne ignotum pro magnifico*;[191] and so with heavy hearts we start to find what ships leave for the Black Sea last night. He was in sailing ship, since Madam Mina tell of sails being set. These not so important as to go in your list of the shipping in *The Times*, and so we go, by suggestion of my Lord Godalming, to your Lloyd's, where are note of all ships that sail, however so small. There we find that only one Black Sea bound ship go out with the tide. She is the *Czarina Catherine*, and she sail from Doolittle's Wharf for Varna,[192] and thence on to other parts and up the Danube. "Soh!" said I, "this is the ship whereon is the Count." So off we go to Doolittle's Wharf, and there we find a man in an office of wood so small that the man look bigger than the office. From him we inquire of the goings of the *Czarina Catherine*. He swear much and he red face and loud of voice, but he good fellow all the same; and when Quincey give him something from his pocket which crackle as he roll it up, and put it in a so small bag which he have hid deep in his clothing, he still better fellow and humble servant to us. He come with us, and ask many men who are rough and hot; these be better fellows too when they have been no more thirsty. They say much of blood and bloom and of others which I comprehend not, though I guess what they mean; but nevertheless they tell us all things which we want to know.

'They make known to us among them, how last afternoon at about five o'clock comes a man so hurry. A tall man, thin and pale, with high nose and teeth so white, and eyes that seem to be burning. That he be all in black, except that he have a hat of straw which suit not him or the time. That he scatter his money in making quick inquiry as to what ship sails for the Black Sea and for where. Some took him to the office and then to the ship, where he will not go aboard but halt at shore end of gang-plank, and ask that the captain come to him. The captain come, when told that he will be pay well; and though he swear much at the first he agree to term. Then the thin man go and someone tell him where horse and cart can be hired. He go there, and soon he come again, himself driving cart on which is a great box; this he himself lift down, though it take several to put it on truck for the ship. He give much talk to captain as to how and where his box is to be place; but the captain like it not and swear at him in many tongues, and tell him that if he like he can come and see where it shall be. But he say, "no;" that he come not yet, for that he have much to do. Whereupon the captain tell him that he had better be quick – with blood – for that his ship will leave the place – of blood – before the turn of the tide – with blood. Then the thin man smile, and say that of course he must go when he think fit; but he will be surprise if he go quite so soon. The captain swear again, polyglot, and the thin man make him bow, and thank him, and say that he will so far intrude on his kindness as to come aboard before the sailing. Final the captain, more red than ever, and in more tongues, tell him that he doesn't want no Frenchmen – with bloom upon them and also with blood – in his ship – with blood on her also. And so, after asking where there might be close at hand a shop where he might purchase ship forms, he departed.

'No one knew where he went "or bloomin' well cared", as they said, for they had something else to think of – well with blood again– for it soon became apparent to all that the *Czarina Catherine* would not sail as was expected. A thin mist began to creep up from the river, and it grew, and grew; till soon a dense fog. He must have come off by himself, for none notice him. Polyglot – very polyglot – polyglot with bloom and blood; but he could do nothing. The water rose and rose; and he began to fear that he would lose the tide altogether. He was in no friendly mood, when just at full tide, the thin man came up the gangplank again and asked to see where his box had been stowed. Then the captain replied that he wished that he and his box – old and with much bloom and blood – were in hell. But the thin man did not be offend, and went down with the mate and saw where it was place, and came up and stood awhile on deck in fog. He must have come off by himself, for none notice him. Indeed they thought not of him; for soon the fog begin to melt away, and all was clear again. My friends of the thirst and the language that was of bloom and blood laughed, as they told how the captain's swears exceeded even his usual polyglot, and was more than ever full of picturesque, when on questioning other mariners who were in movement up and down on the river that hour, he found that few of them had seen any of fog at all, except where it lay round the wharf. However the ship went out on the ebb tide, and was doubtless by morning far down the river mouth. She was by then, when they told us, well out to sea.

'And so, my dear Madam Mina, it is that we have to rest for a time, for our enemy is on the sea, with the fog at his command, on his way to the Danube mouth. To sail a ship takes time, go she never so quick; and when we start we go on land more quick, and we meet him there. Our best hope is to come on him when in the box between sunrise and sunset; for then he can make no struggle, and we may deal with him as we should. There are days for us, in which we can make ready our plan. We know all about where he go; for we have seen the owner of the ship, who have shown us invoices and all papers that can be. The box we seek is to be landed in Varna, and to be given to an agent, one Ristics, who will there present his credentials; and so our merchant friend will have done his part. When he ask if there be any wrong, for that so, he can telegraph and have inquiry made at Varna, we say, "no," for what is to be done is not for police or of the customs. It must be done by us alone and in our own way.'

When Dr Van Helsing had done speaking, I asked him if it were certain that the Count had remained on board the ship. He replied: 'We have the best proof of that: your own evidence when in the hypnotic trance this morning.' I asked him again if it were really necessary that they should pursue the Count, for oh! I dread Jonathan leaving me, and I know that he would surely go if the others went. He answered in growing passion, at first quietly. As he went on, however, he grew more angry and more forceful, till in the end we could not but see wherein was at least some of that personal dominance which made him so long a master amongst men:

'Yes, it is necessary – necessary – necessary! For your sake in the first, and then for the sake of humanity. This monster has done much harm already, in the narrow scope where he find himself, and in the short time when as yet he was only as a body groping his so small measure in darkness and not knowing. All this have I told these others; you, my dear Madam Mina, will learn it in the phonograph of my friend John, or in that of your husband. I have told them how the measure of leaving his own barren land – barren of peoples – and coming to a new land where life of man teems till they are like the multitude of standing corn, was the work of centuries. Were another of the Un-Dead, like him, try to do what he has done, perhaps not all the centuries of the world that have been, or that will be, could aid him. With this one, all the forces of nature that are occult and deep and strong must have worked together in some wondrous way. The very place where he have been alive, Un-

Dead for all these centuries, is full of strangeness of the geologic and chemical world. There are deep caverns and fissures that reach none know whither. There have been volcanoes, some of whose openings still send out waters of strange properties, and gases that kill or make to vivify. Doubtless, there is something magnetic or electric in some of these combinations of occult forces which work for physical life in strange way; and in himself were from the first some great qualities. In a hard and warlike time he was celebrate that he have more iron nerve, more subtle brain, more braver heart, than any man. In him some vital principle have in strange way found their utmost; and as his body keep strong and grow and thrive so his brain grow too. All this without that diabolic aid which is surely to him; for it have to yield to the powers that come from, and are, symbolic of good. And now this is what he is to us. He have infect you – oh, forgive me, my dear, that I must say such; but it is for good of you that I speak. He infect you in such wise, that even if he do no more, you have only to live – to live in your own old, sweet way; and so in time, death, which is of man's common lot and with God's sanction, shall make you like to him. This must not be! We have sworn together that it must not. Thus are we ministers of God's own wish: that the world, and men for whom His Son die, will not be given over to monsters, whose very existence would defame Him. He have allowed us to redeem one soul already, and we go out as the old knights of the Cross to redeem more. Like them we shall travel towards the sunrise; and like them, if we fall, we fall in good cause.' He paused and I said:

'But will not the Count take his rebuff wisely? Since he has been driven from England, will he not avoid it, as a tiger does the village from which he has been hunted?'

'Aha!' he said, 'your simile of the tiger good, for me, and I shall adopt him. Your man-eater, as they of India call the tiger who has once taste blood of the human, care no more for other prey, but prowl unceasing till he get him. This that we hunt from our village is a tiger, too, a man-eater, and he never cease to prowl. Nay, in himself he is not one to retire and stay afar. In his life, his living life, he go over the Turkey frontier and attack his enemy on his own ground; he be beaten back, but did he stay? No! He come again, and again, and again. Look at his persistence and endurance. With the child-brain that was to him he have long since conceive the idea of coming to a great city. What does he do? He find out the place of all the world most of promise for him. Then he deliberately set himself down to prepare for the task. He find in patience just how is his strength, and what are his powers. He study

new tongues. He learn new social life; new environment of old ways,
the politic, the law, the finance, the science, the habit of a new land and
a new people who have come to be since he was. His glimpse that he
have had, whet his appetite only and enkeen his desire. Nay, it help him
to grow as to his brain; for it all prove to him how right he was at the
first in his surmises. He have done this alone; all alone! from a ruin
tomb in a forgotten land. What more may he not do when the greater
world of thought is open to him? He that can smile at death, as we
know him; who can flourish in the midst of diseases that kill off whole
peoples. Oh! If such an one was to come from God, and not the Devil,
what a force for good might he not be in this old world of ours! But we
are pledged to set the world free. Our toil must be in silence, and our
efforts all in secret; for in this enlightened age, when men believe not
even what they see, the doubting of wise men would be his greatest
strength. It would be at once his sheath and his armour, and his
weapons to destroy us, his enemies, who are willing to peril even our
own souls for the safety of one we love – for the good of mankind, and
for the honour and glory of God.' [193]

After a general discussion it was determined that for tonight nothing
be definitely settled; that we should all sleep on the facts, and try to
think out the proper conclusions. Tomorrow at breakfast we are to
meet again, and, after making our conclusions known to one another,
we shall decide on some course of action.

I feel a wonderful peace and rest tonight. It is as if some haunting
presence were removed from me. Perhaps . . .

My surmise was not finished, could not be; for I caught sight in the
mirror of the red mark upon my forehead; and I knew that I was still
unclean.

Dr Seward's Diary

5 October. – We all rose early, and I think that sleep did much for each
and all of us. When we met at early breakfast there was more general
cheerfulness than any of us had ever expected to experience again.

It is really wonderful how much resilience there is in human nature.
Let any obstructing cause, no matter what, be removed in any way –
even by death – and we fly back to first principles of hope and
enjoyment. More than once, as we sat around the table, my eyes opened
in wonder whether the whole of the past days had not been a dream. It
was only when I caught sight of the red blotch on Mrs Harker's

forehead that I was brought back to reality. Even now, when I am gravely resolving the matter, it is almost impossible to realise that the cause of all our trouble is still existent. Even Mrs Harker seems to lose sight of her trouble for whole spells; it is only now and again, when something recalls it to her mind, that she thinks of her terrible scar. We are to meet here in my study in half an hour and decide on our course of action. I see only one immediate difficulty, I know it by instinct rather than reason: we shall all have to speak frankly; and yet I fear that in some mysterious way poor Mrs Harker's tongue is tied. I *know* that she forms conclusions of her own, and from all that has been I can guess how brilliant and how true they must be; but she will not, or cannot, give them utterance. I have mentioned this to Van Helsing, and he and I are to talk it over when we are alone. I suppose it is some of that horrid poison which has got into her veins beginning to work. The Count had his own purposes when he gave her what Van Helsing called 'the Vampire's baptism of blood'. Well, there may be a poison that distils itself out of good things; in an age when the existence of ptomaines[194] is a mystery we should not wonder at anything! One thing I know: that if my instinct be true regarding poor Mrs Harker's silences, then there is a terrible difficulty – an unknown danger – in the work before us. The same power that compels her silence may compel her speech. I dare not think further; for so I should in my thoughts dishonour a noble woman!

Van Helsing is coming to my study a little before the others. I shall try to open the subject with him.

Later. – When the Professor came in, we talked over the state of things. I could see that he had something on his mind which he wanted to say, but felt some hesitancy about broaching the subject. After beating about the bush a little, he said suddenly:

'Friend John, there is something that you and I must talk of alone, just at the first at any rate. Later, we may have to take the others into our confidence,' then he stopped. So I waited; he went on:

'Madam Mina, our poor, dear Madam Mina is changing.' A cold shiver ran through me to find my worst fears thus endorsed. Van Helsing continued:

'With the sad experience of Miss Lucy, we must this time be warned before things go too far. Our task is now in reality more difficult than ever, and this new trouble makes every hour of the direst importance. I can see the characteristics of the vampire coming in her face. It is now but very, very slight; but it is to be seen if we have eyes to notice without to prejudge. Her teeth are some sharper, and at times her eyes are more hard. But these are not all, there is to her the silence now often; as so it was with Miss Lucy. She did not speak, even when she wrote that which she wished to be known later. Now my fear is this. If it be that she can, by our hypnotic trance, tell what the Count see and hear, is it not more true that he who have hypnotise her first, and who have drink of her very blood and make her drink of his, should, if he will, compel her mind to disclose to him that which she know?' I nodded acquiescence; he went on:

'Then, what we must do is to prevent this; we must keep her ignorant of our intent, and so she cannot tell what she know not. This is a painful task! Oh! so painful that it heartbreak me to think of; but it must be. When today we meet, I must tell her that for reason which we will not to speak she must not more be of our council, but be simply guarded by us.' He wiped his forehead, which had broken out in profuse perspiration at the thought of the pain which he might have to inflict upon the poor soul already so tortured. I knew that it would be some sort of comfort to him if I told him that I also had come to the same conclusion; for at any rate it would take away the pain of doubt. I told him, and the effect was as I expected.

It is now close to the time of our general gathering. Van Helsing has gone away to prepare for the meeting, and his painful part of it. I really believe his purpose is to be able to pray alone.

Later. – At the very outset of our meeting a great personal relief was experienced by both Van Helsing and myself. Mrs Harker had sent a message by her husband to say that she would not join us at present, as she thought it better that we should be free to discuss our movements without her presence to embarrass us. The Professor and I looked at each other for an instant, and somehow we both seemed relieved. For my own part, I thought that if Mrs Harker realised the danger herself, it was much pain as well as much danger averted. Under the circumstances we agreed, by a questioning look and answer, with finger on lip, to preserve silence of our suspicions, until we should have been able to confer alone again. We went at once into our Plan of Campaign. Van Helsing roughly put the facts before us first:

'The *Czarina Catherine* left the Thames yesterday morning. It will take her at the quickest speed she has ever made at least three weeks to reach Varna; but we can travel overland to the same place in three days. Now, if we allow for two days less for the ship's voyage, owing to such weather influences as we know that the Count can bring to bear; and if we allow a whole day and night for any delays which may occur to us, then we have a margin of nearly two weeks. Thus, in order to be quite safe, we must leave here on 17th at latest. Then we shall at any rate be in

Varna a day before the ship arrives, and able to make such preparations as may be necessary. Of course we shall all go armed – armed against evil things, spiritual as well as physical.' Here Quincey Morris added:

'I understand that the Count comes from a wolf country, and it may be that he will get there before us. I propose that we add Winchesters[195] to our armament. I have a kind of belief in a Winchester when there is any trouble of that sort around. Do you remember, Art, when we had the pack after us at Tobolsk?[196] What wouldn't we have given then for a repeater apiece!'

'Good!' said Van Helsing, 'Winchesters it shall be. Quincey's head is level at all times, but most so when there is to hunt, though my metaphor be more dishonour to science than wolves be of danger to man. In the meantime we can do nothing here; and as I think that Varna is not familiar to any of us, why not go there more soon? It is as long to wait here as there. Tonight and tomorrow we can get ready, and then, if all be well, we four can set out on our journey.'

'We four?' said Harker interrogatively, looking from one to another of us.

'Of course!' answered the Professor quickly. 'You must remain to take care of your so sweet wife!' Harker was silent for a while and then said in a hollow voice:

'Let us talk of that part of it in the morning. I want to consult with Mina.' I thought that now was the time for Van Helsing to warn him not to disclose our plans to her; but he took no notice. I looked at him significantly and coughed. For answer he put his finger on his lip and turned away.

Jonathan Harker's journal

5 October, afternoon. – For some time after our meeting this morning I could not think. The new phases of things leave my mind in a state of wonder which allows no room for active thought. Mina's determination not to take any part in the discussion set me thinking; and as I could not argue the matter with her, I could only guess. I am as far as ever from a solution now. The way the others received it, too, puzzled me; the last time we talked of the subject we agreed that there was to be no more concealment of anything amongst us. Mina is sleeping now, calmly and sweetly like a little child. Her lips are curved and her face beams with happiness. Thank God there are such moments still for her.

Later. – How strange it all is! I sat watching Mina's happy sleep, and came as near to being happy myself as I suppose I shall ever be. As the evening drew on, and the earth took its shadows from the sun sinking lower, the silence of the room grew more and more solemn to me. All at once Mina opened her eyes, and looking at me tenderly said:

'Jonathan, I want you to promise me something on your word of honour. A promise made to me, but made holily in God's hearing, and not to be broken though I should go down on my knees and implore you with bitter tears. Quick, you must make it to me at once.'

'Mina,' I said, 'a promise like that, I cannot make at once. I may have no right to make it.'

'But, dear one,' she said, with such spiritual intensity that her eyes were like pole stars, 'it is I who wish it; and it is not for myself. You can ask Dr Van Helsing if I am not right; if he disagrees you may do as you will. Nay more, if you all agree, later, you are absolved from the promise.'

'I promise!' I said, and for a moment she looked supremely happy; though to me all happiness for her was denied by the red scar on her forehead. She said:

'Promise me that you will not tell me anything of the plans formed for the campaign against the Count. Not by word, or inference, or implication; not at any time whilst this remains to me!' and she solemnly pointed to the scar. I saw that she was in earnest, and said solemnly:

'I promise!' and as I said it I felt that from that instant a door had been shut between us.

Later, midnight. – Mina has been bright and cheerful all the evening. So much so that all the rest seemed to take courage, as if infected somewhat with her gaiety; as a result even I myself felt as if the pall of gloom which weighs us down were somewhat lifted. We all retired early. Mina is now sleeping like a little child, it is a wonderful thing that her faculty of sleep remains to her in the midst of her terrible trouble. Thank God for it, for then at least she can forget her care. Perhaps her example may affect me as her gaiety did tonight. I shall try it. Oh! for a dreamless sleep.

6 October, morning. – Another surprise. Mina woke me early, about the same time as yesterday, and asked me to bring Dr Van Helsing. I thought that it was another occasion for hypnotism, and without question went for the Professor. He had evidently expected some such call, for I found him dressed in his room. His door was ajar, so that he could hear the opening of the door of our room. He came at once; as he passed into the room, he asked Mina if the others might come too.

'No,' she said quite simply, 'it will not be necessary. You can tell them just as well. I must go with you on your journey.'

Dr Van Helsing was as startled as I was. After a moment's pause he asked:

'But why?'

'You must take me with you. I am safer with you, and you shall be safer too.'

'But why dear Madam Mina? You know that your safety is our solemnest duty. We go into danger, to which you are, or may be, more liable than any of us from – from circumstances – things that have been.' He paused embarrassed.

As she replied, she raised her finger and pointed to her forehead:

'I know. That is why I must go. I can tell you now, whilst the sun is coming up; I may not be able again. I know that when the Count wills me I must go. I know that if he tells me to come in secret, I must come by wile, by any device to hoodwink – even Jonathan.' God saw the look that she turned on me as she spoke, and if there be indeed a Recording Angel that look is noted to her everlasting honour. I could only clasp her hand. I could not speak; my emotion was too great for even the relief of tears. She went on:

'You men are brave and strong. You are strong in your numbers, for you can defy that which would break down the human endurance of one who had to guard alone. Besides, I may be of service, since you can hypnotise me and so learn that which even I myself do not know.' Dr Van Helsing said very gravely:

'Madam Mina, you are, as always, most wise. You shall with us come; and together we shall do that which we go forth to achieve.' When he had spoken, Mina's long spell of silence made me look at her. She had fallen back on her pillow asleep; she did not even wake when I had pulled up the blind and let in the sunlight which flooded the room. Van Helsing motioned to me to come with him quietly. We went to his room, and within a minute Lord Godalming, Dr Seward, and Mr Morris were with us also. He told them what Mina had said, and went on:

'In the morning we shall leave for Varna. We have now to deal with a new factor: Madam Mina. Oh, but her soul is true. It is to her an agony to tell us so much as she has done but it is most right, and we are warned in time. There must be no chance lost, and in Varna we must be ready to act the instant when that ship arrives.'

'What shall we do exactly?' asked Mr Morris laconically. The Professor paused before replying:

'We shall at the first board that ship; then, when we have identified the box, we shall place a branch of the wild rose on it. This we shall fasten, for when it is there none can emerge, so at least says the superstition. And to superstition must we trust at the first, it was man's faith in the early, and it have its root in faith still. Then, when we get the opportunity that we seek when none are near to see, we shall open the box, and – and all will be well.'

'I shall not wait for any opportunity,' said Morris. 'When I see the box I shall open it and destroy the monster, though there were a thousand men looking on, and if I am to be wiped out for it the next moment!' I grasped his hand instinctively and found it as firm as a piece of steel. I think he understood my look; I hope he did.

'Good boy,' said Dr Van Helsing. 'Brave boy. Quincey is all man, God bless him for it. My child, believe me, none of us shall lag behind or pause from any fear. I do but say what we may do – what we must do. But, indeed, indeed we cannot say what we shall do. There are so many things which may happen, and their ways and their ends are so various that until the moment we may not say. We shall all be armed, in all ways, and when the time for the end has come, our effort shall not be lack. Now let us today put all our affairs in order. Let all things which touch on others dear to us, and who on us depend, be complete for none of us can tell what, or when, or how, the end may be. As for me, my own affairs are regulate; and as I have nothing else to do, I shall go make arrangement for the travel. I shall have all tickets and so forth for our journey.'

There was nothing further to be said, and we parted. I shall now settle up all my affairs of earth, and be ready for whatever may come . . .

Later. – It is all done; my will is made, and all complete. Mina if she survive is my sole heir. If it should not be so, then the others who have been so good to us will have remainder.

It is now drawing towards the sunset; Mina's uneasiness calls my attention to it. I am sure that there is something on her mind which the time of exact sunset will reveal. These occasions are becoming harrowing times for us all, for each sunrise and sunset opens up some new danger – some new pain, which, however may in God's will be means to a good end. I write all these things in the diary since my darling must not hear them now; but if it may be that she can see them again, they shall be ready.

She is calling to me.

Chapter 25

Dr Seward's Diary

11 October, evening. – Jonathan Harker has asked me to note this, as he says he is hardly equal to the task, and he wants an exact record kept.

I think that none of us were surprised when we were asked to see Mrs Harker a little before the time of sunset. We have of late come to understand that sunrise and sunset are to her times of peculiar freedom; when her old self can be manifest without any controlling force subduing or restraining her, or inciting her to action. This mood or condition begins some half-hour or more before actual sunrise or sunset, and lasts till either the sun is high, or whilst the clouds are still aglow with the rays streaming above the horizon. At first there is a sort of negative condition, as if some tie were loosened, and then the absolute freedom quickly follows; when, however, the freedom ceases the change-back or relapse comes quickly, preceded only by a spell of warning silence.

Tonight, when we met she was somewhat constrained, and bore all the signs of an internal struggle. I put it down myself to her making a violent effort at the earliest instant she could do so. A very few minutes, however, gave her complete control of herself; then, motioning her husband to sit beside her on the sofa where she was half reclining, she made the rest of us bring chairs up close. Taking her husband's hand in hers she began:

'We are all here together in freedom, for perhaps the last time! I know, dear; I know that you will always be with me to the end.' This was to her husband, whose hand had, as we could see, tightened upon hers. 'In the morning we go out upon our task, and God alone knows what may be in store for any of us. You are going to be so good to me as to take me with you. I know that all that brave earnest men can do for a poor weak woman, whose soul perhaps is lost – no, no, not yet, but is at any rate at stake – you will do. But you must remember that I am not as you are. There is a poison in my blood, in my soul, which may destroy me; which must destroy me, unless some relief come to us. Oh, my friends, you know as well as I do, that my soul is at stake; and though I know there is one way out for me you must not and I must not take it!' She looked appealingly at us all in turn, beginning and ending with her husband.

'What is that way?' asked Van Helsing in a hoarse voice. 'What is that way, which we must not – may not – take?'

'That I may die now, either by my own hand or that of another, before the greater evil is entirely wrought. I know, and you know, that were I once dead you could and would set free my immortal spirit, even as you did my poor Lucy's. Were death, or the fear of death, the only thing that stood in the way I would not shrink to die here, now, amidst the friends who love me. But death is not all. I cannot believe that to die in such a case, when there is hope before us and a better task to be done, is God's will. Therefore, I on my part give up here the certainty of eternal rest, and go out into the dark where may be the blackest things that the world or the nether world holds!' We were all silent, for we knew instinctively that this was only a prelude. The faces of the others were set, and Harker's grew ashen grey; perhaps he guessed better than any of us what was coming. She continued:

'This is what I can give into the hotch-pot.'[197] I could not but note the quaint legal phrase which she used in such a place and with all seriousness. 'What will each of you give? Your lives, I know,' she went on quickly; 'that is easy for brave men. Your lives are God's, and you can give them back to Him; but what will you give to me?' She looked again questioningly but this time avoided her husband's face. Quincey seemed to understand; he nodded, and her face lit up. 'Then I shall tell you plainly what I want, for there must be no doubtful matter in this connection between us now. You must promise me, one and all – even you, my beloved husband – that, should the time come, you will kill me.'

'What is that time?' The voice was Quincey's, but it was low and strained.

'When you shall be convinced that I am so changed that it is better that I die that I may live. When I am thus dead in the flesh, then you will, without a moment's delay, drive a stake through me and cut off my head; or do whatever else may be wanting to give me rest!'

Quincey was the first to rise after the pause. He knelt down before her and taking her hand in his said solemnly:

'I'm only a rough fellow, who hasn't, perhaps, lived as a man should to win such a distinction, but I swear to you by all that I hold sacred and dear that, should the time ever come, I shall not flinch from the duty that you have set us. And I promise you, too, that I shall make all certain, for if I am only doubtful I shall take it that the time has come!'

'My true friend!' was all she could say amid her fast-falling tears, as, bending over, she kissed his hand.

'I swear the same, my dear Madam Mina!' said Van Helsing.

'And I!' said Lord Godalming, each of them in turn kneeling to her to take the oath. I followed, myself. Then her husband turned to her, wan-eyed and with a greenish pallor which subdued the snowy whiteness of his hair, and asked:

'And must I, too, make such a promise, oh, my wife?'

'You too, my dearest,' she said, with infinite yearning of pity in her voice and eyes. 'You must not shrink. You are nearest and dearest and all the world to me; our souls are knit into one, for all life and all time. Think, dear, that there have been times when brave men have killed their wives and their womenkind, to keep them from falling into the hands of the enemy. Their hands did not falter any the more because those that they loved implored them to slay them. It is men's duty towards those whom they love, in such times of sore trial! And oh, my dear, if it is to be that I must meet death at any hand, let it be at the hand of him that loves me best. Dr Van Helsing, I have not forgotten your mercy in poor Lucy's case to him who loved' – she stopped with a flying blush, and changed her phrase – 'to him who had best right to give her peace. If that time shall come again, I look to you to make it a happy memory of my husband's life that it was his loving hand which set me free from the awful thrall upon me.'

'Again I swear!' came the Professor's resonant voice. Mrs Harker smiled, positively smiled, as with a sigh of relief she leaned back and said:

'And now one word of warning, a warning which you must never forget: this time, if it ever come, may come quickly and unexpectedly, and in such case you must lose no time in using your opportunity. At such a time I myself might be – nay! if the time ever comes, *shall* be – leagued with your enemy against you.'

'One more request;' she became very solemn as she said this, 'it is not vital and necessary like the other, but I want you to do one thing for me, if you will.' We all acquiesced, but no one spoke; there was no need to speak:

'I want you to read the Burial Service.' She was interrupted by a deep groan from her husband taking his hand in hers, she held it over her heart, and continued. 'You must read it over me some day. Whatever may be the issue of all this fearful state of things, it will be a sweet thought to all or some of us. You, my dearest, will, I hope, read it, for then it will be in your voice in my memory for ever – come what may!'

'But oh, my dear one,' he pleaded, 'death is afar off from you.'

'Nay,' she said, holding up a warning hand. 'I am deeper in death at this moment than if the weight of an earthly grave lay heavy upon me!'

'Oh, my wife, must I read it?' he said, before he began.

'It would comfort me, my husband!' was all she said; and he began to read when she had got the book ready.

How can I – how could anyone – tell of that strange scene, its solemnity, its gloom, its sadness, its horror; and, withal, its sweetness. Even a sceptic, who can see nothing but a travesty of bitter truth in anything holy or emotional, would have been melted to the heart had he seen that little group of loving and devoted friends kneeling round that stricken and sorrowing lady; or heard the tender passion of her husband's voice, as in tones so broken with emotion that often he had to pause, he read the simple and beautiful service for the Burial of the Dead. 'I – I cannot go on – words – and – v-voice – f-fail m-me!' . . .

She was right in her instinct. Strange as it all was, bizarre as it may hereafter seem even to us who felt its potent influence at the time, it comforted us much; and the silence, which showed Mrs Harker's coming relapse from her freedom of soul, did not seem so full of despair to any of us as we had dreaded.

JONATHAN HARKER'S JOURNAL

15 October. Varna. – We left Charing Cross[198] on the morning of the 12th, got to Paris the same night, and took the places secured for us in the Orient Express.[199] We travelled night and day, arriving here at about five o'clock. Lord Godalming went to the Consulate to see if any telegram had arrived for him, whilst the rest of us came on to this hotel – the Odessus. The journey may have had incidents; I was, however, too eager to get on, to care for them. Until the *Czarina Catherine* comes into port there will be no interest for me in anything in the wide world. Thank God! Mina is well, and looks to be getting stronger; her colour is coming back. She sleeps a great deal; throughout the journey she slept nearly all the time. Before sunrise and sunset, however, she is very wakeful and alert; and it has become a habit for Van Helsing to hypnotise her at such times. At first, some effort was needed, and he had to make many passes; but now, she seems to yield at once, as if by habit, and scarcely any action is needed. He seems to have power at these particular moments to simply will, and her thoughts obey him. He always asks her what she can see and hear. She answers to the first:

'Nothing; all is dark.' And to the second:

'I can hear the waves lapping against the ship, and the water rushing by. Canvas and cordage strain and masts and yards creak. The wind is high – I can hear it in the shrouds, and the bow throws back the foam.' It is evident that the *Czarina Catherine* is still at sea, hastening on her way to Varna. Lord Godalming has just returned. He had four telegrams, one each day since we started, and all to the same effect: that the *Czarina Catherine* had not been reported to Lloyd's[200] from anywhere. He had arranged before leaving London that his agent should send him every day a telegram saying if the ship had been reported. He was to have a message even if she were not reported, so that he might be sure that there was a watch being kept at the other end of the wire.

We had dinner and went to bed early. Tomorrow we are to see the Vice-Consul, and to arrange, if we can, about getting on board the ship as soon as she arrives. Van Helsing says that our chance will be to get on board between sunrise and sunset. The Count, even if he takes the form of a bat, cannot cross the running water of his own volition, and so cannot leave the ship. As he dare not change to man's form without suspicion – which he evidently wishes to avoid – he must remain in the box. If, then, we can come on board after sunrise, he is at our mercy; for we can open the box and make sure of him, as we did of poor Lucy, before he wakes. What mercy he will get from us will not count for much. We think that we shall not have much trouble with officials or the seamen. Thank God! this is the country where bribery can do anything, and we are well supplied with money. We have only to make sure that the ship cannot come into port between sunset and sunrise without our being warned, and we shall be safe. Judge Moneybag will settle this case. I think!

16 October. – Mina's report still the same: lapping waves and rushing water, darkness and favouring winds. We are evidently in good time, and when we hear of the *Czarina Catherine* we shall be ready. As she must pass the Dardanelles we are sure to have some report.

17 October. – Everything is pretty well fixed now, I think, to welcome the Count on his return from his tour. Godalming told the shippers that he fancied that the box sent aboard might contain something stolen from a friend of his, and got a half consent that he might open it at his own risk. The owner gave him a paper telling the captain to give him every facility in doing whatever he chose on board the ship, and also a similar authorisation to his agent at Varna. We have seen the agent, who was much impressed with Godalming's kindly manner to him, and we are all satisfied that whatever he can do to aid our wishes will be done. We have already arranged what to do in case we get the box open. If the Count is there, Van Helsing and Seward will cut off his head at once and drive a stake through his heart. Morris and Godalming and I shall prevent interference, even if we have to use the arms which we shall have ready. The Professor says that if we can so treat the Count's body, it will soon after fall into dust. In such case there would be no evidence against us, in case any suspicion of murder were aroused. But even if it did not, we should stand or fall by our act, and perhaps some day this very script may be evidence to come between some of us and a rope. For myself, I should take the chance only too thankfully if it were to come. We mean to leave no stone unturned to carry out our intent. We have arranged with certain officials that the instant the *Czarina Catherine* is seen, we are to be informed by a special messenger.

24 October. – A whole week of waiting. Daily telegrams to Godalming, but only the same story: 'Not yet reported.' Mina's hypnotic answer is unvaried: 'Lapping waves, rushing water, and creaking masts.'

*Telegram, Rufus Smith, Lloyd's, London, to Lord Godalming,
care of H.B.M.*[201] *Vice-Consul, Varna.*

October 24.

Czarina Catherine reported this morning from Dardanelles.

Dr Seward's Diary

24 October. – How I miss my phonograph! To write diary with a pen is irksome to me; but Van Helsing says I must. We were all wild with excitement today when Godalming got his telegram from Lloyd's. I know now what men feel in battle when the call to action is heard. Mrs Harker, alone of our party, did not show any signs of emotion. After all, it is not strange that she did not; for we took special care not to let her know anything about it, and we all tried not to show any excitement when we were in her presence. In old days she would, I am sure have noticed, no matter how we might have tried to conceal it; but in this way she is greatly changed during the past three weeks. The lethargy grows upon her, and though she seems strong and well, and is getting back some of her colour, Van Helsing and I am not satisfied. We talk of her often; we have not, however, said a word to the others. It would break poor Harker's heart – certainly his nerve – if he knew that we had even a suspicion on the subject. Van Helsing examines he tells me, her teeth very carefully, whilst she is in the hypnotic condition, for he says that so long as they do not begin to sharpen there is no active danger of a change in her. If this change should come, it would be necessary to take steps! . . . We both know what those steps would have to be, though we do not mention our thoughts to each other. We should neither of us shrink from the task – awful though it be to contemplate. 'Euthanasia'[202] is an excellent and a comforting word! I am grateful to whoever invented it.

It is only about 24 hours' sail from the Dardanelles to here, at the rate the *Czarina Catherine* has come from London. She should therefore arrive some time in the morning; but as she cannot possibly get in before then, we are all about to retire early. We shall get up at one o'clock, so as to be ready.

25 October, noon. – No news yet of the ship's arrival. Mrs Harker's hypnotic report this morning was the same as usual, so it is possible that we may get news at any moment. We men are all in a fever of excitement, except Harker, who is calm; his hands are as cold as ice, and an hour ago I found him whetting the edge of the great Ghoorka knife which he now always carries with him. It will be a bad look-out for the Count if the edge of that 'Kukri' ever touches his throat, driven by that stern, ice-cold hand!

Van Helsing and I were a little alarmed about Mrs Harker today. About noon she got into a sort of lethargy which we did not like; although we kept silence to the others, we were neither of us happy about it. She had been restless all the morning, so that we were at first glad to know that she was sleeping. When, however, her husband mentioned casually that she was sleeping so soundly that he could not wake her, we went to her room to see for ourselves. She was breathing naturally and looked so well and peaceful that we agreed that the sleep was better for her than anything else. Poor girl, she has so much to forget that it is no wonder that sleep, if it brings oblivion to her, does her good.

Later. – Our opinion was justified, for when after a refreshing sleep of some hours she woke up, she seemed brighter and better than she has been for days. At sunset she made the usual hypnotic report. Wherever he may be in the Black Sea, the Count is hurrying to his destination. To his doom, I trust!

26 October. – Another day and no tidings of the *Czarina Catherine*. She ought to be here by now. That she is still journeying *somewhere* is apparent, for Mrs Harker's hypnotic report at sunrise was still the same. It is possible that the vessel may be lying by, at times, for fog; some of the steamers which came in last evening reported patches of fog both to north and south of the port. We must continue our watching, as the ship may now be signalled any moment.

27 October, noon. – Most strange; no news yet of the ship we wait for. Mrs Harker reported last night and this morning as usual: 'Lapping waves and rushing water,' though she added that 'the waves were very faint'. The telegrams from London have been the same: 'No further report.' Van Helsing is terribly anxious, and told me just now that he fears the Count is escaping us. He added significantly:

'I did not like that lethargy of Madam Mina's. Souls and memories can do strange things during trance.' I was about to ask him more, but Harker just then came in, and he held up a warning hand. We must try tonight, at sunset, to make her speak more fully when in her hypnotic state.

Telegram. Rufus Smith, London, to Lord Godalming,
care of H.B.M. Vice-Consul, Varna.

October 28.

Czarina Catherine reported entering Galatz[203] at one o'clock today.

Dr Seward's Diary

28 October. – When the telegram came announcing the arrival in Galatz I do not think it was such a shock to any of us as might have been expected. True, we did not know whence, or how, or when, the bolt would come; but I think we all expected that something strange would happen. The delay of arrival at Varna made us individually satisfied that things would not be just as we had expected; we only waited to learn where the change would occur. None the less, however, was it a surprise. I suppose that nature works on such a hopeful basis that we believe against ourselves that things will be as they ought to be, not as we should know that they will be. Transcendentalism[204] is a beacon to the angels, even if it be a will-o'-the-wisp to man. It was an odd experience, and we all took it differently. Van Helsing raised his hands over his head for a moment, as though in remonstrance with the Almighty; but he said not a word, and in a few seconds stood up with his face sternly set. Lord Godalming grew very pale, and sat breathing heavily. I was myself half stunned and looked in wonder at one after another. Quincey Morris tightened his belt with that quick movement which I knew so well; in our old wandering days it meant 'action'. Mrs Harker grew ghastly white, so that the scar on her forehead seemed to burn, but she folded her hands meekly and looked up in prayer. Harker smiled – actually smiled – the dark bitter smile of one who is without hope; but at the same time his action belied his words, for his hands instinctively sought the hilt of the great Kukri knife and rested there.

'When does the next train start for Galatz?' said Van Helsing to us generally.

'At 6.30 tomorrow morning!' We all stared, for the answer came from Mrs Harker.

'How on earth do you know?' said Art.

'You forget – or perhaps you do not know, though Jonathan does and so does Dr Van Helsing – that I am a train fiend. At home in Exeter I always used to make up the time-tables, so as to be helpful to my husband. I found it so useful sometimes, that I always make a study of the time-tables now. I knew that if anything were to take us to Castle Dracula we should go by Galatz, or at any rate through Bucharest, so I learned the times very carefully. Unhappily there are not many to learn, as the only train tomorrow leaves as I say.'

'Wonderful woman!' murmured the Professor.

'Can't we get a special?' asked Lord Godalming.

Van Helsing shook his head: 'I fear not. This land is very different from yours or mine; even if we did have a special, it would probably not arrive as soon as our regular train. Moreover, we have something to prepare. We must think. Now let us organise. You, friend Arthur, go to the train and get the tickets and arrange that all be ready for us to go in the morning. Do you, friend Jonathan, go to the agent of the ship and get from him letters to the agent in Galatz, with authority to make search the ship just as it was here. Quincey Morris, you see the Vice-Consul, and get his aid with his fellow in Galatz and all he can do to make our way smooth, so that no times be lost when over the Danube. John will stay with Madam Mina and me, and we shall consult. For so if time be long you may be delayed; and it will not matter when the sun set, since I am here with Madam to make report.'

'And I,' said Mrs Harker brightly, and more like her old self than she had been for many a long day, 'shall try to be of use in all ways, and shall think and write for you as I used to do. Something is shifting from me in some strange way, and I feel freer than I have been of late!' The three younger men looked happier at the moment as they seemed to realise the significance of her words; but Van Helsing and I, turning to each other, met each a grave and troubled glance. We said nothing at the time, however.

When the three men had gone out to their tasks Van Helsing asked Mrs Harker to look up the copy of the diaries and find him the part of Harker's journal at the Castle. She went away to get it; when the door was shut upon her he said to me:

'We mean the same! speak out!'

'There is some change. It is a hope that makes me sick for it may deceive us.'

'Quite so. Do you know why I asked her to get the manuscript?'

'No!' said I, 'unless it was to get an opportunity of seeing me alone.'

'You are in part right, friend John, but only in part. I want to tell you something. And oh, my friend, I am taking a great – a terrible – risk, but I believe it is right. In the moment when Madam said those words that arrest both our understanding, an inspiration come to me. In the trance of three days ago the Count sent her his spirit to read her mind; or more like he took her to see him in his earth-box in the ship with water rushing, just as it go free at rise and set of sun. He learn then that we are here; for she have more to tell in her open life with eyes to see and ears to hear than he, shut, as he is, in his coffin-box. Now he make his most effort to escape us. At present he want her not. He is sure with his so great knowledge that she will come at his call; but he cut her off – take her, as he can do, out of his own power, that so she come not to him. Ah! there I have hope that our man-brains that have been of man so long and that have not lost the grace of God, will come higher than his child-brain that lie in his tomb for centuries, that grow not yet to our stature, and that do only work selfish and therefore small. Here comes Madam Mina; not a word to her of her trance! She know it not; and it would overwhelm her and make despair just when we want all her hope, all her courage; when most we want all her great brain which is trained like man's brain, but is of sweet woman and have a special power which the Count give her, and which he may not take away altogether – though he think not so. Hush! let me speak, and you shall learn. Oh, John, my friend, we are in awful straits. I fear, as I never feared before. We can only trust the good God. Silence! here she comes!'

I thought that the Professor was going to break down and have hysterics, just as he had when Lucy died, but with a great effort he controlled himself and was at perfect nervous poise when Mrs Harker tripped into the room, bright and happy-looking and, in the doing of work, seemingly forgetful of her misery. As she came in, she handed a number of sheets of typewriting to Van Helsing. He looked over them gravely, his face brightening up as he read. Then, holding the pages between his finger and thumb, he said:

'Friend John, to you with so much of experience already – and you too, dear Madam Mina, that are young – here is a lesson: do not fear ever to think. A half-thought has been buzzing often in my brain, but I fear to let him loose his wings. Here now, with more knowledge, I go back to where that half-thought come from, and I find that he be no half-thought at all; that he be a whole thought, though so young that he is not yet strong to use his little wings. Nay, like the "Ugly Duck" of my friend Hans Andersen,[205] he be no duck-thought at all, but a big swan-thought that sail nobly on big wings, when the time come for him to try them. See I read here what Jonathan have written:

' "That other of his race who, in a later age, again and again, brought his forces over The Great River into Turkey-land who when he was beaten back, came again, and again, and again though he had to come alone from the bloody field where his troops were being slaughtered, since he knew that he alone could ultimately triumph."

'What does this tell us? Not much! no! The Count's child-thought see nothing; therefore he speak so free. Your man-thought see nothing; my man-thought see nothing, till just now. No! But there comes another word from someone who speak without thought because she too know not what it mean – what it *might* mean. Just as there are elements which rest, yet when in nature's course they move on their way and they touch – then pouf! and there comes a flash of light, heaven's wide, that blind and kill and destroy some; but that show up all earth below for leagues and leagues. Is it not so? Well, I shall explain. To begin, have you ever study the philosophy of crime. "Yes" and "No". You, John, yes; for it is a study of insanity. You, no, Madam Mina; for crime touch you not – not but once. Still, your mind works true, and argues not *a particulari ad universale*.[206] There is this peculiarity in criminals. It is so constant, in all countries and at all times, that even police, who know not much from philosophy, come to know it empirically, that *it is*. That is to be empiric. The criminal always work at one crime – that is the true criminal who seems predestinate to crime, and who will of none other. This criminal has not full man-brain. He is clever and cunning and resourceful; but he be not of man-stature as to brain. He be of child-brain in much. Now this criminal of ours is predestinate to crime also; he too have child-brain, and it is of the child to do what he have done. The little bird, the little fish, the little animal learn not by principle, but empirically; and when he learn to do, then there is to him the ground to start from to do more. "*Dos pou sto*,"[207] said Archimedes. "Give me a fulcrum, and I shall move the world!" To do once, is the fulcrum whereby child-brain become man-brain; and until he have the purpose to do more, he continue to do the same again every time, just as he have done before! Oh, my dear, I see that your eyes are opened, and that to you the lightning flash show all the leagues,' for Mrs Harker began to clap her hands, and her eyes sparkled. He went on:

'Now you shall speak. Tell us two dry men of science what you see with those so bright eyes.' He took her hand and held it whilst she spoke. His finger and thumb closed on her pulse, as I thought instinctively and unconsciously, as she spoke:

'The Count is a criminal and of criminal type. Nordau and Lombroso[208] would so classify him, and *quâ* criminal he is of imperfectly formed mind. Thus, in a difficulty he has to seek resource in habit. His past is a clue, and the one page of it that we know – and that from his own lips – tells that once before when in what Mr Morris would call a "tight place", he went back to his own country from the land he had tried to invade, and thence, without losing purpose, prepared himself for a new effort. He came again, better equipped for his work; and won. So he came to London to invade a new land. He was beaten and when all hope of success was lost, and his existence in danger, he fled back over the sea to his home; just as formerly he had fled back over the Danube from Turkey-land.'

'Good, good! oh, you so clever lady!' said Van Helsing, enthusiastically, as he stooped and kissed her hand. A moment later he said to me, as calmly as though we had been having a sick-room consultation:

'Seventy-two only; and in all this excitement. I have hope.' Turning to her again, he said with keen expectation:

'But go on. Go on! there is more to tell if you will. Be not afraid; John and I know. I do in any case, and shall tell you if you are right. Speak, without fear!'

'I will try to; but you will forgive me if I seem egotistical.'

'Nay! fear not, you must be egotist, for it is of you that we think.'

'Then, as he is criminal he is selfish; and as his intellect is small and his action is based on selfishness, he confines himself to one purpose. That purpose is remorseless. As he fled back over the Danube, leaving his forces to be cut to pieces, so now he is intent on being safe, careless of all. So, his own selfishness frees my soul somewhat of the terrible power which he acquired over me on that dreadful night. I felt it, oh! I felt it. Thank God for His great mercy! My soul is freer than it has been since that awful hour; and all that haunts me is a fear lest in some trance or dream he may have used my knowledge for his ends.'

The Professor stood up: 'He has so used your mind; and by it he has left us here in Varna, whilst the ship that carried him rushed through enveloping fog up to Galatz, where, doubtless, he had made preparation for escaping from us. But his child-mind only saw so far; and it may be that, as ever is in God's Providence, the very thing that the evil doer most reckoned on for his selfish good, turns out to be his chiefest harm. The hunter is taken in his own snare, as the great Psalmist says.[209] For now that he think he is free from every trace of us all, and that he has escaped us with so many hours to him, then his selfish child-brain will whisper him to sleep. He think, too, that as he cut himself off from knowing your mind, there can be no knowledge of him to you; there is where he fail! That terrible baptism of blood which he give you makes you free to go to him in spirit, as you have as yet done in your times of freedom, when the sun rise and set. At such times you go by my volition and not by his; and this power to good of you and others, you have won from your suffering at his hands. This is now all more precious that he know it not, and to guard himself have even cut himself off from his knowledge of our where. We, however, are not all selfish, and we believe that God is with us through all this blackness, and these many dark hours. We shall follow him; and we shall not flinch; even if we peril ourselves that we become like him. Friend John, this has been a great hour; and it have done much to advance us on our way. You must be scribe and write him all down so that when the others return from their work you can give it to them; then they shall know as we do.'

And so I have written it whilst we wait their return, and Mrs Harker has written with her typewriter all since she brought the MS. to us.

Chapter 26

Dr Seward's Diary

29 October. – This is written in the train from Varna to Galatz. Last night we all assembled a little before the time of sunset. Each of us had done his work as well as he could; so far as thought, and endeavour, and opportunity go, we are prepared for the whole of our journey and for our work when we get to Galatz. When the usual time came round Mrs Harker prepared herself for her hypnotic effort; and after a longer and more strenuous effort on the part of Van Helsing than has been usually necessary, she sank into the trance. Usually she speaks on a hint; but this time the Professor had to ask her questions, and to ask them pretty resolutely, before we could learn anything; at last her answer came:

'I can see nothing; we are still; there are no waves lapping, but only a steady swirl of water softly running against the hawser.[210] I can hear men's voices calling, near and far, and the roll and creak of oars in the rowlocks. A gun is fired somewhere; the echo of it seems far away. There is tramping of feet overhead and ropes and chains are dragged along. What is this? There is a gleam of light; I can feel the air blowing upon me.'

Here she stopped. She had risen, as if impulsively, from where she lay on the sofa, and raised both her hands, palms upwards, as if lifting a weight. Van Helsing and I looked at each other with understanding. Quincey raised his eyebrows slightly and looked at her intently, whilst Harker's hand instinctively closed round the hilt of his Kukri. There was a long pause. We all knew that the time when she could speak was passing; but we felt that it was useless to say anything. Suddenly she sat up, and, as she opened her eyes, said sweetly:

'Would none of you like a cup of tea? You must all be so tired!' We could only make her happy, and so acquiesced. She bustled off to get tea; when she had gone Van Helsing said:

'You see, my friends. *He* is close to land; he has left his earth-chest. But he has yet to get on shore. In the night he may lie hidden somewhere; but if he be not carried on shore, or if the ship do not touch it, he cannot achieve the land. In such case he can, if it be in the night, change his form and can jump or fly on shore, as he did at Whitby. But if the day come before he get on shore, then, unless he be carried he cannot escape. And if he be carried, then the customs men may discover what the box contains. Thus in fine, if he escape not on shore tonight, or before dawn, there will be the whole day lost to him. We may then arrive in time; for if he escape not at night we shall come on him in daytime, boxed up and at our mercy; for he dare not be his true self, awake and visible, lest he be discovered.'

There was no more to be said, so we waited in patience until the dawn; at which time we might learn more from Mrs Harker.

Early this morning we listened, with breathless anxiety, for her response in her trance. The hypnotic stage was even longer in coming than before; and when it came the time remaining until full sunrise was so short that we began to despair. Van Helsing seemed to throw his whole soul into the effort; at last, in obedience to his will she made reply: 'All is dark. I hear lapping water, level with me, and some creaking as of wood on wood.' She paused, and the red sun shot up. We must wait till tonight.

And so it is that we are travelling towards Galatz in an agony of expectation. We are due to arrive between two and three in the morning; but already, at Bucharest, we are three hours late, so we cannot possibly get in till well after sun-up. Thus we shall have two more hypnotic messages from Mrs Harker; either or both may possibly throw more light on what is happening.

Later. – Sunset has come and gone. Fortunately it came at a time when there was no distraction; for had it occurred whilst we were at a station, we might not have secured the necessary calm and isolation. Mrs Harker yielded to the hypnotic influence even less readily than this morning. I am in fear that her power of reading the Count's sensations may die away, just when we want it most. It seems to me that her imagination is beginning to work. Whilst she has been in the trance hitherto she has confined herself to the simplest of facts. If this goes on it may ultimately mislead us. If I thought that the Count's power over her would die away equally with her power of knowledge it would be a happy thought; but I am afraid that it may not be so. When she did speak, her words were enigmatical:

'Something is going out; I can feel it pass me like a cold wind. I can hear, far off, confused sounds as of men talking in strange tongues, fierce-falling water, and the howling of wolves.' She stopped, and a shudder ran through her, increasing in intensity for a few seconds, till, at the end, she shook as though in a palsy. She said no more, even in answer to the Professor's imperative questioning. When she woke from the trance, she was cold, and exhausted, and languid; but her mind was all alert. She could not remember anything, but asked what she had said; when she was told, she pondered over it deeply for a long time and in silence.

30 *October, 7.a.m.* – We are near Galatz now, and I may not have time to write later. Sunrise this morning was anxiously looked for by us all. Knowing of the increasing difficulty of procuring the hypnotic trance, Van Helsing began his passes earlier than usual. They produced no effect, however, until the regular time, when she yielded with a still greater difficulty, only a minute before the sun rose. The Professor lost no time in his questioning; her answer came with equal quickness:

'All is dark. I hear the water swirling by, level with my ears, and the creaking of wood on wood. Cattle low far off. There is another sound, a queer one like – ' she stopped and grew white, and whiter still.

'Go on! Go on! Speak, I command you!' said Van Helsing in an agonised voice. At the same time there was despair in his eyes, for the risen sun was reddening even Mrs Harker's pale face. She opened her eyes, and we all started as she said, sweetly and seemingly with the utmost concern:

'Oh, Professor, why ask me to do what you know I can't? I don't remember anything.' Then, seeing the look of amazement on our faces, she said, turning from one to the other:

'What have I said? What have I done? I know nothing only that I was lying here, half asleep, and I heard you say "Go on! speak, I command you!" It seemed so funny to hear you order me about, as if I were a bad child!'

'Oh, Madam Mina,' he said sadly, 'it is proof, if proof be needed, of how I love and honour you, when a word for your good, spoken more earnest than ever, can seem so strange because it is to order her whom I am proud to obey!'

The whistles are sounding; we are nearing Galatz. We are on fire with anxiety and eagerness.

MINA HARKER'S JOURNAL

30 October. – Mr Morris took me to the hotel where our rooms had been ordered by telegraph, he being the one who could best be spared, since he does not speak any foreign language. The forces were distributed much as they had been at Varna, except that Lord Godalming went to the Vice-Consul, as his rank might serve as an immediate guarantee of some sort to the official, we being in extreme hurry. Jonathan and the two doctors went to the shipping agent to learn particulars of the arrival of the *Czarina Catherine*.

Later. – Lord Godalming has returned. The Consul is away, and the Vice-Consul sick; so the routine work has been attended to by a clerk. He was very obliging, and offered to do anything in his power.

JONATHAN HARKER'S JOURNAL

30 October. – At nine o'clock Dr Van Helsing, Dr Seward, and I called on Messrs. Mackenzie & Steinkoff, the agents of the London firm of Hapgood. They had received a wire from London, in answer to Lord Godalming's telegraphed request, asking them to show us any civility in their power. They were more than kind and courteous, and took us at once on board the *Czarina Catherine*, which lay at anchor out in the river harbour. There we saw the captain, Donelson by name, who told us of his voyage. He said that in all his life he had never had so favourable a run.

'Man!' he said, 'but it made us afeared, for we expeckit that we should have to pay for it wi' some rare piece o' ill luck, so as to keep up the average. It's no canny[211] to run frae London to the Black Sea wi' a wind ahint[212] ye, as though the Deil himself were blawin' on yer sail for his ain purpose. An' a' the time we could no' speer[213] a thing. Gin[214] we were nigh a ship, or a port, or a headland, a fog fell on us and travelled wi' us, till when after it had lifted and we looked out, the deil a thing could we

see. We ran by Gibraltar wi'oot bein' able to signal; an' till we came to the
Dardanelles and had to wait to get our permit to pass, we never were
within hail o' aught. At first I inclined to slack off sail and beat about till
the fog was lifted; but whiles, I thocht that if the Deil was minded to get us
into the Black Sea quick, he was like to do it whether we would or no. If
we had a quick voyage it would be no' to our miscredit wi' the owners, or
no hurt to our traffic; an' the Old Mon[215] who had served his ain purpose
wad be decently grateful to us for no hinderin' him.' This mixture of
simplicity and cunning, of superstition and commercial reasoning, aroused
Van Helsing, who said: 'Mine friend, that Devil is more clever than he is
thought by some; and he know when he meet his match!' The skipper was
not displeased with the compliment, and went on:

'When we got past the Bosphorus the men began to grumble; some o'
them, the Roumanians, came and asked me to heave overboard a big
box which had been put on board by a queer-lookin' old man just before
we had started frae London. I had seen them speer at the fellow, and put
out their twa fingers when they saw him, to guard against the evil eye.
Man! but the supersteetion of foreigners is pairfectly rideeculous! I sent
them aboot their business pretty quick; but as just after a fog closed in
on us, I felt a wee bit as they did anent[216] something, though I wouldn't
say it was agin[217] the big box. Well, on we went, and as the fog didn't let
up for five days I joost let the wind carry us; for if the Deil wanted to get
somewhere – well, he would fetch it up a'reet. An' if he didn't, well,
we'd keep a sharp look-out anyhow. Sure enuch, we had a fair way and
deep water all the time; and two days ago, when the mornin' sun came
through the fog, we found ourselves just in the river opposite Galatz.
The Roumanians were wild, and wanted me right or wrong to take out
the box and fling it in the river. I had to argy wi' them aboot it wi' a
handspike; an' when the last o' them rose off the deck, wi' his head in his
hand, I had convinced them that, evil eye or no evil eye, the property
and the trust of my owners were better in my hands than in the river
Danube. They had, mind ye, taken the box on the deck ready to fling in,
and as it was marked Galatz *via* Varna, I thocht I'd let it lie till we
discharged in the port an' get rid o't athegither. We didn't do much
clearin' that day, an' had to remain the nicht at anchor; but in the
mornin', braw an' airly, an hour before sun-up, a man came aboord wi'
an order, written to him from England, to receive a box marked for one
Count Dracula. Sure enuch the matter was one ready to his hand. He
had his papers a' reet, an' glad I was to be rid o' the dam thing, for I was
beginnin' masel' to feel uneasy at it. If the Deil did have any luggage
aboord the ship, I'm thinkin' it was nane ither than that same!'

'What was the name of the man who took it?' asked Dr Van Helsing, with restrained eagerness.

'I'll be tellin' ye quick!' he answered, and, stepping down to his cabin, produced a receipt signed 'Immanuel Hildesheim'. Burgen-strasse 16 was the address. We found out that this was all the captain knew; so with thanks we came away.

We found Hildesheim in his office, a Hebrew of rather the Adelphi type, with a nose like a sheep, and a fez. His arguments were pointed with specie[218] – we doing the punctuation – and with a little bargaining he told us what he knew. This turned out to be simple but important. He had received a letter from Mr de Ville of London, telling him to receive, if possible before sunrise so as to avoid customs, a box which would arrive at Galatz in the *Czarina Catherine*. This he was to give in charge to a certain Petrof Skinsky, who dealt with Slovaks who traded down the river to the port. He had been paid for his work by an English bank note, which had been duly cashed for gold at the Danube International Bank. When Skinsky had come to him, he had taken him to the ship and handed over the box, so as to save porterage. That was all he knew.

We then sought for Skinsky, but were unable to find him. One of his neighbours, who did not seem to bear him any affection, said that he had gone away two days before, no one knew whither. This was corroborated by his landlord, who had received by messenger the key of the house together with the rent due, in English money. This had been between ten and eleven o'clock last night. We were at a standstill again.

Whilst we were talking, one came running and breathlessly gasped out that the body of Skinsky had been found inside the wall of the churchyard of St Peter, and that the throat had been torn open as if by some wild animal. Those we had been speaking with ran off to see the horror, the women crying out, 'This is the work of a Slovak!' We hurried away lest we should have been in some way drawn into the affair, and so detained.

As we came home we could arrive at no definite conclusion. We were all convinced that the box was on its way, by water, to somewhere; but where that might be we would have to discover. With heavy hearts we came home to the hotel to Mina.

When we met together, the first thing was to consult as to taking Mina again into our confidence. Things are getting desperate, and it is at least a chance, though a hazardous one. As a preliminary step, I was released from my promise to her.

Mina Harker's Journal

30 October, evening. – They were so tired and worn-out and dispirited that there was nothing to be done till they had some rest; so I asked them all to lie down for half an hour whilst I should enter everything up to the moment. I feel so grateful to the man who invented the 'Traveller's' typewriter, and to Mr Morris for getting this one for me. I should have felt quite astray doing the work if I had to write with a pen . . .

It is all done; poor dear, dear Jonathan, what he must have suffered, what must he be suffering now! He lies on the sofa hardly seeming to breathe, and his whole body appears in collapse. His brows are knit; his face is drawn with pain. Poor fellow, maybe he is thinking, and I can see his face all wrinkled up with the concentration of his thoughts. Oh! if I could only help at all . . . I shall do what I can . . .

I have asked Dr Van Helsing, and he has got me all the papers that I have not yet seen . . . Whilst they are resting, I shall go over all carefully, and perhaps I may arrive at some conclusion. I shall try to follow the Professor's example, and think without prejudice on the facts before me . . .

I do believe that under God's providence I have made a discovery. I shall get the maps and look over them . . .

I am more than ever sure that I am right. My new conclusion is ready, so I shall get our party together and read it. They can judge it; it is well to be accurate, and every minute is precious.

Mina Harker's Memorandum
(Entered in her Journal)

Ground of inquiry. – Count Dracula's problem is to get back to his own place.

(a) He must be *brought back* by someone. This is evident; for, had he power to move himself as he wished, he could go either as man, or wolf, or bat, or in some other way. He evidently fears discovery or interference, in the state of helplessness in which he must be – confined as he is between dawn and sunset in his wooden box.

(b) How is he to be taken? – Here a process of exclusion may help us. By road, by rail, by water?

1. *By Road.* – There are endless difficulties, especially in leaving a city.

(a) There are people; and people are curious, and investigate. A hint, a surmise, a doubt as to what might be in the box would destroy him.

(*b*) There are, or there might be, customs and octroi[219] officers to pass.

(*c*) His pursuers might follow. This is his greatest fear; and in order to prevent his being betrayed he has repelled, so far as he can, even his victim – me!

2. *By Rail*. – There is no one in charge of the box. It would have to take its chance of being delayed; and delay would be fatal, with enemies on the track. True, he might escape at night; but where would he be, if left in a strange place with no refuge that he could fly to? This is not what he intends; and he does not mean to risk it.

3. *By Water*. – Here is the safest way, in one respect, but with most danger in another. On the water he is powerless except at night; even then he can only summon fog and storm and snow and his wolves. But were he wrecked, the living water would engulf him, helpless; and he would indeed be lost. He could have the vessel drive to land; but if it were unfriendly land, wherein he was not free to move, his position would still be desperate.

We know from the record that he was on the water; so what we have to do is to ascertain *what* water.

The first thing is to realise exactly what he has done as yet; we may, then, get a light on what his later task is to be.

Firstly, we must consider what he did in London as part of his general plan of action, when he was pressed for moments and had to arrange as best he could.

Secondly, we must see, as well as we can surmise it from the facts we know of what he has done here.

As to the first he evidently intended to arrive at Galatz, and sent invoice to Varna to deceive us lest we should ascertain his means of exit from England; his immediate and sole purpose then was to escape. The proof of this is the letter of instructions sent to Immanuel Hildesheim to clear and take away the box *before sunrise*. There is also the instruction to Petrof Skinsky. This we must only guess at; but there must have been some letter or message, since Skinsky came to Hildesheim.

That, so far, his plans were successful, we know. The *Czarina Catherine* made a phenomenally quick journey – so much so that Captain Donelson's suspicions were aroused; but his superstition united with his canniness played the Count's game for him, and he ran with his favouring wind through fogs and all till he brought up blindfold at Galatz. That the Count's arrangements were well made, has been proved. Hildesheim cleared the box, took it off, and gave it to Skinsky. Skinsky took it – and here we lose the trail. We only know that the box is somewhere on the water, moving along. The customs and the octroi, if there be any, have been avoided.

Now we come to what the Count must have done after his arrival – *on land*, at Galatz.

The box was given to Skinsky before sunrise. At sunrise the Count could appear in his own form. Here, we ask why Skinsky was chosen at all to aid in the work? In my husband's diary, Skinsky is mentioned as dealing with the Slovaks who trade down the river to the port; and the man's remark, that the murder was the work of a Slovak, showed the general feeling against his class. The Count wanted isolation.

My surmise is this: that in London the Count decided to get back to his Castle by water, as the most safe and secret way. He was brought from the Castle by Szgany, and probably they delivered their cargo to Slovaks who took the boxes to Varna, for there they were shipped for London. Thus the Count had knowledge of the persons who could arrange this service. When the box was on land, before sunrise or after sunset, he came out from his box, met Skinsky and instructed him what to do as to arranging the carriage of the box up some river. When this was done, and he knew that all was in train, he blotted out his traces, as he thought, by murdering his agent.

I have examined the map, and find that the river most suitable for the Slovaks to have ascended is either the Pruth[220] or the Sereth.[221] I read in the typescript that in my trance I heard cows low and water swirling level with my ears and the creaking of wood. The Count in his box, then, was on a river in an open boat – propelled probably either by oars or poles, for the banks are near and it is working against stream. There would be no such sound if floating down stream.

Of course it may not be either the Sereth or the Pruth, but we may possibly investigate further. Now of these two, the Pruth is the more easily navigated, but the Sereth is, at Fundu, joined by the Bistritza, which runs up round the Borgo Pass. The loop it makes is manifestly as close to Dracula's Castle as can be got by water.

MINA HARKER'S JOURNAL (*continued*)

When I had done reading, Jonathan took me in his arms and kissed me. The others kept shaking me by both hands, and Dr Van Helsing said:

'Our dear Madam Mina is once more our teacher. Her eyes have seen where we were blinded. Now we are on the track once again, and this time we may succeed. Our enemy is at his most helpless; and if we can come on him by day, on the water, our task will be over. He has a start, but he is powerless to hasten, as he may not leave his box lest those who carry him may suspect; for them to suspect would be to prompt them to throw him in the stream, where he perish. This he knows, and will not. Now, men, to our Council of War, for, here and now, we must plan what each and all shall do.'

'I shall get a steam launch and follow him,' said Lord Godalming.

'And I, horses to follow on the bank lest by chance he land,' said Mr Morris.

'Good!' said the Professor, 'both good. But neither must go alone. There must be force to overcome force if need be; the Slovak is strong and rough, and he carries rude arms.' All the men smiled, for amongst them they carried a small arsenal. Said Mr Morris:

'I have brought some Winchesters; they are pretty handy in a crowd, and there may be wolves. The Count, if you remember, took some other precautions; he made some requisitions on others that Mrs Harker could not quite hear or understand. We must be ready at all points.' Dr Seward said:

'I think I had better go with Quincey. We have been accustomed to hunt together, and we two well armed, will be a match for whatever may come along. You must not be alone, Art. It may be necessary to fight the Slovaks, and a chance thrust – for I don't suppose these fellows carry guns – would undo all our plans. There must be no chances, this time; we shall not rest until the Count's head and body have been separated, and we are sure that he cannot reincarnate.' He looked at Jonathan as he spoke, and Jonathan looked at me. I could see that the poor dear was torn about in his mind. Of course he wanted to be with me; but then the boat service would, most likely, be the one which would destroy the . . . the . . . the . . . Vampire. (Why did I hesitate to write the word?) He was silent awhile, and during his silence Dr Van Helsing spoke:

'Friend Jonathan, this is to you for twice reasons. First, because you are young and brave and can fight, and all energies may be needed at the last; and again that it is your right to destroy him – that – which has wrought such woe to you and yours. Be not afraid for Madam Mina; she will be my care, if I may. I am old. My legs are not so quick to run as once; and I am not used to ride so long or to pursue as need be, or to fight with lethal weapons. But I can be of other service; I can fight in other way. And I can die, if need be, as well as younger men. Now let me say that what I would is this: while you, my Lord Godalming, and friend Jonathan go in your so swift little steam-boat up the river, and whilst John and Quincey guard the bank where perchance he might be landed, I will take Madam Mina right into the heart of the enemy's country. Whilst the old fox is tied in his box, floating on the running

stream whence he cannot escape to land – where he dares not raise the
lid of his coffin-box lest his Slovak carriers should in fear leave him to
perish – we shall go in the track where Jonathan went – from Bistritz
over the Borgo – and find our way to the Castle of Dracula. Here,
Madam Mina's hypnotic power will surely help, and we shall find our
way – all dark and unknown otherwise – after the first sunrise when we
are near that fateful place. There is much to be done, and other places
to be made sanctify, so that that nest of vipers be obliterated.' Here
Jonathan interrupted him hotly:

'Do you mean to say, Professor Van Helsing, that you would bring
Mina, in her sad case and tainted as she is with that devil's illness, right
into the jaws of his death-trap? Not for the world! Not for Heaven or
Hell!' He became almost speechless for a minute, and then went on:

'Do you know what the place is? Have you seen that awful den of
hellish infamy – with the very moonlight alive with grisly shapes, and
every speck of dust that whirls in the wind a devouring monster in
embryo? Have you felt the Vampire's lips upon your throat?' Here he
turned to me, and as his eyes lit on my forehead, he threw up his arms
with a cry: 'Oh, my God, what have we done to have this terror upon
us!' and he sank down on the sofa in a collapse of misery. The
Professor's voice, as he spoke in clear, sweet tones, which seemed to
vibrate in the air, calmed us all:

'Oh, my friend, it is because I would save Madam Mina from that
awful place that I would go. God forbid that I should take her into that
place! There is work – wild work – to be done there, that her eyes may
not see. We men here, all save Jonathan, have seen with their own eyes
what is to be done before that place can be purify. Remember that we
are in terrible straits. If the Count escape us this time – and he is strong
and subtle and cunning – he may choose to sleep him for a century; and
then in time our dear one' – he took my hand – 'would come to him to
keep him company, and would be as those others that you, Jonathan,
saw. You have told us of their gloating lips; you heard their ribald laugh
as they clutched the moving bag that the Count threw to them. You
shudder; and well may it be. Forgive me that I make you so much pain,
but it is necessary. My friend, is it not a dire need for the which I am
giving, if need be, my life? If it were that anyone went into that place to
stay, it is I who would have to go, to keep them company.'

'Do as you will,' said Jonathan, with a sob that shook him all over, 'we
are in the hands of God!'

Later. – Oh, it did me good to see the way that these brave men
worked. How can women help loving men when they are so earnest,

and so true, and so brave! And, too, it made me think of the wonderful power of money! What can it not do when it is properly applied; and what might it do when basely used! I felt so thankful that Lord Godalming is rich, and that both he and Mr Morris, who also has plenty of money, are willing to spend it so freely. For if they did not, our little expedition could not start, either so promptly or so well equipped, as it will within another hour. It is not three hours since it was arranged what part each of us was to do; and now Lord Godalming and Jonathan have a lovely steam launch, with steam up, ready to start at a moment's notice. Dr Seward and Mr Morris have half a dozen beautiful horses, well appointed. We have all the maps and appliances of various kinds that can be had. Professor Van Helsing and I are to leave by the 11.40 train tonight for Veresti, where we are to get a carriage to drive to the Borgo Pass. We are bringing a good deal of ready money, as we are to buy a carriage and horses. We shall drive ourselves, for we have no one whom we can trust in the matter. The Professor knows something of a great many languages, so we shall get on all right. We have all got arms, even for me a large-bore revolver; Jonathan would not be happy unless I was armed like the rest. Alas! I cannot carry one arm that the rest do; the scar on my forehead forbids that. Dear Dr Van Helsing comforts me by telling me that I am fully armed as there may be wolves; the weather is getting colder every hour, and there are snow-flurries which come and go as warnings.

Later. – It took all my courage to say good-bye to my darling. We may never meet again. Courage, Mina! the Professor is looking at you keenly; his look is a warning. There must be no tears now – unless it may be that God will let them fall in gladness.

JONATHAN HARKER'S JOURNAL

October 30, night. – I am writing this in the light from the furnace door of the steam launch; Lord Godalming is firing up. He is an experienced hand at the work, as he has had for years a launch of his own on the Thames, and another on the Norfolk Broads.[222] Regarding our plans, we finally decided that Mina's guess was correct, and that if any waterway was chosen for the Count's escape back to his Castle, the Sereth, and then the Bistritza at its junction, would be the one. We took it, that somewhere about the 47th degree, north latitude, would be the place chosen for crossing the country between the river and the Carpathians. We have no fear in running at good speed up the river at night; there is plenty of water and the banks are wide enough apart to make steaming, even in the dark, easy enough. Lord Godalming tells me to sleep for a while, as it is enough for the present for one to be on watch. But I cannot sleep – how can I with the terrible danger hanging over my darling, and her going out into that awful place . . . My only comfort is that we are in the hands of God. Only for that faith it would be easier to die than to live, and so be quit of all the trouble. Mr Morris and Dr Seward were off on their long ride before we started; they are to keep up the right bank, far enough off to get on higher lands, where they can see a good stretch of river and avoid the following of its curves. They have, for the first stages, two men to ride and lead their spare horse – four in all, so as not to excite curiosity. When they dismiss the men, which will be shortly, they will themselves look after the horses. It may be necessary for us to join forces; if so they can mount our whole party. One of the saddles has a movable horn, and can be easily adapted for Mina, if required.

It is a wild adventure we are on. Here, as we are rushing along through the darkness, with the cold from the river seeming to rise up and strike us; with all the mysterious voices of the night around us, it all comes home. We seem to be drifting into unknown places and unknown ways; into a whole world of dark and dreadful things. Godalming is shutting the furnace door . . .

31 October. – Still hurrying along. The day has come, and Godalming is sleeping. I am on watch. The morning is bitterly cold; the furnace heat is grateful, though we have heavy fur coats. As yet we have passed only a few open boats, but none of them had on board any box or package of anything like the size of the one we seek. The men were scared every time we turned our electric lamp on them, and fell on their knees and prayed.

1 November, evening. – No news all day; we have found nothing of the kind we seek. We have now passed into the Bistritza; and if we are wrong in our surmise our chance is gone. We have overhauled every boat, big and little. Early this morning, one crew took us for a Government boat, and treated us accordingly. We saw in this a way of smoothing matters, so at Fundu, where the Bistritza runs into the Sereth, we got a Roumanian flag which we now fly conspicuously. With every boat which we have overhauled since then this trick has succeeded; we have had every deference shown to us, and not once any objection to whatever we chose to ask or do. Some of the Slovaks tell us that a big boat passed them, going at more than usual speed as she had a double crew on board. This was before they came to Fundu, so they could not tell us whether the boat turned into the Bistritza or continued on up the Sereth. At Fundu we could not hear of any such boat, so she must have passed there in the night. I am feeling very sleepy; the cold is perhaps beginning to tell upon me, and nature must have rest some time. Godalming insists that he shall keep the first watch. God bless him for all his goodness to poor dear Mina and me.

2 November, morning. – It is broad daylight. That good fellow would not wake me. He says it would have been a sin to, for I slept so peacefully and was forgetting my trouble. It seems brutally selfish of me to have slept so long, and let him watch all night; but he was quite right. I am a new man this morning; and, as I sit here and watch him sleeping, I can do all that is necessary both as to minding the engine, steering, and keeping watch. I can feel that my strength and energy are coming back to me. I wonder where Mina is now, and Van Helsing. They should have got to Veresti about noon on Wednesday. It would take them some time to get the carriage and horses; so if they had started and travelled hard, they would be about now at the Borgo Pass. God guide and help them! I am afraid to think what may happen. If we could only go faster! but we cannot, the engines are throbbing and doing their utmost. I wonder how Dr Seward and Mr Morris are getting on. There seem to be endless streams running down from the mountains into this river but as none of them are very large – at present, at all events, though they are terrible doubtless in winter and when the snow melts – the horsemen may not have met much obstruction. I hope that before we get to Strasba we may see them; for if by that time we have not overtaken the Count, it may be necessary to take counsel together what to do next.

Dr Seward's Diary

2 November. – Three days on the road. No news, and no time to write it if there had been, for every moment is precious. We have had only the rest needful for the horses, but we are both bearing it wonderfully. Those adventurous days of ours are turning up useful. We must push on; we shall never feel happy till we get the launch in sight again.

3 November. – We heard at Fundu that the launch had gone up the Bistritza. I wish it wasn't so cold. There are signs of snow coming; and if it falls heavy it will stop us. In such case we must get a sledge and go on, Russian fashion.

4 November. – Today we heard of the launch having been detained by an accident when trying to force a way up the rapids. The Slovak boats get up all right, by aid of a rope, and steering with knowledge. Some went up only a few hours before. Godalming is an amateur fitter[223] himself, and evidently it was he who put the launch in trim again. Finally, they got up the rapids all right, with local help, and are off on the chase afresh. I fear that the boat is not any better for the accident; the peasantry tell us that after she got upon the smooth water again, she kept stopping every now and again so long as she was in sight. We must push on harder than ever; our help may be wanted soon.

MINA HARKER'S JOURNAL

1 November. – Arrived at Veresti at noon. The Professor tells me that this morning at dawn he could hardly hypnotise me at all, and that all I could say was: 'Dark and quiet.' He is off now buying a carriage and horses. He says that he will later on try to buy additional horses, so that we may be able to change them on the way. We have something more than seventy miles before us. The country is lovely, and most interesting; if only we were under different conditions, how delightful it would be to see it all! If Jonathan and I were driving through it alone what a pleasure it would be! To stop and see people, and learn something of their life, and to fill our minds and memories with all the colour and picturesqueness of the whole wild, beautiful country and the quaint people! But, alas! –

Later. – Dr Van Helsing has returned. He has got the carriage and horses; we are to have some dinner, and to start in an hour. The landlady is putting us up a huge basket of provisions; it seems enough for a company of soldiers. The Professor encourages her, and whispers to me that it may be a week before we can get any good food again. He has been shopping too, and has sent home such a wonderful lot of fur coats and wraps, and all sorts of warm things. There will not be any chance of our being cold.

We shall soon be off. I am afraid to think what may happen to us. We are truly in the hands of God. He alone knows what may be, and I pray Him, with all the strength of my sad and humble soul, that He will watch over my beloved husband; that whatever may happen, Jonathan may know that I loved him and honoured him more than I can say, and that my latest and truest thought will be always for him.

Chapter 27

MINA HARKER'S JOURNAL

1 November. – All day long we have travelled, and at a good speed. The horses seem to know that they are being kindly treated, for they go willingly their full stage at best speed. We have now had so many changes and find the same thing so constantly that we are encouraged to think that the journey will be an easy one. Dr Van Helsing is laconic; he tells the farmers that he is hurrying to Bistritz, and pays them well to make the exchange of horses. We get hot soup, or coffee, or tea; and off we go. It is a lovely country; full of beauties of all imaginable kinds, and the people are brave, and strong, and simple, and seem full of nice qualities. They are *very, very* superstitious. In the first house where we stopped, when the woman who served us saw the scar on my forehead, she crossed herself and put out two fingers towards me, to keep off the evil eye. I believe they went to the trouble of putting an extra amount of garlic into our food; and I can't abide garlic. Ever since then I have taken care not to take off my hat or veil, and so have escaped their suspicions. We are travelling fast, and as we have no driver with us to carry tales, we go ahead of scandal; but I daresay that fear of the evil eye will follow hard behind us all the way. The Professor seems tireless; all day he would not take any rest, though he made me sleep for a long spell. At sunset time he hypnotised me, and he says that I answered as usual 'Darkness, lapping water and creaking wood;' so our enemy is still on the river. I am afraid to think of Jonathan, but somehow I have now no fear for him, or for myself. I write this whilst we wait in a farmhouse for the horses to be got ready. Dr Van Helsing is sleeping. Poor dear, he looks very tired and old and grey, but his mouth is set as firmly as a conqueror's; even in his sleep he is instinct with resolution. When we have well started I must make him rest whilst I drive. I shall tell him that we have days before us, and he must not break down when most of all his strength will be needed . . . All is ready; we are off shortly.

2 November, morning. – I was successful, and we took turns driving all night; now the day is on us, bright though cold. There is a strange heaviness in the air – I say heaviness for want of a better word; I mean that it oppresses us both. It is very cold, and only our warm furs keep us comfortable. At dawn Van Helsing hypnotised me; he says I answered

'Darkness, creaking wood and roaring water,' so the river is changing as they ascend. I do hope that my darling will not run any chance of danger – more than need be; but we are in God's hands.

2 *November, night.* – All day long driving. The country gets wilder as we go, and the great spurs of the Carpathians, which at Veresti seemed so far from us and so low on the horizon, now seem to gather round us and tower in front. We both seem in good spirits; I think we make an effort each to cheer the other; in the doing so we cheer ourselves. Dr Van Helsing says that by morning we shall reach the Borgo Pass. The houses are very few here now, and the Professor says that the last horses we got will have to go on with us, as we may not be able to change. He got two in addition to the two we changed, so that now we have a rude four-in-hand. The dear horses are patient and good, and they give us no trouble. We are not worried with other travellers, and so even I can drive. We shall get to the Pass in daylight; we do not want to arrive before. So we take it easy, and have each a long rest in turn. Oh, what will tomorrow bring to us? We go to seek the place where my poor darling suffered so much. God grant that we may be guided aright, and that He will deign to watch over my husband and those dear to us both, and who are in such deadly peril. As for me, I am not worthy in His sight. Alas! I am unclean to His eyes, and shall be until He may deign to let me stand forth in His sight as one of those who have not incurred His wrath.

Memorandum by Abraham Van Helsing

4 *November.* – This to my old and true friend John Seward, M.D., of Purfleet, London, in case I may not see him. It may explain. It is morning, and I write by a fire which all the night I have kept alive – Madam Mina aiding me. It is cold, cold; so cold that the grey heavy sky is full of snow, which when it falls will settle for all winter as the ground is hardening to receive it. It seems to have affected Madam Mina; she has been so heavy of head all day that she was not like herself. She sleeps, and sleeps, and sleeps! She, who is usual so alert, have done literally nothing all the day; she even have lost her appetite. She make no entry into her little diary, she who write so faithful at every pause. Something whisper to me that all is not well. However, tonight she is more *vif*.[224] Her long sleep all day have refresh and restore her, for now she is all sweet and bright as ever. At sunset I try to hypnotise her, but alas! with no effect; the power has grown less and less with each day, and tonight it fail me altogether. Well. God's will be done – whatever it may be, and whithersoever it may lead!

Now to the historical, for as Madam Mina write not in her stenography, I must, in my cumbrous old fashion, that so each day of us may not go unrecorded.

We got to the Borgo Pass just after sunrise yesterday morning. When I saw the signs of the day I got ready for the hypnotism. We stopped our carriage, and got down so that there might be no disturbance. I made a couch with furs, and Madam Mina, lying down, yield herself as usual, but more slow and more short time than ever, to the hypnotic sleep. As before, came the answer: 'Darkness and the swirling of water.' Then she woke, bright and radiant, and we go on our way and soon reach the Pass. At this time and place she become all on fire with zeal; some new guiding power be in her manifested, for she point to a road and say: 'This is the way.'

'How know you it?' I ask.

'Of course I know it,' she answer, and with a pause add: 'Have not my Jonathan travel it and wrote of his travel?'

At first I think somewhat strange, but soon I see that there be only one such by-road. It is used but little, and very different from the coach road from Bukovina to Bistritz, which is more wide and hard, and more of use.

So we came down this road; when we meet other ways – not always were we sure that they were roads at all, for they be neglect and light snow have fallen – the horses know and they only. I give rein to them, and they go on so patient. By-and-by we find all the things which Jonathan have note in that wonderful diary of him. Then we go on for long, long hours and hours. At the first, I tell Madam Mina to sleep; she try, and she succeed. She sleep all the time; till at the last, I feel myself to suspicious grow, and attempt to wake her. But she sleep on, and I may not wake her though I try. I do not wish to try too hard lest I harm her; for I know that she have suffer much, and sleep at times be all-in-all to her. I think I drowse myself, for all of sudden I feel guilt, as though I have done something; I find myself bolt up, with the reins in my hand, and the good horses go along jog, jog, just as ever. I look down and find Madam Mina still sleep. It is now not far off sunset time, and over the snow the light of the sun flow in big yellow flood, so that we throw great long shadow on where the mountain rise so steep. For we are going up, and up; and all is oh! so wild and rocky, as though it were the end of the world.

Then I arouse Madam Mina. This time she wake with not much trouble, and then I try to put her to hypnotic sleep. But she sleep not, being as though I were not. Still I try and try, till all at once I find her and myself in dark, so I look round, and find that the sun have gone down.

Madam Mina laugh, and I turn and look at her. She is now quite awake, and look so well as I never saw her since that night at Carfax when we first enter the Count's house. I am amaze, and not at ease then; but she is so bright and tender and thoughtful for me that I forget all fear. I light a fire, for we have brought supply of wood with us, and she prepare food while I undo the horses and set them, tethered in shelter, to feed. Then when I return to the fire she have my supper ready. I go to help her; but she smile, and tell me that she have eat already – that she was so hungry that she would not wait. I like it not, and I have grave doubts; but I fear to affright her, and so I am silent of it. She help me and I eat alone; and then we wrap in fur and lie beside the fire, and I tell her to sleep while I watch. But presently I forget all of watching; and when I sudden remember that I watch, I find her lying quiet, but awake, and looking at me with so bright eyes. Once, twice more the same occur, and I get much sleep till before morning. When I wake I try to hypnotise her; but alas! though she shut her eyes obedient, she may not sleep. The sun rise up, and up, and up; and then sleep come to her too late, but so heavy that she will not wake. I have to lift her up and place her sleeping in the carriage when I have harnessed the horses and made all ready. Madam still sleep, and sleep; and she look in her sleep more healthy and more redder than before. And I like it not. And I am afraid, afraid, afraid! – I am afraid of all things – even to think; but I must go on my way. The stake we play for is life and death, or more than these, and we must not flinch.

5 November, morning. – Let me be accurate in everything, for though you and I have seen some strange things together, you may at the first think that I, Van Helsing, am mad – that the many horrors and the so long strain on nerves has at the last turn my brain.

All yesterday we travel, ever getting closer to the mountains, and moving into a more and more wild and desert land. There are great, frowning precipices and much falling water, and Nature seemed to have held sometime her carnival. Madam Mina still sleep and sleep; and though I did have hunger and appeased it, I could not waken her – even for food. I began to fear that the fatal spell of the place was upon her, tainted as she is with that Vampire baptism. 'Well,' said I to myself 'if it be that she sleep all the day, it shall also be that I do not sleep at night.' As we travel on the rough road, for a road of an ancient and imperfect kind there was, I held down my head and slept. Again I waked with a sense of guilt and of time passed, and found Madam Mina still sleeping, and the sun low down. But all was indeed changed; the frowning mountains seemed further away, and we were near the top of a steep-rising hill on summit of which was such a castle as Jonathan tell of in his diary. At once

I exulted and feared; for now, for good or ill, the end was near. I woke
Madam Mina, and again tried to hypnotise her; but alas! unavailing till
too late. Then, ere the great dark came upon us – for even after down-
sun the heavens reflected the gone sun on the snow, and all was for a time
in a great twilight – I took out the horses and fed them in what shelter I
could. Then I make a fire; and near it I make Madam Mina, now wake
and more charming than ever, sit comfortable amid her rugs. I got ready
food; but she would not eat, simply saying that she had not hunger. I did
not press her, knowing her unavailingness. But I myself eat, for I must
needs now be strong for all. Then, with the fear on me of what might be,
I drew a ring so big for her comfort, round where Madam Mina sat; and
over the ring I passed some of the Wafer, and I broke it fine so that all
was well guarded. She sat still all the time – so still as one dead; and she
grew whiter and ever whiter till the snow was not more pale; and no word
she said. But when I drew near, she clung to me, and I could know that
the poor soul shook her from head to feet with a tremor that was pain to
feel. I said to her presently, when she had grown more quiet:

'Will you not come over to the fire?' for I wished to make a test of
what she could. She rose obedient, but when she have made a step she
stopped, and stood as one stricken.

'Why not go on?' I asked. She shook her head and coming back, sat
down in her place. Then, looking at me with open eyes, as of one waked
from sleep, she said simply:

'I cannot!' and remained silent. I rejoiced, for I knew that what she
could not, none of those that we dreaded could. Though there might be
danger to her body, yet her soul was safe!

Presently the horses began to scream and tore at their tethers till I
came to them and quieted them. When they did feel my hands on them,
they whinnied low as in joy, and licked at my hands and were quiet for a
time. Many times through the night did I come to them, till it arrive to
the cold hour when all nature is at lowest; and every time my coming
was with quiet of them. In the cold hour the fire began to die, and I was
about stepping forth to replenish it, for now the snow came in flying
sweeps and with it a chill mist. Even in the dark there was a light of
some kind, as there ever is over snow; and it seemed as though the
snow-flurries and the wreaths of mist took shape as of women with
trailing garments. All was in dead, grim silence, only that the horses
whinnied and cowered, as if in terror of the worst. I began to fear –
horrible fears, but then came to me the sense of safety in that ring
wherein I stood. I began, too, to think that my imaginings were of the
night, and the gloom, and the unrest that I have gone through, and all

the terrible anxiety. It was as though my memories of all Jonathan's horrid experience were befooling me; for the snowflakes and the mist began to wheel and circle round, till I could get as though a shadowy glimpse of those women that would have kissed him. And then the horses cowered lower and lower, and moaned in terror as men do in pain. Even the madness of fright was not to them, so that they could break away. I feared for my dear Madam Mina when these weird figures drew near and circled round. I looked at her, but she sat calm, and smiled at me; when I would have stepped to the fire to replenish it, she caught me and held me back, and whispered, like a voice that one bears in a dream, so low it was:

'No! no! Do not go without. Here you are safe!' I turned to her, and looking in her eyes, said:

'But you? It is for you that I fear!' whereat she laughed – a laugh low and unreal, and said:

'Fear for *me*! Why fear for me? None safer in all the world from them than I am,' and as I wondered at the meaning of her words, a puff of wind made the flame leap up, and I see the red scar on her forehead. Then, alas! I knew. Did I not, I would soon have learned, for the wheeling figures of mist and snow came closer, but keeping ever without the Holy circle. Then they began to materialise, till – if God have not take away my reason, for I saw it through my eyes – there were before me in actual flesh the same three women that Jonathan saw in the room, when they would have kissed his throat. I knew the swaying round forms, the bright hard eyes, the white teeth, the ruddy colour, the voluptuous lips. They smiled ever at poor dear Madam Mina; and as their laugh came through the silence of the night, they twined their arms and pointed to her, and said in those so sweet tingling tones that Jonathan said were of the intolerable sweetness of the water-glasses:

'Come, sister. Come to us. Come! Come!' In fear I turned to my poor Madam Mina, and my heart with gladness leapt like flame; for oh! the terror in her sweet eyes, the repulsion, the horror, told a story to my heart that was all of hope. God be thanked she was not, yet, of them. I seized some of the firewood which was by me, and holding out some of the Wafer, advanced on them towards the fire. They drew back before me, and laughed their low horrid laugh. I fed the fire, and feared them not; for I knew that we were safe within our protections. They could not approach me, whilst so armed, nor Madam Mina whilst she remained within the ring, which she could not leave no more than they could enter. The horses had ceased to moan, and lay still on the ground; the snow fell on them softly, and they grew whiter. I knew that there was for the poor beasts no more of terror.

And so we remained till the red of the dawn began to fall through the snow-gloom. I was desolate and afraid, and full of woe and terror; but when that beautiful sun began to climb the horizon life was to me again. At the first coming of the dawn the horrid figures melted in the whirling mist and snow; the wreaths of transparent gloom moved away towards the castle, and were lost.

Instinctively, with the dawn coming, I turned to Madam Mina, intending to hypnotise her; but she lay in a deep and sudden sleep, from which I could not wake her. I tried to hypnotise through her sleep, but she made no response, none at all, and the day broke. I fear yet to stir. I have made my fire and have seen the horses; they are all dead. Today I have much to do here, and I keep waiting till the sun is up high; for there may be places where I must go, where that sunlight, though snow and mist obscure it, will be to me a safety.

I will strengthen me with breakfast, and then I will to my terrible work. Madam Mina still sleeps; and, God be thanked! she is calm in her sleep . . .

JONATHAN HARKER'S JOURNAL

4 November, evening. – The accident to the launch has been a terrible thing for us. Only for it we should have overtaken the boat long ago; and by now my dear Mina would have been free. I fear to think of her, off on the wolds near that horrid place. We have got horses, and we follow on the track. I note this whilst Godalming is getting ready. We have our arms. The Szgany must look out if they mean fight. Oh, if only Morris and Seward were with us. We must only hope! If I write no more. Good-bye, Mina! God bless and keep you.

DR SEWARD'S DIARY

5 November. – With the dawn we saw the body of Szgany before us dashing away from the river with their leiter-waggon. They surrounded it in a cluster, and hurried along as though beset. The snow is falling lightly and there is a strange excitement in the air. It may be our own excited feelings, but the depression is strange. Far off I hear the howling of wolves; the snow brings them down from the mountains, and there are dangers to all of us, and from all sides. The horses are nearly ready, and we are soon off. We ride to death of someone. God alone knows who, or where, or what, or when, or how it may be . . .

Dr Van Helsing's Memorandum

5 November, afternoon. – I am at least sane. Thank God for that mercy at all events, though the proving it has been dreadful. When I left Madam Mina sleeping within the Holy circle, I took my way to the castle. The blacksmith hammer which I took in the carriage from Veresti was useful; though the doors were all open I broke them off the rusty hinges, lest some ill-intent or ill-chance should close them, so that being entered I might not get out. Jonathan's bitter experience served me here. By memory of his diary I found my way to the old chapel, for I knew that here my work lay. The air was oppressive; it seemed as if there was some sulphurous fume, which at times made me dizzy. Either there was a roaring in my ears or I heard afar off the howl of wolves. Then I bethought me of my dear Madam Mina, and I was in terrible plight. The dilemma had me between his horns. Her, I had not dare to take into this place, but left safe from the Vampire in that Holy circle; and yet even there would be the wolf! I resolve me that my work lay here, and that as to the wolves we must submit, if it were God's Will. At any rate it was only death and freedom beyond. So did I choose for her. Had it but been for myself the choice had been easy; the maw of the wolf were better to rest in than the grave of the Vampire! So I make my choice to go on with my work.

I knew that there were at least three graves to find – graves that are inhabit; so I search and search, and I find one of them. She lay in her Vampire sleep, so full of life and voluptuous beauty that I shudder as though I have come to do murder. Ah, I doubt not that in old time, when such things were, many a man who set forth to do such a task as mine, found at the last his heart fail him, and then his nerve. So he delay, and delay, and delay, till the mere beauty and the fascination of the wanton Un-Dead have hypnotise him; and he remain on, and on, till sunset come, and the Vampire sleep be over. Then the beautiful eyes of the fair woman open and look love, and the voluptuous mouth present to a kiss – and man is weak. And there remain one more victim in the Vampire fold; one more to swell the grim and grisly ranks of the Un-Dead! . . .

There is some fascination, surely, when I am moved by the mere presence of such an one, even lying as she lay in a tomb fretted with age and heavy with the dust of centuries, though there be that horrid odour such as the lairs of the Count have had. Yes, I was moved – I, Van Helsing, with all my purpose and with my motive for hate – I was moved to a yearning for delay which seemed to paralyse my faculties and to clog my very soul. It may have been that the need of natural sleep, and the strange oppression of the air were beginning to overcome me. Certain it was that I was lapsing into sleep, the open-eyed sleep of one who yields to a sweet fascination, when there came through the snow-stilled air a long, low wail, so full of woe and pity that it woke me like the sound of a clarion.

For it was the voice of my dear Madam Mina that I heard. Then I braced myself again to my horrid task, and found by wrenching away tomb-tops one other of the sisters, the other dark one. I dared not pause to look on her as I had on her sister, lest once more I should begin to be enthral; but I go on searching until, presently, I find in a high great tomb as if made to one much beloved that other fair sister which, like Jonathan, I had seen to gather herself out of the atoms of the mist. She was so fair to look on, so radiantly beautiful, so exquisitely voluptuous, that the very instinct of man in me, which calls some of my sex to love and to protect one of hers, made my head whirl with new emotion. But, God be thanked, that soul-wail of my dear Madam Mina had not died out of my ears; and, before the spell could be wrought further upon me, I had nerved myself to my wild work. By this time I had searched all the tombs in the chapel, so far as I could tell; and as there had been only three of these Un-Dead phantoms around us in the night, I took it that there were no more of active Un-Dead existent. There was one great tomb more lordly than all the rest; huge it was, and nobly proportioned. On it was but one word,

DRACULA.

This then was the Un-Dead home of the King-Vampire, to whom so many more were due. Its emptiness spoke eloquent to make certain what I knew. Before I began to restore these women to their dead selves through my awful work, I laid in Dracula's tomb some of the Wafer, and so banished him from it, Un-Dead, for ever.

Then began my terrible task, and I dreaded it. Had it been but one, it had been easy, comparative. But three! To begin twice more after I had been through a deed of horror; for if it was terrible with the sweet Miss Lucy, what would it not be with these strange ones who had survived through centuries, and who had been strengthened by the passing of the years, who would, if they could, have fought for their foul lives . . .

Oh, my friend John, but it was butcher work; had I not been nerved by thoughts of other dead, and of the living over whom hung such a pall of fear, I could not have gone on. I tremble and tremble even yet, though till all was over, God be thanked, my nerve did stand. Had I not seen the repose in the first face, and the gladness that stole over it just ere the final dissolution came, as realisation that the soul had been won, I could not have gone further with my butchery. I could not have endured the horrid screeching as the stake drove home; the plunging of writhing form, and lips of bloody foam. I should have fled in terror and left my work undone. But it is over! And the poor souls, I can pity them now and weep, as I think of them placid each in her full sleep of death, for a short moment ere fading. For, friend John, hardly had my knife severed the head of each, before the whole body began to melt away and crumble into its native dust, as though the death that should have come centuries agone had at last assert himself and say at once and loud 'I am her!'

Before I left the castle I so fixed its entrances that never more can the Count enter there Un-Dead.

When I stepped into the circle where Madam Mina slept, she woke from her sleep, and, seeing me, cried out in pain that I had endured too much.

'Come!' she said, 'come away from this awful place! Let us go to meet my husband, who is, I know, coming towards us.' She was looking thin and pale and weak; but her eyes were pure and glowed with fervour. I was glad to see her paleness and her illness, for my mind was full of the fresh horror of that ruddy Vampire sleep.

And so with trust and hope, and yet full of fear, we go eastward to meet our friends – and *him* – whom Madam Mina tell me that she *know* are coming to meet us.

MINA HARKER'S JOURNAL

6 November. – It was late in the afternoon when the Professor and I took our way towards the east whence I knew Jonathan was coming. We did not go fast, though the way was steeply downhill, for we had to take heavy rugs and wraps with us; we dared not face the possibility of being left without warmth in the cold and the snow. We had to take some of our provisions too, for we were in a perfect desolation, and, so far as we could see through the snowfall, there was not even the sign of a habitation. When we had gone about a mile, I was tired with the heavy walking and sat down to rest. Then we looked back and saw where the clear line of Dracula's castle cut the sky; for we were so deep under the hill whereon it was set that the angle of perspective of the Carpathian mountains was far below it. We saw it in all its grandeur, perched a thousand feet on the summit of a sheer precipice, and with seemingly a great gap between it and the steep of the adjacent mountain on any side. There was something wild and uncanny about the place. We could hear the distant howling of wolves. They were far off, but the sound, even though coming muffled through the deadening snowfall, was full of terror. I knew from the way Dr Van Helsing was searching about that he was trying to seek some strategic point, where we would be less exposed in case of attack. The rough roadway still led downwards; we could trace it through the drifted snow.

In a little while the Professor signalled to me, so I got up and joined him. He had found a wonderful spot, a sort of natural hollow in a rock, with an entrance like a doorway between two boulders. He took me by the hand and drew me in: 'See!' he said, 'here you will be in shelter; and if the wolves do come I can meet them one by one.' He brought in our furs, and made a snug nest for me, and got out some provisions and forced them upon me. But I could not eat; to even try to do so was repulsive to me, and, much as I would have liked to please him, I could not bring myself to the attempt. He looked very sad, but did not reproach me. Taking his field-glasses from the case, he stood on the top of the rock, and began to search the horizon. Suddenly he called out:

'Look! Madam Mina, look! look!' I sprang up and stood beside him on the rock; he handed me his glasses and pointed. The snow was now falling more heavily, and swirled about fiercely, for a high wind was beginning to blow. However, there were times when there were pauses between the snow-flurries, and I could see a long way round. From the height where we were it was possible to see a great distance; and far off, beyond the white waste of snow, I could see the river lying like a black ribbon in kinks and curls as it wound its way. Straight in front of us and not far off – in fact so near that I wondered we had not noticed before – came a group of mounted men hurrying along. In the midst of them was a cart, a long leiter-waggon, which swept from side to side, like a dog's tail wagging, with each stern inequality of the road. Outlined against the snow as they were, I could see from the men's clothes that they were peasants or gipsies of some kind.

On the cart was a great square chest. My heart leaped as I saw it, for I felt that the end was coming. The evening was now drawing close, and well I knew that at sunset the Thing, which was till then imprisoned there, would take new freedom and could in any of many forms elude all pursuit. In fear I turned to the Professor; to my consternation, however, he was not there. An instant later, I saw him below me. Round the rock he had drawn a circle, such as we had found shelter in last night. When he had completed it he stood beside me again, saying:

'At least you shall be safe here from *him*!' He took the glasses from me, and at the next lull of the snow swept the whole space below us. 'See,' he said, 'they come quickly; they are flogging the horses, and galloping as hard as they can.' He paused and went on in a hollow voice:

'They are racing for the sunset. We may be too late. God's Will be done!' Down came another blinding rush of driving snow, and the whole landscape was blotted out. It soon passed, however, and once more his glasses were fixed on the plain. Then came a sudden cry:

'Look! Look! Look! See, two horsemen follow fast, coming up from the south. It must be Quincey and John. Take the glass. Look, before the snow blots it all out!' I took it and looked. The two men might be Dr Seward and Mr Morris. I knew at all events that neither of them was Jonathan. At the same time I *knew* that Jonathan was not far off; looking around I saw on the north side of the coming party two other men, riding at break-neck speed. One of them I knew was Jonathan, and the other I took, of course, to be Lord Godalming. They, too, were pursuing the party with the cart. When I told the Professor he shouted in glee like a schoolboy, and, after looking intently till snowfall made sight impossible, he laid his Winchester rifle ready for use against the boulder at the opening of our shelter. 'They are all converging,' he said. 'When the time comes we shall have the gipsies on all sides.' I got out my revolver ready to hand, for whilst we were speaking the howling of wolves came louder and closer. When the snowstorm abated a moment we looked again. It was strange to see the snow falling in such heavy flakes close to us, and beyond, the sun shining more and more brightly as it sank down towards the far mountain tops. Sweeping the glass all around us I could see here and there dots moving singly and in twos and threes and larger numbers – the wolves were gathering for their prey.

Every instant seemed an age whilst we waited. The wind came now in fierce bursts, and the snow was driven with fury as it swept upon us in circling eddies. At times we could not see an arm's length before us; but at others as the hollow-sounding wind swept by us, it seemed to clear the air-space around us so that we could see afar off. We had of late been so accustomed to watch for sunrise and sunset, that we knew with fair accuracy when it would be, and we knew that before long the sun would set.

It was hard to believe that by our watches it was less than an hour that we waited in that rocky shelter before the various bodies began to converge close upon us. The wind came now with fiercer and more bitter sweeps, and more steadily from the north. It seemingly had driven the snow-clouds from us, for, with only occasional bursts, the snow fell. We could distinguish clearly the individuals of each party, the pursued and the pursuers. Strangely enough those pursued did not seem to realise, or at least to care, that they were pursued; they seemed, however, to hasten with redoubled speed as the sun dropped lower and lower on the mountain-tops.

Closer and closer they drew. The Professor and I crouched down behind our rock, and held our weapons ready; I could see that he was determined that they should not pass. One and all were quite unaware of our presence.

All at once two voices shouted out to 'Halt!' One was my Jonathan's, raised in a high key of passion; the other, Mr Morris's strong resolute tone of quiet command. The gipsies may not have known the language, but there was no mistaking the tone, in whatever tongue the words were spoken. Instinctively they reined in, and at the instant Lord Godalming and Jonathan dashed up at one side and Dr Seward and Mr Morris on the other. The leader of the gipsies, a splendid-looking fellow, who sat his horse like a centaur, waved them back, and in a fierce voice gave to his companions some word to proceed. They lashed the horses, which sprang forward; but the four men raised their Winchester rifles, and in an unmistakable way commanded them to stop. At the same moment Dr Van Helsing and I rose behind the rock and pointed our weapons at them. Seeing that they were surrounded, the men tightened their reins and drew up. The leader turned to them and gave a word, at which every man of the gipsy party drew what weapon he carried, knife or pistol, and held himself in readiness to attack. Issue was joined in an instant.

The leader, with a quick movement of his rein, threw his horse out in front, and pointing first to the sun – now close down on the hill-tops – and then to the castle, said something which I did not understand. For answer all four men of our party threw themselves from their horses and dashed towards the cart. I should have felt terrible fear at seeing Jonathan in such danger, but that the ardour of battle must have been upon me as well as the rest of them; I felt no fear, but only a wild surging desire to do something. Seeing the quick movement of our parties, the leader of the gipsies gave a command; his men instantly formed round the cart in a sort of undisciplined endeavour, each one shouldering and pushing the other in his eagerness to carry out the order.

In the midst of this I could see that Jonathan on one side of the ring of men, and Quincey on the other, were forcing a way to the cart; it was evident that they were bent on finishing their task before the sun should set. Nothing seemed to stop or even to hinder them. Neither the levelled weapons or the flashing knives of the gipsies in front, or the howling of the wolves behind, appeared to even attract their attention. Jonathan's impetuosity, and the manifest singleness of his purpose, seemed to overawe those in front of him; instinctively they cowered aside and let him pass. In an instant he had jumped upon the cart, and, with a strength which seemed incredible, raised the great box and flung it over the wheel to the ground. In the meantime, Mr Morris had had to use force to pass through his side of the ring of Szgany. All the time I had been breathlessly watching Jonathan I had, with the tail of my eye, seen him pressing desperately forward, and had seen the knives of the gipsies flash as he won a way through them, and they cut at him. He parried with his great bowie knife, and at first I thought that he too had come through in safety; but as he sprang beside Jonathan, who had by now jumped from the cart, I could see that with his left hand he was clutching at his side, and that the blood was spurting through his fingers. He did not delay notwithstanding this, for as Jonathan, with desperate energy, attacked one end of the chest, attempting to prise off the lid with his great Kukri knife, he attacked the other frantically with his bowie. Under the efforts of both men the lid began to yield; the nails drew with a quick screeching sound, and the top of the box was thrown back.

By this time the gipsies, seeing themselves covered by the Winchesters, and at the mercy of Lord Godalming and Dr Seward, had given in and made no further resistance. The sun was almost down on the mountain-tops, and the shadows of the whole group fell long upon the snow. I saw the Count lying within the box upon the earth, some of which the rude falling from the cart had scattered over him. He was deathly pale, just like a waxen image, and the red eyes glared with the horrible vindictive look which I knew too well.

As I looked, the eyes saw the sinking sun, and the look of hate in them turned to triumph.

But, on the instant, came the sweep and flash of Jonathan's great knife. I shrieked as I saw it shear through the throat; whilst at the same moment Mr Morris's bowie knife plunged into the heart.

It was like a miracle; but before our very eyes, and almost in the drawing of a breath, the whole body crumbled into dust and passed from our sight.

I shall be glad as long as I live that even in that moment of final dissolution there was in the face a look of peace, such as I never could have imagined might have rested there.

The Castle of Dracula now stood out against the red sky, and every stone of its broken battlements was articulated against the light of the setting sun.

The gipsies, taking us as in some way the cause of the extraordinary disappearance of the dead man, turned, without a word, and rode away as if for their lives. Those who were unmounted jumped upon the leiter-waggon and shouted to the horsemen not to desert them. The wolves which had withdrawn to a safe distance, followed in their wake leaving us alone.

Mr Morris, who had sunk to the ground, leaned on his elbow, holding his hand pressed to his side; the blood still gushed through his fingers. I flew to him, for the Holy circle did not now keep me back; so did the two doctors. Jonathan knelt behind him and the wounded man laid back his head on his shoulder. With a sigh he took, with a feeble effort, my hand in that of his own which was unstained. He must have seen the anguish of my heart in my face, for he smiled at me and said:

'I am only too happy to have been of any service! Oh, God!' he cried suddenly, struggling up to a sitting posture and pointing to me, 'it was worth this to die! Look! look!'

The sun was now right down upon the mountain-top, and the red gleams fell upon my face, so that it was bathed in rosy light. With one impulse the men sank on their knees, and a deep and earnest 'Amen' broke from all as their eyes followed the pointing of his finger as the dying man spoke:

'Now God be thanked that all has not been in vain! See! the snow is not more stainless than her forehead! The curse has passed away!'

And, to our bitter grief, with a smile and in silence, he died, a gallant gentleman.

Note

Seven years ago we all went through the flames; and the happiness of some of us since then is, we think, well worth the pain we endured. It is an added joy to Mina and to me that our boy's birthday is the same day as that on which Quincey Morris died. His mother holds, I know, the secret belief that some of our brave friend's spirit has passed into him. His bundle of names links all our little band of men together; but we call him Quincey.

In the summer of this year we made a journey to Transylvania and went over the old ground which was, and is, to us so full of vivid and terrible memories. It was almost impossible to believe that the things which we had seen with our own eyes and heard with our own ears were living truths. Every trace of all that had been was blotted out. The castle stood as before, reared high above a waste of desolation.

When we got home we got to talking of the old time – which we could all look back on without despair, for Godalming and Seward are both happily married. I took the papers from the safe where they have been ever since our return so long ago. We were struck with the fact, that in all the mass of material of which the record is composed, there is hardly one authentic document; nothing but a mass of type-writing, except the later note-books of Mina and Seward and myself, and Van Helsing's memorandum. We could hardly ask anyone, even did we wish to, to accept these as proofs of so wild a story. Van Helsing summed it all up as he said, with our boy on his knee:

'We want no proofs; we ask none to believe us! This boy will some day know what a brave and gallant woman his mother is. Already he knows her sweetness and loving care; later on he will understand how some men so loved her, that they did dare much for her sake.'

Jonathan Harker

NOTES

1 (p. 25) *Bistritz* or Bistrita, a town in Transylvania, which means 'the Land Beyond the Forest' and which refers to a high plateau region in central and northwest Romania. In Stoker's day, Transylvania was a Hungarian province noted mainly for its orchards, wheatfields and vineyards. Bistrita is today a town in eastern Hungary.

2 (p. 25) *Buda-Pesth* Budapest, an industrial city on the Danube River that is now the capital city of Hungary. Buda, which is situated on the right bank of the Danube, became the capital in 1867. It was joined with Pest, on the left bank, in 1872.

3 (p. 25) *Danube* the second longest river in Europe, flowing from the east slopes of the Black Forest to the Black Sea in Romania and separating Buda from Pest

4 (p. 25) *Klausenburgh* town in Transylvania, which is now the provincial capital Cluj

5 (p. 25) *British Museum* the largest museum in England, opened in 1759 in Montagu House, Bloomsbury. Stoker used its circular reading room, added in 1857, to learn about the history of Eastern Europe and its legends.

6 (p. 25) *Moldavia and Bukovina* The former, once a principality, was the eastern district of Romania from 1861 to 1940; the latter, once an Austrian possession, is a region in northeast Romania.

7 (p. 25) *Ordnance Survey maps* military maps

8 (p. 25) *Saxons; Wallachs; Dacians; Magyars; Szekleys* respectively, peoples of West Germany who occupied Transylvania in the twelfth and thirteenth centuries; inhabitants of the one-time principality Wallachia, now the southern province of Romania; inhabitants of an ancient region generally equivalent to Romania; the dominant ethnic group of Hungary who also reside in southwest Siberia; an ancient Transylvanian family.

9 (p. 26) *forcemeat* poultry, fish or meat ground finely and highly spiced and sometimes used in stuffing

10 (p. 28) *English Churchman* Victorian Anglicanism disliked anything seemingly associated with Catholic relics and rituals, particularly following the Oxford Movement's attempt to restore some Roman Catholic practices during the 1830s and 1840s.

DRACULA 347

11 (p. 30) *Borgo Prund* Angelicised version of Borgóprund, which is the Hungarian name for a Romanian village and rail junction, Prundul-Bărgăului, located near Bistrita

12 (p. 30) *Hospadars* rulers of Wallachia and Moldavia between the fifteenth century and 1866

13 (p. 33) *Denn die Todten* well-known poem published in 1773 by the German poet Gottfried August Burger (1747–94) and translated into English by William Taylor in 1796. Harker misquotes the line, 'the dead ride fast', which is a refrain in the poem.

14 (p. 34) *blue flame* Emanating in medieval folklore from those who died from the plague, it acquired mystical properties though association with St George's Eve, which occurs on 23 April and commemorates the Christian knight and slayer of dragons.

15 (p. 36) *solicitor* legal term for someone who in British legal practice prepares court cases for barristers but who rarely appears in court him or herself

16 (p. 39) *Tokay* a sweet white wine produced in Hungary near the town of Tokaj

17 (p. 40) *Hampton Court* a royal residence until eighteenth century founded by Cardinal Wolsey in 1515 and lying approximately fifteen miles from London appropriated by Henry VIII after Wolsey's fall

18 (p. 41) *London Dictionary; the 'Red' and 'Blue' books; the Army and Navy Lists; the Law List* respectively, a comprehensive list of commercial traders in London and surrounding suburbs; government reports of a committee or royal commission and directories of those people serving or pensioned by the state; official lists of all serving commissioned officers in both branches and reserve officers subject to recall; and directory of professional lawyers

19 (p. 41) *boyar* refers to a nobleman in Russia and to a member of the upper class in Romania

20 (p. 41) *stranger in a strange land* see Exodus 2:22. Moses' son by Zipporah is named Gershom because 'he said, I have been a stranger in a strange land'.

21 (p. 42) *artificial avalanches* reference to battle in November 1330 when the army of the Hungarian king invading Romania was trapped in the narrow pass of Posada by Wallachians led by Prince Basarab who threw boulders down upon them

22 (p. 43) *Bradshaw's Guide* annual book of English railway timetables published between 1839 and 1961

23 (p. 43) *Purfleet* a town in the county of Essex, approximately twenty miles from London

24 (p. 44) *Kodak*   trademark name for the portable photographic camera invented by George Eastman in 1888 which has a continuous roll of sensitised film upon which successive negatives are made

25 (p. 48) *Ugric tribe*   a division of Ural-Altaic people including Siberians, Magyars and Finns

26 (p. 48) *Berserkers*   ancient Norse fighters renowned for their courage and ferocity

27 (p. 48) *Scythia*   ancient region north of the Black and Caspian Seas

28 (p. 48) *Honofoglalas*   refers to Arpad, Magyar chieftain elected to succeed Attila the Hun, who conquered Hungary in the ninth century, and means 'conquest of the homeland'. The thousandth anniversary of the Honofoglalas was still being celebrated in 1896 as Stoker was writing *Dracula*.

29 (p. 49) *Cassova*   refers to a 1448 battle of Kossovso in which Hungarians and Wallachs were defeated for the second time by the Turks, the first defeat having taken place in 1389

30 (p. 49) *Viovode*   Governor or (Romanian) prince

31 (p. 49) *brother*   Radu, brother of Vlad the Impaler, who assumed the throne of Wallachia in 1462

32 (p. 49) *Mohacs*   defeated by the Turks in 1526, Hungary became a Turkish province; Transylvania gained semi-autonomous status until re-conquered by the Austrians.

33 (p. 49) *Hapsburgs and Romanoffs*   respectively, ruling house of Austria from 1282–1918 (during Stoker's time they ruled the Austro-Hungarian Empire) and Russian dynastic rulers from 1613 to 1917 (the royal family executed by Bolsheviks in 1918)

34 (p. 49) *Lincoln's Inn*   an old legal training establishment in London

35 (p. 54) *culverin*   a kind of handgun; later a large cannon that was very long in proportion to its bore

36 (p. 55) *My tablets!* . . .   See *Hamlet*, 1, 5, 107.

37 (p. 58) *in the toils*   like a trapped animal

38 (p. 59) *band of Szgany*   Romany gypsies, usually referred to as *Tsigane*

39 (p. 61) *hetman*   Polish, from the German *Hauptmann*, meaning captain or commander

40 (p. 65) *weird sisters*   refers to *Macbeth*

41 (p. 66) *parting guest*   from Alexander Pope's translation of Homer's *Odyssey*, 15, l. 84

42 (p. 69) *typewriter*   invented in America in 1867

43 (p. 70) *last Pop*   a popular concert

44 (p. 70) *parti*   a marriageable person, considered in reference to means, etc., or as a 'match'.

45 (p. 73) *Desdemona*   tragic heroine of Shakespeare's *Othello*

46 (p. 75) *phonograph*   invented by Thomas Edison in 1877

47 (p. 75) *Omnia Romæ vernalia sunt*   All Romans are venal.

48 (p. 75) *verb sap*   short for *verbum sapienti sat est*, meaning 'a word is sufficient to a wise man'

49 (p. 75) *ætat*   Latin for 'age'

50 (p. 76) *Marquesas*   volcanic islands northeast of Tahiti in the South Pacific

51 (p. 76) *Titicaca*   large lake in the Andes

52 (p. 76) *Korea*   country where United States and Europe tried and failed to curb the burgeoning commercial control of Japan near the turn of the nineteenth century

53 (p. 77) *Whitby*   port city in Yorkshire on the North Sea coast of England

54 (p. 77) *Whitby Abbey*   founded in 658 and destroyed in 867 by the Danes

55 (p. 77) *Marmion*   refers to the narrative of the same name by Sir Walter Scott published in 1808, and the fate of Constance de Beverley, who forswears her nun's vows for the love of the knight Marmion

56 (p. 78) *Waterloo*   battle fought on 18 June 1815 in which the British commander Wellington defeated the French emperor Napoleon near the village of Waterloo in Belgium. Wellington was supported in the last stages by Prussians led by General Blücher.

57 (p. 78) *fash masel*   Whitby dialect for 'fuss myself'. Stoker relied on *A Glossary of Words Used in the Neighbourhood of Whitby*, published by F. K. Robinson in 1875–6.

58 (p. 78) *feet-folks*   derogatory slang for tourists who travel by foot rather than by carriage as do the wealthy passengers

59 (p. 78) *York and Leeds*   large industrial and manufacturing cities in the north of England

60 (p. 78) *crammle aboon the grees*   hobble down the stairs

61 (p. 78) *belly-timber*   food

62 (p. 78) *Sir Oracle*   from Gratiano in *The Merchant of Venice* 1, 1, 93–4 'I am Sir Oracle,/And when I ope my lips let no dog bark!'

63 (p. 79) . . . *a-belderin*   . . . curses and ghosts and apparitions and harbingers of death and hobgoblins and all concerning them is only fit to set children and half-witted women a-crying.

64 (p. 79) *beuk-bodies*   learned people

65 (p. 79) *skeer an' scunner hafflin's*   scare half-wits

66 (p. 79) *scowderment*   odd commotion

67 (p. 79) *Yabblins!*   Possibly!

68 (p. 80) *I have me antherums aboot it!*   I doubt it!

69 (p. 80) *jommlin'*   shoving

70 (p. 80) *thruffstean*   a table-shaped tombstone covering the complete length of a grave

71 (p. 81) *gawm*   know

72 (p. 81) *acrewk'd*   twisted or crooked

73 (p. 81) *lamiter*   cripple

74 (p. 81) *the clegs and the dowps*   horse flies and carrion crows

75 (p. 81) *addle*   collect earnings

76 (p. 81) *keckle*   chuckle

77 (p. 83) *madness*   See *Hamlet*, 2, 2, 207.

78 (p. 84) *brain-knowledge*   respectively, Burdon-Sanderson (1828–1905), an English physician who first measured the electrical impulses coming from the heart, and David Ferrier (1843–1928), physician who conducted experiments on the brain structures of primates; both were criticised by anti-vivisectionists; the latter was prosecuted under the Cruelty to Animals Act of 1876 but acquitted.

79 (p. 86) *'brool'*   a deep, murmuring sound

80 (p. 86) *trees walking*   refers to Mark 8:24

81 (p. 86) *scuppers*   opening in the side of a ship on a level with the deck designed to allow water to escape

82 (p. 87) *krok-hooal*   grave

83 (p. 87) *caffin'*   chafing

84 (p. 87) *chafts*   jaws

85 (p. 88) *Mulgrave Woods . . . Staithes*   towns and spots of beauty around Whitby

86 (p. 88) *R. A. and R. I.*   the Royal Academy of Arts (1786) and the Royal Institution of Great Britain (1799), founded respectively to
encourage painting, sculpture and architecture and to promote, diffuse and extend science and knowledge

87 (p. 89) *ocean*   See *The Rime of the Ancient Mariner*, II, 113–8, by Samuel Taylor Coleridge.

88 (p. 90) *gunwale*   upper part of a boat or a ship

89 (p. 90) *mirabile dictu*   wonderful to relate

90 (p. 91) *'top-hammer'*   rigging, sails, upper masts, etc. that provide weight on the upper parts of the ship

91 (p. 92) *mortmain*   legal term signifying ownership in perpetuity of real estate by institutions such as churches that cannot sell or transfer it

92 (p. 92) *Casabianca*   the boy in a well-known poem published by Felicia Hemans in 1827

93 (p. 92) *wolds*   open, elevated stretches of land

94 (p. 92) *Demeter*   Greek goddess of fertility whose daughter Perse-phone was kidnapped by the lord of the Underworld

95 (p. 93) *cum grano*   short for *cum grano salis*, which means 'with a grain of salt'

96 (p. 93) *Backsheesh*   money reputedly given in former times for a bribe or tip in some Eastern countries

97 (p. 95) *round robin*   petition or protest signed in a circle to conceal the identity of its initiators

98 (p. 95) *yawing*   nautical term meaning to travel off course temporarily

99 (p. 99) *dusty miller*   the auricula (Primula Auricula), from the fine powder on the leaves and flowers; a kind of artificial fly

100 (p. 100) *diorama*   large, nineteenth-century theatres that featured grand artistic or natural spectacles

101 (p. 103) *Spohr and Mackenzie*   German violinist Louis Spohr (1784–1859) and Scottish violinist Sir Alexander Campbell Mackenzie respectively

102 (p. 109) *rejoice*   suggests a passage in John 3:29

103 (p. 110) *Morpheus*   god of dreams

104 (p. 111) *fishes*   refers to the story of the loaves and fishes told in Matthew 15:32–9; Mark 6:37–44; Luke 9:13–17; and John 6:9–13

105 (p. 112) *Hull and Hamburg*   important nineteenth-century English and German port, respectively

106 (p. 114) *Whitby, 30 August*   should probably read 20 August

107 (p. 116) *happens*   refers to a line in chapter 4, Book II of *Egymion* by Benjamin Disraeli, prime minister from 1874 to 1880, which reads 'What we anticipate seldom occurs; what we least expect generally happens.'

108 (p. 119) *ice-brook*   See *Othello*, 5, 2, 256.

109 (p. 119) *Stores*   slang for the fashionable London department store Harrod's

110 (p. 120) *smuts*   smog

111 (p. 125) *corn is grown*   see Luke 8:8 and 8:15

112 (p. 132) *Gott in Himmel*   German for God in Heaven

113 (p. 134) *Lethe*   according to Greek mythology the river in Hades that caused those who drank its waters to fall into a state of for-getfulness. See too the beginning of John Keats's *Ode to Melancholy*.

114 (p. 135) *fly*   lightweight, one-horse carriage

115 (p. 136) *strewments*   See *Hamlet*, 5, 1, 226–7.

116 (p. 136) *Berkeley*   hotel near Piccadilly Circus

117 (p. 139) *Pall Mall Gazette*   Victorian evening newspaper and review

118 (p. 139) *arf-quid*   slang for ten shillings or half a pound; i.e. fifty pence

119 (p. 140) *anceterer*   Cockney slang for 'etcetera'

120 (p. 141) *'armony*   a sing-song

121 (p. 141) *garding 'edges*   Stoker's Cockney version of 'garden hedges'

122 (p. 142) *quondam friend*   former friend

123 (p. 143) *blood is the life*   most likely refers to Deuteronomy 12:23 – 'Only be sure that thou eat not the blood; for the blood is the life, and thou mayest not eat the life with the flesh.' See too Deuteronomy 12:16; Genesis 9:4; and Leviticus 17:12.

124 (p. 145) *simoom*   suffocating, sandy wind that occurs often in the deserts of North Africa

125 (p. 151) *in camera*   to speak in the judge's chamber as opposed to open court

126 (p. 151) *Pampas*   flat, treeless plains in Argentina lying between the Andes and the Atlantic

127 (p. 151) *go to grass*   to die or to be ruined

128 (p. 152) *19 September*   to be consistent, Stoker should have made this date 20 September

129 (p. 155) *M.D., M.R.C.S., L.K.Q.C.P.I., etc. etc.*   Doctor of Medicine; Member of the Royal College of Surgeons; Licentiate of the King's and Queen's College of Physicians, Ireland

130 (p. 156) *grog*   rum and water

131 (p. 158) *chaplet*   garland

132 (p. 161) *. . . she died*   from 'The Death Bed' by Thomas Hood (1799–1845)

133 (p. 162) *chapelle ardente*   temporary mortuary, sometimes used as a chapel to mourn the dead

134 (p. 162) *'decay's effacing fingers'*   See Lord George Byron's poem *The Giaour*, line 72.

135 (p. 168) *Hyde Park Corner*   area of Hyde Park, one of the largest open spaces in London, that adjoins Kensington Gardens and occupies nearly 350 acres in Westminster.

136 (p. 168) *the Row*   wide track for horse riders in Hyde Park called Rotten Row

137 (p. 168) *Piccadilly*   district in central London

138 (p. 169) *victoria*   a horse-drawn carriage built for two people with a front seat for the driver

139 (p. 169) *Green Park*   a small park across from the east end of Hyde Park

140 (p. 173) *Westminster Gazette*   founded in 1893

141 (p. 173) *'bloofer lady'*   beautiful lady

142 (p. 173) *Ellen Terry*   British actress (1847–1928) who was the most

famous leading lady to Henry Irving from 1878 and excelled in Shakespearian roles

143 (p. 177) *à deux mains* in both hands

144 (p. 181) *Paddington* west-central London railway station near Kensington Gardens

145 (p. 182) *Launceston* a market city in Cornwall approximately fifty miles from Exeter

146 (p. 185) *Charcot* Jean-Martin Charcot (1825–93), a French neurologist who studied diseases of the nervous system and became known for his work in sclerosis, locomotor ataxia, hysteria and senile diseases; in Paris he studied how certain mental illnesses cause physical changes in the brain. Sigmund Freud was one of his pupils.

147 (p. 185) *Methuselah* Old Testament Hebrew patriarch who lived before the Flood and whose reputed age of 969 years made him a byword for longevity

148 (p. 185) '*Old Parr*' the legendary figure Thomas Parr who was reputed to have lived between 1483 and 1635, but whose legend probably developed from a succession of men of the same name and not just a single person

149 (p. 187) *American* most likely refers to the nineteenth-century American novelist and humorist Mark Twain and this saying from his *Pudd'nhead Wilson's New Calender*: 'Faith is believing what you know ain't so.'

150 (p. 188) . . . *abhorred* a slight misquote of Byron's *Don Juan*, 1, 39, 1112, which reads: 'To prove himself the thing he most abhor'd.'

151 (p. 189) '*Jack Straw's Castle*' an inn on Hampstead Heath

152 (p. 192) *Spaniards* an old pub near Hampstead Heath called the Spaniards Inn

153 (p. 197) *pourparlers* informal discussions that are preliminary to any actual negotiations

154 (p. 197) *Kingstead* fictional churchyard that may be an alias for 'Hampstead'

155 (p. 201) *Host* Catholic communion wafer

156 (p. 201) *Indulgence* in Catholic doctrine

157 (p. 203) *Medusa's snakes* in Greek mythology, the beautiful woman Medusa was changed into a Gorgon by the jealous goddess Althea. Her hair became a nest of serpents, and she turned into stone anyone who looked at her. She was killed by Perseus, who then used her severed head to fend off other monsters.

158 (p. 206) *Thor* Norse god of thunder whose weapon was a hammer

159 (p. 208) *ploughshare* See Luke 9:62.

160 (p. 209) *Liverpool Street*   central London railway terminus

161 (p. 209) *Fenchurch Street*   small London terminus. The first electric subway or underground began operation in 1890.

162 (p. 221) *non causæ* and *ignoratio elenchi* respectively, 'there is no reason' and 'ignorance of the charge'

163 (p. 226) *Chersonese*   the Thracian peninsula west of the Hellespont

164 (p. 227) *Arminius*   Arminius Vambéry (1832–1913), whom Stoker met in 1890, was Professor of Oriental Languages at Budapest.

165 (p. 227) *Scholomance*   according to Emily Gerard, a school where 'the secrets of nature, the language of animals, and all magic spells' were taught by the Devil himself.

166 (p. 227) *Lake Hermanstadt*   an 'immeasurably deep' lake, according to legend, wherein lived the thunder and a sleeping dragon. On its banks lived the descendants of the children mesmerised by the Pied Piper.

167 (p. 230) *Derby night*   Held at the Epsom Downs, southwest of London, the Derby is the most famous of the classic horseraces run annually in England.

168 (p. 230) *Union*   the United States. Texas became a state in 1845.

169 (p. 230) *Pole and the Tropics*   Alaska and Hawaii, respectively.

170 (p. 230) *Monroe doctrine*   doctrine of American foreign policy, set out by James Monroe, the fifth president, which warned European powers not to attempt to control the future of the Spanish-American states in the Western Hemisphere and which remained government policy from 1823 to 1895

171 (p. 235) *In manus tuas, Domine*   'Into thy hands, O Lord!' See Luke 23:46. Also see the last words of Alfred Tennyson's play *Becket*.

172 (p. 242) *fire by night*   See Exodus 13:21–2.

173 (p. 244) *Bethnal Green*   manufacturing area in the East End of London

174 (p. 244) *Bermondsey*   neighbourhood in southeast London

175 (p. 244) *the City*   self-governing district of central London usually identified with banking and financial interests

176 (p. 246) *Poplar*   industrial and shipping area in east London

177 (p. 247) *Piccadilly Circus*   centre of the theatre, club, shopping and hotel district of London in Stoker's day.

178 (p. 247) *Constitutional*   Conservative club located at 101 Piccadily

179 (p. 248) *Sackville Street*   west of Piccadilly Circus

180 (p. 249) *Aerated Bread Company*   a chain of tea shops

181 (p. 252) *Malvolio*   Olivia's steward in Shakespeare's *Twelfth Night*

182 (p. 252) *Enoch*   Old Testament figure. In the Cainite genealogy of Genesis 4, Enoch is the son of Cain and therefore the third from Adam. In the Sethite genealogy in Genesis 5, he is the son of Jared and

thus the seventh from Adam. He is also the father of Methuselah. Because of his perfect fellowship with God, Enoch was taken directly to heaven and spared the experience of death. In apocaplytic literature, Enoch, whose lifespan of 365 years associated him with the Babylonian sun god, appears as a preacher of repentance, a prophet of future events and recipient of supernatural knowledge about the secrets of heaven and earth.

183 (p. 252) *to be kind*   See *Hamlet*, 3, 4, 178.

184 (p. 253) *small deer*   See *King Lear*, 3, 4, 142.

185 (p. 267) *flesh of my flesh*   See Genesis 2:23.

186 (p. 272) *en règle*   according to rule

187 (p. 275) *Unclean!*   See Leviticus 13:45.

188 (p. 280) *Festina lente*   hasten slowly

189 (p. 282) *Nota bene*   note well

190 (p. 290) *double entente*   literally, especially good harmony or rapport, but perhaps malapropism for *double entendre*

191 (p. 292) *magnifico*   'That which is not known is enchanting [or wonderful]'; see Chapter 30 of *Agricola* by Tacitus.

192 (p. 292) *Varna*   a major port city on the Black Sea ruled by the Turks between 1391 and 1878 when it became part of Bulgaria

193 (p. 296) *Glory of God*   echoes the motto of the Society of Jesus, which is *Ad majoram Dei gloriam*: 'For the greater glory of God'

194 (p. 297) *ptomaines*   poisonous alkaloid substances found in decaying animal and vegetable bodies

195 (p. 299) *Winchesters*   rifles first used in the United States and Canada in 1866

196 (p. 299) *Tobolsk*   city in western Siberia

197 (p. 304) *hotch-pot*   legal terms referring to the property of a deceased person that is to be divided

198 (p. 306) *Charing Cross*   large railway terminus in London near Trafalgar Square

199 (p. 306) *Orient Express*   luxurious express train operating between Paris and Istanbul

200 (p. 307) *Lloyd's*   the insurance company Lloyd's of London

201 (p. 308) *H. B. M.*   Her Britannia Majesty

202 (p. 309) '*Euthenasia*'   According to the *Oxford English Dictionary*, *euthanasia* began to be used to refer to the *act* of inducing a quiet and easy death in 1869.

203 (p. 310) *Galatz*   Romanian port on the Black Sea

204 (p. 310) *Transcendalism*   nineteenth-century secular philosophy associated mainly with the American essayist and poet Ralph Waldo

Emerson and based on an interfusion of spirituality between nature and humankind

205 (p. 313) *Hans Andersen*   Danish writer Hans Christian Andersen (1805–1875)

206 (p. 313) *particulari ad universale*   from the particular to the general

207 (p. 313) *Dos pou sto*   refers to a line in Archimedes' *Geometra* which reads *Dos moi pou sto Kai ten gen kineso*: 'Give me a place to stand and I will move the earth.'

208 (p. 314) *Nordau and Lombroso*   Hungarian physician, novelist and Zionist leader Max Nordau (1849–1923), who wrote a book called *Degeneration* (1892–3) which attempts to show a link between genius and moral degeneracy, and Cesare Lombroso (1836–1909), sometimes called the father of modern criminology

209 (p. 314) *Psalmist says*   See Psalm 69:22.

210 (p. 315) *hawser*   ship's cable or rope

211 (p. 318) *no canny*   not natural

212 (p. 318) *ahint*   behind

213 (p. 318) *speer*   see

214 (p. 318) *Gin*   when

215 (p. 319) *Old Mon*   old man; the devil

216 (p. 319) *anent*   about

217 (p. 319) *agin*   against

218 (p. 320) *specie*   coins

219 (p. 322) *octroi*   a tax levied on certain articles on their admission into a town; the barrier at which such a tax is paid; also, the service or the body of officials who collect the tax

220 (p. 323) *Pruth or the Sereth*   respectively, the River Prut, which joins the Danube just above Reni, and the River Sereth that merges with it above Galati

221 (p. 323) *Sereth*   the Pruth flows into the Danube near Reni, the Sereth near Galati

222 (p. 326) *Norfolk Broads*   located on the coast of England north east of London

223 (p. 328) *fitter*   person able to install or repair steam-driven equipment; a steamfitter

224 (p. 331) *vif*   bright, lively, alive

DRACULA'S GUEST

and Other Stories

Bram Stoker

with an Introduction by
DAVID STUART DAVIES

CONTENTS

INTRODUCTION

The collection of nine stories entitled *Dracula's Guest & Other Supernatural Tales* was originally published in 1914. This new Wordsworth edition has the bonus of four extra stories written by Stoker but not previously anthologised in this form.

* * *

Bram Stoker was a unique individual. Not only was he a gothic story-teller of great power, ensuring his own immortality by creating the arch-vampire Dracula, one of the most famous of all literary characters whose influence on the world of supernatural fiction and horror movies is incalculable; but he also worked ceaselessly and successfully as the business manager of Henry Irving, the great Victorian actor (the first actor to be granted a knighthood). So demanding were his managerial duties, it is great wonder that Stoker had any time left for his own writing. The fact that he completed twelve novels and many short stories as well as several non-fiction works before his comparatively early death at the age of sixty-four, is a testament to his dedication and industry.

Abraham (Bram) Stoker was born on 8 November 1847 in Dublin, Ireland. He was denied the joys and pleasures of a normal childhood for it was marred by illness. He spent much of his time in bed and he was often carried about the house from room to room because he was not able to walk properly until he was seven. To entertain her sickly child, Charlotte Stoker spent many hours relating grim tales of Irish folklore and real-life horrors, including all the grisly details of the 1832 outbreak of cholera in Sligo. Her memories of this tragedy were strong and would form the subject of gruesome accounts. These peopled the boy's nascent Celtic imagination with terrifying and haunting images which would later help to shape much of his mature literary output. The almost surreal existence of his early years had a great influence on his fiction, all of which is tinged with strange, dreamlike qualities.

Remarkably, to the bafflement of doctors, Stoker overcame his illnesses to grow into a sturdy youth who became an athlete and football star at the University of Dublin, where he studied history, literature, mathematics and physics at Trinity College. On leaving university he followed in his father's footsteps and became a civil servant, a career which did not satisfy him.

To provide some diversion from his mundane chores in the office, Stoker took to writing short stories for publication in various magazines, as well as taking on the role of theatre critic for Dublin's *Evening Mail*. Although this was an unpaid position, it allowed him to see a vast array of exciting dramatic productions playing in the city. In 1876 his eloquent and favourable review of Henry Irving's version of *Hamlet* prompted the actor to invite Stoker to dine with him one evening. The two men liked each other immediately and they sat and talked until dawn, thus forging a lifelong friendship. Stoker himself wrote in his journal, 'From that hour began a friendship so profound, as close and lasting as can be between two men.' Irving, too, must have felt the significance of the occasion for he presented Stoker with a photograph of himself inscribed, 'My dear friend Stoker, God Bless You! God Bless You! Henry Irving. Dublin, December 3, 1876.'

Their partnership solidified in 1878 when Irving persuaded Stoker to move to England to manage both his Lyceum Theatre and the actor himself. This was also the year that Stoker married the Irish beauty Florence Balcombe who had been a great love of Oscar Wilde. Stoker's only son, Noel, was born in 1879.

Once settled in England with his beautiful wife and his onerous but exciting duties as Irving's right-hand man, Stoker began to write fiction again and in 1881 published his first book, a collection of macabre fairy tales, *Under the Sunset*; his first full-length novel, *The Snake's Pass*, a romance set in Ireland, followed some years later in 1890. In the meantime, his association with Irving brought him into contact with many of the noted men of letters of the day including Arthur Conan Doyle, George Bernard Shaw, Wilkie Collins, William S. Gilbert and Walt Whitman. In the course of Irving's tours, Stoker had the opportunity to travel to many places around the world. All these experiences provided the raw material for his writing.

Then in 1890 he began working on what was to be his masterpiece, *Dracula*. He laboured almost seven years on the novel, researching European folklore and vampire tales from around the world. His

visits to Whitby were also influential and he incorporated into the
novel a real shipwreck which occurred in the bay there. He also
delved back into his childhood and the traumas of his illness to create
scenes of dark, nightmare quality. And at the heart of the book, like a
hypnotic dark fire, stands the figure of Count Dracula, a tall, lean,
mesmeric character who, it has been suggested, exhibited the same
gaunt appearance and commanding presence of Henry Irving himself. The actor was described as 'a tall, slender figure – about 6ft 2 –
a long, strikingly sensitive face and a dominant, rather sardonic,
presence which both fascinated and intimidated'. Indeed, Stoker
hoped Irving would play Dracula in a stage version of the story, but
the actor disliked the work intensely. He attended a private dramatised reading of the book at the Lyceum Theatre, held to establish
the copyright of the work. The audience for this reading was made
up of friends, relatives, staff and cleaners at the theatre. After the
show, Stoker asked Irving what he thought of it. His employer
dismissed the work with one memorable word: 'Dreadful.' Possibly
this crudely adapted version of the novel *was* dreadful – it lasted over
four hours – but it is strange that Irving failed to see the magical
dramatic potency of the original work. Sadly, Stoker never lived to
see any other dramatised form of *Dracula*.

The Dead Un-Dead was one of Stoker's original titles for *Dracula*,
and up until a few weeks before publication the manuscript was titled
simply *The Un-Dead*. The name of Stoker's count was originally
going to be Count Vampyre, but while carrying out his research
Stoker ran across an intriguing name: 'Dracula', meaning 'Son of the
Order of the Dragon'. This name belonged to a real fifteenth-century
nobleman, Prince Vlad Dracula, also known as Vlad the Impaler.
Stoker took the name for his own aristocratic bogeyman.

After Stoker's death in 1912, a man called Jarvis was appointed as
his literary executor and while sorting through the author's papers
he discovered a dramatic tale entitled 'Dracula's Guest', which he
believed was a missing chapter from *Dracula*. It was assumed that
it had been omitted from the final version at the request of the
publisher, Constable, as the book needed to come in under 400
pages, otherwise sixpence would have been added to the price and
this increase would have affected sales adversely. However several
Stoker scholars, including Sir Christopher Frayling, author of *Vampires, Lord Byron to Count Dracula*, and Clive Leatherdale believe that
'Dracula's Guest' was written as a free-standing narrative based on
Stoker's manuscript notes. This seems to be the most feasible theory

for not only does 'Dracula's Guest' hold up as an effective story in its own right, but it is difficult to see where exactly it would fit with ease into the tight narrative of the orginal novel. Its locale is Austria rather than Transylvania and the use of a single narrator is at odds with the style of the published novel, which involves an epistolatory, multi-narrator approach.

In her Preface to this collection, Florence Stoker states that, 'Had my husband lived longer, he might have seen fit to revise this work from the earlier years of his strenuous life. But, as fate has entrusted me the issuing of it, I consider it proper to let it go forth practically as it was left by him.' This statement raises two other interesting points. Her final words suggest the possibility that the story was edited after Stoker's death, which further muddies the waters. Also the fact that she claims this is an early work of her husband's suggests that the incidents in the story are ideas that the author played around with while formulating the narrative for *Dracula*. This might explain why he never published the story at the time of its conception. As further support for this idea, 'Dracula's Guest' contains strong echoes of Sheridan Le Fanu's vampire tale *Carmilla* (1872), which anticipated Stoker's aristocratic female vampire theme and Styrian location. Stoker would be conscious of this and perhaps worried that comparisons could be drawn and criticisms levelled at the story for being unduly derivative.

While there is a mystery surrounding the genesis and construction of 'Dracula's Guest', there is no doubt that it is a chilling excursion into the gothic and a rattling good tale which was far too good to leave mouldering with Stoker's papers.

The story has all the elements of a wild nightmare where reality shrinks into the shadows as fantastic and frightening events hold sway. The scene where the storyteller (one must presume this to be Jonathan Harker, the character from Stoker's novel who travels to Dracula's castle) wakes to find a wolf lying on him 'licking' at his throat is one of the most chilling in all gothic fiction. While 'Dracula's Guest' is linked tenuously to the famous novel, it can be enjoyed as an entity on its own.

If there are some influences from the work of Sheridan Le Fanu to be found in 'Dracula's Guest', they are far stronger in the second story in this collection, 'The Judge's House'. The notion of a revenging judge represented by the figure of a rat and a strange hanging can be found in Le Fanu's story, 'An Account of Some Strange Disturbances in Aungier Street' (1853). However, while the

Le Fanu piece has the charm and the gentle chill of the Victorian ghost story, 'The Judge's House' has more of a direct visceral force and a modern theatricality which takes it into the realms of horror fiction. Stoker's tale has a gruesome and fascinating inevitability about it which makes it a gripping read. We can see that in the recounting of the events which take place in the haunted chamber in 'The Judge's House' Stoker's dramatic style looks forward to the kind of supernatural fiction created by the twentieth-century masters rather than echoing his earlier literary influences.

However, it is true that most of what Stoker wrote was in fact influenced directly either by the work of other authors or by his own experiences. Like so many Victorian writers he was a collector of trifles, whether from works of fiction or from his own life. Ideas, memories, incidents, concepts were stored away in his memory bank ready to be withdrawn when the creative urge was upon him. Take for example 'The Squaw', which some anthologists rate as his most grotesque story, probably on the basis that it includes two cruel undeserved deaths – one at the beginning of the story and one at the end. This was a product of a trip Stoker took to Nuremberg where he was impressed by the medieval German city and its more bizarre relics. The determination of the cat to wreak revenge also has echoes of Poe's 'The Black Cat' (1843).

Similarly, 'The Burial of the Rats', which is set in the rubbish dumps of Paris, is the result of a visit he made to the city in 1874. Stoker called upon the impressions gathered at the time to provide the authentic backdrop for this tale, one in which, yet again, the malevolent figure of a rat features. The story also contains a fragment of biography. The narrator states, 'In this year I was very much in love with a young lady who, though she returned my passion, so far yielded to the wishes of her parents that she promised not to see me or correspond with me for a year.' Stoker's biographers have established that the author did indeed have what we might term 'a holiday romance' at this time with a certain 'Miss Henry'. The affair fizzled out but Stoker was able to refer to the liaison years later in this story.

'The Secret of the Growing Gold' may well have been inspired by the exhumation of the poet Dante Gabriel Rossetti's wife, Elizabeth Siddal. On her death Rossetti had buried the only copies of his unpublished poems in the coffin with his beloved wife. Seven years later, in 1869, Rossetti ordered an exhumation to recover the note-book. When the coffin was opened it is said that her hair was still golden and growing. A friend of Stoker was shown some of her hair which was recovered from the perfectly preserved body. It was fine and lustrous as though it had been cut from a living head. This macabre account prompted Stoker to create his story of haunting and revenge from beyond the grave – a plot that was also reminiscent of *The Bells*, the famous melodrama which was one of Irving's greatest successes.

Stoker plays around with fate in the very satisfying twist-in-the-tail story, 'The Gypsy's Prophecy'. All the elements are familiar and yet he manages to surprise the reader in the final pages. It is this ability to turn predictability on its head that makes Stoker such an entertaining writer.

At first glance 'The Coming of Abel Behenna' is merely an anecdoctal tale of frustrated passion, the machinations of rivals in love, but the narrative drive is fierce and propels the reader on to find out what happens to this triangular love affair. The ending is subtle and, as one might imagine, tragic in the extreme. The Cornish port of Pencastle, so well detailed in the opening of the story, is based on the small fishing village of Boscastle which Stoker discovered by accident on a long walking tour of the area during Holy Week on 1892. The location inspired him to create this unsettling narrative. Indeed Stoker fell in love with Boscastle and gave such a glowing account of it to his employer that Irving spent two vacations there himself.

'A Dream of Red Hands' is in essence a morality tale and was well received at the time of its publication in 1894. Again we are in 'love triangle' territory with only the dream element suggesting touches of the supernatural. It has been suggested that the themes of unrequited love which feature in several of the stories in this collection are a reflection of Stoker's own marriage. Evidence indicates that after the birth of their son Noel, Florence Stoker became frigid towards her husband and he sought comfort elsewhere. Some scholars maintain that Stoker contracted syphillis, probably around the turn of the century in Paris, and that this disease contributed to his death.

The 'Crooken Sands', the final tale of the original collection, ends on a comparatively light-hearted note. The real target of the story is pseudo-Celticism, those sassenachs who travel north of the border and dress and behave in a far more Scottish fashion than the Scots themselves. It has been suggested that Stoker got his inspiration for the central character, Arthur Markham, from the elderly nineteenth Earl of Erroll who was in the habit of parading pompously round Cruden Bay in a 'tweed suit of antique cut and a high Glengarry bonnet with the Hay falcon in silver on it', and insisting that all the villagers doff their caps and curtsey to him as he passed by.

*   *   *

The four remaining stories have been added to the original collection in this edition as they are rare and neglected little gems. 'The Crystal Cup' creates a wonderful surreal air with its strange multi-voiced narration. The story seems to be an experiment in form and one can note the influences of Oscar Wilde's prose work in Stoker's style and ideas.

The beauty of 'The Chain of Destiny' is its oddness. The piece refuses to be categorised. Although it is part love story, part ghost story, Stoker creates a powerful dreamlike atmosphere that pervades the whole narrative, imbuing it with a strangeness as though one is witnessing events through a misty mirror where reality is kept at bay.

'The Dualitists; or, The Death-Doom of the Double-Born' is like a fairytale told by a wicked uncle who has a dubious sense of humour. This is a rare foray into the realms of satire for Stoker and surely this tale cannot fail to bring a dark smile to the face of the reader.

Finally, for good measure, we have a rumbustious tale of pirates and drama on the high seas in 'The Red Stockade'. To be honest, there really are no supernatural elements in this yarn, but it is full-blooded, rather gory at times and highly dramatic. A fitting end to this bright and unique collection.

*   *   *

In October 1905, Sir Henry Irving died suddenly while on tour in Bradford. His death was such a shock to Stoker that he suffered a stroke from which he never fully recovered. His ability to walk was impaired – a return almost to his infant self – and his eyesight deteriorated so much that he needed a magnifying glass to write. His last years were ones of illness and suffering. He died in April 1912.

It is fair to say that Bram Stoker was not in the first division of the literary men of his time, but he has made an indelible mark in the world of storytelling by his creation of the gothic masterpiece *Dracula*, and for writing a series of highly entertaining supernatural tales, a choice selection of which feature in this volume. Turn down the lights, turn the page and be prepared to be chilled.

DAVID STUART DAVIES

PREFACE

A few months before the lamented death of my husband – I might say even as the shadow of death was over him – he planned three series of short stories for publication, and the present volume is one of them. To his original list of stories in this book, I have added a hitherto unpublished episode from *Dracula*. It was originally excised owing to the length of the book, and may prove of interest to the many readers of what is considered my husband's most remarkable work. The other stories have already been published in English and American periodicals. Had my husband lived longer, he might have seen fit to revise this work, which is mainly from the earlier years of his strenuous life. But, as fate has entrusted to me the issuing of it, I consider it fitting and proper to let it go forth practically as it was left by him.

FLORENCE BRAM STOKER

Dracula's Guest

When we started for our drive the sun was shining brightly on Munich, and the air was full of the joyousness of early summer. Just as we were about to depart, Herr Delbrück (the maître d'hôtel of the Quatre Saisons, where I was staying) came down, bareheaded, to the carriage and, after wishing me a pleasant drive, said to the coachman, still holding his hand on the handle of the carriage door: 'Remember you are back by nightfall. The sky looks bright but there is a shiver in the north wind that says there may be a sudden storm. But I am sure you will not be late.' Here he smiled, and added, 'for you know what night it is.'

Johann answered with an emphatic, 'Ja, mein Herr,' and, touching his hat, drove off quickly. When we had cleared the town, I said, after signalling to him to stop: 'Tell me, Johann, what is tonight?'

He crossed himself, as he answered laconically: 'Walpurgis-Nacht.' Then he took out his watch, a great, old-fashioned German silver thing as big as a turnip, and looked at it, with his eyebrows gathered together and a little impatient shrug of his shoulders. I realised that this was his way of respectfully protesting against the unnecessary delay, and sank back in the carriage, merely motioning him to pro-ceed. He started off rapidly, as if to make up for lost time. Every now and then the horses seemed to throw up their heads and sniffed the air suspiciously. On such occasions I often looked round in alarm. The road was pretty bleak, for we were traversing a sort of high, wind-swept plateau. As we drove, I saw a road that looked but little used, and which seemed to dip through a little, winding valley. It looked so inviting that, even at the risk of offending him, I called Johann to stop – and when he had pulled up, I told him I would like to drive down that road. He made all sorts of excuses, and frequently crossed himself as he spoke. This somewhat piqued my curiosity, so I asked him various questions. He answered fencingly, and repeatedly looked at his watch in protest. Finally I said: 'Well, Johann, I want to go down this road. I shall not ask you to come unless you like; but tell

me why you do not like to go, that is all I ask.' For answer he seemed
to throw himself off the box, so quickly did he reach the ground.
Then he stretched out his hands appealingly to me, and implored me
not to go. There was just enough of English mixed with the German
for me to understand the drift of his talk. He seemed always
just about to tell me something – the very idea of which evidently
frightened him; but each time he pulled himself up, saying, as he
crossed himself: 'Walpurgis-Nacht!'

I tried to argue with him, but it was difficult to argue with a man
when I did not know his language. The advantage certainly rested
with him, for although he began to speak in English, of a very crude
and broken kind, he always got excited and broke into his native
tongue – and every time he did so, he looked at his watch. Then the
horses became restless and sniffed the air. At this he grew very
pale, and, looking around in a frightened way, he suddenly jumped
forward, took them by the bridles and led them on some twenty feet.
I followed, and asked why he had done this. For answer he crossed
himself, pointed to the spot we had left and drew his carriage in the
direction of the other road, indicating a cross, and said, first in
German, then in English: 'Buried him – him what killed themselves.'

I remembered the old custom of burying suicides at crossroads:
'Ah! I see, a suicide. How interesting!' But for the life of me I could
not make out why the horses were frightened.

Whilst we were talking, we heard a sort of sound between a yelp
and a bark. It was far away; but the horses got very restless, and it
took Johann all his time to quiet them. He was pale, and said, 'It
sounds like a wolf – but yet there are no wolves here now.'

'No?' I said, questioning him; 'isn't it long since the wolves were so
near the city?'

'Long, long,' he answered, 'in the spring and summer; but with the
snow the wolves have been here not so long.'

Whilst he was petting the horses and trying to quiet them, dark
clouds drifted rapidly across the sky. The sunshine passed away, and
a breath of cold wind seemed to drift past us. It was only a breath,
however, and more in the nature of a warning than a fact, for the sun
came out brightly again. Johann looked under his lifted hand at the
horizon and said: 'The storm of snow, he comes before long time.'
Then he looked at his watch again, and, straightway holding his reins
firmly – for the horses were still pawing the ground restlessly and
shaking their heads – he climbed to his box as though the time had
come for proceeding on our journey.

I felt a little obstinate and did not at once get into the carriage.

'Tell me,' I said, 'about this place where the road leads,' and I pointed down.

Again he crossed himself and mumbled a prayer, before he answered, 'It is unholy.'

'What is unholy?' I enquired.

'The village.'

'Then there is a village?'

'No, no. No one lives there hundreds of years.' My curiosity was piqued, 'But you said there was a village.'

'There was.'

'Where is it now?'

Whereupon he burst out into a long story in German and English, so mixed up that I could not quite understand exactly what he said, but roughly I gathered that long ago, hundreds of years, men had died there and been buried in their graves; and sounds were heard under the clay, and when the graves were opened, men and women were found rosy with life, and their mouths red with blood. And so, in haste to save their lives (aye, and their souls! – and here he crossed himself) those who were left fled away to other places, where the living lived, and the dead were dead and not – not something. He was evidently afraid to speak the last words. As he proceeded with his narration, he grew more and more excited. It seemed as if his imagination had got hold of him, and he ended in a perfect paroxysm of fear – white-faced, perspiring, trembling and looking round him, as if expecting that some dreadful presence would manifest itself there in the bright sunshine on the open plain. Finally, in an agony of desperation, he cried: 'Walpurgis-Nacht!' and pointed to the carriage for me to get in. All my English blood rose at this, and, standing back, I said: 'You are afraid, Johann – you are afraid. Go home; I shall return alone; the walk will do me good.' The carriage door was open. I took from the seat my oak walking-stick – which I always carry on my holiday excursions – and closed the door, pointing back to Munich, and said, 'Go home, Johann – Walpurgis-Nacht doesn't concern Englishmen.'

The horses were now more restive than ever, and Johann was trying to hold them in, while excitedly imploring me not to do anything so foolish. I pitied the poor fellow, he was deeply in earnest; but all the same I could not help laughing. His English was quite gone now. In his anxiety he had forgotten that his only means of making me understand was to talk my language, so he jabbered away in his native German. It began to be a little tedious. After giving the direction, 'Home!' I turned to go down the cross-road into the valley.

With a despairing gesture, Johann turned his horses towards Munich. I leaned on my stick and looked after him. He went slowly along the road for a while: then there came over the crest of the hill a man tall and thin. I could see so much in the distance. When he drew near the horses, they began to jump and kick about, then to scream with terror. Johann could not hold them in; they bolted down the road, running away madly. I watched them out of sight, then looked for the stranger, but I found that he, too, was gone.

With a light heart I turned down the side road through the deepening valley to which Johann had objected. There was not the slightest reason, that I could see, for his objection; and I dare say I tramped for a couple of hours without thinking of time or distance, and certainly without seeing a person or a house. So far as the place was concerned, it was desolation itself. But I did not notice this particularly till, on turning a bend in the road, I came upon a scattered fringe of wood; then I recognised that I had been impressed unconsciously by the desolation of the region through which I had passed.

I sat down to rest myself, and began to look around. It struck me that it was considerably colder than it had been at the commencement of my walk – a sort of sighing sound seemed to be around me, with, now and then, high overhead, a sort of muffled roar. Looking upwards I noticed that great thick clouds were drifting rapidly across the sky from north to south at a great height. There were signs of coming storm in some lofty stratum of the air. I was a little chilly, and, thinking that it was the sitting still after the exercise of walking, I resumed my journey.

The ground I passed over was now much more picturesque. There were no striking objects that the eye might single out; but in all there was a charm of beauty. I took little heed of time and it was only when the deepening twilight forced itself upon me that I began to think of how I should find my way home. The brightness of the day had gone. The air was cold, and the drifting of clouds high overhead was more marked. They were accompanied by a sort of far-away rushing sound, through which seemed to come at intervals that mysterious cry which the driver had said came from a wolf. For a while I hesitated. I had said I would see the deserted village, so on I went, and presently came on a wide stretch of open country, shut in by hills all around. Their sides were covered with trees which spread down to the plain, dotting, in clumps, the gentler slopes and hollows which showed here and there. I followed with my eye the winding of the road, and saw that it curved close to one of the densest of these clumps and was lost behind it.

As I looked there came a cold shiver in the air, and the snow began to fall. I thought of the miles and miles of bleak country I had passed, and then hurried on to seek the shelter of the wood in front. Darker and darker grew the sky, and faster and heavier fell the snow, till the earth before and around me was a glistening white carpet, the further edge of which was lost in misty vagueness. The road was here but crude, and when on the level its boundaries were not so marked, as when it passed through the cuttings; and in a little while I found that I must have strayed from it, for I missed underfoot the hard surface, and my feet sank deeper in the grass and moss. Then the wind grew stronger and blew with ever increasing force, till I was fain to run before it. The air became icy-cold, and in spite of my exercise I began to suffer. The snow was now falling so thickly and whirling around me in such rapid eddies that I could hardly keep my eyes open. Every now and then the heavens were torn asunder by vivid lightning, and in the flashes I could see ahead of me a great mass of trees, chiefly yew and cypress all heavily coated with snow.

I was soon amongst the shelter of the trees, and there, in comparative silence, I could hear the rush of the wind high overhead. Presently the blackness of the storm had become merged in the darkness of the night By-and-by the storm seemed to be passing away: it now only came in fierce puffs or blasts. At such moments the weird sound of the wolf appeared to be echoed by many similar sounds around me.

Now and again, through the black mass of drifting cloud, came a straggling ray of moonlight, which lit up the expanse, and showed me that I was at the edge of a dense mass of cypress and yew trees. As the snow had ceased to fall, I walked out from the shelter and began to investigate more closely. It appeared to me that, amongst so many old foundations as I had passed, there might be still standing a house in which, though in ruins, I could find some sort of shelter for a while. As I skirted the edge of the copse, I found that a low wall encircled it, and following this, I presently found an opening. Here the cypresses formed an alley leading up to a square mass of some kind of building. Just as I caught sight of this, however, the drifting clouds obscured the moon, and I passed up the path in darkness. The wind must have grown colder, for I felt myself shiver as I walked; but there was hope of shelter, and I groped my way blindly on.

I stopped, for there was a sudden stillness. The storm had passed; and, perhaps in sympathy with nature's silence, my heart seemed to cease to beat. But this was only momentarily; for suddenly the moonlight broke through the clouds, showing me that I was in a graveyard, and that the square object before me was a great massive tomb of marble, as white as the snow that lay on and all around it. With the moonlight there came a fierce sigh of the storm, which appeared to resume its course with a long, low howl, as of many dogs or wolves. I was awed and shocked, and felt the cold perceptibly grow upon me till it seemed to grip me by the heart. Then while the flood of moonlight still fell on the marble tomb, the storm gave further evidence of renewing, as though it was returning on its track. Impelled by some sort of fascination, I approached the sepulchre to see what it was, and why such a thing stood alone in such a place. I walked around it, and read, over the Doric door, in German:

COUNTESS DOLINGEN OF GRATZ
IN STYRIA
SOUGHT AND FOUND DEAD
1801

On the top of the tomb, seemingly driven through the solid marble – for the structure was composed of a few vast blocks of stone – was a great iron spike or stake. On going to the back I saw, graven in great Russian letters:

THE DEAD TRAVEL FAST

There was something so weird and uncanny about the whole thing that it gave me a turn and made me feel quite faint. I began to wish, for the first time, that I had taken Johann's advice. Here a thought struck me, which came under almost mysterious circumstances and with a terrible shock. This was Walpurgis Night!

Walpurgis Night, when, according to the belief of millions of people, the devil was abroad – when the graves were opened and the dead came forth and walked. When all evil things of earth and air and water held revel. This very place the driver had specially shunned. This was the depopulated village of centuries ago. This was where the suicide lay; and this was the place where I was alone – unmanned, shivering with cold in a shroud of snow with a wild storm gathering again upon me! It took all my philosophy, all the religion I had been taught, all my courage, not to collapse in a paroxysm of fright.

And now a perfect tornado burst upon me. The ground shook as though thousands of horses thundered across it; and this time the storm bore on its icy wings, not snow, but great hailstones which drove with such violence that they might have come from the thongs of Balearic slingers – hailstones that beat down leaf and branch and made the shelter of the cypresses of no more avail than though their stems were standing-corn. At the first I had rushed to the nearest tree; but I was soon fain to leave it and seek the only spot that seemed to afford refuge, the deep Doric doorway of the marble tomb. There, crouching against the massive bronze door, I gained a certain amount of protection from the beating of the hailstones, for now they only drove against me as they ricocheted from the ground and the side of the marble.

As I leaned against the door, it moved slightly and opened inwards. The shelter of even a tomb was welcome in that pitiless tempest, and I was about to enter it when there came a flash of forked-lightning that lit up the whole expanse of the heavens. In the instant, as I am a living man, I saw, as my eyes were turned into the darkness of the tomb, a beautiful woman, with rounded cheeks and red lips, seemingly sleeping on a bier. As the thunder broke overhead, I was grasped as by the hand of a giant and hurled out into the storm. The whole thing was so sudden that, before I could realise the shock, moral as well as physical, I found the hailstones beating me down. At the same time I had a strange, dominating feeling that I was not alone. I looked towards the tomb. Just then there came another blinding flash, which seemed to strike the iron stake that surmounted the tomb and to pour through to the earth, blasting and crumbling the marble, as in a burst of flame. The dead woman rose for a moment of agony, while she was lapped in the flame, and her bitter scream of pain was drowned in the thundercrash. The last thing I heard was this mingling of dreadful sound, as again I was seized in the giant-grasp and dragged away, while the hailstones beat on me, and the air around seemed reverberant with the howling of wolves. The last sight that I remembered was a vague, white, moving mass, as if all the graves around me had sent out the phantoms of their sheeted-dead, and that they were closing in on me through the white cloudiness of the driving hail.

Gradually there came a sort of vague beginning of consciousness; then a sense of weariness that was dreadful. For a time I remembered nothing; but slowly my senses returned. My feet seemed positively racked with pain, yet I could not move them. They seemed to be numbed. There was an icy feeling at the back of my neck and all down my spine, and my ears, like my feet, were dead, yet in torment; but there was in my breast a sense of warmth which was, by comparison, delicious. It was as a nightmare – a physical nightmare, if one may use such an expression; for some heavy weight on my chest made it difficult for me to breathe.

This period of semi-lethargy seemed to remain a long time, and as it faded away I must have slept or swooned. Then came a sort of loathing, like the first stage of sea-sickness, and a wild desire to be free from something – I knew not what. A vast stillness enveloped me, as though all the world were asleep or dead – only broken by the low panting as of some animal close to me. I felt a warm rasping at my throat, then came a consciousness of the awful truth, which chilled me to the heart and sent the blood surging up through my brain. Some great animal was lying on me and now licking my throat. I feared to stir, for some instinct of prudence bade me lie still; but the brute seemed to realise that there was now some change in me, for it raised its head. Through my eyelashes I saw above me the two great flaming eyes of a gigantic wolf. Its sharp white teeth gleamed in the gaping red mouth, and I could feel its hot breath fierce and acrid upon me.

For another spell of time I remembered no more. Then I became conscious of a low growl, followed by a yelp, renewed again and again. Then, seemingly very far away, I heard a 'Holloa! holloa!' as of many voices calling in unison. Cautiously I raised my head and looked in the direction whence the sound came; but the cemetery blocked my view. The wolf still continued to yelp in a strange way, and a red glare began to move round the grove of cypresses, as though following the sound. As the voices drew closer, the wolf yelped faster and louder. I feared to make either sound or motion. Nearer came the red glow, over the white pall which stretched into the darkness around me. Then all at once from beyond the trees there came at a trot a troop of horsemen bearing torches. The wolf rose from my breast and made for the cemetery. I saw one of the horsemen (soldiers by their caps and their long military cloaks) raise his carbine and take aim. A companion knocked up his arm, and I heard the ball whizz over my head. He had evidently taken my body for that of the wolf. Another sighted the animal as it slunk away, and a shot followed. Then, at a gallop, the troop rode forward – some towards me, others following the wolf as it disappeared amongst the snow-clad cypresses.

As they drew nearer I tried to move, but was powerless, although I could see and hear all that went on around me. Two or three of the soldiers jumped from their horses and knelt beside me. One of them raised my head, and placed his hand over my heart.

'Good news, comrades!' he cried. 'His heart still beats!'

Then some brandy was poured down my throat; it put vigour into me, and I was able to open my eyes fully and look around. Lights and shadows were moving among the trees, and I heard men call to one another. They drew together, uttering frightened exclamations; and the lights flashed as the others came pouring out of the cemetery pell-mell, like men possessed. When the further ones came close to us, those who were around me asked them eagerly: 'Well, have you found him?'

The reply rang out hurriedly: 'No! no! Come away quick – quick! This is no place to stay, and on this of all nights!'

'What was it?' was the question, asked in all manner of keys. The answer came variously and all indefinitely as though the men were moved by some common impulse to speak, yet were restrained by some common fear from giving their thoughts.

'It – it – indeed!' gibbered one, whose wits had plainly given out for the moment.

'A wolf – and yet not a wolf!' another put in shudderingly.

'No use trying for him without the sacred bullet,' a third remarked in a more ordinary manner.

'Serve us right for coming out on this night! Truly we have earned our thousand marks!' were the ejaculations of a fourth.

'There was blood on the broken marble,' another said after a pause – 'the lightning never brought that there. And for him – is he safe? Look at his throat! See, comrades, the wolf has been lying on him and keeping his blood warm.'

The officer looked at my throat and replied: 'He is all right; the skin is not pierced. What does it all mean? We should never have found him but for the yelping of the wolf.'

'What became of it?' asked the man who was holding up my head, and who seemed the least panic-stricken of the party, for his hands were steady and without tremor. On his sleeve was the chevron of a petty officer.

'It went to its home,' answered the man, whose long face was pallid, and who actually shook with terror as he glanced around him fearfully. 'There are graves enough there in which it may lie. Come, comrades – come quickly! Let us leave this cursed spot.'

The officer raised me to a sitting posture, as he uttered a word of command; then several men placed me upon a horse. He sprang to the saddle behind me, took me in his arms, gave the word to advance; and, turning our faces away from the cypresses, we rode away in swift, military order.

As yet my tongue refused its office, and I was perforce silent. I must have fallen asleep; for the next thing I remembered was finding myself standing up, supported by a soldier on each side of me. It was almost broad daylight, and to the north a red streak of sunlight was reflected, like a path of blood, over the waste of snow. The officer was telling the men to say nothing of what they had seen, except that they found an English stranger, guarded by a large dog.

'Dog! that was no dog,' cut in the man who had exhibited such fear. 'I think I know a wolf when I see one.'

The young officer answered calmly: 'I said a dog.'

'Dog!' reiterated the other ironically. It was evident that his courage was rising with the sun; and, pointing to me, he said, 'Look at his throat. Is that the work of a dog, master?'

Instinctively I raised my hand to my throat, and as I touched it I cried out in pain. The men crowded round to look, some stooping down from their saddles; and again there came the calm voice of the young officer: 'A dog, as I said. If aught else were said we should only be laughed at.'

I was then mounted behind a trooper, and we rode on into the suburbs of Munich. Here we came across a stray carriage, into which I was lifted, and it was driven off to the Quatre Saisons – the young officer accompanying me, whilst a trooper followed with his horse, and the others rode off to their barracks.

When we arrived, Herr Delbrück rushed so quickly down the steps to meet me, that it was apparent he had been watching within. Taking me by both hands he solicitously led me in. The officer saluted me and was turning to withdraw, when I recognised his purpose, and insisted that he should come to my rooms. Over a glass of wine I warmly thanked him and his brave comrades for saving me. He replied simply that he was more than glad, and that Herr Delbrück had at the first taken steps to make all the searching party pleased; at which ambiguous utterance the maître d'hôtel smiled, while the officer pleaded duty and withdrew.

'But Herr Delbrück,' I enquired, 'how and why was it that the soldiers searched for me?'

He shrugged his shoulders, as if in depreciation of his own deed, as he replied: 'I was so fortunate as to obtain leave from the commander of the regiment in which I served, to ask for volunteers.'

'But how did you know I was lost?' I asked.

'The driver came hither with the remains of his carriage, which had been upset when the horses ran away.'

'But surely you would not send a search-party of soldiers merely on this account?'

'Oh, no!' he answered; 'but even before the coachman arrived, I had this telegram from the Boyar whose guest you are,' and he took from his pocket a telegram which he handed to me, and I read:

Bistritz

Be careful of my guest – his safety is most precious to me. Should aught happen to him, or if he be missed, spare nothing to find him and ensure his safety. He is English and therefore adventurous. There are often dangers from snow and wolves and night. Lose not a moment if you suspect harm to him. I answer your zeal with my fortune.

DRACULA

As I held the telegram in my hand, the room seemed to whirl around me; and, if the attentive *maître d'hôtel* had not caught me, I think I should have fallen. There was something so strange in all this, something so weird and impossible to imagine, that there grew on me a sense of my being in some way the sport of opposite forces – the mere vague idea of which seemed in a way to paralyse me. I was certainly under some form of mysterious protection. From a distant country had come, in the very nick of time, a message that took me out of the danger of the snow-sleep and the jaws of the wolf.

The Judge's House

When the time for his examination drew near, Malcolm Malcolmson made up his mind to go somewhere to read by himself. He feared the attractions of the seaside, and also he feared completely rural isolation, for of old he knew its charms, and so he determined to find some unpretentious little town where there would be nothing to distract him. He refrained from asking suggestions from any of his friends, for he argued that each would recommend some place of which he had knowledge, and where he had already acquaintances. As Malcolmson wished to avoid friends, he had no wish to encumber himself with the attention of friends' friends, and so he determined to look out for a place for himself. He packed a portmanteau with some clothes and all the books he required, and then took a ticket for the first name on the local time-table which he did not know.

When at the end of three hours' journey he alighted at Benchurch, he felt satisfied that he had so far obliterated his tracks as to be sure of having a peaceful opportunity of pursuing his studies. He went straight to the one inn which the sleepy little place contained, and put up for the night. Benchurch was a market town, and once in three weeks was crowded to excess, but for the remainder of the twenty-one days it was as attractive as a desert, Malcolmson looked around the day after his arrival to try to find quarters more isolated than even so quiet an inn as 'The Good Traveller' afforded. There was only one place which took his fancy, and it certainly satisfied his wildest ideas regarding quiet; in fact, quiet was not the proper word to apply to it – desolation was the only term conveying any suitable idea of its isolation. It was an old rambling, heavy-built house of the Jacobean style, with heavy gables and windows, unusually small, and set higher than was customary in such houses, and was surrounded with a high brick wall massively built. Indeed, on examination, it looked more like a fortified house than an ordinary dwelling. But all these things pleased Malcolmson. 'Here,' he thought, 'is the very spot I have been looking for, and if I can get opportunity of using it I shall be happy.' His joy was increased when he realised beyond doubt that it was not at present inhabited.

From the post-office he got the name of the agent, who was rarely surprised at the application to rent a part of the old house. Mr Carnford, the local lawyer and agent, was a genial old gentleman, and frankly confessed his delight at anyone being willing to live in the house.

'To tell you the truth,' said he, 'I should be only too happy, on behalf of the owners, to let anyone have the house rent free for a term of years if only to accustom the people here to see it inhabited. It has been so long empty that some kind of absurd prejudice has grown up about it, and this can be best put down by its occupation – if only,' he added with a sly glance at Malcolmson, 'by a scholar like yourself, who wants its quiet for a time.'

Malcolmson thought it needless to ask the agent about the 'absurd prejudice'; he knew he would get more information, if he should require it, on that subject from other quarters. He paid his three months' rent, got a receipt, and the name of an old woman who would probably undertake to 'do' for him, and came away with the keys in his pocket. He then went to the landlady of the inn, who was a cheerful and most kindly person, and asked her advice as to such stores and provisions as he would be likely to require. She threw up her hands in amazement when he told her where he was going to settle himself.

'Not in the Judge's House!' she said, and grew pale as she spoke. He explained the locality of the house, saying that he did not know its name. When he had finished she answered: 'Aye, sure enough – sure enough the very place! It is the Judge's House sure enough.' He asked her to tell him about the place, why so called, and what there was against it. She told him that it was so called locally because it had been many years before – how long she could not say, as she was herself from another part of the country, but she thought it must have been a hundred years or more – the abode of a judge who was held in great terror on account of his harsh sentences and his hostility to prisoners at Assizes. As to what there was against the house itself she could not tell. She had often asked, but no one could inform her; but there was a general feeling that there was *something*, and for her own part she would not take all the money in Drinkwater's Bank and stay in the house an hour by herself. Then she apologised to Malcolmson for her disturbing talk.

'It is too bad of me, sir, and you – and a young gentlemen, too – if you will pardon me saying it, going to live there all alone. If you were my boy – and you'll excuse me for saying it – you wouldn't sleep there a night, not if I had to go there myself and pull the big alarm bell that's on the roof!' The good creature was so manifestly in earnest, and was so kindly in her intentions, that Malcolmson, although amused, was touched. He told her kindly how much he appreciated her interest in him, and added: 'But, my dear Mrs Witham, indeed you need not be concerned about me! A man who is reading for the Mathematical Tripos has too much to think of to be disturbed by any of these mysterious "somethings", and his work is of too exact and prosaic a kind to allow of his having any corner in his mind for mysteries of any kind. Harmonical Progression, Permutations and Combinations, and Elliptic Functions have suffi-cient mysteries for me!' Mrs Witham kindly undertook to see after his commissions, and he went himself to look for the old woman who had been recommended to him. When he returned to the Judge's House with her, after an interval of a couple of hours, he found Mrs Witham herself waiting with several men and boys carrying parcels, and an upholsterer's man with a bed in a car, for she said, though tables and chairs might be all very well, a bed that hadn't been aired for mayhap fifty years was not proper for young bones to lie on. She was evidently curious to see the inside of the house; and though manifestly so afraid of the 'somethings' that at the slightest sound she clutched on to Malcolmson, whom she never left for a moment, went over the whole place.

After his examination of the house, Malcolmson decided to take up his abode in the great dining-room, which was big enough to serve for all his requirements; and Mrs Witham, with the aid of the charwoman, Mrs Dempster, proceeded to arrange matters. When the hampers were brought in and unpacked, Malcolmson saw that with much kind fore-thought she had sent from her own kitchen sufficient provisions to last for a few days. Before going she expressed all sorts of kind wishes; and at the door turned and said: 'And perhaps, sir, as the room is big and draughty it might be well to have one of those big screens put round your bed at night – though, truth to tell, I would die myself if I were to be so shut in with all kinds of – of "things", that put their heads round the sides, or over the top, and look on me!' The image which she had called up was too much for her nerves, and she fled incontinently.

Mrs Dempster sniffed in a superior manner as the landlady dis-appeared, and remarked that for her own part she wasn't afraid of all the bogies in the kingdom.

'I'll tell you what it is, sir,' she said; 'bogies is all kinds and sorts of things – except bogies! Rats and mice, and beetles; and creaky doors, and loose slates, and broken panes, and stiff drawer handles, that stay out when you pull them and then fall down in the middle of the night. Look at the wainscot of the room! It is old – hundreds of years old! Do you think there's no rats and beetles there! And do you imagine, sir, that you won't see none of them? Rats is bogies, I tell you, and bogies is rats; and don't you get to think anything else!'

'Mrs Dempster,' said Malcolmson gravely, making her a polite bow, 'you know more than a Senior Wrangler! And let me say, that, as a mark of esteem for your indubitable soundness of head and heart, I shall, when I go, give you possession of this house, and let you stay here by yourself for the last two months of my tenancy, for four weeks will serve my purpose.'

'Thank you kindly, sir!' she answered, 'but I couldn't sleep away from home a night. I am in Greenhow's Charity, and if I slept a night away from my rooms I should lose all I have got to live on. The rules is very strict; and there's too many watching for a vacancy for me to run any risks in the matter. Only for that, sir, I'd gladly come here and attend on you altogether during your stay.'

'My good woman,' said Malcolmson hastily, 'I have come here on purpose to obtain solitude; and believe me that I am grateful to the late Greenhow for having so organised his admirable charity – whatever it is – that I am perforce denied the opportunity of suffering from such a form of temptation! Saint Anthony himself could not be more rigid on the point!'

The old woman laughed harshly. 'Ah, you young gentlemen,' she said, 'you don't fear for naught; and belike you'll get all the solitude you want here.' She set to work with her cleaning; and by nightfall, when Malcolmson returned from his walk – he always had one of his books to study as he walked – he found the room swept and tidied, a fire burning in the old hearth, the lamp lit, and the table spread for supper with Mrs Witham's excellent fare. 'This is comfort, indeed,' he said, as he rubbed his hands.

When he had finished his supper, and lifted the tray to the other end of the great oak dining-table, he got out his books again, put fresh wood on the fire, trimmed his lamp, and set himself down to a spell of real hard work. He went on without pause till about eleven o'clock, when he knocked off for a bit to fix his fire and lamp, and to make himself a cup of tea. He had always been a tea-drinker, and during his college life had sat late at work and had taken tea late. The rest was a great luxury to him, and he enjoyed it with a sense of delicious, voluptuous ease. The renewed fire leaped and sparkled, and threw quaint shadows through the great old room; and as he sipped his hot tea he revelled in the sense of isolation from his kind. Then it was that he began to notice for the first time what a noise the rats were making.

'Surely,' he thought, 'they cannot have been at it all the time I was reading. Had they been, I must have noticed it!' Presently, when the noise increased, he satisfied himself that it was really new. It was evident that at first the rats had been frightened at the presence of a stranger, and the light of fire and lamp; but that as the time went on they had grown bolder and were now disporting themselves as was their wont.

How busy they were! and hark to the strange noises! Up and down behind the old wainscot, over the ceiling and under the floor they raced, and gnawed, and scratched! Malcolmson smiled to himself as he recalled to mind the saying of Mrs Dempster, 'Bogies is rats, and rats is bogies!' The tea began to have its effect of intellectual and nervous stimulus; he saw with joy another long spell of work to be done before the night was past, and in the sense of security which it gave him, he allowed himself the luxury of a good look round the room. He took his lamp in one hand, and went all around, wondering that so quaint and beautiful an old house had been so long neglected. The carving of the oak on the panels of the wainscot was fine, and on and round the doors and windows it was beautiful and of rare merit. There were some old pictures on the walls, but they were coated so thick with dust and dirt that he could not distinguish any detail of them, though he held his lamp as high as he could over his head. Here and there as he went round he saw some crack or hole blocked for a moment by the face of a rat with its bright eyes glittering in the light, but in an instant it was gone, and a squeak and a scamper followed. The thing that most struck him, however, was the rope of the great alarm bell on the roof, which hung down in a corner of the room on the right-hand side of the fireplace. He pulled up close to the hearth a great high-backed carved oak chair, and sat down to his last cup of tea. When this was done he made up the fire, and went back to his work, sitting at the corner of the table, having the fire to his left. For a little while the rats disturbed him somewhat with their perpetual scampering, but he got accustomed to the noise as one does to the ticking of a clock or to the roar of moving water; and he became so immersed in his work that everything in the world, except the problem which he was trying to solve, passed away from him.

He suddenly looked up, his problem was still unsolved, and there was in the air that sense of the hour before the dawn, which is so dread to doubtful life. The noise of the rats had ceased. Indeed it seemed to him that it must have ceased but lately and that it was the sudden cessation which had disturbed him. The fire had fallen low, but still it threw out a deep red glow. As he looked he started in spite of his *sang froid*.

There on the great high-backed carved oak chair by the right side of the fireplace sat an enormous rat, steadily glaring at him with baleful eyes. He made a motion to it as though to hunt it away, but it did not stir. Then he made the motion of throwing something. Still it did not stir, but showed its great white teeth angrily, and its cruel eyes shone in the lamplight with an added vindictiveness.

Malcolmson felt amazed, and seizing the poker from the hearth ran at it to kill it. Before, however, he could strike it, the rat, with a squeak that sounded like the concentration of hate, jumped upon the floor, and, running up the rope of the alarm bell, disappeared in the darkness beyond the range of the green-shaded lamp. Instantly, strange to say, the noisy scampering of the rats in the wainscot began again.

By this time Malcolmson's mind was quite off the problem; and as a shrill cock-crow outside told him of the approach of morning, he went to bed and to sleep.

He slept so sound that he was not even waked by Mrs Dempster coming in to make up his room. It was only when she had tidied up the place and got his breakfast ready and tapped on the screen which closed in his bed that he woke. He was a little tired still after his night's hard work, but a strong cup of tea soon freshened him up and, taking his book, he went out for his morning walk, bringing with him a few sandwiches lest he should not care to return till dinner time. He found a quiet walk between high elms some way outside the town, and here he spent the greater part of the day studying his Laplace. On his return he looked in to see Mrs Witham and to thank her for her kindness. When she saw him coming through the diamond-paned bay window of her sanctum she came out to meet him and asked him in. She looked at him searchingly and shook her head as she said: 'You must not overdo it, sir. You are paler this morning than you should be. Too late hours and too hard work on the brain isn't good for any man! But tell me, sir, how did you pass the night? Well, I hope? But my heart! sir, I was glad when Mrs Dempster told me this morning that you were all right and sleeping sound when she went in.'

'Oh, I was all right,' he answered smiling, 'the "somethings" didn't worry me, as yet. Only the rats; and they had a circus, I tell you, all over the place. There was one wicked looking old devil that sat up on my own chair by the fire, and wouldn't go till I took the poker to him, and then he ran up the rope of the alarm bell and got to somewhere up the wall or the ceiling – I couldn't see where, it was so dark.'

'Mercy on us,' said Mrs Witham, 'an old devil, and sitting on a chair by the fireside! Take care, sir! take care! There's many a true word spoken in jest.'

'How do you mean? 'Pon my word I don't understand.'

'An old devil! The old devil, perhaps. There! sir, you needn't laugh,' for Malcolmson had broken into a hearty peal. 'You young folks thinks it easy to laugh at things that makes older ones shudder. Never mind, sir! never mind! Please God, you'll laugh all the time. It's what I wish you myself!' and the good lady beamed all over in sympathy with his enjoyment, her fears gone for a moment.

'Oh, forgive me!' said Malcolmson presently. 'Don't think me rude; but the idea was too much for me – that the old devil himself was on the chair last night! And at the thought he laughed again. Then he went home to dinner.

This evening the scampering of the rats began earlier; indeed it had been going on before his arrival, and only ceased whilst his presence by its freshness disturbed them. After dinner he sat by the fire for a while and had a smoke; and then, having cleared his table, began to work as before. Tonight the rats disturbed him more than they had done on the previous night. How they scampered up and down and under and over! How they squeaked, and scratched, and gnawed! How they, getting bolder by degrees, came to the mouths of their holes and to the chinks and cracks and crannies in the wainscoting till their eyes shone like tiny lamps as the firelight rose and fell. But to him, now doubtless accustomed to them, their eyes were not wicked; only their playfulness touched him. Sometimes the boldest of them made sallies out on the floor or along the mouldings of the wainscot. Now and again as they disturbed him Malcolmson made a sound to frighten them, smiting the table with his hand or giving a fierce 'Hsh, hsh,' so that they fled straightway to their holes.

And so the early part of the night wore on; and despite the noise Malcolmson got more and more immersed in his work.

All at once he stopped, as on the previous night, being overcome by a sudden sense of silence. There was not the faintest sound of gnaw, or scratch, or squeak. The silence was as of the grave. He remembered the odd occurrence of the previous night, and instinctively he looked at the chair standing close by the fireside. And then a very odd sensation thrilled through him.

There, on the great old high-backed carved oak chair beside the fireplace, sat the same enormous rat, steadily glaring at him with baleful eyes.

Instinctively he took the nearest thing to his hand, a book of logarithms, and flung it at it. The book was badly aimed and the rat did not stir, so again the poker performance of the previous night was repeated; and again the rat, being closely pursued, fled up the rope of the alarm bell. Strangely too, the departure of this rat was instantly followed by the renewal of the noise made by the general rat community. On this occasion, as on the previous one, Malcolmson could not see at what part of the room the rat disappeared, for the green shade of his lamp left the upper part of the room in darkness, and the fire had burned low.

On looking at his watch he found it was close on midnight; and, not sorry for the *divertissement*, he made up his fire and made himself his nightly pot of tea. He had got through a good spell of work, and thought himself entitled to a cigarette; and so he sat on the great oak chair before the fire and enjoyed it. Whilst smoking he began to think that he would like to know where the rat disappeared to, for he had certain ideas for the morrow not entirely disconnected with a rat-trap. Accordingly he lit another lamp and placed it so that it would shine well into the right-hand corner of the wall by the fireplace. Then he got all the books he had with him, and placed them handy to throw at the vermin. Finally he lifted the rope of the alarm bell and placed the end of it on the table, fixing the extreme end under the lamp. As he handled it he could not help noticing how pliable it was, especially for so strong a rope, and one not in use. 'You could hang a man with it,' he thought to himself. When his preparations were made he looked around, and said complacently: 'There now, my friend, I think we shall learn something of you this time!' He began his work again, and though as before somewhat disturbed at first by the noise of the rats, soon lost himself in his propositions and problems.

Again he was called to his immediate surroundings suddenly. This time it might not have been the sudden silence only which took his attention; there was a slight movement of the rope, and the lamp moved. Without stirring, he looked to see if his pile of books was within range, and then cast his eye along the rope. As he looked he saw the great rat drop from the rope on the oak armchair and sit there glaring at him. He raised a book in his right hand, and taking careful aim, flung it at the rat. The latter, with a quick movement, sprang aside and dodged the missile. He then took another book, and a third, and flung them one after another at the rat, but each time unsuccessfully. At last, as he stood with a book poised in his hand to throw, the rat squeaked and seemed afraid. This made Malcolmson more than ever eager to strike, and the book flew and struck the rat a resounding blow. It gave a terrified squeak, and turning on his pursuer a look of terrible malevolence, ran up the chair-back and made a great jump to the rope of the alarm bell and ran up it like lightning. The lamp rocked under the sudden strain, but it was a heavy one and did not topple over. Malcolmson kept his eyes on the rat, and saw it by the light of the second lamp leap to a moulding of the wainscot and disappear through a hole in one of the great pictures which hung on the wall, obscured and invisible through its coating of dirt and dust.

'I shall look up my friend's habitation in the morning,' said the student, as he went over to collect his books. 'The third picture from the fireplace; I shall not forget.' He picked up the books one by one, commenting on them as he lifted them. '*Conic Sections* he does not mind, nor *Cycloidal Oscillations*, nor the *Principia*, nor *Quaternions*, nor *Thermodynamics*. Now for the book that fetched him!' Malcolmson took it up and looked at it. As he did so he started, and a sudden pallor overspread his face. He looked round uneasily and shivered slightly, as he murmured to himself: 'The Bible my mother gave me! What an odd coincidence.' He sat down to work again, and the rats in the wainscot renewed their gambols. They did not disturb him, however; somehow their presence gave him a sense of companionship. But he could not attend to his work, and after striving to master the subject on which he was engaged gave it up in despair, and went to bed as the first streak of dawn stole in through the eastern window.

He slept heavily but uneasily, and dreamed much; and when Mrs Dempster woke him late in the morning he seemed ill at ease, and for a few minutes did not seem to realise exactly where he was. His first request rather surprised the servant.

'Mrs Dempster, when I am out today I wish you would get the steps and dust or wash those pictures – specially that one the third from the fireplace – I want to see what they are.'

Late in the afternoon Malcolmson worked at his books in the shaded walk, and the cheerfulness of the previous day came back to him as the day wore on, and he found that his reading was progressing well. He had worked out to a satisfactory conclusion all the problems which had as yet baffled him, and it was in a state of jubilation that he paid a visit to Mrs Witham at 'The Good Traveller'. He found a stranger in the cosy sitting-room with the landlady, who was introduced to him as Dr Thornhill. She was not quite at ease, and this, combined with the doctor's plunging at once into a series of questions, made Malcolmson come to the conclusion that his presence was not an accident, so without preliminary he said: 'Dr Thornhill, I shall with pleasure answer you any question you may choose to ask me if you will answer me one question first.'

The doctor seemed surprised, but he smiled and answered at once, 'Done! What is it?'

'Did Mrs Witham ask you to come here and see me and advise me?'

Dr Thornhill for a moment was taken aback, and Mrs Witham got fiery red and turned away; but the doctor was a frank and ready man, and he answered at once and openly.

'She did: but she didn't intend you to know it. I suppose it was my clumsy haste that made you suspect. She told me that she did not like the idea of your being in that house all by yourself, and that she thought you took too much strong tea. In fact, she wants me to advise you if possible to give up the tea and the very late hours. I was a keen student in my time, so I suppose I may take the liberty of a college man, and without offence, advise you not quite as a stranger.'

Malcolmson with a bright smile held out his hand. 'Shake! as they say in America,' he said. 'I must thank you for your kindness and Mrs Witham too, and your kindness deserves a return on my part. I promise to take no more strong tea – no tea at all till you let me – and I shall go to bed tonight at one o'clock at latest. Will that do?'

'Capital,' said the doctor. 'Now tell us all that you noticed in the old house,' and so Malcolmson then and there told in minute detail all that had happened in the last two nights. He was interrupted every now and then by some exclamation from Mrs Witham, till finally when he told of the episode of the Bible the landlady's pent-up emotions found vent in a shriek; and it was not till a stiff glass of brandy and water had been administered that she grew composed again. Dr Thornhill listened with a face of growing gravity, and when the narrative was complete and Mrs Witham had been restored he asked: 'The rat always went up the rope of the alarm bell?'

'Always.'

'I suppose you know,' said the Doctor after a pause, 'what the rope is?'

'No!'

'It is,' said the Doctor slowly, 'the very rope which the hangman used for all the victims of the Judge's judicial rancour!' Here he was interrupted by another scream from Mrs Witham, and steps had to be taken for her recovery. Malcolmson having looked at his watch, and found that it was close to his dinner hour, had gone home before her complete recovery.

When Mrs Witham was herself again she almost assailed the Doctor with angry questions as to what he meant by putting such horrible ideas into the poor young man's mind. 'He has quite enough there already to upset him,' she added. Dr Thornhill replied: 'My dear madam, I had a distinct purpose in it! I wanted to draw his attention to the bell rope, and to fix it there. It may be that he is in a highly overwrought state, and has been studying too much, although I am bound to say that he seems as sound and healthy a young man, mentally and bodily, as ever I saw – but then the rats – and that suggestion of the devil.' The doctor shook his head and went on. 'I would have offered to go and stay the first night with him but that I felt sure it would have been a cause of offence. He may get in the night some strange fright or hallucination; and if he does I want him to pull that rope. All alone as he is it will give us warning, and we may reach him in time to be of service. I shall be sitting up pretty late tonight and shall keep my ears open. Do not be alarmed if Benchurch gets a surprise before morning.'

'Oh, Doctor, what do you mean? What do you mean?'

'I mean this; that possibly – nay, more probably – we shall hear the great alarm bell from the Judge's House tonight,' and the Doctor made about as effective an exit as could be thought of.

When Malcolmson arrived home he found that it was a little after his usual time, and Mrs Dempster had gone away – the rules of Greenhow's Charity were not to be neglected. He was glad to see that the place was bright and tidy with a cheerful fire and a well-trimmed lamp. The evening was colder than might have been expected in April, and a heavy wind was blowing with such rapidly

increasing strength that there was every promise of a storm during
the night. For a few minutes after his entrance the noise of the rats
ceased; but so soon as they became accustomed to his presence they
began again. He was glad to hear them, for he felt once more the
feeling of companionship in their noise, and his mind ran back to the
strange fact that they only ceased to manifest themselves when that
other – the great rat with the baleful eyes – came upon the scene.
The reading-lamp only was lit and its green shade kept the ceiling
and the upper part of the room in darkness, so that the cheerful light
from the hearth spreading over the floor and shining on the white
cloth laid over the end of the table was warm and cheery. Malcolmson sat down to his dinner with a good appetite and a buoyant
spirit. After his dinner and a cigarette he sat steadily down to work,
determined not to let anything disturb him, for he remembered his
promise to the doctor, and made up his mind to make the best of the
time at his disposal.

For an hour or so he worked all right, and then his thoughts began
to wander from his books. The actual circumstances around him, the
calls on his physical attention, and his nervous susceptibility were
not to be denied. By this time the wind had become a gale, and the
gale a storm. The old house, solid though it was, seemed to shake to
its foundations, and the storm roared and raged through its many
chimneys and its queer old gables, producing strange, unearthly
sounds in the empty rooms and corridors. Even the great alarm bell
on the roof must have felt the force of the wind, for the rope rose and
fell slightly, as though the bell were moved a little from time to time
and the limber rope fell on the oak floor with a hard and hollow
sound.

As Malcolmson listened to it he bethought himself of the doctor's
words, 'It is the rope which the hangman used for the victims of the
Judge's judicial rancour,' and he went over to the corner of the
fireplace and took it in his hand to look at it. There seemed a sort of
deadly interest in it, and as he stood there he lost himself for a
moment in speculation as to who these victims were, and the grim
wish of the Judge to have such a ghastly relic ever under his eyes. As
he stood there the swaying of the bell on the roof still lifted the rope
now and again; but presently there came a new sensation – a sort of
tremor in the rope, as though something was moving along it.

Looking up instinctively Malcolmson saw the great rat coming
slowly down towards him, glaring at him steadily. He dropped the
rope and started back with a muttered curse, and the rat turning

ran up the rope again and disappeared, and at the same instant Malcolmson became conscious that the noise of the rats, which had ceased for a while, began again.

All this set him thinking, and it occurred to him that he had not investigated the lair of the rat or looked at the pictures, as he had intended. He lit the other lamp without the shade, and, holding it up, went and stood opposite the third picture from the fireplace on the right-hand side where he had seen the rat disappear on the previous night.

At the first glance he started back so suddenly that he almost dropped the lamp, and a deadly pallor overspread his face. His knees shook, and heavy drops of sweat came on his forehead, and he trembled like an aspen. But he was young and plucky, and pulled himself together, and after the pause of a few seconds stepped forward again, raised the lamp, and examined the picture which had been dusted and washed, and now stood out clearly.

It was of a judge dressed in his robes of scarlet and ermine. His face was strong and merciless, evil, crafty, and vindictive, with a sensual mouth, hooked nose of ruddy colour, and shaped like the beak of a bird of prey. The rest of the face was of a cadaverous colour. The eyes were of peculiar brilliance and with a terribly malignant expression. As he looked at them, Malcolmson grew cold, for he saw there the very counterpart of the eyes of the great rat. The lamp almost fell from his hand, he saw the rat with its baleful eyes peering out through the hole in the corner of the picture, and noted the sudden cessation of the noise of the other rats. However, he pulled himself together, and went on with his examination of the picture.

The Judge was seated in a great high-backed carved oak chair, on the right-hand side of a great stone fireplace where, in the corner, a rope hung down from the ceiling, its end lying coiled on the floor. With a feeling of something like horror, Malcolmson recognised the scene of the room as it stood, and gazed around him in an awe-struck manner as though he expected to find some strange presence behind him. Then he looked over to the corner of the fireplace – and with a loud cry he let the lamp fall from his hand.

There, in the Judge's armchair, with the rope hanging behind, sat the rat with the Judge's baleful eyes, now intensified and with a fiendish leer. Save for the howling of the storm without there was silence.

The fallen lamp recalled Malcolmson to himself. Fortunately it was of metal, and so the oil was not spilt. However, the practical need of attending to it settled at once his nervous apprehensions.

When he had turned it out, he wiped his brow and thought for a moment.

'This will not do,' he said to himself. 'If I go on like this I shall become a crazy fool. This must stop! I promised the doctor I would not take tea. Faith, he was pretty right! My nerves must have been getting into a queer state. Funny I did not notice it. I never felt better in my life. However, it is all right now, and I shall not be such a fool again.'

Then he mixed himself a good stiff glass of brandy and water and resolutely sat down to his work.

It was nearly an hour when he looked up from his book, disturbed by the sudden stillness. Without, the wind howled and roared louder than ever, and the rain drove in sheets against the windows, beating like hail on the glass; but within there was no sound whatever save the echo of the wind as it roared in the great chimney, and now and then a hiss as a few raindrops found their way down the chimney in a lull of the storm. The fire had fallen low and had ceased to flame, though it threw out a red glow. Malcolmson listened attentively, and presently heard a thin, squeaking noise, very faint. It came from the corner of the room where the rope hung down, and he thought it was the creaking of the rope on the floor as the swaying of the bell raised and lowered it. Looking up, however, he saw in the dim light the great rat clinging to the rope and gnawing it. The rope was already nearly gnawed through – he could see the lighter colour where the strands were laid bare. As he looked the job was completed, and the severed end of the rope fell clattering on the oaken floor, whilst for an instant the great rat remained like a knob or tassel at the end of the rope, which now began to sway to and fro. Malcolmson felt for a moment another pang of terror as he thought that now the possibility of calling the outer world to his assistance was cut off, but an intense anger took its place, and seizing the book he was reading he hurled it at the rat. The blow was well aimed, but before the missile could reach him the rat dropped off and struck the floor with a soft thud. Malcolmson instantly rushed over towards him, but it darted away and disappeared in the darkness of the shadows of the room. Malcolmson felt that his work was over for the night, and determined then and there to vary the monotony of the proceedings by a hunt for the rat, and took off the green shade of the lamp so as to insure a wider spreading light. As he did so the gloom of the upper part of the room was relieved, and in the new flood of light, great by comparison with the previous darkness, the pictures on the wall stood out boldly. From where he stood, Malcolmson saw right opposite to him the third picture on the wall from the right of the fireplace. He rubbed his eyes in surprise, and then a great fear began to come upon him.

In the centre of the picture was a great irregular patch of brown canvas, as fresh as when it was stretched on the frame. The background was as before, with chair and chimney-corner and rope, but the figure of the Judge had disappeared.

Malcolmson, almost in a chill of horror, turned slowly round, and then he began to shake and tremble like a man in a palsy. His strength seemed to have left him, and he was incapable of action or movement, hardly even of thought. He could only see and hear.

There, on the great high-backed carved oak chair sat the Judge in his robes of scarlet and ermine, with his baleful eyes glaring vindictively, and a smile of triumph on the resolute, cruel mouth, as he lifted with his hands a *black cap*. Malcolmson felt as if the blood was running from his heart, as one does in moments of prolonged suspense. There was a singing in his ears. Without, he could hear the roar and howl of the tempest, and through it, swept on the storm, came the striking of midnight by the great chimes in the market place. He stood for a space of time that seemed to him endless still as a statue, and with wide-open, horror-struck eyes, breathless. As the clock struck, so the smile of triumph on the Judge's face intensified, and at the last stroke of midnight he placed the black cap on his head.

Slowly and deliberately the Judge rose from his chair and picked up the piece of the rope of the alarm bell which lay on the floor, drew it through his hands as if he enjoyed its touch, and then deliberately began to knot one end of it, fashioning it into a noose. This he tightened and tested with his foot, pulling hard at it till he was satisfied and then making a running noose of it, which he held in his hand. Then he began to move along the table on the opposite side to Malcolmson keeping his eyes on him until he had passed him, when with a quick movement he stood in front of the door. Malcolmson then began to feel that he was trapped, and tried to think of what he should do. There was some fascination in the Judge's eyes, which he never took off him, and he had, perforce, to look. He saw the Judge approach – still keeping between him and the door – and raise the noose and throw it towards him as if to entangle him. With a great effort he made a quick movement to one side, and saw the rope fall beside him, and heard it strike the oaken floor. Again the Judge raised the noose and tried to ensnare him, ever keeping his baleful eyes fixed on him, and each time by a mighty effort the student just managed to evade it. So this went on for many times, the Judge seeming never discouraged nor discomposed at failure, but playing as a cat does with a mouse. At last in despair, which had reached its climax, Malcolmson cast a quick glance round him. The lamp seemed to have blazed up, and there was a fairly good light in the room. At the many rat-holes and in the chinks and crannies of the wainscot he saw the rats' eyes; and this aspect, that was purely physical, gave him a gleam of comfort. He looked around and saw that the rope of the great alarm bell was laden with rats. Every inch of it was covered with them, and more and more were pouring through the small circular hole in the ceiling whence it emerged, so that with their weight the bell was beginning to sway.

Hark! it had swayed till the clapper had touched the bell. The sound was but a tiny one, but the bell was only beginning to sway, and it would increase.

At the sound the Judge, who had been keeping his eyes fixed on Malcolmson, looked up, and a scowl of diabolical anger over-spread his face. His eyes fairly glowed like hot coals, and he stamped his foot with a sound that seemed to make the house shake. A dreadful peal of thunder broke overhead as he raised the rope again, whilst the rats kept running up and down the rope as though working against time. This time, instead of throwing it, he drew close to his victim, and held open the noose as he approached. As he came closer there seemed something para-lysing in his very presence, and Malcolmson stood rigid as a corpse. He felt the Judge's icy fingers touch his throat as he adjusted the rope. The noose tightened – tightened. Then the Judge, taking the rigid form of the student in his arms, carried him over and placed him standing in the oak chair, and stepping up beside him, put his hand up and caught the end of the swaying rope of the alarm bell. As he raised his hand the rats fled squeak-ing, and disappeared through the hole in the ceiling. Taking the end of the noose which was round Malcolmson's neck he tied it to the hanging-bell rope, and then descending pulled away the chair.

*   *   *

When the alarm bell of the Judge's House began to sound a crowd soon assembled. Lights and torches of various kinds appeared, and soon a silent crowd was hurrying to the spot. They knocked loudly at the door, but there was no reply. Then they burst in the door, and poured into the great dining-room, the doctor at the head.

There at the end of the rope of the great alarm bell hung the body of the student, and on the face of the Judge in the picture was a malignant smile.

The Squaw

Nürnberg at the time was not so much exploited as it has been since then. Irving had not been playing *Faust*, and the very name of the old town was hardly known to the great bulk of the travelling public. My wife and I being in the second week of our honeymoon, naturally wanted someone else to join our party, so that when the cheery stranger, Elias P. Hutcheson, hailing from Isthmian City, Bleeding Gulch, Maple Tree County, Nebraska, turned up at the station at Frankfort, and casually remarked that he was going on to see the most all-fired old Methuselah of a town in Yurrup, and that he guessed that so much travelling alone was enough to send an intelligent, active citizen into the melancholy ward of a daft house, we took the pretty broad hint and suggested that we should join forces. We found, on comparing notes afterwards, that we had each intended to speak with some diffidence or hesitation so as not to appear too eager, such not being a good compliment to the success of our married life; but the effect was entirely marred by our both beginning to speak at the same instant – stopping simultaneously and then going on together again. Anyhow, no matter how, it was done; and Elias P. Hutcheson became one of our party. Straightway Amelia and I found the pleasant benefit; instead of quarrelling, as we had been doing, we found that the restraining influence of a third party was such that we now took every opportunity of spooning in odd corners. Amelia declares that ever since she has, as the result of that experience, advised all her friends to take a friend on the honeymoon. Well, we 'did' Nürnberg together, and much enjoyed the racy remarks of our Transatlantic friend, who, from his quaint speech and his wonderful stock of adventures, might have stepped out of a novel. We kept for the last object of interest in the city to be visited the Burg, and on the day appointed for the visit strolled round the outer wall of the city by the eastern side.

The Burg is seated on a rock dominating the town and an immensely deep fosse guards it on the northern side. Nürnberg has been happy in that it was never sacked; had it been it would certainly not be so spick and span perfect as it is at present. The ditch has not been used for centuries, and now its base is spread with tea-gardens and orchards, of which some of the trees are of quite respectable growth. As we wandered round the wall, dawdling in the hot July sunshine, we often paused to admire the views spread before us, and in especial the great plain covered with towns and villages and bounded with a blue line of hills, like a landscape of Claude Lorraine. From this we always turned with new delight to the city itself, with its myriad of quaint old gables and acre-wide red roofs dotted with dormer windows, tier upon tier. A little to our right rose the towers of the Burg, and nearer still, standing grim, the Torture Tower, which was, and is, perhaps, the most interesting place in the city. For centuries the tradition of the Iron Virgin of Nürnberg has been handed down as an instance of the horrors of cruelty of which man is capable; we had long looked forward to seeing it; and here at last was its home.

In one of our pauses we leaned over the wall of the moat and looked down. The garden seemed quite fifty or sixty feet below us, and the sun pouring into it with an intense, moveless heat like that of an oven. Beyond rose the grey, grim wall seemingly of endless height, and losing itself right and left in the angles of bastion and counterscarp. Trees and bushes crowned the wall, and above again towered the lofty houses on whose massive beauty Time has only set the hand of approval. The sun was hot and we were lazy; time was our own, and we lingered, leaning on the wall. Just below us was a pretty sight – a great black cat lying stretched in the sun, whilst round her gambolled prettily a tiny black kitten. The mother would wave her tail for the kitten to play with, or would raise her feet and push away the little one as an encouragement to further play. They were just at the foot of the wall, and Elias P. Hutcheson, in order to help the play, stooped and took from the walk a moderate-sized pebble.

'See!' he said, 'I will drop it near the kitten, and they will both wonder where it came from.'

'Oh, be careful,' said my wife; 'you might hit the dear little thing!'

'Not me, ma'am,' said Elias P. 'Why, I'm as tender as a Maine cherry tree. Lor, bless ye. I wouldn't hurt the poor pooty little critter more'n I'd scalp a baby. An' you may bet your variegated socks on that! See, I'll drop it fur away on the outside so's not to go near her!' Thus saying, he leaned over and held his arm out at full length and dropped the stone. It may be that there is some attractive force which draws lesser matters to greater; or more probably that the wall was not plump but sloped to its base – we not noticing the inclination from above; but the stone fell with a sickening thud that came up to us through the hot air, right on the kitten's head, and shattered out its little brains then and there. The black cat cast a swift upward glance, and we saw her eyes like green fire fixed an instant on Elias P. Hutcheson; and then her attention was given to the kitten, which lay still with just a quiver of her tiny limbs, whilst a thin red stream trickled from a gaping wound. With a muffled cry, such as a human being might give, she bent over the kitten licking its wounds and moaning. Suddenly she seemed to realise that it was dead, and again threw her eyes up at us. I shall never forget the sight, for she looked the perfect incarnation of hate. Her green eyes blazed with lurid fire, and the white, sharp teeth seemed to almost shine through the blood which dabbled her mouth and whiskers. She gnashed her teeth, and her claws stood out stark and at full length on every paw. Then she made a wild rush up the wall as if to reach us, but when the momentum ended fell back, and further added to her horrible appearance for she fell on the kitten, and rose with her black fur smeared with its brains and blood. Amelia turned quite faint, and I had to lift her back from the wall. There was a seat close by in shade of a spreading plane tree, and here I placed her whilst she composed herself. Then I went back to Hutcheson, who stood without moving, looking down on the angry cat below.

As I joined him, he said: 'Wall, I guess that am the savagest beast I ever see – 'cept once when an Apache squaw had an edge on a half-breed what they nicknamed "Splinters" 'cos of the way he fixed up her papoose which he stole on a raid just to show that he appreciated the way they had given his mother the fire torture. She got that kinder look so set on her face that it jest seemed to grow there. She followed Splinters mor'n three year till at last the braves got him and handed him over to her. They did say that no man, white or Injun, had ever been so long a-dying under the tortures of the Apaches. The only time I ever see her smile was when I wiped her out. I kem on the camp just in time to see Splinters pass in his checks, and he wasn't sorry to go either. He was a hard citizen, and though I never could shake with him after that papoose business – for it was bitter bad, and he should have been a white man, for he looked like one – I see he had got paid out in full. Durn me, but I took a piece of his hide from one of his

skinnin' posts an' had it made into a pocket-book. It's here now!'
and he slapped the breast pocket of his coat.

Whilst he was speaking the cat was continuing her frantic efforts
to get up the wall. She would take a run back and then charge up,
sometimes reaching an incredible height. She did not seem to mind
the heavy fall which she got each time but started with renewed
vigour; and at every tumble her appearance became more horrible.
Hutcheson was a kind-hearted man – my wife and I had both
noticed little acts of kindness to animals as well as to persons – and
he seemed concerned at the state of fury to which the cat had
wrought herself.

'Wall, now!' he said, 'I du declare that that poor critter seems quite
desperate. There! there! poor thing, it was all an accident – though
that won't bring back your little one to you. Say! I wouldn't have had
such a thing happen for a thousand! Just shows what a clumsy fool of
a man can do when he tries to play! Seems I'm too darned slipper-
handed to even play with a cat. Say Colonel!' – it was a pleasant way
he had to bestow titles freely – 'I hope your wife don't hold no grudge
against me on account of this unpleasantness? Why, I wouldn't have
had it occur on no account.'

He came over to Amelia and apologised profusely, and she with
her usual kindness of heart hastened to assure him that she quite
understood that it was an accident. Then we all went again to the
wall and looked over.

The cat missing Hutcheson's face had drawn back across the moat,
and was sitting on her haunches as though ready to spring. Indeed,
the very instant she saw him she did spring, and with a blind un-
reasoning fury, which would have been grotesque, only that it was
so frightfully real. She did not try to run up the wall, but simply
launched herself at him as though hate and fury could lend her wings
to pass straight through the great distance between them. Amelia,
womanlike, got quite concerned, and said to Elias P. in a warning
voice: 'Oh! you must be very careful. That animal would try to kill
you if she were here; her eyes look like positive murder.'

He laughed out jovially. 'Excuse me, ma'am,' he said, 'but I can't
help laughin'. Fancy a man that has fought grizzlies an' Injuns bein'
careful of bein' murdered by a cat!'

When the cat heard him laugh, her whole demeanour seemed to
change. She no longer tried to jump or run up the wall, but went
quietly over, and sitting again beside the dead kitten began to lick
and fondle it as though it were alive.

'See!' said I, 'the effect of a really strong man. Even that animal in the midst of her fury recognises the voice of a master, and bows to him!'

'Like a squaw!' was the only comment of Elias P. Hutcheson, as we moved on our way round the city fosse. Every now and then we looked over the wall and each time saw the cat following us. At first she had kept going back to the dead kitten, and then as the distance grew greater took it in her mouth and so followed. After a while, however, she abandoned this, for we saw her following all alone; she had evidently hidden the body somewhere.

Amelia's alarm grew at the cat's persistence, and more than once she repeated her warning; but the American always laughed with amusement, till finally, seeing that she was beginning to be worried, he said: 'I say, ma'am, you needn't be skeered over that cat. I go heeled, I du!' Here he slapped his pistol pocket at the back of his lumbar region. 'Why sooner'n have you worried, I'll shoot the critter, right here, an' risk the police interferin' with a citizen of the United States for carryin' arms contrairy to reg'lations!' As he spoke he looked over the wall, but the cat on seeing him, retreated, with a growl, into a bed of tall flowers, and was hidden. He went on: 'Blest if that thar critter ain't got more sense of what's good for her than most Christians. I guess we've seen the last of her! You bet, she'll go back now to that busted kitten and have a private funeral of it, all to herself!'

Amelia did not like to say more, lest he might, in mistaken kindness to her, fulfil his threat of shooting the cat: and so we went on and crossed the little wooden bridge leading to the gateway whence ran the steep paved roadway between the Burg and the pentagonal Torture Tower. As we crossed the bridge we saw the cat again down below us. When she saw us her fury seemed to return, and she made frantic efforts to get up the steep wall. Hutcheson laughed as he looked down at her, and said: 'Goodbye, old girl. Sorry I injured your feelin's, but you'll get over it in time! So long!' And then we passed through the long, dim archway and came to the gate of the Burg.

When we came out again after our survey of this most beautiful old place which not even the well-intentioned efforts of the gothic restorers of forty years ago have been able to spoil – though their restoration was then glaring white – we seemed to have quite forgotten the unpleasant episode of the morning. The old lime tree with its great trunk gnarled with the passing of nearly nine centuries, the deep well cut through the heart of the rock by those captives of old, and the lovely view from the city wall whence we heard, spread over almost a full quarter of an hour, the multitudinous chimes of the city, had all helped to wipe out from our minds the incident of the slain kitten.

We were the only visitors who had entered the Torture Tower that morning – so at least said the old custodian – and as we had the place all to ourselves were able to make a minute and more satisfactory survey than would have otherwise been possible. The custodian, looking to us as the sole source of his gains for the day, was willing to meet our wishes in any way. The Torture Tower is truly a grim place, even now when many thousands of visitors have sent a stream of life, and the joy that follows life, into the place; but at the time I mention it wore its grimmest and most gruesome aspect. The dust of ages seemed to have settled on it, and the darkness and the horror of its memories seem to have become sentient in a way that would have satisfied the Pantheistic souls of Philo or Spinoza. The lower chamber where we entered was seemingly, in its normal state, filled with incarnate darkness; even the hot sunlight streaming in through the door seemed to be lost in the vast thickness of the walls, and only showed the masonry rough as when the builder's scaffolding had come down, but coated with dust and marked here and there with patches of dark stain which, if walls could speak, could have given their own dread memories of fear and pain. We were glad to pass up the dusty wooden staircase, the custodian leaving the outer door open to light us somewhat on our way; for to our eyes the one long-wick'd, evil-smelling candle stuck in a sconce on the wall gave an inadequate light. When we came up through the open trap in the corner of the chamber overhead, Amelia held on to me so tightly that I could actually feel her heart beat. I must say for my own part that I was not surprised at her fear, for this room was even more gruesome than that below. Here there was certainly more light, but only just sufficient to realise the horrible surroundings of the place. The builders of the tower had evidently intended that only they who should gain the top should have any of the joys of light and prospect. There, as we had noticed from below, were ranges of windows, albeit of mediaeval smallness, but elsewhere in the tower were only a very few narrow slits such as were habitual in places of mediaeval defence. A few of these only lit the chamber, and these so high up in the wall that from no part could the sky be seen through the thickness of the walls. In racks, and leaning in disorder against the walls, were a

number of headsmen's swords, great double-handed weapons with
broad blade and keen edge. Hard by were several blocks whereon the
necks of the victims had lain, with here and there deep notches where
the steel had bitten through the guard of flesh and shored into the
wood. Round the chamber, placed in all sorts of irregular ways, were
many implements of torture which made one's heart ache to see –
chairs full of spikes which gave instant and excruciating pain; chairs
and couches with dull knobs whose torture was seemingly less, but
which, though slower, were equally efficacious; racks, belts, boots,
gloves, collars, all made for compressing at will; steel baskets in
which the head could be slowly crushed into a pulp if necessary;
watchmen's hooks with long handle and knife that cut at resistance –
this a speciality of the old Nürnberg police system; and many, many
other devices for man's injury to man. Amelia grew quite pale with
the horror of the things, but fortunately did not faint, for being a
little overcome she sat down on a torture chair, but jumped up again
with a shriek, all tendency to faint gone. We both pretended that
it was the injury done to her dress by the dust of the chair, and the
rusty spikes which had upset her, and Mr Hutcheson acquiesced in
accepting the explanation with a kind-hearted laugh.

But the central object in the whole of this chamber of horrors was
the engine known as the Iron Virgin, which stood near the centre of
the room. It was a rudely-shaped figure of a woman, something of
the bell order, or, to make a closer comparison, of the figure of Mrs
Noah in the children's Ark, but without that slimness of waist and
perfect *rondeur* of hip which marks the aesthetic type of the Noah
family. One would hardly have recognised it as intended for a human
figure at all had not the founder shaped on the forehead a rude
semblance of a woman's face. This machine was coated with rust
without, and covered with dust; a rope was fastened to a ring in the
front of the figure, about where the waist should have been, and
was drawn through a pulley, fastened on the wooden pillar which
sustained the flooring above. The custodian pulling this rope showed
that a section of the front was hinged like a door at one side; we then
saw that the engine was of considerable thickness, leaving just room
enough inside for a man to be placed. The door was of equal thickness and of great weight, for it took the custodian all his strength,
aided though he was by the contrivance of the pulley, to open it. This
weight was partly due to the fact that the door was of manifest
purpose hung so as to throw its weight downwards, so that it might
shut of its own accord when the strain was released. The inside

was honeycombed with rust – nay more, the rust alone that comes through time would hardly have eaten so deep into the iron walls; the rust of the cruel stains was deep indeed! It was only, however, when we came to look at the inside of the door that the diabolical intention was manifest to the full. Here were several long spikes, square and massive, broad at the base and sharp at the points, placed in such a position that when the door should close the upper ones would pierce the eyes of the victim, and the lower ones his heart and vitals. The sight was too much for poor Amelia, and this time she fainted dead off, and I had to carry her down the stairs, and place her on a bench outside till she recovered. That she felt it to the quick was afterwards shown by the fact that my eldest son bears to this day a rude birthmark on his breast, which has, by family consent, been accepted as representing the Nürnberg Virgin.

When we got back to the chamber we found Hutcheson still opposite the Iron Virgin; he had been evidently philosophising, and now gave us the benefit of his thought in the shape of a sort of exordium.

'Wall, I guess I've been learnin' somethin' here while madam has been gettin' over her faint. 'Pears to me that we're a long way behind the times on our side of the big drink. We uster think out on the plains that the Injun could give us points in tryin' to make a man uncomfortable; but I guess your old mediaeval law-and-order party could raise him every time. Splinters was pretty good in his bluff on the squaw, but this here young miss held a straight flush all high on him. The points of them spikes air sharp enough still, though even the edges air eaten out by what uster be on them. It'd be a good thing for our Indian section to get some specimens of this here play-toy to send round to the Reservations jest to knock the stuffin' out of the bucks, and the squaws too, by showing them as how old civilisation lays over them at their best. Guess but I'll get in that box a minute jest to see how it feels!'

'Oh no! no!' said Amelia. 'It is too terrible!'

'Guess, ma'am, nothin's too terrible to the explorin' mind. I've been in some queer places in my time. Spent a night inside a dead horse while a prairie fire swept over me in Montana Territory – an' another time slept inside a dead buffler when the Comanches was on the war path an' I didn't keer to leave my kyard on them. I've been two days in a caved-in tunnel in the Billy Broncho gold mine in New Mexico, an' was one of the four shut up for three parts of a day in the caisson what slid over on her side when we was settin' the foundations of the Buffalo Bridge. I've not funked an odd experience yet, an' I don't propose to begin now!'

We saw that he was set on the experiment, so I said: 'Well, hurry up, old man, and get through it quick!'

'All right, General,' said he, 'but I calculate we ain't quite ready yet. The gentlemen, my predecessors, what stood in that thar canister, didn't volunteer for the office – not much! And I guess there was some ornamental tyin' up before the big stroke was made. I want to go into this thing fair and square, so I must get fixed up proper first. I dare say this old galoot can rise some string and tie me up accordin' to sample?'

This was said interrogatively to the old custodian, but the latter, who understood the drift of his speech, though perhaps not appreciating to the full the niceties of dialect and imagery, shook his head. His protest was, however, only formal and made to be overcome. The American thrust a gold piece into his hand, saying: 'Take it, pard! it's your pot; and don't be skeer'd. This ain't no necktie party that you're asked to assist in!' He produced some thin frayed rope and proceeded to bind our companion with sufficient strictness for the purpose. When the upper part of his body was bound, Hutcheson said: 'Hold on a moment, Judge. Guess I'm too heavy for you to tote into the canister. You jest let me walk in, and then you can wash up regardin' my legs!'

Whilst speaking he had backed himself into the opening which was just enough to hold him. It was a close fit and no mistake. Amelia looked on with fear in her eyes, but she evidently did not like to say anything. Then the custodian completed his task by tying the American's feet together so that he was now absolutely helpless and fixed in his voluntary prison. He seemed to really enjoy it, and the incipient smile which was habitual to his face blossomed into actuality as he said: 'Guess this here Eve was made out of the rib of a dwarf! There ain't much room for a full-grown citizen of the United States to hustle. We uster make our coffins more roomier in Idaho territory. Now, Judge, you jest begin to let this door down, slow, on to me. I want to feel the same pleasure as the other jays had when those spikes began to move toward their eyes!'

'Oh no! no! no!' broke in Amelia hysterically. 'It is too terrible! I can't bear to see it! – I can't! I can't!' But the American was obdurate. 'Say, Colonel,' said he, 'why not take Madame for a little promenade? I wouldn't hurt her feelin's for the world; but now that I am here, havin' kem eight thousand miles, wouldn't it be too hard to give up the very experience I've been pinin' an' pantin' fur? A man can't get to feel like canned goods every time! Me and the Judge here'll fix up this thing in no time, an' then you'll come back, an' we'll all laugh together!'

Once more the resolution that is born of curiosity triumphed, and Amelia stayed holding tight to my arm and shivering whilst the custodian began to slacken slowly inch by inch the rope that held back the iron door. Hutcheson's face was positively radiant as his eyes followed the first movement of the spikes.

'Wall!' he said, 'I guess I've not had enjoyment like this since I left Noo York. Bar a scrap with a French sailor at Wapping – an' that warn't much of a picnic neither – I've not had a show fur real pleasure in this dod-rotted Continent, where there ain't no b'ars nor no Injuns, an' wheer nary man goes heeled. Slow there, Judge! Don't you rush this business! I want a show for my money this game – I du!'

The custodian must have had in him some of the blood of his predecessors in that ghastly tower, for he worked the engine with a deliberate and excruciating slowness which after five minutes, in which the outer edge of the door had not moved half as many inches, began to overcome Amelia. I saw her lips whiten, and felt her hold upon my arm relax. I looked around an instant for a place whereon to lay her, and when I looked at her again found that her eye had become fixed on the side of the Virgin. Following its direction I saw the black cat crouching out of sight. Her green eyes shone like danger lamps in the gloom of the place, and their colour was heightened by the blood which still smeared her coat and reddened her mouth. I cried out: 'The cat! look out for the cat!' for even then she sprang out before the engine. At this moment she looked like a triumphant demon. Her eyes blazed with ferocity, her hair bristled out till she seemed twice her normal size, and her tail lashed about as does a tiger's when the quarry is before it.

Elias P. Hutcheson when he saw her was amused, and his eyes positively sparkled with fun as he said: 'Darned if the squaw hain't got on all her war paint! Jest give her a shove off if she comes any of her tricks on me, for I'm so fixed everlastingly by the boss, that durn my skin if I can keep my eyes from her if she wants them! Easy there, Judge! don't you slack that ar rope or I'm euchered!'

At this moment Amelia completed her faint, and I had to clutch hold of her round the waist or she would have fallen to the floor. Whilst attending to her I saw the black cat crouching for a spring, and jumped up to turn the creature out.

But at that instant, with a sort of hellish scream, she hurled herself, not as we expected at Hutcheson, but straight at the face of the custodian. Her claws seemed to be tearing wildly as one sees in the Chinese drawings of the dragon rampant, and as I looked I saw one of them light on the poor man's eye, and actually tear through it and down his cheek, leaving a wide band of red where the blood seemed to spurt from every vein.

With a yell of sheer terror which came quicker than even his sense of pain, the man leaped back, dropping as he did so the rope which held back the iron door. I jumped for it, but was too late, for the cord ran like lightning through the pulley-block, and the heavy mass fell forward from its own weight.

As the door closed I caught a glimpse of our poor companion's face. He seemed frozen with terror. His eyes stared with a horrible anguish as if dazed, and no sound came from his lips.

And then the spikes did their work. Happily the end was quick, for when I wrenched open the door they had pierced so deep that they had locked in the bones of the skull through which they had crushed, and actually tore him – it – out of his iron prison till, bound as he was, he fell at full length with a sickly thud upon the floor, the face turning upward as he fell.

I rushed to my wife, lifted her up and carried her out, for I feared for her very reason if she should wake from her faint to such a scene. I laid her on the bench outside and ran back. Leaning against the wooden column was the custodian moaning in pain whilst he held his reddening handkerchief to his eyes. And sitting on the head of the poor American was the cat, purring loudly as she licked the blood which trickled through the gashed socket of his eyes.

I think no one will call me cruel because I seized one of the old executioner's swords and shore her in two as she sat.

The Secret of the Growing Gold

When Margaret Delandre went to live at Brent's Rock the whole neighbourhood awoke to the pleasure of an entirely new scandal. Scandals in connection with either the Delandre family or the Brents of Brent's Rock, were not few; and if the secret history of the county had been written in full both names would have been found well represented. It is true that the status of each was so different that they might have belonged to different continents – or to different worlds for the matter of that – for hitherto their orbits had never crossed. The Brents were accorded by the whole section of the country a unique social dominance, and had ever held themselves as high above the yeoman class to which Margaret Delandre belonged, as a blue-blooded Spanish hidalgo out-tops his peasant tenantry.

The Delandres had an ancient record and were proud of it in their way as the Brents were of theirs. But the family had never risen above yeomanry; and although they had been once well-to-do in the good old times of foreign wars and protection, their fortunes had withered under the scorching of the free trade sun and the 'piping times of peace'. They had, as the elder members used to assert, 'stuck to the land', with the result that they had taken root in it, body and soul. In fact, they, having chosen the life of vegetables, had flourished as vegetation does – blossomed and thrived in the good season and suffered in the bad. Their holding, Dander's Croft, seemed to have been worked out, and to be typical of the family which had inhabited it. The latter had declined generation after generation, sending out now and again some abortive shoot of unsatisfied energy in the shape of a soldier or sailor, who had worked his way to the minor grades of the services and had there stopped, cut short either from unheeding gallantry in action or from that destroying cause to men without breeding or youthful care – the recognition of a position above them which they feel unfitted to fill. So, little by little, the family dropped lower and lower, the men brooding and dissatisfied, and drinking themselves into the grave, the women drudging at home, or marrying beneath them – or worse. In process of time all disappeared, leaving only two in the Croft, Wykham Delandre and his sister Margaret. The man and woman seemed to have inherited in masculine and feminine form respectively the evil tendency of their race, sharing in common the principles, though manifesting them in different ways, of sullen passion, voluptuousness and recklessness.

The history of the Brents had been something similar, but showing the causes of decadence in their aristocratic and not their plebeian forms. They, too, had sent their shoots to the wars; but their positions had been different and they had often attained honour – for without flaw they were gallant, and brave deeds were done by them before the selfish dissipation which marked them had sapped their vigour.

The present head of the family – if family it could now be called when one remained of the direct line – was Geoffrey Brent. He was almost a type of worn out race, manifesting in some ways its most brilliant qualities, and in others its utter degradation. He might be fairly compared with some of those antique Italian nobles whom the painters have preserved to us with their courage, their unscrupulousness, their refinement of lust and cruelty – the voluptuary actual with the fiend potential. He was certainly handsome, with that dark, aquiline, commanding beauty which women so generally recognise as dominant. With men he was distant and cold; but such a bearing never deters womankind. The inscrutable laws of sex have so arranged that even a timid woman is not afraid of a fierce and haughty man. And so it was that there was hardly a woman of any kind or degree, who lived within view of Brent's Rock, who did not cherish some form of secret admiration for the handsome wastrel. The category was a wide one, for Brent's Rock rose up steeply from the midst of a level region and for a circuit of a hundred miles it lay on the horizon, with its high old towers and steep roofs cutting the level edge of wood and hamlet, and far-scattered mansions.

So long as Geoffrey Brent confined his dissipations to London and Paris and Vienna – anywhere out of sight and sound of his home – opinion was silent. It is easy to listen to far off echoes unmoved, and we can treat them with disbelief, or scorn, or disdain, or whatever attitude of coldness may suit our purpose. But when the scandal came close home it was another matter; and the feelings of independence and integrity which are in people of every community which is not utterly spoiled, asserted itself and demanded that condemnation should be expressed. Still there was a certain reticence in all, and no more notice was taken of the existing facts than was absolutely necessary. Margaret Delandre bore herself so fearlessly and so open-ly – she accepted her position as the justified companion of Geoffrey Brent so naturally that people came to believe that she was secretly married to him, and therefore thought it wiser to hold their tongues lest time should justify her and also make her an active enemy.

The one person who, by his interference, could have settled all doubts was debarred by circumstances from interfering in the matter. Wykham Delandre had quarrelled with his sister – or per-haps it was that she had quarrelled with him – and they were on terms not merely of armed neutrality but of bitter hatred. The quarrel had been antecedent to Margaret going to Brent's Rock. She and Wykham had almost come to blows. There had certainly been threats on one side and on the other; and in the end Wykham, overcome with passion, had ordered his sister to leave his house. She had risen straightway, and, without waiting to pack up even her own personal belongings, had walked out of the house. On the threshold she had paused for a moment to hurl a bitter threat at Wykham that he would rue in shame and despair to the last hour of his life his act of that day. Some weeks had since passed; and it was understood in the neighbourhood that Margaret had gone to London, when she suddenly appeared driving out with Geoffrey Brent, and the entire neighbourhood knew before nightfall that she had taken up her abode at the Rock. It was no subject of surprise that Brent had come back unexpectedly, for such was his usual custom. Even his own servants never knew when to expect him, for there was a private door, of which he alone had the key, by which he sometimes entered without anyone in the house being aware of his coming. This was his usual method of appearing after a long absence.

Wykham Delandre was furious at the news. He vowed vengeance – and to keep his mind level with his passion drank deeper than ever. He tried several times to see his sister, but she contemptuously refused to meet him. He tried to have an interview with Brent and was refused by him also. Then he tried to stop him in the road, but without avail, for Geoffrey was not a man to be stopped against his will. Several actual encounters took place between the two men, and many more were threatened and avoided. At last Wykham Delandre settled down to a morose, vengeful acceptance of the situation.

Neither Margaret nor Geoffrey was of a pacific temperament, and it was not long before there began to be quarrels between them. One thing would lead to another, and wine flowed freely at Brent's Rock.

Now and again the quarrels would assume a bitter aspect, and threats would be exchanged in uncompromising language that fairly awed the listening servants. But such quarrels generally ended where domestic altercations do, in reconciliation, and in a mutual respect for the fighting qualities proportionate to their manifestation. Fighting for its own sake is found by a certain class of persons, all the world over, to be a matter of absorbing interest, and there is no reason to believe that domestic conditions minimise its potency. Geoffrey and Margaret made occasional absences from Brent's Rock, and on each of these occasions Wykham Delandre also absented himself; but as he generally heard of the absence too late to be of any service, he returned home each time in a more bitter and discontented frame of mind than before.

At last there came a time when the absence from Brent's Rock became longer than before. Only a few days earlier there had been a quarrel, exceeding in bitterness anything which had gone before; but this, too, had been made up, and a trip on the Continent had been mentioned before the servants. After a few days Wykham Delandre also went away, and it was some weeks before he returned. It was noticed that he was full of some new importance – satisfaction, exaltation – they hardly knew how to call it. He went straightway to Brent's Rock, and demanded to see Geoffrey Brent, and on being told that he had not yet returned, said, with a grim decision which the servants noted: 'I shall come again. My news is solid – it can wait!' and turned away.

Week after week went by, and month after month; and then there came a rumour, certified later on, that an accident had occurred in the Zermatt valley. Whilst crossing a dangerous pass the carriage containing an English lady and the driver had fallen over a precipice, the gentleman of the party, Mr Geoffrey Brent, having been fortunately saved as he had been walking up the hill to ease the horses. He gave information, and search was made. The broken rail, the excoriated roadway, the marks where the horses had struggled on the decline before finally pitching over into the torrent – all told the sad tale. It was a wet season, and there had been much snow in the winter, so that the river was swollen beyond its usual volume, and the eddies of the stream were packed with ice. All search was made, and finally the wreck of the carriage and the body of one horse were found in an eddy of the river. Later on the body of the driver was found on the sandy, torrent-swept waste near Täsch; but the body of the lady, like that of the other horse, had quite disappeared, and was –

what was left of it by that time – whirling amongst the eddies of the Rhone on its way down to the Lake of Geneva.

Wykham Delandre made all the enquiries possible, but could not find any trace of the missing woman. He found, however, in the books of the various hotels the name of 'Mr and Mrs Geoffrey Brent'. And he had a stone erected at Zermatt to his sister's memory, under her married name, and a tablet put up in the church at Bretten, the parish in which both Brent's Rock and Dander's Croft were situated.

There was a lapse of nearly a year, after the excitement of the matter had worn away, and the whole neighbourhood had gone on its accustomed way. Brent was still absent, and Delandre more drunken, more morose, and more revengeful than before.

Then there was a new excitement. Brent's Rock was being made ready for a new mistress. It was officially announced by Geoffrey himself in a letter to the Vicar, that he had been married some months before to an Italian lady, and that they were then on their way home. Then a small army of workmen invaded the house; and hammer and plane sounded, and a general air of size and paint pervaded the atmosphere. One wing of the old house, the south, was entirely re-done; and then the great body of the workmen departed, leaving only materials for the doing of the old hall when Geoffrey Brent should have returned, for he had directed that the decoration was only to be done under his own eyes. He had brought with him accurate drawings of a hall in the house of his bride's father, for he wished to reproduce for her the place to which she had been accustomed. As the moulding had all to be re-done, some scaffolding poles and boards were brought in and laid on one side of the great hall, and also a great wooden tank or box for mixing the lime, which was laid in bags beside it.

When the new mistress of Brent's Rock arrived the bells of the church rang out, and there was a general jubilation. She was a beautiful creature, full of the poetry and fire and passion of the South; and the few English words which she had learned were spoken in such a sweet and pretty broken way that she won the hearts of the people almost as much by the music of her voice as by the melting beauty of her dark eyes.

Geoffrey Brent seemed more happy than he had ever before appeared; but there was a dark, anxious look on his face that was new to those who knew him of old, and he started at times as though at some noise that was unheard by others.

And so months passed and the whisper grew that at last Brent's Rock was to have an heir. Geoffrey was very tender to his wife, and the new bond between them seemed to soften him. He took more interest in his tenants and their needs than he had ever done; and works of charity on his part as well as on his sweet young wife's were not lacking. He seemed to have set all his hopes on the child that was coming, and as he looked deeper into the future the dark shadow that had come over his face seemed to die gradually away.

All the time Wykham Delandre nursed his revenge. Deep in his heart had grown up a purpose of vengeance which only waited an opportunity to crystallise and take a definite shape. His vague idea was somehow centred in the wife of Brent, for he knew that he could strike him best through those he loved, and the coming time seemed to hold in its womb the opportunity for which he longed. One night he sat alone in the living-room of his house. It had once been a handsome room in its way, but time and neglect had done their work and it was now little better than a ruin, without dignity or picturesqueness of any kind. He had been drinking heavily for some time and was more than half stupefied. He thought he heard a noise as of someone at the door and looked up. Then he called half-savagely to come in; but there was no response. With a muttered blasphemy he renewed his potations. Presently he forgot all around him, sank into a daze, but suddenly awoke to see standing before him someone or something like a battered, ghostly edition of his sister. For a few moments there came upon him a sort of fear. The woman before him, with distorted features and burning eyes seemed hardly human, and the only thing that seemed a reality of his sister, as she had been, was her wealth of golden hair, and this was now streaked with grey. She eyed her brother with a long, cold stare; and he, too, as he looked and began to realise the actuality of her presence, found the hatred of her which he had had, once again surging up in his heart. All the brooding passion of the past year seemed to find a voice at once as he asked her: 'Why are you here? You're dead and buried.'

'I am here, Wykham Delandre, for no love of you, but because I hate another even more than I do you!' A great passion blazed in her eyes.

'Him?' he asked, in so fierce a whisper that even the woman was for an instant startled till she regained her calm.

'Yes, him!' she answered. 'But make no mistake, my revenge is my own; and I merely use you to help me to it.'

Wykham asked suddenly: 'Did he marry you?'

The woman's distorted face broadened out in a ghastly attempt at a smile. It was a hideous mockery, for the broken features and seamed scars took strange shapes and strange colours, and queer lines of white showed out as the straining muscles pressed on the old cicatrices.

'So you would like to know! It would please your pride to feel that your sister was truly married! Well, you shall not know. That was my revenge on you, and I do not mean to change it by a hair's breadth. I have come here tonight simply to let you know that I am alive, so that if any violence be done me where I am going there may be a witness.'

'Where are you going?' demanded her brother.

'That is my affair! and I have not the least intention of letting you know!' Wykham stood up, but the drink was on him and he reeled and fell. As he lay on the floor he announced his intention of following his sister; and with an outburst of splenetic humour told her that he would follow her through the darkness by the light of her hair, and of her beauty. At this she turned on him, and said that there were others beside him that would rue her hair and her beauty too. 'As he will,' she hissed; 'for the hair remains though the beauty be gone. When he withdrew the lynch-pin and sent us over the precipice into the torrent, he had little thought of my beauty. Perhaps his beauty would be scarred like mine were he whirled, as I was, among the rocks of the Visp, and frozen on the ice pack in the drift of the river. But let him beware! His time is coming!' and with a fierce gesture she flung open the door and passed out into the night.

* * *

Later on that night, Mrs Brent, who was but half-asleep, became suddenly awake and spoke to her husband: 'Geoffrey, was not that the click of a lock somewhere below our window?'

But Geoffrey – though she thought that he, too, had started at the noise – seemed sound asleep, and breathed heavily. Again Mrs Brent dozed; but this time awoke to the fact that her husband had arisen and was partially dressed. He was deadly pale, and when the light of the lamp which he had in his hand fell on his face, she was frightened at the look in his eyes.

'What is it, Geoffrey? What dost thou?' she asked.

'Hush! little one,' he answered, in a strange, hoarse voice. 'Go to sleep. I am restless, and wish to finish some work I left undone.'

'Bring it here, my husband,' she said; 'I am lonely and I fear when thou art away.'

For reply he merely kissed her and went out, closing the door behind him. She lay awake for a while, and then nature asserted itself, and she slept.

Suddenly she started broad awake with the memory in her ears of a smothered cry from somewhere not far off. She jumped up and ran to the door and listened, but there was no sound. She grew alarmed for her husband, and called out: 'Geoffrey! Geoffrey!'

After a few moments the door of the great hall opened, and Geoffrey appeared at it, but without his lamp.

'Hush!' he said, in a sort of whisper, and his voice was harsh and stern. 'Hush! Get to bed! I am working, and must not be disturbed. Go to sleep, and do not wake the house!'

With a chill in her heart – for the harshness of her husband's voice was new to her – she crept back to bed and lay there trembling, too frightened to cry, and listened to every sound. There was a long pause of silence, and then the sound of some iron implement striking muffled blows! Then there came a clang of a heavy stone falling, followed by a muffled curse. Then a dragging sound, and then more noise of stone on stone. She lay all the while in an agony of fear, and her heart beat dreadfully. She heard a curious sort of scraping sound; and then there was silence. Presently the door opened gently, and Geoffrey appeared. His wife pretended to be asleep; but through her eyelashes she saw him wash from his hands something white that looked like lime.

In the morning he made no allusion to the previous night, and she was afraid to ask any question.

From that day there seemed some shadow over Geoffrey Brent. He neither ate nor slept as he had been accustomed, and his former habit of turning suddenly as though someone were speaking from behind him revived. The old hall seemed to have some kind of fascination for him. He used to go there many times in the day, but grew impatient if anyone, even his wife, entered it. When the builder's foreman came to enquire about continuing his work Geoffrey was out driving; the man went into the hall, and when Geoffrey returned the servant told him of his arrival and where he was. With a frightful oath he pushed the servant aside and hurried up to the old hall. The workman met him almost at the door; and as Geoffrey burst into the room he ran against him. The man apologised: 'Beg pardon, sir, but I was just going out to make some enquiries. I directed twelve sacks of lime to be sent here, but I see there are only ten.'

'Damn the ten sacks and the twelve too!' was the ungracious and incomprehensible rejoinder.

The workman looked surprised, and tried to turn the conversation.

'I see, sir, there is a little matter which our people must have done; but the governor will of course see it set right at his own cost.'

'What do you mean?'

'That 'ere 'arth-stone, sir. Some idiot must have put a scaffold pole on it and cracked it right down the middle, and it's thick enough you'd think to stand hanythink.' Geoffrey was silent for quite a minute, and then said in a constrained voice and with much gentler manner: 'Tell your people that I am not going on with the work in the hall at present. I want to leave it as it is for a while longer.'

'All right sir. I'll send up a few of our chaps to take away these poles and lime bags and tidy the place up a bit.'

'No! No!' said Geoffrey, 'leave them where they are. I shall send and tell you when you are to get on with the work.' So the foreman went away, and his comment to his master was: 'I'd send in the bill, sir, for the work already done. 'Pears to me that money's a little shaky in that quarter.'

Once or twice Delandre tried to stop Brent on the road, and at last, finding that he could not attain his object, rode after the carriage, calling out: 'What has become of my sister, your wife?' Geoffrey lashed his horses into a gallop, and the other, seeing from his white face and from his wife's collapse almost into a faint that his object was attained, rode away with a scowl and a laugh.

That night when Geoffrey went into the hall he passed over to the great fireplace, and all at once started back with a smothered cry. Then with an effort he pulled himself together and went away, returning with a light. He bent down over the broken hearth-stone to see if the moonlight falling through the storied window had in any way deceived him. Then with a groan of anguish he sank to his knees.

There, sure enough, through the crack in the broken stone were protruding a multitude of threads of golden hair just tinged with grey!

He was disturbed by a noise at the door, and looking round, saw his wife standing in the doorway. In the desperation of the moment he took action to prevent discovery, and lighting a match at the lamp, stooped down and burned away the hair that rose through the broken stone. Then rising nonchalantly as he could, he pretended surprise at seeing his wife beside him.

For the next week he lived in an agony; for, whether by accident or design, he could not find himself alone in the hall for any length of time. At each visit the hair had grown afresh through the crack, and he had to watch it carefully lest his terrible secret should be discovered. He tried to find a receptacle for the body of the murdered woman outside the house, but someone always interrupted him; and once, when he was coming out of the private doorway, he was met by his wife, who began to question him about it, and manifested surprise that she should not have before noticed the key which he now reluctantly showed her. Geoffrey dearly and passionately loved his wife, so that any possibility of her discovering his dread secrets, or even of doubting him, filled him with anguish; and after a couple of days had passed, he could not help coming to the conclusion that, at least, she suspected something.

That very evening she came into the hall after her drive and found him there sitting moodily by the deserted fireplace. She spoke to him directly.

'Geoffrey, I have been spoken to by that fellow Delandre, and he says horrible things. He tells to me that a week ago his sister returned to his house, the wreck and ruin of her former self, with only her golden hair as of old, and announced some fell intention. He asked me where she is – and oh, Geoffrey, she is dead, she is dead! So how can she have returned? Oh! I am in dread, and I know not where to turn!'

For answer, Geoffrey burst into a torrent of blasphemy which made her shudder. He cursed Delandre and his sister and all their kind, and in especial he hurled curse after curse on her golden hair.

'Oh, hush! hush!' she said, and was then silent, for she feared her husband when she saw the evil effect of his humour. Geoffrey in the torrent of his anger stood up and moved away from the hearth; but suddenly stopped as he saw a new look of terror in his wife's eyes. He followed their glance, and then he too, shuddered – for there on the broken hearth-stone lay a golden streak as the point of the hair rose though the crack.

'Look, look!' she shrieked. 'Is it some ghost of the dead! Come away – come away!' and seizing her husband by the wrist with the frenzy of madness, she pulled him from the room.

That night she was in a raging fever. The doctor of the district attended her at once, and special aid was telegraphed for to London.

Geoffrey was in despair, and in his anguish at the danger of his young wife almost forgot his own crime and its consequences. In the evening the doctor had to leave to attend to others; but he left Geoffrey in charge of his wife. His last words were: 'Remember, you must humour her till I come in the morning, or till some other doctor has her case in hand. What you have to dread is another attack of emotion. See that she is kept warm. Nothing more can be done.'

Late in the evening, when the rest of the household had retired, Geoffrey's wife got up from her bed and called to her husband.

'Come!' she said. 'Come to the old hall! I know where the gold comes from! I want to see it grow!'

Geoffrey would fain have stopped her, but he feared for her life or reason on the one hand, and lest in a paroxysm she should shriek out her terrible suspicion, and seeing that it was useless to try to prevent her, wrapped a warm rug around her and went with her to the old hall. When they entered, she turned and shut the door and locked it.

'We want no strangers amongst us three tonight!' she whispered with a wan smile.

'We three! nay we are but two,' said Geoffrey with a shudder; he feared to say more.

'Sit here,' said his wife as she put out the light. 'Sit here by the hearth and watch the gold growing. The silver moonlight is jealous! See, it steals along the floor towards the gold – our gold!' Geoffrey looked with growing horror, and saw that during the hours that had passed the golden hair had protruded further through the broken hearth-stone. He tried to hide it by placing his feet over the broken place; and his wife, drawing her chair beside him, leant over and laid her head on his shoulder.

'Now do not stir, dear,' she said; 'let us sit still and watch. We shall find the secret of the growing gold!' He passed his arm round her and sat silent; and as the moonlight stole along the floor she sank to sleep.

He feared to wake her; and so sat silent and miserable as the hours stole away.

Before his horror-struck eyes the golden hair from the broken stone grew and grew; and as it increased, so his heart got colder and colder, till at last he had not power to stir, and sat with eyes full of terror watching his doom.

* * *

In the morning when the London doctor came, neither Geoffrey nor his wife could be found. Search was made in all the rooms, but without avail. As a last resource the great door of the old hall was broken open, and those who entered saw a grim and sorry sight.

There by the deserted hearth Geoffrey Brent and his young wife sat cold and white and dead. Her face was peaceful, and her eyes were closed in sleep; but his face was a sight that made all who saw it shudder, for there was on it a look of unutterable horror. The eyes were open and stared glassily at his feet, which were twined with tresses of golden hair, streaked with grey, which came through the broken hearth-stone.

The Gypsy Prophecy

'I really think,' said the Doctor, 'that, at any rate, one of us should go and try whether or not the thing is an imposture.'

'Good!' said Considine. 'After dinner we will take our cigars and stroll over to the camp.'

Accordingly, when the dinner was over, and the *La Tour* finished, Joshua Considine and his friend, Dr Burleigh, went over to the east side of the moor, where the gypsy encampment lay. As they were leaving, Mary Considine, who had walked as far as the end of the garden where it opened into the laneway, called after her husband: 'Mind, Joshua, you are to give them a fair chance, but don't give them any clue to a fortune – and don't you get flirting with any of the gypsy maidens – and take care to keep Gerald out of harm.'

For answer Considine held up his hand, as if taking a stage oath, and whistled the air of the old song, 'The Gypsy Countess'. Gerald joined in the strain, and then, breaking into merry laughter, the two men passed along the laneway to the common, turning now and then to wave their hands to Mary, who leaned over the gate, in the twilight, looking after them.

It was a lovely evening in the summer; the very air was full of rest and quiet happiness, as though an outward type of the peacefulness and joy which made a heaven of the home of the young married folk. Considine's life had not been an eventful one. The only disturbing element which he had ever known was in his wooing of Mary Winston, and the long-continued objection of her ambitious parents, who expected a brilliant match for their only daughter. When Mr and Mrs Winston had discovered the attachment of the young barrister, they had tried to keep the young people apart by sending their daughter away for a long round of visits, having made her promise not to correspond with her lover during her absence. Love, however, had stood the test. Neither absence nor neglect seemed to cool the passion of the young man, and jealousy seemed a thing unknown to his sanguine nature; so, after a long period of waiting, the parents had given in, and the young folk were married.

They had been living in the cottage a few months, and were just beginning to feel at home. Gerald Burleigh, Joshua's old college chum, and himself a sometime victim of Mary's beauty, had arrived a week before, to stay with them for as long a time as he could tear himself away from his work in London.

When her husband had quite disappeared Mary went into the house, and, sitting down at the piano, gave an hour to Mendelssohn.

It was but a short walk across the common, and before the cigars required renewing the two men had reached the gypsy camp. The place was as picturesque as gypsy camps – when in villages and when business is good – usually are. There were some few persons round the fire, investing their money in prophecy, and a large number of others, poorer or more parsimonious, who stayed just outside the bounds but near enough to see all that went on.

As the two gentlemen approached, the villagers, who knew Joshua, made way a little, and a pretty, keen-eyed gypsy girl tripped up and asked to tell their fortunes. Joshua held out his hand, but the girl, without seeming to see it, stared at his face in a very odd manner. Gerald nudged him: 'You must cross her hand with silver,' he said. 'It is one of the most important parts of the mystery.'

Joshua took from his pocket a half-crown and held it out to her, but, without looking at it, she answered: 'You have to cross the gypsy's hand with gold.'

Gerald laughed. 'You are at a premium as a subject,' he said. Joshua was of the kind of man – the universal kind – who can tolerate being stared at by a pretty girl; so, with some little deliberation, he answered: 'All right; here you are, my pretty girl; but you must give me a real good fortune for it,' and he handed her a half-sovereign, which she took, saying: 'It is not for me to give good fortune or bad, but only to read what the Stars have said.' She took his right hand and turned it palm upward; but the instant her eyes met it she dropped it as though it had been red hot, and, with a startled look, glided swiftly away. Lifting the curtain of the large tent, which occupied the centre of the camp, she disappeared within.

'Sold again!' said the cynical Gerald. Joshua stood a little amazed, and not altogether satisfied. They both watched the large tent. In a few moments there emerged from the opening not the young girl, but a stately looking woman of middle age and commanding presence.

The instant she appeared the whole camp seemed to stand still. The clamour of tongues, the laughter and noise of the work were, for a second or two, arrested, and every man or woman who sat, or crouched, or lay, stood up and faced the imperial-looking gypsy.

'The Queen, of course,' murmured Gerald. 'We are in luck tonight.'

The gypsy Queen threw a searching glance around the camp, and then, without hesitating an instant, came straight over and stood before Joshua.

'Hold out your hand,' she said in a commanding tone.

Again Gerald spoke, *sotto voce*: 'I have not been spoken to in that way since I was at school.'

'Your hand must be crossed with gold.'

'A hundred per cent, at this game,' whispered Gerald, as Joshua laid another half-sovereign on his upturned palm.

The gypsy looked at the hand with knitted brows; then suddenly looking up into his face, said: 'Have you a strong will – have you a true heart that can be brave for one you love?'

'I hope so; but I am afraid I have not vanity enough to say "yes".'

'Then I will answer for you; for I read resolution in your face – resolution desperate and determined if need be. You have a wife you love?'

'Yes,' emphatically.

'Then leave her at once – never see her face again. Go from her now, while love is fresh and your heart is free from wicked intent. Go quick – go far, and never see her face again!'

Joshua drew away his hand quickly, and said, 'Thank you!' stiffly but sarcastically, as he began to move away.

'I say!' said Gerald, 'you're not going like that, old man; no use in being indignant with the Stars or their prophet – and, moreover, your sovereign – what of it? At least, hear the matter out.'

'Silence, ribald!' commanded the Queen, 'you know not what you do. Let him go – and go ignorant, if he will not be warned.'

Joshua immediately turned back. 'At all events, we will see this thing out,' he said. 'Now, madam, you have given me advice, but I paid for a fortune.'

'Be warned!' said the gypsy. 'The Stars have been silent for long; let the mystery still wrap them round.'

'My dear madam, I do not get within touch of a mystery every day, and I prefer for my money knowledge rather than ignorance. I can get the latter commodity for nothing when I want any of it.'

Gerald echoed the sentiment. 'As for me I have a large and un-saleable stock on hand.'

The gypsy Queen eyed the two men sternly, and then said: 'As you wish. You have chosen for yourself, and have met warning with scorn, and appeal with levity. On your own heads be the doom!'

'Amen!' said Gerald.

With an imperious gesture the Queen took Joshua's hand again, and began to tell his fortune.

'I see here the flowing of blood; it will flow before long; it is running in my sight. It flows through the broken circle of a severed ring.'

'Go on!' said Joshua, smiling. Gerald was silent.

'Must I speak plainer?'

'Certainly; we commonplace mortals want something definite. The Stars are a long way off, and their words get somewhat dulled in the message.'

The gypsy shuddered, and then spoke impressively. 'This is the hand of a murderer – the murderer of his wife!' She dropped the hand and turned away.

Joshua laughed. 'Do you know,' said he, 'I think if I were you I should prophesy some jurisprudence into my system. For instance, you say "this hand is the hand of a murderer". Well, whatever it may be in the future – or potentially – it is at present not one. You ought to give your prophecy in such terms as "the hand which will be a murderer's", or, rather, "the hand of one who will be the murderer of his wife". The Stars are really not good on technical questions.'

The gypsy made no reply of any kind, but, with drooping head and despondent mien, walked slowly to her tent, and, lifting the curtain, disappeared.

Without speaking the two men turned homewards, and walked across the moor. Presently, after some little hesitation, Gerald spoke: 'Of course, old man, this is all a joke; a ghastly one, but still a joke. But would it not be well to keep it to ourselves?'

'How do you mean?'

'Well, not tell your wife. It might alarm her.'

'Alarm her! My dear Gerald, what are you thinking of? Why, she would not be alarmed or afraid of me if all the gypsies that ever didn't come from Bohemia agreed that I was to murder her, or even to have a hard thought of her, whilst so long as she was saying "Jack Robinson". '

Gerald remonstrated. 'Old fellow, women are superstitious – far more than we men are; and, also they are blessed – or cursed – with a nervous system to which we are strangers. I see too much of it in my work not to realise it. Take my advice and do not let her know, or you will frighten her.'

Joshua's lips unconsciously hardened as he answered: 'My dear fellow, I would not have a secret from my wife. Why, it would be the beginning of a new order of things between us. We have no secrets from each other. If we ever have, then you may begin to look out for something odd between us.'

'Still,' said Gerald, 'at the risk of unwelcome interference, I say again be warned in time.'

'The gypsy's very words,' said Joshua. 'You and she seem quite of one accord. Tell me, old man, is this a put-up thing? You told me of the gypsy camp – did you arrange it all with Her Majesty?' This was said with an air of bantering earnestness. Gerald assured him that he only heard of the camp that morning; but he made fun of every answer of his friend, and, in the process of this raillery, the time passed, and they entered the cottage.

Mary was sitting at the piano but not playing. The dim twilight had waked some very tender feelings in her breast, and her eyes were full of gentle tears. When the men came in she stole over to her husband's side and kissed him. Joshua struck a tragic attitude.

'Mary,' he said in a deep voice, 'before you approach me, listen to the words of Fate. The Stars have spoken and the doom is sealed.'

'What is it, dear? Tell me the fortune, but do not frighten me.'

'Not at all, my dear; but there is a truth which it is well that you should know. Nay, it is necessary so that all your arrangements can be made beforehand, and everything be decently done and in order.'

'Go on, dear; I am listening.'

'Mary Considine, your effigy may yet be seen at Madame Tussaud's. The juris-imprudent Stars have announced their fell tidings that this hand is red with blood – your blood. Mary! Mary! my God!' He sprang forward, but too late to catch her as she fell fainting on the floor.

'I told you,' said Gerald. 'You don't know them as well as I do.'

After a little while Mary recovered from her swoon, but only to fall into strong hysterics, in which she laughed and wept and raved and cried, 'Keep him from me – from me, Joshua, my husband,' and many other words of entreaty and of fear.

Joshua Considine was in a state of mind bordering on agony, and when at last Mary became calm he knelt by her and kissed her feet and hands and hair and called her all the sweet names and said all the tender things his lips could frame. All that night he sat by her bedside and held her hand. Far through the night and up to the early morning she kept waking from sleep and crying out as if in fear, till she was comforted by the consciousness that her husband was watching beside her.

Breakfast was late the next morning, but during it Joshua received a telegram which required him to drive over to Withering, nearly twenty miles. He was loth to go; but Mary would not hear of his remaining, and so before noon he drove off in his dog-cart alone.

When he was gone Mary retired to her room. She did not appear at lunch, but when afternoon tea was served on the lawn under the great weeping willow, she came to join her guest. She was looking quite recovered from her illness of the evening before. After some casual remarks, she said to Gerald: 'Of course it was very silly about last night, but I could not help feeling frightened. Indeed I would feel so still if I let myself think of it. But, after all these people may only imagine things, and I have got a test that can hardly fail to show that the prediction is false – if indeed it be false,' she added sadly.

'What is your plan?' asked Gerald.

'I shall go myself to the gypsy camp, and have my fortune told by the Queen.'

'Capital. May I go with you?'

'Oh, no! That would spoil it. She might know you and guess at me, and suit her utterance accordingly. I shall go alone this afternoon.'

When the afternoon was gone Mary Considine took her way to the gypsy encampment. Gerald went with her as far as the near edge of the common, and returned alone.

Half-an-hour had hardly elapsed when Mary entered the drawing-room, where he lay on a sofa reading. She was ghastly pale and was in a state of extreme excitement. Hardly had she passed over the threshold when she collapsed and sank moaning on the carpet. Gerald rushed to aid her, but by a great effort she controlled herself and motioned him to be silent. He waited, and his ready attention to her wish seemed to be her best help, for, in a few minutes, she had somewhat recovered, and was able to tell him what had passed.

'When I got to the camp,' she said, 'there did not seem to be a soul about. I went into the centre and stood there. Suddenly a tall woman stood beside me. "Something told me I was wanted!" she said. I held out my hand and laid a piece of silver on it. She took from her neck a small golden trinket and laid it there also; and then, seizing the two, threw them into the stream that ran by. Then she took my hand in hers and spoke: "Naught but blood in this guilty place," and turned away. I caught hold of her and asked her to tell me more. After some hesitation, she said: "Alas! alas! I see you lying at your husband's feet, and his hands are red with blood." '

Gerald did not feel at all at ease, and tried to laugh it off. 'Surely,' he said, 'this woman has a craze about murder.'

'Do not laugh,' said Mary, 'I cannot bear it,' and then, as if with a sudden impulse, she left the room.

Not long after Joshua returned, bright and cheery, and as hungry as a hunter after his long drive. His presence cheered his wife, who seemed much brighter, but she did not mention the episode of the visit to the gypsy camp, so Gerald did not mention it either. As if by tacit consent the subject was not alluded to during the evening. But there was a strange, settled look on Mary's face, which Gerald could not but observe.

In the morning Joshua came down to breakfast later than usual. Mary had been up and about the house from an early hour; but as the time drew on she seemed to get a little nervous and now and again threw around an anxious look.

Gerald could not help noticing that none of those at breakfast could get on satisfactorily with their food. It was not altogether that the chops were tough, but that the knives were all so blunt. Being a guest, he, of course, made no sign; but presently saw Joshua draw his thumb across the edge of his knife in an unconscious sort of way. At the action Mary turned pale and almost fainted.

After breakfast they all went out on the lawn. Mary was making up a bouquet, and said to her husband, 'Get me a few of the tea-roses, dear.'

Joshua pulled down a cluster from the front of the house. The stem bent, but was too tough to break. He put his hand in his pocket to get his knife; but in vain. 'Lend me your knife, Gerald,' he said. But Gerald had not got one, so he went into the breakfast room and took one from the table. He came out feeling its edge and grumbling. 'What on earth has happened to all the knives – the edges seem all ground off?' Mary turned away hurriedly and entered the house.

Joshua tried to sever the stalk with the blunt knife as country cooks sever the necks of fowl – as schoolboys cut twine. With a little effort he finished the task. The cluster of roses grew thick, so he determined to gather a great bunch.

He could not find a single sharp knife in the sideboard where the cutlery was kept, so he called Mary, and when she came, told her the state of things. She looked so agitated and so miserable that he could not help knowing the truth, and, as if astounded and hurt, asked her: 'Do you mean to say that *you* have done it?'

She broke in, 'Oh, Joshua, I was so afraid.'

He paused, and a set, white look came over his face. 'Mary!' said he, 'is this all the trust you have in me? I would not have believed it.'

'Oh, Joshua! Joshua!' she cried entreatingly, 'forgive me,' and wept bitterly.

Joshua thought a moment and then said: 'I see how it is. We shall better end this or we shall all go mad.'

He ran into the drawing-room.

'Where are you going?' almost screamed Mary.

Gerald saw what he meant – that he would not be tied to blunt instruments by the force of a superstition, and was not surprised when he saw him come out through the French window, bearing in his hand a large Ghourka knife, which usually lay on the centre table, and which his brother had sent him from Northern India. It was one of those great hunting-knives which worked such havoc, at close quarters with the enemies of the loyal Ghourkas during the mutiny, of great weight but so evenly balanced in the hand as to seem light, and with an edge like a razor. With one of these knives a Ghourka can cut a sheep in two.

When Mary saw him come out of the room with the weapon in his hand she screamed in an agony of fright, and the hysterics of last night were promptly renewed.

Joshua ran toward her, and, seeing her falling, threw down the knife and tried to catch her.

However, he was just a second too late, and the two men cried out in horror simultaneously as they saw her fall upon the naked blade.

When Gerald rushed over he found that in falling her left hand had struck the blade, which lay partly upwards on the grass. Some of the small veins were cut through, and the blood gushed freely from the wound. As he was tying it up he pointed out to Joshua that the wedding ring was severed by the steel.

They carried her fainting to the house. When, after a while, she came out, with her arm in a sling, she was peaceful in her mind and happy. She said to her husband: 'The gypsy was wonderfully near the truth; too near for the real thing ever to occur now, dear.'

Joshua bent over and kissed the wounded hand.

The Coming of Abel Behenna

The little Cornish port of Pencastle was bright in the early April, when the sun had seemingly come to stay after a long and bitter winter. Boldly and blackly the rock stood out against a background of shaded blue, where the sky fading into mist met the far horizon. The sea was of true Cornish hue – sapphire, save where it became deep emerald green in the fathomless depths under the cliffs, where the seal caves opened their grim jaws. On the slopes the grass was parched and brown. The spikes of furze bushes were ashy grey, but the golden yellow of their flowers streamed along the hillside, dipping out in lines as the rock cropped up, and lessening into patches and dots till finally it died away all together where the sea winds swept round the jutting cliffs and cut short the vegetation as though with ever-working aerial shears. The whole hillside, with its body of brown and flashes of yellow, was just like a colossal yellow-hammer.

The little harbour opened from the sea between towering cliffs, and behind a lonely rock, pierced with many caves and blow-holes through which the sea in storm time sent its thunderous voice, together with a fountain of drifting spume. Hence, it wound west-wards in a serpentine course, guarded at its entrance by two little curving piers to left and right. These were roughly built of dark slates placed endways and held together with great beams bound with iron bands. Thence, it flowed up the rocky bed of the stream whose winter torrents had of old cut out its way amongst the hills. This stream was deep at first, with here and there, where it widened, patches of broken rock exposed at low water, full of holes where crabs and lobsters were to be found at the ebb of the tide. From amongst the rocks rose sturdy posts, used for warping in the little coasting vessels which frequented the port. Higher up, the stream still flowed deeply, for the tide ran far inland, but always calmly for all the force of the wildest storm was broken below. Some quarter mile inland the stream was deep at high water, but at low tide there were at each side patches of the same broken rock as lower down, through the chinks of which the sweet water of the natural stream trickled and murmured after the tide had ebbed away. Here, too, rose mooring posts for the fishermen's boats. At either side of the river was a row of cottages down almost on the level of high tide. They were pretty cottages, strongly and snugly built, with trim narrow gardens in front, full of old-fashioned plants, flowering currants, coloured primroses, wallflower, and stonecrop. Over the fronts of many of them climbed clematis and wisteria. The window sides and door posts of all were as white as snow, and the little pathway to each was paved with light coloured stones. At some of the doors were tiny porches, whilst at others were rustic seats cut from tree trunks or from old barrels; in nearly every case the window ledges were filled with boxes or pots of flowers or foliage plants.

Two men lived in cottages exactly opposite each other across the stream. Two men, both young, both good-looking, both prosperous, and who had been companions and rivals from their boyhood. Abel Behenna was dark with the gypsy darkness which the Phoenician mining wanderers left in their track; Eric Sanson – which the local antiquarian said was a corruption of Sagamanson – was fair, with the ruddy hue which marked the path of the wild Norseman. These two seemed to have singled out each other from the very beginning to work and strive together, to fight for each other and to stand back to back in all endeavours. They had now put the coping-stone on their Temple of Unity by falling in love with the same girl. Sarah Trefusis was certainly the prettiest girl in Pencastle, and there was many a young man who would gladly have tried his fortune with her, but that there were two to contend against, and each of these the strongest and most resolute man in the port – except the other. The average young man thought that this was very hard, and on account of it bore no good will to either of the three principals: whilst the average young woman who had, lest worse should befall, to put up with the grumbling of her sweetheart, and the sense of being only second best which it implied, did not either, be sure, regard Sarah with friendly eye. Thus it came, in the course of a year or so, for rustic courtship is a slow process, that the two men and woman found themselves thrown much together. They were all satisfied, so it did not matter, and Sarah, who was vain and something frivolous, took care to have her revenge on both men and women in a quiet way. When a young woman in her 'walking out' can only boast one not-quite-satisfied young man, it is no particular pleasure to her to see her escort cast sheep's eyes at a better-looking girl supported by two devoted swains.

At length there came a time which Sarah dreaded, and which she had tried to keep distant – the time when she had to make her choice between the two men. She liked them both, and, indeed, either of them might have satisfied the ideas of even a more exacting girl. But her mind was so constituted that she thought more of what she might lose, than of what she might gain; and whenever she thought she had made up her mind she became instantly assailed with doubts as to the wisdom of her choice. Always the man whom she had presumably lost became endowed afresh with a newer and more bountiful crop of advantages than had ever arisen from the possibility of his acceptance. She promised each man that on her birthday she would give him his answer, and that day, the 11th of April, had now arrived. The promises had been given singly and confidentially, but each was given to a man who was not likely to forget. Early in the morning she found both men hovering round her door. Neither had taken the other into his confidence, and each was simply seeking an early opportunity of getting his answer, and advancing his suit if necessary. Damon, as a rule, does not take Pythias with him when making a proposal; and in the heart of each man his own affairs had a claim far above any requirements of friendship. So, throughout the day, they kept seeing each other out. The position was doubtless somewhat embarrassing to Sarah, and though the satisfaction of her vanity that she should be thus adored was very pleasing, yet there were moments when she was annoyed with both men for being so persistent. Her only consolation at such moments was that she saw, through the elaborate smiles of the other girls when in passing they noticed her door thus doubly guarded, the jealousy which filled their hearts. Sarah's mother was a person of commonplace and sordid ideas, and, seeing all along the state of affairs, her one intention, persistently expressed to her daughter in the plainest words, was to so arrange matters that Sarah should get all that was possible out of both men. With this purpose she had cunningly kept herself as far as possible in the background in the matter of her daughter's wooings, and watched in silence. At first Sarah had been indignant with her for her sordid views; but, as usual, her weak nature gave way before persistence, and she had now got to the stage of acceptance. She was not surprised when her mother whispered to her in the little yard behind the house: 'Go up the hillside for a while; I want to talk to these two. They're both red-hot for ye, and now's the time to get things fixed!' Sarah began a feeble remonstrance, but her mother cut her short.

'I tell ye, girl, that my mind is made up! Both these men want ye, and only one can have ye, but before ye choose it'll be so arranged that ye'll have all that both have got! Don't argy, child! Go up the hillside, and when ye come back I'll have it fixed – I see a way quite easy!' So Sarah went up the hillside through the narrow paths between the golden furze, and Mrs Trefusis joined the two men in the living-room of the little house.

She opened the attack with the desperate courage which is in all mothers when they think for their children, howsoever mean the thoughts may be.

'Ye two men, ye're both in love with my Sarah!'

Their bashful silence gave consent to the barefaced proposition. She went on.

'Neither of ye has much!' Again they tacitly acquiesced in the soft impeachment.

'I don't know that either of ye could keep a wife!' Though neither said a word their looks and bearing expressed distinct dissent. Mrs Trefusis went on: 'But if ye'd put what ye both have together ye'd make a comfortable home for one of ye – and Sarah!' She eyed the men keenly, with her cunning eyes half shut, as she spoke; then satisfied from her scrutiny that the idea was accepted she went on quickly, as if to prevent argument: 'The girl likes ye both, and mayhap it's hard for her to choose. Why don't ye toss up for her? First put your money together – ye've each got a bit put by, I know. Let the lucky man take the lot and trade with it a bit, and then come home and marry her. Neither of ye's afraid, I suppose! And neither of ye'll say that he won't do that much for the girl that ye both say ye love!'

Abel broke the silence: 'It don't seem the square thing to toss for the girl! She wouldn't like it herself, and it doesn't seem – seem respectful like to her – '

Eric interrupted. He was conscious that his chance was not so good as Abel's in case Sarah should wish to choose between them: 'Are ye afraid of the hazard?'

'Not me!' said Abel, boldly. Mrs Trefusis, seeing that her idea was beginning to work, followed up the advantage.

'It is settled that ye put yer money together to make a home for her, whether ye toss for her or leave it for her to choose?'

'Yes,' said Eric quickly, and Abel agreed with equal sturdiness. Mrs Trefusis' little cunning eyes twinkled. She heard Sarah's step in the yard, and said: 'Well! here she comes, and I leave it to her.' And she went out.

During her brief walk on the hillside Sarah had been trying to make up her mind. She was feeling almost angry with both men for being the cause of her difficulty, and as she came into the room said shortly: 'I want to have a word with you both – come to the Flagstaff Rock, where we can be alone.' She took her hat and went out of the house up the winding path to the steep rock crowned with a high flagstaff, where once the wreckers' fire basket used to burn. This was the rock which formed the northern jaw of the little harbour. There was only room on the path for two abreast, and it marked the state of things pretty well when, by a sort of implied arrangement, Sarah went first, and the two men followed, walking abreast and keeping step. By this time, each man's heart was boiling with jealousy. When they came to the top of the rock, Sarah stood against the flagstaff, and the two young men stood opposite her. She had chosen her position with knowledge and intention, for there was no room for anyone to stand beside her.

They were all silent for a while; then Sarah began to laugh and said: 'I promised the both of you to give you an answer today. I've been thinking and thinking and thinking, till I began to get angry with you both for plaguing me so; and even now I don't seem any nearer than ever I was to making up my mind.'

Eric said suddenly: 'Let us toss for it, lass!'

Sarah showed no indignation whatever at the proposition; her mother's eternal suggestion had schooled her to the acceptance of something of the kind, and her weak nature made it easy to her to grasp at any way out of the difficulty. She stood with downcast eyes idly picking at the sleeve of her dress, seeming to have tacitly acquiesced in the proposal. Both men instinctively realising this pulled each a coin from his pocket, spun it in the air, and dropped his other hand over the palm on which it lay. For a few seconds they remained thus, all silent; then Abel, who was the more thoughtful of the men, spoke: 'Sarah! is this good?' As he spoke he removed the upper hand from the coin and placed the latter back in his pocket. Sarah was nettled.

'Good or bad, it's good enough for me! Take it or leave it as you like,' she said, to which he replied quickly: 'Nay lass! Aught that concerns you is good enow for me. I did but think of you lest you might have pain or disappointment hereafter. If you love Eric better nor me, in God's name say so, and I think I'm man enow to stand aside. Likewise, if I'm the one, don't make us both miserable for life!' Face to face with a difficulty, Sarah's weak nature proclaimed itself; she put her hands before her face and began to cry, saying: 'It was my mother. She keeps telling me!'

The silence which followed was broken by Eric, who said hotly to Abel: 'Let the lass alone, can't you? If she wants to choose this way, let her. It's good enough for me – and for you, too! She's said it now, and must abide by it!'

Hereupon Sarah turned upon him in sudden fury, and cried: 'Hold your tongue! what is it to you, at any rate?' and she resumed her crying. Eric was so flabbergasted that he had not a word to say, but stood looking particularly foolish, with his mouth open and his hands held out with the coin still between them. All were silent till Sarah, taking her hands from her face laughed hysterically and said: 'As you two can't make up your minds, I'm going home!' and she turned to go.

'Stop,' said Abel, in an authoritative voice. 'Eric, you hold the coin, and I'll cry. Now, before we settle it, let us clearly understand: the man who wins takes all the money that we both have got, brings it to Bristol and ships on a voyage and trades with it. Then he comes back and marries Sarah, and they two keep all, whatever there may be, as the result of the trading. Is this what we understand?'

'Yes,' said Eric.

'I'll marry him on my next birthday,' said Sarah. Having said it the intolerably mercenary spirit of her action seemed to strike her, and impulsively she turned away with a bright blush. Fire seemed to sparkle in the eyes of both men. Said Eric: 'A year so be! The man that wins is to have one year.'

'Toss!' cried Abel, and the coin spun in the air. Eric caught it, and again held it between his outstretched hands.

'Heads!' cried Abel, a pallor sweeping over his face as he spoke. As he leaned forward to look Sarah leaned forward too, and their heads almost touched. He could feel her hair blowing on his cheek, and it thrilled through him like fire. Eric lifted his upper band; the coin lay with its head up. Abel stepped forward and took Sarah in his arms. With a curse Eric hurled the coin far into the sea. Then he leaned against the flagstaff and scowled at the others with his hands thrust deep into his pockets. Abel whispered wild words of passion and delight into Sarah's ears, and as she listened she began to believe that fortune had rightly interpreted the wishes of her secret heart, and that she loved Abel best.

Presently Abel looked up and caught sight of Eric's face as the last ray of sunset struck it. The red light intensified the natural ruddiness of his complexion, and he looked as though he were steeped in blood. Abel did not mind his scowl, for now that his own heart was at rest he could feel unalloyed pity for his friend. He stepped over meaning to comfort him, and held out his hand, saying: 'It was my chance, old lad. Don't grudge it me. I'll try to make Sarah a happy woman, and you shall be a brother to us both!'

'Brother be damned!' was all the answer Eric made, as he turned away. When he had gone a few steps down the rocky path he turned and came back. Standing before Abel and Sarah, who had their arms round each other, he said: 'You have a year. Make the most of it! And be sure you're in time to claim your wife! Be back to have your banns up in time to be married on the 11th April. If you're not, I tell you I shall have my banns up, and you may get back too late.'

'What do you mean, Eric? You are mad!'

'No more mad than you are, Abel Behenna. You go, that's your chance! I stay, that's mine! I don't mean to let the grass grow under my feet. Sarah cared no more for you than for me five minutes ago, and she may come back to that five minutes after you're gone! You won by a point only – the game may change.'

'The game won't change!' said Abel shortly. 'Sarah, you'll be true to me? You won't marry till I return?'

'For a year!' added Eric, quickly, 'that's the bargain.'

'I promise for the year,' said Sarah. A dark look came over Abel's face, and he was about to speak, but he mastered himself and smiled.

'I mustn't be too hard or get angry tonight! Come, Eric! we played and fought together. I won fairly. I played fairly all the game of our wooing! You know that as well as I do; and now when I am going away, I shall look to my old and true comrade to help me when I am gone!'

'I'll help you none,' said Eric, 'so help me God!'

'It was God helped me,' said Abel simply.

'Then let Him go on helping you,' said Eric angrily. 'The Devil is good enough for me!' and without another word he rushed down the steep path and disappeared behind the rocks.

When he had gone Abel hoped for some tender passage with Sarah, but the first remark she made chilled him.

'How lonely it all seems without Eric!' and this note sounded till he had left her at home – and after.

Early on the next morning Abel heard a noise at his door, and on going out saw Eric walking rapidly away: a small canvas bag full of gold and silver lay on the threshold; on a small slip of paper pinned to it was written: 'Take the money and go. I stay. God for you! The Devil for me! Remember the 11th of April. ERIC SANSON'.

That afternoon Abel went off to Bristol, and a week later sailed on the *Star of the Sea* bound for Pahang. His money – including that which had been Eric's – was on board in the shape of a venture of cheap toys. He had been advised by a shrewd old mariner of Bristol whom he knew, and who knew the ways of the Chersonese, who predicted that every penny invested would be returned with a shilling to boot.

As the year wore on Sarah became more and more disturbed in her mind. Eric was always at hand to make love to her in his own persistent, masterful manner, and to this she did not object. Only one letter came from Abel, to say that his venture had proved successful, and that he had sent some two hundred pounds to the bank at Bristol, and was trading with fifty pounds still remaining in goods for China, whither the *Star of the Sea* was bound and whence she would return to Bristol. He suggested that Eric's share of the venture should be returned to him with his share of the profits. This proposition was treated with anger by Eric, and as simply childish by Sarah's mother.

More than six months had since then elapsed, but no other letter had come, and Eric's hopes which had been dashed down by the letter from Pahang, began to rise again. He perpetually assailed Sarah with an 'if!' If Abel did not return, would she then marry him? If the 11th April went by without Abel being in the port, would she give him over? If Abel had taken his fortune, and married another girl on the head of it, would she marry him, Eric, as soon as the truth were known? And so on in an endless variety of possibilities. The power of the strong will and the determined purpose over the woman's weaker nature became in time manifest. Sarah began to lose her faith in Abel and to regard Eric as a possible husband; and a possible husband is in a woman's eye different to all other men. A new affection for him began to arise in her breast, and the daily familiarities of permitted courtship furthered the growing affection. Sarah began to regard Abel as rather a rock in the road of her life, and had it not been for her mother's constantly reminding her of the good fortune already laid by in the Bristol Bank she would have tried to have shut her eyes altogether to the fact of Abel's existence.

The 11th April was Saturday, so that in order to have the marriage on that day it would be necessary that the banns should be called on Sunday, 22nd March. From the beginning of that month Eric kept perpetually on the subject of Abel's absence, and his outspoken opinion that the latter was either dead or married began to become a reality to the woman's mind. As the first half of the month wore on Eric became more jubilant, and after church on the 15th he took Sarah for a walk to the Flagstaff Rock. There he asserted himself strongly: 'I told Abel, and you too, that if he was not here to put up his banns in time for the eleventh, I would put up mine for the twelfth. Now the time has come when I mean to do it. He hasn't kept his word' – here Sarah struck in out of her weakness and indecision: 'He hasn't broken it yet!' Eric ground his teeth with anger.

'If you mean to stick up for him,' he said, as he smote his hands savagely on the flagstaff, which sent forth a shivering murmur, 'well and good. I'll keep my part of the bargain. On Sunday I shall give notice of the banns, and you can deny them in the church if you will. If Abel is in Pencastle on the eleventh, he can have them cancelled, and his own put up; but till then, I take my course, and woe to anyone who stands in my way!' With that he flung himself down the rocky pathway, and Sarah could not but admire his Viking strength and spirit, as, crossing the hill, he strode away along the cliffs towards Bude.

During the week no news was heard of Abel, and on Saturday Eric gave notice of the banns of marriage between himself and Sarah Trefusis. The clergyman would have remonstrated with him, for although nothing formal had been told to the neighbours, it had been understood since Abel's departure that on his return he was to marry Sarah; but Eric would not discuss the question.

'It is a painful subject, sir,' he said with a firmness which the parson, who was a very young man, could not but be swayed by. 'Surely there is nothing against Sarah or me. Why should there be any bones made about the matter?' The parson said no more, and on the next day he read out the banns for the first time amidst an audible buzz from the congregation. Sarah was present, contrary to custom, and though she blushed furiously enjoyed her triumph over the other girls whose banns had not yet come. Before the week was over she began to make her wedding dress. Eric used to come and look at her at work and the sight thrilled through him. He used to say all sorts of pretty things to her at such times, and there were to both delicious moments of love-making.

The banns were read a second time on the 29th, and Eric's hope grew more and more fixed though there were to him moments of acute despair when he realised that the cup of happiness might be dashed from his lips at any moment, right up to the last. At such times he was full of passion – desperate and remorseless – and he ground his teeth and clenched his hands in a wild way as though some taint of the old Berserker fury of his ancestors still lingered in his blood. On the Thursday of that week he looked in on Sarah and found her, amid a flood of sunshine, putting finishing touches to her white wedding gown. His own heart was full of gaiety, and the sight of the woman who was so soon to be his own so occupied, filled him with a joy unspeakable, and he felt faint with languorous ecstasy. Bending over he kissed Sarah on the mouth, and then whispered in her rosy ear – 'Your wedding dress, Sarah! And for me!'

As he drew back to admire her she looked up saucily, and said to him – 'Perhaps not for you. There is more than a week yet for Abel!' and then cried out in dismay, for with a wild gesture and a fierce oath Eric dashed out of the house, banging the door behind him. The incident disturbed Sarah more than she could have thought possible, for it awoke all her fears and doubts and indecision afresh. She cried a little, and put by her dress, and to soothe herself went out to sit for a while on the summit of the Flagstaff Rock. When she arrived she found there a little group anxiously discussing the weather. The sea was calm and the sun bright, but across the sea were strange lines of darkness and light, and close in to shore the rocks were fringed with foam, which spread out in great white curves and circles as the currents drifted. The wind had backed, and came in sharp, cold puffs. The blow-hole, which ran under the Flagstaff Rock, from the rocky bay without to the harbour within, was booming at intervals, and the seagulls were screaming ceaselessly as they wheeled about the entrance of the port.

'It looks bad,' she heard an old fisherman say to the coastguard. 'I seen it just like this once before, when the East Indiaman *Coromandel* went to pieces in Dizzard Bay!' Sarah did not wait to hear more. She was of a timid nature where danger was concerned, and could not bear to hear of wrecks and disasters. She went home and resumed the completion of her dress, secretly determined to appease Eric when she should meet him with a sweet apology – and to take the earliest opportunity of being even with him after her marriage.

The old fisherman's weather prophecy was justified. That night at dusk a wild storm came on. The sea rose and lashed the western coasts from Skye to Scilly and left a tale of disaster everywhere. The sailors and fishermen of Pencastle all turned out on the rocks and cliffs and watched eagerly. Presently, by a flash of lightning, a 'ketch' was seen drifting under only a jib about half-a-mile outside the port. All eyes and all glasses were concentrated on her, waiting for the next flash, and when it came a chorus went up that it was the *Lovely Alice*, trading between Bristol and Penzance, and touching at all the little ports between. 'God help them!' said the harbour-master, 'for nothing in this world can save them when they are between Bude and Tintagel and the wind on shore!' The coastguards exerted themselves, and, aided by brave hearts and willing hands, they brought the rocket apparatus up on the summit of the Flagstaff Rock. Then they burned blue lights so that those on board might see the harbour opening in case they could make any effort to reach it. They worked gallantly enough on board; but no skill or strength of man could avail. Before many minutes were over the *Lovely Alice* rushed to her doom on the great island rock that guarded the mouth of the port. The screams of those on board were faintly borne on the tempest as they flung themselves into the sea in a last chance for life. The blue lights were kept burning, and eager eyes peered into the depths of the waters in case any face could be seen; and ropes were held ready to fling out in aid. But never a face was seen, and the willing arms rested idle. Eric was there amongst his fellows. His old Icelandic origin was never more apparent than in that wild hour. He took a rope, and shouted in the ear of the harbour-master: 'I shall go down on the rock over the seal cave. The tide is running up, and someone may drift in there!'

'Keep back, man!' came the answer. 'Are you mad? One slip on that rock and you are lost: and no man could keep his feet in the dark on such a place in such a tempest!'

'Not a bit,' came the reply. 'You remember how Abel Behenna saved me there on a night like this when my boat went on the Gull Rock. He dragged me up from the deep water in the seal cave, and now someone may drift in there again as I did,' and he was gone into the darkness. The projecting rock hid the light on the Flagstaff Rock, but he knew his way too well to miss it. His boldness and sureness of foot standing to him, he shortly stood on the great round-topped rock cut away beneath by the action of the waves over the entrance of the seal cave, where the water was fathomless. There he stood in comparative safety, for the concave shape of the rock beat back the waves with their own force, and though the water below him seemed to boil like a seething cauldron, just beyond the spot there was a space of almost calm. The rock, too, seemed here to shut off the sound of the gale, and he listened as well as watched. As he stood there ready, with his coil of rope poised to throw, he thought he heard below him, just beyond the whirl of the water, a faint, despairing cry. He echoed it with a shout that rang into the night. Then he waited for the flash of lightning, and as it passed flung his rope out into the darkness where he had seen a face rising through the swirl of the foam. The rope was caught, for he felt a pull on it, and he shouted again in his mighty voice: 'Tie it round your waist, and I shall pull you up.' Then when he felt that it was fast he moved along the rock to the far side of the sea cave, where the deep water was something stiller, and where he could get foothold secure enough to drag the rescued man on the overhanging rock. He began to pull, and shortly he knew from the rope taken in that the man he was now rescuing must soon be close to the top of the rock. He steadied himself for a moment, and drew a long breath, that he might at the next effort complete the rescue. He had just bent his back to the work when a flash of lightning revealed to each other the two men – the rescuer and the rescued.

Eric Sanson and Abel Behenna were face to face – and none knew of the meeting save themselves; and God.

On the instant a wave of passion swept through Eric's heart. All his hopes were shattered, and with the hatred of Cain his eyes looked out. He saw in the instant of recognition the joy in Abel's face that his was the hand to succour him, and this intensified his hate. Whilst the passion was on him he started back, and the rope ran out between his hands. His moment of hate was followed by an impulse of his better manhood, but it was too late.

Before he could recover himself, Abel, encumbered with the rope that should have aided him, was plunged with a despairing cry back into the darkness of the devouring sea.

Then, feeling all the madness and the doom of Cain upon him, Eric rushed back over the rocks, heedless of the danger and eager only for one thing – to be amongst other people whose living noises would shut out that last cry which seemed to ring still in his ears. When he regained the Flagstaff Rock the men surrounded him, and through the fury of the storm he heard the harbour-master say: 'We feared you were lost when we heard a cry! How white you are! Where is your rope? Was there anyone drifted in?'

'No one,' he shouted in answer, for he felt that he could never explain that he had let his old comrade slip back into the sea, and at the very place and under the very circumstances in which that comrade had saved his own life. He hoped by one bold lie to set the matter at rest for ever. There was no one to bear witness – and if he should have to carry that still white face in his eyes and that despairing cry in his ears for evermore – at least none should know of it. 'No one,' he cried, more loudly still. 'I slipped on the rock, and the rope fell into the sea!' So saying he left them, and, rushing down the steep path, gained his own cottage and locked himself within.

The remainder of that night he passed lying on his bed – dressed and motionless – staring upwards, and seeming to see through the darkness a pale face gleaming wet in the lightning, with its glad recognition turning to ghastly despair, and to hear a cry which never ceased to echo in his soul.

In the morning the storm was over and all was smiling again, except that the sea was still boisterous with its unspent fury. Great pieces of wreck drifted into the port, and the sea around the island rock was strewn with others. Two bodies also drifted into the harbour – one the master of the wrecked ketch, the other a strange seaman whom no one knew.

Sarah saw nothing of Eric till the evening, and then he only looked in for a minute. He did not come into the house, but simply put his head in through the open window.

'Well, Sarah,' he called out in a loud voice, though to her it did not ring truly, 'is the wedding dress done? Sunday week, mind! Sunday week!'

Sarah was glad to have the reconciliation so easy; but, womanlike, when she saw the storm was over and her own fears groundless, she at once repeated the cause of offence.

'Sunday so be it,' she said without looking up, 'if Abel isn't there on Saturday!' Then she looked up saucily, though her heart was full of fear of another outburst on the part of her impetuous lover. But the window was empty; Eric had taken himself off, and with a pout she resumed her work. She saw Eric no more till Sunday afternoon, after the banns had been called the third time, when he came up to her before all the people with an air of proprietorship which half-pleased and half-annoyed her.

'Not yet, mister!' she said, pushing him away, as the other girls giggled. 'Wait till Sunday next, if you please – the day after Saturday!' she added, looking at him saucily. The girls giggled again, and the young men guffawed. They thought it was the snub that touched him so that he became as white as a sheet as he turned away. But Sarah, who knew more than they did, laughed, for she saw triumph through the spasm of pain that overspread his face.

The week passed uneventfully; however, as Saturday drew nigh Sarah had occasional moments of anxiety, and as to Eric he went about at night-time like a man possessed. He restrained himself when others were by, but now and again he went down amongst the rocks and caves and shouted aloud. This seemed to relieve him somewhat, and he was better able to restrain himself for some time after. All Saturday he stayed in his own house and never left it. As he was to be married on the morrow, the neighbours thought it was shyness on his part, and did not trouble or notice him.

Only once was he disturbed, and that was when the chief boatman came to him and sat down, and after a pause said: 'Eric, I was over in Bristol yesterday. I was in the ropemaker's getting a coil to replace the one you lost the night of the storm, and there I saw Michael Heavens of this place, who is a salesman there. He told me that Abel Behenna had come home the week ere last on the *Star of the Sea* from Canton, and that he had lodged a sight of money in the Bristol Bank in the name of Sarah Behenna. He told Michael so himself – and that he had taken passage on the *Lovely Alice* to Pencastle. Bear up, man,' for Eric had with a groan dropped his head on his knees, with his face between his hands. 'He was your old comrade, I know, but you couldn't help him. He must have gone down with the rest that awful night. I thought I'd better tell you, lest it might come some other way, and you might keep Sarah Trefusis from being frightened. They were good friends once, and women take these things to heart. It would not do to let her be pained with such a thing on her wedding day!' Then he rose and went away, leaving Eric still sitting disconsolately with his head on his knees.

'Poor fellow!' murmured the chief boatman to himself; 'he takes it to heart. Well, well! right enough! They were true comrades once, and Abel saved him!'

The afternoon of that day, when the children had left school, they strayed as usual on half-holidays along the quay and the paths by the cliffs. Presently some of them came running in a state of great excitement to the harbour, where a few men were unloading a coal ketch, and a great many were superintending the operation. One of the children called out: 'There is a porpoise in the harbour mouth! We saw it come through the blow-hole! It had a long tail, and was deep under the water!'

'It was no porpoise,' said another; 'it was a seal; but it had a long tail! It came out of the seal cave!' The other children bore various testimony, but on two points they were unanimous – it, whatever 'it' was, had come through the blow-hole deep under the water, and had a long, thin tail – a tail so long that they could not see the end of it. There was much unmerciful chaffing of the children by the men on this point, but as it was evident that they had seen something, quite a number of persons, young and old, male and female, went along the high paths on either side of the harbour mouth to catch a glimpse of this new addition to the fauna of the sea, a long-tailed porpoise or seal. The tide was now coming in. There was a slight breeze, and the surface of the water was rippled so that it was only at moments that anyone could see clearly into the deep water. After a spell of watching a woman called out that she saw something moving up the channel, just below where she was standing. There was a stampede to the spot, but by the time the crowd had gathered the breeze had freshened, and it was impossible to see with any distinctness below the surface of the water. On being questioned the woman described what she had seen, but in such an incoherent way that the whole thing was put down as an effect of imagination; had it not been for the children's report she would not have been credited at all. Her semi-hysterical statement that what she saw was 'like a pig with the entrails out' was only thought anything of by an old coastguard, who shook his head but did not make any remark. For the remainder of the daylight this man was seen always on the bank, looking into the water, but always with disappointment manifest on his face.

Eric arose early on the next morning – he had not slept all night, and it was a relief to him to move about in the light. He shaved himself with a hand that did not tremble, and dressed himself in his wedding clothes. There was a haggard look on his face, and he seemed as though he had grown years older in the last few days. Still there was a wild, uneasy light of triumph in his eyes, and he kept murmuring to himself over and over again: 'This is my wedding-day! Abel cannot claim her now – living or dead! – living or dead! Living or dead!' He sat in his armchair, waiting with an uncanny quietness for the church hour to arrive.

When the bell began to ring he arose and passed out of his house, closing the door behind him. He looked at the river and saw the tide had just turned. In the church he sat with Sarah and her mother, holding Sarah's hand tightly in his all the time, as though he feared to lose her. When the service was over they stood up together, and were married in the presence of the entire congregation; for no one left the church. Both made the responses clearly – Eric's being even on the defiant side. When the wedding was over Sarah took her husband's arm, and they walked away together, the boys and younger girls being cuffed by their elders into a decorous behaviour, for they would fain have followed close behind their heels.

The way from the church led down to the back of Eric's cottage, a narrow passage being between it and that of his next neighbour. When the bridal couple had passed through this the remainder of the congregation, who had followed them at a little distance, were startled by a long, shrill scream from the bride. They rushed through the passage and found her on the bank with wild eyes, pointing to the river bed opposite Eric Sanson's door.

The falling tide had deposited there the body of Abel Behenna stark upon the broken rocks. The rope trailing from its waist had been twisted by the current round the mooring post, and had held it back whilst the tide had ebbed away from it. The right elbow had fallen in a chink in the rock, leaving the hand outstretched toward Sarah, with the open palm upward as though it were extended to receive hers, the pale drooping fingers open to the clasp.

All that happened afterwards was never quite known to Sarah Sanson. Whenever she would try to recollect there would become a buzzing in her ears and a dimness in her eyes, and all would pass away. The only thing that she could remember of it all – and this she never forgot – was Eric's breathing heavily, with his face whiter than that of the dead man, as he muttered under his breath: 'Devil's help! Devil's faith! Devil's price!'

The Burial of the Rats

Leaving Paris by the Orleans road, cross the Enceinte, and, turning to the right, you find yourself in a somewhat wild and not at all savoury district. Right and left, before and behind, on every side rise great heaps of dust and waste accumulated by the process of time.

Paris has its night as well as its day life, and the sojourner who enters his hotel in the Rue de Rivoli or the Rue Saint-Honoré late at night or leaves it early in the morning, can guess, in coming near Montrouge – if he has not done so already – the purpose of those great waggons that look like boilers on wheels which he finds halting everywhere as he passes.

Every city has its peculiar institutions created out of its own needs; and one of the most notable institutions of Paris is its rag-picking population. In the early morning – and Parisian life commences at an early hour – may be seen in most streets standing on the pathway opposite every court and alley and between every few houses, as still in some American cities, even in parts of New York, large wooden boxes into which the domestics or tenement-holders empty the accumulated dust of the past day. Round these boxes gather and pass on, when the work is done, to fresh fields of labour and pastures new, squalid hungry-looking men and women, the implements of whose craft consist of a coarse bag or basket slung over the shoulder and a little rake with which they turn over and probe and examine in the minutest manner the dustbins. They pick up and deposit in their baskets, by aid of their rakes, whatever they may find, with the same facility as a China-man uses his chopsticks.

Paris is a city of centralisation – and centralisation and classification are closely allied. In the early times, when centralisation is becoming a fact, its forerunner is classification. All things which are similar or analogous become grouped together, and from the grouping of groups rises one whole or central point. We see radiating many long arms with innumerable tentaculae, and in the centre rises a gigantic head with a comprehensive brain and keen eyes to look on every side and ears sensitive to hear – and a voracious mouth to swallow.

Other cities resemble all the birds and beasts and fishes whose appetites and digestions are normal. Paris alone is the analogical apotheosis of the octopus. Product of centralisation carried to an *ad absurdum*, it fairly represents the devil fish; and in no respects is the resemblance more curious than in the similarity of the digestive apparatus.

Those intelligent tourists who, having surrendered their individuality into the hands of Messrs Cook or Gaze, 'do' Paris in three days, are often puzzled to know how it is that the dinner which in London would cost about six shillings, can be had for three francs in a café in the Palais Royal. They need have no more wonder if they will but consider the classification which is a theoretic speciality of Parisian life, and adopt all round the fact from which the *chiffonier* has his genesis.

The Paris of 1850 was not like the Paris of today, and those who see the Paris of Napoleon and Baron Hausseman can hardly realise the existence of the state of things forty-five years ago.

Amongst other things, however, which have not changed are those districts where the waste is gathered. Dust is dust all the world over, in every age, and the family likeness of dustheaps is perfect. The traveller, therefore, who visits the environs of Montrouge can go back in fancy without difficulty to the year 1850.

In this year I was making a prolonged stay in Paris. I was very much in love with a young lady who, though she returned my passion, so far yielded to the wishes of her parents that she had promised not to see me or to correspond with me for a year. I, too, had been compelled to accede to these conditions under a vague hope of parental approval. During the term of probation I had promised to remain out of the country and not to write to my dear one until the expiration of the year.

Naturally the time went heavily with me. There was not one of my own family or circle who could tell me of Alice, and none of her own folk had, I am sorry to say, sufficient generosity to send me even an occasional word of comfort regarding her health and well-being. I spent six months wandering about Europe, but as I could find no satisfactory distraction in travel, I determined to come to Paris, where, at least, I would be within easy hail of London in case any good fortune should call me thither before the appointed time. That 'hope deferred maketh the heart sick' was never better exemplified than in my case, for in addition to the perpetual longing to see the

face I loved there was always with me a harrowing anxiety lest some
accident should prevent me showing Alice in due time that I had,
throughout the long period of probation, been faithful to her trust
and my own love. Thus, every adventure which I undertook had a
fierce pleasure of its own, for it was fraught with possible consequences greater than it would have ordinarily borne.

Like all travellers I exhausted the places of most interest in the first
month of my stay, and was driven in the second month to look for
amusement whithersoever I might. Having made sundry journeys
to the better-known suburbs, I began to see that there was a
terra incognita, in so far as the guide book was concerned, in the
social wilderness lying between these attractive points. Accordingly I
began to systematise my researches, and each day took up the thread
of my exploration at the place where I had on the previous day
dropped it.

In the process of time my wanderings led me near Montrouge, and
I saw that hereabouts lay the Ultima Thule of social exploration – a
country as little known as that round the source of the White Nile.
And so I determined to investigate philosophically the *chiffonier* – his
habitat, his life, and his means of life.

The job was an unsavoury one, difficult of accomplishment,
and with little hope of adequate reward. However, despite reason,
obstinacy prevailed, and I entered into my new investigation with
a keener energy than I could have summoned to aid me in any
investigation leading to any end, valuable or worthy.

One day, late in a fine afternoon, toward the end of September, I
entered the holy of holies of the city of dust. The place was evidently
the recognised abode of a number of *chiffoniers*, for some sort of
arrangement was manifested in the formation of the dust heaps near
the road. I passed amongst these heaps, which stood like orderly
sentries, determined to penetrate further and trace dust to its ultimate location.

As I passed along I saw behind the dust heaps a few forms that
flitted to and fro, evidently watching with interest the advent of any
stranger to such a place. The district was like a small Switzerland,
and as I went forward my tortuous course shut out the path behind
me.

Presently I got into what seemed a small city or community of
chiffoniers. There were a number of shanties or huts, such as may be
met with in the remote parts of the Bog of Allan – rude places with
wattled walls, plastered with mud and roofs of rude thatch made

from stable refuse – such places as one would not like to enter for any consideration, and which even in water-colour could only look picturesque if judiciously treated. In the midst of these huts was one of the strangest adaptations – I cannot say habitations – I had ever seen. An immense old wardrobe, the colossal remnant of some boudoir of Charles VII, or Henry II, had been converted into a dwelling-house. The double doors lay open, so that the entire ménage was open to public view. In the open half of the wardrobe was a common sitting-room of some four feet by six, in which sat, smoking their pipes round a charcoal brazier, no fewer than six old soldiers of the First Republic, with their uniforms torn and worn threadbare. Evidently they were of the *mauvais sujet* class; their bleary eyes and limp jaws told plainly of a common love of absinthe; and their eyes had that haggard, worn look of slumbering ferocity which follows hard in the wake of drink. The other side stood as of old, with its shelves intact, save that they were cut to half their depth, and in each shelf, of which there were six, was a bed made with rags and straw. The half-dozen of worthies who inhabited this structure looked at me curiously as I passed; and when I looked back after going a little way I saw their heads together in a whispered conference. I did not like the look of this at all, for the place was very lonely, and the men looked very, very villainous. However, I did not see any cause for fear, and went on my way, penetrating further and further into the Sahara. The way was tortuous to a degree, and from going round in a series of semi-circles, as one goes in skating with the Dutch roll, I got rather confused with regard to the points of the compass.

When I had penetrated a little way I saw, as I turned the corner of a half-made heap, sitting on a heap of straw an old soldier with threadbare coat.

'Hallo!' said I to myself; 'the First Republic is well represented here in its soldiery.'

As I passed him the old man never even looked up at me, but gazed on the ground with stolid persistency. Again I remarked to myself: 'See what a life of rude warfare can do! This old man's curiosity is a thing of the past.'

When I had gone a few steps, however, I looked back suddenly, and saw that curiosity was not dead, for the veteran had raised his head and was regarding me with a very queer expression. He seemed to me to look very like one of the six worthies in the press. When he saw me looking he dropped his head; and without thinking further of him I went on my way, satisfied that there was a strange likeness between these old warriors.

Presently I met another old soldier in a similar manner. He, too, did not notice me whilst I was passing.

By this time it was getting late in the afternoon, and I began to think of retracing my steps. Accordingly I turned to go back, but could see a number of tracks leading between different mounds and could not ascertain which of them I should take. In my perplexity I wanted to see someone of whom to ask the way, but could see no one. I determined to go on a few mounds further and so try to see someone – not a veteran.

I gained my object, for after going a couple of hundred yards I saw before me a single shanty such as I had seen before – with, however, the difference that this was not one for living in, but merely a roof with three walls open in front. From the evidences which the neighbourhood exhibited I took it to be a place for sorting. Within it was an old woman wrinkled and bent with age; I approached her to ask the way.

She rose as I came close and I asked her my way. She immediately commenced a conversation; and it occurred to me that here in the very centre of the Kingdom of Dust was the place to gather details of the history of Parisian rag-picking – particularly as I could do so from the lips of one who looked like the oldest inhabitant.

I began my enquiries, and the old woman gave me most interesting answers – she had been one of the *tricoteuses* who sat daily before the guillotine and had taken an active part among the women who signalised themselves by their violence in the revolution. While we were talking she said suddenly: 'But m'sieur must be tired standing,' and dusted a rickety old stool for me to sit down. I hardly liked to do so for many reasons; but the poor old woman was so civil that I did not like to run the risk of hurting her by refusing, and moreover the conversation of one who had been at the taking of the Bastille was so interesting that I sat down and so our conversation went on.

While we were talking an old man – older and more bent and wrinkled even than the woman – appeared from behind the shanty. 'Here is Pierre,' said she. 'M'sieur can hear stories now if he wishes, for Pierre was in everything, from the Bastille to Waterloo.' The old man took another stool at my request and we plunged into a sea of revolutionary reminiscences. This old man, albeit clothed like a scarecrow, was like any one of the six veterans.

I was now sitting in the centre of the low hut with the woman on
my left hand and the man on my right, each of them being somewhat
in front of me. The place was full of all sorts of curious objects of
lumber, and of many things that I wished far away. In one corner was
a heap of rags which seemed to move from the number of vermin it
contained, and in the other a heap of bones whose odour was something shocking. Every now and then, glancing at the heaps, I could
see the gleaming eyes of some of the rats which infested the place.
These loathsome objects were bad enough, but what looked even
more dreadful was an old butcher's axe with an iron handle stained
with clots of blood leaning up against the wall on the right hand side.
Still, these things did not give me much concern. The talk of the two
old people was so fascinating that I stayed on and on, till the evening
came and the dust heaps threw dark shadows over the vales between
them.

After a time I began to grow uneasy. I could not tell how or why,
but somehow I did not feel satisfied. Uneasiness is an instinct and
means warning. The psychic faculties are often the sentries of
the intellect, and when they sound alarm the reason begins to act,
although perhaps not consciously.

This was so with me. I began to bethink me where I was and by
what surrounded, and to wonder how I should fare in case I should
be attacked; and then the thought suddenly burst upon me, although
without any overt cause, that I was in danger. Prudence whispered:
'Be still and make no sign', and so I was still and made no sign, for
I knew that four cunning eyes were on me. 'Four eyes – if not
more.' My God, what a horrible thought! The whole shanty might
be surrounded on three sides with villains! I might be in the midst
of a band of such desperadoes as only half a century of periodic
revolution can produce.

With a sense of danger my intellect and observation quickened,
and I grew more watchful than was my wont. I noticed that the
old woman's eyes were constantly wandering towards my hands. I
looked at them too, and saw the cause – my rings. On my left little
finger I had a large signet and on the right a good diamond.

I thought that if there was any danger my first care was to avert
suspicion. Accordingly I began to work the conversation round to
rag-picking – to the drains – of the things found there; and so by easy
stages to jewels. Then, seizing a favourable opportunity, I asked the
old woman if she knew anything of such things. She answered that
she did, a little. I held out my right hand, and, showing her the

diamond, asked her what she thought of that. She answered that her eyes were bad, and stooped over my hand. I said as nonchalantly as I could: 'Pardon me! You will see better thus!' and taking it off handed it to her. An unholy light came into her withered old face, as she touched it. She stole one glance at me swift and keen as a flash of lightning.

She bent over the ring for a moment, her face quite concealed as though examining it. The old man looked straight out of the front of the shanty before him, at the same time fumbling in his pockets and producing a screw of tobacco in a paper and a pipe, which he proceeded to fill. I took advantage of the pause and the momentary rest from the searching eyes on my face to look carefully round the place, now dim and shadowy in the gloaming. There still lay all the heaps of varied reeking foulness; there the terrible blood-stained axe leaning against the wall in the right hand corner, and everywhere, despite the gloom, the baleful glitter of the eyes of the rats. I could see them even through some of the chinks of the boards at the back low down close to the ground. But stay! these latter eyes seemed more than usually large and bright and baleful!

For an instant my heart stood still, and I felt in that whirling condition of mind in which one feels a sort of spiritual drunkenness, and as though the body is only maintained erect in that there is no time for it to fall before recovery. Then, in another second, I was calm – coldly calm, with all my energies in full vigour, with a self-control which I felt to be perfect and with all my feeling and instincts alert.

Now I knew the full extent of my danger: I was watched and surrounded by desperate people! I could not even guess at how many of them were lying there on the ground behind the shanty, waiting for the moment to strike. I knew that I was big and strong, and they knew it, too. They knew also, as I did, that I was an Englishman and would make a fight for it; and so we waited. I had, I felt, gained an advantage in the last few seconds, for I knew my danger and understood the situation. Now, I thought, is the test of my courage – the enduring test: the fighting test may come later!

The old woman raised her head and said to me in a satisfied kind of way: 'A very fine ring, indeed – a beautiful ring! Oh, me! I once had such rings, plenty of them, and bracelets and earrings! Oh! for in those fine days I led the town a dance! But they've forgotten me now! They've forgotten me! They? Why they never heard of me! Perhaps their grandfathers remember me, some of them!' and she laughed a harsh, croaking laugh. And then I am bound to say that she astonished me, for she handed me back the ring with a certain suggestion of old-fashioned grace which was not without its pathos.

The old man eyed her with a sort of sudden ferocity, half rising from his stool, and said to me suddenly and hoarsely: 'Let me see!'

I was about to hand the ring when the old woman said: 'No! no, do not give it to Pierre! Pierre is eccentric. He loses things; and such a pretty ring!'

'Cat!' said the old man, savagely. Suddenly the old woman said, rather more loudly than was necessary: 'Wait! I shall tell you something about a ring.' There was something in the sound of her voice that jarred upon me. Perhaps it was my hyper-sensitiveness, wrought up as I was to such a pitch of nervous excitement, but I seemed to think that she was not addressing me. As I stole a glance round the place I saw the eyes of the rats in the bone heaps, but missed the eyes along the back. But even as I looked I saw them again appear. The old woman's 'Wait!' had given me a respite from attack, and the men had sunk back to their reclining posture.

'I once lost a ring – a beautiful diamond hoop that belonged to a queen, and which was given to me by a farmer of the taxes, who afterwards cut his throat because I sent him away. I thought it must have been stolen, and taxed my people; but I could get no trace. The police came and suggested that it had found its way to the drain. We descended – I in my fine clothes, for I would not trust them with my beautiful ring! I know more of the drains since then, and of rats, too! but I shall never forget the horror of that place – alive with blazing eyes, a wall of them just outside the light of our torches. Well, we got beneath my house. We searched the outlet of the drain, and there in the filth found my ring, and we came out.

'But we found something else also before we came! As we were coming toward the opening a lot of sewer rats – human ones this time – came towards us. They told the police that one of their number had gone into the drain, but had not returned. He had gone in only shortly before we had, and, if lost, could hardly be far off. They asked help to seek him, so we turned back. They tried to prevent me going, but I insisted. It was a new excitement, and had I not recovered my ring? Not far did we go till we came on something. There was but little water, and the bottom of the drain was raised with brick, rubbish, and much matter of the kind. He had made a fight for it, even when his torch had gone out. But they were too many for him! They had not been long about it! The bones were still warm; but they were picked clean. They had even eaten their own dead ones and there were bones of rats as well as of the man. They took it cool enough those other – the human ones – and joked of their comrade when they found him dead, though they would have helped him living. Bah! what matters it – life or death?'

'And had you no fear?' I asked her.

'Fear!' she said with a laugh. 'Me have fear? Ask Pierre! But I was younger then, and, as I came through that horrible drain with its wall of greedy eyes, always moving with the circle of the light from the torches, I did not feel easy. I kept on before the men, though! It is a way I have! I never let the men get it before me. All I want is a chance and a means! And they ate him up – took every trace away except the bones; and no one knew it, nor no sound of him was ever heard!' Here she broke into a chuckling fit of the ghastliest merriment which it was ever my lot to hear and see. A great poetess describes her heroine singing: 'Oh! to see or hear her singing! Scarce I know which is the divinest.'

And I can apply the same idea to the old crone – in all save the divinity, for I scarce could tell which was the most hellish – the harsh, malicious, satisfied, cruel laugh, or the leering grin, and the horrible square opening of the mouth like a tragic mask, and the yellow gleam of the few discoloured teeth in the shapeless gums. In that laugh and with that grin and the chuckling satisfaction I knew as well as if it had been spoken to me in words of thunder that my murder was settled, and the murderers only bided the proper time for its accomplishment. I could read between the lines of her gruesome story the commands to her accomplices. 'Wait,' she seemed to say, 'bide your time. I shall strike the first blow. Find the weapon for me, and I shall make the opportunity! He shall not escape! Keep him quiet, and then no one will be wiser. There will be no outcry, and the rats will do their work!'

It was growing darker and darker; the night was coming. I stole a glance round the shanty, still all the same! The bloody axe in the corner, the heaps of filth, and the eyes on the bone heaps and in the crannies of the floor.

Pierre had been still ostensibly filling his pipe; he now struck a light and began to puff away at it. The old woman said: 'Dear heart, how dark it is! Pierre, like a good lad, light the lamp!'

Pierre got up and with the lighted match in his hand touched the wick of a lamp which hung at one side of the entrance to the shanty, and which had a reflector that threw the light all over the place. It was evidently that which was used for their sorting at night.

'Not that, stupid! Not that! the lantern!' she called out to him.

He immediately blew it out, saying: 'All right, mother, I'll find it,' and he hustled about the left corner of the room – the old woman saying through the darkness: 'The lantern! the lantern! Oh! That is the light that is most useful to us poor folks. The lantern was the friend of the revolution! It is the friend of the *chiffonier*! It helps us when all else fails.'

Hardly had she said the word when there was a kind of creaking of the whole place, and something was steadily dragged over the roof.

Again I seemed to read between the lines of her words. I knew the lesson of the lantern.

'One of you get on the roof with a noose and strangle him as he passes out if we fail within.'

As I looked out of the opening I saw the loop of a rope outlined black against the lurid sky. I was now, indeed, beset!

Pierre was not long in finding the lantern. I kept my eyes fixed through the darkness on the old woman. Pierre struck his light, and by its flash I saw the old woman raise from the ground beside her where it had mysteriously appeared, and then hide in the folds of her gown, a long sharp knife or dagger. It seemed to be like a butcher's sharpening iron fined to a keen point.

The lantern was lit.

'Bring it here, Pierre,' she said. 'Place it in the doorway where we can see it. See how nice it is! It shuts out the darkness from us; it is just right!'

Just right for her and her purposes! It threw all its light on my face, leaving in gloom the faces of both Pierre and the woman, who sat outside of me on each side.

I felt that the time of action was approaching, but I knew now that the first signal and movement would come from the woman, and so watched her.

I was all unarmed, but I had made up my mind what to do. At the first movement I would seize the butcher's axe in the right-hand corner and fight my way out. At least, I would die hard. I stole a glance round to fix its exact locality so that I could not fail to seize it at the first effort, for then, if ever, time and accuracy would be precious.

Good God! It was gone! All the horror of the situation burst upon me; but the bitterest thought of all was that if the issue of the terrible position should be against me Alice would infallibly suffer. Either she would believe me false – and any lover, or anyone who has ever been one, can imagine the bitterness of the thought – or else she would go on loving long after I had been lost to her and to the world, so that her life would be broken and embittered, shattered with disappointment and despair. The very magnitude of the pain braced me up and nerved me to bear the dread scrutiny of the plotters.

I think I did not betray myself. The old woman was watching me as a cat does a mouse; she had her right hand hidden in the folds of her gown, clutching, I knew, that long, cruel-looking dagger. Had she seen any disappointment in my face she would, I felt, have known that the moment had come, and would have sprung on me like a tigress, certain of taking me unprepared.

I looked out into the night, and there I saw new cause for danger. Before and around the hut were at a little distance some shadowy forms; they were quite still, but I knew that they were all alert and on guard. Small chance for me now in that direction.

Again I stole a glance round the place. In moments of great excitement and of great danger, which is excitement, the mind works very quickly, and the keenness of the faculties which depend on the mind grows in proportion. I now felt this. In an instant I took in the whole situation. I saw that the axe had been taken through a small hole made in one of the rotten boards. How rotten they must be to allow of such a thing being done without a particle of noise.

The hut was a regular murder-trap, and was guarded all around. A garroter lay on the roof ready to entangle me with his noose if I should escape the dagger of the old hag. In front the way was guarded by I know not how many watchers. And at the back was a row of desperate men – I had seen their eyes still through the crack in the boards of the floor, when last I looked – as they lay prone waiting for the signal to start erect. If it was to be ever, now for it!

As nonchalantly as I could I turned slightly on my stool so as to get my right leg well under me. Then with a sudden jump, turning my head, and guarding it with my hands, and with the fighting instinct of the knights of old, I breathed my lady's name, and hurled myself against the back wall of the hut.

Watchful as they were, the suddenness of my movement surprised both Pierre and the old woman. As I crashed through the rotten timbers I saw the old woman rise with a leap like a tiger and heard her low gasp of baffled rage. My feet lit on something that moved, and as I jumped away I knew that I had stepped on the back of one of the row of men lying on their faces outside the hut. I was torn with nails and splinters, but otherwise unhurt. Breathless I rushed up the mound in front of me, hearing as I went the dull crash of the shanty as it collapsed into a mass.

It was a nightmare climb. The mound, though but low, was awfully steep, and with each step I took the mass of dust and cinders tore down with me and gave way under my feet. The dust rose and choked me; it was sickening, foetid, awful; but my climb was, I felt, for life or death, and I struggled on. The seconds seemed hours; but the few moments I had in starting, combined with my youth and strength, gave me a great advantage, and, though several forms struggled after me in deadly silence which was more dreadful than any sound, I easily reached the top. Since then I have climbed the cone of Vesuvius, and as I struggled up that dreary steep amid the sulphurous fumes the memory of that awful night at Montrouge came back to me so vividly that I almost grew faint.

The mound was one of the tallest in the region of dust, and as I struggled to the top, panting for breath and with my heart beating like a sledge-hammer, I saw away to my left the dull red gleam of the sky, and nearer still the flashing of lights. Thank God! I knew where I was now and where lay the road to Paris!

For two or three seconds I paused and looked back. My pursuers were still well behind me, but struggling up resolutely, and in deadly silence. Beyond, the shanty was a wreck – a mass of timber and moving forms. I could see it well, for flames were already bursting out; the rags and straw had evidently caught fire from the lantern. Still silence there! Not a sound! These old wretches could die game, anyhow.

I had no time for more than a passing glance, for as I cast an eye round the mound preparatory to making my descent I saw several dark forms rushing round on either side to cut me off on my way. It was now a race for life. They were trying to head me on my way to Paris, and with the instinct of the moment I dashed down to the right-hand side. I was just in time, for, though I came as it seemed to me down the steep in a few steps, the wary old men who were watching me turned back, and one, as I rushed by into the opening between the two mounds in front, almost struck me a blow with that terrible butcher's axe. There could surely not be two such weapons about!

Then began a really horrible chase. I easily ran ahead of the old men, and even when some younger ones and a few women joined in the hunt I easily distanced them. But I did not know the way, and I could not even guide myself by the light in the sky, for I was running away from it. I had heard that, unless of conscious purpose, hunted men turn always to the left, and so I found it now; and so, I suppose, knew also my pursuers, who were more animals than men, and with cunning or instinct had found out such secrets for themselves: for on finishing a quick spurt, after which I intended to take a moment's breathing space, I suddenly saw ahead of me two or three forms swiftly passing behind a mound to the right.

I was in the spider's web now indeed! But with the thought of this new danger came the resource of the hunted, and so I darted down the next turning to the right. I continued in this direction for some hundred yards, and then, making a turn to the left again, felt certain that I had, at any rate, avoided the danger of being surrounded.

But not of pursuit, for on came the rabble after me, steady, dogged, relentless, and still in grim silence.

In the greater darkness the mounds seemed now to be somewhat smaller than before, although – for the night was closing – they looked bigger in proportion. I was now well ahead of my pursuers, so I made a dart up the mound in front.

Oh joy of joys! I was close to the edge of this inferno of dustheaps. Away behind me the red light of Paris was in the sky, and towering up behind rose the heights of Montmartre – a dim light, with here and there brilliant points like stars.

Restored to vigour in a moment, I ran over the few remaining mounds of decreasing size, and found myself on the level land beyond. Even then, however, the prospect was not inviting. All before me was dark and dismal, and I had evidently come on one of those dank, low-lying waste places which are found here and there in the neighbourhood of great cities. Places of waste and desolation, where the space is required for the ultimate agglomeration of all that is noxious, and the ground is so poor as to create no desire of occupancy even in the lowest squatter. With eyes accustomed to the gloom of the evening, and away now from the shadows of those dreadful dustheaps, I could see much more easily than I could a little while ago. It might have been, of course, that the glare in the sky of the lights of Paris, though the city was some miles away, was reflected here. Howsoever it was, I saw well enough to take bearings for certainly some little distance around me.

In front was a bleak, flat waste that seemed almost dead level, with here and there the dark shimmering of stagnant pools. Seemingly far off on the right, amid a small cluster of scattered lights, rose a dark mass of Fort Montrouge, and away to the left in the dim distance, pointed with stray gleams from cottage windows, the lights in the sky showed the locality of Bicêtre. A moment's thought decided me to take to the right and try to reach Montrouge. There at least would be some sort of safety, and I might possibly long before come on some of the cross roads which I knew. Somewhere, not far off, must lie the strategic road made to connect the outlying chain of forts circling the city.

Then I looked back. Coming over the mounds, and outlined black against the glare of the Parisian horizon, I saw several moving figures, and still a way to the right several more deploying out between me and my destination. They evidently meant to cut me off in this direction, and so my choice became constricted; it lay now between going straight ahead or turning to the left. Stooping to the ground, so as to get the advantage of the horizon as a line of sight, I looked carefully in this direction, but could detect no sign of my enemies. I argued that as they had not guarded or were not trying to guard that point, there was evidently danger to me there already. So I made up my mind to go straight on before me.

It was not an inviting prospect, and as I went on the reality grew worse. The ground became soft and oozy, and now and again gave way beneath me in a sickening kind of way. I seemed somehow to be going down, for I saw round me places seemingly more elevated than where I was, and this in a place which from a little way back seemed dead level. I looked around, but could see none of my pursuers. This was strange, for all along these birds of the night had followed me through the darkness as well as though it was broad daylight. How I blamed myself for coming out in my light-coloured tourist suit of tweed. The silence, and my not being able to see my enemies, whilst I felt that they were watching me, grew appalling, and in the hope of someone not of this ghastly crew hearing me I raised my voice and shouted several times. There was not the slightest response; not even an echo rewarded my efforts. For a while I stood stock still and kept my eyes in one direction. On one of the rising places around me I saw something dark move along, then another, and another. This was to my left, and seemingly moving to head me off.

I thought that again I might with my skill as a runner elude my enemies at this game, and so with all my speed darted forward.

Splash!

My feet had given way in a mass of slimy rubbish, and I had fallen headlong into a reeking, stagnant pool. The water and the mud in which my arms sank up to the elbows was filthy and nauseous beyond description, and in the suddenness of my fall I had actually swallowed some of the filthy stuff, which nearly choked me, and made me gasp for breath. Never shall I forget the moments during which I stood trying to recover myself almost fainting from the foetid odour of the filthy pool, whose white mist rose ghostlike around. Worst of all, with the acute despair of the hunted animal when he sees the pursuing pack closing on him, I saw before my eyes whilst I stood helpless the dark forms of my pursuers moving swiftly to surround me.

It is curious how our minds work on odd matters even when the energies of thought are seemingly concentrated on some terrible and pressing need. I was in momentary peril of my life: my safety depended on my action, and my choice of alternatives coming now with almost every step I took, and yet I could not but think of the strange dogged persistency of these old men. Their silent resolution, their steadfast, grim, persistency even in such a cause commanded, as well as fear, even a measure of respect. What must they have been in the vigour of their youth. I could understand now that whirlwind rush on the bridge of Arcola, that scornful exclamation of the Old Guard at Waterloo! Unconscious cerebration has its own pleasures, even at such moments; but fortunately it does not in any way clash with the thought from which action springs.

I realised at a glance that so far I was defeated in my object, my enemies as yet had won. They had succeeded in surrounding me on three sides, and were bent on driving me off to the left-hand, where there was already some danger for me, for they had left no guard. I accepted the alternative – it was a case of Hobson's choice and run. I had to keep the lower ground, for my pursuers were on the higher places. However, though the ooze and broken ground impeded me my youth and training made me able to hold my ground, and by keeping a diagonal line I not only kept them from gaining on me but even began to distance them. This gave me new heart and strength, and by this time habitual training was beginning to tell and my second wind had come. Before me the ground rose slightly. I rushed up the slope and found before me a waste of watery slime, with a low dyke or bank looking black and grim beyond. I felt that if I could but reach that dyke in safety I could there, with solid ground under my feet and some kind of path to guide me, find with comparative ease a way out of my troubles. After a glance right and left and seeing no one near, I kept my eyes for a few minutes to their rightful work of aiding my feet whilst I crossed the swamp. It was rough, hard work, but there was little danger, merely toil; and a short time took me to the dyke. I rushed up the slope exulting; but here again I met a new shock. On either side of me rose a number of crouching figures. From right and left they rushed at me. Each body held a rope.

The cordon was nearly complete. I could pass on neither side, and the end was near.

There was only one chance, and I took it. I hurled myself across the dyke, and escaping out of the very clutches of my foes threw myself into the stream.

At any other time I should have thought that water foul and filthy, but now it was as welcome as the most crystal stream to the parched traveller. It was a highway of safety!

My pursuers rushed after me. Had only one of them held the rope it would have been all up with me, for he could have entangled me before I had time to swim a stroke; but the many hands holding it embarrassed and delayed them, and when the rope struck the water I heard the splash well behind me. A few minutes' hard swimming took me across the stream. Refreshed with the immersion and encouraged by the escape, I climbed the dyke in comparative gaiety of spirits.

From the top I looked back. Through the darkness I saw my assailants scattering up and down along the dyke. The pursuit was evidently not ended, and again I had to choose my course. Beyond the dyke where I stood was a wild, swampy space very similar to that which I had crossed. I determined to shun such a place, and thought for a moment whether I would take up or down the dyke. I thought I heard a sound – the muffled sound of oars, so I listened, and then shouted.

No response; but the sound ceased. My enemies had evidently got a boat of some kind. As they were on the up side of me I took the down path and began to run. As I passed to the left of where I had entered the water I heard several splashes, soft and stealthy, like the sound a rat makes as he plunges into the stream, but vastly greater; and as I looked I saw the dark sheen of the water broken by the ripples of several advancing heads. Some of my enemies were swimming the stream also.

And now behind me, up the stream, the silence was broken by the quick rattle and creak of oars; my enemies were in hot pursuit. I put my best leg foremost and ran on. After a break of a couple of minutes I looked back, and by a gleam of light through the ragged clouds I saw several dark forms climbing the bank behind me. The wind had now begun to rise, and the water beside me was ruffled and beginning to break in tiny waves on the bank. I had to keep my eyes pretty well on the ground before me, lest I should stumble, for I knew that to stumble was death. After a few minutes I looked back behind me. On the dyke were only a few dark figures, but crossing the waste, swampy ground were many more. What new danger this portended I did not know – could only guess. Then as I ran it seemed to me that my track kept ever sloping away to the right. I looked up ahead and saw that the river was much wider than before, and that the dyke on which I stood fell quite away, and beyond it was another stream on whose near bank I saw some of the dark forms now across the marsh. I was on an island of some kind.

My situation was now indeed terrible, for my enemies had hemmed me in on every side. Behind came the quickening roll of the oars, as though my pursuers knew that the end was close. Around me on every side was desolation; there was not a roof or light, as far as I could see. Far off to the right rose some dark mass, but what it was I knew not. For a moment I paused to think what I should do, not for more, for my pursuers were drawing closer. Then my mind was made up. I slipped down the bank and took to the water. I struck out straight ahead so as to gain the current by clearing the backwater of the island, for such I presume it was, when I had passed into the stream. I waited till a cloud came driving across the moon and leaving all in darkness. Then I took off my hat and laid it softly on the water floating with the stream, and a second after dived to the right and struck out under water with all my might. I was, I suppose, half a minute under water, and when I rose came up as softly as I could, and turning, looked back. There went my light brown hat floating merrily away. Close behind it came a rickety old boat, driven furiously by a pair of oars. The moon was still partly obscured by the drifting clouds, but in the partial light I could see a man in the bows holding aloft ready to strike what appeared to me to be that same dreadful pole-axe which I had before escaped. As I looked the boat drew closer, closer, and the man struck savagely. The hat disappeared. The man fell forward, almost out of the boat. His comrades dragged him in but without the axe, and then as I turned with all my energies bent on reaching the farther bank, I heard the fierce whirr of the muttered 'Sacré!' which marked the anger of my baffled pursuers.

That was the first sound I had heard from human lips during all this dreadful chase, and full as it was of menace and danger to me it was a welcome sound for it broke that awful silence which shrouded and appalled me. It was as though an overt sign that my opponents were men and not ghosts, and that with them I had, at least, the chance of a man, though but one against many.

But now that the spell of silence was broken the sounds came thick and fast. From boat to shore and back from shore to boat came quick question and answer, all in the fiercest whispers. I looked back – a fatal thing to do – for in the instant someone caught sight of my face, which showed white on the dark water, and shouted. Hands pointed to me, and in a moment or two the boat was under weigh, and following hard after me. I had but a little way to go, but quicker and quicker came the boat after me. A few more strokes and I would be on the shore, but I felt the oncoming of the boat, and expected each second to feel the crash of an oar or other weapon on my head. Had I not seen that dreadful axe disappear in the water I do not think that I could have won the shore. I heard the muttered curses of those not rowing and the laboured breath of the rowers. With one supreme effort for life or liberty I touched the bank and sprang up it. There was not a single second to spare, for hard behind me the boat grounded and several dark forms sprang after me. I gained the top of the dyke, and keeping to the left ran on again. The boat put off and followed down the stream. Seeing this I feared danger in this direction, and quickly turning, ran down the dyke on the other side, and after passing a short stretch of marshy ground gained a wild, open flat country and sped on.

Still behind me came on my relentless pursuers. Far away, below me, I saw the same dark mass as before, but now grown closer and greater. My heart gave a great thrill of delight, for I knew that it must be the fortress of Bicêtre, and with new courage I ran on. I had heard that between each and all of the protecting forts of Paris there are strategic ways, deep sunk roads where soldiers marching should be sheltered from an enemy. I knew that if I could gain this road I would be safe, but in the darkness I could not see any sign of it, so, in blind hope of striking it, I ran on.

Presently I came to the edge of a deep cut, and found that down below me ran a road guarded on each side by a ditch of water fenced on either side by a straight, high wall.

Getting fainter and dizzier, I ran on; the ground got more broken – more and more still, till I staggered and fell, and rose again, and ran on in the blind anguish of the hunted. Again the thought of

Alice nerved me. I would not be lost and wreck her life: I would fight and struggle for life to the bitter end. With a great effort I caught the top of the wall. As, scrambling like a catamount, I drew myself up, I actually felt a hand touch the sole of my foot. I was now on a sort of causeway, and before me I saw a dim light. Blind and dizzy, I ran on, staggered, and fell, rising, covered with dust and blood.

'*Halt là!*'

The words sounded like a voice from heaven. A blaze of light seemed to enwrap me, and I shouted with joy.

'*Qui va là?*' The rattle of musketry, the flash of steel before my eyes. Instinctively I stopped, though close behind me came a rush of my pursuers.

Another word or two, and out from a gateway poured, as it seemed to me, a tide of red and blue, as the guard turned out. All around seemed blazing with light, and the flash of steel, the clink and rattle of arms, and the loud, harsh voices of command. As I fell forward, utterly exhausted, a soldier caught me. I looked back in dreadful expectation, and saw the mass of dark forms disappearing into the night. Then I must have fainted. When I recovered my senses I was in the guard room. They gave me brandy, and after a while I was able to tell them something of what had passed. Then a commissary of police appeared, apparently out of the empty air, as is the way of the Parisian police officer. He listened attentively, and then had a moment's consultation with the officer in command. Apparently they were agreed, for they asked me if I were ready now to come with them.

'Where to?' I asked, rising to go.

'Back to the dust heaps. We shall, perhaps, catch them yet!'

'I shall try!' said I.

He eyed me for a moment keenly, and said suddenly: 'Would you like to wait a while or till tomorrow, young Englishman?' This touched me to the quick, as, perhaps, he intended, and I jumped to my feet.

'Come now!' I said; 'now! now! An Englishman is always ready for his duty!'

The commissary was a good fellow, as well as a shrewd one; he slapped my shoulder kindly. '*Brave garçon!*' he said. 'Forgive me, but I knew what would do you most good. The guard is ready. Come!'

And so, passing right through the guard room, and through a long vaulted passage, we were out into the night. A few of the men in front had powerful lanterns. Through courtyards and down a sloping way we passed out through a low archway to a sunken road, the same that I had seen in my flight. The order was given to get at the double, and with a quick, springing stride, half run, half walk, the soldiers went swiftly along. I felt my strength renewed again – such is the difference between hunter and hunted. A very short distance took us to a low-lying pontoon bridge across the stream, and evidently very little higher up than I had struck it. Some effort had evidently been made to damage it, for the ropes had all been cut, and one of the chains had been broken. I heard the officer say to the commissary: 'We are just in time! A few more minutes, and they would have destroyed the bridge. Forward, quicker still!' and on we went. Again we reached a pontoon on the winding stream; as we came up we heard the hollow boom of the metal drums as the efforts to destroy the bridge was again renewed. A word of command was given, and several men raised their rifles.

'Fire!' A volley rang out. There was a muffled cry, and the dark forms dispersed. But the evil was done, and we saw the far end of the pontoon swing into the stream. This was a serious delay, and it was nearly an hour before we had renewed ropes and restored the bridge sufficiently to allow us to cross.

We renewed the chase. Quicker, quicker we went towards the dust heaps.

After a time we came to a place that I knew. There were the remains of a fire – a few smouldering wood ashes still cast a red glow, but the bulk of the ashes were cold. I knew the site of the hut and the hill behind it up which I had rushed, and in the flickering glow the eyes of the rats still shone with a sort of phosphorescence. The commissary spoke a word to the officer, and he cried: 'Halt!'

The soldiers were ordered to spread around and watch, and then we commenced to examine the ruins. The commissary himself began to lift away the charred boards and rubbish. These the soldiers took and piled together. Presently he started back, then bent down and rising beckoned me.

'See!' he said.

It was a gruesome sight. There lay a skeleton face downwards, a woman by the lines – an old woman by the coarse fibre of the bone. Between the ribs rose a long spike-like dagger made from a butcher's sharpening knife, its keen point buried in the spine.

'You will observe,' said the commissary to the officer and to me as he took out his note book, 'that the woman must have fallen on her dagger. The rats are many here – see their eyes glistening among that heap of bones – and you will also notice' – I shuddered as he placed his hand on the skeleton – 'that but little time was lost by them, for the bones are scarcely cold!'

There was no other sign of anyone near, living or dead; and so deploying again into line the soldiers passed on. Presently we came to the hut made of the old wardrobe. We approached. In five of the six compartments was an old man sleeping – sleeping so soundly that even the glare of the lanterns did not wake them. Old and grim and grizzled they looked, with their gaunt, wrinkled, bronzed faces and their white moustaches.

The officer called out harshly and loudly a word of command, and in an instant each one of them was on his feet before us and standing at 'attention!'

'What do you here?'

'We sleep,' was the answer.

'Where are the other *chiffoniers*?' asked the commissary.

'Gone to work.'

'And you?'

'We are on guard!'

'Peste!' laughed the officer grimly, as he looked at the old men one after the other in the face and added with cool deliberate cruelty: 'Asleep on duty! Is this the manner of the Old Guard? No wonder, then, a Waterloo!'

By the gleam of the lantern I saw the grim old faces grow deadly pale, and almost shuddered at the look in the eyes of the old men as the laugh of the soldiers echoed the grim pleasantry of the officer.

I felt in that moment that I was in some measure avenged.

For a moment they looked as if they would throw themselves on the taunter, but years of their life had schooled them and they remained still.

'You are but five,' said the commissary; 'where is the sixth?' The answer came with a grim chuckle.

'He is there!' and the speaker pointed to the bottom of the wardrobe. 'He died last night. You won't find much of him. The burial of the rats is quick!'

The commissary stooped and looked in. Then he turned to the officer and said calmly: 'We may as well go back. No trace here now; nothing to prove that man was the one wounded by your soldiers' bullets! Probably they murdered him to cover up the trace. See!' again he stooped and placed his hands on the skeleton. 'The rats work quickly and they are many. These bones are warm!'

I shuddered, and so did many more of those around me.

'Form!' said the officer, and so in marching order, with the lan-terns swinging in front and the manacled veterans in the midst, with steady tramp we took ourselves out of the dustheaps and turned backward to the fortress of Bicêtre.

*   *   *

My year of probation has long since ended, and Alice is my wife. But when I look back upon that trying twelvemonth one of the most vivid incidents that memory recalls is that associated with my visit to the City of Dust.

A Dream of Red Hands

The first opinion given to me regarding Jacob Settle was a simple descriptive statement, 'He's a down-in-the-mouth chap': but I found that it embodied the thoughts and ideas of all his fellow-workmen. There was in the phrase a certain easy tolerance, an absence of positive feeling of any kind, rather than any complete opinion, which marked pretty accurately the man's place in public esteem. Still, there was some dissimilarity between this and his appearance which unconsciously set me thinking, and by degrees, as I saw more of the place and the workmen, I came to have a special interest in him. He was, I found, for ever doing kindnesses, not involving money expenses beyond his humble means, but in the manifold ways of forethought and forbearance and self-repression which are of the truer charities of life. Women and children trusted him implicitly, though, strangely enough, he rather shunned them, except when anyone was sick, and then he made his appearance to help if he could, timidly and awkwardly. He led a very solitary life, keeping house by himself in a tiny cottage, or rather hut, of one room, far on the edge of the moorland. His existence seemed so sad and solitary that I wished to cheer it up, and for the purpose took the occasion when we had both been sitting up with a child, injured by me through accident, to offer to lend him books. He gladly accepted, and as we parted in the grey of the dawn I felt that something of mutual confidence had been established between us.

The books were always most carefully and punctually returned, and in time Jacob Settle and I became quite friends. Once or twice as I crossed the moorland on Sundays I looked in on him; but on such occasions he was shy and ill at ease so that I felt diffident about calling to see him. He would never under any circumstances come into my own lodgings.

One Sunday afternoon, I was coming back from a long walk beyond the moor, and as I passed Settle's cottage stopped at the door to say 'How do you do?' to him. As the door was shut, I thought that he was out, and merely knocked for form's sake, or through habit, not expecting to get any answer. To my surprise, I heard a feeble voice from within, though what was said I could not hear. I entered at once, and found Jacob lying half-dressed upon his bed. He was as pale as death, and the sweat was simply rolling off his face. His hands were unconsciously gripping the bedclothes as a drowning man holds on to whatever he may grasp. As I came in he half arose, with a wild, hunted look in his eyes, which were wide open and staring, as though something of horror had come before him; but when he recognised me he sank back on the couch with a smothered sob of relief and closed his eyes. I stood by him for a while, quite a minute or two, while he gasped. Then he opened his eyes and looked at me, but with such a despairing, woeful expression that, as I am a living man, I would have rather seen that frozen look of horror. I sat down beside him and asked after his health. For a while he would not answer me except to say that he was not ill; but then, after scrutinising me closely, he half arose on his elbow and said: 'I thank you kindly, sir, but I'm simply telling you the truth. I am not ill, as men call it, though God knows whether there be not worse sick- nesses than doctors know of. I'll tell you, as you are so kind, but I trust that you won't ever mention such a thing to a living soul, for it might work me more and greater woe. I am suffering from a bad dream.'

'A bad dream!' I said, hoping to cheer him; 'but dreams pass away with the light – even with waking.' There I stopped, for before he spoke I saw the answer in his desolate look round the little place.

'No! no! that's all well for people that live in comfort and with those they love around them. It is a thousand times worse for those who live alone and have to do so. What cheer is there for me, waking here in the silence of the night, with the wide moor around me full of voices and full of faces that make my waking a worse dream than my sleep? Ah, young sir, you have no past that can send its legions to people the darkness and the empty space, and I pray the good God that you may never have!' As he spoke, there was such an almost irresistible gravity of conviction in his manner that I abandoned my remonstrance about his solitary life. I felt that I was in the presence of some secret influence which I could not fathom. To my relief, for I knew not what to say, he went on: 'Two nights past have I dreamed it. It was hard enough the first night, but I came through it. Last night the expectation was in itself almost worse than the dream – until the dream came, and then it swept away every remembrance of lesser pain. I stayed awake till just before the dawn, and then it came again, and ever since I have been in such an agony as I am sure the dying feel, and with it all the dread of tonight.' Before he had got to the end of the sentence my mind was made up, and I felt that I could speak to him more cheerfully.

'Try and get to sleep early tonight – in fact, before the evening has passed away. The sleep will refresh you, and I promise you there will not be any bad dreams after tonight.' He shook his head hopelessly, so I sat a little longer and then left him.

When I got home I made my arrangements for the night, for I had made up my mind to share Jacob Settle's lonely vigil in his cottage on the moor. I judged that if he got to sleep before sunset he would wake well before midnight, and so, just as the bells of the city were striking eleven, I stood opposite his door armed with a bag, in which were my supper, an extra large flask, a couple of candles, and a book. The moonlight was bright, and flooded the whole moor, till it was almost as light as day; but ever and anon black clouds drove across the sky, and made a darkness which by comparison seemed almost tangible. I opened the door softly, and entered without waking Jacob, who lay asleep with his white face upward. He was still, and again bathed in sweat. I tried to imagine what visions were passing before those closed eyes which could bring with them the misery and woe which were stamped on the face, but fancy failed me, and I waited for the awakening. It came suddenly, and in a fashion which touched me to the quick, for the hollow groan that broke from the man's white lips as he half arose and sank back was manifestly the realisation or completion of some train of thought which had gone before.

'If this be dreaming,' said I to myself, 'then it must be based on some very terrible reality. What can have been that unhappy fact that he spoke of?'

While I thus spoke, he realised that I was with him. It struck me as strange that he had no period of that doubt as to whether dream or reality surrounded him which commonly marks an expected environment of waking men. With a positive cry of joy, he seized my hand and held it in his two wet, trembling hands, as a frightened child clings on to someone whom it loves. I tried to soothe him: 'There, there! it is all right. I have come to stay with you tonight, and together we will try to fight this evil dream.' He let go my hand suddenly, and sank back on his bed and covered his eyes with his hands.

'Fight it? – the evil dream! Ah! no, sir, no! No mortal power can fight that dream, for it comes from God – and is burned in here;' and he beat upon his forehead. Then he went on: 'It is the same dream, ever the same, and yet it grows in its power to torture me every time it comes.'

'What is the dream?' I asked, thinking that the speaking of it might give him some relief, but he shrank away from me, and after a long pause said: 'No, I had better not tell it. It may not come again.'

There was manifestly something to conceal from me – something that lay behind the dream, so I answered: 'All right. I hope you have seen the last of it. But if it should come again, you will tell me, will you not? I ask, not out of curiosity, but because I think it may relieve you to speak.' He answered with what I thought was almost an undue amount of solemnity: 'If it comes again, I shall tell you all.'

Then I tried to get his mind away from the subject to more mundane things, so I produced supper, and made him share it with me, including the contents of the flask. After a little he braced up, and when I lit my cigar, having given him another, we smoked a full hour, and talked of many things. Little by little the comfort of his body stole over his mind, and I could see sleep laying her gentle hands on his eyelids. He felt it, too, and told me that now he felt all right, and I might safely leave him; but I told him that, right or wrong, I was going to see in the daylight. So I lit my other candle, and began to read as he fell asleep.

By degrees I got interested in my book, so interested that presently I was startled by its dropping out of my hands. I looked and saw that Jacob was still asleep, and I was rejoiced to see that there was on his face a look of unwonted happiness, while his lips seemed to move with unspoken words. Then I turned to my work again, and again woke, but this time to feel chilled to my very marrow by hearing the voice from the bed beside me: 'Not with those red hands! Never! never!'

On looking at him, I found that he was still asleep. He woke, however, in an instant, and did not seem surprised to see me; there was again that strange apathy as to his surroundings. Then I said: 'Settle, tell me your dream. You may speak freely, for I shall hold your confidence sacred. While we both live I shall never mention what you may choose to tell me.'

He replied: 'I said I would; but I had better tell you first what goes before the dream, that you may understand. I was a schoolmaster when I was a very young man; it was only a parish school in a little

village in the West Country. No need to mention any names. Better
not. I was engaged to be married to a young girl whom I loved and
almost reverenced. It was the old story. While we were waiting for
the time when we could afford to set up house together, another man
came along. He was nearly as young as I was, and handsome, and a
gentleman, with all a gentleman's attractive ways for a woman of our
class. He would go fishing, and she would meet him while I was at my
work in school. I reasoned with her and implored her to give him up.
I offered to get married at once and go away and begin the world in a
strange country; but she would not listen to anything I could say, and
I could see that she was infatuated with him. Then I took it on myself
to meet the man and ask him to deal well with the girl, for I thought
he might mean honestly by her, so that there might be no talk or
chance of talk on the part of others. I went where I should meet him
with none by, and we met!' Here Jacob Settle had to pause, for
something seemed to rise in his throat, and he almost gasped for
breath. Then he went on: 'Sir, as God is above us, there was no
selfish thought in my heart that day, I loved my pretty Mabel too
well to be content with a part of her love, and I had thought of my
own unhappiness too often not to have come to realise that, whatever
might come to her, my hope was gone. He was insolent to me – you,
sir, who are a gentleman, cannot know, perhaps, how galling can be
the insolence of one who is above you in station – but I bore with
that. I implored him to deal well with the girl, for what might be only
a pastime of an idle hour with him might be the breaking of her
heart. For I never had a thought of her truth, or that the worst of
harm could come to her – it was only the unhappiness to her heart I
feared. But when I asked him when he intended to marry her his
laughter galled me so that I lost my temper and told him that I would
not stand by and see her life made unhappy. Then he grew angry too,
and in his anger said such cruel things of her that then and there I
swore he should not live to do her harm. God knows how it came
about, for in such moments of passion it is hard to remember the
steps from a word to a blow, but I found myself standing over his
dead body, with my hands crimson with the blood that welled from
his torn throat. We were alone and he was a stranger, with none of
his kin to seek for him and murder does not always out – not all at
once. His bones may be whitening still, for all I know, in the pool of
the river where I left him. No one suspected his absence, or why it
was, except my poor Mabel, and she dared not speak. But it was all in
vain, for when I came back again after an absence of months – for I

could not live in the place – I learned that her shame had come and that she had died in it. Hitherto I had been borne up by the thought that my ill deed had saved her future, but now, when I learned that I had been too late, and that my poor love was smirched with that man's sin, I fled away with the sense of my useless guilt upon me more heavily than I could bear. Ah! sir, you that have not done such a sin don't know what it is to carry it with you. You may think that custom makes it easy to you, but it is not so. It grows and grows with every hour, till it becomes intolerable, and with it growing, too, the feeling that you must for ever stand outside Heaven. You don't know what that means, and I pray God that you never may. Ordinary men, to whom all things are possible, don't often, if ever, think of Heaven. It is a name, and nothing more, and they are content to wait and let things be, but to those who are doomed to be shut out for ever you cannot think what it means, you cannot guess or measure the terrible endless longing to see the gates opened, and to be able to join the white figures within.

'And this brings me to my dream. It seemed that the portal was before me, with great gates of massive steel with bars of the thickness of a mast, rising to the very clouds, and so close that between them was just a glimpse of a crystal grotto, on whose shining walls were figured many white-clad forms with faces radiant with joy. When I stood before the gate my heart and my soul were so full of rapture and longing that I forgot. And there stood at the gate two mighty angels with sweeping wings, and, oh! so stern of countenance. They held each in one hand a flaming sword, and in the other the latchet, which moved to and fro at their lightest touch. Nearer were figures all draped in black, with heads covered so that only the eyes were seen, and they handed to each who came white garments such as the angels wear. A low murmur came that told that all should put on their own robes, and without soil, or the angels would not pass them in, but would smite them down with the flaming swords. I was eager to don my own garment, and hurriedly threw it over me and stepped swiftly to the gate; but it moved not, and the angels, loosing the latchet, pointed to my dress; I looked down, and was aghast, for the whole robe was smeared with blood. My hands were red; they glittered with the blood that dripped from them as on that day by the river bank. And then the angels raised their flaming swords to smite me down, and the horror was complete – I awoke. Again, and again, and again, that awful dream comes to me. I never learn from the experience, I never remember, but at the beginning the hope is ever there to make the end more appalling; and I know that the dream does not come out of the common darkness where the dreams abide, but that it is sent from God as a punishment! Never, never shall I be able to pass the gate, for the soil on the angel garments must ever come from these bloody hands!'

I listened as in a spell as Jacob Settle spoke. There was something so far away in the tone of his voice – something so dreamy and mystic in the eyes that looked as if through me at some spirit beyond – something so lofty in his very diction and in such marked contrast to his workworn clothes and his poor surroundings that I wondered if the whole thing were not a dream.

We were both silent for a long time. I kept looking at the man before me in growing wonderment. Now that his confession had been made, his soul, which had been crushed to the very earth, seemed to leap back again to uprightness with some resilient force. I suppose I ought to have been horrified with his story, but, strange to say, I was not. It certainly is not pleasant to be made the recipient of the confidence of a murderer, but this poor fellow seemed to have had, not only so much provocation, but so much self-denying purpose in his deed of blood that I did not feel called upon to pass judgement upon him. My purpose was to comfort, so I spoke out with what calmness I could, for my heart was beating fast and heavily: 'You need not despair, Jacob Settle. God is very good, and His mercy is great. Live on and work on in the hope that some day you may feel that you have atoned for the past.' Here I paused, for I could see that sleep, natural sleep this time, was creeping upon him. 'Go to sleep,' I said; 'I shall watch with you here and we shall have no more evil dreams tonight.'

He made an effort to pull himself together, and answered: 'I don't know how to thank you for your goodness to me this night, but I think you had best leave me now, I'll try and sleep this out; I feel a weight off my mind since I have told you all. If there's anything of the man left in me, I must try and fight out life alone.'

'I'll go tonight, as you wish it,' I said; 'but take my advice, and do not live in such a solitary way. Go among men and women; live among them. Share their joys and sorrows, and it will help you to forget. This solitude will make you melancholy mad.'

'I will!' he answered, half-unconsciously, for sleep was overmastering him.

I turned to go, and he looked after me. When I had touched the latch I dropped it, and, coming back to the bed, held out my hand.

He grasped it with both his as he rose to a sitting posture, and I said my goodnight, trying to cheer him: 'Heart, man, heart! There is work in the world for you to do, Jacob Settle. You can wear those white robes yet and pass through that gate of steel!'

Then I left him.

A week after I found his cottage deserted, and on asking at the works was told that he had 'gone north', no one exactly knew whither.

Two years afterwards, I was staying for a few days with my friend Dr Munro in Glasgow. He was a busy man, and could not spare much time for going about with me, so I spent my days in excursions to the Trossachs and Loch Katrine and down the Clyde. On the second last evening of my stay I came back somewhat later than I had arranged, but found that my host was late too. The maid told me that he had been sent for to the hospital – a case of accident at the gasworks, and the dinner was postponed an hour; so telling her I would stroll down to find her master and walk back with him, I went out. At the hospital I found him washing his hands preparatory to starting for home. Casually, I asked him what his case was.

'Oh, the usual thing! A rotten rope and men's lives of no account. Two men were working in a gasometer, when the rope that held their scaffolding broke. It must have occurred just before the dinner hour, for no one noticed their absence till the men had returned. There was about seven feet of water in the gasometer, so they had a hard fight for it, poor fellows. However, one of them was alive, just alive, but we have had a hard job to pull him through. It seems that he owes his life to his mate, for I have never heard of greater heroism. They swam together while their strength lasted, but at the end they were so done up that even the lights above, and the men slung with ropes, coming down to help them, could not keep them up. But one of them stood on the bottom and held up his comrade over his head, and those few breaths made all the difference between life and death. They were a shocking sight when they were taken out, for that water is like a purple dye with the gas and the tar. The man upstairs looked as if he had been washed in blood. Ugh!'

'And the other?'

'Oh, he's worse still. But he must have been a very noble fellow. That struggle under the water must have been fearful; one can see that by the way the blood has been drawn from the extremities. It makes the idea of the *Stigmata* possible to look at him. Resolution like this could, you would think, do anything in the world. Ay! it might almost unbar the gates of Heaven. Look here, old man, it is not a very pleasant sight, especially just before dinner, but you are a writer, and this is an odd case. Here is something you would not like to miss, for in all human probability you will never see anything like it again.' While he was speaking he had brought me into the mortuary of the hospital.

On the bier lay a body covered with a white sheet, which was wrapped close round it.

'Looks like a chrysalis, don't it? I say, Jack, if there be anything in the old myth that a soul is typified by a butterfly, well, then the one that this chrysalis sent forth was a very noble specimen and took all the sunlight on its wings. See here!' He uncovered the face. Horrible, indeed, it looked, as though stained with blood. But I knew him at once, Jacob Settle! My friend pulled the winding sheet farther down.

The hands were crossed on the purple breast as they had been reverently placed by some tender-hearted person. As I saw them my heart throbbed with a great exultation, for the memory of his harrowing dream rushed across my mind. There was no stain now on those poor, brave hands, for they were blanched white as snow.

And somehow as I looked I felt that the evil dream was all over. That noble soul had won a way through the gate at last. The white robe had now no stain from the hands that had put it on.

Crooken Sands

Mr Arthur Fernlee Markam, who took what was known as the Red
House above the Mains of Crooken, was a London merchant, and
being essentially a cockney, thought it necessary when he went for
the summer holidays to Scotland to provide an entire rig-out as a
Highland chieftain, as manifested in chromolithographs and on the
music-hall stage. He had once seen in the Empire the Great Prince –
'The Bounder King' – bring down the house by appearing as 'The
MacSlogan of that Ilk', and singing the celebrated Scotch song,
'There's naething like haggis to mak a mon dry!' and he had ever
since preserved in his mind a faithful image of the picturesque
and warlike appearance which he presented. Indeed, if the true in-
wardness of Mr Markam's mind on the subject of his selection of
Aberdeenshire as a summer resort were known, it would be found
that in the foreground of the holiday locality which his fancy painted
stalked the many hued figure of the MacSlogan of that Ilk. However,
be this as it may, a very kind fortune – certainly so far as external
beauty was concerned – led him to the choice of Crooken Bay. It is a
lovely spot, between Aberdeen and Peterhead, just under the rock-
bound headland whence the long, dangerous reefs known as the
Spurs run out into the North Sea. Between this and the 'Mains of
Crooken' – a village sheltered by the northern cliffs – lies the deep
bay, backed with a multitude of bent-grown dunes where the rabbits
are to be found in thousands. Thus at either end of the bay is a rocky
promontory, and when the dawn or the sunset falls on the rocks of
red syenite the effect is very lovely. The bay itself is floored with
level sand and the tide runs far out, leaving a smooth waste of hard
sand on which are dotted here and there the stake nets and bag nets
of the salmon fishers. At one end of the bay there is a little group or
cluster of rocks whose heads are raised something above high water,
except when in rough weather the waves come over them green. At
low tide they are exposed down to sand level; and here is perhaps the
only little bit of dangerous sand on this part of the eastern coast.

Between the rocks, which are apart about some fifty feet, is a small quicksand, which, like the Goodwins, is dangerous only with the incoming tide. It extends outwards till it is lost in the sea, and inwards till it fades away in the hard sand of the upper beach. On the slope of the hill which rises beyond the dunes, midway between the Spurs and the Port of Crooken, is the Red House. It rises from the midst of a clump of fir trees which protect it on three sides, leaving the whole seafront open. A trim old-fashioned garden stretches down to the roadway, on crossing which a grassy path, which can be used for light vehicles, threads a way to the shore, winding amongst the sand-hills.

When the Markam family arrived at the Red House after their thirty-six hours of pitching on the Aberdeen steamer *Ban Righ* from Blackwall, with the subsequent train to Yellon and drive of a dozen miles, they all agreed that they had never seen a more delightful spot. The general satisfaction was more marked as at that very time none of the family were, for several reasons, inclined to find favourable anything or any place over the Scottish border. Though the family was a large one, the prosperity of the business allowed them all sorts of personal luxuries, amongst which was a wide latitude in the way of dress. The frequency of the Markam girls' new frocks was a source of envy to their bosom friends and of joy to themselves.

Arthur Fernlee Markam had not taken his family into his confidence regarding his new costume. He was not quite certain that he should be free from ridicule, or at least from sarcasm, and as he was sensitive on the subject, he thought it better to be actually in the suitable environment before he allowed the full splendour to burst upon them. He had taken some pains to ensure the completeness of the Highland costume. For the purpose he had paid many visits to 'The Scotch All-Wool Tartan Clothing Mart' which had been lately established in Copthall Court by the Messrs. MacCallum More and Roderick MacDhu. He had anxious consultations with the head of the firm – MacCallum as he called himself, resenting any such additions as 'Mr' or 'Esquire'. The known stock of buckles, buttons, straps, brooches and ornaments of all kinds were examined in critical detail; and at last an eagle's feather of sufficiently magnificent proportions was discovered, and the equipment was complete. It was only when he saw the finished costume, with the vivid hues of the tartan seemingly modified into comparative sobriety by the multitude of silver fittings, the cairngorm brooches, the filibeg, dirk and sporran, that he was fully and absolutely satisfied with his choice. At first he had thought of the Royal Stuart dress tartan, but abandoned it on the MacCallum pointing out that if he should happen to be in the neighbourhood of Balmoral it might lead to complications. The MacCallum, who, by the way, spoke with a remarkable cockney accent, suggested other plaids in turn; but now that the other question of accuracy had been raised, Mr Markam foresaw difficulties if he should by chance find himself in the locality of the clan whose colours he had usurped. The MacCallum at last undertook to have, at Markam's expense, a special pattern woven which would not be exactly the same as any existing tartan, though partaking of the characteristics of many. It was based on the Royal Stuart, but contained suggestions as to simplicity of pattern from the Macalister and Ogilvie clans, and as to neutrality of colour from the clans of Buchanan, Macbeth, Chief of Macintosh and Macleod. When the specimen had been shown to Markam he had feared somewhat lest it should strike the eye of his domestic circle as gaudy; but as Roderick MacDhu fell into perfect ecstasies over its beauty he did not make any objection to the completion of the piece. He thought, and wisely, that if a genuine Scotchman like MacDhu liked it, it must be right – especially as the junior partner was a man very much of his own build and appearance. When the MacCallum was receiving his cheque – which, by the way, was a pretty stiff one – he remarked: 'I've taken the liberty of having some more of the stuff woven in case you or any of your friends should want it.' Markam was gratified, and told him that he should be only too happy if the beautiful stuff which they had originated between them should become a favourite, as he had no doubt it would in time. He might make and sell as much as he would.

Markam tried the dress on in his office one evening after the clerks had all gone home. He was pleased, though a little frightened, at the result. The MacCallum had done his work thoroughly, and there was nothing omitted that could add to the martial dignity of the wearer.

'I shall not, of course, take the claymore and the pistols with me on ordinary occasions,' said Markam to himself as he began to undress. He determined that he would wear the dress for the first time on landing in Scotland, and accordingly on the morning when the *Ban Righ* was hanging off the Girdle Ness lighthouse, waiting for the tide to enter the port of Aberdeen, he emerged from his cabin in all the gaudy splendour of his new costume. The first comment he heard was from one of his own sons, who did not recognise him at first.

'Here's a guy! Great Scott! It's the governor!' And the boy fled forthwith and tried to bury his laughter under a cushion in the saloon. Markam was a good sailor and had not suffered from the pitching of the boat, so that his naturally rubicund face was even more rosy by the conscious blush which suffused his cheeks when he had found himself at once the cynosure of all eyes. He could have wished that he had not been so bold for he knew from the cold that there was a big bare spot under one side of his jauntily worn Glengarry cap. However, he faced the group of strangers boldly. He was not, outwardly, upset even when some of the comments reached his ears.

'He's off his bloomin' chump,' said a cockney in a suit of exaggerated plaid.

'There's flies on him,' said a tall thin Yankee, pale with seasickness, who was on his way to take up his residence for a time as close as he could get to the gates of Balmoral.

'Happy thought! Let us fill our mulls; now's the chance!' said a young Oxford man on his way home to Inverness. But presently Mr Markam heard the voice of his eldest daughter.

'Where is he? Where is he?' and she came tearing along the deck with her hat blowing behind her. Her face showed signs of agitation, for her mother had just been telling her of her father's condition; but when she saw him she instantly burst into laughter so violent that it ended in a fit of hysterics. Something of the same kind happened to each of the other children. When they had all had their turn Mr Markam went to his cabin and sent his wife's maid to tell each member of the family that he wanted to see them at once. They all made their appearance, suppressing their feelings as well as they could. He said to them very quietly: 'My dears, don't I provide you all with ample allowances?'

'Yes, father!' they all answered gravely, 'no one could be more generous!'

'Don't I let you dress as you please?'

'Yes, father!' – this a little sheepishly.

'Then, my dears, don't you think it would be nicer and kinder of you not to try and make me feel uncomfortable, even if I do assume a dress which is ridiculous in your eyes, though quite common enough in the country where we are about to sojourn?' There was no answer except that which appeared in their hanging heads. He was a good father and they all knew it. He was quite satisfied and went on: 'There, now, run away and enjoy yourselves! We shan't have another word about it.' Then he went on deck again and stood bravely the fire of ridicule which he recognised around him, though nothing more was said within his hearing.

The astonishment and the amusement which his get-up occasioned on the *Ban Righ* was, however, nothing to that which it created in Aberdeen. The boys and loafers, and women with babies, who waited at the landing shed, followed *en masse* as the Markam party took their way to the railway station; even the porters with their old-fashioned knots and their new-fashioned barrows, who await the traveller at the foot of the gang-plank, followed in wondering delight. Fortunately the Peterhead train was just about to start, so that the martyrdom was not unnecessarily prolonged. In the carriage the glorious Highland costume was unseen, and as there were but few persons at the station at Yellon, all went well there. When, however, the carriage drew near the Mains of Crooken and the fisher folk had run to their doors to see who it was that was passing, the excitement exceeded all bounds. The children with one impulse waved their bonnets and ran shouting behind the carriage; the men forsook their nets and their baiting and followed; the women clutched their babies, and followed also. The horses were tired after their long journey to Yellon and back, and the hill was steep, so that there was ample time for the crowd to gather and even to pass on ahead.

Mrs Markam and the elder girls would have liked to make some protest or to do something to relieve their feelings of chagrin at the ridicule which they saw on all faces, but there was a look of fixed determination on the face of the seeming Highlander which awed them a little, and they were silent. It might have been that the eagle's feather, even when arising above the bald head, the cairngorm brooch even on the fat shoulder, and the claymore, dirk and pistols, even when belted round the extensive paunch and protruding from the stocking on the sturdy calf, fulfilled their existence as symbols of martial and terrifying import! When the party arrived at the gate of the Red House there awaited them a crowd of Crooken inhabitants, hatless and respectfully silent; the remainder of the population was painfully toiling up the hill. The silence was broken by only one sound, that of a man with a deep voice.

'Man! but he's forgotten the pipes!'

The servants had arrived some days before, and all things were in readiness. In the glow consequent on a good lunch after a hard journey all the disagreeableness of travel and all the chagrin consequent on the adoption of the obnoxious costume were forgotten.

That afternoon Markam, still clad in full array, walked through the Mains of Crooken. He was all alone, for, strange to say, his wife and both daughters had sick headaches, and were, as he was told, lying down to rest after the fatigue of the journey. His eldest son, who claimed to be a young man, had gone out by himself to explore the surroundings of the place, and one of the boys could not be found. The other boy, on being told that his father had sent for him to come for a walk, had managed – by accident, of course – to fall into the water butt, and had to be dried and rigged out afresh. His clothes not having been as yet unpacked this was of course impossible without delay.

Mr Markam was not quite satisfied with his walk. He could not meet any of his neighbours. It was not that there were not enough people about, for every house and cottage seemed to be full; but the people when in the open were either in their doorways some distance behind him, or on the roadway a long distance in front. As he passed he could see the tops of heads and the whites of eyes in the windows or round the corners of doors. The only interview which he had was anything but a pleasant one. This was with an odd sort of old man who was hardly ever heard to speak except to join in the 'Amens' in the meeting-house. His sole occupation seemed to be to wait at the window of the post-office from eight o'clock in the morning till the arrival of the mail at one, when he carried the letter-bag to a neighbouring baronial castle. The remainder of his day was spent on a seat in a draughty part of the port, where the offal of the fish, the refuse of the bait, and the house rubbish was thrown, and where the ducks were accustomed to hold high revel.

When Saft Tammie beheld him coming he raised his eyes, which were generally fixed on the nothing which lay on the roadway opposite his seat, and, seeming dazzled as if by a burst of sunshine, rubbed them and shaded them with his hand. Then he started up and raised his hand aloft in a denunciatory manner as he spoke: '"Vanity of vanities, saith the preacher. All is vanity." Mon, be warned in time! "Behold the lilies of the field, they toil not, neither do they spin, yet Solomon in all his glory was not arrayed like one of these." Mon! Mon! Thy vanity is as the quicksand which swallows up all which comes within its spell. Beware vanity! Beware the quicksand, which yawneth for thee, and which will swallow thee up! See thyself! Learn thine own vanity! Meet thyself face to face, and then in that moment thou shalt learn the fatal force of thy vanity. Learn it, know it, and repent ere the quicksand swallow thee!' Then without another word he went back to his seat and sat there immovable and expressionless as before.

Markam could not but feel a little upset by this tirade. Only that it was spoken by a seeming madman, he would have put it down to some eccentric exhibition of Scottish humour or impudence; but the gravity of the message – for it seemed nothing else – made such a reading impossible. He was, however, determined not to give in to ridicule, and although he had not yet seen anything in Scotland to remind him even of a kilt, he determined to wear his Highland dress. When he returned home, in less than half-an-hour, he found that every member of the family was, despite the headaches, out taking a walk. He took the opportunity afforded by their absence of locking himself in his dressing-room, took off the Highland dress, and, putting on a suit of flannels, lit a cigar and had a snooze. He was awakened by the noise of the family coming in, and at once donning his dress made his appearance in the drawing-room for tea.

He did not go out again that afternoon; but after dinner he put on his dress again – he had, of course dressed for dinner as usual – and went by himself for a walk on the sea-shore. He had by this time come to the conclusion that he would get by degrees accustomed to the Highland dress before making it his ordinary wear. The moon was up and he easily followed the path through the sand-hills, and shortly struck the shore. The tide was out and the beach firm as a rock, so he strolled southwards to nearly the end of the bay. Here he was attracted by two isolated rocks some little way out from the edge of the dunes, so he strolled towards them. When he reached the nearest one he climbed it, and, sitting there elevated some fifteen or twenty feet over the waste of sand, enjoyed the lovely, peaceful prospect. The moon was rising behind the headland of Pennyfold, and its light was just touching the top of the furthermost rock of the Spurs some three-quarters of a mile out; the rest of the rocks were in dark shadow. As the moon rose over the headland, the rocks of the Spurs and then the beach by degrees became flooded with light.

For a good while Mr Markam sat and looked at the rising moon and the growing area of light which followed its rise. Then he turned and faced eastwards and sat with his chin in his hand looking sea-wards, and revelling in the peace and beauty and freedom of the scene. The roar of London – the darkness and the strife and weariness of London life – seemed to have passed quite away, and he lived at the moment a freer and higher life. He looked at the glistening water as it stole its way over the flat waste of sand, coming closer and closer insensibly – the tide had turned. Presently he heard a distant shouting along the beach very far off.

'The fishermen calling to each other,' he said to himself and looked around. As he did so he got a horrible shock, for though just then a cloud sailed across the moon he saw, in spite of the sudden darkness around him, his own image. For an instant, on the top of the opposite rock he could see the bald back of the head and the Glengarry cap with the immense eagle's feather. As he staggered back his foot slipped, and he began to slide down towards the sand between the two rocks. He took no concern as to failing, for the sand was really only a few feet below him, and his mind was occupied with the figure or simulacrum of himself, which had already disappeared. As the easiest way of reaching *terra firma* he prepared to jump the remainder of the distance. All this had taken but a second, but the brain works quickly, and even as he gathered himself for the spring he saw the sand below him lying so marbly level shake and shiver in an odd way. A sudden fear overcame him; his knees failed, and instead of jumping he slid miserably down the rock, scratching his bare legs as he went. His feet touched the sand – went through it like water – and he was down below his knees before he realised that he was in a quicksand. Wildly he grasped at the rock to keep himself from sinking further, and fortunately there was a jutting spur or edge which he was able to grasp instinctively. To this he clung in grim desperation. He tried to shout, but his breath would not come, till after a great effort his voice rang out. Again he shouted, and it seemed as if the sound of his own voice gave him new courage, for he was able to hold on to the rock for a longer time than he thought possible – though he held on only in blind desperation. He was, however, beginning to find his grasp weakening, when, joy of joys! his shout was answered by a rough voice from just above him.

'God be thankit, I'm nae too late!' and a fisherman with great thigh-boots came hurriedly climbing over the rock. In an instant he recognised the gravity of the danger, and with a cheering 'Haud fast, mon! I'm comin'!' scrambled down till he found a firm foothold. Then with one strong hand holding the rock above, he leaned down, and catching Markam's wrist, called out to him, 'Haud to me, mon! Haud to me wi' ither hond!'

Then he lent his great strength, and with a steady, sturdy pull, dragged him out of the hungry quicksand and placed him safe upon the rock. Hardly giving him time to draw breath, he pulled and pushed him – never letting him go for an instant – over the rock into the firm sand beyond it, and finally deposited him, still shaking from the magnitude of his danger, high upon the beach. Then he began to speak: 'Mon! but I was just in time. If I had no laucht at yon foolish lads and begun to rin at the first you'd a bin sinkin' doon to the bowels o' the airth be the noo! Wully Beagrie thocht you was a ghaist, and Tom MacPhail swore ye was only like a goblin on a puddick-steel! "Na!" said I. "Yon's but the daft Englishman – the loony that had escapit frae the waxworks." I was thinkin' that bein' strange and silly – if not a whole-made feel – ye'd no ken the ways o' the quicksan'! I shouted till warn ye, and then ran to drag ye aff, if need be. But God be thankit, be ye fule or only half-daft wi' yer vanity, that I was no that late!' and he reverently lifted his cap as he spoke.

Mr Markam was deeply touched and thankful for his escape from a horrible death; but the sting of the charge of vanity thus made once more against him came through his humility. He was about to reply angrily, when suddenly a great awe fell upon him as he remembered the warning words of the half-crazy letter-carrier: 'Meet thyself face to face, and repent ere the quicksand shall swallow thee!'

Here, too, he remembered the image of himself that he had seen and the sudden danger from the deadly quicksand that had followed. He was silent a full minute, and then said: 'My good fellow, I owe you my life!'

The answer came with reverence from the hardy fisherman, 'Na! Na! Ye owe that to God; but, as for me, I'm only too glad till be the humble instrument o' His mercy.'

'But you will let me thank you,' said Mr Markam, taking both the great hands of his deliverer in his and holding them tight. 'My heart is too full as yet, and my nerves are too much shaken to let me say much; but, believe me, I am very, very grateful!' It was quite evident that the poor old fellow was deeply touched, for the tears were running down his cheeks.

The fisherman said, with a rough but true courtesy: 'Ay, sir! thank me and ye will – if it'll do yer poor heart good. An' I'm thinking that if it were me I'd be thankful too. But, sir, as for me I need no thanks. I am glad, so I am!'

That Arthur Fernlee Markam was really thankful and grateful was shown practically later on. Within a week's time there sailed into Port Crooken the finest fishing smack that had ever been seen in the harbour of Peterhead. She was fully found with sails and gear of all kinds, and with nets of the best. Her master and men went away by the coach, after having left with the salmon-fisher's wife the papers which made her over to him.

As Mr Markam and the salmon-fisher walked together along the shore the former asked his companion not to mention the fact that he had been in such imminent danger, for that it would only distress his dear wife and children. He said that he would warn them all of the quicksand, and for that purpose he, then and there, asked questions about it till he felt that his information on the subject was complete. Before they parted he asked his companion if he had happened to see a second figure, dressed like himself on the other rock as he had approached to succour him.

'Na! Na!' came the answer, 'there is nae sic another fule in these parts. Nor has there been since the time o' Jamie Fleeman – him that was fule to the Laird o' Udny. Why, mon! sic a heathenish dress as ye have on till ye has nae been seen in these pairts within the memory o' mon. An' I'm thinkin' that sic a dress never was for sittin' on the cauld rock, as ye done beyont. Mon! but do ye no fear the rheumatism or the lumbagy wi' floppin' doon on to the cauld stanes wi' yer bare flesh? I was thinking that it was daft ye waur when I see ye the mornin' doon be the port, but it's fule or eediot ye maun be for the like o' thot!' Mr Markam did not care to argue the point, and as they were now close to his own home he asked the salmon-fisher to have a glass of whisky – which he did – and they parted for the night. He took good care to warn all his family of the quicksand, telling them that he had himself been in some danger from it.

All that night he never slept. He heard the hours strike one after the other; but try how he would he could not get to sleep. Over and over again he went through the horrible episode of the quicksand, from the time that Saft Tammie had broken his habitual silence to preach to him of the sin of vanity and to warn him. The question kept ever arising in his mind: 'Am I then so vain as to be in the ranks of the foolish?' and the answer ever came in the words of the crazy prophet: '"Vanity of vanities! All is vanity." Meet thyself face to face, and repent ere the quicksand shall swallow thee!' Somehow a feeling of doom began to shape itself in his mind that he would yet perish in that same quicksand, for there he had already met himself face to face.

In the grey of the morning he dozed off, but it was evident that he continued the subject in his dreams, for he was fully awakened by his wife, who said: 'Do sleep quietly! That blessed Highland suit has got on your brain. Don't talk in your sleep, if you can help it!' He was somehow conscious of a glad feeling, as if some terrible weight had been lifted from him, but he did not know any cause of it. He asked his wife what he had said in his sleep, and she answered: 'You said it often enough, goodness knows, for one to remember it – "Not face to face! I saw the eagle plume over the bald head! There is hope yet! Not face to face!" Go to sleep! Do!' And then he did go to sleep, for he seemed to realise that the prophecy of the crazy man had not yet been fulfilled. He had not met himself face to face – as yet at all events.

He was awakened early by a maid who came to tell him that there was a fisherman at the door who wanted to see him. He dressed himself as quickly as he could – for he was not yet expert with the Highland dress – and hurried down, not wishing to keep the salmon-fisher waiting. He was surprised and not altogether pleased to find that his visitor was none other than Saft Tammie, who at once opened fire on him: 'I maun gang awa' t' the post; but I thocht that I would waste an hour on ye, and ca' roond just to see if ye waur still that fou wi' vanity as on the nicht gane by. An I see that ye've no learned the lesson. Well! the time is comin', sure eneucht! However I have all the time i' the marnins to my ain sel', so I'll aye look roond jist till see how ye gang yer ain gait to the quicksan', and then to the de'il! I'm aff till ma wark the noo!' And he went straightway, leaving Mr Markam considerably vexed, for the maids within earshot were vainly trying to conceal their giggles. He had fairly made up his mind to wear on that day ordinary clothes, but the visit of Saft Tammie reversed his decision. He would show them all that he was not a coward, and he would go on as he had begun – come what might. When he came to breakfast in full martial panoply the children, one and all, held down their heads and the backs of their necks became very red indeed. As, however, none of them laughed – except Titus, the youngest boy, who was seized with a fit of hysterical choking and was promptly banished from the room – he could not reprove them, but began to break his egg with a sternly determined air. It was unfortunate that as his wife was handing him a cup of tea one of the buttons of his sleeve caught in the lace of her morning wrapper, with the result that the hot tea was spilt over his bare knees. Not unnaturally, he made use of a swear word, whereupon his wife, somewhat nettled, spoke out: 'Well, Arthur, if you will make such an idiot of yourself with that ridiculous costume what else can you expect? You are not accustomed to it – and you never will be!' In answer he began an indignant speech with: 'Madam!' but he got no further, for now that the subject was broached, Mrs Markam intended to have her say out. It was not a pleasant say, and, truth to tell, it was not said in a pleasant manner. A wife's manner seldom is pleasant when she undertakes to tell what she considers 'truths' to her husband. The result was that Arthur Fernlee Markam undertook, then and there, that during his stay in Scotland he would wear no other costume than the one she abused. Woman-like his wife had the last word – given in this case with tears: 'Very well, Arthur! Of course you will do as you choose. Make me as ridiculous as you can, and spoil the poor girls' chances in life. Young men don't seem to care, as a general rule, for an idiot father-in-law! But I must warn you that your vanity will some day get a rude shock – if indeed you are not before then in an asylum or dead!'

It was manifest after a few days that Mr Markam would have to take the major part of his outdoor exercise by himself. The girls now and again took a walk with him, chiefly in the early morning or late at night, or on a wet day when there would be no one about; they professed to be willing to go out at all times, but somehow something always seemed to occur to prevent it. The boys could never be found at all on such occasions, and as to Mrs Markam she sternly refused to go out with him on any consideration so long as he should continue to make a fool of himself. On the Sunday he dressed himself in his habitual broadcloth, for he rightly felt that church was not a place for angry feelings; but on Monday morning he resumed his Highland garb. By this time he would have given a good deal if he had never thought of the dress, but his British obstinacy was strong, and he would not give in. Saft Tammie called at his house every morning, and, not being able to see him nor to have any message taken to him, used to call back in the afternoon when the letter-bag had been delivered and watched for his going out. On such occasions he never failed to warn him against his vanity in the same words which he had used at the first. Before many days were over Mr Markam had come to look upon him as little short of a scourge.

By the time the week was out the enforced partial solitude, the constant chagrin, and the never-ending brooding which was thus engendered, began to make Mr Markam quite ill. He was too proud to take any of his family into his confidence since they had in his view treated him very badly. Then he did not sleep well at night, and when he did sleep he had constantly bad dreams. Merely to assure himself that his pluck was not failing him he made it a practice to visit the quicksand at least once every day, he hardly ever failed to go there the last thing at night. It was perhaps this habit that wrought the quicksand with its terrible experience so perpetually into his dreams. More and more vivid these became, till on waking at times he could hardly realise that he had not been actually in the flesh to visit the fatal spot. He sometimes thought that he might have been walking in his sleep.

One night his dream was so vivid that when he awoke he could not believe that it had only been a dream. He shut his eyes again and again, but each time the vision, if it was a vision, or the reality, if it was a reality, would rise before him. The moon was shining full and yellow over the quicksand as he approached it; he could see the expanse of light shaken and disturbed and full of black shadows as the liquid sand quivered and trembled and wrinkled and eddied as was its wont between its pauses of marble calm. As he drew close to it another figure came towards it from the opposite side with equal footsteps. He saw that it was his own figure, his very self, and in silent terror, compelled by what force he knew not, he advanced – charmed as the bird is by the snake, mesmerised or hypnotised – to meet this other self. As he felt the yielding sand closing over him he awoke in the agony of death, trembling with fear, and, strange to say, with the silly man's prophecy seeming to sound in his ears: "'Vanity of vanities! All is vanity!' See thyself and repent ere the quicksand swallow thee!'

So convinced was he that this was no dream that he arose, early as it was, and dressing himself without disturbing his wife took his way to the shore. His heart fell when he came across a series of footsteps on the sands, which he at once recognised as his own. There was the same wide heel, the same square toe; he had no doubt now that he had actually been there, and half horrified, and half in a state of dreamy stupor, he followed the footsteps, and found them lost in the edge of the yielding quicksand. This gave him a terrible shock, for there were no return steps marked on the sand, and he felt that there was some dread mystery which he could not penetrate, and the penetration of which would, he feared, undo him.

In this state of affairs he took two wrong courses. Firstly he kept his trouble to himself, and, as none of his family had any clue to it, every innocent word or expression which they used supplied fuel to the consuming fire of his imagination. Secondly he began to read books professing to bear upon the mysteries of dreaming and of mental phenomena generally, with the result that every wild imagination of every crank or half-crazy philosopher became a living germ of unrest in the fertilising soil of his disordered brain. Thus negatively and positively all things began to work to a common end. Not the least of his disturbing causes was Saft Tammie, who had now become at certain times of the day a fixture at his gate. After a while, being interested in the previous state of this individual, he made enquiries regarding his past with the following result.

Saft Tammie was popularly believed to be the son of a laird in one of the counties round the Firth of Forth. He had been partially educated for the ministry, but for some cause which no one ever knew threw up his prospects suddenly, and, going to Peterhead in its days of whaling prosperity, had there taken service on a whaler. Here off and on he had remained for some years, getting gradually more and more silent in his habits, till finally his shipmates protested against so taciturn a mate, and he had found service amongst the fishing smacks of the northern fleet. He had worked for many years at the fishing with always the reputation of being 'a wee bit daft', till at length he had gradually settled down at Crooken, where the laird, doubtless knowing something of his family history, had given him a job which practically made him a pensioner. The minister who gave the information finished thus: 'It is a very strange thing, but the man seems to have some odd kind of gift. Whether it be that "second sight" which we Scotch people are so prone to believe in, or some other occult form of knowledge, I know not, but nothing of a disastrous tendency ever occurs in this place but the men with whom he lives are able to quote after the event some saying of his which certainly appears to have foretold it. He gets uneasy or excited – wakes up, in fact – when death is in the air!'

This did not in any way tend to lessen Mr Markam's concern, but on the contrary seemed to impress the prophecy more deeply on his mind. Of all the books which he had read on his new subject of study none interested him so much as a German one, *Die Döppleganger*, by Dr Heinrich von Aschenberg, formerly of Bonn. Here he learned for the first time of cases where men had led a double existence – each nature being quite apart from the other – the body being always a reality with one spirit, and a simulacrum with the other. Needless to say that Mr Markam realised this theory as exactly suiting his own case. The glimpse which he had of his own back the night of his escape from the quicksand – his own footmarks disappearing into the quicksand with no return steps visible – the prophecy of Saft Tammie about his meeting himself and perishing in the quicksand –

all lent aid to the conviction that he was in his own person an instance of the döppleganger. Being then conscious of a double life he took steps to prove its existence to his own satisfaction. To this end on one night before going to bed he wrote his name in chalk on the soles of his shoes. That night he dreamed of the quicksand, and of his visiting it – dreamed so vividly that on walking in the grey of the dawn he could not believe that he had not been there. Arising, without disturbing his wife, he sought his shoes.

The chalk signatures were undisturbed! He dressed himself and stole out softly. This time the tide was in, so he crossed the dunes and struck the shore on the further side of the quicksand. There, oh, horror of horrors! he saw his own footprints dying into the abyss!

He went home a desperately sad man. It seemed incredible that he, an elderly commercial man, who had passed a long and uneventful life in the pursuit of business in the midst of roaring, practical London, should thus find himself enmeshed in mystery and horror, and that he should discover that he had two existences. He could not speak of his trouble even to his own wife, for well he knew that she would at once require the fullest particulars of that other life – the one which she did not know; and that she would at the start not only imagine but charge him with all manner of infidelities on the head of it. And so his brooding grew deeper and deeper still. One evening – the tide then going out and the moon being at the full – he was sitting waiting for dinner when the maid announced that Saft Tammie was making a disturbance outside because he would not be let in to see him. He was very indignant, but did not like the maid to think that he had any fear on the subject, and so told her to bring him in. Tammie entered, walking more briskly than ever with his head up and a look of vigorous decision in the eyes that were so generally cast down. As soon as he entered he said: 'I have come to see ye once again – once again; and there ye sit, still just like a cockatoo on a pairch. Weel, mon, I forgie ye! Mind ye that, I forgie ye!' And without a word more he turned and walked out of the house, leaving the master in speechless indignation.

After dinner he determined to pay another visit to the quicksand – he would not allow even to himself that he was afraid to go. And so, about nine o'clock, in full array, he marched to the beach, and passing over the sands sat on the skirt of the nearer rock. The full moon was behind him and its light lit up the bay so that its fringe of foam, the dark outline of the headland, and the stakes of the salmon-nets were all emphasised. In the brilliant yellow glow the lights in the windows of Port Crooken and in those of the distant castle of the laird trembled like stars through the sky. For a long time he sat and drank in the beauty of the scene, and his soul seemed to feel a peace that it had not known for many days. All the pettiness and annoyance and silly fears of the past weeks seemed blotted out, and a new holy calm took the vacant place. In this sweet and solemn mood he reviewed his late action calmly, and felt ashamed of himself for his vanity and for the obstinacy which had followed it. And then and there he made up his mind that the present would be the last time he would wear the costume which had estranged him from those whom he loved, and which had caused him so many hours and days of chagrin, vexation, and pain.

But almost as soon as he arrived at this conclusion another voice seemed to speak within him and mockingly to ask him if he should ever get the chance to wear the suit again – that it was too late – he had chosen his course and must now abide the issue.

'It is not too late,' came the quick answer of his better self; and full of the thought, he rose up to go home and divest himself of the now hateful costume right away. He paused for one look at the beautiful scene. The light lay pale and mellow, softening every outline of rock and tree and house-top, and deepening the shadows into velvety-black, and lighting, as with a pale flame, the incoming tide, that now crept fringe-like across the flat waste of sand. Then he left the rock and stepped out for the shore.

But as he did so a frightful spasm of horror shook him, and for an instant the blood rushing to his head shut out all the light of the full moon. Once more he saw that fatal image of himself moving beyond the quicksand from the opposite rock to the shore. The shock was all the greater for the contrast with the spell of peace which he had just enjoyed; and, almost paralysed in every sense, he stood and watched the fatal vision and the wrinkly, crawling quicksand that seemed to writhe and yearn for something that lay between. There could be no mistake this time, for though the moon behind threw the face into shadow he could see there the same shaven cheeks as his own, and the small stubby moustache of a few weeks' growth. The light shone on the brilliant tartan, and on the eagle's plume. Even the bald space at one side of the Glengarry cap glistened, as did the cairngorm brooch on the shoulder and the tops of the silver buttons. As he looked he felt his feet slightly sinking, for he was still near the edge of the belt of quicksand, and he stepped back. As he did so the other figure stepped forward, so that the space between them was preserved.

So the two stood facing each other, as though in some weird fascination; and in the rushing of the blood through his brain Markam seemed to hear the words of the prophecy: 'See thyself face to face, and repent ere the quicksand swallow thee.' He did stand face to face with himself, he had repented – and now he was sinking in the quicksand! The warning and prophecy were coming true.

Above him the seagulls screamed, circling round the fringe of the incoming tide, and the sound being entirely mortal recalled him to himself. On the instant he stepped back a few quick steps, for as yet only his feet were merged in the soft sand. As he did so the other figure stepped forward, and coming within the deadly grip of the quicksand began to sink. It seemed to Markam that he was looking at himself going down to his doom, and on the instant the anguish of his soul found vent in a terrible cry. There was at the same instant a terrible cry from the other figure, and as Markam threw up his hands the figure did the same. With horror-struck eyes he saw him sink deeper into the quicksand; and then, impelled by what power he knew not, he advanced again towards the sand to meet his fate. But as his more forward foot began to sink he heard again the cries of the seagulls which seemed to restore his benumbed faculties. With a mighty effort he drew his foot out of the sand which seemed to clutch it, leaving his shoe behind, and then in sheer terror he turned and ran from the place, never stopping till his breath and strength failed him, and he sank half-swooning on the grassy path through the sand-hills.

*   *   *

Arthur Markam made up his mind not to tell his family of his terrible adventure – until at least such time as he should be complete master of himself. Now that the fatal double – his other self – had been engulfed in the quicksand he felt something like his old peace of mind.

That night he slept soundly and did not dream at all; and in the morning was quite his old self. It really seemed as though his newer and worser self had disappeared for ever; and strangely enough Saft Tammie was absent from his post that morning and never appeared there again, but sat in his old place watching nothing, as of old, with lack-lustre eye. In accordance with his resolution he did not wear his Highland suit again, but one evening tied it up in a bundle, claymore, dirk and philibeg and all, and bringing it secretly with him threw it into the quicksand. With a feeling of intense pleasure he saw it sucked below the sand, which closed above it into marble smooth-ness. Then he went home and announced cheerily to his family assembled for evening prayers: 'Well! my dears, you will be glad to hear that I have abandoned my idea of wearing the Highland dress. I see now what a vain old fool I was and how ridiculous I made myself! You shall never see it again!'

'Where is it, father?' asked one of the girls, wishing to say some-thing so that such a self-sacrificing announcement as her father's should not be passed in absolute silence. His answer was so sweetly given that the girl rose from her seat and came and kissed him. It was: 'In the quicksand, my dear! and I hope that my worser self is buried there along with it – for ever.'

* * *

The remainder of the summer was passed at Crooken with delight by all the family, and on his return to town Mr Markam had almost forgotten the whole of the incident of the quicksand, and all touching on it, when one day he got a letter from the MacCallum More which caused him much thought, though he said nothing of it to his family, and left it, for certain reasons, unanswered. It ran as follows:

The MacCallum More and Roderick MacDhu.
The Scotch All-Wool Tartan Clothing Mart.
Copthall Court, E.C.
30th September, 1892

DEAR SIR – I trust you will pardon the liberty which I take in writing to you, but I am desirous of making an enquiry, and I am informed that you have been sojourning during the summer in Aberdeenshire (Scotland, N.B.). My partner, Mr Roderick MacDhu – as he appears for business reasons on our bill-heads and in our advertisements, his real name being Emmanuel Moses Marks of London – went early last month to Scotland (N.B.) for a tour, but as I have only once heard from him, shortly after his departure, I am anxious lest any misfortune may have befallen him. As I have been unable to obtain any news of him on making all enquiries in my power, I venture to appeal to you. His letter was written in deep dejection of spirit, and mentioned that he feared a judgement had come upon him for wishing to appear as a Scotchman on Scottish soil, as he had one moonlight night shortly after his arrival seen his 'wraith'. He evidently alluded to the fact that before his departure he had procured for himself a Highland costume similar to that which we had the honour to supply to you, with which, as perhaps you will remember, he was much struck. He may, however, never have worn it, as he was, to my own knowledge, diffident about putting it on, and even went so far as to tell me that he would at first only venture to wear it late at night or very early in the morning, and then only in remote places, until such time as he should get accustomed to it. Unfortunately he did not advise me of his route so that I am in complete ignorance of his whereabouts; and I venture to ask if you may have seen or heard of a Highland costume similar to your own having been seen anywhere in the neighbourhood in which I am told you have recently purchased the estate which you temporarily occupied. I shall not expect an answer to this letter unless you can give me some information regarding my friend and partner, so pray do not trouble to reply unless there be cause. I am encouraged to think that he may have been in your neighbourhood as, though his letter is not dated, the envelope is marked with the postmark of 'Yellon' which I find is in Aberdeenshire, and not far from the Mains of Crooken.

I have the honour to be, dear sir,
Yours very respectfully

JOSHUA SHEENY COHEN BENJAMIN
(*The MacCallum More*)

The Crystal Cup

1   The Dream-Birth

The blue waters touch the walls of the palace; I can hear their soft, lapping wash against the marble whenever I listen. Far out at sea I can see the waves glancing in the sunlight, ever-smiling, ever-glancing, ever-sunny. Happy waves! Happy in your gladness, thrice happy that ye are free!

I rise from my work and spring up the wall till I reach the embrasure. I grasp the corner of the stonework and draw myself up till I crouch in the wide window. Sea, sea, out away as far as my vision extends. There I gaze till my eyes grow dim; and in the dimness of my eyes my spirit finds its sight. My soul flies on the wings of memory away beyond the blue, smiling sea – away beyond the glancing waves and the gleaming sails, to the land I call my home. As the minutes roll by, my actual eyesight seems to be restored, and I look round me in my old birth-house. The rude simplicity of the dwelling comes back to me as something new. There I see my old books and manuscripts and pictures, and there, away on their old shelves, high up above the door, I see my first rude efforts in art.

How poor they seem to me now! And yet, were I free, I would not give the smallest of them for all I now possess. Possess? How I dream.

The dream calls me back to waking life. I spring down from my window-seat and work away frantically, for every line I draw on paper, every new form that springs on the plaster, brings me nearer freedom. I will make a vase whose beauty will put to shame the glorious works of Greece in her golden prime! Surely a love like mine and a hope like mine must in time make some form of beauty spring to life! When He beholds it he will exclaim with rapture, and will order my instant freedom. I can forget my hate, and the deep debt of revenge which I owe him when I think of liberty – even from his hands. Ah! then on the wings of the morning shall I fly beyond the sea to my home – her home – and clasp her to my arms, never more to be separated!

But, oh Spirit of Day! if she should be – No, no, I cannot think of it, or I shall go mad. Oh Time, Time! maker and destroyer of men's fortunes, why hasten so fast for others whilst thou laggest so slowly for me? Even now my home may have become desolate, and she – my bride of an hour – may sleep calmly in the cold earth. Oh this suspense will drive me mad! Work, work! Freedom is before me; Aurora is the reward of my labour!

So I rush to my work; but to my brain and hand, heated alike, no fire or no strength descends. Half mad with despair, I beat myself against the walls of my prison, and then climb into the embrasure, and once more gaze upon the ocean, but find there no hope. And so I stay till night, casting its pall of blackness over nature, puts the possibility of effort away from me for yet another day.

So my days go on, and grow to weeks and months. So will they grow to years, should life so long remain an unwelcome guest within me; for what is man without hope? and is not hope nigh dead within this weary breast?

*   *   *

Last night, in my dreams, there came, like an inspiration from the Day-Spirit, a design for my vase.

All day my yearning for freedom – for Aurora, or news of her – had increased tenfold, and my heart and brain were on fire. Madly I beat myself, like a caged bird, against my prison bars. Madly I leaped to my window-seat, and gazed with bursting eyeballs out on the free, open sea. And there I sat till my passion had worn itself out; and then I slept, and dreamed of thee, Aurora – of thee and freedom. In my ears I heard again the old song we used to sing together, when as children we wandered on the beach; when, as lovers, we saw the sun sink in the ocean, and I would see its glory doubled as it shone in thine eyes, and was mellowed against thy cheek; and when, as my bride, you clung to me as my arms went round you on that desert tongue of land whence rushed that band of sea-robbers that tore me away. Oh! how my heart curses those men – not men, but fiends! But one solitary gleam of joy remains from that dread encounter – that my struggle stayed those hellhounds, and that, ere I was stricken down, this right hand sent one of them to his home. My spirit rises as I think of that blow that saved thee from a life worse than death. With the thought I feel my cheeks burning, and my forehead swelling with mighty veins. My eyes burn, and I rush wildly round my prisonhouse, 'Oh! for one of my enemies, that I might dash out his brains against these marble walls, and trample his heart out as he lay before me!' These walls would spare him not. They are pitiless, alas! I know too well. 'Oh, cruel mockery of kindness, to make a palace a prison, and to taunt a captive's aching heart with forms of beauty and sculptured marble!' Wondrous, indeed, are these sculptured walls! Men call them passing fair; but oh, Aurora! with thy beauty ever before my eyes, what form that men call lovely can be fair to me? Like him who gazes sunwards, and then sees no light on earth, from the glory that dyes his iris, so thy beauty or its memory has turned the fairest things of earth to blackness and deformity.

In my dream last night, when in my ears came softly, like music stealing across the waters from afar, the old song we used to sing together, then to my brain, like a ray of light, came an idea whose grandeur for a moment struck me dumb. Before my eyes grew a vase of such beauty that I knew my hope was born to life, and that the Great Spirit had placed my foot on the ladder that leads from this my palace dungeon to freedom and to thee. Today I have got a block of crystal – for only in such pellucid substance can I body forth my dream – and have commenced my work.

I found at first that my hand had lost its cunning, and I was beginning to despair, when, like the memory of a dream, there came back in my ears the strains of the old song. I sang it softly to myself, and as I did so I grew calmer; but oh! how differently the song sounded to me when thy voice, Aurora, rose not in unison with my own! But what avails pining? To work! To work! Every touch of my chisel will bring me nearer thee.

* * *

My vase is daily growing nearer to completion. I sing as I work, and my constant song is the one I love so well. I can hear the echo of my voice in the vase; and as I end, the wailing song note is prolonged in sweet, sad music in the crystal cup. I listen, ear down, and sometimes I weep as I listen, so sadly comes the echo to my song. Imperfect though it be, my voice makes sweet music, and its echo in the cup guides my hand towards perfection as I work. Would that thy voice rose and fell with mine, Aurora, and then the world would behold a vase of such beauty as never before woke up the slumbering fires of man's love for what is fair; for if I do such work in sadness, imperfect as I am in my solitude and sorrow, what would I do in joy, perfect when with thee? I know that my work is good as an artist, and I feel that it is as a man; and the cup itself, as it daily grows in beauty, gives back a clearer echo. Oh! if I worked in joy how gladly would it give back our voices! Then would we hear an echo and music such as mortals seldom hear; but now the echo, like my song, seems imperfect. I grow daily weaker; but still I work on – work with my whole soul – for am I not working for freedom and for thee?

*   *   *

My work is nearly done. Day by day, hour by hour, the vase grows more finished. Ever clearer comes the echo whilst I sing; ever softer, ever more sad and heart-rending comes the echo of the wail at the end of the song. Day by day I grow weaker and weaker; still I work on with all my soul. At night the thought comes to me, whilst I think of thee, that I will never see thee more – that I breathe out my life into the crystal cup, and that it will last there when I am gone.

So beautiful has it become, so much do I love it, that I could gladly die to be maker of such a work, were it not for thee – for my love for thee, and my hope of thee, and my fear for thee, and my anguish for thy grief when thou knowest I am gone.

*   *   *

My work requires but few more touches. My life is slowly ebbing away, and I feel that with my last touch my life will pass out for ever into the cup. Till that touch is given I must not die – I will not die. My hate has passed away. So great are my wrongs that revenge of mine would be too small a compensation for my woe. I leave revenge to a juster and a mightier than I. Thee, oh Aurora, I will await in the land of flowers, where thou and I will wander, never more to part, never more! Ah, never more! Farewell, Aurora – Aurora – Aurora!

2   *The Feast of Beauty*

The Feast of Beauty approaches rapidly, yet hardly so fast as my royal master wishes. He seems to have no other thought than to have this feast greater and better than any ever held before. Five summers ago his Feast of Beauty was nobler than all held in his sire's reign together; yet scarcely was it over, and the rewards given to the victors, when he conceived the giant project whose success is to be tested when the moon reaches her full. It was boldly chosen and boldly done; chosen and done as boldly as the project of a monarch should be. But still I cannot think that it will end well. This yearning after completeness must be unsatisfied in the end – this desire that makes a monarch fling his kingly justice to the winds, and strive to reach his Mecca over a desert of blighted hopes and lost lives. But hush! I must not dare to think ill of my master or his deeds; and besides, walls have ears. I must leave alone these dangerous topics, and confine my thoughts within proper bounds.

The moon is waxing quickly, and with its fullness comes the Feast of Beauty, whose success as a whole rests almost solely on my watch-fulness and care; for if the ruler of the feast should fail in his duty, who could fill the void? Let me see what arts are represented, and what works compete. All the arts will have trophies: poetry in its various forms, and prose-writing; sculpture with carving in various metals, and glass, and wood, and ivory, and engraving gems, and setting jewels; painting on canvas, and glass, and wood, and stone and metal; music, vocal and instrumental; and dancing. If that woman will but sing, we will have a real triumph of music; but she appears sickly too. All our best artists either get ill or die, although we promise them freedom or rewards or both if they succeed.

Surely never yet was a Feast of Beauty so fair or so richly dowered as this which the full moon shall behold and hear; but ah! the crown-ing glory of the feast will be the crystal cup. Never yet have these eyes beheld such a form of beauty, such a wondrous mingling of substance and light. Surely some magic power must have helped to draw such loveliness from a cold block of crystal. I must be careful that no harm happens to the vase. Today when I touched it, it gave forth such a ringing sound that my heart jumped with fear lest it should sustain any injury. Henceforth, till I deliver it up to my master, no hand but my own shall touch it lest any harm should happen to it.

Strange story has that cup. Born to life in the cell of a captive torn from his artist home beyond the sea, to enhance the splendour of a feast by his labour – seen at work by spies, and traced and followed till a chance – cruel chance for him – gave him into the hands of the emissaries of my master. He too, poor moth, fluttered about the flame: the name of freedom spurred him on to exertion till he wore away his life. The beauty of that cup was dearly bought for him. Many a man would forget his captivity whilst he worked at such a piece of loveliness; but he appeared to have some sorrow at his heart, some sorrow so great that it quenched his pride.

How he used to rave at first! How he used to rush about his

chamber, and then climb into the embrasure of his window, and gaze out away over the sea! Poor captive! perhaps over the sea some one waited for his coming who was dearer to him than many cups, even many cups as beautiful as this, if such could be on earth . . . Well, well, we must all die soon or late, and who dies first escapes the more sorrow, perhaps, who knows? How, when he had commenced the cup, he used to sing all day long, from the moment the sun shot its first fiery arrow into the retreating hosts of night-clouds, till the shades of evening advancing drove the lingering sunbeams into the west – and always the same song!

How he used to sing, all alone! Yet sometimes I could almost imagine I heard not one voice from his chamber, but two . . . No more will it echo again from the wall of a dungeon, or from a hillside in free air. No more will his eyes behold the beauty of his crystal cup.

It was well he lived to finish it. Often and often have I trembled to think of his death, as I saw him day by day grow weaker as he worked at the unfinished vase. Must his eyes never more behold the beauty that was born of his soul? Oh, never more! Oh Death, grim King of Terrors, how mighty is thy sceptre! All-powerful is the wave of thy hand that summons us in turn to thy kingdom away beyond the poles!

Would that thou, poor captive, hadst lived to behold thy triumph, for victory will be thine at the Feast of Beauty such as man never before achieved. Then thou mightst have heard the shout that hails the victor in the contest, and the plaudits that greet him as he passes out, a free man, through the palace gates. But now thy cup will come to light amid the smiles of beauty and rank and power, whilst thou liest there in thy lonely chamber, cold as the marble of its walls.

And, after all, the feast will be imperfect, since the victors cannot all be crowned. I must ask my master's direction as to how a blank place of a competitor, should he prove a victor, is to be filled up. So late? I must see him ere the noontide hour of rest be past.

*   *   *

Great Spirit! how I trembled as my master answered my question!

I found him in his chamber, as usual in the noontide. He was lying on his couch disrobed, half-sleeping; and the drowsy zephyr, scented with rich odours from the garden, wafted through the windows at either side by the fans, lulled him to complete repose. The darkened chamber was cool and silent. From the vestibule came the murmuring of many fountains, and the pleasant splash of falling waters.

'Oh, happy,' said I, in my heart, 'Oh, happy great King, that has such pleasures to enjoy!' The breeze from the fans swept over the strings of the Aeolian harps, and a sweet, confused, happy melody arose like the murmuring of children's voices singing afar off in the valleys, and floating on the wind.

As I entered the chamber softly, with muffled footfall and pent-in breath, I felt a kind of awe stealing over me. To me who was born and have dwelt all my life within the precincts of the court – to me who talk daily with my royal master, and take his minutest directions as to the coming feast – to me who had all my life looked up to my king as to a spirit, and had venerated him as more than mortal – came a feeling of almost horror; for my master looked then, in his quiet chamber, half-sleeping amid the drowsy music of the harps and fountains, more like a common man than a God. As the thought came to me I shuddered in affright, for it seemed to me that I had been guilty of sacrilege. So much had my veneration for my royal master become a part of my nature, that but to think of him as another man seemed like the anarchy of my own soul.

I came beside the couch, and watched him in silence. He seemed to be half-listening to the fitful music; and as the melody swelled and died away his chest rose and fell as he breathed in unison with the sound.

After a moment or two he appeared to become conscious of the presence of some one in the room, although by no motion of his face could I see that he heard any sound, and his eyes were shut. He opened his eyes, and, seeing me, asked, 'Was all right about the Feast of Beauty?' for that is the subject ever nearest to his thoughts. I answered that all was well, but that I had come to ask his royal pleasure as to how a vacant place amongst the competitors was to be filled up. He asked, 'How vacant?' and on my telling him, 'From death,' he asked again, quickly, 'Was the work finished?' When I told him that it was, he lay back again on his couch with a sigh of relief, for he had half arisen in his anxiety as he asked the question. Then he said, after a minute, 'All the competitors must be present at the feast.' 'All?' said I. 'All,' he answered again, 'alive or dead; for the old custom must be preserved, and the victors crowned.' He stayed still for a minute more, and then said, slowly, 'Victors or martyrs.' And I could see that the kingly spirit was coming back to him.

Again he went on, 'This will be my last Feast of Beauty; and all the captives shall be set free. Too much sorrow has sprung already from my ambition. Too much injustice has soiled the name of king.'

He said no more, but lay still and closed his eyes. I could see by the working of his hands and the heaving of his chest that some violent emotion troubled him, and the thought arose, 'He is a man, but he is yet a king; and, though a king as he is, still happiness is not for him. Great Spirit of Justice! thou metest out his pleasures and his woes to man, to king and slave alike! Thou lovest best to whom thou givest peace!'

Gradually my master grew more calm, and at length sunk into a gentle slumber; but even in his sleep he breathed in unison with the swelling murmur of the harps.

'To each is given,' said I gently, 'something in common with the world of actual things. Thy life, oh King, is bound by chains of sympathy to the voice of Truth, which is Music! Tremble, lest in the presence of a master-strain thou shouldst feel thy littleness, and die!' and I softly left the room.

3 *The Story of the Moonbeam*

Slowly I creep along the bosom of the waters.

Sometimes I look back as I rise upon a billow, and see behind me many of my kin sitting each upon a wave-summit as upon a throne. So I go on for long, a power that I wist not forcing me onward, without will or purpose of mine.

At length, as I rise upon a mimic wave, I see afar a hazy light that springs from a vast palace, through whose countless windows flame lamps and torches. But at the first view, as if my coming had been the signal, the lights disappear in an instant.

Impatiently I await what may happen; and as I rise with each heartbeat of the sea, I look forward to where the torches had gleamed. Can it be a deed of darkness that shuns the light?

*   *   *

The time has come when I can behold the palace without waiting to mount upon the waves. It is built of white marble, and rises steep from the brine. Its sea front is glorious with columns and statues; and from the portals the marble steps sweep down, broad and wide to the waters, and below them, down as deep as I can see.

No sound is heard, no light is seen. A solemn silence abounds, a perfect calm.

Slowly I climb the palace walls, my brethren following as soldiers up a breach. I slide along the roofs, and as I look behind me walls and roofs are glistening as with silver. At length I meet with something smooth and hard and translucent; but through it I pass and enter a vast hall, where for an instant I hang in midair and wonder.

My coming has been the signal for such a burst of harmony as brings back to my memory the music of the spheres as they rush through space; and in the full-swelling anthem of welcome I feel that I am indeed a sun-spirit, a child of light, and that this is homage to my master.

I look upon the face of a great monarch, who sits at the head of a banquet-table. He has turned his head upwards and backwards, and looks as if he had been awaiting my approach. He rises and fronts me with the ringing out of the welcome-song, and all the others in the great hall turn towards me as well. I can see their eyes gleaming. Down along the immense table, laden with plate and glass and flowers, they stand holding each a cup of ruby wine, with which they pledge the monarch when the song is ended, as they drink success to him and to the 'Feast of Beauty'.

I survey the hall. An immense chamber, with marble walls covered with bas-reliefs and frescoes and sculptured figures, and panelled by great columns that rise along the surface and support a dome ceiling painted wondrously; in its centre the glass lantern by which I entered.

On the walls are hung pictures of various forms and sizes, and down the centre of the table stretches a raised platform on which are placed works of art of various kinds.

At one side of the hall is a dais on which sit persons of both sexes with noble faces and lordly brows, but all wearing the same expression – care tempered by hope. All these hold scrolls in their hands.

At the other side of the hall is a similar dais, on which sit others fairer to earthly view, less spiritual and more marked by surface passion. They hold music-scores. All these look more joyous than those on the other platform, all save one, a woman, who sits with downcast face and dejected mien, as of one without hope. As my light falls at her feet she looks up, and I feel happy. The sympathy between us has called a faint gleam of hope to cheer that poor pale face.

Many are the forms of art that rise above the banquet-table, and all are lovely to behold. I look on all with pleasure one by one, till I see the last of them at the end of the table away from the monarch, and then all the others seem as nothing to me. What is this that makes other forms of beauty seem as nought when compared with it, when brought within the radius of its lustre? A crystal cup, wrought with such wondrous skill that light seems to lose its individual glory as it shines upon it and is merged in its beauty. 'Oh Universal Mother, let me enter there. Let my life be merged in its beauty, and no more will I regret my sun-strength hidden deep in the chasms of my moon-mother. Let me live there and perish there, and I will be joyous whilst it lasts, and content to pass into the great vortex of nothing-ness to be born again when the glory of the cup has fled.'

Can it be that my wish is granted, that I have entered the cup and become a part of its beauty? 'Great Mother, I thank thee.'

Has the cup life? or is it merely its wondrous perfectness that makes it tremble, like a beating heart, in unison with the ebb and flow, the great wave-pulse of nature? To me it feels as if it had life.

I look through the crystal walls and see at the end of the table, isolated from all others, the figure of a man seated. Are those cords that bind his limbs? How suits that crown of laurel those wide, dim eyes, and that pallid hue? It is passing strange. This Feast of Beauty holds some dread secrets, and sees some wondrous sights.

I hear a voice of strange, rich sweetness, yet wavering – the voice of one almost a king by nature. He is standing up; I see him through my palace wall. He calls a name and sits down again.

Again I hear a voice from the platform of scrolls, the Throne of Brows; and again I look and behold a man who stands trembling yet flushed, as though the morning light shone bright upon his soul. He reads in cadenced measure a song in praise of my moon-mother, the Feast of Beauty, and the king. As he speaks, he trembles no more, but seems inspired, and his voice rises to a tone of power and grandeur, and rings back from walls and dome. I hear his words distinctly, though saddened in tone, in the echo from my crystal home. He concludes and sits down, half-fainting, amid a whirlwind of applause, every note, every beat of which is echoed as the words had been.

Again the monarch rises and calls 'Aurora', that she may sing for freedom. The name echoes in the cup with a sweet, sad sound. So sad, so despairing seems the echo, that the hall seems to darken and the scene to grow dim.

'Can a sun-spirit mourn, or a crystal vessel weep?'

She, the dejected one, rises from her seat on the Throne of Sound, and all eyes turn upon her save those of the pale one, laurel-crowned. Thrice she essays to begin, and thrice nought comes from her lips but a dry, husky sigh, till an old man who has been moving round the hall settling all things, cries out, in fear lest she should fail, 'Freedom!'

The word is re-echoed from the cup. She hears the sound, turns towards it and begins.

Oh, the melody of that voice! And yet it is not perfect alone; for after the first note comes an echo from the cup that swells in unison with the voice, and the two sounds together seem as if one strain came ringing sweet from the lips of the All-Father himself. So sweet it is, that all throughout the hall sit spellbound, and scarcely dare to breathe.

In the pause after the first verses of the song, I hear the voice of the old man speaking to a comrade, but his words are unheard by any other: 'Look at the king. His spirit seems lost in a trance of melody. Ah! I fear me some evil: the nearer the music approaches to perfection the more rapt he becomes. I dread lest a perfect note shall prove his death-call.' His voice dies away as the singer commences the last verse.

Sad and plaintive is the song; full of feeling and tender love, but love overshadowed by grief and despair. As it goes on the voice of the singer grows sweeter and more thrilling, more real; and the cup, my crystal time-home, vibrates more and more as it gives back the echo. The monarch looks like one entranced, and no movement is within the hall . . . The song dies away in a wild wail that seems to tear the heart of the singer in twain; and the cup vibrates still more as it gives back the echo. As the note, long-swelling, reaches its highest, the cup, the Crystal Cup, my wondrous home, the gift of the All-Father, shivers into millions of atoms, and passes away.

Ere I am lost in the great vortex I see the singer throw up her arms and fall, freed at last, and the king sitting, glory-faced, but pallid with the hue of Death.

The Chain of Destiny

1   A Warning

It was so late in the evening when I arrived at Scarp that I had but little opportunity of observing the external appearance of the house; but, as far as I could judge in the dim twilight, it was a very stately edifice of seemingly great age, built of white stone. When I passed the porch, however, I could observe its internal beauties much more closely, for a large wood fire burned in the hall and all the rooms and passages were lighted. The hall was almost baronial in its size, and opened on to a staircase of dark oak so wide and so generous in its slope that a carriage might almost have been driven up it. The rooms were large and lofty, with their walls, like those of the staircase, panelled with oak black from age. This sombre material would have made the house intensely gloomy but for the enormous width and height of both rooms and passages. As it was, the effect was a homely combination of size and warmth. The windows were set in deep embrasures, and, on the ground story, reached from quite level with the floor to almost the ceiling. The fireplaces were quite in the old style, large and surrounded with massive oak carvings, representing on each some scene from biblical history, and at the side of each fireplace rose a pair of massive carved iron firedogs. It was altogether just such a house as would have delighted the heart of Washington Irving or Nathaniel Hawthorne.

The house had been lately restored; but in effecting the restoration comfort had not been forgotten, and any modern improvement which tended to increase the homelike appearance of the rooms had been added. The old diamond-paned casements, which had remained probably from the Elizabethan age, had given place to more useful plate glass; and, in like manner, many other changes had taken place. But so judiciously had every change been effected that nothing of the new clashed with the old, but the harmony of all the parts seemed complete.

I thought it no wonder that Mrs Trevor had fallen in love with Scarp the first time she had seen it. Mrs Trevor's liking the place was tantamount to her husband's buying it, for he was so wealthy that he could get almost anything money could purchase. He was himself a man of good taste, but still he felt his inferiority to his wife in this respect so much that he never dreamt of differing in opinion from her on any matter of choice or judgement. Mrs Trevor had, without exception, the best taste of any one whom I ever knew, and, strange to say, her taste was not confined to any branch of art. She did not write, or paint, or sing; but still her judgement in writing, painting, or music, was unquestioned by her friends. It seemed as if nature had denied to her the power of execution in any separate branch of art, in order to make her perfect in her appreciation of what was beautiful and true in all. She was perfect in the art of harmonising the art of everyday life. Her husband used to say, with a far-fetched joke, that her star must have been in the House of Libra, because everything which she said and did showed such a nicety of balance.

Mr and Mrs Trevor were the most model couple I ever knew – they really seemed not twain, but one. They appeared to have adopted something of the French idea of man and wife – that they should not be the less like friends because they were linked together by indissoluble bonds – that they should share their pleasures as well as their sorrows. The former outbalanced the latter, for both husband and wife were of that happy temperament which can take pleasure from everything, and find consolation even in the chastening rod of affliction.

Still, through their web of peaceful happiness ran a thread of care. One that cropped up in strange places, and disappeared again, but which left a quiet tone over the whole fabric – they had no child.

They had their share of sorrow, for when time was ripe
The still affection of the heart became an outward breathing type,
That into stillness passed again,
But left a want unknown before.

There was something simple and holy in their patient endurance of their lonely life – for lonely a house must ever be without children to those who love truly. Theirs was not the eager, disappointed longing of those whose union had proved fruitless. It was the simple, patient, hopeless resignation of those who find that a common sorrow draws them more closely together than many common joys.

I myself could note the warmth of their hearts and their strong
philoprogenitive feeling in their manner towards me.

From the time when I lay sick in college when Mrs Trevor appeared to my fever-dimmed eyes like an angel of mercy, I felt myself
growing in their hearts. Who can imagine my gratitude to the lady
who, merely because she heard of my sickness and desolation from a
college friend, came and nursed me night and day till the fever left
me. When I was sufficiently strong to be moved she had me brought
away to the country, where good air, care, and attention soon made
me stronger than ever. From that time I became a constant visitor at
the Trevors' house; and as month after month rolled by I felt that I
was growing in their affections. For four summers I spent my long
vacation in their house, and each year I could feel Mr Trevor's shake
of the hand grow heartier, and his wife's kiss on my forehead – for so
she always saluted me – grow more tender and motherly.

Their liking for me had now grown so much that in their heart of
hearts – and it was a sanctum common to them both – they secretly
loved me as a son. Their love was returned manifold by the lonely
boy, whose devotion to the kindest friends of his youth and his
trouble had increased with his growth into manhood. Even in my
own heart I was ashamed to confess how I loved them both – how I
worshipped Mrs Trevor as I adored the mother whom I had lost so
young, and whose eyes shone sometimes even then upon me, like
stars, in my sleep.

It is strange how timorous we are when our affections are concerned. Merely because I had never told her how I loved her as a
mother, because she had never told me how she loved me as a son, I
used sometimes to think of her with a sort of lurking suspicion that I
was trusting too much to my imagination. Sometimes even I would
try to avoid thinking of her altogether, till my yearning would grow
too strong to be repelled, and then I would think of her long and
silently, and would love her more and more. My life was so lonely
that I clung to her as the only thing I had to love. Of course I loved
her husband, too, but I never thought about him in the same way; for
men are less demonstrative about their affections to each other, and
even acknowledge them to themselves less.

Mrs Trevor was an excellent hostess. She always let her guests see
that they were welcome, and, unless in the case of casual visitors, that
they were expected. She was, as may be imagined, very popular with
all classes; but what is more rare, she was equally popular with both
sexes. To be popular with her own sex is the touchstone of a woman's

worth. To the houses of the peasantry she came, they said, like an angel, and brought comfort wherever she came. She knew the proper way to deal with the poor; she always helped them materially, but never offended their feelings in so doing. Young people all adored her.

My curiosity had been aroused as to the sort of place Scarp was; for, in order to give me a surprise, they would not tell me anything about it, but said that I must wait and judge it for myself. I had looked forward to my visit with both expectation and curiosity.

When I entered the hall, Mrs Trevor came out to welcome me and kissed me on the forehead, after her usual manner. Several of the old servants came near, smiling and bowing, and wishing welcome to 'Master Frank'. I shook hands with several of them, whilst their mistress looked on with a pleased smile.

As we went into a snug parlour, where a table was laid out with the materials for a comfortable supper, Mrs Trevor said to me: 'I am glad you came so soon, Frank. We have no one here at present, so you will be quite alone with us for a few days; and you will be quite alone with me this evening, for Charley is gone to a dinner party at Westholm.'

I told her that I was glad that there was no one else at Scarp, for that I would rather be with her and her husband than any one else in the world. She smiled as she said: 'Frank, if any one else said that, I would put it down as a mere compliment; but I know you always speak the truth. It is all very well to be alone with an old couple like Charley and me for two or three days; but just you wait till Thursday, and you will look on the intervening days as quite wasted.'

'Why?' I enquired.

'Because, Frank, there is a girl coming to stay with me then, with whom I intend you to fall in love.'

I answered jocosely: 'Oh, thank you, Mrs Trevor, very much for your kind intentions – but suppose for a moment that they should be impracticable. "One man may lead a horse to the pond's brink." "The best laid schemes o' mice an' men." Eh?'

'Frank, don't be silly. I do not want to make you fall in love against your inclination; but I hope and I believe that you will.'

'Well, I'm sure I hope you won't be disappointed; but I never yet heard a person praised that I did not experience a disappointment when I came to know him or her.'

'Frank, did I praise any one?'

'Well, I am vain enough to think that your saying that you knew I would fall in love with her was a sort of indirect praise.'

'Dear, me, Frank, how modest you have grown.' A sort of indirect praise! 'Your humility is quite touching.'

'May I ask who the lady is, as I am supposed to be an interested party?'

'I do not know that I ought to tell you on account of your having expressed any doubt as to her merits. Besides, I might weaken the effect of the introduction. If I stimulate your curiosity it will be a point in my favour.'

'Oh, very well; I suppose I must only wait?'

'Ah, well, Frank, I will tell you. It is not fair to keep you waiting. She is a Miss Fothering.'

'Fothering? Fothering? I think I know that name. I remember hearing it somewhere, a long time ago, if I do not mistake. Where does she come from?'

'Her father is a clergyman in Norfolk, but he belongs to the Warwickshire family. I met her at Winthrop, Sir Harry Blount's place, a few months ago, and took a great liking for her, which she returned, and so we became fast friends. I made her promise to pay me a visit this summer, so she and her sister are coming here on Thursday to stay for some time.'

'And, may I be bold enough to enquire what she is like?'

'You may enquire if you like, Frank; but you won't get an answer. I shall not try to describe her. You must wait and judge for yourself.'

'Wait,' said I, 'three whole days? How can I do that? Do, tell me.'

She remained firm to her determination. I tried several times in the course of the evening to find out something more about Miss Fothering, for my curiosity was roused; but all the answer I could get on the subject was: 'Wait, Frank; wait, and judge for yourself.'

When I was bidding her good night, Mrs Trevor said to me: 'By the bye, Frank, you will have to give up the room which you will sleep in tonight, after tomorrow. I will have such a full house that I cannot let you have a doubled-bedded room all to yourself; so I will give that room to the Miss Fotherings, and move you up to the second floor. I just want you to see the room, as it has a romantic look about it, and has all the old furniture that was in it when we came here. There are several pictures in it worth looking at.'

My bedroom was a large chamber – immense for a bedroom – with two windows opening level with the floor, like those of the parlours and drawing-rooms. The furniture was old-fashioned, but not old enough to be curious, and on the walls hung many pictures – portraits – the house was full of portraits – and landscapes. I just glanced at these, intending to examine them in the morning, and went to bed. There was a fire in the room, and I lay awake for some time looking dreamily at the shadows of the furniture flitting over the walls and ceiling as the flames of the wood fire leaped and fell, and the red embers dropped whitening on the hearth. I tried to give the rein to my thoughts, but they kept constantly to the one subject – the mysterious Miss Fothering, with whom I was to fall in love. I was sure that I had heard her name somewhere, and I had at times lazy recollections of a child's face. At such times I would start awake from my growing drowsiness, but before I could collect my scattered thoughts the idea had eluded me. I could remember neither when nor where I had heard the name, nor could I recall even the expression of the child's face. It must have been long, long ago, when I was young. When I was young my mother was alive. My mother – mother – mother. I found myself half awakening, and repeating the word over and over again. At last I fell asleep.

I thought that I awoke suddenly to that peculiar feeling which we sometimes have on starting from sleep, as if some one had been speaking in the room, and the voice is still echoing through it. All was quite silent, and the fire had gone out. I looked out of the window that lay straight opposite the foot of the bed, and observed a light outside, which gradually grew brighter till the room was almost as light as by day. The window looked like a picture in the framework formed by the cornice over the foot of the bed, and the massive pillars shrouded in curtains which supported it.

With the new accession of light I looked round the room, but nothing was changed. All was as before, except that some of the objects of furniture and ornament were shown in stronger relief than hitherto. Amongst these, those most in relief were the other bed, which was placed across the room, and an old picture that hung on the wall at its foot. As the bed was merely the counterpart of the one in which I lay, my attention became fixed on the picture. I observed it closely and with great interest. It seemed old, and was the portrait of a young girl, whose face, though kindly and merry, bore signs of thought and a capacity for deep feeling – almost for passion. At some moments, as I looked at it, it called up before my mind a vision of Shakespeare's Beatrice, and once I thought of Beatrice Cenci. But this was probably caused by the association of ideas suggested by the similarity of names.

The light in the room continued to grow even brighter, so I looked again out of the window to seek its source, and saw there a lovely sight. It seemed as if there were grouped without the window three lovely children, who seemed to float in midair. The light seemed to spring from a point far behind them, and by their side was something dark and shadowy, which served to set off their radiance.

The children seemed to be smiling in upon something in the room, and, following their glances, I saw that their eyes rested upon the other bed. There, strange to say, the head which I had lately seen in the picture rested upon the pillow. I looked at the wall, but the frame was empty, the picture was gone. Then I looked at the bed again, and saw the young girl asleep, with the expression of her face constantly changing, as though she were dreaming.

As I was observing her, a sudden look of terror spread over her face, and she sat up like a sleepwalker, with her eyes wide open, staring out of the window.

Again turning to the window, my gaze became fixed, for a great and weird change had taken place. The figures were still there, but their features and expressions had become woefully different. Instead of the happy innocent look of childhood was one of malignity. With the change the children had grown old, and now three hags, decrepit and deformed, like typical witches, were before me.

But a thousand times worse than this transformation was the change in the dark mass that was near them. From a cloud, misty and undefined, it became a sort of shadow with a form. This gradually, as I looked, grew darker and fuller, till at length it made me shudder. There stood before me the phantom of the Fiend.

There was a long period of dead silence, in which I could hear the beating of my heart; but at length the phantom spoke to the others. His words seemed to issue from his lips mechanically, and without expression: 'Tomorrow, and tomorrow, and tomorrow. The fairest and the best.' He looked so awful that the question arose in my mind: 'Would I dare to face him without the window – would any one dare to go amongst those fiends?' A harsh, strident, diabolical laugh from without seemed to answer my unasked question in the negative.

But as well as the laugh I heard another sound – the tones of a sweet sad voice in despair coming across the room.

'Oh, alone, alone! is there no human thing near me? No hope – no hope. I shall go mad – or die.'

The last words were spoken with a gasp.

I tried to jump out of bed, but could not stir, my limbs were bound in sleep. The young girl's head fell suddenly back upon the pillow, and the limp-hanging jaw and wide-open, purposeless mouth spoke but too plainly of what had happened.

Again I heard from without the fierce, diabolical laughter, which swelled louder and louder, till at last it grew so strong that in very horror I shook aside my sleep and sat up in bed. I listened and heard a knocking at the door, but in another moment I became more awake, and knew that the sound came from the hall. It was, no doubt, Mr Trevor returning from his party.

The hall door was opened and shut, and then came a subdued sound of tramping and voices, but this soon died away, and there was silence throughout the house.

I lay awake for long thinking, and looking across the room at the picture and at the empty bed; for the moon now shone brightly, and the night was rendered still brighter by occasional flashes of summer lightning. At times the silence was broken by an owl screeching outside.

As I lay awake, pondering, I was very much troubled by what I had seen; but at length, putting several things together, I came to the conclusion that I had had a dream of a kind that might have been expected. The lightning, the knocking at the hall door, the screeching of the owl, the empty bed, and the face in the picture, when grouped together, supplied materials for the main facts of the vision. The rest was, of course, the offspring of pure fancy, and the natural consequence of the component elements mentioned acting with each other in the mind.

I got up and looked out of the window, but saw nothing but the broad belt of moonlight glittering on the bosom of the lake, which extended miles and miles away, till its farther shore was lost in the night haze, and the green sward, dotted with shrubs and tall grasses, which lay between the lake and the house.

The vision had utterly faded. However, the dream – for so, I suppose, I should call it – was very powerful, and I slept no more till the sunlight was streaming broadly in at the window, and then I fell into a doze.

2   *More Links*

Late in the morning I was awakened by Parks, Mr Trevor's man, who always used to attend on me when I visited my friends. He brought me hot water and the local news; and, chatting with him, I forgot for a time my alarm of the night.

Parks was staid and elderly, and a type of a class now rapidly disappearing – the class of old family servants who are as proud of their hereditary loyalty to their masters, as those masters are of name and rank. Like all old servants he had a great loving for all sorts of traditions. He believed them, and feared them, and had the most profound reverence for anything which had a story.

I asked him if he knew anything of the legendary history of Scarp. He answered with an air of doubt and hesitation, as of one carefully delivering an opinion which was still incomplete.

'Well, you see, Master Frank, that Scarp is so old that it must have any number of legends; but it is so long since it was inhabited that no one in the village remembers them. The place seems to have become in a kind of way forgotten, and died out of people's thoughts, and so I am very much afraid, sir, that all the genuine history is lost.'

'What do you mean by the genuine history?' I enquired.

'Well, sir, I mean the true tradition, and not the inventions of the village folk. I heard the sexton tell some stories, but I am quite sure that they were not true, for I could see, Master Frank, that he did not believe them himself, but was only trying to frighten us.'

'And could you not hear of any story that appeared to you to be true?'

'No, sir, and I tried very hard. You see, Master Frank, that there is a sort of club held every week in the tavern down in the village, composed of very respectable men, sir – very respectable men, indeed – and they asked me to be their chairman. I spoke to the master about it, and he gave me leave to accept their proposal. I accepted it as they made a point of it; and from my position I have of course a fine opportunity of making enquiries. It was at the club, sir, that I was, last night, so that I was not here to attend on you, which I hope that you will excuse.'

Parks's air of mingled pride and condescension, as he made the announcement of the club, was very fine, and the effect was heightened by the confiding frankness with which he spoke. I asked him if he could find no clue to any of the legends which must have existed about such an old place. He answered with a very slight reluctance: 'Well, sir, there was one woman in the village who was awfully old and doting, and she evidently knew something about Scarp, for when she heard the name she mumbled out something about "awful stories" and "times of horror", and such like things, but I couldn't make her understand what it was I wanted to know, or keep her up to the point.'

'And have you tried often, Parks? Why do you not try again?'

'She is dead, sir!'

I had felt inclined to laugh at Parks when he was telling me of the old woman. The way in which he gloated over the words 'awful stories', and 'times of horror', was beyond the power of description; it should have been heard and seen to have been properly appreciated. His voice became deep and mysterious, and he almost smacked his lips at the thought of so much pabulum for nightmares. But when he calmly told me that the woman was dead, a sense of blankness, mingled with awe, came upon me. Here, the last link between myself and the mysterious past was broken, never to be mended. All the rich stores of legend and tradition that had arisen from strange conjunctures of circumstances, and from the belief and imagination of long lines of villagers, loyal to their suzerain lord, were lost forever. I felt quite sad and disappointed; and no attempt was made either by Parks or myself to continue the conversation. Mr Trevor came presently into my room, and having greeted each other warmly we went together to breakfast.

At breakfast Mrs Trevor asked me what I thought of the girl's portrait in my bedroom. We had often had discussions as to characters in faces for we were both physiognomists, and she asked the question as if she were really curious to hear my opinion. I told her that I had only seen it for a short time, and so would rather not attempt to give a final opinion without a more careful study; but from what I had seen of it I had been favourably impressed.

'Well, Frank, after breakfast go and look at it again carefully, and then tell me exactly what you think about it.'

After breakfast I did as directed and returned to the breakfast room, where Mrs Trevor was still sitting.

'Well, Frank, what is your opinion – mind, correctly. I want it for a particular reason.'

I told her what I thought of the girl's character; which, if there be any truth in physiognomy, must have been a very fine one.

'Then you like the face?'

I answered: 'It is a great pity that we have none such nowadays. They seem to have died out with Sir Joshua and Greuze. If I could meet such a girl as I believe the prototype of that portrait to have been I would never be happy till I had made her my wife.'

To my intense astonishment my hostess jumped up and clapped her hands. I asked her why she did it, and she laughed as she replied in a mocking tone imitating my own voice: 'But suppose for a moment that your kind intentions should be frustrated. "One man may lead a horse to the pond's brink." "The best laid schemes o' mice an' men." Eh?'

'Well,' said I, 'there may be some point in the observation. I suppose there must be since you have made it. But for my part I don't see it.'

'Oh, I forgot to tell you, Frank, that that portrait might have been painted for Diana Fothering.'

I felt a blush stealing over my face. She observed it and took my hand between hers as we sat down on the sofa, and said to me tenderly: 'Frank, my dear boy, I intend to jest with you no more on the subject. I have a conviction that you will like Diana, which has been strengthened by your admiration for her portrait, and from what I know of human nature I am sure that she will like you. Charley and I both wish to see you married, and we would not think of a wife for you who was not in every way eligible. I have never in my life met a girl like Di; and if you and she fancy each other it will be Charley's pleasure and my own to enable you to marry – as far as means are concerned. Now, don't speak. You must know perfectly well how much we both love you. We have always regarded you as our son, and we intend to treat you as our only child when it pleases God to separate us. There now, think the matter over, after you have seen Diana. But, mind me, unless you love each other well and truly, we would far rather not see you married. At all events, whatever may happen you have our best wishes and prayers for your happiness. God bless you, Frank, my dear, dear boy.'

There were tears in her eyes as she spoke. When she had finished she leaned over, drew down my head and kissed my forehead very, very tenderly, and then got up softly and left the room. I felt inclined to cry myself. Her words to me were tender, and sensible, and womanly, but I cannot attempt to describe the infinite tenderness and gentleness of her voice and manner. I prayed for every blessing on her in my secret heart, and the swelling of my throat did not prevent my prayers finding voice. There may have been women in the world like Mrs Trevor, but if there had been I had never met any of them, except herself.

As may be imagined, I was most anxious to see Miss Fothering, and for the remainder of the day she was constantly in my thoughts. That evening a letter came from the younger Miss Fothering apologising for her not being able to keep her promise with reference to her visit, on account of the unexpected arrival of her aunt, with whom she was obliged to go to Paris for some months. That night I slept in my new room, and had neither dream nor vision. I awoke in the morning half ashamed of having ever paid any attention to such a silly circumstance as a strange dream in my first night in an old house.

After breakfast next morning, as I was going along the corridor, I saw the door of my old bedroom open, and went in to have another look at the portrait. Whilst I was looking at it I began to wonder how it could be that it was so like Miss Fothering as Mrs Trevor said it was. The more I thought of this the more it puzzled me, till suddenly the dream came back – the face in the picture, and the figure in the bed, the phantoms out in the night, and the ominous words: 'The fairest and the best'. As I thought of these things all the possibilities of the lost legends of the old house thronged so quickly into my mind that I began to feel a buzzing in my ears and my head began to swim, so that I was obliged to sit down.

'Could it be possible,' I asked myself, 'that some old curse hangs over the race that once dwelt within these walls, and can she be of that race? Such things have been before now!'

The idea was a terrible one for me, for it made to me a reality that which I had come to look upon as merely the dream of a distempered imagination. If the thought had come to me in the darkness and stillness of the night it would have been awful. How happy I was that it had come by daylight, when the sun was shining brightly, and the air was cheerful with the trilling of the song birds, and the lively, strident cawing from the old rookery.

I stayed in the room for some little time longer, thinking over the scene, and, as is natural, when I had got over the remnants of my fear, my reason began to question the genuineness of the dream. I began to look for the internal evidence of the untruth to facts; but, after thinking earnestly for some time the only fact that seemed to me of any importance was the confirmatory one of the younger Miss Fothering's apology. In the dream the frightened girl had been alone, and the mere fact of two girls coming on a visit had seemed a sort of disproof of its truth. But, just as if things were conspiring to force on the truth of the dream, one of the sisters was not to come, and the other was she who resembled the portrait whose prototype I had seen sleeping in a vision. I could hardly imagine that I had only dreamt.

I determined to ask Mrs Trevor if she could explain in any way Miss Fothering's resemblance to the portrait, and so went at once to seek her.

I found her in the large drawing room alone, and, after a few casual remarks, I broached the subject on which I had come to seek for information. She had not said anything further to me about marrying since our conversation on the previous day, but when I mentioned Miss Fothering's name I could see a glad look on her face which gave me great pleasure. She made none of those vulgar commonplace remarks which many women find it necessary to make when talking to a man about a girl for whom he is supposed to have an affection, but by her manner she put me entirely at my ease, as I sat fidgeting on the sofa, pulling purposelessly the woolly tufts of an antimacassar, painfully conscious that my cheeks were red, and my voice slightly forced and unnatural.

She merely said, 'Of course, Frank, I am ready if you want to talk about Miss Fothering, or any other subject.' She then put a marker in her book and laid it aside, and, folding her arms, looked at me with a grave, kind, expectant smile.

I asked her if she knew anything about the family history of Miss Fothering. She answered: 'Not further than I have already told you. Her father's is a fine old family, although reduced in circumstances.'

'Has it ever been connected with any family in this county? With the former owners of Scarp, for instance?'

'Not that I know of. Why do you ask?'

'I want to find out how she comes to be so like that portrait.'

'I never thought of that. It may be that there was some remote connection between her family and the Kirks who formerly owned Scarp. I will ask her when she comes. Or stay. Let us go and look if there is any old book or tree in the library that will throw a light upon the subject. We have rather a good library now, Frank, for we have all our own books, and all those which belonged to the Scarp library also. They are in great disorder, for we have been waiting till you came to arrange them, for we knew that you delighted in such work.'

'There is nothing I should enjoy more than arranging all these splendid books. What a magnificent library. It is almost a pity to keep it in a private house.'

We proceeded to look for some of those old books of family history which are occasionally to be found in old county houses. The library of Scarp, I saw, was very valuable, and as we prosecuted our search I came across many splendid and rare volumes which I determined to examine at my leisure, for I had come to Scarp for a long visit.

We searched first in the old folio shelves, and, after some few disappointments, found at length a large volume, magnificently printed and bound, which contained views and plans of the house, illuminations of the armorial bearings of the family of Kirk, and all the families with whom it was connected, and having the history of all these families carefully set forth. It was called on the title page 'The Book of Kirk', and was full of anecdotes and legends, and contained a large stock of family tradition. As this was exactly the book which we required, we searched no further, but, having carefully dusted the volume, bore it to Mrs Trevor's boudoir where we could look over it quite undisturbed.

On looking in the index, we found the name of Fothering mentioned, and on turning to the page specified, found the arms of Kirk quartered on those of Fothering. From the text we learned that one of the daughters of Kirk had, in the year 1573, married the brother of Fothering against the united wills of her father and brother, and that after a bitter feud of some ten or twelve years, the latter, then master of Scarp, had met the brother of Fothering in a duel and had killed him. Upon receiving the news Fothering had sworn a great oath to revenge his brother, invoking the most fearful curses upon himself and his race if he should fail to cut off the hand that had slain his brother, and to nail it over the gate of Fothering. The feud then became so bitter that Kirk seems to have gone quite mad on the subject. When he heard of Fothering's oath he knew that he had but little chance of escape, since his enemy was his master at every weapon; so he determined upon a mode of revenge which, although costing him his own life, he fondly hoped would accomplish the eternal destruction of his brother-in-law through his violated oath. He sent Fothering a letter cursing him and his race, and praying for the consummation of his own curse invoked in case of failure. He concluded his missive by a prayer for the complete destruction, soul, mind, and body, of the first Fothering who should enter the gate of Scarp, who he hoped would be the fairest and best of the race. Having despatched this letter he cut off his right hand and threw it into the centre of a roaring fire, which he had made for the purpose. When it was entirely consumed he threw himself upon his sword, and so died.

A cold shiver went through me when I read the words 'fairest and best'. All my dream came back in a moment, and I seemed to hear in my ears again the echo of the fiendish laughter. I looked up at Mrs Trevor, and saw that she had become very grave. Her face had a half-frightened look, as if some wild thought had struck her. I was more frightened than ever, for nothing increases our alarms so much as the sympathy of others with regard to them; however, I tried to conceal my fear. We sat silent for some minutes, and then Mrs Trevor rose up saying: 'Come with me, and let us look at the portrait.'

I remember her saying the and not that portrait, as if some concealed thought of it had been occupying her mind. The same dread had assailed her from a coincidence as had grown in me from a vision. Surely – surely I had good grounds for fear!

We went to the bedroom and stood before the picture, which seemed to gaze upon us with an expression which reflected our own fears. My companion said to me in slightly excited tones: 'Frank, lift down the picture till we see its back.' I did so, and we found written in strange old writing on the grimy canvas a name and a date, which, after a great deal of trouble, we made out to be 'Margaret Kirk, 1572'. It was the name of the lady in the book.

Mrs Trevor turned round and faced me slowly, with a look of horror on her face.

'Frank, I don't like this at all. There is something very strange here.'

I had it on my tongue to tell her my dream, but was ashamed to do so. Besides, I feared that it might frighten her too much, as she was already alarmed.

I continued to look at the picture as a relief from my embarrassment, and was struck with the excessive griminess of the back in comparison to the freshness of the front. I mentioned my difficulty to my companion, who thought for a moment, and then suddenly said: 'I see how it is. It has been turned with its face to the wall.'

I said no word but hung up the picture again; and we went back to the boudoir.

On the way I began to think that my fears were too wildly improbable to bear to be spoken about. It was so hard to believe in the horrors of darkness when the sunlight was falling brightly around me. The same idea seemed to have struck Mrs Trevor, for she said, when we entered the room: 'Frank, it strikes me that we are both rather silly to let our imaginations carry us away so. The story is merely a tradition, and we know how report distorts even the most innocent facts. It is true that the Fothering family was formerly connected with the Kirks, and that the picture is that of the Miss Kirk who married against her father's will; it is likely that he quarrelled with her for so doing, and had her picture turned to the wall – a common trick of angry fathers at all times – but that is all. There can be nothing beyond that. Let us not think any more upon the subject, as it is one likely to lead us into absurdities. However, the picture is a really beautiful one – independent of its being such a likeness of Diana, and I will have it placed in the dining-room.'

The change was effected that afternoon, but she did not again allude to the subject. She appeared, when talking to me, to be a little constrained in manner – a very unusual thing with her, and seemed to fear that I would renew the forbidden topic. I think that she did not wish to let her imagination lead her astray, and was distrustful of herself. However, the feeling of constraint wore off before night – but she did not renew the subject.

I slept well that night, without dreams of any kind; and next morning – the third tomorrow promised in the dream – when I came down to breakfast, I was told that I would see Miss Fothering before that evening.

I could not help blushing, and stammered out some commonplace remark, and then glancing up, feeling very sheepish, I saw my hostess looking at me with her kindly smile intensified. She said: 'Do you know, Frank, I felt quite frightened yesterday when we were looking at the picture; but I have been thinking the matter over since, and have come to the conclusion that my folly was perfectly unfounded. I am sure you agree with me. In fact, I look now upon our fright as a good joke, and will tell it to Diana when she arrives.'

Once again I was about to tell my dream; but again was restrained by shame. I knew, of course, that Mrs Trevor would not laugh at me or even think little of me for my fears, for she was too well-bred, and kind-hearted, and sympathetic to do anything of the kind, and, besides, the fear was one which we had shared in common.

But how could I confess my fright at what might appear to others to be a ridiculous dream, when she had conquered the fear that had been common to us both, and which had arisen from a really strange conjuncture of facts. She appeared to look on the matter so lightly that I could not do otherwise. And I did it honestly for the time.

3   *The Third Tomorrow*

In the afternoon I was out in the garden lying in the shadow of an immense beech, when I saw Mrs Trevor approaching. I had been reading Shelley's 'Stanzas Written in Dejection', and my heart was full of melancholy and a vague yearning after human sympathy.

I had thought of Mrs Trevor's love for me, but even that did not seem sufficient. I wanted the love of some one more nearly of my own level, some equal spirit, for I looked on her, of course, as I would have regarded my mother. Somehow my thoughts kept returning to Miss Fothering till I could almost see her before me in my memory of the portrait. I had begun to ask myself the question: 'Are you in love?' when I heard the voice of my hostess as she drew near.

'Ha! Frank, I thought I would find you here. I want you to come to my boudoir.'

'What for?' I enquired, as I rose from the grass and picked up my volume of Shelley.

'Di has come ever so long ago; and I want to introduce you and have a chat before dinner,' said she, as we went towards the house.

'But won't you let me change my dress? I am not in correct costume for the afternoon.'

I felt somewhat afraid of the unknown beauty when the introduction was imminent. Perhaps it was because I had come to believe too firmly in Mrs Trevor's prediction.

'Nonsense, Frank, just as if any woman worth thinking about cares how a man is dressed.'

We entered the boudoir and found a young lady seated by a window that overlooked the croquet ground. She turned round as we came in, so Mrs Trevor introduced us, and we were soon engaged in a lively conversation. I observed her, as may be supposed, with more than curiosity, and shortly found that she was worth looking at. She was very beautiful, and her beauty lay not only in her features but in her expression. At first her appearance did not seem to me so perfect as it afterwards did, on account of her wonderful resemblance to the portrait with whose beauty I was already acquainted. But it was not long before I came to experience the difference between the portrait and the reality. No matter how well it may be painted a picture falls far short of its prototype. There is something in a real face which cannot exist on canvas – some difference far greater than that contained in the contrast between the one expression, however beautiful, of the picture, and the moving features and varying expression of the reality. There is something living and lovable in a real face that no art can represent.

When we had been talking for a while in the usual conventional style, Mrs Trevor said, 'Di, my love, I want to tell you of a discovery Frank and I have made. You must know that I always call

Mr Stanford, Frank – he is more like my own son than my friend, and that I am very fond of him.'

She then put her arms round Miss Fothering's waist, as they sat on the sofa together, and kissed her, and then, turning towards me, said, 'I don't approve of kissing girls in the presence of gentlemen, but you know that Frank is not supposed to be here. This is my sanctum, and who invades it must take the consequences. But I must tell you about the discovery.'

She then proceeded to tell the legend, and about her finding the name of Margaret Kirk on the back of the picture.

Miss Fothering laughed gleefully as she heard the story, and then said, suddenly, 'Oh, I had forgotten to tell you, dear Mrs Trevor, that I had such a fright the other day. I thought I was going to be prevented coming here. Aunt Deborah came to us last week for a few days, and when she heard that I was about to go on a visit to Scarp she seemed quite frightened, and went straight off to papa and asked him to forbid me to go. Papa asked her why she made the request, so she told a long family legend about any of us coming to Scarp – just the same story that you have been telling me. She said she was sure that some misfortune would happen if I came; so you see that the tradition exists in our branch of the family too. Oh, you can't fancy the scene there was between papa and Aunt Deborah. I must laugh whenever I think of it, although I did not laugh then, for I was greatly afraid that aunty would prevent me coming. Papa got very grave, and aunty thought she had carried her point when he said, in his dear, old, pompous manner, "Deborah, Diana has promised to pay Mrs Trevor, of Scarp, a visit, and, of course, must keep her engagement. And if it were for no other reason than the one you have just alleged, I would strain a point of convenience to have her go to Scarp. I have always educated my children in such a manner that they ought not to be influenced by such vain superstitions; and with my will their practice shall never be at variance with the precepts which I have instilled into them." Poor aunty was quite overcome. She seemed almost speechless for a time at the thought that her wishes had been neglected, for you know that Aunt Deborah's wishes are commands to all our family.'

Mrs Trevor said: 'I hope Mrs Howard was not offended?'

'Oh, no. Papa talked to her seriously, and at length – with a great deal of difficulty I must say – succeeded in convincing her that her fears were groundless – at least, he forced her to confess that such things as she was afraid of could not be.'

I thought of the couplet:

> A man convinced against his will
> Is of the same opinion still

but said nothing.

Miss Fothering finished her story by saying: 'Aunty ended by hoping that I might enjoy myself, which I am sure, my dear Mrs Trevor, that I will do.'

'I hope you will, my love.'

I had been struck during the above conversation by the mention of Mrs Howard. I was trying to think of where I had heard the name, Deborah Howard, when suddenly it all came back to me. Mrs Howard had been Miss Fothering, and was an old friend of my mother's. It was thus that I had been accustomed to her name when I was a child. I remembered now that once she had brought a nice little girl, almost a baby, with her to visit. The child was her niece, and it was thus that I now accounted for my half-recollection of the name and the circumstance on the first night of my arrival at Scarp. The thought of my dream here recalled me to Mrs Trevor's object in bringing Miss Fothering to her boudoir, so I said to the latter: 'Do you believe these legends?'

'Indeed I do not, Mr Stanford; I do not believe in anything half so silly.'

'Then you do not believe in ghosts or visions?'

'Most certainly not.'

How could I tell my dream to a girl who had such profound disbelief? And yet I felt something whispering to me that I ought to tell it to her. It was, no doubt, foolish of me to have this fear of a dream, but I could not help it. I was just going to risk being laughed at, and unburden my mind, when Mrs Trevor started up, after looking at her watch, saying: 'Dear me, I never thought it was so late. I must go and see if any others have come. It will not do for me to neglect my guests.'

We all left the boudoir, and as we did so the gong sounded for dressing for dinner, and so we each sought our rooms.

When I came down to the drawing room I found assembled a number of persons who had arrived during the course of the afternoon. I was introduced to them all, and chatted with them till dinner was announced. I was given Miss Fothering to take into dinner, and when it was over I found that we had improved our acquaintance very much. She was a delightful girl, and as I looked at her I thought with a glow of pleasure of Mrs Trevor's prediction. Occasionally I saw our hostess observing us, and as she saw us chatting pleasantly together as though we enjoyed it a more than happy look came into her face. It was one of her most fascinating points that in the midst of gaiety, while she never neglected anyone, she specially remembered her particular friends. No matter what position she might be placed in she would still remember that there were some persons who would treasure up her recognition at such moments.

After dinner, as I did not feel inclined to enter the drawing room with the other gentlemen, I strolled out into the garden by myself, and thought over things in general, and Miss Fothering in particular. The subject was such a pleasant one that I quite lost myself in it, and strayed off farther than I had intended. Suddenly I remembered myself and looked around. I was far away from the house, and in the midst of a dark, gloomy walk between old yew trees. I could not see through them on either side on account of their thickness, and as the walk was curved I could see but a short distance either before or behind me. I looked up and saw a yellowish, luminous sky with heavy clouds passing sluggishly across it. The moon had not yet risen, and the general gloom reminded me forcibly of some of the weird pictures which William Blake so loved to paint. There was a sort of vague melancholy and ghostliness in the place that made me shiver, and I hurried on.

At length the walk opened and I came out on a large sloping lawn, dotted here and there with yew trees and tufts of pampas grass of immense height, whose stalks were crowned with large flowers. To the right lay the house, grim and gigantic in the gloom, and to the left the lake which stretched away so far that it was lost in the evening shadow. The lawn sloped from the terrace round the house down to the water's edge, and was only broken by the walk which continued to run on round the house in a wide sweep.

As I came near the house a light appeared in one of the windows which lay before me, and as I looked into the room I saw that it was the chamber of my dream.

Unconsciously I approached nearer and ascended the terrace, from the top of which I could see across the deep trench which surrounded the house, and looked earnestly into the room. I shivered as I looked. My spirits had been damped by the gloom and desolation of the yew walk, and now the dream and all the subsequent revelations came before my mind with such vividness that the horror of the thing again seized me, but more forcibly than before. I looked at the sleeping arrangements, and groaned as I saw that the bed where the dying woman had seemed to lie was alone prepared, while the other bed, that in which I had slept, had its curtains drawn all round. This was but another link in the chain of doom. Whilst I stood looking, the servant who was in the room came and pulled down one of the blinds, but, as she was about to do the same with the other, Miss Fothering entered the room, and, seeing what she was about, evidently gave her contrary directions, for she let go the window string, and then went and pulled up again the blind which she had let down. Having done so she followed her mistress out of the room. So wrapped up was I in all that took place with reference to that chamber, that it never even struck me that I was guilty of any impropriety in watching what took place.

I stayed there for some little time longer purposeless and terrified. The horror grew so great to me as I thought of the events of the last few days, that I determined to tell Miss Fothering of my dream, in order that she might not be frightened in case she should see anything like it, or at least that she might be prepared for anything that might happen. As soon as I had come to this determination the inevitable question 'when?' presented itself. The means of making the communication was a subject most disagreeable to contemplate, but as I had made up my mind to do it, I thought that there was no time like the present. Accordingly I was determined to seek the drawing room, where I knew I should find Miss Fothering and Mrs Trevor, for, of course, I had determined to take the latter into our confidence. As I was really afraid to go through the awful yew walk again, I completed the half circle of the house and entered the backdoor, from which I easily found my way to the drawing room.

When I entered Mrs Trevor, who was sitting near the door, said to me, 'Good gracious, Frank, where have you been to make you look so pale? One would think you had seen a ghost!'

I answered that I had been strolling in the garden, but made no other remark, as I did not wish to say anything about my dream before the persons to whom she was talking, as they were strangers to me. I waited for some time for an opportunity of speaking to her alone, but her duties, as hostess, kept her so constantly occupied that I waited in vain. Accordingly I determined to tell Miss Fothering at all events, at once, and then to tell Mrs Trevor as soon as an opportunity for doing so presented itself.

With a good deal of difficulty – for I did not wish to do anything marked – I succeeded in getting Miss Fothering away from the persons by whom she was surrounded, and took her to one of the embrasures, under the pretence of looking out at the night view. Here we were quite removed from observation, as the heavy window curtains completely covered the recess, and almost isolated us from the rest of the company as perfectly as if we were in a separate chamber. I proceeded at once to broach the subject for which I had sought the interview; for I feared lest contact with the lively company of the drawing room would do away with my present fears, and so break down the only barrier that stood between her and Fate.

'Miss Fothering, do you ever dream?'

'Oh, yes, often. But I generally find that my dreams are most ridiculous.'

'How so?'

'Well, you see, that no matter whether they are good or bad they appear real and coherent whilst I am dreaming them; but when I wake I find them unreal and incoherent, when I remember them at all. They are, in fact, mere disconnected nonsense.'

'Are you fond of dreams?'

'Of course I am. I delight in them, for whether they are sense or gibberish when you wake, they are real whilst you are asleep.'

'Do you believe in dreams?'

'Indeed, Mr Stanford, I do not.'

'Do you like hearing them told?'

'I do, very much, when they are worth telling. Have you been dreaming anything? If you have, do tell it to me.'

'I will be glad to do so. It is about a dream which I had that concerns you, that I came here to tell you.'

'About me. Oh, how nice. Do go on.'

I told her all my dream, after calling her attention to our conversation in the boudoir as a means of introducing the subject. I did not attempt to heighten the effect in any way or to draw any inferences. I tried to suppress my own emotion and merely to let the facts speak for themselves. She listened with great eagerness, but, as far as I could see, without a particle of either fear or belief in the dream as a warning. When I had finished she laughed a quiet, soft laugh, and said: 'That is delicious. And was I really the girl that you saw afraid of ghosts? If papa heard of such a thing as that even in a dream what a lecture he would give me! I wish I could dream anything like that.'

'Take care,' said I, 'you might find it too awful. It might indeed prove the fulfilling of the ban which we saw in the legend in the old book, and which you heard from your aunt.'

She laughed musically again, and shook her head at me wisely and warningly.

'Oh, pray do not talk nonsense and try to frighten me – for I warn you that you will not succeed.'

'I assure you on my honour, Miss Fothering, that I was never more in earnest in my whole life.'

'Do you not think that we had better go into the room?' said she, after a few moments' pause.

'Stay just a moment, I entreat you,' said I. 'What I say is true. I am really in earnest.'

'Oh, pray forgive me if what I said led you to believe that I doubted your word. It was merely your inference which I disagreed with. I thought you had been jesting to try and frighten me.'

'Miss Fothering, I would not presume to take such a liberty. But I am glad that you trust me. May I venture to ask you a favour? Will you promise me one thing?'

Her answer was characteristic: 'No. What is it?'

'That you will not be frightened at anything which may take place tonight?'

She laughed softly again.

'I do not intend to be. But is that all?'

'Yes, Miss Fothering, that is all; but I want to be assured that you will not be alarmed – that you will be prepared for anything which may happen. I have a horrid foreboding of evil – some evil that I dread to think of – and it will be a great comfort to me if you will do one thing.'

'Oh, nonsense. Oh, well, if you really wish it I will tell you if I will do it when I hear what it is.'

Her levity was all gone when she saw how terribly in earnest I was. She looked at me boldly and fearlessly, but with a tender, half-pitying glance as if conscious of the possession of strength superior to mine. Her fearlessness was in her free, independent attitude, but her pity was in her eyes. I went on: 'Miss Fothering, the worst part of my dream was seeing the look of agony on the face of the girl when she looked round and found herself alone. Will you take some token and keep it with you till morning to remind you, in case anything should happen, that you are not alone – that there is one thinking of you, and one human intelligence awake for you, though all the rest of the world should be asleep or dead?'

In my excitement I spoke with fervour, for the possibility of her enduring the horror which had assailed me seemed to be growing more and more each instant. At times since that awful night I had disbelieved the existence of the warning, but when I thought of it by night I could not but believe, for the very air in the darkness seemed to be peopled by phantoms to my fevered imagination. My belief had been perfected tonight by the horror of the yew walk, and all the sombre, ghostly thoughts that had arisen amid its gloom.

There was a short pause. Miss Fothering leaned on the edge of the window, looking out at the dark, moonless sky. At length she turned and said to me, with some hesitation, 'But really, Mr Stanford, I do not like doing anything from fear of supernatural things, or from a belief in them. What you want me to do is so simple a thing in itself that I would not hesitate a moment to do it, but that papa has always taught me to believe that such occurrences as you seem to dread are quite impossible, and I know that he would be very much displeased if any act of mine showed a belief in them.'

'Miss Fothering, I honestly think that there is not a man living who would wish less than I would to see you or anyone else disobeying a father either in word or spirit, and more particularly when that father is a clergyman; but I entreat you to gratify me on this one point. It cannot do you any harm; and I assure you that if you do not I will be inexpressibly miserable. I have endured the greatest tortures of suspense for the last three days, and tonight I feel a nervous horror of which words can give you no conception. I know that I have not the smallest right to make the request, and no reason for doing it except that I was fortunate, or unfortunate, enough to get the warning. I apologise most sincerely for the great liberty which I have taken, but believe me that I act with the best intentions.'

My excitement was so great that my knees were trembling, and large drops of perspiration rolling down my face.

There was a long pause, and I had almost made up my mind for a refusal of my request when my companion spoke again.

'Mr Stanford, on that plea alone I will grant your request. I can see that for some reason which I cannot quite comprehend you are deeply moved; and that I may be the means of saving pain to any one, I will do what you ask. Just please to state what you wish me to do.'

I thought from her manner that she was offended with me; however I explained my purpose: 'I want you to keep about you, when you go to bed, some token which will remind you in an instant of what has passed between us, so that you may not feel lonely or frightened – no matter what may happen.'

'I will do it. What shall I take?'

She had her handkerchief in her hand as she spoke. So I put my hand upon it and blessed it in the name of the Father, Son, and Holy Ghost. I did this to fix its existence in her memory by awing her slightly about it. 'This,' said I, 'shall be a token that you are not alone.' My object in blessing the handkerchief was fully achieved, for she did seem somewhat awed, but still she thanked me with a sweet smile. 'I feel that you act from your heart,' said she, 'and my heart thanks you.' She gave me her hand as she spoke, in an honest, straightforward manner, with more the independence of a man than the timorousness of a woman. As I grasped it I felt the blood rushing to my face, but before I let it go an impulse seized me and I bent down and touched it with my lips. She drew it quickly away, and said more coldly than she had yet spoken: 'I did not mean you to do that.'

'Believe me I did not mean to take a liberty – it was merely the natural expression of my gratitude. I feel as if you had done me some great personal service. You do not know how much lighter my heart is now than it was an hour ago, or you would forgive me for having so offended.'

As I made my apologetic excuse, I looked at her wistfully. She returned my glance fearlessly, but with a bright, forgiving smile. She then shook her head slightly, as if to banish the subject.

There was a short pause, and then she said: 'I am glad to be of any service to you; but if there be any possibility of what you fear happening it is I who will be benefited. But mind, I will depend upon you not to say a word of this to anybody. I am afraid that we are both very foolish.'

'No, no, Miss Fothering. I may be foolish, but you are acting nobly in doing what seems to you to be foolish in order that you may save me from pain. But may I not even tell Mrs Trevor?'

'No, not even her. I should be ashamed of myself if I thought that anyone except ourselves knew about it.'

'You may depend upon me. I will keep it secret if you wish.'

'Do so, until morning at all events. Mind, if I laugh at you then I will expect you to join in my laugh.'

'I will,' said I. 'I will be only too glad to be able to laugh at it.' And we joined the rest of the company.

When I retired to my bedroom that night I was too much excited to sleep – even had my promise not forbidden me to do so. I paced up and down the room for some time, thinking and doubting. I could not believe completely in what I expected to happen, and yet my heart was filled with a vague dread. I thought over the events of the evening – particularly my stroll after dinner through that awful yew walk and my looking into the bedroom where I had dreamed. From these my thoughts wandered to the deep embrasure of the window where I had given Miss Fothering the token. I could hardly realise that whole interview as a fact. I knew that it had taken place, but that was all. It was so strange to recall a scene that, now that it was enacted, seemed half comedy and half tragedy, and to remember that it was played in this practical nineteenth century, in secret, within earshot of a room full of people, and only hidden from them by a curtain. I felt myself blushing, half from excitement, half from shame, when I thought of it. But then my thoughts turned to the way in which Miss Fothering had acceded to my request, strange as it was; and as I thought of her my blundering shame changed to a deeper glow of hope. I remembered Mrs Trevor's prediction – 'From what I know of human nature I think that she will like you' – and as I did so I felt how dear to me Miss Fothering was already becoming. But my joy was turned to anger on thinking what she might be called on to endure; and the thought of her suffering pain or fright caused me greater distress than any suffered myself. Again my thoughts flew back to the time of my own fright and my dream, with all the subsequent revelations concerning it, rushed across my mind. I felt again the feeling of extreme terror – as if something was about to happen – as if the tragedy was approaching its climax. Naturally I thought of the time of night and so I looked at my watch. It was within a few minutes of one o'clock. I remembered that the clock had struck twelve after Mr Trevor had come home on the night of my dream. There was a large clock at Scarp which tolled the hours so loudly that for a long way round the estate the country people all regulated their affairs by it. The next few minutes passed so slowly that each moment seemed an age.

I was standing, with my watch in my hand, counting the moments when suddenly a light came into the room that made the candle on the table appear quite dim, and my shadow was reflected on the wall by some brilliant light which streamed in through the window. My heart for an instant ceased to beat, and then the blood rushed so violently to my temples that my eyes grew dim and my brain began to reel. However, I shortly became more composed, and then went to the window expecting to see my dream again repeated.

The light was there as formerly, but there were no figures of children, or witches, or fiends. The moon had just risen, and I could see its reflection upon the far end of the lake. I turned my head in trembling expectation to the ground below where I had seen the children and the hags, but saw merely the dark yew trees and tall crested pampas tufts gently moving in the night wind. The light caught the edges of the flowers of the grass, and made them most conspicuous.

As I looked a sudden thought flashed like a flame of fire through my brain. I saw in one second of time all the folly of my wild fancies. The moonlight and its reflection on the water shining into the room was the light of my dream, or phantasm as I now understood it to be. Those three tufts of pampas grass clumped together were in turn the fair young children and the withered leaves and the dark foliage of the yew beside them gave substance to the semblance of the fiend. For the rest, the empty bed and the face of the picture, my half-recollection of the name of Fothering, and the long-forgotten legend of the curse. Oh, fool! fool that I had been! How I had been the victim of circumstances, and of my own wild imagination! Then came the bitter reflection of the agony of mind which Miss Fothering might be compelled to suffer. Might not the recital of my dream, and my strange request regarding the token, combined with the natural causes of night and scene, produce the very effect which I so dreaded? It was only at that bitter, bitter moment that I realised how foolish I had been. But what was my anguish of mind to hers? For an instant I conceived the idea of rousing Mrs Trevor and telling her all the facts of the case so that she might go to Miss Fothering and tell her not to be alarmed. But I had no time to act upon my thought. As I was hastening to the door the clock struck one and a moment later I heard from the room below me a sharp scream – a cry of surprise rather than fear. Miss Fothering had no doubt been awakened by the striking of the clock, and had seen outside the window the very figures which I had described to her.

I rushed madly down the stairs and arrived at the door of her bedroom, which was directly under the one which I now occupied. As I was about to rush in I was instinctively restrained from so doing by the thoughts of propriety; and so for a few moments I stood silent, trembling, with my hand upon the door handle.

Within I heard a voice – her voice – exclaiming, in tones of stupefied surprise: 'Has it come then? Am I alone?' She then continued joyously,

'No, I am not alone. His token! Oh, thank God for that. Thank God for that.'

Through my heart at her words came a rush of wild delight. I felt my bosom swell and the tears of gladness spring to my eyes. In that moment I knew that I had strength and courage to face the world, alone, for her sake. But before my hopes had time to manifest themselves they were destroyed, for again the voice came wailing from the room of blank despair that made me cold from head to foot.

'Ah–h–h! still there? Oh! God, preserve my reason. Oh! for some human thing near me.' Then her voice changed slightly to a tone of entreaty: 'You will not leave me alone? Your token. Remember your token. Help me. Help me now.' Then her voice became more wild, and rose to an inarticulate, wailing scream of horror.

As I heard that agonised cry, I realised the idea that it was madness to delay – that I had hesitated too long already – I must cast aside the shackles of conventionality if I wished to repair my fatal error. Nothing could save her from some serious injury – perhaps madness – perhaps death; save a shock which would break the spell which was over her from fear and her excited imagination. I flung open the door and rushed in, shouting loudly: 'Courage, courage. You are not alone. I am here. Remember the token.'

She grasped the handkerchief instinctively, but she hardly comprehended my words, and did not seem to heed my presence. She was sitting up in bed, her face being distorted with terror, and was gazing out upon the scene. I heard from without the hooting of an owl as it flew across the border of the lake. She heard it also, and screamed: 'The laugh, too! Oh, there is no hope. Even he will not dare to go amongst them.'

Then she gave vent to a scream, so wild, so appalling that, as I heard it, I trembled, and the hair on the back of my head bristled up. Throughout the house I could hear screams of affright, and the ringing of bells, and the banging of doors, and the rush of hurried feet; but the poor sufferer comprehended not these sounds; she still continued gazing out of the window awaiting the consummation of the dream.

I saw that the time for action and self-sacrifice was come. There was but one way now to repair my fatal error. To burst through the window and try by the shock to wake her from her trance of fear.

I said no word but rushed across the room and hurled myself, back foremost, against the massive plate glass. As I turned I saw Mrs

Trevor rushing into the room, her face wild with excitement. She was calling out: 'Diana, Diana, what is it?'

The glass crashed and shivered into a thousand pieces, and I could feel its sharp edges cutting me like so many knives. But I heeded not the pain, for above the rushing of feet and crashing of glass and the shouting both within and without the room I heard her voice ring forth in a joyous, fervent cry, 'Saved. He has dared,' as she sank down in the arms of Mrs Trevor, who had thrown herself upon the bed.

Then I felt a mighty shock, and all the universe seemed filled with sparks of fire that whirled around me with lightning speed, till I seemed to be in the centre of a world of flame, and then came in my ears the rushing of a mighty wind, swelling ever louder, and then came a blackness over all things and a deadness of sound as if all the earth had passed away, and I remembered no more.

4   *Afterwards*

When I next became conscious I was lying in bed in a dark room. I wondered what this was for, and tried to look around me, but could hardly stir my head. I attempted to speak, but my voice was without power – it was like a whisper from another world. The effort to speak made me feel faint, and again I felt a darkness gathering round me.

*   *   *

I became gradually conscious of something cool on my forehead. I wondered what it was. All sorts of things I conjectured, but could not fix my mind on any of them. I lay thus for some time, and at length opened my eyes and saw my mother bending over me – it was her hand which was so deliciously cool on my brow. I felt amazed somehow. I expected to see her; and yet I was surprised, for I had not seen her for a long time – a long, long time. I knew that she was dead – could I be dead, too? I looked at her again more carefully, and as I looked, the old features died away, but the expression remained the same. And then the dear, well-known face of Mrs Trevor grew slowly before me. She smiled as she saw the look of recognition in my eyes, and, bending down, kissed me very tenderly. As she drew back her head something warm fell on my face. I wondered what this could be, and after thinking for a long time, to do which I closed my eyes, I came to the conclusion that it was a tear. After some more thinking I opened my eyes to see why she was crying; but she was gone, and I could see that although the window-blinds were pulled up the room was almost dark. I felt much more awake and much stronger than I had been before, and tried to call Mrs Trevor. A woman got up from a chair behind the bed-curtains and went to the door, said something, and came back and settled my pillows.

'Where is Mrs Trevor?' I asked, feebly. 'She was here just now.'

The woman smiled at me cheerfully, and answered: 'She will be here in a moment. Dear heart! but she will be glad to see you so strong and sensible.'

After a few minutes she came into the room, and, bending over me, asked me how I felt. I said that I was all right – and then a thought struck me, so I asked, 'What was the matter with me?'

I was told that I had been ill, very ill, but that I was now much better. Something, I know not what, suddenly recalled to my memory all the scene of the bedroom, and the fright which my folly had caused, and I grew quite dizzy with the rush of blood to my head. But Mrs Trevor's arm supported me, and after a time the faintness passed away, and my memory was completely restored. I started violently from the arm that held me up, and called out: 'Is she all right? I heard her say, "saved". Is she all right?'

'Hush, dear boy, hush – she is all right. Do not excite yourself.'

'Are you deceiving me?' I enquired. 'Tell me all – I can bear it. Is she well or no?'

'She has been very ill, but she is now getting strong and well, thank God.'

I began to cry, half from weakness and half from joy, and Mrs Trevor seeing this, and knowing with the sweet instinct of woman-hood that I would rather be alone, quickly left the room, after making a sign to the nurse, who sank again to her old place behind the bed-curtain.

I thought for long; and all the time from my first coming to Scarp to the moment of unconsciousness after I sprung through the window came back to me as in a dream. Gradually the room became darker and darker, and my thoughts began to give semblance to the objects around me, till at length the visible world passed away from my wearied eyes, and in my dreams I continued to think of all that had been. I have a hazy recollection of taking some food and then relapsing into sleep; but remember no more distinctly until I woke fully in the morning and found Mrs Trevor again in the room. She came over to my bedside, and sitting down said gaily: 'Ah, Frank, you look bright and strong this morning, dear boy. You will soon be well now I trust.'

Her cool deft fingers settled my pillow and brushed back the hair from my forehead. I took her hand and kissed it, and the doing so made me very happy. By and by I asked her how was Miss Fothering.

'Better, much better this morning. She has been asking after you ever since she has been able; and today when I told her how much better you were she brightened up at once.'

I felt a flush painfully strong rushing over my face as she spoke, but she went on: 'She has asked me to let her see you as soon as both of you are able. She wants to thank you for your conduct on that awful night. But there, I won't tell any more tales – let her tell you what she likes herself.'

'To thank me – me – for what? For having brought her to the verge of madness or perhaps death through my silly fears and imagination. Oh, Mrs Trevor, I know that you never mock anyone – but to me that sounds like mockery.'

She leaned over me as she sat on my bedside and said, oh, so sweetly, yet so firmly that a sense of the truth of her words came at once upon me: 'If I had a son I would wish him to think as you have thought, and to act as you have acted. I would pray for it night and day and if he suffered as you have done, I would lean over him as I lean over you now and feel glad, as I feel now, that he had thought and acted as a true-hearted man should think and act. I would rejoice that God had given me such a son; and if he should die – as I feared at first that you should – I would be a prouder and happier woman kneeling by his dead body than I would in clasping a different son, living, in my arms.'

Oh, how my weak fluttering heart did beat as she spoke. With pity for her blighted maternal instincts, with gladness that a true-hearted woman had approved of my conduct toward a woman whom I loved, and with joy for the deep love for myself. There was no mistaking the honesty of her words – her face was perfectly radiant as she spoke them.

I put up my arms – it took all my strength to do it – round her neck, and whispered softly in her ear one word, 'mother'.

She did not expect it, for it seemed to startle her; but her arms tightened around me convulsively. I could feel a perfect rain of tears falling on my upturned face as I looked into her eyes, full of love and long-sought joy. As I looked I felt stronger and better; my sympathy for her joy did much to restore my strength.

For some little time she was silent, and then she spoke as if to herself, 'God has given me a son at last. I thank thee, O Father;

forgive me if I have at any time repined. The son I prayed for might have been different from what I would wish. Thou doest best in all things.'

For some time after this she stayed quite silent, still supporting me in her arms. I felt inexpressibly happy. There was an atmosphere of love around me, for which I had longed all my life. The love of a mother, for which I had pined since my orphan childhood, I had got at last, and the love of a woman to become far dearer to me than a mother I felt was close at hand.

At length I began to feel tired, and Mrs Trevor laid me back on my pillow. It pleased me inexpressibly to observe her kind motherly manner with me now. The ice between us had at last been broken, we had declared our mutual love, and the white-haired woman was as happy in the declaration as the young man.

The next day I felt a shade stronger, and a similar improvement was manifested on the next. Mrs Trevor always attended me herself, and her good reports of Miss Fothering's progress helped to cheer me not a little. And so the days wore on, and many passed away before I was allowed to rise from bed.

One day Mrs Trevor came into the room in a state of suppressed delight. By this time I had been allowed to sit up a little while each day, and was beginning to get strong, or rather less weak, for I was still very helpless.

'Frank, the doctor says that you may be moved into another room tomorrow for a change, and that you may see Di.'

As may be supposed I was anxious to see Miss Fothering. Whilst I had been able to think during my illness, I had thought about her all day long, and sometimes all night long. I had been in love with her even before that fatal night. My heart told me that secret whilst I was waiting to hear the clock strike, and saw all my folly about the dream; but now I not only loved the woman but I almost worshipped my own bright ideal which was merged in her. The constant series of kind messages that passed between us tended not a little to increase my attachment, and now I eagerly looked forward to a meeting with her face to face.

I awoke earlier than usual next morning, and grew rather feverish as the time for our interview approached. However, I soon cooled down upon a vague threat being held out, that if I did not become more composed I must defer my visit.

The expected time at length arrived, and I was wheeled in my chair into Mrs Trevor's boudoir. As I entered the door I looked eagerly round and saw, seated in another chair near one of the windows, a girl, who, turning her head round languidly, disclosed the features of Miss Fothering. She was very pale and ethereal looking, and seemed extremely delicate; but in my opinion this only heightened her natural beauty. As she caught sight of me a beautiful blush rushed over her poor, pale face, and even tinged her alabaster forehead. This passed quickly, and she became calm again, and paler than before. My chair was wheeled over to her, and Mrs Trevor said, as she bent over and kissed her, after soothing the pillow in her chair: 'Di, my love, I have brought Frank to see you. You may talk together for a little while; but, mind, the doctor's orders are very strict, and if either of you excite yourselves about anything I must forbid you to meet again until you are both much stronger.'

She said the last words as she was leaving the room.

I felt red and pale, hot and cold by turns. I looked at Miss Fothering and faltered. However, in a moment or two I summoned up courage to address her.

'Miss Fothering, I hope you forgive me for the pain and danger I caused you by that foolish fear of mine. I assure you that nothing I ever did – '

Here she interrupted me. 'Mr Stanford, I beg you will not talk like that. I must thank you for the care you thought me worthy of. I will not say how proud I feel of it, and for the generous courage and wisdom you displayed in rescuing me from the terror of that awful scene.'

She grew pale, even paler than she had been before, as she spoke the last words, and trembled all over. I feared for her, and said as cheerfully as I could: 'Don't be alarmed. Do calm yourself. That is all over now and past. Don't let its horror disturb you ever again.'

My speaking, although it calmed her somewhat, was not sufficient to banish her fear, and, seeing that she was really excited, I called to Mrs Trevor, who came in from the next room and talked to us for a little while. She gradually did away with Miss Fothering's fear by her pleasant cheery conversation. She, poor girl, had received a sad shock, and the thought that I had been the cause of it gave me great anguish. After a little quiet chat, however, I grew more cheerful, but presently feeling faintish, was wheeled back to my own room and put to bed.

For many long days I continued very weak, and hardly made any advance. I saw Miss Fothering every day, and each day I loved her more and more. She got stronger as the days advanced, and after a few weeks was comparatively in good health, but still I continued weak. Her illness had been merely the result of the fright she had sustained on that unhappy night; but mine was the nervous prostration consequent on the long period of anxiety between the dream and its seeming fulfilment, united with the physical weakness resulting from my wounds caused by jumping through the window. During all this time of weakness Mrs Trevor was, indeed, a mother to me. She watched me day and night, and as far as a woman could, made my life a dream of happiness. But the crowning glory of that time was the thought that sometimes forced itself upon me – that Diana cared for me. She continued to remain at Scarp by Mrs Trevor's request, as her father had gone to the Continent for the winter, and with my adopted mother she shared the attendance on me. Day after day her care for my every want grew greater, till I came to fancy her like a guardian angel keeping watch over me. With the peculiar delicate sense that accompanies extreme physical prostration I could see that the growth of her pity kept pace with the growth of her strength. My love kept pace with both. I often wondered if it could be sympathy and not pity that so forestalled my wants and wishes; or if it could be love that answered in her heart when mine beat for her. She only showed pity and tenderness in her acts and words, but still I hoped and longed for something more.

Those days of my long-continued weakness were to me sweet, sweet days. I used to watch her for hours as she sat opposite to me reading or working, and my eyes would fill with tears as I thought how hard it would be to die and leave her behind me. So strong was the flame of my love that I believed, in spite of my religious teaching, that, should I die, I would leave the better part of my being behind me. I used to think in a vague imaginative way, that was no less powerful because it was undefined, of what speeches I would make to her – if I were well. How I would talk to her in nobler language than that in which I would now allow my thoughts to mould themselves. How, as I talked, my passion, and honesty, and purity would make me so eloquent that she would love to hear me speak. How I would wander with her through the sunny gladed woods that stretched away before me through the open window, and sit by her feet on a mossy bank beside some purling brook that rippled gaily over the stones, gazing into the depths of her eyes, where my future life was pictured in one long sheen of light. How I would whisper in her ear sweet words that would make me tremble to speak them, and her tremble to hear. How she would bend to me and show me her love by letting me tell her mine without reproof. And then would come, like the shadow of a sudden rain – cloud over an April landscape, the bitter, bitter thought that all this longing was but a dream, and that when the time had come when such things might have been, I would, most likely, be sleeping under the green turf. And she might, perhaps, be weeping in the silence of her chamber sad, sad tears for her blighted love and for me.

Then my thoughts would become less selfish, and I would try to imagine the bitter blow of my death – if she loved me – for I knew that a woman loves not by the value of what she loves, but by the strength of her affection and admiration for her own ideal, which she thinks she sees bodied forth in some man. But these thoughts had always the proviso that the dreams of happiness were prophetic. Alas! I had altogether lost faith in dreams. Still, I could not but feel that even if I had never frightened Miss Fothering by telling my vision, she might, nevertheless, have been terrified by the effect of the moonlight upon the flowers of the pampas tufts, and that, under Providence, I was the instrument of saving her from a shock even greater than that which she did experience, for help might not have come to her so soon. This thought always gave me hope. Whenever I thought of her sorrow for my death, I would find my eyes filled with a sudden rush of tears which would shut out from my waking vision the object of my thoughts and fears. Then she would come over to me and place her cool hand on my forehead, and whisper sweet words of comfort and hope in my ears. As I would feel her warm breath upon my cheek and wafting my hair from my brow, I would lose all sense of pain and sorrow and care, and live only in the brightness of the present. At such times I would cry silently from very happiness, for I was sadly weak, and even trifling things touched me deeply. Many a stray memory of some tender word heard or some gentle deed done, or of some sorrow or distress, would set me thinking for hours and stir all the tender feelings of my nature.

Slowly – very slowly – I began to get stronger, but for many days more I was almost completely helpless. With returning strength came the strengthening of my passion – for passion my love for Diana had become. She had been so woven into my thoughts that my love for her was a part of my being, and I felt that away from her my future life would be but a bare existence and no more. But strange to say, with increasing strength and passion came increasing diffidence. I felt in her presence so bashful and timorous that I hardly dared to look at her, and could not speak save to answer an occasional question. I had ceased to dream entirely, for such daydreams as I used to have seemed now wild and almost sacrilegious to my overexcited imagination. But when she was not looking at me I would be happy in merely seeing her or hearing her speak. I could tell the moment she left the house or entered it, and her footfall was the music sweetest to my ears – except her voice. Sometimes she would catch sight of my bashful looks at her, and then, at my conscious blushing, a bright smile would flit over her face. It was sweet and womanly, but sometimes I would think that it was no more than her pity finding expression. She was always in my thoughts and these doubts and fears constantly assailed me, so that I could feel that the brooding over the subject – a matter which I was powerless to prevent – was doing me an injury; perhaps seriously retarding my recovery.

One day I felt very sad. There had a bitter sense of loneliness come over me which was unusual. It was a good sign of returning health, for it was like the waking from a dream to a world of fact, with all its troubles and cares. There was a sense of coldness and loneliness in the world, and I felt that I had lost something without gaining anything in return – I had, in fact, lost somewhat of my sense of dependence, which is a consequence of prostration, but had not yet regained my strength. I sat opposite a window itself in shade, but looking over a garden that in the summer had been bright with flowers, and sweet with their odours, but which, now, was lit up only in patches by the quiet mellow gleams of the autumn sun, and brightened by a few stray flowers that had survived the first frosts.

As I sat I could not help thinking of what my future would be. I felt that I was getting strong, and the possibilities of my life seemed very real to me. How I longed for courage to ask Diana to be my wife! Any certainty would be better than the suspense I now constantly endured. I had but little hope that she would accept me, for she seemed to care less for me now than in the early days of my illness. As I grew stronger she seemed to hold somewhat aloof from me; and as my fears and doubts grew more and more, I could hardly bear to think of my joy should she accept me, or of my despair should she refuse. Either emotion seemed too great to be borne.

Today when she entered the room my fears were vastly increased. She seemed much stronger than usual, for a glow, as of health, ruddied her cheeks, and she seemed so lovely that I could not conceive that such a woman would ever condescend to be my wife. There was an unusual constraint in her manner as she came and spoke to me, and flitted round me, doing in her own graceful way all the thousand little offices that only a woman's hand can do for an invalid. She turned to me two or three times, as if she was about to speak; but turned away again, each time silent, and with a blush. I could see that her heart was beating violently. At length she spoke.

'Frank.'

Oh! what a wild throb went through me as I heard my name from her lips for the first time. The blood rushed to my head, so that for a moment I was quite faint. Her cool hand on my forehead revived me.

'Frank, will you let me speak to you for a few minutes as honestly as I would wish to speak, and as freely?'

'Go on.'

'You will promise me not to think me unwomanly or forward, for indeed I act from the best motives – promise me?'

This was said slowly with much hesitation, and a convulsive heaving of the chest.

'I promise.'

'We can see that you are not getting as strong as you ought, and the doctor says that there is some idea too much in your mind – that you brood over it, and that it is retarding your recovery. Mrs Trevor and I have been talking about it. We have been comparing notes, and I think we have found out what your idea is. Now, Frank, you must not pale and red like that, or I will have to leave off.'

'I will be calm – indeed, I will. Go on.'

'We both thought that it might do you good to talk to you freely, and we want to know if our idea is correct. Mrs Trevor thought it better that I should speak to you than she should.'

'What is the idea?'

Hitherto, although she had manifested considerable emotion, her voice had been full and clear, but she answered this last question very faintly, and with much hesitation.

'You are attached to me, and you are afraid I – I don't love you.'

Here her voice was checked by a rush of tears, and she turned her head away.

'Diana,' said I, 'dear Diana,' and I held out my arms with what strength I had.

The colour rushed over her face and neck, and then she turned, and with a convulsive sigh laid her head upon my shoulder. One weak arm fell round her waist, and my other hand rested on her head. I said nothing. I could not speak, but I felt the beating of her heart against mine, and thought that if I died then I must be happy for ever, if there be memory in the other world.

For a long, long, blissful time she kept her place, and gradually our hearts ceased to beat so violently, and we became calm.

Such was the confession of our love. No plighted faith, no passionate vows, but the silence and the thrill of sympathy through our hearts were sweeter than words could be.

Diana raised her head and looked fearlessly but appealingly into my eyes as she asked me: 'Oh, Frank, did I do right to speak? Could it have been better if I had waited?'

She saw my wishes in my eyes, and bent down her head to me. I kissed her on the forehead and fervently prayed, 'Thank God that all was as it has been. May He bless my own darling wife for ever and ever.'

'Amen,' said a sweet, tender voice.

We both looked up without shame, for we knew the tones of my second mother. Her face, streaming with tears of joy, was lit up by a sudden ray of sunlight through the casement.

The Dualitists
or, the Death-Doom of the Double-Born

I

Bis Dat Qui Non Cito Dat
(He gives twice who does not give quickly)

There was joy in the house of Bubb.

For ten long years had Ephraim and Sophonisba Bubb mourned in vain the loneliness of their life. Unavailingly had they gazed into the emporia of baby-linen, and fixed their searching glances on the basket-makers' warehouses where the cradles hung in tempting rows. In vain had they prayed, and sighed, and groaned, and wished, and waited, and wept, but never had even a ray of hope been held out by the family physician.

* * *

But now at last the wished-for moment had arrived. Month after month had flown by on leaden wings, and the destined days had slowly measured their course. The months had become weeks; the weeks had dwindled down to days; the days had been attenuated to hours; the hours had lapsed into minutes, the minutes had slowly died away, and but seconds remained.

Ephraim Bubb sat cowering on the stairs, and tried with high-strung ears to catch the strain of blissful music from the lips of his first-born. There was silence in the house – silence as of the deadly calm before the cyclone. Ah! Ephra Bubb, little thinkest thou that another moment may for ever destroy the peaceful, happy course of thy life, and open to thy too craving eyes the portals of that wondrous land where Childhood reigns supreme, and where the tyrant infant with the wave of his tiny hand and the imperious treble of his tiny voice sentences his parent to the deadly vault beneath the castle moat. As the thought strikes thee thou becomest pale. How thou tremblest as thou findest thyself upon the brink of the abyss! Wouldst that thou could recall the past!

But hark! the die is cast for good or ill. The long years of praying and hoping have found an end at last. From the chamber within comes a sharp cry, which shortly after is repeated. Ah! Ephraim, that cry is the feeble effort of childish lips as yet unused to the rough, worldly form of speech to frame the word Father. In the glow of thy transport all doubts are forgotten; and when the doctor cometh forth as the harbinger of joy he findeth thee radiant with new-found delight.

'My dear sir, allow me to congratulate you – to offer twofold felicitations. Mr Bubb, sir, you are the father of Twins!'

2   *Halcyon Days*

The twins were the finest children that ever were seen – so at least said the *cognoscenti*, and the parents were not slow to believe. The nurse's opinion was in itself a proof.

It was not, ma'am, that they was fine for twins, but they was fine for singles, and she had ought to know, for she had nussed a many in her time, both twins and singles. All they wanted was to have their dear little legs cut off and little wings on their dear little shoulders, for to be put one on each side of a white marble tombstone, cut beautiful, sacred to the relic of Ephraim Bubb, that they might, sir, if so be that missus was to survive the father of two such lovely twins – although she would make bold to say, and no offence intended, that a handsome gentleman, though a trifle or two older than his good lady, though for the matter of that she heerd that gentlemen was never too old at all, and for her own part she liked them the better for it: not like bits of boys that didn't know their own minds – that a gentleman what was the father of two such 'eavenly twins (God bless them!) couldn't be called anything but a boy; though for the matter of that she never knowed in her experience – which it was much – of a boy as had such twins, or any twins at all so much for the matter of that.

The twins were the idols of their parents, and at the same time their pleasure and their pain. Did Zerubbabel cough, Ephraim would start from his balmy slumbers with an agonised cry of consternation, for visions of innumerable twins black in the face from croup haunted his nightly pillow. Did Zacariah rail at ethereal expansion, Sophonisba with pallid hue and dishevelled locks would

fly to the cradle of her offspring. Did pins torture or strings afflict, or
flannel or flies tickle, or light dazzle, or darkness affright, or hunger
or thirst assail the synchronous productions, the household of Bubb
would be roused from quiet slumbers or the current of its manifold
workings changed.

The twins grew apace; were weaned; teethed; and at length arrived
at the stage of three years!

> They grew in beauty side by side,
> They filled one home, etc.

3   *Rumours of Wars*

Harry Merford and Tommy Santon lived in the same range of villas
as Ephraim Bubb. Harry's parents had taken up their abode in
No 25, No 27 was happy in the perpetual sunshine of Tommy's
smiles, and between these two residences Ephraim Bubb reared his
blossoms, the number of his mansion being 26. Harry and Tommy
had been accustomed from the earliest times to meet each other daily.
Their primal method of communication had been by the housetops,
till their respective sires had been obliged to pay compensation to
Bubb for damages to his roof and dormer windows; and from that
time they had been forbidden by the home authorities to meet,
whilst their mutual neighbour had taken the precaution of having his
garden walls pebbledashed and topped with broken glass to prevent
their incursions. Harry and Tommy, however, being gifted with
daring souls, lofty ambitions, impetuous natures, and strong seats to
their trousers, defied the rugged walls of Bubb and continued to
meet in secret.

Compared with these two youths, Castor and Pollux, Damon and
Pythias, Eloisa and Abelard are but tame examples of duality or
constancy and friendship. All the poets from Hyginus to Schiller
might sing of noble deeds done and desperate dangers held as naught
for friendship's sake, but they would have been mute had they but
known of the mutual affection of Harry and Tommy. Day by day,
and often night by night, would these two brave the perils of nurse,
and father, and mother, of whip and imprisonment, and hunger
and thirst, and solitude and darkness to meet together. What they
discussed in secret none other knew. What deeds of darkness were
perpetrated in their symposia none could tell. Alone they met, alone
they remained, and alone they departed to their several abodes.

There was in the garden of Bubb a summer house overgrown with trailing plants, and surrounded by young poplars which the fond father had planted on his children's natal day, and whose rapid growth he had proudly watched. These trees quite obscured the summerhouse, and here Harry and Tommy, knowing after a careful observation that none ever entered the place, held their conclaves. Time after time they met in full security and followed their customary pursuit of pleasure. Let us raise the mysterious veil and see what was the great Unknown at whose shrine they bent the knee.

Harry and Tommy had each been given as a Christmas box a new knife; and for a long time – nearly a year – these knives, similar in size and pattern, were their chief delights. With them they cut and hacked in their respective homes all things which would not be likely to be noticed; for the young gentlemen were wary and had no wish that their moments of pleasure should be atoned for by moments of pain. The insides of drawers, and desks, and boxes, and under parts of tables and chairs, the backs of picture frames, even the floors, where corners of the carpets could surreptitiously be turned up, all bore marks of their craftsmanship; and to compare notes on these artistic triumphs was a source of joy. At length, however, a critical time came, some new field of action should be opened up, for the old appetites were sated, and the old joys had begun to pall. It was absolutely necessary that the existing schemes of destruction should be enlarged; and yet this could hardly be done without a terrible risk of discovery, for the limits of safety had long since been reached and passed. But, be the risk great or small, some new ground should be broken – some new joy found, for the old earth was barren, and the craving for pleasure was growing fiercer with each successive day.

The crisis had come: who could tell the issue?

4   *The Tucket Sounds*

They met in the arbour, determined to discuss this grave question. The heart of each was big with revolution, the head of each was full of scheme and strategy, and the pocket of each was full of sweetstuff, the sweeter for being stolen. After having despatched the sweets, the conspirators proceeded to explain their respective views with regard to the enlargement of their artistic operations. Tommy unfolded with much pride a scheme which he had in contemplation of cutting a series of holes in the sounding board of the piano, so as to destroy its musical properties. Harry was in no wise behindhand in his ideas of reform. He had conceived the project of cutting the canvas at the back of his great grandfather's portrait, which his father held in high regard among his lares and penates, so that in time when the picture should be moved the skin of paint would be broken, the head fall bodily out from the frame.

At this point of the council a brilliant thought occurred to Tommy. 'Why should not the enjoyment be doubled, and the musical instruments and family pictures of both establishments be sacrificed on the altar of pleasure?' This was agreed to nem. con.; and then the meeting adjourned for dinner. When they next met it was evident that there was a screw loose somewhere – that there was 'something rotten in the state of Denmark'. After a little fencing on both sides, it came out that all the schemes of domestic reform had been foiled by maternal vigilance, and that so sharp had been the reprimand consequent on a partial discovery of the schemes that they would have to be abandoned – till such time, at least, as increased physical strength would allow the reformers to laugh to scorn parental threats and injunctions.

Sadly the two forlorn youths took out their knives and regarded them; sadly, sadly they thought, as erst did Othello, of all the fair chances of honour and triumph and glory gone for ever. They compared knives with almost the fondness of doting parents. There they were – so equal in size and strength and beauty – dimmed by no corrosive rust, tarnished by no stain, and with unbroken edges of the keenness of Saladin's sword.

So like were the knives that but for the initials scratched in the handles neither boy could have been sure which was his own. After a little while they began mutually to brag of the superior excellence of their respective weapons. Tommy insisted that his was the sharper, Harry asserted that his was the stronger of the two. Hotter and hotter grew the war of words. The tempers of Harry and Tommy got inflamed, and their boyish bosoms glowed with manly thoughts of daring and of hate. But there was abroad in that hour a spirit of a bygone age – one that penetrated even to that dim arbour in the grove of Bubb. The world-old scheme of ordeal was whispered by the spirit in the ear of each, and suddenly the tumult was allayed. With one impulse the boys suggested that they should test the quality of their knives by the ordeal of the Hack.

No sooner said than done. Harry held out his knife edge uppermost; and Tommy, grasping his firmly by the handle, brought down the edge of the blade crosswise on Harry's. The process was then reversed, and Harry became in turn the aggressor. Then they paused and eagerly looked for the result. It was not hard to see; in each knife were two great dents of equal depth; and so it was necessary to renew the contest, and seek a further proof.

What needs it to relate seriatim the details of that direful strife? The sun had long since gone down, and the moon with fair, smiling face had long risen over the roof of Bubb, when, wearied and jaded, Harry and Tommy sought their respective homes. Alas! the splendour of the knives was gone for ever. Ichabod! Ichabod! The glory had departed and naught remained but two useless wrecks, with keen edges destroyed, and now like unto nothing save the serried hills of Spain.

But though they mourned for their fondly cherished weapons, the hearts of the boys were glad; for the bygone day had opened to their gaze a prospect of pleasure as boundless as the limits of the world.

5   *The First Crusade*

From that day a new era dawned in the lives of Harry and Tommy. So long as the resources of the parental establishments could hold out, so long would their new amusement continue. Subtly they obtained surreptitious possession of articles of family cutlery not in general use, and brought them one by one to their rendezvous. These came fair and spotless from the sanctity of the butler's pantry. Alas! they returned not as they came.

But in course of time the stock of available cutlery became exhausted, and again the inventive faculties of the youths were called into requisition. They reasoned thus: 'The knife game, it is true, is played out, but the excitement of the Hack is not to be dispensed with. Let us carry, then, this Great Idea into new worlds; let us still live in the sunshine of pleasure; let us continue to hack, but with objects other than knives.'

It was done. Not knives now engaged the attention of the ambitious youths. Spoons and forks were daily flattened and beaten out of shape; pepper castor met pepper castor in combat, and both were borne dying from the field; candlesticks met in fray to part no more on this side of the grave; even epergnes were used as weapons in the crusade of Hack.

At last all the resources of the butler's pantry became exhausted, and then began a system of miscellaneous destruction that proved in a little time ruinous to the furniture of the respective homes of Harry and Tommy. Mrs Santon and Mrs Merford began to notice

that the wear and tear in their households became excessive. Day
after day some new domestic calamity seemed to have occurred.
Today a valuable edition of some book whose luxurious binding
made it an object for public display would appear to have suffered
some dire misfortune, for the edges were frayed and broken and
the back loose if not altogether displaced; tomorrow the same
awful fate would seem to have followed some miniature frame; the
day following the legs of some chair or spider-table would show
signs of extraordinary hardship. Even in the nursery the sounds of
lamentation were heard. It was a thing of daily occurrence for the
little girls to state that when going to bed at night they had laid their
dear dollies in their beds with tender care, but that when again
seeking them in the period of recess they had found them with all
their beauty gone, with legs and arms amputated and faces beaten
from all semblance of human form.

Then articles of crockery began to be missed. The thief could in
no case be discovered, and the wages of the servants, from constant
stoppages, began to be nominal rather than real. Mrs Merford and
Mrs Santon mourned their losses, but Harry and Tommy gloated
day after day over their spoils, which lay in an ever-increasing heap
in the hidden grove of Bubb. To such an extent had the fondness of
the Hack now grown that with both youths it was an infatuation – a
madness – a frenzy.

At length one awful day arrived. The butlers of the houses of
Merford and Santon, harassed by constant losses and complaints,
and finding that their breakage account was in excess of their wages,
determined to seek some sphere of occupation where, if they did not
meet with a suitable reward or recognition of their services, they
would, at least, not lose whatever fortune and reputation they had
already acquired. Accordingly, before rendering up their keys and
the goods entrusted to their charge, they proceeded to take a preliminary stock of their own accounts, to make sure of their accredited
accuracy. Dire indeed was their distress when they knew to the full
the havoc which had been wrought; terrible their anguish of the
present, bitter their thoughts of the future. Their hearts, bowed
down with weight of woe, failed them quite; reeled the strong brains
that had erst overcome foes of deadlier spirit than grief; and fell
their stalwart forms prone on the floors of their respective sancta
sanctorum.

Late in the day when their services were required they were sought
for in bower and hall, and at length discovered where they lay.

But alas for justice! They were accused of being drunk and for having, whilst in that degraded condition, deliberately injured all the property on which they could lay hands. Were not the evidences of their guilt patent to all in the hecatombs of the destroyed? Then they were charged with all the evils wrought in the houses, and on their indignant denial Harry and Tommy, each in his own home, according to their concerted scheme of action, stepped forward and relieved their minds of the deadly weight that had for long in secret borne them down. The story of each ran that time after time he had seen the butler, when he thought that nobody was looking, knocking knives together in the pantry, chairs and books and pictures in the drawing-room and study, dolls in the nursery, and plates in the kitchen. Then, indeed, was the master of each household stern and uncompromising in his demands for justice. Each butler was committed to the charge of myrmidons of the law under the double charge of drunkenness and wilful destruction of property.

*   *   *

Softly and sweetly slept Harry and Tommy in their little beds that night. Angels seemed to whisper to them, for they smiled as though lost in pleasant dreams. The rewards given by proud and grateful parents lay in their pockets, and in their hearts the happy consciousness of having done their duty.

Truly sweet should be the slumbers of the just.

6   'Let the Dead Past Bury Its Dead'

It might be supposed that now the operations of Harry and Tommy would be obliged to be abandoned.

Not so, however. The minds of these youths were of no common order, nor were their souls of such weak nature as to yield at the first summons of necessity. Like Nelson, they knew not fear; like Napoleon, they held 'impossible' to be the adjective of fools; and they revelled in the glorious truth that in the lexicon of youth is no such word as 'fail'. Therefore on the day following the *éclaircissement* of the butlers' misdeeds, they met in the arbour to plan a new campaign.

In the hour when all seemed blackest to them, and when the narrowing walls of possibility hedged them in on every side, thus ran the deliberations of these dauntless youths: 'We have played out the meaner things that are inanimate and inert; why not then trench on the domains of life? The dead have lapsed into the regions of the forgotten past – let the living look to themselves.'

That night they met when all households had retired to balmy sleep, and naught but the amorous wailings of nocturnal cats told of the existence of life and sentience. Each bore into the arbour in his arms a pet rabbit and a piece of sticking plaster. Then, in the peaceful, quiet moonlight, commenced a work of mystery, blood, and gloom. The proceedings began by the fixing of a piece of sticking plaster over the mouth of each rabbit to prevent it making a noise, if so inclined. Then Tommy held up his rabbit by its scutty tail, and it hung wriggling, a white mass in the moonlight. Slowly Harry raised his rabbit holding it in the same manner, and when level with his head brought it down on Tommy's client.

But the chances had been miscalculated. The boys held firmly to the tails, but the chief portions of the rabbits fell to earth. Ere the doomed beasts could escape, however, the operators had pounced upon them, and this time holding them by the hind legs renewed the trial.

Deep into the night the game was kept up, and the Eastern sky began to show signs of approaching day as each boy bore triumphantly the dead corse of his favourite bunny and placed it within its sometime hutch.

Next night the same game was renewed with a new rabbit on each side, and for more than a week – so long as the hutches supplied the wherewithal – the battle was sustained. True that there were sad hearts and red eyes in the juveniles of Santon and Merford as one by one the beloved pets were found dead, but Harry and Tommy, with the hearts of heroes steeled to suffering and deaf to the pitiful cries of childhood, still fought the good fight on to the bitter end.

When the supply of rabbits was exhausted, other munition was not wanting, and for some days the war was continued with white mice, dormice, hedgehogs, guinea pigs, pigeons, lambs, canaries, parroqueets, linnets, squirrels, parrots, marmots, poodles, ravens, tortoises, terriers, and cats. Of these, as might be expected, the most difficult to manipulate were the terriers and the cats, and of these two classes the proportion of the difficulties in the way of terrier-hacking was, when compared with those of cat-hacking, about that which the simple Lac of the *British Pharmacopoeia* bears to water in the compound which dairymen palm off upon a too confiding public as milk. More than once when engaged in the rapturous delights of cat-hacking had Harry and Tommy wished that the silent tomb could open its ponderous and massy jaws and engulf them, for the feline victims were not patient in their death agonies, and often broke the bonds in which the security of the artists rested, and turned fiercely on their executioners.

At last, however, all the animals available were sacrificed; but the passion for hacking still remained. How was it all to end?

7   *A Cloud with Golden Lining*

Tommy and Harry sat in the arbour dejected and disconsolate. They wept like two Alexanders because there were no more worlds to conquer. At last the conviction had been forced upon them that the resources available for hacking were exhausted. That very morning they had had a desperate battle, and their attire showed the ravages of direful war. Their hats were battered into shapeless masses, their shoes were soleless and heelless and had the uppers broken, the ends of their braces, their sleeves, and their trousers were frayed, and had they indulged in the manly luxury of coat tails these too would have gone.

Truly, hacking had become an absorbing passion with them. Long and fiercely had they been swept onward on the wings of the demon of strife, and powerless at the best of times had been the promptings of good; but now, heated with combat, maddened by the equal success of arms, and with the lust for victory still unsated, they longed more fiercely than ever for some new pleasure: like tigers that have tasted blood they thirsted for a larger and more potent libation.

As they sat, with their souls in a tumult of desire and despair, some evil genius guided into the garden the twin blossoms of the tree of Bubb. Hand in hand Zacariah and Zerubbabel advanced from the back door; they had escaped from their nurses, and with the exploring instinct of humanity, advanced boldly into the great world – the *terra incognita*, the *Ultima Thule* of the paternal domain.

In the course of time they approached the hedge of poplars, from behind which the anxious eyes of Harry and Tommy looked for their approach, for the boys knew that where the twins were the nurses were accustomed to be gathered together, and they feared discovery if their retreat should be cut off.

It was a touching sight, these lovely babes, alike in form, feature, size, expression, and dress; in fact, so like each other that one 'might not have told either from which.' When the startling similarity was recognised by Harry and Tommy, each suddenly turned, and, grasping the other by the shoulder, spoke in a keen whisper: 'Hack! They are exactly equal! This is the very apotheosis of our art!'

With excited faces and trembling hands they laid their plans to lure the unsuspecting babes within the precincts of their charnel house, and they were so successful in their efforts that in a little time the twins had toddled behind the hedge and were lost to the sight of the parental mansion.

Harry and Tommy were not famed for gentleness within the immediate precincts of their respective homes, but it would have delighted the heart of any philanthropist to see the kindly manner in which they arranged for the pleasures of the helpless babes. With smiling faces and playful words and gentle wiles they led them within the arbour, and then, under pretence of giving them some of those sudden jumps in which infants rejoice, they raised them from the ground. Tommy held Zacariah across his arm with his baby moon-face smiling up at the cobwebs on the arbour roof, and Harry, with a mighty effort, raised the cherubic Zerubbabel aloft.

Each nerved himself for a great endeavour, Harry to give, Tommy to endure a shock, and then the form of Zerubbabel was seen whirling through the air round Harry's glowing and determined face. There was a sickening crash and the arm of Tommy yielded visibly.

The pasty face of Zerubbabel had fallen fair on that of Zacariah, for Tommy and Harry were by this time artists of too great experience to miss so simple a mark. The putty-like noses collapsed, the putty-like cheeks became for a moment flattened, and when in an instant more they parted, the faces of both were dabbled in gore. Immediately the firmament was rent with a series of such yells as might have awakened the dead. Forthwith from the house of Bubb came the echoes in parental cries and footsteps. As the sounds of scurrying feet rang through the mansion, Harry cried to Tommy: 'They will be on us soon. Let us cut to the roof of the stable and draw up the ladder.'

Tommy answered by a nod, and the two boys, regardless of consequences, and bearing each a twin, ascended to the roof of the stable by means of a ladder which usually stood against the wall, and which they pulled up after them.

As Ephraim Bubb issued from his house in pursuit of his lost darlings, the sight which met his gaze froze his very soul. There, on the coping of the stable roof, stood Harry and Tommy renewing their game. They seemed like two young demons forging some diabolical implement, for each in turn the twins were lifted high

in air and let fall with stunning force on the supine form of its
fellow. How Ephraim felt none but a tender and imaginative
father can conceive. It would be enough to wring the heart of even
a callous parent to see his children, the darlings of his old age –
his own beloved twins – being sacrificed to the brutal pleasure of
unregenerate youths, without being made unconsciously and helplessly guilty of the crime of fratricide.

Loudly did Ephraim and also Sophonisba, who, with dishevelled
locks, had now appeared upon the scene, bewail their unhappy lot
and shriek in vain for aid; but by rare ill chance no eyes save their
own saw the work of butchery or heard the shrieks of anguish and
despair. Wildly did Ephraim, mounting on the shoulders of his
spouse, strive, but in vain, to scale the stable wall.

Baffled in every effort, he rushed into the house and appeared in a
moment bearing in his hands a double-barrelled gun, into which he
poured the contents of a shot pouch as he ran. He came anigh the
stable and hailed the murderous youths: 'Drop them twins and come
down here or I'll shoot you like a brace of dogs.'

'Never!' exclaimed the heroic two with one impulse, and continued their awful pastime with a zest tenfold as they knew that the
agonised eyes of parents wept at the cause of their joy.

'Then die!' shrieked Ephraim, as he fired both barrels, right – left,
at the hackers.

But, alas! love for his darlings shook the hand that never shook
before. As the smoke cleared off and Ephraim recovered from the
kick of his gun, he heard a loud twofold laugh of triumph and saw
Harry and Tommy, all unhurt, waving in the air the trunks of the
twins – the fond father had blown the heads completely off his own
offspring.

Tommy and Harry shrieked aloud in glee, and after playing catch
with the bodies for some time, seen only by the agonised eyes of the
infanticide and his wife, flung them high in the air. Ephraim leaped
forward to catch what had once been Zacariah, and Sophonisba
grabbed wildly for the loved remains of her Zerubbabel.

But the weight of the bodies and the height from which they fell
were not reckoned by either parent, and from being ignorant of a
simple dynamical formula each tried to effect an object which calm,
common sense, united with scientific knowledge, would have told
them was impossible. The masses fell, and Ephraim and Sophonisba
were stricken dead by the falling twins, who were thus posthumously
guilty of the crime of parricide.

An intelligent coroner's jury found the parents guilty of the crimes of infanticide and suicide, on the evidence of Harry and Tommy, who swore, reluctantly, that the inhuman monsters, maddened by drink, had killed their offspring by shooting them into the air out of a cannon – since stolen – whence like curses they had fallen on their own heads; and that then they had slain themselves *suis manibus*, with their own hands.

Accordingly Ephraim and Sophonisba were denied the solace of Christian burial, and were committed to the earth with 'maimed rites', and had stakes driven through their middles to pin them down in their unhallowed graves till the Crack of Doom.

Harry and Tommy were each rewarded with National honours and were knighted, even at their tender years.

Fortune seemed to smile upon them all the long after years, and they lived to a ripe old age, hale of body, and respected and beloved of all.

Often in the golden summer eves, when all nature seemed at rest, when the oldest cask was opened and the largest lamp was lit, when the chestnuts glowed in the embers and the kid turned on the spit, when their great-grandchildren pretended to mend fictional armour and to trim an imaginary helmet's plume, when the shuttles of the good wives of their grandchildren went flashing each through its proper loom, with shouting and with laughter they were accustomed to tell the tale of *The Dualitists; or, the Death-Doom of the Double-Born*.

The Red Stockade

A Story Told by the Old Coastguard

We was on the southern part of the China station, when the 'George Ranger' was ordered to the Straits of Malacca, to put down the pirates that had been showing themselves of late. It was in the forties, when ships was ships, not iron kettles full of wheels, and other devilments, and there was a chance of hand-to-hand fighting – not being blown up in an iron cellar by you don't know who. Ships was ships in them days!

There had been a lot of throat-cutting and scuttling, for them devils stopped at nothing. Some of us had been through the straits before, when we was in the 'Polly Phemus', seventy-four, going to the China station, and although we had never come to quarters with the Malays, we had seen some of their work, and knew what kind they was. So, when we had left Singapore in the 'George Ranger' – for that was our saucy, little thirty-eight-gun frigate – the place wasn't in them days what it is now – many and many's the yarn was told in the fo'c'sle, and on the watches, of what the yellow devils could do, and had done. Some of us took it one way, and some another, but all, save a few, wanted to get into hand-grips with the pirates, for all their kreeses, and their stinkpots, and the devil's engines what they used. There was some that didn't mind cold steel of an ordinary kind, and would have faced cutlasses and boarding-pikes, any day, for a holiday, but that didn't like the idea of those knives like crooked flames, and that sliced a man in two, and hacked through the bowels of him. Naturally, we didn't take much stock of this kind; and many's the joke we had on them, and some of them cruel enough jokes, too.

You may be sure there was good stories, with plenty of cutting, and blood, and tortures in them, told in their watches, and nigh the whole ship's crew was busy, day and night, remembering and inventing things that'd make them gasp and grow white. I think that, somehow, the captain and the officers must have known what was goin' on, for there came tales from the wardroom that was worse nor any of ours. The midshipmen used to delight in them, like the ship's boys did, and one of them, that had a kreese, used to bring it out when he could, and show how the pirates used it when they cut the hearts out of men and women, and ripped them up to the chins. It was a bit cruel, at times, on them poor, white-livered chaps – a man can't help his liver, I suppose – but, anyhow, there's no place for them in a warship, for they're apt to do more harm by living where there's men of all sorts, than they can do by dying. So there wasn't any mercy for them, and the captain was worse on them than any. Captain Wynyard was him that commanded the corvette 'Sentinel' on the China station, and was promoted to the 'George Ranger' for cutting up a fleet of junks that was hammering at the 'Rajah', from Canton, racing for Southampton with the first of the season's tea. He was a man, if you like, a bulldog full of hellfire, when he was on for fighting; he wouldn't have a white liver at any price. 'God hates a coward,' he said once, 'and under Her Britannic Majesty I'm here to carry out God's will. Trice him up, and give him a dozen!' At least, that's the story they tell of him when he was round Shanghai, and one of his men had held back when the time came for boarding a fire-junk that was coming down the tide. And with that he went in, and steered her off with his own hands.

Well, the captain knew what work there was before us, and that it weren't no time for kid gloves and hair oil, much less a bokey in your buttonhole and a top hat, and he didn't mean that there should be any funk on his ship. So you take your davy that it wasn't his fault if things was made too pleasant aboard for men what feared fallin' into the clutches of the Malays.

Now and then he went out of his way to be nasty over such folk, and, boy or man, he never checked his tongue on a hard word when any one's face was pale before him. There was one old chap on board that we called 'Old Land's End', for he came from that part, and that had a boy of his on the 'Billy Ruffian', when he sailed on her, and after got lost, one night, in cutting out a Greek sloop at Navarino, in 1827. We used to chaff him when there was trouble with any of the boys, for he used to say that his boy might have been in that trouble, too. And now, when the chaff was on about bein' afeered of the Malays, we used to rub it into the old man; but he would flame up, and answer us that his boy died in his duty, and that he couldn't be afeered of nought.

One night there was a row on among the midshipmen, for they said that one of them, Tempest by name, owned up to being afraid of being kreesed. He was a rare bright little chap of about thirteen, that was always in fun and trouble of some kind; but he was soft-hearted, and sometimes the other lads would tease him. He would own up truthfully to anything he thought, or felt, and now they had drawn him to own something that none of them would – no matter how true it might be. Well, they had a rare fight, for the boy was never backward with his fists, and by accident it came to the notice of the captain. He insisted on being told what it was all about, and when young Tempest spoke out, and told him, he stamped on the deck, and called out: 'I'll have no cowards in this ship,' and was going on, when the boy cut in: 'I'm no coward, sir; I'm a gentleman!'

'Did you say you were afraid? Answer me – yes, or no?'

'Yes, sir, I did, and it was true! I said I feared the Malay kreeses; but I did not mean to shirk them, for all that. Henry of Navarre was afraid, but, all the same, he – '

'Henry of Navarre be damned,' shouted the captain, 'and you, too! You said you were afraid, and that, let me tell you, is what we call a coward in the Queen's navy. And if you are one, you can, at least, have the grace to keep it to yourself! No answer to me! To the masthead for the remainder of the day! I want my crew to know what to avoid, and to know it when they see it!' and he walked away, while the lad, without a word, ran up the maintop.

Some way, the men didn't say much about this. The only one that said anything to the point was Old Land's End, and says he: 'That may be a coward, but I'd chance it that he was a boy of mine.'

As we went up the straits and got the sun on us, and the damp heat of that kettle of a place – Lor' bless ye! Ye steam there, all day and all night like a copper at the galley – we began to look around for the pirates, and there wasn't a man that got drowsy on the watch. We coasted along as we went up north, and took a look into the creeks and rivers as we went. It was up these that the Malays hid themselves; for the fevers and such that swept off their betters like flies, didn't seem to have any effect on them. There was pretty bad bits, I tell you, up some of them rivers through the mango groves, where the marshes spread away, mile after mile, as far as you could see, and where everything that is noxious, both beast, and bird, and fish, and crawling thing, and insect, and tree, and bush, and flower, and creeper, is most at home.

But the pirate ships kept ahead of us; or, if they came south again, passed us by in the night, and so we ran up till about the middle of the peninsula, where the worst of the piracies had happened. There we got up as well as we could to look like a ship in distress; and, sure enough, we deceived the beggars, for two of them came out one early dawn and began to attack us. They was ugly looking craft, too – long, low hull and lateen sails, and a double crew twice told in every one of them.

But if the crafts was ugly the men was worse, for uglier devils I never saw. Swarthy, yellow chaps, some of them, and some with shaven crowns and white eyeballs, and others as black as your shoe, with one or two white men, more shame, among them, but all carrying kreeses as long as your arm, and pistols in their belts.

They didn't get much change from us, I tell you. We let them get close, and then gave them a broadside that swept their decks like a hailstorm; but we was unlucky that we didn't grapple them, for they managed to shift off and ran for it. Our boats was out quick, but we daren't follow them where they ran into a wide creek, with mango swamps on each side as far as the eye could reach. The boat came back after a bit and reported that they had run up the river which was deep enough but with a winding channel between great mudbanks, where alligators lay in hundreds. There seemed some sort of fort where the river narrowed, and the pirates ran in behind it and disappeared up the bend of the river.

Then the preparations began. We knew that we had got two craft, at any rate, caged in the river, and there was every chance that we had found their lair. Our captain wasn't one that let things go asleep, and by daylight the next morning we was ready for an attack. The pinnace and four other boats started out under the first lieutenant to prospect, and the rest that was left on board waited, as well as they could, till we came back.

That was an awful day. I was in the second boat, and we all kept well together when we began to get into the narrows of the mouth of the river. When we started, we went in a couple of hours after the flood tide, and so all we saw when the light came seemed fresh and watery. But as the tide ran out, and the big black mudbanks began to show their heads above everywhere, it wasn't nice, I can tell you. It was hardly possible for us to tell the channels, for everywhere the tide raced quick, and it was only when the boat began to touch the black slime that you knew that you was on a bank. Twice our boat was almost caught this way, but by good luck we pulled and pushed off in time into the ebbing tide; and hardly a boat but touched somewhere. One that was a bit out from the rest of us got stuck at last in a nasty cut between two mudbanks, and as the water ran away the boat turned over on the slope, despite all her crew could do, and we saw the poor fellows thrown out into the slime. More than one of them began to swim toward us, but behind each came a rush of something dark, and though we shouted and made what noise we could, and fired many shots, the alligators was too close, and with shriek after shriek they went down to the bottom of the filth and slime. Oh, man! it was a dreadful sight, and none the better that it was new to nigh all of us. How it would have taken us if we had time to think about it, I hardly know, but I doubt that more than a few would have grown cold over it; but just then there flew amongst us a hail of small shot from a fleet of boats that had stolen down on us. They drove out from behind a big mudbank that rose steeper than the others and that seemed solider, too, for the gravel of it showed, as the scour of the tide washed the mud away. We was not sorry, I tell you, to have men to fight with, instead of alligators and mudbanks, in an ebbing tide, in a strange tropical river.

We gave chase at once, and the pinnace fired the twelve-pounder which she carried in the bows, in among the huddle of the boats, and the yells arose as the rush of the alligators turned to where the Malay heads bobbed up and down in the drift of the tide. Then the pirates turned and ran, and we after them as hard as we could pull, till round a sharp bend of the river we came to a narrow place, where one side was steep for a bit and then tailed away to a wilderness of marsh, worse than we had seen. The other side was crowned by a sort of fort, built on the top of a high bank, but guarded by a stockade and a mudbank which lay at its base. From this there came a rain of bullets, and we saw some guns turned toward us. We was hardly strong enough to attack such a position without reconnoitring, and so we drew away; but not quite quick enough, for before we could get out of range of their guns a round shot carried away the whole of the starboard oars of one of our boats.

It was a dreary pull to the ship, and the tide was agin us, for we all got thinking of what we had to tell – one boat and crew lost entirely, and a set of oars shot away – and no work done.

The captain was furious; and, in the wardroom, and in the fo'c'sle that night, there was nothing that wasn't flavoured with anger and curses. Even the boys, of all sorts, from the cabin-boys to the mid-shipmen, was wanting to get at the Malays. However, sharp was the order; and by daylight three boats was up at the stockaded fort, making an accurate survey. I was again in one of the boats; and, in spite of what the captain had said to make us all so angry – and he had a tongue like vitriol, I tell you – we all felt pretty down and cold when we got again amongst those terrible mudbanks and saw the slime that shone on them bubble up, when the grey of the morning let us see anything.

We found that the fort was one that we would have to take if we wanted to follow the pirates up the river, for it barred the way without a chance. There was a gut of the river between the two great ridges of gravel, and this was the only channel where there was a chance of passing. But it had been staked on both sides, so that only the centre was left free. Why, from the fort they could have stoned any one in the boats passing there, only that there wasn't any stone, that we could see, in their whole blasted country!

When we got back, with two cases of sunstroke among us, and reported, the captain ordered preparations for an attack on the fort, and the next morning the ball began. It was ugly work. We got close up to the fort, but, as the tide ran out, we had to sheer away some-what so as not to get stranded. The whole place swarmed with those grinning devils. They evidently had some way of getting to and from their boats behind the stockade. They did not fire a shot at us – not at first – and that was the most aggravating thing that you can imagine. They seemed to know something that we did not, and they only just waited. As the tide sank lower and lower, and the mudbanks grew steeper, and the sun on them began to fizzle, a steam arose that nigh turned our stomachs. Why, the sight of them alone would make your heart sink!

The slime shimmered in all kinds of colours, like the water when there's tarring work on hand, and the whole place seemed alive with all that was horrible. The alligators kept off the boats and the banks close to us, but the thick water was full of eels and watersnakes, and the mud was alive with water-worms and leeches, and horrible, gaudy-coloured crabs. The very air was filled with pests – flies of all kinds, and a sort of big-striped insect that they call the 'tiger mosquito', which comes out in the daytime and bites you like red-hot pincers. It was bad enough, I tell you, for us men with hair on our faces, but some of the boys got very white and pale, and they was all pretty silent for a while. All at once the crowd of Malays behind the stockade began to roll their eyes and wave their kreeses and to shout. We knew that there was some cause for it, but couldn't make it out, and this exasperated us more than ever. Then the captain sings out to us to attack the stockade; so out we all jumped into the mud. We knew it couldn't be very deep just there, on account of the gravel beneath. We was knee-deep in a moment, but we struggled, and slipped, and fell over each other; and, when we got to the top of that bank, we was the queerest, filthiest-looking crowd you ever see. But the mud hadn't took the heart out of us, and the Malays, with their necks craned over the stockade, and with the nearest thing to a laugh or a smile that the devil lets them have, drew back and fell, one on another, when they heard our cheer.

Between them and us there was a bit of a dip where the water had been running in the ebb tide, but which seemed now as dry as the rest, and the foremost of our men charged down the slope, and then we knew why they had kept silent and waited! We was in a regular trap. The first ranks disappeared at once in the mud and ooze in the hollow, and those next were up to their armpits before they could stop. Then those Malay devils opened on us, and while we tried to pull our chaps out, they mowed us down with every kind of small arm they had – and they had a queer assortment, I tell you.

It was all we could do to get back over the slope and to the boats again – what was left of us – and, as we hadn't hands enough left even to row with full strength, we had to make for the ship as fast as we could, for their boats began to pass out in a cloud through the narrow by the stockade. But before we went we saw them dragging the live and dead out of the mud with hooks on the end of long bamboos; and there was terrible shrieks from some poor fellows when the kreeses gashed through them. We daren't wait; but we saw enough to make us swear revenge. When we saw them devils stick the bleeding heads of our comrades on the spikes of the stockade, there was nigh a mutiny because the captain wouldn't let us go back and have another try for it. He was cool enough now; and those of us that knew him and understood what was in his mind, when the smile on him showed the white teeth in the corners of his mouth, felt that it was no good day's work that the pirates had done for themselves.

When we got back to the ship and told our tale, it wasn't long till the men was all on fire; and nigh every man took a turn with the grindstone at his cutlass, till they was all like razors. The captain mustered every one on board, and detailed every man to his work in the boats, ready for the next time; and we knew that, by daylight, we were to have another slap at the pirates. We got six-pounders and twelve-pounders in most of the boats, for we was to give them a dose of big shot before we came to close quarters.

When we got up near the stockade, the tide had turned, and we thought it better to wait till dawn, for it was bad work among the mudbanks at the ebb in the dark. So we hung on a while, and then when the sky began to lighten, we made for the fort. When we got nigh enough to see it, there wasn't a man of us who didn't want to have some bloody revenge, for there, on the spikes of the stockade, were the heads of all the poor fellows that we had lost the day before, with a cloud of mosquitoes and flies already beginning to buzz around them in the dawn. But beyond that again, they had painted the outside of the stockade with blood, so that the whole place was a crimson mass. You could smell it as the sun came up!

Well, that day was a hard one. We opened fire with our guns, and the Malays returned it, with all they had got. A fleet of boats came out from beyond the fort, and for a while we had to turn our attention to these. The small guns served us well, and we made a rare havoc among the boats, for our shot went crashing through them, and quite a half of them were sunk. The water was full of bobbing heads; but the tide carried them away from us, and their cries and shrieks came from beyond the fort and then died away. The other boats recognized their danger, and turned and ran in through the narrow, and let us alone for hours after. Then we went at the fort again. We turned our guns at the piles of the stockade, and, of course, every shot told – but their fire was at too close quarters, and with their rifles and matchlocks, and the rest, they picked us off too fast, and we had to sheer off where our heavy metal could tell without our being within their range. Before we sheered off, we could see that the hole we had knocked in the stockade was only in the outer work, and that the real fort was within. We had to go down the river, as we couldn't go far enough across without danger from the banks, and this only gave us a side view, and, do what we would, we couldn't make an impression – at least any that we could see.

That was a long and awful day! The sun was blazing on us like a furnace, and we was nigh mad with heat, and flies, and drouth, and anger. It was that hot that if you touched metal it fairly burned you. When the tide was near the flood, the captain ordered up the boats in the wide water now opposite the fort; and there, for a while, we got a fair chance, till, when the ebb began, we should have to sheer off again. By this time our shot was nearly run out, and we thought that we should have to give over; but all at once came order to prepare for attack, and in a few minutes we was working for dear life across the river, straight for the stockade. The men set up a cheer, and the pirates showed over the top of the stockade and waved their kreeses, and more than one of them sliced off pieces of the heads on the spikes, and jeered at us, as much as to say that they would do the same for us in our turn! When we got close up, every one of them had disappeared, and there was a silence of the grave. We knew that there was something up, but what the move was we could not tell, till from behind the fort came rushing again a fleet of boats. We turned on them, and, like we did before, we made mincemeat of them. This time the tide made for us, and the bobbing heads went by us in dozens. Now and then there was a wild yell, as an alligator pulled some one down into the mud. This went on for a little, and we had beaten them off enough to be able to get our grappling-irons ready for climbing the stockade, when the second lieutenant, who was in the outer boat, called out: 'Back with the boats! Back, quick, the tide is falling!' and with one impulse we began to shove off. Then, in an instant, the place became alive again with the Malays, and they began firing on us so quickly that before we could get out into the whirl of tide there was many a dead man in our boats.

There was no use trying to do any more that day, and after we had done what could be done for the wounded, and patched up our boats, for there was plenty of shot-holes to plug, we pulled back to the ship. The alligators had had a good day, and as we went along, and the mudbanks grew higher and higher with the falling of the tide, we could see them lie out lazily, as if they had been gorged. Aye! And there was enough left for the ground-sharks out in the offing; for the men on board told us that every while on the ebb something would go along, bobbing up and down in the swell, till presently there would be a swift ripple of a fin, and then there was no more pirate.

Well! when we got aboard, the rest was mighty anxious to know what had been done; and when we began, with the heads on spikes of the red stockade, the men ground their teeth, and Old Land's End up, and says he: 'The Red Stockade! We'll not forget the name! It'll be our turn next, and then we'll paint it inside this time.' And so it was that we came to know the place by that name. That night the captain was like a man that would do murder. His face was like steel, and his eyes was as red as flames. He didn't seem to have a thought for any one; and everything he did was as hard as though his heart were brass. He ordered all that was needful to be done for the wounded, but he added to the doctor: 'And, mind you, get them well as soon as you can. We're too short-handed already!'

Up to now, we all had known him treat men as men, but now

he only thought of us as machines for fighting! True enough, he thought the same of himself. Twice that very night he cut up rough in a new way. Of course, the men was talking of the attack, and there was lots of brag and chaff, for all they was so grim earnest, and some of the old fooling went on about blood and tortures. The captain came on deck, and as he walked along, he saw one of the men that didn't like the kreeses, and he didn't evidently like the looks of him, for he turned on his heel and said savagely: 'Send the doctor here!' So the doctor came, and the captain he says to him, cold as ice, and as polite as you please: 'Dr Fairbrother, there is a sick man here! look at his pale face. Something wrong with his liver, I suppose. It's the only thing that makes a seaman's face white when there's fighting ahead. Take him down to sick bay, and do something for him. I'd like to cut the accursed white liver out of him altogether!' and with that he went down to his cabin.

Well if we was hot for fighting before, we was boiling after that, and we all came to know that the next attack on the Red Stockade would be the last, one way or the other! We had to wait two more days before that could come off, for the boats and tackle had to be made ready, and there wasn't going to be any mistakes made this time.

It was just after midnight when we began to get ready. Every man was to his post. The moon was up, and it was lighter nor a London day, and the captain stood by and saw every man to his place, and nothing escaped him. By and by, as No 6 boat was filling, and before the officer in charge of it got in, came the midshipman, young Tempest, and when the captain saw him he called him up and hissed out before all the crew: 'Why are you so white? What's wrong with you, anyway? Is your liver out of order, too?'

True enough, the boy was white, but at the flaming insult the blood rushed to his face and we could see it red in the starlight. Then in another moment it passed away and left him paler than ever, and he said with a gentle voice, though standing as straight as a ramrod: 'I can't help the blood in my face, sir. If I'm a coward because I'm pale, perhaps you are right. But I shall do my duty all the same!' and with that he pulled himself up, touched his cap, and went down into the boat.

Old Land's End was behind me in the boat with him, number five to my six, and he whispered to me through his shut teeth: 'Too rough that! He might have thought a bit that he's only a child. And he came all the same, even if he was afeer'd!'

We stole away with muffled oars, and dropped silently into the river on the floodtide. If any man had had any doubts as to whether we was in earnest at other times, he had none then, anyhow. It was a pretty grim time, I tell you, for the most of us felt that whether we won or not this time, there would be many empty hammocks that night in the 'George Ranger', but we meant to win even if we went into the maws of the sharks and crocodiles for it. When we came up close on the flood we lost no time but went slap at the fort. At first, of course, we had crawled up the river in silence, and I think that we took the beggars by surprise, for we was there before the time they expected us. Howsomever, they turned out quick enough and there was soon music on both sides of the stockade. We didn't want to take any chance on the mudbanks this time, so we ran in close under the stockade at once and hooked on. We found that they had repaired the breach we had made the last time. They fought like devils, for they knew that we could beat them hand to hand, if we could once get in, and they sent round the boats to take us on the flank, as they had done each time before. But this time we wasn't to be drawn away from our attack, and we let our boats outside tackle them, while we minded our own business closer home.

It was a long fight and a bloody one. They was sheltered inside, and they knew that time was with them, for when the tide should have fallen, if we hadn't got in we should have our old trouble with the mudbanks all over again. But we knew it, too, and we didn't lose no time. Still, men is only men, after all, and we couldn't fly up over a stockade out of a boat, and them as did get up was sliced about dreadful – they are handy workmen with their kreeses, and no doubt! We was so hot on the job we had on hand that we never took no note of time at all, and all at once we found the boat fixed tight under us.

The tide had fallen and left us on the bank under the Red Stockade, and the best half of the boats was cut off from us. We had some thirty men left, and we knew we had to fight whether we liked it or not. It didn't much matter, anyhow, for we was game to go through with it. The captain, when he seen the state of things, gave his orders to take the boats out into midstream, and shell and shot the fort, whilst we was to do what we could to get in. It was no use trying to bridge over the slobs, for the masts of an old seventy-four wouldn't have done it. We was in a tight place, then, I can tell you, between two fires, for the guns in the boats couldn't fire high enough to clear us every time, without going over the fort altogether, and more than one of our own shots did some of us a harm. The cutter came into the game, and began sending the war-rockets from the tubes. The pirates didn't like that, I tell you, and more betoken, no more did we, for we got as much of them as they did, till the captain saw the harm to us, and bade them cease. But he knew his business, and he kept all the fire of the guns on the one side of the stockade, till he knocked a hole that we could get in by. When this was done, the Malays left the outer wall and went within the fort proper. This gave us some protection, since they couldn't fire right down on us, and our guns kept the boats away that would have taken us from the riverside. But it was hot work, and we began dropping away with stray shots, and with the stinkpots and hand grenades that they kept hurling over the stockade on to us.

So the time came when we found that we must make a dash for the fort, or get picked out, one by one, where we stood. By this time some of our boats was making for the opening, and there seemed less life behind the stockade; some of them was up to some move, and was sheering off to make up some other devilment. Still, they had their guns in the fort, and there was danger to our boats if they tried to cross the opening between the piles. One did, and went down with a hole in her within a minute. So we made a burst inside the stockade, and found ourselves in a narrow place between the two walls of piles. Anyhow, the place was drier, and we felt a relief in getting out of up to our knees in steaming mud. There was no time to lose, and the second lieutenant, Webster by name, told us to try to scale the stockade in front.

It wasn't high, but it was slimy below and greasy above, and do what we would, we couldn't get no nigher. A shot from a pistol wiped out the lieutenant, and for a moment we thought we was without a leader. Young Tempest was with us, silent all the time, with his face as white as a ghost, though he done his best, like the rest of us. Suddenly he called out: 'Here, lads! take and throw me in. I'm light enough to do it, and I know that when I'm in you'll all follow.'

Ne'er a man stirred. Then the lad stamped his foot and called again, and I remember his young, high voice now: 'Seamen to your duty! I command here!'

At the word we all stood at attention, just as if we was at quarters. Then Jack Pring, that we called the Giant, for he was six feet four and as strong as a bullock, spoke out: 'It's no duty, sir, to fling an officer into hell!' The lad looked at him and nodded.

'Volunteers for dangerous duty!' he called, and every man of the crowd stepped out.

'All right, boys!' says he. 'Now take me up and throw me in. We'll get down that flag, anyhow,' and he pointed to the black flag that the pirates flew on the flagstaff in the fort. Then he took the small flag of the float and put it on his breast, and says he: 'This'll suit better.'

'Won't I do, sir?' said Jack, and the lad laughed a laugh that rang again.

'Oh, my eye!' says he, 'has any one got a crane to hoist in the Giant?' The lad told us to catch hold of him, and when Jack hesitated, says he: 'We've always been friends, Jack, and I want you to be one of the last to touch me!' So Jack laid hold of him by one side, and Old Land's End stepped out and took him by the other. The rest of us was, by this time, kicking off our shoes and pulling off our shirts, and getting our knives open in our teeth. The two men gave a great heave together and they sent the boy clean over the top of the stockade. We heard across the river a cheer from our boats, as we began to scramble. There was a pause within the fort for a few seconds, and then we saw the lad swarm up the bamboo flagstaff that swayed under him, and tear down the black flag. He pulled our own flag from his breast and hung it over the top of the post. And he waved his hand and cheered, and the cheer was echoed in thunder across the river. And then a shot fetched him down, and with a wild yell they all went for him, while the cheering from the boats came like a storm.

We never knew quite how we got over that stockade. To this day I can't even imagine how we done it! But when we leaped down, we saw something lying at the foot of the flagstaff all red – and the kreeses was red, too! The devils had done their work! But it was their last, for we came at them with our cutlasses – there was never a sound from the lips of any of us – and we drove them like a hailstorm beats down standing corn! We didn't leave a living thing within the Red Stockade that day, and we wouldn't if there had been a million there!

It was a while before we heard the shouting again, for the boats was coming up the river, now that the fort was ours, and the men had other work for their breath than cheering.

Between us, we made a rare clearance of the pirates' nest that day. We destroyed every boat on the river, and the two ships that we was looking for, and one other that was careened. We tore down and burned every house, and jetty, and stockade in the place, and there was no quarter for them we caught. Some of them got away by a path they knew through the swamp where we couldn't follow them. The sun was getting low when we pulled back to the ship. It would have been a merry enough homecoming, despite our losses – all but for one thing, and that was covered up with a Union Jack in the captain's own boat. Poor lad! when they lifted him on deck, and the men came round to look at him, his face was pale enough now, and, one and all, we felt that it was to make amends, as the captain stooped over and kissed him on the forehead.

'We'll bury him tomorrow,' he said, 'but in blue water, as becomes a gallant seaman.'

At the dawn, next day, he lay on a grating, sewn in his hammock, with the shot at his feet, and the whole crew was mustered, and the chaplain read the service for the dead. Then he spoke a bit about him – how he had done his duty, and was an example to all – and he said how all loved and honoured him. Then the men told off for the duty stood ready to slip the grating and let the gallant boy go plunging down to join the other heroes under the sea; but Old Land's End stepped out and touched his cap to the captain, and asked if he might say a word.

'Say on, my man!' said the captain, and he stood, with his cocked hat in his hand, whilst Old Land's End spoke: 'Mates! ye've heerd what the chaplain said. The boy done his duty, and died like the brave gentleman he was! And we wish he was here now. But, for all that, we can't be sorry for him, or for what he done, though it cost him his life. I had a lad once of my own, and I hoped for him what I never wanted for myself – that he would win fame and honour, and become an admiral of the fleet, as others have done before. But, so help me God! I'd rather see him lying under the flag as we see that brave boy lie now, and know why he was there, than I'd see him in his epaulettes on the quarterdeck of the flagship! He died for his Queen and country, and for the honour of the flag! And what more would you have him do!'